Fury

The Earth is long dead and the human survivors live in huge citadels beneath the Venusian seas, ruled by the Immortals, genetic mutations with a lifespan of 1000 years. Sam Reed was born an immortal, but his deranged father had him mutilated as a baby. Now, at the age of 80, he learns what he is.

Mutant

People called them 'baldies'.

A race of hairless mutants with egg-like skulls and lashless eyes …

A race hated by normal human beings, who hunted them with animal ferocity and killed them with religious fervour …

But the baldies had an extraordinary talent: the power of telepathy. So they disguised themselves and waited for the day when there would be enough of them to stop their persecution by normal men.

The Best of Henry Kuttner

These seventeen classic stories create their own unique galaxy of vain, protective and murderous robots; devilish angels; and warm and angry aliens. Ray Bradbury called Henry Kuttner 'a man who shaped science fiction and fantasy in its most important years'.

This definitive collection will be a revelation to those who wish to discover or rediscover Henry Kuttner, a true master of the universe.

Also by Henry Kuttner

Novels

Fury (1950)
Mutant (1953)
The Well of the Worlds (1953)
Valley of the Flame (1964)
Earth's Last Citadel (1964)
The Dark World (1965)
The Time Axis (1965)
The Creature From Beyond Infinity (1968)
The Mask of Circe (1971)

Collections

Dr Cyclops (1967)
Elak of Atlantis (1985)
Prince Raynor (1987)

Henry Kuttner

SF GATEWAY OMNIBUS

FURY

MUTANT

THE BEST OF HENRY KUTTNER

GOLLANCZ
LONDON

This omnibus copyright © 2013 Carole Ann Rodriguez, the Executor of the Estate of Henry Kuttner and C. L. Moore
Fury copyright © Henry Kuttner 1950
Mutant copyright © Henry Kuttner 1953
The Best of Henry Kuttner copyright © Catherine Moore Kuttner, executrix for the Estate of Henry Kuttner 1975
Introduction copyright © SFE Ltd 2013

All rights reserved

The right of Henry Kuttner to be identified as the author of this work has been asserted by him in accordance with the Copyright, Designs and Patents Act 1988.

First published in Great Britain in 2013 by
Gollancz
An imprint of the Orion Publishing Group
Orion House, 5 Upper St Martin's Lane,
London WC2H 9EA

An Hachette UK Company

A CIP catalogue record for this book is available from the British Library

ISBN 978 0 575 12886 6

1 3 5 7 9 10 8 6 4 2

Typeset by Jouve (UK), Milton Keynes

Printed and bound by CPI Group (UK) Ltd, Croydon, CR0 4YY

The Orion Publishing Group's policy is to use papers that are natural, renewable and recyclable products and made from wood grown in sustainable forests. The logging and manufacturing processes are expected to conform to the environmental regulations of the country of origin.

www.orionbooks.co.uk
www.gollancz.co.uk

CONTENTS

ENTER THE SF GATEWAY . . .

Towards the end of 2011, in conjunction with the celebration of fifty years of coherent, continuous science fiction and fantasy publishing, Gollancz launched the SF Gateway.

Over a decade after launching the landmark SF Masterworks series, we realised that the realities of commercial publishing are such that even the Masterworks could only ever scratch the surface of an author's career. Vast troves of classic SF and fantasy were almost certainly destined never again to see print. Until very recently, this meant that anyone interested in reading any of those books would have been confined to scouring second-hand bookshops. The advent of digital publishing changed that paradigm for ever.

Embracing the future even as we honour the past, Gollancz launched the SF Gateway with a view to utilising the technology that now exists to make available, for the first time, the entire backlists of an incredibly wide range of classic and modern SF and fantasy authors. Our plan, at its simplest, was – and still is! – to use this technology to build on the success of the SF and Fantasy Masterworks series and to go even further.

The SF Gateway was designed to be the new home of classic science fiction and fantasy – the most comprehensive electronic library of classic SFF titles ever assembled. The programme has been extremely well received and we've been very happy with the results. So happy, in fact, that we've decided to complete the circle and return a selection of our titles to print, in these omnibus editions.

We hope you enjoy this selection. And we hope that you'll want to explore more of the classic SF and fantasy we have available. These are wonderful books you're holding in your hand, but you'll find much, much more … through the SF Gateway.

www.sfgateway.com

INTRODUCTION

from The Encyclopedia of Science Fiction

Henry Kuttner (1915–1958) was a US author, married to C. L. Moore from 1940 until his death; from 1940 at the latest, the two authors collaborated constantly. Kuttner's childhood interest in *Weird Tales* had early led him to correspond with H. P. Lovecraft and others: his first sale to the magazine was a poem, 'Ballad of the Gods', in February 1936, followed by 'The Graveyard Rats' (1936). His stories for the magazine included a Robert E. Howard-like Sword-and-Sorcery series from 1938 to 1941, eventually collected as *Elak of Atlantis* (1985). As with many of his fellow authors of the 1930s, much of his output, whether fantasy or SF, only reached book form in later years. Further examples of his early solo work have been assembled as *Prince Raynor* (1987), *Book of Iod* (1995), and *The Graveyard Rats and Other Stories* (2010); a more systematic coverage of these years has begun with *The Early Kuttner, Volume One: Terror in the House* (2010).

Kuttner began to publish SF stories in October 1937 with 'When the Earth Lived', remaining a prolific contributor in several modes, including Space Opera, a substantial selection of the latter being assembled as *Thunder in the Void* (2012); nearly 300 stories are credited to him in all, under his own name and various pseudonyms, between 1936 and the early 1950s, though much of his later work is inextricably entwined with that of his wife and partner. The two wrote very many stories together; all the stories assembled as *The Best of Henry Kuttner* (1975) (see below) seem to have been collaborations, though they were all first issued as by Kuttner alone. The two authors also used many pseudonyms; Kuttner himself also published stories under various House Names.

Early in their marriage, Kuttner and Moore made what became a very well-known claim: that each could pick up and smoothly continue any story from wherever the other had left off typing on the single typewriter they seem to have used for at least some of their work together. Moore seems to have been the more fluent stylist, and perhaps the more ambitious writer (though in the end this is very difficult to demonstrate), but Kuttner's wit, deftly audacious deployment of ideas and neat exposition complemented her talents very well. The two together wrote many colourful novels for *Startling Stories* during the 1940s, which became archetypes of the hybrid genre Science Fantasy, neatly fusing Kuttner's vigorous plotting with Moore's romanticism.

Two of the best – *Beyond Earth's Gates* (1954) and *Well of the Worlds* (1953) – reached book form while Kuttner was still alive. Most of them, however, were made available to the large paperback audience only after his early death: they include *Earth's Last Citadel* (1964), *Valley of the Flame* (1964), *The Dark World* (1965), *The Time Axis* (1965) and *The Mask of Circe* (1971). For *Startling*'s companion *Thrilling Wonder Stories*, Kuttner (possibly with Moore) wrote the humorous Hogben series about an ill-assorted family of weirdly gifted Mutant hillbillies between 1947 and 1949; Neil Gaiman has acknowledged that they supplied a model for characters in his novel, *The Ocean at the End of the Lane* (2013).

It was also during this period that the team became part of John W. Campbell Jr's stable of writers, publishing much of their work in *Astounding*, much of it appearing initially as by K. M. O'Donnell or Lewis Padgett, their best known pseudonyms. The Padgett stories are ingenious and slickly written, often deploying offbeat Humour: Kuttner may have been the sole author of the Galloway Gallegher series collected as *Robots Have No Tails* (1952), and of other notable Padgett stories including 'The Twonky' (1942), filmed as *The Twonky* (1952). Two Padgett short novels, also likely by Kuttner alone, *Tomorrow and Tomorrow* and *The Fairy Chessmen* (1951), are intensely recomplicated tales in the tradition of A. E. Van Vogt, whose influence is also less directly evident in the Baldy series assembled as *Mutant* (1953) (see below). But probably the finest work Kuttner published in *Astounding*, almost certainly with Moore, is the Keeps sequence comprising *Clash by Night* (1952) and *Fury* (1950) (see below).

In 1950 Kuttner and Moore went to study at the University of Southern California; they wrote a number of mystery novels thereafter but very few SF stories. Kuttner graduated in 1954 and went on to work for his MA, but died of a heart attack before it was completed. During his career Kuttner rarely received the credit his work merited, being to an extent overshadowed by his own pseudonyms; his posthumous stature was similarly overshadowed, in this case by an understandable desire to give fair credit to C. L. Moore, the absence of whose name on many shared publications being perhaps attributable to her sex: for women in the 1940s and 1950s were not seen by editors as attractive to SF readers (SF readers themselves seemed less concerned). This argument may have stretched a point with regard to the Kuttner/Moore partnership, but clearly needed making.

Since the correction, the process of evaluation has calmed down, and Kuttner's reputation as one of the most able and versatile of modern SF writers, and as a competent partner to his wife, has become easier to think was in fact fully earned; *Two-Handed Engine* (2005) as by both authors is a balanced presentation of their work together. Kuttner's own influence on the young Ray Bradbury – who introduced *The Best of Henry Kuttner* – was considerable, and many later writers have acknowledged their debt to him. If in the end Kuttner was a journeyman writer, he was a journeyman of genius; and more.

The first of three titles presented here is perhaps the darkest of any Kuttner story, and for that reason may reflect a strong input from Moore. It is the main section of the Keeps sequence which begins with a preliminary sketch, *Clash by Night* (magazine 1943; as novella 1950), not vital to the central tale, and not reprinted here. The heart of the series is *Fury* (magazine 1947; 1950). Over and above its virtues as a Planetary Romance set on a vividly romantic ocean-drenched Venus, the sequence is notable for the clarity and power of its depiction of the Keeps – self-contained defendable submarine cities – which house complex strata of human dwellers. The term Keep has since been used by other writers to designate armoured enclaves, whether or not submerged. The novel itself, through glorious twists and turns of plot, seems to glimpse forward.

The second title to appear here, *Mutant* (1953); it would be the last SF book Kuttner and Moore would write together (she continued to publish after his death). It is set in a Ruined Earth America, a considerable time after a nuclear catastrophe has savaged the world, and created a Mutant strain of human telepaths. They are persecuted by the 'normal' majority; *Mutant* describes, in engaging and realistic detail, the lives they live over several generations as they attempt (in the end successfully) to survive. Though the tale reflects the apprehensions almost everyone suffered in the decade after the dropping of the first atomic bombs, a textured humanness suffuses each episode. We end the book wishing to read more. Perhaps that was Henry Kuttner's cleverest trick of all: he made us want him never to stop.

The third title selected, *The Best of Henry Kuttner*, provides a wide and carefully chosen selection from the prime decade, from 1939 to 1950. It includes tales like 'The Voice of the Lobster' (1950) by Kuttner alone; 'Mimsy Were the Borogoves' (1943), which Moore may have had a hand in, about deadly educational toys that have Timeslipped from the future; plus undoubted collaborations like 'Absalom' (1946). Because they are so competent, and surprising, and flippant, and wise, these stories have a habit of staying in the memory. They are a pleasure to return to.

For a more detailed version of the above, see Henry Kuttner's author entry in *The Encyclopedia of Science Fiction*: http://sf-encyclopedia.com/entry/kuttner_henry

Some terms above are capitalised when they would not normally be so rendered; this indicates that the terms represent discrete entries in *The Encyclopedia of Science Fiction*.

FURY

FOREWORD

This is no story for the lily-livered ...

Fury is a novel of violence. It describes the tortured struggle of the human race to aspire once again to the stars from the deeps of the Venusian seas. The struggle is organized around the career of Sam Reed, an Immortal.

It is a career which finally, through chicanery, desire for self-aggrandizement, and murder – and yet, beyond it all, a distorted vision of the glowing future of man – brings all the human race up from the safe Venusian seas and out into the open terrors of the biologically furious land surface of the planet, there to struggle and achieve once again a noble destiny.

Fury shows how under conditions incomprehensibly different from those we now experience, mankind once again starts up the long climb from decay to greatness.

GROFF CONKLIN

PART ONE

Despair thy charm;
And let the angel whom thou still hast serv'd
Tell thee, Macduff was from his mother's womb
Untimely ripp'd.

– *Shakespeare*

Sam Harker's birth was a double prophecy. It showed what was happening to the great Keeps where civilization's lights still burned, and it foreshadowed Sam's life in those underwater fortresses and out of them. His mother Bessi was a fragile, pretty woman who should have known better than to have a child. She was narrow-hipped and tiny, and she died in the emergency Caesarean that released Sam into a world that he had to smash before it could smash him.

That was why Blaze Harker hated his son with such a blind, vicious hatred. Blaze could never think of the boy without remembering what had happened that night. He could never hear Sam's voice without hearing Bessi's thin, frightened screams. The caudal anesthesia hadn't helped much, because Bessi was psychologically as well as physically unfit for motherhood.

Blaze and Bessi – it was a Romeo and Juliet story with a happy ending, up to the time Sam was conceived. They were casual, purposeless hedonists. In the Keeps you had to choose. You could either find a drive, an incentive – be one of the technicians or artists – or you could drift. The technologies made a broad field, everything from thalassopolitics to the rigidly limited nuclear physics. But drifting was easy, if you could afford it. Even if you couldn't, lotus-eating was cheap in the Keeps. You simply didn't go in for the expensive pleasures like the Olympus rooms and the arenas.

Still, Blaze and Bessi could afford the best. Their idyll could make a saga of hedonism. And it seemed that it would have a happy ending, for in the Keeps it wasn't the individual who paid. It was the race that was paying.

After Bessi died, Blaze had nothing left except hatred.

These were the generations of Harker:

Geoffery begat Raoul; Raoul begat Zachariah; Zachariah begat Blaze; and Blaze begat Sam.

Blaze relaxed in the cushioned seat and looked at his great-great-grandfather.

'You can go to the devil,' he said. 'All of you.'

Geoffery was a tall, muscular, blond man with curiously large ears and feet. He said, 'You talk like that because you're young, that's all. How old are you now? Not twenty!'

'It's my affair,' Blaze said.

'I'll be two hundred in another twenty years,' Geoffery said. 'I had sense enough to wait till I was past fifty before fathering a son. I had sense enough not to use my common-law wife for breeding. Why blame the child?'

Blaze stubbornly looked at his fingers.

His father Zachariah, who had been glaring silently, sprang up and snapped, 'He's psychotic! Where he belongs is in a psych-hospital. They'd get the truth out of him!'

Blaze smiled. 'I took precautions, Father,' he said mildly, 'I took a number of tests and exams before I came here today. Administration's approved my I.Q. and my sanity. I'm thoroughly compos mentis. Legally, too. There's nothing any of you can do, and you know it.'

'Even a two-week-old child has his civil rights,' said Raoul, who was thin, dark, elegantly tailored in soft celoflex, and seemed wryly amused by the entire scene. 'But you've been careful not to admit anything, eh, Blaze?'

'Very careful.'

Geoffery hunched his buffalo shoulders forward, met Blaze's eyes with his own cool blue ones, and said, 'Where's the boy?'

'I don't know.'

Zachariah said furiously, 'My grandson – we'll find him! Be sure of that! If he's in Delaware Keep we'll find him – or if he's on Venus!'

'Exactly,' Raoul agreed. 'The Harkers are rather powerful, Blaze. You should know that. That's why you've been allowed to do exactly as you wanted all your life. But that's stopping now.'

'I don't think it is stopping,' Blaze said. 'I've a great deal of money of my own. As for your finding … *him* … have you thought that it might be difficult?'

'We're a powerful family,' Geoffery said steadily.

'So we are,' Blaze said. 'But what if you can't recognize the boy when you find him?' He smiled.

The first thing they did was to give him a depilatory treatment. Blaze couldn't endure the possibility that dyed hair would grow back red. The baby's scanty growth of auburn fuzz was removed. It would never grow again.

A culture catering to hedonism has its perversions of science. And Blaze could pay well. More than one technician had been wrecked by pleasure-addiction; such men were usually capable – when they were sober. But it was a woman Blaze found, finally, and she was capable only when alive. She lived when she was wearing the Happy Cloak. She wouldn't live long; Happy Cloak addicts lasted about two years, on the average. The thing was a biological adaptation of an organism found in the Venusian seas. It had been illegally developed, after its potentialities were first realized. In its native state, it got its prey by touching it. After that neuro-contact had been established, the prey was quite satisfied to be ingested.

It was a beautiful garment, a living white like the white of a pearl, shivering softly with rippling lights, stirring with a terrible, ecstatic movement of its own as the lethal symbiosis was established. It was beautiful as the woman technician wore it, as she moved about the bright, quiet room in a tranced concentration upon the task that would pay her enough to insure her death within two years. She was very capable. She knew endocrinology. When she had finished, Sam Harker had forever lost his heritage. The matrix had been set – or, rather, altered from its original pattern.

Thalamus, thyroid, pineal – tiny lumps of tissue, some already active, some waiting till the trigger of approaching maturity started the secretions. The infant was unformed, a somewhat larger lump of tissue, with cartilage for bones and his soft skull imperfectly sutured as yet.

'Not a monster,' Blaze had said, thinking about Bessi all the time. 'No, nothing extreme. Short, fleshy – *thick!*'

The bandaged lump of tissue lay still on the operating table. Germicidal lamps focused on the anaesthetized form.

The woman, swimming in anticipated ecstasy, managed to touch a summoning signal-button. Then she lay down quietly on the floor, the shining pearly garment caressing her. Her tranced eyes looked up, flat and empty as mirrors. The man who came in gave the Happy Cloak a wide berth. He began the necessary post-operative routine.

The elder Harkers watched Blaze, hoping they could find the child through the father. But Blaze had refined his plan too thoroughly to leave such loopholes. In a secret place he had Sam's fingerprints and retina-prints, and he knew that through those he could locate his son at any time. He was in no hurry. What would happen would happen. It was inevitable – now. Given the basic ingredients, and the stable environment there was no hope at all for Sam Harker.

Blaze set an alarm clock in his mind, an alarm that would not ring for many years. Meanwhile, having faced reality for the first time in his life, he did his utmost to forget it again. He could never forget Bessi, though he tried. He plunged back into the bright, euphoric spin of hedonism in the Keeps.

The early years merged into the unremembered past. Time moved more slowly for Sam then. Days and hours dragged. The man and woman he knew as father and mother had nothing in common with him, even then. For the operation had not altered his mind; his intelligence, his ingenuity, he had inherited from half-mutant ancestors. Though the mutation was merely one of longevity, that trait had made it possible for the Harkers to rise to dominance on Venus. They were not the only long-lived ones, by any means; there were a few hundred others who had a life-expectancy of from two to seven hundred years, depending on various complicated factors. But the strain bred true. It was easy to identify them.

There was a carnival season once, he remembered, and his foster parents awkwardly donned finery and went to mingle with the rest. He was old enough to be a reasoning animal by then. He had already seen glamour from a distance, but he had never seen it in operation.

Carnival was a respected custom. All Delaware Keep was shining. Colored perfumes hung like a haze above the moving Ways, clinging to the merry-makers as they passed. It was a time when all classes mingled.

Technically there were no lower classes. Actually –

He saw a woman – the loveliest woman he had ever seen. Her gown was blue. That does not describe its color in the least. It was a deep, rich, different blue, so velvety and smooth that the boy ached to touch it. He was too young to understand the subtlety of the gown's cut, its sharp, clean lines, the way it enhanced the woman's face and her corn-yellow hair. He saw her from a distance and was filled with a violent need to know more about her.

His foster mother could not tell him what he wanted.

'That's Kedre Walton. She must be two, three hundred years old by now.'

'Yes.' Years meant nothing. 'But who *is* she?'

'Oh – she runs a lot of things.'

'This is a farewell party, my dear,' she said.

'So soon?'

'Sixty years – hasn't it been?'

'Kedre, Kedre – sometimes I wish our lives weren't so long.'

She smiled at him. 'Then we'd never have met. We Immortals gravitate to the same level – so we *do* meet.'

Old Zachariah Harker reached for her hand. Beneath their terrace the Keep glittered with carnival.

'It's always new,' he said.

'It wouldn't be, though, if we'd stayed together that first time. Imagine being bound together indissolubly for hundreds of years!'

Zachariah gave her a shrewd, questioning stare.

'A matter of proportion, probably,' he said. 'Immortals shouldn't live in the Keeps. The restrictions … the older you grow, the more you've got to expand.'

'Well – I am expanding.'

'Limited by the Keeps. The young men and the short-lived ones don't see the walls around them. We old ones do. We need more room. Kedre, I'm growing afraid. We're reaching our limits.'

'Are we?'

'Coming close to them – we Immortals. I'm afraid of intellectual death. What's the use of longevity if you're not able to use your skills and powers as you gain them? We're beginning to turn inward.'

'Well – what then? Interplanetary?'

'Outposts, perhaps. But on Mars we'd need Keeps, too. And on most of the other planets. I'm thinking of interstellar.'

'It's impossible.'

'It was impossible when man came to Venus. It's theoretically possible now, Kedre. But not practically so. There's no … no symbolic launching-platform. No interstellar ship could be built or launched from an undersea Keep. I'm speaking symbolically.'

'My dear,' she said, 'we have all the time in the world. We'll discuss this again in … oh, fifty years, perhaps.'

'And I won't see you till then?'

'Of course you'll see me, Zachariah. But no more than that. It's time we took our vacation. Then, when we come together again –'

She rose. They kissed. That, too, was symbolic. Both of them felt the ardor fading into gray ash – and, because they were in love, they were wise enough and patient enough to wait till the fire could be rekindled again.

So far the plan had been successful.

After fifty years had passed they would be lovers again.

Sam Harker stared at the gaunt gray-faced man moving purposefully through the throng. He was wearing cheerful celoflex too, but nothing could disguise the fact that he was not a Keep man. He had been sunburned once, so deeply that centuries undersea had not bleached him of that deep tan. His mouth was set in a habitual sneering grin.

'Who's that?'

'What? Where? Oh, I don't know. Don't bother me.'

He hated the compromise that had made him don celoflex. But his old uniform would have been far too conspicuous. Cold, cruel-mouthed, suffering, he let the Way carry him past the enormous globe of the Earth, draped in a black plastic pall, which served in every Keep as a reminder of mankind's greatest achievement. He went to a walled garden and handed in an identification disk at a barred window. Presently he was admitted to the temple.

So this was the Temple of Truth!

It was impressive. He had respect for technicians – logistics, logicians … not logistics, that was behind him now. A priest took him into an inner chamber and showed him a chair.

'You're Robin Hale?'

'Right.'

'Well – you've collated and given us the data we need. But there must be a few clarifying questions. The Logician will ask them himself.'

He went away. Downstairs, in the hydroponic gardens, a tall, thin, bony-faced man was pottering about cheerfully.

'The Logician is needed. Robin Hale's waiting.'

'Ah, rats,' said the tall, thin man, setting down a spray and scratching his long jaw. 'Nothing I can tell the poor fella. He's sunk.'

'Sir!'

'Take it easy. I'll talk to him. Go away and relax. Got his papers ready?'

'Yes, sir.'

'O.K. I'll be along. Don't rush me.' Muttering, the Logician shambled toward a lift. Presently he was in the control room, watching, through a visor, the gaunt sunburned man sitting uncomfortably on his chair.

'Robin Hale,' he said, in a new, deeper voice.

Hale automatically stiffened. 'Yes.'

'You are an Immortal. That means that you have a life-expectancy of up to seven hundred years. But you have no job. Is that right?'

'That's right!'

'What happened to your job?'

'What happened to the Free Companies?'

... They died. They passed, when the Keeps unified under one government, and the token wars between them became unnecessary. In those days, the Free Companions had been the warriors, hired mercenaries paid to fight battles the Keeps dared not fight themselves, for fear of perishing.

The Logician said, 'Not many Free Companies were Immortals. It's been a long time since there was a Free Company. You've outlived your job, Hale.'

'I know.'

'Do you want me to find a job for you?'

'You can't,' Hale said bitterly. 'You can't find one, and I can't face the prospect of hundreds of years – doing nothing. Just enjoying myself. I'm not a hedonist.'

'I can tell you what to do very easily,' the Logician said. 'Die.'

There was silence.

The Logician went on: 'I can't tell you how to do it quite so easily. You're a fighter. You'll want to die fighting for your life. And, preferably, fighting for something you believe.' He paused. When he spoke again, his voice had changed.

'Wait a minute,' he said. 'I'm coming out there. Hang on.'

And a moment later his thin, tall form shambled from behind a curtain in the wall. Hale jumped to his feet, staring at the scarecrow figure confronting him. The Logician waved him back to his seat.

'Lucky I'm the boss,' he said. 'Those priests of mine wouldn't stand for this if they had a thing to say about it. But what could they do without me? *I'm* the Logician. Sit down.' He pulled up a seat opposite, took an odd-looking object from his pocket – it was a pipe – and stuffed it with tobacco.

'Grow it and cure it myself,' he said. 'Look, Hale. This phony stuff is O.K. for the Keeps, but I don't see the point of handing you a line.'

Hale was staring. 'But … the Temple … this is the Temple of Truth? You mean it's all –'

'Phony? Nope. It's on the level. Trouble is, the truth don't always come out dignified. Those old statues of Truth – naked, she was. Well, she had the figger for it. But look at me, now. I'd be a sight. There was a time when we played it straight; it didn't work. People just thought I was giving an opinion. Fair enough; I look like an ordinary guy. But I'm not. I'm a trick mutant. Come full circle. We went around through Plato and Aristotle and Bacon and Korzybski and the truth-machines – and end up right where we started, the best method in the world to use logic on human problems. I know the answers. The right ones.'

Hale found it difficult to understand. 'But … you can't be infallible … don't you use any system?'

'Tried the systems,' the Logician said. 'Lots of four-bit words. Boils down to one thing. Horse sense.'

Hale blinked.

The Logician kindled his pipe. 'I'm over a thousand years old,' he said. 'Kind of hard to believe, I know. But I told you I was a trick mutant. Son, I was born on Earth. I can remember the atomic wars. Not the first ones – that was how I come to be born, my parents got in the way of some secondary radiations. I'm about as close to a real Immortal as they come. But my main talent – do you remember reading about Ben the Prophet? No? Well, he was only one of a lot of prophets, in those days. Plenty of people guessed what was coming. Didn't take much logic. I was Ben the Prophet. Lucky some of the right people listened and started colonizing Venus. I came along. Time on Earth blew up, I was right here being studied. Some technicians found out my brain was a little queer. There was a new sense in it, instinct, or whatever – nobody's ever found out exactly what it is. But it's the same thing that made the thinking-machines give the right answers – when they did! Brother, I just can't help giving the right answers!'

'You're a thousand years old?' Hale asked, fastening on the single point.

'Nigh. I've seen 'em come and go. I've seen how I could get to rule the whole roost, if I wanted to. But preserve me from that! I can see most of the answers to that, and I don't like any of 'em. I just sit here in the Temple of Truth and answer questions.'

Hale said blankly, 'We've always thought … there was a machine –'

'Sure, I know. Funny, people will believe what a machine tells 'em, where they won't believe a fella like themselves. Or maybe it isn't funny at all. Look, son – no matter how you cut it, I know the answers. I turn over the information in my head, and pretty soon I see what they add up to. Common sense is all. Only requirement is that I've got to know all about you and your problem.'

'Then you can read the future.'

'Too many variables,' the Logician said. 'By the way, I hope you won't shoot off your mouth about me. The priests won't like it. Every time I show myself to some client and come off my high horse, they raise the temple roof. Not that it matters. You can talk if you want; nobody'd believe the infallible oracle's anything but a super-machine.' He grinned cheerfully. 'Main thing is, son, I got an idea. I told you I add up the numbers and get the answer. Well, sometimes I get more than one answer. Why don't you go landside?'

'What?'

'Why not?' the Logician said. 'You're pretty tough. Course you may get killed. Probably will, I'll say. But you'll go down fighting. Not much fighting you can do in the Keeps, for anything you believe in. There's some other people feel the way you do. A few Free Companions, I think – Immortals too. Look them up. Go landside.'

Hale said, 'It's impossible.'

'The Companies had their forts, didn't they?'

'It took gangs of technicians to keep the jungle out. And the animals. We had to keep waging a continual war against landside. Besides, the forts – there isn't much left of them now.'

'Pick one out and rebuild it.'

'But – then what?'

'Maybe you can be top man,' the Logician said quietly. 'Maybe you can get to be top man – on Venus.'

The silence drew on and on. Hale's face changed.

'Good enough,' the Logician said, getting up. He put out his hand. 'My name's Ben Crowell, by the way. Come see me if you run into trouble. Or I might even drop in to see you. If I do, don't let on I'm the great brain.' He winked.

He shambled out, sucking at his pipe.

Life in the Keeps was very much like a game of chess. In the barnyard, among fowls, social precedence is measured by length of tenancy. Extension in time is wealth. Pawns have a low life-expectancy; knights and bishops and castles have more. Socially, there was a three-dimensional democracy and a temporal autocracy. There was a reason why the long-lived Biblical patriarchs achieved power. They could hold power.

In the Keeps, the Immortals simply knew more than the non-Immortals. Psychologically a curious displacement became evident. Immortals weren't worshipped as gods in those practical days, but there was definite displacement. Parents have one faculty a child cannot have: maturity. The plus factor. Experience. *Age.*

So there was displacement. Unconsciously the short-lived peoples of the Keeps began to look with dependence upon the Immortals. They knew more, of course. And, too, they were older.

Let George do it.

Besides, it is a regrettably human trait to disclaim unpleasant responsibilities. For centuries the trend had been away from individualism. Social responsibility had been carried to the point where everyone, theoretically, was his brother's keeper.

Eventually they all formed a circle and collapsed gracefully into one another's arms.

The Immortals, who knew what long, empty centuries were ahead of them, took pains to insure that those centuries would not be so empty. They learned. They studied. They had plenty of time.

As they gained in knowledge and experience, they began to take the responsibilities easily delegated to them by the collapsing multitudes.

It was a stable enough culture – for a moribund race.

He was always getting into mischief.

Anything new was fascinating to him. The Harker chromosomes took care of that. His name, though, was Sam Reed.

He kept fighting the invisible bars that he knew prisoned him. There were fourscore and ten of them. Something in his mind, something illogical and inherited, kept rebelling, seeking expression. *What can you do in ninety years?*

Once he tried to get a job in the great hydroponic gardens. His blunt, coarse face, his bald head, his precocious mind – these made it possible for him to lie convincingly about his age. He managed it for a while, till his curiosity got the better of him, and he began experimenting with botanical forced cultures. Since he knew nothing about it, he spoiled a good-sized crop.

Before that, though, he had discovered a blue flower in one of the tanks, and it reminded him of the woman he had seen at carnival. Her gown had been exactly the same color. He asked one of the attendants about it.

'Blasted weeds,' the man said. 'Can't keep 'em out of the tanks. Hundreds of years, and they still show up. We don't have much trouble with these, though. It's the crab grass that's worst.' He pulled up the weed and tossed it aside. Sam rescued it and asked more questions later. It was, he learned, a violet. The unobtrusive, pretty little plant was a far cry from the glamorous hybrid flowers grown in other sections of Hydroponics. He kept it till it broke into dust. He kept its memory after that, as he kept the memory of the woman in the violet-blue gown.

One day he ran away to Canada Keep, far across the Sea of Shallows. He had never been outside a Keep before, and was fascinated as the great, transparent globe drove upward through the bubbling water. He went with a man whom he had bribed – with stolen money – to pretend to be his father. But after he reached Canada Keep he never saw the man again.

He was ingenious at twelve. He worked out various ways to earn a living. But none satisfied him. They were all too dull. Blaze Harker had known what he was doing when he had left the boy's mind untouched in a stunted, warped body.

It was warped only by the aesthetic standards of the time. The long-limbed, tall Immortals had set the standard of beauty. There came to be a stigma of ugliness attached to the stocky, blunt-featured, thick boned, short-lived ones.

There was a tough, violent seed of unfulfillment within Sam. It drove him. It couldn't develop normally, for it was seed of the Immortals, and he obviously was no Immortal. He simply could not qualify for work that might take training of a hundred years or more. Even fifty years training –!

He did it the hard way, and the inevitable way. He got his mentor, his Chiron-Fagin, after he met the Slider.

The Slider was a fat, wicked old man without any name. He had bushy white hair, a carbuncled red nose, and a philosophy of his own. He never proffered advice, but he gave it when it was asked.

'People want fun,' he told the boy. 'Most of 'em. And they don't want to look at a thing that hurts their tender feelings. Use your head, kid. Thieving's out. Best to make yourself useful to people who've got power. Now you take Jim Sheffield's gang. Jim caters to the right people. Don't ask questions; do what you're told – but first get the right connections.'

He sniffled and blinked his watery eyes at Sam.

'I spoke to Jim about you. Go see him. Here's the place.' He thrust a plastic disk at the boy. 'I wouldn't of got you out of that scrape if I hadn't seen something in you. Go see Jim.'

He stopped Sam at the door.

'You'll get along. Likewise, you won't forget old Slider, eh? Some people have. I can make trouble as easy as I can do favors.'

Sam left the fat, malignant old man sniffling and chuckling.

He went to see Jim Sheffield. He was fourteen then, strong, short, scowling. He found Sheffield stronger and larger. Sheffield was seventeen, a graduate of the Slider's twisted school, an independent, shrewd businessman whose gang was already becoming known. The human factor was vital for Keep intrigue. It wasn't merely politics; the mores of the era were as punctilious and complicated as the social life of Machiavelli's Italy. The straight thrust of the knife was not only illegal but in poor taste. Intrigue was the thing. In the continually shifting balance of power, the man who could outwit an opponent, wind him in webs of his own spinning, and force him to ruin himself – that was the game.

Sheffield's gang free-lanced. Sam Reed's – he didn't know the name Harker except to identify it with one of the great Families of his old Keep – first job was to go undersea, with one more-experienced companion, and collect some specimens of bluish algae, illegal within the Keeps. When he got back through the secret lock, he was surprised to find the Slider waiting, with a portable ray-mechanism already set up. The little room had been sealed off.

The Slider was wearing protective armor. His voice came through a diaphragm.

'Stay right there, boys. Catch this.' He tossed a spray-gun to Sam. Now spray that plastibulb. It's sealed, isn't it? Right. Spray it all over – fine. Now turn around slowly.'

'Wait a minute –' said the other boy.

The Slider sniffled. 'Do what I tell you or I'll break your skinny neck,' he said conversationally. 'Raise your arms. Turn slowly, while I use the ray on you ... that's it.'

Afterward, the three of them met Jim Sheffield. Jim was subdued but angry. He tried to argue with the Slider.

The Slider sniffled and rumpled his white hair.

'You shut up,' he said. 'Too big for your boots, you're getting to be. If you'd remember to ask me when you get into something new, you'd save yourself trouble.' He tapped the black-painted globe Sam had set on the table. 'This algae – know why it's forbidden in the Keeps? Didn't your patron tell you to be careful when he commissioned you to get the stuff?'

Sheffield's broad mouth twisted. 'I was careful.'

'The stuff's safe to handle under lab conditions,' the Slider said. 'Only then. It's a metal-eater. Dissolves metal. Once it's been treated with the right re-agents, it's innocuous. But raw like this, it could get loose and cause a lot of trouble here – and it'd be traced back to you, and you'd land in Therapy. See? If you'd come to me first, I'd have told you to have this ultraviolet set up, to burn the daylights out of any algae the boys might bring in stuck to their suits. Next time I won't be so easy on you. *I* don't want to go to Therapy, Jim.'

The old man looked innocuous enough, but Sheffield's rebellious stare wavered and fell. With a word of agreement he rose, picked up the globe and went out, beckoning to the other boys. Sam waited for a moment.

The Slider winked at him.

'You make a lot of mistakes when you don't get advice, kid,' he said.

These were only episodes among many like them along the course of his outward life. Inwardly too he was precocious, amoral, rebellious. Above all, rebellious. He rebelled against the shortness of life that made learning seem futile to him when he thought of the Immortals. He rebelled against his own body, thick and stocky and plebeian. He rebelled obscurely, and without knowing the reasons himself, against all that he had irrevocably become in that first week of his life.

There have always been angry men in the world. Sometimes the anger, like Elijah's, is the fire of God, and the man lives in history as a saint and a reformer whose anger moved mountains to improve the lot of mankind. Sometimes the anger is destructive, and great war-leaders rise to devastate whole nations. Angers like that find outward expression and need not consume their hosts.

But Sam Reed's anger was a rage against intangibles like time and destiny, and the only target it could find to explode against was himself. Granted that such anger is not normal in a man. But Sam Reed was not normal. His father before him could not have been normal, or he would never have taken such disproportionate vengeance on his son. A flaw somewhere in the Harker blood was responsible for the bitter rage in which father and son alike lived out their days, far separate, raging against far different things, but in armed rebellion all their lives, both of them, against life itself.

Sam went through many inward phases that would have astonished the Slider and Jim Sheffield and the others with whom he worked in those days. Because his mind was more complex than theirs, he was able to live on many more levels than they, and able to conceal it. From the day he first discovered the great libraries of the Keeps he became a passionate reader. He was never an intellectual man, and the unrest in him prevented him from ever mastering any one field of knowledge and so rising above his station by the one superiority he possessed – his mind.

But he devoured books as fire devours fuel, as his own discontent devoured himself. He raced through whole courses of reading on any subject that caught his quick, glancing fancy, and emerged with knowledge of that subject stored uselessly away in a chamber of the uselessly capacious brain. Sometimes the knowledge helped him to promote a fraud or consummate a murder. More often it simply lay dormant in the mind that had been meant for the storage of five hundred years' experience, and was doomed to extinction in less than a century.

One great trouble with Sam Reed was that he didn't know what really ailed him. He had long struggles with his own conscience, in which he tried to rationalize his mind out of its own unconscious knowledge of its lost heritage. For a time he hoped to find among books some answer …

In those early days he sought and found in them the respite of escapism which he later tried in so many other forms – drugs among them, a few women, much restless shifting from Keep to Keep – until he came at last to the one great, impossible task which was to resolve his destiny and which he faced with such violent reluctance.

For the next decade and a half he read, quietly and rapidly, through the libraries of whichever Keep he found himself in, as a smooth undercurrent to whatever illicit affair he might currently be involved with. His profound contempt for the people he victimized, directly or indirectly, was one with the contempt he felt for his associates. Sam Reed was not in any sense a nice man.

Even to himself he was unpredictable. He was the victim of his own banked fire of self-hatred, and when that fire burst forth, Sam Reed's lawlessness took very direct forms. His reputation became tricky. No one trusted him very far – how could they, when he didn't even trust himself? – but his hand and his mind were so expert that his services were in considerable demand among those willing to take the chance that their careful plans might blow up in bloody murder if Sam Reed's temper got the better of him. Many were willing. Many found him rather fascinating.

For life in the Keeps had levelled off to an evenness which is not native to the mind of man. In many, many people something like an unrecognized flicker of the rebellion which consumed Sam Reed burned restlessly, coming to the surface in odd ways. Psychological protective screens took strange forms, such as the wave of bloodthirsty ballads which was sweeping the Keeps on a high tide of popularity when Sam was in his formative years. Less strange, but as indicative, was the fad for near-worship of the old Free-Companion days, the good old days of man's last romantic period.

Deep in human minds lies the insistence that war is glamorous, although it never can have been except to a select few, and for nearly a thousand years now has been wholly terrible. Still the tradition clung on – perhaps because terror itself is perversely fascinating, though most of us have to translate it into other terms before we can admire it.

The Free Companions, who had been serious, hard-working men operating a warfare machine, became swaggering heroes in the public fancy and many a man sighed for a day he thought he had missed by a period of heartbreaking briefness.

They sang the wailing ballads the Free Companions had carried over, in changed forms, from the pioneer days on Venus, which in turn had derived from the unimaginably different days on Old Earth. But they sang them with a difference now. Synthetic Free Companions in inaccurate costumes performed for swaying audiences that followed their every intonation without guessing how wrong they were.

The emphasis was off, in words and rhythm alike. For the Keeps were stagnant, and stagnant people do not know how to laugh. Their humor is subtle and devious, evoking the snigger rather than the guffaw. Slyness and innuendo was the basis of their oblique humor, not laughter.

For laughter is cruel and open. The hour was on its way when men would sing again the old bloodthirsty ballads as they were meant to be sung, and laugh again with the full-throated heartiness that comes from the need to laugh – at one's own misfortunes. To laugh because the only alternative is tears – and tears mean defeat. Only pioneers laugh in the primitive fullness of the sense. No one in the Keeps in those days had so much as heard real laughter in its cruelty and courage, except perhaps the very eldest among them, who remembered earlier days.

Sam Reed along with the rest accepted the Free Companions – extinct almost as Old Earth's dinosaurs, and for much the same reason – as the epitome of glamorous romance. But he understood the reasons behind that emotional acceptance, and could jeer at himself for doing it. It was not Free Companionship but free endeavor which, in the last analysis, enchanted them all.

They didn't want it, really. It would have terrified and repelled most of these people who so gracefully collapsed into the arms of anyone willing to offer them moral and mental support. But nostalgia is graceful too, and they indulged themselves in it to the full.

Sam read of the pioneer days on Venus with a sort of savage longing. A man could use all of himself against an adversary like the ravening planet the newcomers had fought. He read of Old Earth with a burning nostalgia for the wider horizons it had offered. He hummed the old songs over to himself and tried to imagine what a free sky must have looked like, terrifyingly studded with the visible worlds of space.

His trouble was that his world was a simple place, made intricate only artificially, for the sake of intricate intrigue, so that one couldn't hurl oneself wholeheartedly into conflict against a barrier – because the barrier was artificial and would collapse. You had to support it with one hand while you battered it with the other.

The only thing that could have offered Sam an opponent worthy of his efforts was time, the long, complex stretch of centuries which he knew he would never live. So he hated men, women, the world, himself. He fought them all indiscriminately and destructively for lack of an opponent he could engage with in a constructive fight.

He fought them for forty years.

One pattern held true through all that time, though he recognized it only dimly and without much interest. Blue was a color that could touch him as nothing else could. He rationalized that, in part, by remembering the stories of Old Earth and a sky inconceivably colored blue.

Here water hemmed one in everywhere. The upper air was heavy with moisture, the clouds above it hung gravid with moisture and the gray seas which were a blanket above the Keeps seemed scarcely wetter than clouds and air. So the blueness of that lost sky was one in his mind with the thought of freedom …

But the first girl he took in free-marriage was a little dancer from one of the Way cafes, who had worn a scanty costume of blue feathers when he saw her first. She had blue eyes, not so blue as the feathers or the unforgotten skies of Earth, but blue. Sam rented a little apartment for them on a back street in Montana Keep, and for six months or so they bickered no more than most domestic couples.

One morning he came in from an all-night job with the Sheffield gang and smelled something strange the moment he pushed the door open. A heavy sweetness in the air, and a sharp, thick, already familiar acridness that not many Keep men would recognize these effete days.

The little dancer lay slumped against the far wall, already stiffening in her slump. Where her face had been was a great palely tinted blossom whose petals gripped like a many-fingered hand, plastering the flower tight against her skull. It had been a yellow flower, but the veins in the petals were bright red now, and more red ran down beneath the blossom over the girl's blue dress.

Beside her on the floor lay the florist's box, spilling green tissue, in which someone had sent her the flower.

Sam never knew who had done it, or why. It might have been some enemy of his, taking revenge for past indignities, it might even have been one of his friends – he suspected the Slider for awhile – afraid of the hold the girl was getting over him, to divert him from profitable business in the dark hours. Or it might have been one of the girl's dancing rivals, for the bitterest sort of struggle went on constantly among people of that profession for the too-few jobs that were open just now in Montana Keep.

Sam made inquiries, found out what he wanted to know, and exacted dispassionate justice from people who may or may not have been guilty. Sam was not very concerned with that. The girl had not been a particularly nice girl in any sense, any more than Sam was a nice man. She had been convenient, and she had blue eyes. It was his own reputation Sam was upholding when he did what he did about her murder.

After that other girls came and went. Sam exchanged the little back-street apartment for a better one in a quieter neighborhood. Then he finished an exceptionally profitable job and forsook girl and apartment for almost elegant quarters high up in a tower looking out over the central Way. He found a pretty blue-eyed singer to share it with him.

By the time our story opens he had three apartments in three Keeps, one quite expensive, one average, and one deliberately chosen down among the port loading streets in the dimmest section of Virginia Keep. The occupants matched the apartments. Sam was an epicure in his own way. By now he could afford to be.

In the expensive apartment he had two rooms sacred to his privacy, stocked with a growing library of books and music, and an elaborate selection of liquors and drugs. This was not known among his business associates. He went here by another name and was generally supposed to be a commercial traveler from some unspecified but distant Keep. It was as close as Sam Reed could come to the life Sam Harker would have led by rights.

The Queen of Air and Darkness
Begins to shrill and cry,
O young man, O my slayer,
Tomorrow you shall die …

On the first day of the annual Carnival which ushered in the last year of Sam Reed's life, he sat across a small, turning table and spoke practically of love and money with a girl in pink velvet. It must have been near noon, for the light filtering down through the Sea of Shallows and the great dome of the Keep fell at its dim maximum upon them. But all clocks were stopped for the three-day Carnival so that no one need worry about time.

To anyone not reared from childhood upon such phenomena as a merry-go-round cafe, the motion of the city around Sam would have been sickening. The whole room turned slowly to slow music within its transparent circular walls. The tables turned each upon its own axis, carrying a perimeter of chairs with it. Behind the girl's soft cloud of hair Sam could see all of the Keep spreading out and out below them and wheeling solemnly in parade past his unheeding vantage point.

A drift of colored perfume floated past them in a long, airy ribbon lifted and dropped by the air currents, Sam felt tiny spatters of scented moisture beading his face as the pink fog drifted past. He dispelled it with an impatient fanning of the hand and narrowed his eyes at the girl across from him.

'Well?' he said.

The girl smiled and bent her head over the tall, narrow, double-horned lyre, streaming with colored ribbons, which she embraced with one arm as she sat there. Her eyes were gentian blue, shadowed with lashes so heavy she seemed to look up at him through them from black eyes.

'I have another number in a minute,' she said. 'I'll tell you later.'

'You'll tell me now,' Sam declared, not harshly as he would have spoken to most other women, but firmly. The expensive apartment, high up at the exclusive peak of the Keep residential section, was vacant just now, and if Sam had his way this girl would be the next dweller there. Perhaps a permanent dweller. He was aware of an uneasy stir in his mind whenever he thought of Rosathe. He didn't like any woman to affect him this deeply.

Rosathe smiled at him. She had a small, soft mouth and a cloud of soft dark hair cut short and haloed all over her head like a dark mist. There was unexpected humor in her face sometimes, a rather disconcerting intelligence behind the gentian eyes, and she sang in a voice like the pink velvet of her gown, a small soft plaintive voice that brushed the nerves with pleasant tremors.

Sam was afraid of her. But being Sam Reed, he was reaching for this particular nettle. He dealt with danger by confronting it, and if there was any way of getting this velvety creature out of his mind, it would be through surfeit, not by trying to forget her. He proposed to surfeit himself, if he could, as soon as possible.

Rosathe plucked one string of the lyre with a thoughtful forefinger. She said, 'I heard something interesting on the grapevine this morning. Jim Sheffield doesn't like you any more. Is it true, Sam?'

Sam said without heat, 'I asked you a question.'

'I asked you one.'

'All right, it's true. I'll leave you a year's income in my will if Jim gets me first – is that what you're after?'

She flushed and twanged the string so that it disappeared in violent vibration. 'I could slap you, Sam Reed. You know I can earn my own money.'

He sighed. She could, which made it rather more difficult to argue with her. Rosathe was a more than popular singer. If she came to him it wouldn't be for the money. That was another thing that made her dangerous to his peace of mind.

The slow music which had been matching the room's slow turns paused. Then a stronger beat rang through the air, making all the perfume drifts shiver. Rosathe stood up, hoisting the tall, narrow lyre against her hip.

'That's me,' she said. 'I'll think it over, Sam. Give me a few days. I might be very bad for you.'

'I know you'll be bad for me. Go sing your song. I'll see you after Carnival, but not for an answer. I know the answer. You'll come.'

She laughed and walked away from him, sweeping her hand across the strings and humming her song as she went. Sam sat there watching, seeing heads turn and faces light up in anticipation.

But before her song was finished, he got up and went out of the turning room, hearing behind him the velvety little voice diminishing in plaintive lament for a fabled Genevieve. Every note was delicately true as she slid up and down the difficult flats which gave the old, old song its minor wailing.

'Oh Genevieve, sweet Genevieve, the days may come, the days may go ...' wailed Rosathe, watching Sam's broad red-velvet back out of the room. When she had finished the song she went quickly to her dressing room and flipped the switch to the communicator, giving Sheffield's call-signal.

'Listen, Jim,' she said rapidly when his dark, scowling face swam into the screen. 'I was just talking to Sam, and ...'

If Sam could have listened, he probably would have killed her then, instead of much later. But, of course, he didn't hear. At the moment the conversation began, he was walking into an important coincidence which was a turning point in his life.

The coincidence was another woman in blue. Sauntering down the moving Way, she lifted an arm and threw the corner of her filmy blue robe over her hair like a veil. The motion and the color caught Sam's eye, and he stopped so suddenly that men on both sides jolted into him, and one turned with a growl, ready to make a quarrel out of it. Then he got a better glimpse of the granite face, long-jawed, with lines of strain etched from nose to mouth, and for no clear reason turned away, giving up the idea.

Because the image of Rosathe was still vivid in his mind, Sam looked at the woman with less enthusiasm than he might have shown a few days earlier. But deep in his mind buried memories stirred and he stood motionless, staring. The breeze of the sliding Way rippled the veil above her face so that shadows moved in her eyes, blue shadows from the blue veil in the heavily shadowed blue of her eyes. She was very beautiful.

Sam brushed aside a haze of pink Carnival perfume, hesitated – which was not normal to him – and then hitched his gilded belt with a gesture of decision and went forward with the long motion of a stride, but his feet falling softly, as was his habit. He didn't know why the woman's face and her violet-blue robe disturbed him. He had forgotten a great deal since the long-ago Carnival when he saw her last.

At Carnival there are no social barriers – in theory. Sam would have spoken anyhow. He came up below her on the sliding street and looked unsmilingly into her face. On a level she would have been taller than he. She was very slender, very elegant, with a look of graceful weariness much cultivated in the Keep. Sam could not know that she had set the style, or that with her weariness and grace were native, not assumed.

The blue robe was wrapped tight over a tighter sheath of flexible gold that gleamed through the filmy blue. Her hair was an extravagant cascade of blue-black ringlets drawn back from her lovely, narrow face and gathered through a broad gold ring at the crown of her head, so that they fell free from the band in a rich cascade to her waist.

With deliberate barbarism her ears had been pierced, and she wore a hooped gold bell through each lobe. It was part of the current fad that aped the vitality of barbarism. Next season might see a gold ring through the nose, and this woman would wear one with the same air of elegant disdain she turned now upon Sam Reed.

He ignored it. He said in a voice of flat command, 'You can come with me now,' and he held out his crooked arm shoulder-high before him, in invitation.

She tilted her head back slightly and looked at him down her narrow nose. She may have been smiling. It was impossible to tell, because she had the same full, delicately curved mouth so many Egyptian portrait heads once had, with the smile implicit in the contour of the lips. If she did smile, it was in disdain. The heavy waterfall of her ringlets seemed to pull her head farther back on the delicate slender neck, so that she looked down on Sam partly in weariness, partly in scorn, partly in sheer contempt for him as he was.

She stood for a prolonged moment, looking at him down her nose, so still the bells in her pierced ears did not jingle.

For Sam, at first glance merely a squat plebeian like the rest of the lower classes, at second glance offered many contrasts to the discerning eye. He had lived nearly forty years now with his all-devouring anger; if he had come to terms with it, it consumed him inwardly all the same. The marks of that violence were on his face, so that even in repose he looked like a man straining against heavy odds. It gave a thrust and drive to his features which went far toward redeeming their heaviness.

The fact that he had no hair was another curious thing. Baldness was ordinary enough, but this man was so completely hairless that he did not seem bald at all. His bare skull had a classical quality, and hair would look anachronistic now upon the well-shaped curve of his head. Much harm had been done the infant forty years past but in some haste and with some carelessness, because of the Happy-Cloak, so that things remained like the well-shaped ears set close against a well-shaped skull, and the good lines of the jaw and neck, which were Harker lines in essence, though well disguised.

The thick neck was no Harker neck, vanishing into a gaudy crimson shirt. No Harker would have dressed even for Carnival in crimson velvet from head to foot, with a gilded belt supporting a gilded holster. And yet, if a Harker had put this costume on – somehow, subtly, this is the way a Harker would have looked in it.

Thick-bodied, barrel-chested, rolling a little with a wide stride as he walked, nevertheless there was in Sam Reed a full tide of Harker blood that showed in subtle ways about him. No one could have said why or how, but he wore his clothes with an air and moved with an assurance that was almost elegance in spite of the squatness which the upper classes so scorned.

The velvet sleeve fell back from his proffered arm. He stood there steady, holding the crooked forearm out, looking up over it at the woman with his eyes narrowed, steel-color in his ruddy face.

After a moment, moved by no impulse she could name, the woman let her lips tuck in at the corners in an acknowledged smile, disdainful, condescending. She moved one shoulder to shrug her robe aside and stretched out a slender arm and a very slender, small-boned hand with plain, thick gold bands pushed down well at the base of every finger. Very delicately she laid the hand on Sam Reed's arm and stepped down beside him. On that thick forearm, hazed with red hair, the muscles interlacing in a hard column toward the wrist, her hand looked waxen and unreal. She felt the muscles tighten beneath her touch, and her smile grew even more condescending.

Sam said, 'Your hair wasn't black the last time I saw you at Carnival.'

She gave him an aloof glance down her delicate thin nose. She did not yet trouble herself to speak. Sam looked at her unsmilingly, inspecting her feature by feature as if this were some portrait and not a breathing, disdainful woman who was here beside him only by a precarious whim.

'It was yellow,' he said finally, with decision. The memory was clear now, wrenched out of the past in almost complete detail, so that he realized how vividly it must have impressed him at the time. 'That was – thirty years ago. You wore blue on that day, too. I remember it very well.'

The woman said disinterestedly, her head turned aside so that she seemed to be addressing someone at her other shoulder, 'That was my daughter's daughter, I expect.'

It jolted Sam. He was well aware of the long-lived aristocracy, of course. But he had never spoken directly to one before. To a man who counts in decades his own life and those of all his friends, the sudden impact of a life that spans centuries unimpaired must strike a disconcerting blow.

He laughed, a short bark of sound. The woman turned her head and looked at him with faint interest, because she had never before heard one of these lower classes make quite such a sound as that, self-assured, indifferent, the laugh of a confident man who doesn't trouble himself with manners.

Many people before Kedre Walton had found Sam rather mysteriously fascinating. Few had Kedre's perception. She knew before very long exactly why. It was the same quality that she and the world of fashion groped for when they hung barbaric ornaments through the pierced flesh of their ears and sang the wailing, forthright ballads of bloodshed and slaughter which were only words to them – yet. A quality of vitality and virility which the world of man had lost, and hungered for obscurely, and would not accept when it was next offered them, if they could avoid the gift.

She looked at him scornfully, turned her head a little to let the black cascading curls caress her shoulders, and said coldly, 'Your name?'

His red brows met above his nose. 'You don't need to know,' he told her with deliberate rudeness.

For an instant she froze. Then, slowly, an almost imperceptible warming seemed to flow down her limbs, relaxing everything about her, muscles, nerves, even the chill of her aloofness. She drew a deep, silent breath and the ringed fingers which had only touched his arm until now moved deliberately, opened out so that her palm lay against his forearm. She let the palm slide gently forward toward the thickly tapered wrist, her rings cold and catching a little in the heavy red hair that thatched his arm.

She said without looking at him, 'You may tell me about yourself – until you bore me.'

'Are you easily bored?'

'Very easily.'

He looked her up and down, liking what he saw, and he thought he understood it. In forty years Sam Reed had gained an immense store of casual knowledge about the Keeps – not only the ordinary life that anyone could see, but the devious, secret methods a race uses to whip its lagging interest in living when life has gone on longer than humans can easily adjust to. He thought he could hold her interest.

'Come along,' he said.

That was the first day of Carnival. On the third and last day, Sam got his first intimation from her that this casual liaison might not come to an end with the festival. It rather surprised him, and he was not pleased. For one thing, there was Rosathe. And for another – well, Sam Reed was locked in the confines of one prison he could never escape, but he would not submit to gyves within the confines of his cell.

Hanging without gravity in empty darkness, they were watching a three-dimensional image. This particular pleasure was expensive. It required skilled operators and at least one robot plane, equipped with special long-view lenses and televisor. Somewhere far above a continent on Venus the plane was hanging, focused on the scene it had tracked down.

A beast fought with a plant.

It was enormous, that beast, and magnificently equipped for fighting. But its great wet body was wetter now with the blood that ran from gashes opened all over it by the saber-thorned vines. They lashed out with calculating accuracy, flirting drops of venom that flashed in the wet gray air. Music, deftly improvised to fit the pulse of the battle, crashed around them.

Kedre touched a stud. The music softened to a whisper. Somewhere far above the plane hovered on ignored above the battle, the improviser fingered his keys unheard. Kedre, in the darkness, turned her head with a faint silken rustling of unseen hair, and said, 'I made a mistake.'

Sam was impatient. He had wanted to see the finish of the fight.

'What?' he demanded brusquely.

'You.' Out of the darkness a finger brushed his cheek lightly, with casual possessiveness. 'I underestimated you, Sam. Or overestimated. Or both.'

He shook his head to evade the finger. He reached out in the dark, feeling his hand slip across a smooth, curved cheek and into the back-drawn hair. He found the ring through which the showering curls were drawn and seized a handful of ringlets, shaking her head roughly from side to side. The hair moved softly over his forearm.

'That's enough of that,' he said. 'I'm not your pet dog. What do you mean?'

She laughed. 'If you weren't so *young*,' she said insultingly.

He released her with such abruptness he unsteadied her on the divan beside him, and she laid a hand on his shoulder to catch herself. He was silent. Then in a remote voice he asked, 'Just how old are you?'

'Two hundred and twenty years.'

'And I bore you. I'm a child.'

Her laughter was flattering. 'Not a child, Sam – not a child! But our viewpoints are so different. No, you don't bore me. That's the trouble, or part of it. I wish you did. Then I could leave you tonight and forget all this had ever happened. But there's something about you, Sam – I don't know.' Her voice grew reflective. Behind it in the darkness the music swelled to a screaming crescendo, but very softly, a muted death-note as one adversary or the other triumphed far up in the swamplands overhead.

'If you were the man you look,' Kedre Walton was saying. 'If you only were! You have a fine mind, Sam – it's a pity you must die too soon to use it. I wish you weren't one of the commons. I'd marry you – for awhile.'

'How does it feel,' Sam asked her savagely, 'to be a god?'

'I'm sorry. That was patronizing, wasn't it? And you deserve better. How does it feel? Well, we *are* immortals, of a sort. We can't help that. It feels – good, and frightening. It's a responsibility. We do much more than just play, you know. I spent my first hundred years maturing and studying, travelling, learning people and things. Then for a hundred years it was intrigue I liked. Learning how to pull strings to make the Council see things my way, for instance. A sort of jujitsu of the mind – touch a man's vanity and make his ego react in just the way I mean it to. I think you know those tricks well enough yourself – only you'll never live long enough to master the art as I know it. It's a pity. There's something about you that I … I … never mind.'

'Don't say again you'd marry me. I wouldn't have you.'

'Oh yes you would. And I might try it, at that, even if you are a common. I might –'

Sam leaned forward across her knees and groped for the light switch. The small, cushioned room sprang into illumination as the switch clicked, and Kedre blinked her beautiful ageless eyes and laughed half in protest and half in surprise.

'Sam! I'm blind. Don't do that.' She reached to extinguish the light. Sam caught her hand, folding the fingers together over their heavy golden rings.

'No. Listen. I'm leaving you right now and I never want to see you again. Understand? You've got nothing I want.' He rose abruptly.

There was something almost serpentine in the way she moved to her feet in one smooth, swift flow, light glinting on the overlapping golden sequins that sheathed her.

'Wait. No, wait! Forget about all this, Sam. I want to show you something. That was just talk, before. I needed to sound you out. Sam, I want you to come with me to Haven. I have a problem for you.'

He looked at her coldly, his eyes steel splinters between the ruddy lashes, under the rough, ruddy brows. He named the sum his listening would cost her. She curled her lip at him and said she would pay it, the subtle Egyptian smile denting in the corners of her mouth.

He followed her out of the room.

Haven approximated man's half-forgotten birthplace. It was Earth, but an Earth glamourized and inaccurately remembered. It was a gigantic half dome honeycombed with cells that made a shell arched over a great public room below. Each cell could be blocked off, or a rearrangement of penetrating rays could give you the illusion of being in the midst of an immense, crowded room. Or you could use the architect's original plan and enjoy the illusion of a terrestrial background.

True, palms and pines seemed to grow out of the same surrogate soil, grapes and roses and blossoming fruit trees shouldered one another; but since these were merely clever images they did not matter except to the purist. And only scholars really knew the difference. Seasons had become an exotic piece of history.

It was a strange and glamorous thought – the rhythmic equinoxes, earth's face changing from green and brown to glittering blue-white, and then the magic of pale green blades pushing up and green buds breaking from the trees, and all hydroponics.

Kedre Walton and Sam Reed came to Haven. From the stage where they entered they could look up at that immense, shining hemisphere, crowded with glittering cells like fragments of a bright, exploded dream, shifting and floating, rising and falling in the intricate light-currents. Down below, very far away, was the bar, a serpentine black shape where men and women made centipede-legs for its twisting body.

Kedre spoke into a microphone. One of the circling cells moved in its orbit and bumped gently against the landing stage. They stepped inside, and the swaying underfoot told Sam that they were afloat again.

Leaning among cushions by the low table were a man and a woman. Sam knew the man by sight. He was Zachariah Harker, oldest of one of the great Immortal families. He was a big man, long-boned, fine of line, his face a curious mixture of – not age – but experience, maturity, contrasting with the ageless youth that kept his features fresh and unlined. He had a smoothness that came from within, smooth assurance, smooth courtesy, smooth and quiet wisdom.

The woman –

'Sari, my dear,' Kedre said, 'I've brought you a guest. Sari is my granddaughter. Zachariah, this is … I don't know his name. He wouldn't tell me.'

Sari Walton had the delicate, disdainful face that was apparently a family characteristic. Her hair was an improbable green-gold, falling with careful disorder loose over her bare shoulders. She wore a tight garment of the very fine fur of a landside beast, plucked down to the undercoat which was as short and thick as velvet and patterned with shadowy stripes like a tiger. Thin and flexible as cloth, it sheathed her tightly to the knees and lay in broad folds about her ankles.

The two Immortals looked up, surprise showing briefly on their faces. Sam was aware of a quick surge of resentment that they should be surprised. He felt suddenly clumsy, conscious of his thick body and his utter unlikeness to these aristocrats. And he felt, too, his immaturity. As a child resents his elders, Sam resented the superior knowledge implicit upon these handsome, quiet features.

'Sit down.' Kedre waved to the cushions. Stiffly Sam lowered himself, accepted a drink, sat watching the averted faces of his hosts with a hot resentment he did not try to hide. Why should he?

Kedre said, 'I was thinking of the Free Companion when I brought him here. He ... what *is* your name? Or shall I give you one?'

Sullenly Sam told her. She lay back among the cushions, the gold rings gleaming softly on her hand as she raised her drink. She looked at ease, gracefully comfortable, but there was a subtle tension in her that Sam could sense. He wondered if the others could.

'I'd better explain to you first, Sam Reed,' she said, 'that for twenty years now I've been in contemplation.'

He knew what that meant – a sort of intellectual nunnery, a high religion of the mind, wherein the acolyte retires from the world in an attempt to find – well, what is indescribable when found. Nirvana? No – stasis, perhaps, peace, balance.

He knew somewhat more of the Immortals than they probably suspected. He realized, as well as a short-lived mortal could, how complete the life that will span up to a thousand years must be. The character must be finely integrated, so that their lives become a sort of close and delicate mosaic, an enormous one, but made up of tiles the same size as those composing an ordinary life. You may live a thousand years, but one second is still exactly one second long at a time. And periods of contemplation were needed to preserve balance.

'What about the Free Companion?' Sam demanded harshly. He knew Robin Hale, last of the warriors, was very much in public interest just now. The deep discontent which was urging popular favor toward the primitive had caught up the Companion, draped him in synthetic glamour, and was eager to follow his project toward colonization of the landside.

Or they thought they were eager. So far most of the idea was still on paper. When it came to an actual struggle with the ravening fury that was continental Venus – well, realists suspected how different a matter that might turn out to be. But just now Robin Hale's crusade for colonization was enjoying a glowing, irrational boom.

'Do you think it could, Sam Reed?'

'What about him?' Zachariah Harker asked. 'It won't work.

Sam gave him a red-browed scowl. He snorted and shook his head, deliberately not troubling to answer aloud. He was conscious of a rising desire to provoke discord among these smoothly civilized Immortals.

'When I came out of contemplation,' Kedre said, 'I found this Free Companion's project the most interesting thing that was happening. And one of the most dangerous. For many reasons, we feel that to attempt colonization now would be disastrous.'

Sam grunted. 'Why?'

Zachariah Harker leaned across the table to set down his drink. 'We aren't ready yet,' he said smoothly. 'It will take careful planning, psychologically and technologically. And we're a declining race, Sam Reed. We can't afford to fail. This Free Companion project will fail. It must not be given the chance.' He lifted his brows and regarded Sam thoughtfully.

Sam squirmed. He had an uncomfortable feeling that the deep, quiet gaze could read more upon his face than he wanted anyone to read. You couldn't tell about these people. They had lived too long. Perhaps they knew too much.

He said bluntly, 'You want me to kill him?'

There was silence in the little room for a moment. Sam had an instant's impression that until he spoke they had not thought the thing through quite so far. He felt a swift rearrangement of ideas going on all about him, as if the Immortals were communicating with one another silently. People who have known each other for so many centuries would surely develop a mild ability at thought-reading, if only through the nuances of facial expression. Silently, then, the three Immortals seemed to exchange confidences above Sam's head.

Then Kedre said, 'Yes. Yes, kill him if you can.'

'It would be the best solution,' Zachariah added slowly. 'To do it now – today. Not later than forty-eight hours from now. The thing's growing too fast to wait. If we can stop him now, there's no one ready to step into his place as figurehead. Tomorrow someone might. Can you handle it, Sam Reed?'

Sam scowled at them. 'Are you all fools?' he demanded. 'Or do you know much more about me than I think?'

Kedre laughed. 'We know. It's been three days, my dear. Do you think I let myself get involved without knowing the man I was with? I had your name before evening of the first day. I knew your record by the next morning. It's quite safe to entrust a job like this to you. You can handle it and for a price you'll keep quiet.'

Sam flushed. He hated her consciously for the first time then. No man cares to be told he has been made a fool of.

'That,' he said, 'will cost you twice what it would cost anyone else in the Keep.' He named a very high price.

Zachariah said, 'No. We can get –'

'Please, Zachariah.' Kedre lifted her hand. 'I'll pay it. I have a reason.'

He looked at her carefully. The reason was plain on her face, and for an instant Zachariah winced. He had hoped the free-marriage she had stepped out of when she went into contemplation might be resumed very soon now. Seeing her eyes upon Sam, he recognized that it would not be soon.

Sari leaned forward and put her pale, narrow hand on his arm.

'Zachariah,' she said, warning and possessiveness in her voice. 'Let her have her way, my dear. There's time enough for everything.'

Grandmother and granddaughter, almost, mirror-images, exchanged a look in which Sam, who had missed nothing, thought he saw both rivalry and understanding.

Zachariah said, 'Look over there.' He moved his hand and the cell wall glowed into transparence. Floating a little distance off among the crowded cells was an enclosure in which a man sat alone. 'He's been there for two hours now,' Zachariah went on.

The cell drifted nearer. The man in it was thin, dark, frowning. He wore a dull brown costume.

'I know him by sight,' Sam said, and stood up. The floor rocked slightly at the motion. 'Drop me at the landing stage. I'll take care of him for you.'

At the long bar he found a vacant seat and ordered a drink. The bartender looked at him sharply. This was a rendezvous for the Immortals and the upper classes; it was not often that a man as squatly plebeian as Sam Reed appeared at the bar. But there was something about Sam's scowl and the imperiousness of his order that after a moment made the bartender mutter, 'Yes, sir,' rather sullenly and bring him his drink.

Sam sat there a long while. He ordered twice more and made the drinks last, while the great shell hummed and spun above him and the crowd filled the dome with music and a vast amorphous murmuring. He watched the floating cell with the brown figure inside drift aimlessly around the vast circle. He was waiting for the Immortal to descend, and he was thinking very fast.

Sam was frightened. It was dangerous to mix in the affairs of the Immortals even politically. To get emotionally involved was sheer suicide and Sam had no illusion about his chances for survival as soon as his usefulness was over. He had seen the look of mild speculation that Zachariah Harker turned on him.

When the Free Companion's cell drifted finally toward the landing stage, Sam Reed was there to meet it. He wasted no words.

'I've just been hired to kill you, Hale,' he said.

They were leaving Haven together an hour later when the Sheffield gang caught up with Sam.

Sam Reed would never have come this far in his career if he hadn't been a glib and convincing talker when he had to be. Robin Hale had certainly been a target for glib promotioners often enough since his colonizing crusade began to know how to brush them off. But here again the Harker blood spoke silently to its kindred Immortality in Hale, and though Sam credited his own glibness, it was the air of quiet conviction carried by his subsurface heritage which convinced the Free Companion.

Sam talked very fast – in a leisurely way. He knew that his life and Hale's were bound together just now by a short rope – a rope perhaps forty-eight hours long. Within those limits both were safe. Beyond them, both would die unless something very, very clever occurred to them. Sam's voice as he explained this carried sincere conviction.

This was the point at which the Sheffield boys picked him up. The two came out of the Haven portal and stepped onto the slow-speed ribbon of a moving Way. Then a deliberate press of the crowd separated them a bit and Sam, turning to fight his way back, saw too late the black bulb in the hand that rose toward his face and smelled the sickening fragrance of an invisible dust too late to hold his breath.

Everything about him slowed and stopped.

A hand slipped through his arm. He was being urged along the Way. Globes and lanterns made patches of color along the street until it curved; there they coalesced into a blob of hypnotic color. The Way slid smoothly along and shining, perfumed mists curled in fog-banks above it. But he saw it all in stopped motion. Dimly he knew that this was his own fault. He had let Kedre distract him; he had allowed himself to take on a new job before he finished an old one that required all his attention. He would pay now.

Then something like a whirlwind in slow motion struck across the moving belts of the Way. Sam was aware only of jostling and shouts and the thud of fists on flesh. He couldn't sort out the faces, though he saw the Free Companion's floating before him time and again in a sort of palimpsest superimposed upon other faces, dimly familiar, all of them shouting.

With a dreamlike smoothness he saw the other faces receding backward along the slower ramp while the lights slipped rapidly away at the edges of the highspeed Way and Robin Hale's hand gripped his arm.

He let the firmness of the hand guide him. He was moving, but not moving. His brain had ceased almost entirely to function. He knew only vaguely that they were mounting the ramp to one of the hydroponic rooms, that Hale was clinking coins into an attendant's hand, that now they had paused before a tank where a heavy, gray-green foliage clustered.

From far off Hale's voice murmured, 'It usually grows on this stuff. Hope they haven't sprayed it too well, but it's hardy. It gets in everywhere. Here!' A sound of scraping fingernails, a glimpse of bluish lichen crushed between Hale's palms and dusted in Sam's face.

Then everything speeded up into sudden accelerated motion timed to Sam's violent sneezes. A stinging pain began in his sinuses and spread through his brain. It exploded there, rose to a crescendo, faded.

Sweating and shaking, he found he could talk again. Time and motion came back to normal and he blinked streaming eyes at Hale.

'All right?' the Free Companion asked.

'I – I guess so.' Sam wiped his eyes.

'What brought that on?' Hale inquired with interest.

'My own fault,' Sam told him shortly. 'Personal matter. I'll settle it later – if I live.'

Hale laughed. 'We'll go up to my place. I want to talk to you.'

'They don't understand what they'll be facing,' the Free Companion said grimly. 'I can't seem to convince anyone of that. They've got a romantic vision of a crusade and not one in a thousand has ever set foot on dry land.'

'Convince me,' Sam said.

'I saw the Logician,' Hale began. 'The crusade was his idea. I needed – something. This is it, and I'm afraid of it now. It's got out of hand. These people are emotional dead-beats. They're pawing me like so many dogs begging for romance. All I can offer them is personal hardship beyond anything they can ever dream, and no hope of success for this generation or the next. That sort of spirit seems to have bred out of the race since we've lived in Keeps. Maybe the underwater horizons are too narrow. They can't see beyond them, or their own noses.' He grinned. 'I offer not peace but a sword,' he said. 'And nobody will believe it.'

'I've never been topside myself,' Sam told him. 'What's it like?'

'You've seen it in the projectors, relayed from planes *above* the jungles. So have most people. And that's the fallacy – seeing it from above. It looks pretty. I'd like to take a projector down into the mud and look up at all that stuff towering over and reaching down, and the mud-wolves erupting underfoot and the poison-vines lashing out. If I did, my whole crusade would fall flat and there'd be an end of the colonizing.' He shrugged.

'I've made a start, you know, in the old fort,' he said. 'The Doonemen had it once. Now the jungle's got it back. The old walls and barriers are deactivated and useless. All that great technology is dead now. Whole rooms are solid blocks of vegetation, alive with vermin and snakes and poison plants. We're cleaning that out, but keeping it clean – well, that's going to take more than these people have got. Why, the lichens alone will eat through wood and glass and steel and flesh! And we don't know enough about the jungle. Here on Venus the ecology has no terrestrial parallel. And it won't be enough simply to hold the fort. It's got to be self-supporting.'

'That'll take money and backing,' Sam reminded him. 'The Families are dead against it – now.'

'I know. I think they're wrong. So does the Logician.'

'Are you working alone on this?'

Hale nodded. 'So far I am.'

'Why? A good promotion man could get you all the backing you need.'

'No good promotion man would. It'd be a swindle. I believe in this, Reed. With me it *is* a crusade. I wouldn't trust a man who'd be willing to tackle it, knowing the truth.'

A beautiful idea was beginning to take voluptuous shape in Sam's mind. He said, 'Would you trust me?'

'Why should I?'

Sam thought back rapidly over how much of the truth he had already told Hale. Not too much. It was safe to go ahead. 'Because I've already risked my neck to warn you,' he said. 'If I'd gone ahead with the job Harker gave me, I'd be collecting a small fortune right now. I didn't. I haven't told you why yet. I guess I don't need to. I feel the way you do about colonizing. I could make some money out of promoting it – I won't deny that. But nothing like the money I could make killing you.'

'I've just told you the thing can't succeed,' Hale pointed out. But there was a light in his eyes and more eagerness in his manner than Sam had yet seen.

'Hooked!' Sam thought. Aloud, he said, 'Maybe not. All it needs is plenty of backing – and I mean plenty! I think I can provide that. And we've got to give the crusaders a substitute goal for the real one, something they think they can collect on in their lifetime. Something they *can* collect on. No cheating. Shall I try?'

Hale pinched his chin thoughtfully. At last he said, 'Come with me to the Logician.'

Sam hedged. He was afraid of the Logician. His own motives were not the kind that could stand the light of clear reason. But Hale, essentially romanticist as he was, had several centuries of experience behind him to bolster up his apparent naiveté. They argued for over an hour.

Then Sam went with him to see the Logician.

A globe spoke to them, a shining white globe on an iron pedestal. It said, 'I told you I can't foretell the future, Hale.'

'But you know the right answers.'

'The right answer for you may not be the right one for Sam Reed.'

Sam moved uneasily. 'Then make it two answers,' he said. He thought it was a machine speaking. He had let down his guard a trifle; machines weren't human. Willy-nilly, he had given the data it required. Now he waited uneasily, knowing the hours of his deadline were slipping away while Kedre and Harker waited for news of the Companion's death.

In the silver globe shadows swam, the distorted reflection of the Logician's long, sardonic face. Robin Hale could trace the likeness but he knew that to one who didn't know the secret the shadows would be meaningless.

'The Keep people aren't pioneers,' the Logician said unnecessarily. 'You need recruits from the reformatories.'

'We need good men,' Hale said.

'Criminals are good men, most of them. They're merely displaced socially or temporally. Any antisocial individual can be thoroughly prosocial in the right environment. Malcontents and criminals will be your best men. You'll want biologists, naturalists, geologists –'

'We'd have to pay tremendous sums to get even second-rate men,' Sam objected.

'No you wouldn't. You'd have to pay – yes. But you'll be surprised how many top-flight men are malcontents. The Keeps are too circumscribed. No good worker is ever happy operating at less than full capacity, and who in the Keeps has ever used more than a fraction of his ability since the undersea was conquered?'

'You think you can go ahead then?' Hale asked specifically.

'If you and Reed can get around this current danger – ask me again.'

'Hale tells me,' Sam put in, 'that the Logician disagrees with the Families about colonization. Why won't you help us against the Families, then?'

The shadows moved in the globe; the Logician was shaking his head.

'I'm not omnipotent. The Families mean well – as they see it. They take a long view. By intrigue and influence they do sway the Council decisions, though the Council is perfectly free. But the Families sit back and decide policy, and then see that their decisions are carried out. Nominally the councils and the governors run the Keeps. Actually the Immortals run them. They've got a good deal of social consciousness, but they're ruthless, too. The laws they promote may seem harsh to the short-lived, but the grandchildren of the apparent victims may live to thank the Families for their harshness. From the Families' viewpoint common good covers a longer period of time. In this case I think they're wrong.

'The race is going downhill fast. The Families argue we can't finance but one colonizing effort. If it fails we're ruined. We'll never try again. We won't have the materials or the human drive. We've got to wait until they give the word, until they're convinced failure won't happen. I say they're wrong. I say the race is declining faster than they think. If we wait for their word, we'll have waited too long …

'But the Families run this planet. Not the Logician. I've opposed their opinions too often in other things for them to believe me now. They figure I'm against them in everything.'

To Robin Hale it was an old story. He said impatiently when the voice paused, 'Can you give us a prognosis, Logician? Is there enough evidence in now to tell us whether we've got a chance to succeed?'

The Logician said nothing for awhile. Then a curious sound came from the globe. It was a chuckle that grew to a laugh which startled Hale and utterly astonished Sam Reed. That a machine could laugh was inconceivable.

'Landside will be colonized,' the Logician said, still chuckling. 'You've got a chance – a good chance. And a better chance, my friend, if this man Reed is with you. That's all I can say, Hale. I think it's enough.'

Sam froze, staring at the shadows swimming in the globe. All his preconceived ideas turned over in his head. Was the Logician after all a fraud? Was it offering them mere guesswork? And if it could be this wrong on the point of Sam's dependability, of what value was anything else it said?

'Thank you, Logician,' the Free Companion was saying, and Sam turned to stare anew at Robin Hale. Why should he thank a machine, and especially as faulty a machine as this had just proved itself to be?

A deep chuckle sounded from the globe as they turned away. It rose again to laughter that followed them out of the hall, wave upon wave of full-throated laughter that had something of sympathy in it and much of irony.

The Logician was laughing from the bottom of his lungs, from the bottom of his thousand-years' experience, at the future of Sam Reed.

'"If we can get around this current danger –"' Sam quoted the Logician. He was sitting beside a transparent plastic table, very dusty, looking at the Free Companion across it. This was a dim secret room the Slider owned. So long as they sat here they were safe, but they couldn't stay forever. Sam had a fair idea of how many of the Families' retainers were reporting on his movements and Hale's.

'Any ideas?' Hale asked.

'You don't seem much worried. What's the matter? Don't you believe me?'

'Oh, yes. I'll admit I mightn't believe just any man who came up to me in a crowd and said he'd been hired to kill me. It's easy to say, if you're working up to a favor. But I've rather been expecting the Families to do something drastic, and – I trust the Logician. How about it – have you any ideas?'

Sam looked at him from under scowling red brows. He had begun to hate Hale for this easy acquiescence. He wanted it. He needed it. But he didn't like Hale's motive. Hale wasn't likely to entrust the success or failure of his crusade to the doubtful integrity of a promoter, which was the role Sam aspired to now. Even though the Logician – moved by flawed logic – had pronounced favorable judgment and even though Hale trusted the Logician implicitly, there was another motive.

Robin Hale was an Immortal.

The thing Sam had sensed and hated in the Waltons and Harker he sensed and hated in Hale, too. A tremendous and supreme self-confidence. He was not the slave of time; time served him. A man with centuries of experience behind him must already have encountered very nearly every combination of social circumstance he was likely to encounter. He had a pattern set for him. There would have been time enough to experiment, to think things over carefully and try out this reaction and until the best treatment for a given set of circumstances would come automatically to mind.

It wasn't fair, Sam thought childishly. Problems that shorter-lived men never solved the infinitely resourceful Immortals must know backward and forward. And there was another unfairness – problems the ordinary man had to meet with drastic solutions or compromise Hale could meet simply by waiting. There was always, with the Immortals, that last, surest philosophy to fall back on: *This too, will pass.*

The Immortals, then, were random factors. They had extensions in time that no non-Immortal could quite understand. You had to experience that long, long life in order to *know* …

Sam drew a deep breath and answered Hale's question, obliquely enough.

'The Families – I mean specifically the Waltons and Harkers – won't strike overtly. They don't want to be publicly connected with your death. They're not afraid of the masses, because the masses have never organized. There's never been any question of a revolt, for there's never been any motive for revolt. The Families are just. It's only with intangibles like this colonizing crusade that a question may come up, and – I hope – that may make it a dangerous question for them. Because for the first time the masses really are organized, in a loose sort of way – they're excited about the crusade.' He squinted at Hale. 'I've got an idea about how to use that, but –' Sam glanced at the dusty televisor screen in the wall above them – 'I can't explain it yet.'

'All right.' Hale sounded comfortable and unexcited. It was normal enough, Sam told himself, with a suddenly quickened pulse as he realized consciously for the first time that to this man warfare – that glamorous thing of the dead past – was a familiar story. He had seen slaughter and wreaked slaughter. The threat of death must by now be so old a tale to him that he faced it with unshaken nerves. Sam hated him anew.

'Meanwhile' – he forced himself to speak calmly – 'I've got to sell myself to you on the crusading idea. Shall I talk awhile?'

Hale grinned and nodded.

'We've got the unique problem of fighting off converts, not recruiting them. We need key men and we need manpower. One's expendable. The other – you *can* protect your key men, can't you?'

'Against some dangers. Not against boredom. Not against a few things, like lichens – they can get into an air vent and eat a man alive. Some of the germs mutate under UV, instead of dying. Oh, it isn't adventure.'

'So we'll need a screening process. Malcontents. Technical successes and personal failures.'

'Up to a point, yes. What do you suggest?' The laconic voice filled Sam with unreasonable resentment. He had a suspicion that this man already knew most of the answers, that he was leading Sam on, like a reciting child, partly to test his knowledge, partly perhaps in the hope that Sam might have ideas to offer which Hale could twist to his own use. And yet – under the confidence, under the resourcefulness that all his experiences had bred, the man showed an unconquerable naïveté which gave Sam hope. Basically Hale was a crusader. Basically he was selfless and visionary. A million years of experience, instead of a few hundred, would never give him something Sam had been born with. Yes, this was worth a try …

'Of course, not all the failures will do,' he went on. 'We've got to find the reasons *why* they're malcontents. You had technicians in the old days, when the wars were going on?'

Hale nodded. 'Yes. But they had the traditions of the Free Companions behind them.'

'We'll start a new tradition. I don't know what. *Ad astra per aspera*, maybe.' Sam considered. 'Can you get access to the psych records and personal histories of those old technicians?'

'Some of them must have been saved. I think I can. Why?'

'This will come later, but I think it's our answer. Break down the factors that made them successful. The big integrators will do that. It'll give us the prime equation. Then break down the factors that make up the current crop of technicians – malcontents preferable. X equals a successful wartime technician, plus the equivalent of the old tradition. Find out who's got X today and give him the new tradition.

'It'll take careful propaganda and semantic build-up. All we need is the right channeling of public opinion now. Catchwords, a banner, a new Peter the Hermit, maybe. The Crusades had a perfect publicity buildup. I've given you a solution for your technicians – now about the manpower and the financial backing.' Sam glanced at the quiet Immortal face and looked away again. But he went on.

'We'll have to screen the volunteers for manpower, too. There are plenty of good men left in the human race. They won't all fold up at the first threat of danger. We'll set up a very rigid series of tests for every potential colonist. Phony them up if we have to. One set of answers for the public, another for us. You can't openly reject a man for potential cowardice, or the rest might not dare take the test. But we've got to know.'

'So far – good,' Hale said. 'What about money?'

'How much have you got?'

Hale shrugged. 'Pennies. I've got a foothold, cleaning out Doone Keep. But it'll take real money to keep the thing going.'

'Form a company and sell stock. People will always gamble. Especially if they get dividends – and the dividends they want aren't merely money. Glamour. Excitement. The romance they've been starved for. The reason they go in for secondhand thrills.'

'Will rejected volunteers buy stock?'

Sam laughed. 'I've got it! Every share of stock will pay a dividend of thrills. All the excitement of volunteering with none of the danger. Every move the colony makes will be covered by televisor – with a direct beam to the receiver of every stockholder!'

Hale gave him a glance in which anger and admiration were mingled. Sam was aware of a little surge of gratification at having startled the man into something like approval. But Hale's next reaction spoiled it.

'No. That's cheap. And it's cheating. This is no Roman holiday for the thrill-hunters. And I've told you it's hard work, not romance. It isn't exciting, it's drudgery.'

'It can be exciting,' Sam assured him. 'It'll have to be. You've got to make compromises. People pay for thrills. Well, thrills can be staged landside, can't they?'

Hale moved his shoulders uncomfortably. 'I don't like it.'

'Yes, but it *could* be done. Just in theory – is there anything going on landside right now that could be built up?'

After a pause, Hale said, 'Well, we've been having trouble with an ambulant vine – it's thermotropic. Body heat attracts it. Refrigerating units in our jungle suits stop it cold, of course. And it's easy to draw it off by tossing thermite or something hot around. It heads for that instead of us, and gets burned into ash.'

'What does it look like?'

Hale went into details. Sam sat back, looking pleased.

'That's the ticket. Perfectly safe, but it'll look ugly as the devil. That ought to help us screen out the unfit by scaring 'em off right at the start. We'll just have your men turn off their refrigerating units and stage a battle with the vines, while somebody stands by out of camera range with thermite ready to throw. We'll send out a message that the vines are breaking through – cover it with televisor – and that does it!'

'No,' Hale said.

'The Crusades started as a publicity stunt,' Sam remarked. But he didn't press the point just yet. Instead he mentioned the fact that both of them would be dead within thirty-six hours now unless something could be worked out. He had seen a flicker in the wall screen. It was time to bring up the next subject on the agenda.

'The Families could get rid of us both in ways that look perfectly innocent. A few germs, for instance. They've got us cold unless we do something drastic. My idea is to try a trick so outrageous they won't know how to meet it until it's had a chance to work.'

'What do you mean?'

'The Families depend tremendously on their own prestige to maintain their power. Their real power is an intangible – longevity. But public faith in their infallibility has kept them on top. Attack that. Put them in a spot where they've got to *defend* us.'

'But how?'

'You're a public darling. Harker gave me a forty-eight hour deadline because he was afraid you might turn up a henchman at any moment who could step into your shoes and carry on the crusade even if he got you out of the way.' Sam tapped his own chest. 'I'm the man. I've got to be, to save my own skin. But it offers you an out, too. We halve the danger if either of us is replaceable – by the other. It wouldn't solve anything to kill either of us if the other lives.'

'But how the devil do you expect to make yourself that important to the public in the few hours you've got left?' Hale was really interested now.

Sam gave him a confident grin. Then he kicked the leg of his chair. An opening widened in the hall and the Slider came in, sniffling.

He lowered his great bulk to a chair and looked curiously at Hale. Sam said, 'First – the Sheffield gang's after me. I can't afford to fight it out right now. Got something really big on the fire. Can you call 'em off?'

'Might manage it,' the Slider said. It was a guarantee. The old poison-master was still a top danger in the underworld of the Keeps.

'Thanks.' Sam turned in his chair to face the Slider. 'Now, the important thing. I need a quick job of sound-track faking.'

'That's easy,' the Slider assured him, and sniffled.

'*And* the faces to match.'

'That's harder. Whose faces?'

'Zachariah Harker, for one. Any other Harkers or Waltons you've got on file, but Zachariah first.'

The Slider stared harder at him, forgetting for the moment even to sniffle. '*Harkers?*' he demanded. And then chuckled unexpectedly. 'Well, guess I can swing it, but it'll cost you. How soon you want the job done?'

Sam told him.

Faking a sound-track was an immemorially old gag, almost as old as sound-tracks themselves. It takes only nominal skill to snip out and rearrange already spoken words into new sequences. But only recently had a technique been developed for illicit extensions of the idea. It took a very deft operator, and a highly skilled one, to break down speech-sounds into their basic sibilants and gutturals and build up again a whole new pattern of speech. It was not usually possible to transpose from one language to another because of different phonetic requirements, but any recorded speech of reasonable length could usually be mined for a large enough number of basic sounds to construct almost any other recorded speech out of its building blocks.

From this it was, of course, only a step to incorporating the speaker visually into the changed speech. The lips that shaped each sound could be stopped in mid-syllable and the pictures transposed with the sounds.

The result was jerky to the ear and eye. There was always a certain amount of reducing and enlarging and adjustment to make the faces from various speeches into a single speech. Some experiments had even been made to produce a missing full-face view, for verisimilitude, by projecting onto a three-dimensional form the two-dimensional images of profile or three-quarter views to blend into the desired face, and photographing that anew. Afterward a high degree of skill was necessary to bend the result into convincing smoothness.

The Slider had access to a technician who knew the job forward and backward. And there were plenty of Harker and Walton records on file. But at best it was a dangerous thing to tamper with and Sam knew it. He had no choice.

It took five hours to talk Robin Hale into the hoax. Sam had to convince him of his own danger first; there were Family agents by now ringing in the building where they hid, so that wasn't too hard. Then he had to convince him of Sam's own trustworthiness, which Sam finally managed by rehearsing his arguments with the straps of a pressure gauge recording his blood-reactions for conscious lies. That took some semantic hedging, for Sam had much to conceal and had to talk around it.

'You and I are as good as dead,' he told Hale, with the recording needles holding steady, for this was true enough. 'Sure, this trick is dangerous. It's practically suicide. But if I've got to die anyhow, I'd as soon do it taking chances. And it's our only chance, unless you can think of something better. Can you?'

The Immortal couldn't.

And so on the evening telecast advance word went out that Robin Hale could make an important announcement about the colony. All through the Keeps, visors were tuned in on the telecast, waiting. What they were really waiting for was a moment when the Harkers and Waltons involved in the faked reel were together and out of the way.

The private lives of the Immortals were never very private, and the Slider had a network of interlocking connections that functioned very efficiently. Hale's influence kept the telecast schedule open and waiting, and presently word came that the Immortals involved were all accounted for.

Then on the great public screens and on countless private ones the driving color-ads gave place to Robin Hale's face. He was dressed for landside, and he spoke his lines with a reluctance and a haste to get it over that gave the words an air of unexpected conviction.

He said he had hoped to tell them in detail of the magnificent idea which his good friend Sam Reed had produced to make full-scale colonizing possible without delay. But trouble landside had just broken out and he had been called up to offer his experience as an old Free Companion to the men who were facing a new and deadly menace up above them all, on the jungle shore. Then he offered them a stiff quick salute and left the screen.

Zachariah Harker's face replaced Hale's. It would have taken a better than expert eye to detect the faint qualities of unevenness which might betray the fact that this was a synthesis of rearranged sound-waves and light-waves. Technically, even Zachariah, watching the screen from wherever he was just now, could not deny he had spoken the words, for every sound he heard and every motion of his own lips was genuine.

The synthetic speech was a triumph in semantics. It was typical of Sam that he should use this boldly suicidal venture not only to clear himself and Hale, if he could, but also to further his plans for the colony. So Harker was made to name Sam – brought forward with modest reluctance to stand beside the Immortal as the speech went on – as the public-spirited, adventurous philanthropist who was going to make the colonizing crusade possible.

Sam Reed, man of the people, short-lived but far-seeing, would lead his fellows to success behind Robin Hale in the great crusade. Landside lay the future of the race. Even the Harkers, Zachariah said, had finally been convinced of that by the persuasions of Sam and Hale. A great adventure lay ahead. Volunteers would be accepted for examination very soon. *Ad astra per aspera!*

He spoke of danger. He went into details, each word carefully chosen and charted to make the listeners discontented. He hinted at the stagnation of the Keeps, of growing racial debility, new vulnerabilities to disease. And most important – man had stopped growing. His destiny was no longer to be found in the Keeps. The great civilizations of Earth must not reach a dead end under the seas of this fertile planet. *Ad astra!*

Zachariah's face left the screen. Sam stepped forward to clinch the matter, nervous and deeply worried under his calm. Now that he had actually done this, he quivered with belated qualms. What would the Harkers do when they discovered how fantastically they had been tricked? How outrageously their innermost convictions had been reversed and repudiated before all the Keeps, apparently in their own words! They must be moving already; the Families were geared to rapid action when the need arose. But what they would do Sam couldn't guess.

He spoke with quiet confidence into the screen. He outlined his ideas of offering the people themselves the opportunity to join in the crusade, financially if not personally. In deft words he referred to the hardships and dangers of landside; he wanted to discourage all but the hardiest from offering as personal volunteers. And to aid in that, as well as to provide a smash finale to his scheme, he made his great announcement.

Something which until today had been a plaything for the wealthy would now be offered to all who owned shares in the magnificent venture before mankind. Each participant could watch the uses to which his money was put, share almost at first hand in the thrills and perils of landside living.

Look!

On the screen flashed a dizzying view of jungle that swooped up toward the beholder with breathtaking swiftness. A ring of velvet-black mud studded the flowery quilt of tree-tops. The ring swung up toward the view and you could see an iridescent serpent slithering across the blackness. The mud erupted and a mud-wolf's jaws closed upon the snake. Blood and mud spattered wildly. Churning and screaming, the combatants sank from sight and the velvety pool quivered into stillness again except for the rings that ran out around it from time to time as bubbles of crimson struggled up and burst on the surface with dull plops which every listener in the Keeps could hear.

Sam thanked his audience. He asked their patience for a few days longer, until the first examination trials could be set up. He observed with arrogant humility that he hoped to earn their trust and faith by his service toward themselves and the Free Companion, who had left all such matters in his hands while Hale himself struggled up there on landside in the jungles he knew so well. We would all, Sam finished, soon be watching such struggles, with men instead of monsters enlisting our sympathy in their brave attempts to conquer Venus as our forebears once conquered Old Earth …

The Families did nothing.

It worried Sam more than any direct action could possibly have done. For there was nothing here he could fight. Profoundly he distrusted that silence. All telecast attempts to interview any of the Immortals on this tremendous subject which was uppermost, overnight, in every mind, came to nothing. They would smile and nod and refuse to comment – yet.

But the plans went on at breakneck rate. And after all, Sam told himself, what could the Harkers do? To deny the public this delightful new toy might be disastrous. You can't give candy to a baby and then snatch it away untasted without rousing yells of protest. The people of the Keeps were much more formidable than babies, and they were used to collapsing into paternalistic hands. Remove the support, and you might expect trouble.

Sam knew he had won a gambit, not the game. But he had too much to do just now to let the future worry him. All this was to be a swindle, of course. He had never intended anything else.

Paradoxically, Sam trusted the judgment of the Harkers. They thought this attempt would fail. Sam was sure they were right. Of course the Logician believed that colonizing *would* succeed, and the Logician normally should be right. How can a machine err? But the machine had erred, very badly, in its analysis of Sam himself, so it isn't strange that he disbelieved all its conclusions now.

The only way to make the scheme succeed as Sam intended it to succeed was to insure its failure. Sam was out this time for really big money. The public clamored to buy, and Sam sold and sold.

He sold three hundred per cent of the stock.

After that he had to fail. If he put the money into landside development there'd be nothing left over for the promoter, and anyhow, how could he pay off on three hundred per cent?

But on paper it looked beautiful. New sources of supply and demand, a booming culture rising from the underseas, shaking off the water from gigantic shoulders, striding onto the shore. And then interplanetary and interstellar travel for the next goal. *Ad astra* was a glorious dream, and Sam worked it for all it was worth.

Two months went by.

Rosathe, like all the other fruits of success, dropped delightfully into his arms. Sam closed all three of his apartments and with Rosathe found a new place, full of undreamed of luxuries, its windows opening out over the hydroponic garden that flourished as lavishly, though not so dangerously, as the jungles overhead. From these windows he could see the lights of the whole Keep spread out below, where every man danced to his piping. It was dreamlike, full of paranoid splendors, megalomaniac grandeur – and all of it true.

Sam didn't realize it yet, though looking back he would surely have seen, but he was spinning faster and faster down a vortex of events which by now were out of his control. Events would have blurred as they whirled by, if he had been given time enough to look back at them when the moment of reckoning came. But he was not given time …

Rosathe was sitting on a low hassock at his feet, her harp on her arm, singing very sweetly to him, when the moment finally came.

Her violet-blue skirts lay about her in a circle on the floor, her cloudy head was bent above the high horns of the lyre and her voice was very soft.

'Oh, slowly, slowly got she up, and slowly she came nigh … him …' How delightfully, the sweet voice soared on the last word! That dip and rise in the old ballads tried every voice but an instrument as true as the lovely instrument in Rosathe's throat. *'But all she said'* – Rosathe reported in that liquid voice – and was stopped by the musical buzzing of the televisor.

Sam knew it must be important, or it would never have been put through to him at this hour. Reluctantly he swung his feet to the floor and got up.

Rosathe did not lift her head. She sat quite motionless for an instant, curiously as if she had been frozen by the sound of the buzzer. Then without glancing up she swept the strings with polished fingertips and sang her final line. '*Young man, I think you're dyin'* ...'

The cloudiness of the visor screen cleared as Sam flipped the switch and a face swam out of it that rocked him back a bit on his heels. It was Kedre Walton's face, and she was very angry. The black ringlets whipped like Medusa-locks as she whirled her head toward the screen. She must have been talking to someone in the background as she waited for Sam to acknowledge the call, for her anger was not wholly for Sam. He could see that. Her words belied it.

'Sam Reed, you're a fool!' she told him flatly and without preamble. The Egyptian calm was gone from her delicate, disdainful face. Even the disdain was gone now. 'Did you really think you could get away with all this?'

'I've got away with it,' Sam assured her. He was very confident at that point in the progress of his scheme.

'You poor fool, you've never fought an Immortal before. Our plans work slowly. We can afford to be slow! But surely you didn't imagine Zachariah Harker would let you do what you did and live! He –'

A voice from behind her said, 'Let me speak for myself, Kedre, my dear,' and the smooth, ageless young face of Zachariah looked out at Sam from the screen. The eyes were quietly speculative as they regarded him. 'In a way I owe you thanks, Reed,' the Immortal's voice said. 'You were clever. You had more resources than I expected. You put me on my mettle, and that's an unexpected pleasure. Also, you've made it possible for me to overthrow Hale's whole ambitious project. So I want to thank you for that, too. I like to be fair when I can afford to be.'

His eyes were the eyes of a man looking at something so impersonally that Sam felt a sudden chill. Such remoteness in time and space and experience – as if Sam were not there at all. Or as if Harker were looking already on death. Something as impersonal and remote from living as a corpse. As Sam Reed.

And Sam knew a moment's profound shaking of his own convictions – he had a flash of insight in which he thought that perhaps Harker had planned it this way from the start, knowing that Sam would doublecross Hale, too. Sam was the weak link in Hale's crusade, the one thing that might bring the whole thing crashing if anyone suspected. Until now, Sam had been sure no one did suspect.

But Zachariah Harker knew.

'Good-by, Reed,' the smooth voice said. 'Kedre, my dear –'

Kedre's face came back into the screen. She was still angry, but the anger had been swallowed up in another emotion as her eyes met Sam's. The long lashes half veiled them, and there were tears on the lashes.

'Good-by, Sam,' she said. 'Good-by.' And the blue glance flickered across his shoulder.

Sam had one moment to turn and see what was coming, but not time enough to stop it. For Rosathe stood at his shoulder, watching the screen, too. And as he turned her pointed fingers which had evoked music from the harp for him this evening pinched together suddenly and evoked oblivion.

He felt the sweet, terrifying odor of dust stinging in his nostrils. He stumbled forward futilely, reaching for her, meaning to break her neck. But she floated away before him, and the whole room floated, and then Rosathe was looking down on him from far above, and there were tears in her eyes, too.

The fragrance of dream-dust blurred everything else. Dream-dust, the narcotic euthanasia dust which was the way of the suicide.

His last vision was the sight of the tear-wet eyes looking down, two women who must have loved him to evoke those tears and who together had worked out his ruin.

He woke. The smell of scented dust died from his nostrils. It was dark here. He felt a wall at his shoulder, and got up stiffly, bracing himself against it. Light showed blurrily a little way off. The end of an alley, he thought. People were passing now and then through the dimness out there.

The alley hurt his feet. His shoes felt queer and loose. Investigating, Sam found that he was in rags, his bare feet pressing the pavement through broken soles. And the fragrance of dream-dust was still a miasma in the air around him.

Dream-dust – that could put a man to sleep for a long, long while. *How long!*

He stumbled toward the mouth of the alley. A passer-by glanced at him with curiosity and distaste. He reached out and collared the man.

'The Colony,' he said urgently. 'Has it – have they opened it yet?'

The man struck his arm away. 'What colony?' he asked impatiently.

'The Colony! The Land Colony!'

'Oh, that.' The man laughed. 'You're a little late.' Clearly he thought Sam was drunk. 'It's been open a long time now – what's left of it.'

'How long?'

'Forty years.'

Sam hung on the bar of a vending machine in the wall at the alley mouth. He had to hold the bar to keep himself upright, for his knees were strengthless beneath him. He was looking into the dusty mirror and into his own eyes. 'Forty years. Forty years!' And the ageless, unchanged face of Sam Harker looked back at him, ruddy-browed, unlined as ever.

'Forty years!' Sam Harker murmured to himself.

PART TWO

And indeed there will be time
For the yellow smoke that slides along the street,
Rubbing its back upon the window panes;
There will be time, there will be time
To prepare a face to meet the faces that you meet,
There will be time to murder and create,
And time for all the works and days of hands
That lift and drop a question on your plate …

– *T. S. Eliot*

The city moved past him in a slow, descending spiral. Sam Harker looked at it blankly, taking in nothing. His brain was too filled already to be anything just now but empty. There was too much to cope with. He could not yet think at all. He had no recollection to span the time between the moment when he looked into his impossibly young face in the glass, and this current moment. Under his broken soles he felt the faint vibration of the Way, and the city was familiar that moved downward beneath him in its slow sweep, street after street swinging into view as the spiral Way glided on. There was nothing to catch hold of and focus, no way to anchor his spinning brain.

'I need a shot,' he told himself, and even the thought came clumsily, as if along rusty channels where no thought had moved before in forty drugged years. But when he tried his ragged pockets, he found them empty. He had nothing. No credits, no memory, not even a past.

'Nothing?' he thought foggily. 'Nothing?' And then for the first time the impact of what he had seen in the mirror struck him hard. *'Nothing? I'm immortal!'*

It could not be true. It was part of the dream-dust fantasy. But the feel of his own firm cheek and hard, smooth neck muscles beneath his shaking fingers – that was no fantasy. That was real. Then the idea of forty years gone by must be the unreality. And that man at the alley-mouth had lied. Looking back now, it seemed to Sam that the man had looked at him oddly, with more than passing interest. He had assumed the man was a passer-by, but when he forced his rusty brain to remember, it seemed to him that the man had been standing there watching him, ready to go or to stay according to the cue Sam's conduct gave him.

He groped for the memory of the man's face, and found nothing. A blur that looked at him and spoke. But looked with clinical interest, and spoke with purpose and interest beyond the casual. This was the first coherent thought that took shape in the dimness of Sam's brain, so the stimulus must have been strong. The man must have been there for a reason. For a reason concerned with Sam.

'Forty years,' Sam murmured. 'I can check that, anyhow.'

The city had not changed at all. But that was no criterion. The Keeps never changed. Far ahead, towering above the buildings, he saw the great globe of dead Earth in its black plastic pall. He could orient himself by that, and the shapes of the streets and buildings fell into familiar place around him. He knew the city. He knew where he was, where his old haunts had been, where that lavish apartment had looked down over these glittering ways, and a girl with blue eyes had blown dust in his face.

Kedre's face swam before him in the remembered screen, tears in the eyes, command in the gesture that brought about his downfall. Kedre and Rosathe. He had a job to do, then. He knew Kedre's had not really been the hand behind that poison dust, any more than Rosathe's had been. Zachariah Harker was the man who gave the orders here. And Zachariah would suffer for it. But Kedre must suffer too, and as for Rosathe – Sam's fingers curved. Rosathe he had trusted. Her crime was the worst – betrayal. Rosathe had better die, he thought.

But wait. Forty years? Had time done that job for him already? The first thing he must learn was the date of this day on which he had awakened. The moving street glided toward one of the big public newscast screens, and he knew he could check the date on that when it came into view. But he thought he did not really need to. He could *feel* time's passage. And though the city had not changed, the people had, a little. Some of the men near him were bearded, so that much was new. Clothes had a more extreme cut than he remembered. Fashions change in rhythm with changed social orders, not meaninglessly but in response to known patterns. He could work it out from that alone, he thought, if his mind were clearer and there was no other way to learn.

The Way swung round slowly so that a corner of the newscast screen loomed into view, and Sam noticed how few faces around him turned toward it. He could remember a time when every neck craned and people jostled one another in their hurry to read the news a little faster than the moving Way would let them. All that was over now. Apathy in direct and easily understood contrast to the extreme new styles showed upon every face. Sam was the only one here who craned to see the big screen.

Yes, it had been forty years.

There was something like a bright explosion in the center of his brain.

Immortality! Immortality! All the possibilities, all the dangers, all the glories lying before him burst outward in one blinding glow. And then the glow faded and he was afraid for a moment of maturity's responsibilities – this new, incredible maturity so far beyond anything that he had ever dreamed of before. And then the last doubts he would feel about this wonderful gift assailed him, and he searched his memory frantically for knowledge of some drug, some treatment that could produce a catalepsy like this, ageless over a span of forty years. He knew of none. No, it must be real. It could not be, but it was true.

It would wait. Sam laughed dryly to himself. This of all things would most certainly wait. There were more urgent things to think of. Something magical had happened to him, and the result was forty years of sleep and then immortality. But what had that something been?

Dream-dust. The remembered fragrance of it was still in his nostrils, and there was an ominous dry thirst beginning to assert itself beneath his tongue, a thirst no liquid would assuage.

I've got to get cured. First of all, I've got to get cured.

He knew dream-dust. It wasn't incurable, but it was habit-forming. Worse than that, really, because once you went under the deadly stuff you didn't come out again. There were no rational periods during which you could commit yourself for cure. Not until the organism built up antibodies, and that took almost a lifetime. Even then the dream-dust virus could mutate so rapidly that the rational term didn't last. You dropped back into dreams, and eventually, you died.

Panic struck Sam for a moment. How long would this rationality last? How long had it lasted already? At any time now would the dusty dreams strike again and his newly emerged identity go under? Immortality was useless if he must sleep it all away.

He had to get cured. The thirst mounted now as he recognized it for what it was, a darker thirst than the average man ever knows. The cure took money. Several thousand korium-credits, at least. And he had nothing. He was rich beyond dreams of avarice if this immortality meant what he believed it meant, but the wealth of his endless years might vanish in any instant now because he had no material wealth at all. Paradox. He owned centuries of the future, but for the lack of a few current hours he might be robbed of his treasure laid up in time.

Panic was no good. He knew that. He forced it down again and considered very quietly what he had to do. What he had to learn. How to go about it. Two things were paramount – his immortality and his dream-dust addiction.

Money.

He hadn't any.

Immortality.

That was an asset quite apart from the future it promised, but he didn't yet know how to spend it most wisely. So – keep it a secret.

How?

Disguise.

As whom?

As himself, of course. As Sam Reed, but not Sam Reed Immortal. Sam as he should have looked at the age of eighty. This tied in with the money angle. For the only way to get money was to return to his old haunts, his oldest practices. And he must not throw away his most precious secret there. Already a dim stirring in his brain hinted at the wonderful use he might make of this secret. Time enough for that later. Time in spilling-over plenty, if he could salvage it soon enough.

But first, a little money, a little knowledge.

Knowledge was easier and safer to acquire. It came first. He must learn immediately what had been happening in the past four decades, what had happened to himself, whether he had dropped out of the public attention, when and how. Clearly he was no longer a public figure, but where he had been the past forty years was still a question.

He stepped off onto a cross-Way and let it carry him toward the nearest library. On the way he considered the problem of money. He had been a very rich man when Rosathe blew the dream-dust in his face. Some of the credits were in his own name, but four caches privately hidden held most of the fortune. It seemed likely that at least one still remained secret, but whether he could collect the money in any identity but his own remained to be seen. That had waited forty years – it would wait a few hours longer.

He had not even the few cents required to buy the privacy of a room or a booth at the library, but he seated himself at one of the long tables and bent forward, hiding his face between the sound-absorbent wings that jutted out from the middle-partition. He lowered his eyes to the viewpiece of the visor. He touched control buttons and waited.

A general newscast forty years old unrolled itself on the magnified screen below him. It was a weekly summary that covered the last seven days he could remember.

Rip van Winkle could have helped his own disorientation by reading a twenty-year-old newspaper. It wouldn't have told him what had happened since he slept, but it would have restored the firmness of the world he woke in. In all the Keep, in all the planet, this odd newscast was the only thing that could have put solidity under Sam Reed's feet. Outside the library danger and unfamiliarity waited everywhere, because the frames of reference had changed so much.

The little things change most – fads, fashions, slang – and lapses from that superficial norm are instantly noticed. But a lapse from a basic can often remain undetected.

Sam watched the past unroll which seemed so vividly the present that he could almost smell dream-dust puffed freshly in his face from Rosathe's hand. When he thought of that the dryness of his thirst suddenly choked him, and he remembered anew how urgent his need for haste was. He pressed his forehead to the viewpiece and sped the roll faster.

SAM REED DREAM-DUSTS! The thin voice from the past shrilled ghostlike in his ears while the tri-di pictures moved swiftly by. *Sam Reed, promoter behind the Land Colony, today gave up his career and dream-dusted, amazing everyone who knew him ... found wandering through the city ...*

It was all there. The investigation that followed his apparent suicide, the scandal as his swindle began to emerge. Four days after Sam Reed disappeared, after a dozen reputable witnesses saw him under the influence of dream-dust, the Colony bubble burst.

Robin Hale, the Free Companion, had no answer to make. What could he say? Three hundred per cent of the stock had been sold, speaking louder than any words of the fact that the Colony's promoters had known it could not succeed. Hale did the only thing he could do – tried to weather the storm as he had weathered so many in his long lifetime, man-made storms and the violent tornadoes of landside. It was impossible, of course. Emotions had been strung too high. Too many men had believed in the Colony.

When the bubble burst, little remained.

Sam Reed's name bore the brunt of the opprobrium. Not only was he a swindler, but he had run out – given up completely and lost himself in the suicidal escape of dream-dust. No one seemed to wonder why. There was no logic behind such a step. But publicity-wise minds behind the telling of the story wasted no time that might give people a chance to think the thing out. If the Colony was foredoomed to failure, Sam had only to wait to collect his illicit three hundred per cent in safe secrecy. His suicide might have argued that he feared the Colony would succeed – but no one thought of that. It seemed only that, fearing exposure, he took the quickest way out.

Investigation followed him, back-tracked and discovered the caches of swindled money that he hadn't concealed quite cleverly enough. Not against the deductive technology of the Keeps and the Immortals. They found the four caches and emptied them – all of them. The old newscasts gave details.

Sam leaned back and blinked in the dim air of the library. Well, he was broke, then.

He could see the hands of the Harker Family moving behind this four-decade-old game. Zachariah's face came back to him like something seen an hour ago, smooth and smiling in the visor screen, remote as a god's face watching ephemeral mortals. Zachariah had known exactly what he was doing, of course. But that was only the start of the game. Sam was a pawn to be used and discarded in the opening move. He turned back to the newscast to learn how the rest of the moves had been carried out.

And he was surprised to find that Robin Hale went ahead and started the Land Colony, in the face of the lack of all popular support – in the face of actual enmity. He had only one weapon. He still had the granted charter, and they couldn't take that away from him, especially since the money Sam stole had been recovered. Doggedly, Hale must have forged ahead, laying his long-term plans as the Families laid theirs, looking forward to the time when these petty scandals would have blown past and he could start anew with a fresh generation and fight the Families to win this generation over as he had won the last – for a while.

Yes, the Colony was started. But remarkably little news had been recorded about it. There was a spectacular murder in Delaware Keep and then a new play was produced that had all undersea Venus scrambling for tickets, and presently Sam found week after week of newscast spinning by with only the briefest references to the fact that a Colony had been started.

That was deliberate, of course. The Harkers knew what they were doing.

Sam stopped the newscast and thought. He would have to rearrange his tentative plans, but not much. He still needed money – fast, He swallowed dryly against the drug-thirst. The cached money was gone. What remained? Only himself, his experience, his priceless secret that must not yet be squandered – and what else? The old land charter issued in his name forty years ago was still on file, he assumed, since the charters were irrevocable. He couldn't claim it in his own name, and in any other name it would be invalid. Well, deal with that later.

Right now – money. Sam's lips tightened. He got up and left the library, walking lightly, seeking a weapon and a victim. He couldn't get two or three thousand credits by robbery without taking long risks, but he could manage a simple blackjacking up an alley for twenty or thirty credits – if he was lucky.

He was lucky. So was the man he stunned, whose skull didn't crack under the impact of a sock filled with pebbles. Sam had taken careful stock of himself, and was surprised to find that physically he seemed to be in better shape than he had any right to expect. Most dream-dust victims are skin-and-bone mummies by the time they die. It raised another mystery – what sort of life had he been leading during these forty dreaming years?

Memory of the man in the alley where Sam woke returned bafflingly. If he had only been clear-headed enough to keep his grip on that collar until he could shake the information he needed out of the watcher who had stood waiting above him. Well, that would come, too, in its time.

With forty-three credits in his pocket, he headed for a certain establishment he had known forty years ago. The attendants there kept their mouths shut and worked efficiently, in the old days, and things did not change fast in the Keeps. He thought they would still be there.

On the way he passed a number of big new salons where men and women were visible being embellished to a high point of perfection. Apparently the demand had increased. Certainly more foppery was evident in the Keep now. Men with exquisitely curled beards and ringlets were everywhere. But privacy and discretion were necessary to Sam's purpose. He went on to his semi-illegal establishment, and was not surprised to find it still in business.

His nerve shook a little as he paused before the entrance. But no one had recognized him on the Ways, apparently. Forty years ago his televised face had been thoroughly familiar in the Keeps, but now –

Rationalization is a set pattern in men's minds. If they looked at him and saw familiarity, they decided automatically that it was a remarkable likeness, no more. The unconscious always steers the conscious toward the most logical conclusion – the one grooved by channels of parallel experience. Sometimes striking resemblances do occur; that is natural. It was not natural to see Sam Reed as he had looked forty years before, moving along a Way. And many of those he passed had been unborn at the time of the Colony fiasco, or had seen Sam Reed with the indifferent eyes of childhood. Those who might remember were old now, dim-sighted, and many faces in public life had superimposed themselves on these failing memories since then.

No, he was safe except for random chance. He went confidently through the glass door and gave his orders to the man assigned to him. It was routine enough.

'Permanent or temporary?'

'Temporary,' Sam said, after a brief pause.

'Quick-change?' There was a call for emergency quick-changes of disguise among the establishment's clientele.

'That's right.'

The artist went to work. He was an anatomist and something of a psychologist as well as a disguise expert. He left Sam's pate bald, as directed; he dyed and bleached the red brows and lashes to pepper-and-salt that could pass for either dark or light, depending on the rest of the ensemble. With the beard, they passed for grimy white. The beard was a dirty, faded mixture.

He built up Sam's nose and ears as time would have built them had it touched Sam. He put a few wrinkles in the right places with surrogate tissues. The beard hid most of Sam's face, but when the artist had finished eighty years of hard living looked out above its grayish mask.

'For a quick change,' he said, 'take off the beard and change your expression. You can't remove the surrogate quickly, but you can iron out those wrinkles by the right expression. Try it, please.' He wheeled Sam's chair around to the mirror and made him practice until both men were satisfied.

'All right,' Sam said finally. 'I'll need a costume.'

They settled on three things only – hat, cloak, shoes. Simplicity and speed were the factors behind the choice. Each item was a special article. The hat could be completely altered in shape by a pull and a twist. The cloak was opaque, but of a texture so thin it could be crumpled and stuffed into a pocket. It was weighted to hang straight when worn, to hide the fact that the body beneath was not an old man's body. Sam had to practice the proper gait. And the shoes were nondescript in color, like the hat, but their large, dull buckles could be opened to release puffy blue bows.

Sam went out by the back way. Moving stiffly, like one who felt the weight of his eighty years, he returned to the library. He was a remarkably well-preserved eighty, he concluded, watching his reflection in windows as he passed, a hale and hearty old man, but old – old. It would do.

Now he wanted to study the current crime news.

In a way the criminal classes are agrarian – if you look at them over a span as broad as Sam's. They move as they feed, drifting from pasture to greener pasture. The Blue Way had been a skid-row forty years ago, but no more, Sam realized, listening to reports from the telecast. As for the crimes themselves, they hadn't altered much. That pattern was basic. Vice, through the ages, changes less than virtue.

Finally he located the present green pasture. He bought a vial of water-soluble red dye and a high-powered smoke bomb. The instructions on the bomb told how to use it in hydroponic gardens to destroy insect pests. Sam didn't read them; he had used these bombs before.

Then he had to locate the right place for his trap.

He needed two alleys, close together, opening on a Way not too well-traveled. In one of the alleys was a cellar Sam remembered. It was deserted now, as in the old days. He hid near the entrance several fist-sized chunks of metal he had picked up, and he made a hiding-place for the smoke bomb in the cellar. After that he was ready for the next step.

He did not let himself think how many steps the stairway contained altogether. When he thought of that, he remembered that he had all the time he needed – now! – and that sent him into drunken, elated dreams far divorced from the immediate necessity of redeeming his future. Instead, he reminded himself on his drug-addiction and the need for money and curative treatment.

He went to the current green pasture and drank rotgut whisky, the cheapest available. And he kept in mind always the fact that he was a very old man. There were little tricks. He remembered never to fill his lungs with air before speaking; old men are short of breath and their voices lack resonance. The result was convincing. Also he moved slowly and carefully, making himself think of each move before he made it. A hobble doesn't indicate age, but action that is the result of old thought-processes does indicate it. The old have to move slowly because it's necessary to consider whether the stiff legs and weak muscles can manage obstacles. The world is as dangerous to the very old as to the very young, but a baby doesn't know the peril of gravity.

So Sam didn't creak or hobble. But he didn't seem to have much breath and he apparently wasn't conditioned to fast moving any more – and it was an old man who sat in Gem o' Venus drinking rotgut and getting quietly drunk.

It was a dive. A colorful dive, just as many of the dives of Imperial Rome must have been, the jetsam of costumes and customs drifting down from the higher levels, so that the eye caught here and there the flash of a gilded belt, the blood-brilliant scarlet of a feather-pierced cap, the swirl of a rainbow cloak.

But basically Gem o' Venus was for drinking and gaming and more sordid uses. In the upper levels men gambled with fantastic devices, tricky so-called improvements on the ancient games of chance. There you might encounter such dubious streamlined tricks as roulette which employed a slightly radioactive ball and Geiger counters; there you had the game of Empire with its gagged-up cards and counters, where men played at winning imaginary galactic empires.

In Gem o' Venus there were some gadgety games too, but the basics remained constant – dice and cards. Faces were not familiar to Sam here, but types were. Some of the customers didn't care where they sat; others always faced the door. These interested Sam. So did a card game on the verge of breaking up. The players were too drunk to be wary. Sam picked up his drink and kibitzed. After a while he slid into the game.

He was rather surprised to find that the cards they were using were not the familiar pipped and face cards of the old days. They were larger, patterned with the esoteric pictures of the tarot. The old, old cards of Earth's cloudy past had been drifting back into favor in Sam's earlier life, but it was a little surprising to find they had reached such depths as these in forty years.

He had chosen these players carefully, so he was able to win without making it obvious, though the cards were distracting enough to lend verisimilitude to his game. It was confusing to play with pentacles and cups instead of diamonds and hearts, though, when you thought of it objectively, no more exotic.

These stakes weren't high, but Sam didn't expect to make his killing here. Cards were too uncertain, in any case. He needed only enough money to make an impression, and he managed to put over the idea that he had quite a lot more tucked away in his pockets. Shabbiness was no criterion of a man's financial status in this fluctuating half-world.

He let the game break up presently, protesting in his thin old voice. Then he made his way slowly out of Gem o' Venus and stood considering, letting himself sway a trifle. To the man who followed, it must have appeared as though libation had induced libration.

'Look, grandpa – want to sit in on another game?'

Sam gave him a wary glance. 'Floater?'

'No.'

Sam was pleased. The backer of a floating game might be too penny ante for his needs. He let himself be talked into it, remaining obviously wary until he found the destination wasn't a dark alley, but a third-rate gambling-and-pleasure house he remembered as a restaurant forty years past.

He was steered into poker, this time with more familiar cards. Playing against sober men, he tried no tricks, with the result that he lost what money he had and ended up with a stack of chips he couldn't pay for. As usual, Sam Reed had sold three hundred per cent of his stock issue.

So they took him to a man named Doc Mallard, a short, neckless man with curly fair hair and a face bronzed with scented skin-oil. Doc Mallard gave Sam a cold look. 'What's this about? I don't take IOUs.'

Sam had the sudden, strange realization that forty years ago this man had been a raw kid, learning the angles that he himself had mastered long before that. He knew a queer moment of toppling, almost frightening psychological perspective, as though, somehow, he looked down at Mallard from the enormous height of years. *He was immortal* –

But vulnerable. He let the drunkenness die out of his voice, but not the age. He said, 'Let's talk privately.' Mallard regarded him with a shrewdness that made Sam want to smile. When they were alone he said deliberately, 'Ever hear of Sam Reed?'

'Reed? Reed? Oh, the Colony boy. Sure. Dream-dust, wasn't it?'

'Not exactly. Not for very long, anyhow. I'm Sam Reed.'

Mallard did not take it in for a moment. He was obviously searching his memory for details of that long-ago scandal of his boyhood days. But because the Colony bubble had been unique in Keep history, apparently he remembered after a while.

'Reed's dead,' he said presently. 'Everybody knows –'

'I'm Sam Reed. I'm not dead. Sure, I dream-dusted, but that can be cured. I've been landside for a long time. Just got back.'

'What's the angle?'

'Nothing's in it for you, Mallard. I've retired. I just mentioned it to prove I'm good for my IOUs.'

Mallard sneered. 'You haven't proved a thing. Nobody comes back rich from landside.'

'I made my money right here, before I left.' Sam looked crafty.

'I remember all about that. The government found your caches. You haven't got a penny left from *that*.' Mallard was goading him.

Sam made his voice crack. 'You call seventy thousand credits nothing?' he cried in senile anger.

Mallard grinned at the ease with which he was trapping the old fool.

'How do I know you're Sam Reed? Can you prove it?'

'Fingerprints –'

'Too easy to fake. Eyeprints, though –' Mallard hesitated. Clearly he was of two minds. But after a moment he turned and spoke into a mike. The door opened and a man came in with a bulky camera. Sam, on request, looked into the eyepiece and was briefly blinded. They waited in silence, a long time.

Then the desk-mike buzzed before Mallard. Out of it a tinny voice said, 'O.K., Doc. The patterns check with the library files. That's your man.'

Mallard clicked the switch and said, 'All right, boys, come on in.' The door opened and four men entered. Mallard spoke to them over his shoulder. 'This is Sam Reed, boys. He wants to give us seventy-thousand credits. Talk him into it, will you?'

The four moved competently toward Sam Reed.

Third-degree methods hadn't changed much. Here along Skid Row you depended on the basic, physical pain, and generally it worked. It worked with Sam. He stood it as long as an old man might, and then broke down and talked.

There had been one bad moment when he was afraid his beard would come off. But the artist knew his business. The surrogate tissue stuck firm and would continue to do so until Sam used the contents of the bottle in his pocket, the bottle that looked like the stub of a stylus.

Breathing short and hard, he answered Doc Mallard's questions.

'I had – double cache. Opened with a korium key –'

'How much?'

'One point … one point three four –'

'Why haven't you got that seventy thousand before now?'

'I just … just got back from landside. They'd found – all the other caches. All but that – and I can't open it without the korium key. Where can – I get that much korium? I'm broke. Seventy thousand credits – and I can't buy the key to open the lock!' Sam let his voice break.

Mallard scratched his ear.

'That's a lot of korium,' he said. 'Still, it's the safest kind of lock in the world.'

Sam nodded with an old man's eager quickness at the crumb of implied praise. 'It won't open – without the exact amount of radioactivity focused on the lock. I was smart in the old days. You've got to know just the right amount. Can't stand the exposure – hit-or-miss. Got to know –'

'One point three four, eh?' Mallard interrupted him. He spoke to one of his men. 'Find out how much that would cost.'

Sam sank back, muffling his smile in his beard. It was a cold smile. He did not like Mallard or Mallard's methods. The old, familiar anger with which he had lived his forty earlier years was beginning to come back – the familiar impatience, the desire to smash everything that stood in his path. Mallard, now – he curled his fingers in the depths of his cloak, thinking how satisfying it would be to sink them into that thick, bronze-oiled neck.

And then a strange new thought came to him for the first time. Was murder satisfactory vengeance – for an Immortal? For him other methods lay open now. He could watch his enemies die slowly. He could let them grow old.

He played with the idea, biding his time. Time – how much of it he had, and how little! But he must take it step by step, until he could use his immortality.

One step at a time he went with the gang to the cache.

One stiff, eighty-year-old step at a time.

In the cellar, Sam reluctantly showed Doc where to expose the korium key. Korium was U233 – activated thorium – and definitely not a plaything. They didn't have much of it. Not much was needed. It was in a specially-insulated box, just too big to fit a man's pocket, and Doc had brought along a folding shield – the only protection necessary against a brief one-time exposure. He set it up at the spot Sam indicated.

There were four men in the cellar besides Sam – Doc Mallard and three of his associates. They were all armed. Sam wasn't. Outside in the alley, was another man, the lookout. The only preparation Sam had been able to make was to seize an opportunity to rub the 'defixer' liquid into the roots of his beard. That appendage would come off at a tug now.

It was so silent the sound of breathing was very audible. Sam began taking long breaths, storing the oxygen-reserve he would probably need very soon. He watched Mallard's careful adjustment of the shield and the korium box, which looked like an old fashioned camera, and, like a camera, had a shutter and a timing attachment.

'Right here?' Mallard asked, jabbing his finger at the plasti-brick wall.

Sam nodded.

Mallard pressed the right button and stepped back, behind the shield. *Click – click!*

That was all.

Sam said hastily, 'The cache is over here, where I said. Not by the lock.' He stumbled forward, reaching, but one of the men caught his shoulder.

'Just show us,' he said. 'There might be a gun stashed away with the dough.'

Sam showed them. Mallard tested the loose brick with his finger tips. He exhaled in satisfaction.

'I think –' he began – and pulled the brick toward him.

Sam drew a long breath and kept his eyes open just long enough to see the smoke-cloud begin to explode outward from the cache. With the tail-end of his glance he made certain of the korium box's location. Then he moved.

He moved fast, hearing the sound of startled voices and then the explosive *sssssh-slam* of a gun. The beam didn't touch him. He felt the sharp corners of the korium box against his palm, and he bent and used his free hand to pull another loose brick from the wall. The korium went into this emergency cache, and the brick slipped back easily into its socket.

'Hold your fire!' Mallard's voice shouted. 'Head for the door. *Pollard!* Don't come in here! Stop Reed –'

Sam was already at the door and had opened his eyes. He could see nothing at all in the thick smoke that was billowing across the threshold, but he could hear a plaintive query from the lookout – Pollard. He crouched, searching for the jagged lump of metal he had planted here. It was gone. No – he touched it; his fingers curled lovingly around the cold, hard alloy, and he brought his arm up and back as, through the thinning edges of the smoke, he saw Pollard.

The man's gun was out. Sam said, 'Where's Reed? Did he –'

That was enough. It made Pollard's finger hesitate on the trigger button, as he tried to make certain of the identity of the vague figure emerging from the smoke. Sam's weapon was already poised. He smashed it into Pollard's face. He felt the crunching of bone and he heard a muffled, choking bleat as Pollard arched backward and began to fall. Sam hurdled the body before it struck. He ran fourteen feet and whipped around the corner. Instantly he snatched off his cloak and beard. They went into his pockets, making no noticeable bulges. He was still running. He tore off his hat, twisted it deftly, and thrust it back on his head. It had a new shape and a different color. He dropped to the pavement and spun around, facing in the direction from which he had come. Two hasty motions opened the buckles on his shoes so that the bright bows leaped out, disguising them. There was no need for the surrogate red dye; he had blood on his hand – not his own. He wiped this across his mouth and chin.

Then he twisted his head and looked behind him, until he heard thudding footsteps.

Doc Mallard and one of his associates burst out of the alley mouth. They paused, staring around, and, as they saw Sam, sprinted toward him. Another man came out of the alley and ran after Mallard. His gun was out.

Sam dabbed feebly at his chin, blinked, and made a vague gesture behind him. He said, 'Wh … what –' His voice wasn't senile any more.

The fourth man came out of the alley. 'Pollard's dead,' he called.

'Shut up,' Mallard said, his mouth twisting. He stared at Sam. 'Where'd he go? The old man –'

'That passage up there,' Sam said, pointing. He – bumped into me from behind. I … my nose is bleeding.' He dabbed experimentally and eyed his wet fingers. 'Yes. That passage –'

Mallard didn't wait. He herded his men on and turned into the alley Sam had indicated. Sam glanced around. The Way wasn't crowded, but one man was coming crosswise toward Sam.

He got up and waved the good Samaritan back. 'It's all right,' he called. 'I'm not hurt.' Wiping the blood from his face, he started to walk away.

He turned back into the alley from which he had emerged. There was no special hurry. Mallard would be chasing an old man, and feeling certain he could overtake the slow-moving octogenarian. Later he would return to the cellar, but not immediately, Sam decided.

Smoke was still billowing out. He stumbled over Pollard's body, and that gave him the location of the door. Inside the cellar, he oriented himself in the darkness and then found the loose brick. He pried it out, removed the korium box, and replaced the brick. Carrying the korium, he went out, and thirty seconds later was on the fastest Way-strip, moving rapidly away from Doc Mallard and company.

What next?

Korium was negotiable. But not on a no-questions-asked basis. This loot would have to be disposed of through illegal channels. Sam was no longer recognizable as the old man who had bilked Mallard. Nevertheless, he dared not appear in this transaction – not until he had fortified his position. Mallard would be watching for an underground korium sale, and he would check back.

What channels would have remained unchanged after forty years?

The same ones – but administered by different individuals. That was no help, since in such transactions it was vital to know the right people. The right ones wouldn't be at the top any more – after forty years. Except, of course, the Harkers – the Immortal families. Sam grimaced and licked his lips, conscious again of the dry thirst under his tongue.

Who, then?

He rode the Ways for three hours, increasingly furious at this simple, easy problem that had him stopped cold. He had swindled Doc Mallard out of several thousand credits. He had the korium under his arm. But he had lost all his contacts.

Hunger grew, and thirst grew. He had no money at all. He had lost it all at the gaming table. To be distracted by such a trivial matter as hunger was infuriating. He was an Immortal!

Nevertheless Immortals could starve.

These petty details! There was so much to do, so much he could do now – an endless road opening down for his feet – and he couldn't do a thing till he got cured of the dream-dust addiction.

So, groping, he came at last to the one man who had stood *in loco parentis* to him many years before.

It was not surprising that the Slider still lived in the same dingy apartment in a corner of the Keep. What was surprising was the fact that the Slider still lived.

Sam hadn't expected that. He had expected it so little, unconsciously, that he hadn't put on his disguise again.

The Slider was in bed, a monstrously corpulent figure sagging the mattress, his dropsical face bluish. He sniffed painfully. His malevolent little eyes regarded Sam steadily.

'All right,' he wheezed. 'Come on in, kid.'

The room was filthy. In the bed the old man puffed and blinked and tried to prop himself upright. He gave up the impossible task and sank back, staring at Sam.

'Give me a drink,' he said, breathlessly.

Sam found a bottle on the table and uncapped it. The invalid drank greedily. A flush spread over the sagging cheeks.

'Woman never does anything I tell her,' he mumbled. 'What you want?'

Sam regarded him in distance and amazement. The monstrous creature seemed almost as immortal as the Immortals themselves, but a Tithonian sort of immortality that no sane man would covet. He must be close to a hundred years old now, Sam thought, marveling.

He stepped forward and took the bottle from the Slider's lax hand.

'Don't do that. Give it back. I need –'

'Answer some questions first.'

'The bottle – let's have it.'

'When you've told me what I want to know.'

The Slider groped among his dirty bedding. His hand came out with a needle-pistol half engulfed by the flesh. The tiny muzzle held steady on Sam.

'Gimme the bottle, kid,' the Slider said softly.

Sam shrugged and held it out, feeling reassured. The old man hadn't quite lost his touch, then. Perhaps he had come to the right place, after all.

'Slider,' he said, 'do you know how long since you saw me last?'

The shapeless lips mumbled a moment. 'Long time, son. Long time. Thirty – no, close on to forty years, eh?'

'But – you knew me. I haven't changed. I haven't grown older. And you weren't even surprised. Slider, you must have known about me. *Where have I been?*'

A subterranean chuckle heaved the great wallowing bulk. The bed creaked.

'You think you're real?' the Slider demanded. 'Don't be a fool. I'm dreaming of you, ain't I?' He reached out and patted an opalescent globe the size of a man's fist. 'This is the stuff, kid. You don't need to feel any pain no matter what ails you, long as you got Orange Devil around.'

Sam stepped closer, looking down at the bright powder in the globe.

'Oh,' he said.

The Slider peered up at him out of little shrewd eyes in their fat creases. The eyes cleared a bit as they stared. 'You're real, ain't you?' he murmured. 'Yes, I guess you are. All right, son, now I'm surprised.'

Sam eyed the orange powder. He knew what it was, yes. A drug of sorts, weakening the perception between objective and subjective, so that a man's mental images and ideations became almost tangible to him. The hope that had roused for a moment sank back in his mind. No, he was not likely to learn from the Slider where he had spent that vanished forty years.

'What's happened to you, Sam?' the Slider wheezed. 'You ought to be dead long ago.'

'The last thing I remember is having dream-dust blown in my face. That was forty years ago. But I haven't changed!'

'Dream-dust – that don't keep you young.'

'Is there anything that will? Any sort of preservation at all that could have kept me – like this?'

The bed heaved again with the enormous chuckling.

'Sure,' he said. 'Sure! Get yourself born of the right stock – you live a thousand years.'

'What do you mean?' Suddenly Sam found that he was shaking. Until now he had had no time to reason the thing out. He awoke, he was young when he should have been old – ergo, he was immortal. But how and why he had not yet considered. Out of some unconscious well of sureness, he had assumed that like the long-limbed Immortals, he, too, was the heir of a millennium of life. But all Immortals until now had been slender, tall, fine-boned...

'You've always been bald?' the Slider asked obliquely. At Sam's mystified nod he went on, 'Might have been sickness when you were a baby. Then it might not. When I first knew you, you had a few little scars here and there. They're mostly gone now, I see. But the Slider's smart, kid. I heard some talk a long time ago – didn't connect it with you till now. There was a woman, a medic, who did some work on a baby once and got herself a happy-cloak for pay.'

'What kind of work?' Sam asked tightly.

'Mostly glands. That give you any ideas?'

'Yes,' Sam said. His voice was thick. His throat felt tight and the blood throbbed in his temples and his neck. He took two forward steps, picked up a plastic chair and broke it across his knee. The tough plastic broke hard, cutting his hands a little, bruising his knee. The final snap at the chair gave way was satisfying. Not enough, but satisfying. With a tremendous effort he choked back his useless rage, fettering it as Fenris Wolf was fettered, to bide its time. Carefully he set down the chair and faced the Slider.

'I'm an Immortal,' he said. 'That's what it means. I'd have grown up like them if … if someone hadn't paid that medic. Who paid her?'

A vast seismographic shrug rippled the bedding. 'I never heard.' The Slider wallowed restlessly. 'Give me another drink.'

'You've got the bottle,' Sam pointed out. 'Slider – forget about this immortality. I'll take care of – everything. I came to you about something else. Slider, have you still got your contacts?'

'I'm still with it,' the Slider said, tilting the bottle.

Sam showed him the box he had taken from Mallard's men. 'This is korium. I want two thousand credits. Keep all you get above that. Make sure the transaction can't be traced.'

'Hijacked?' the Slider demanded. 'Better give me a name, so I can play it close.'

'Doc Mallard.'

The Slider chuckled. 'Sure, kid. I'll fix it. Shove that visor over here.'

'I'm in a hurry.'

'Come back in an hour.'

'Good. One thing more – you're the only one who knows I'm young.' Sam pulled the ragged beard from his pocket and dangled it.

'I get it. Trust the Slider, kid. See you in an hour.'

Sam went out.

At the hospital he would have to give a name. Would they recognize him as the old-time Colony swindler? Someone might. His eye-pattern records were on file, so must his other identifying marks be recorded. The average man, seeing a baffling familiarity in Sam, would chalk it up to some accidental resemblance. But in the sanitarium he would be under much closer observation. Too close to maintain the octogenarian disguise – that was certain.

Suddenly it occurred to Sam that there was one man who could very logically resemble him and yet seem the age he looked now. His own son.

He had none, it was true. But he might have had. And everyone knew that short physiques weren't Immortal, couldn't tap the fountain of youth. He could preserve his precious secret and get by with a minimal disguise as Sam Reed's son.

What name? Out of the depths of his omnivorous reading in those years which still seemed hardly an hour ago he dredged up the memory of the prophet Samuel, whose eldest son was Joel. *Now the name of his first-born was Joel.*

As good a name as any. He was Joel Reed …

Thirty-five minutes after that he stood before the hospital reception desk, shocked into immobility with surprise, able only to stare, while the circuits of his brain tried frantically to close their contacts again. But the disorientation was too abrupt and complete. All he could do was stand there, repeating stupidly, 'What? What did you say?'

The competent young man behind the desk said patiently, 'We discharged you as cured early this morning.'

Sam opened his mouth and closed it. No sound came out.

The young man regarded him thoughtfully. 'Amnesia?' he suggested. 'It hardly ever happens, but – do you want to see one of the doctors?'

Sam nodded.

'Six weeks ago,' the man in the quiet office said, 'you were brought here for the regulation cure. A man who gave the name of Evans delivered you and signed you in. He gave us no permanent address – said he was a transient at one of the hotels. You can try to trace him later if you like. The fee was paid anonymously, by special delivery, just before you arrived. You seemed in good physical condition on admission.' The doctor referred again to the ledger page before him. 'Apparently adequate care had been taken of you while you were dream-dusting. You were discharged this morning. You seemed quite normal. Another man called for you – not the same one, though he gave the name of Evans, too. That's all I can tell you, Mr Reed.'

'But' – Sam rubbed his forehead dazedly – 'why have I forgotten? What does it mean? I –'

'There are a good many amnesic preparations on the underworld market, unfortunately,' the doctor said. 'You left here in a suit of good clothes, with a hundred credits in your pocket. Did you wake with them?'

'No. I –'

'You were probably robbed.'

'Yes, I … of course that was it.' Sam's eyes went blank as he thought of the many ways in which a man might be rendered unconscious – a puff of dust in the face in some alleyway, a crack on the head. Robbers rarely bothered to stuff a stripped victim into their own discarded rags, but aside from that the story was plausible enough.

Except for that man who had been waiting when he woke.

He got up, still slightly dazed. 'If I could have the address the Evans man gave you –'

It would lead nowhere, he knew, looking down on the scrawled slip as the moving Way glided slowly beneath him, carrying him away from the hospital. Whoever was responsible for the chain of mysteries which had led him here would have covered any tracks efficiently.

Someone had fed him dream-dust forty years ago. Zachariah Harker –

that much he knew. Kedre Walton gave the signal, but Zachariah was the man behind her. *The voice is Jacob's voice, but the hand is the hand of Esau.*

Had Harker watched over him these forty years? Had Kedre? Someone did a careful job of it, according to the doctor. Someone paid to have him cured at last, and discharged – and robbed and stripped, so that when he woke he possessed materially as little as he had possessed when he came into the world.

Less – for then he came with a birthright. Well, of that they had not cheated him after all. And if there were a Joel Reed, Sam realized with a sudden gust of pride, he would stand head and shoulders above his father, on long, straight legs, slender and elegant as Zachariah himself – an Immortal in body as well as in heritage.

The stretching of his mind was almost painful as he surveyed the years before him. And when he thought now of the Slider he saw him through a new temporal perspective that was almost frightening. It was oddly similar to the attitude he might have toward a cat or a dog. There was always, and there must always be from now on, the knowledge that the life-span of an ordinary man was too short.

No wonder the Families had formed a tight clique. How could you feel deep friendship, or love untouched by pity, except for an equal? It was the old, old gulf between gods and men. Nothing – immortal – was alien.

That didn't solve his current problem. He was here on sufferance – by grace of somebody's indulgence. Whose? If only he had kept his grip on the collar of that man in the alley until his own wits returned to him! Someone had deliberately redeemed him from oblivion and set him free, penniless and in rags – why? To watch what he would do? It was a godlike concept. Zachariah? He looked around hopelessly at the uninterested crowds that moved with him along the Way. Did one of these faces mask an absorbed interest in his behavior? Or had his unknown guardian tired of the burden and set him on his own feet again, to go his own way?

Well, in time he would know. Or he would never know.

One excellent result of the past few hours was the money in his pocket, two thousand credits, free and clear. He had hurdled the next step without realizing it. Now there were a few old scores to settle, a few details to attend to, and then – Immortality!

He refused to think of it. His mind shrank from the infinite complexities, the fantastic personal applications of his new extended life. Instead, he concentrated on the two men named Evans who had shepherded him to and from the hospital. The Slider would start investigations on those – he made a mental note. Rosathe. The Slider would be useful there, too. Other things he would attend to himself.

His throat was dry. He laughed to himself. Not the pseudo-thirst of dream-dust, after all. He had simply played a trick on himself. Water could have quenched his thirst at any time, had he allowed himself to believe it. He stepped off the Way at the nearest Public Aid station and drank cool water, freshly cold, ecstatically quenching, until he could drink no more.

He looked up at the brightness of the Way, the towering buildings beyond, twinkling with lights, and something within him began to expand, growing and growing until it seemed the Keep could not contain this strange new vastness. He stared up at the impervium dome and pierced the shallow seas above it, and the clouds and the twinkling void beyond which he had never seen. There was so much to do now. And no need to hurry. He had time. All the time in the world.

Time to kill.

His bones are full of the sin of his youth, which shall lie down with him in the dust. Though wickedness be sweet in his mouth … – Job

He turned from his contemplation of the city and into the arms of the two men in uniform who had come up behind him on the Way platform. The uniforms had not changed – they were private government police and Sam knew before a word had been uttered that there was no point in trying to argue.

In a way he was rather more pleased than otherwise as the older of the two flashed an engraved plaque at him and said, 'Come along.' At least, someone else had finally made a tangible move. Perhaps now he would learn the answers to some of the questions that had been tantalizing him.

They took him along the high-speed Ways toward the center of the Keep. People glanced curiously at the three as the city flashed past around them. Sam held the railing to keep steady, aware of the unaccustomed flutter around his face as his red wig blew in the wind of their speed. He was watching with interest and anticipation the destination toward which they seemed headed.

The Immortals of every Keep lived in a group of high, colored towers built at the city's center and guarded by a ring of walled gardens. The police were taking Sam straight toward the tall, shining quarters of the Harker Family. Sam was not surprised. It seemed unlikely that Zachariah would have ordered his ruin forty years ago and then let him wander unguarded for the next forty. On the other hand, it seemed unlikely that Zachariah would have let him live at all. Sam shrugged. He should know the truth, soon.

They took him in through a small door at the back of the highest tower, down transparent plastic steps under which a stream of gray water flowed toward the gardens beyond. Red and gold fish went by with the stream, a long blue ribboneel, a strand of flowering seaweed.

At the foot of the steps a small gilded lift was waiting. The two policemen put

Sam into it, closed the door without a word behind him. He had a glimpse through the glass of their impassive faces sliding down outside; then he was alone in the gently sighing cage as it rose toward the height of the Harker tower.

The lift's walls were mirrored. Sam considered himself in the role of Joel Reed, feeling rather foolish about it, wondering whether whoever it was that waited for him above knew him already as Sam Reed. The disguise was good. He couldn't look exactly like his supposed father, but there was a naturally strong likeness. A red wig matched the heavy red brows, trimmed and smoothed a little now. A set of tooth caps altered the contour of his lower face. There were eye shells with bright blue irises instead of gray. Nothing else.

The eye shells served the same psychological purpose as dark glasses – unconsciously Sam felt himself masked. He could look out, but nobody could look in. It is difficult to meet a straight stare, unprotected, when you have something to hide.

The pressure on Sam's soles decreased; the lift was slowing. It stopped, the door slid open and he stepped out into a long hall whose walls and ceiling were a constant rustle of green leaves. A glow of simulated daylight poured softly through them from luminous walls. The vines sprang from hydroponic tanks under the floor and met in a trellislike tunnel overhead. Flowers and fruit swayed among the leaves in a scented, continuing breeze that soughed down the arbor. To a Keep-bred man it was exotic beyond all imagining.

Sam went warily down the silent hall, shrinking a little from the leaves that brushed his face. Like all Venus-bred people he feared and mistrusted by instinct the dangerous products of the landside world.

From the other end of the hall came the pleasant tinkle and splash of falling water. Sam paused on the threshold of the room upon which the trellis opened, staring in amazement.

This room was an arbor, too. Vines looped down festooned with clustering blossoms; the air was heavy with their fragrance. And the floor of the room was water. Blue water, a shallow lake of it perhaps a foot deep, filling the room from wall to wall. Flowers mirrored themselves in its surface, other flowers floated upon it. Tiny fish darted among their drifting leaves. A luminous jellyfish or two lay motionless on the blue water, dangling dangerous-looking jeweled webs.

There was a bridge of filigreed glass, insubstantial-looking as frost, that spanned the pool. One end lay at Sam's feet, the other at a low platform, cushion-covered, on the far side of the room. A woman lay face-down among the cushions, elbow on the edge of the pool, one arm submerged to the elbow as she splashed in the shining water. Her hair hid her face, its curled ends dipping in the ripples. The hair was a very pale green-gold, wholly unreal in its color and its water-smooth lustrousness.

Sam knew her. The long lines of Kedre Walton's body, her leisured motions, the shape of her head and her hands, were unmistakable even though the face was hidden. Why she should be here in the Harker stronghold, and why she had summoned him, remained to be seen.

'Kedre?' he said.

She looked up. Sam's mind spun dizzily for an instant. It was Kedre – it was not. The same delicate, narrow, disdainful face, with the veiled eyes and the secret Egyptian mouth – but a different personality looking out at him. A malicious, essentially unstable personality, he thought in his first glimpse of the eyes.

'No, I'm Sari Walton,' the pale-haired woman said, smiling her malicious smile. 'Kedre's my grandmother. Remember?'

He remembered. Sari Walton, leaning possessively on Zachariah's shoulder long ago, while Zachariah spoke with him about the murder of Robin Hale. Sam had scarcely noticed her then. He searched his memory quickly – antagonism was what returned to it first, antagonism between Sari and Kedre, submerged but potent as the two beautiful women watched each other across the table with mirror-image faces.

'All right,' he said. 'What does that mean?' He knew well enough. Joel Reed could not be expected to remember a scene in which Sam Reed had figured. She knew who he was. She knew, then, that he, too, was immortal.

'Come here,' Sari said, gesturing with a dripping white arm. She sat up among the cushions, swinging her feet around beneath her. Sam looked dubiously at the glass bridge. 'It'll hold you. Come on.' Derision was in Sari's voice.

It did, though it sang with faint music at the pressure of every step. At Sari's gesture he sank hesitantly to a seat among the cushions beside her, sitting stiffly, every angle of his posture rejecting this exotic couch, this fantastic, water-floored bower.

'How did you locate me?' he demanded bluntly.

She laughed at him, putting her head to one side so that the green-gold hair swayed between them like a veil. There was something about her eyes and the quality of her laughter that he did not like at all.

'Kedre's had a watch out for you for the past forty years,' she said. 'I think they traced you through an inquiry at the library archives about your eye patterns today. Anyhow, they found you – that's all that matters, isn't it?'

'Why isn't Kedre here now?'

Again she laughed, that faintly malicious laughter. 'She doesn't know. That's why. Nobody knows but me.'

Sam regarded her thoughtfully. There was a challenge in her eyes, an unpredictable capriciousness in her whole manner that he could not quite make up his mind about. In the old days he had known one solution for all such problems as that. He reached out with a quick, smooth gesture and closed his fingers about her wrist, jerking her off balance so that she fell with an almost snakelike gracefulness across his knees. She twisted, unpleasantly lithe in his grasp, and laughed up at him derisively.

There was a man's aggressive sureness in the way she reached up to take his cheek in the cup of her palm and pull his head down to hers. He let her do it, but he made the kiss she was demanding a savage one. Then he pushed her off his knee with an abrupt thrust and sat looking at her angrily.

Again she laughed. 'Kedre's not such a fool after all,' she said, running a delicate forefinger across her lip.

Sam got to his feet, kicking a cushion out of the way. Without a word he set his foot on the ringing bridge and started back across it. From the corner of his eye he saw the serpentine twist with which Sari Walton got to her feet.

'Come back,' she said.

Sam did not turn. An instant later he heard a hissing past his ear, felt the searing heat of a needle-gun's beam. He stopped dead still, not daring to stir for fear another beam was on the way. It was. The hiss and the heat stung his other ear. It was fine shooting – too fine for Sam's liking. He said without moving his head, 'All right, I'm coming. Let me hear the gun drop.'

There was a soft thud among the cushions and Sari's laughter sounded almost as softly. Sam turned and went back to her.

When they were standing like this he had to tip his head back to look into her eyes. He did not like it. He liked nothing about her, least of all her air of self-confident aggressiveness which from time immemorial has belonged to man, not woman. She looked as fragile as the frost-patterned bridge, as delicately feminine as the most sheltered woman alive – but she was an Immortal and the world belonged to her and her kind. There had been generations of time for her to set in this pattern of malice and self-assurance.

Or – had there been? Sam squinted at her thoughtfully, an idea beginning to take shape in his mind that blotted everything else out for a moment. In contrast to Kedre, this beautiful, fragile creature seemed amazingly immature. That was it – immaturity. It explained the capriciousness, the air of experimental malice he had sensed in her. And he realized that for the Immortals maturity must be a long, long time in forming fully. Probably he himself was very far from it, but his early training had hardened him into the pattern of an adult.

But Sari – sheltered and indulged, wielding almost godlike powers – it was no wonder she seemed unstable in these years before her final matrix of centuries-old maturity had set. It would never set quite properly, he thought. She was not essentially a stable person. She would never be a woman to like or trust. But now she was more vulnerable than she knew. And one of Sam's devious schemes for making use of an adversary's weakness started to spin a web in his mind.

'Sit down,' Sam told her.

She lifted both hands over her green-gold head to pluck a cluster of pale fruit like grapes that dangled from a vine. Sam could see her cradling fingers through them, they were so nearly transparent, the blue seeds making a pattern of shadows inside the tiny globes. She smiled at him and sank to her knees with her unpleasantly boneless litheness.

Sam looked down at her. 'All right,' he said. 'Now. Why did you get me up here? If Kedre sent the orders out, why isn't she here instead of you?'

Sari put a pale glassy globe into her mouth and bit down on it. She spat out blue seeds. 'Kedre doesn't know, I told you.' She looked up at him under heavy lashes. Her eyes were a paler blue than Kedre's. 'The warrant's been out for forty years. She's in Nevada Keep this week.'

'Has she been notified?'

Sari shook her head, the lustrous, improbable hair swinging softly. 'Nobody knows but me. I wanted to see you. If Zachariah knew he'd be furious. He –'

'Zachariah ordered me dream-dusted,' Sam broke in impatiently, eager to get the story clear in his head. 'Was Kedre behind it?'

'Zachariah ordered you poisoned,' Sari corrected, smiling up at him. 'He meant you to die. Kedre said no. They had a terrible quarrel about it.' Her smile grew secret; she seemed to hug herself with a pleasant memory. 'Kedre made it dream-dust,' she went on after a moment. 'No one could understand why, really. You wouldn't be any use to her after that, alive or dead, young or old.' Her voice failed gently; she sat with a transparent fruit between thumb and finger halfway to her lips, and did not move for a long second.

Sam had a sudden, dazzling idea. He dropped to his knees before her and put a finger under her chin, turning her head toward him, looking into her eyes. And a surge of triumph made his throat close for an instant.

'Narco-dust!' he said softly. 'I'll be damned! Narco-dust!'

Sari gurgled with laughter and leaned forward to rub her forehead against his shoulder, her eyes glazed with that strange luminous lustre which is unmistakable in the addict.

It explained a great deal – her instability, her curious indifference, the fact that she had not yet quite realized Sam's strange youth. How odd, he thought – and how significant – that the two people he had met who remembered him from long ago were both under a haze of drug-induced dreams.

Sari pushed him away. She put the fruit in her mouth without knowing her gesture had been interrupted, and spat out the seeds and smiled at him with that sharp, glittering malice that had no reason behind it. Of course his inexplicable youth had not struck her. She was quite accustomed to seeing unchanging faces about her as the decades went by. And under narco-dust a serene, unquestioning acceptance of all one sees is a major factor. But at any moment now she might have a flash of clarity. And Sam still had much to learn.

'Kedre substituted dream-dust for the poison,' he said. 'Did she have someone guard me after that?'

The greenish hair spread out like a shawl as Sari shook her head.

'She meant to. Zachariah fixed that, I think. Kedre always thought he did. You'd disappeared when her men went to look for you. You've been missing ever since – until now. Where were you, Sam Reed? I think I could like you, Sam. I think I see now what was in Kedre's mind when she sent her people out to find you and cure you. I –'

'What are you doing here in the Harker house?'

'I live here.' Sari laughed, and then an ugly timbre crept into the laughter and she closed her delicate, long-fingered hand suddenly over the cluster of fruit. Colorless juice spurted through her fingers. 'I live here with Zachariah,' she said. 'He wants Kedre. But if he can't have her – I'll do instead. Some day I think I'll kill Zachariah.' She smiled again, sweetly enough, and Sam wondered if Zachariah knew how she felt about him, and that she was a narco-addict. He rather doubted it. The combination was dynamite.

He was beginning to realize what a ripe plum of opportunity had dropped into his lap – but an instant later the familiar doubt crept in. How opportunely had it dropped, after all? How much reasoned planning lay behind all that had happened to him since he woke? There was still no explanation of the watcher in the alley. And that man had known what he was doing. There was no drug-dream behind the precise pattern of what had so far happened to Sam Reed.

'Why did you send for me?' he demanded. Sari was splashing her hand in the water to wash away the sticky juice. He had to ask her twice before she appeared to hear him. Then she looked up and smiled her bright, vacant smile.

'I was curious. I've been watching Kedre's private visor for a long time now. She doesn't know. When word came in that they'd found you I thought I'd see … I thought I could use you. Against Kedre or against Zachariah – I'm not sure yet. After awhile I'll think about it. Not now. I'm thinking about Zachariah now. And the Harkers. I hate the Harkers, Sam. I hate all Harkers. I even hate myself, because I'm half a Harker. Yes, I think I'll use you against Zachariah.' She leaned forward, brushing Sam's shoulder with a fan of green-gold hair, looking up at him with a pale-blue flash under the heavy lashes.

'You hate Zachariah too, don't you, Sam? You should. He wanted you poisoned. What do you think would hurt him most, Sam? I think for Kedre to know you're alive – and young. Young?' Her narrow brows drew together in brief bewilderment. But that was a subject that required thought, and she was in no condition now to attack serious problems. Her mind was not working except in its deepest levels at this moment, the primitive levels that move automatically, without conscious effort.

Suddenly she threw back her head and laughed, choked on the laughter, looked at Sam with swimming eyes. 'It's wonderful!' she said. 'I can punish them both, can't I? Zachariah will have to wait until Kedre's tired of you, now that you're alive again. And Kedre can't have you if she doesn't know where you are. Could you go away and hide, Sam? Some place where Kedre's men couldn't find you? Oh, please, Sam, do go and hide! For Sari. It would make Sari so happy!'

Sam rose. The bridge rang musically as he crossed it, a series of faint, sweet undernotes to Sari's laughter. The scented breeze blew in his face as he went back down the trellised hall. The lift stood waiting where he had left it. There was no one in sight when he came out at the foot of the shaft and went back up the glass steps over the swimming stream and into the street.

Moving almost in a daze, he stepped onto the nearest Way and let it carry him at random through the city. The episode just past had all the qualities of a dream; he had to focus hard upon it to convince himself it had happened at all. But the seed of a great opportunity lay in it, if he could only isolate what was important.

The Harkers had a weakness they did not suspect – Sari. And beyond that lay implicit an even deeper weakness, if Sari was really a Harker, too. For she was definitely not a normal person. The narco-dust and the possible immaturity of her mind explained only partly that shuddering instability at the very core of her being. It opened new vistas for Sam's thought. So even Immortals were not wholly invulnerable, even they had hidden weaknesses in the fabric of their heritage.

There were two secret paths now by which he might ambush Zachariah. The paths would need exploring. That must come later.

Just now the most important thing was to hide while he thought things over. And the more he considered this, the more inclined Sam felt to visit the Colony where Robin Hale administered his sterile jurisdiction.

Hale would probably shoot him on sight. Or would he, as Joel Reed? No one knew Sam yet except Sari, but who could guess what wild caprices might move her between now and the time he was face to face with Hale? He had better act fast.

He did.

The most striking thing about the Colony was that it might just as well have been undersea.

At no time since Sam Reed had left the Keep was the open sky ever above his head. First there was the Keep's impervium dome and above that a mile of water. Then the plane, with its alloy and plastic shell. After that, the great Colony locks, with their safeguards against infection – UV, acid spray, and so on – and now he stood on the land of Venus, with a transparent impervium dome catching rainbows wherever the fugitive sun broke through the cloud blanket. The air smelt the same. That was a tip-off. The free air of Venus was short on oxygen and long on carbon dioxide; it was breathable, but not vintage atmosphere. And it was unmistakable. Here, under the dome, the atmospheric ingredients were carefully balanced. Necessary, of course – just as the impervium shell itself seemed necessary against the fecund insanity that teemed the Venusian lands – flora and fauna bursting up toward the light, homicidally and fratricidally determined to bud and seed, to mate and breed, in an environment so fertile that it made its own extraordinary imbalance.

On the shore stood the old Fort, one-time stronghold of the Doonemen Free Companions. It had been rehabilitated. It, too, was enclosed under the impervium, the great shell a quarter of a mile in diameter. There were small houses arranged here and there, with no attempt at planning. The houses themselves were of all shapes, sizes, and colors. With no rainfall or winds here, the architects had a free hand. The only limitations were those of natural gravity, and paragravatic shields made even Pisa-towers possible. Still, there was nothing really extravagant in material or design. No lavishness. The whole Colony had an air of faint attrition.

There was no open land visible beneath the dome.

The ground had been floored over with plastic materials. Protection against the ground-lichens? Probably. Great hydroponic tanks were the gardens, though a few shallow tanks held sterilized soil. Men were working, rather lazily. It seemed a siesta hour.

Sam walked along one of the paths, following the sign that pointed toward Administration. A mild agoraphobia afflicted him. All his life he had dwelt under an opaque dome, knowing the weight of water above it, shutting out the upper air. Now through the translucent impervium above he had glimpses of watery sunlight, and the illumination was not artificial, though it seemed a bad imitation of the surrogate daylight of the Keep lamps.

His mind was very busy. He was taking in all he saw, evaluating it, packing facts and impressions away against the moment when his innate opportunism saw its chance. He had for the moment dismissed Sari and the Harkers. Let that group of ideas settle and incubate. How Robin Hale would receive Sam Reed, or Sam's son, was the important question now. He did not consider that he owed Hale any debt. Sam did not think in terms like that. He thought only in terms of what would best benefit Sam Reed – and the Colony was something that still looked promising to him.

A girl in a pink smock, bending over a tank of growing things, looked up as he passed. It was curious to see the effect even diluted sunlight made upon the faces of these Landsiders. Her skin was creamy, not milk-white as Sari's in the Keep. She had smooth brown hair, brushed sleek, and her eyes were brown, with a subtly different focus from the eyes of Keep people. An impervium dome shut in her life as fully as any undersea Keep life, but light from the sun came through it, and the jungle pressed ravenously against the gates – a hungry, animate jungle, not the dead weight of sea water. You could tell by her eyes that she was aware of it.

Sam lingered a little. 'Administration?' he asked unnecessarily.

'That way.' Her voice was pleasant.

'Like it here?'

She shrugged. 'I was born here. The Keeps must be wonderful. I've never seen a Keep.'

'You wouldn't know the difference – there isn't any,' Sam assured her, and went on with a troubling thought in his mind. She had been born here. She could be no more than twenty. She was pretty, but not wholly to his taste. And the idea had come to him that if she had only partially the qualities he liked in a woman, he could afford to wait for her daughter, or her daughter's daughter – if he chose the parents of the final product with reasonable care. An Immortal could work out a strain of humanity as a mortal could breed for elegance in cats or speed in horses. Except that the product would be only a cut flower, lovely but perishing in a day. He wondered how many of the Immortals did just that, maintaining in effect a harem in time as well as in space. It would be excellent, so long as one's emotions were unengaged.

The Governor of the Land Colony should have been busy. He wasn't. A minute after Sam sent in his assumed name, the door opened with an automatic click and he walked into Robin Hale's office.

'Joel Reed?' Hale said slowly. His stare was intent, and it took all Sam's hardihood to meet it without shrinking a little.

'Yes. Sam Reed was my father.' He said it with a bit of bravado.

'All right,' Hale said. 'Sit down.'

Sam looked at him through the thin protection of his eye shields. It might have been yesterday they met last, Hale had changed so little. Or – no, he had changed, but in ways too subtle for the eye to catch. The voice told more of the story. He was still thin, still brown, still quiet, a man whose mind was attuned to patience because of the years behind him and the centuries ahead. He could accept any defeat as temporary, and any victory as evanescent.

This change in him was temporary too, but no less real for that. He had not quite the quiet enthusiasm of voice and manner that Sam remembered. The thing he had been working toward with high hope when they parted was an accomplished fact now, and a finished failure. But it was so brief a thing in the total of Hale's experience – that was it, Sam realized, staring at the man.

Robin Hale remembered the Free Companion days, the long war years, the time generations past when the last vestiges of mankind had been free to roam the seas, free to face danger. It had been matter-of-fact enough, Sam knew. A business, not a swashbuckling romance. But emotions had run high and the life the Free Companions led was nomadic, the last nomads before mankind returned wholly to the shelter of the Keeps, the stagnation of the underseas. The Keeps were the tomb, or the womb, or both, for the men of Venus, who had begun their life as wild tribesmen on Earth.

Sam was beginning to feel the first stirrings of interest in his own kind as a long-term investment for a long-lived Immortal.

'Are you a volunteer?' Hale asked.

Sam came back to himself with something of a jolt. 'No,' he said.

'I didn't know Sam Reed had a son.' Hale was still looking at him with that quiet, speculative stare that Sam found hard to meet. Could one Immortal know another, through any disguise, simply by those mannerisms no man could wholly hide? He thought it likely. It didn't apply to himself – yet, for he was not yet immortal in the sense that these others were. He had not acquired the long-term view with which they kept life at bay.

'I didn't know myself until just lately,' he said, making his voice matter-of-fact. 'My mother changed my name after the Colony scandal.'

'I see.' Hale was noncommittal.

'Do you know what happened to my father?' That was pushing things. If Hale said, 'Yes – you're Sam Reed,' it would at least settle this uncertainty. But if he didn't, it need not mean he had failed to recognize Sam.

The Free Companion shook his head. 'He dream-dusted. I suppose he's dead by now. He'd made enemies after the bubble burst.'

'I know. You … you must have been one of them.'

Hale shook his head again, smiling faintly. Sam knew what the smile meant. One neither hates nor loves the ephemeral short-lived. Temporary annoyance is the worst they can evoke. Nevertheless Sam was not tempted to reveal himself. Olympians had the god-prerogative of being unpredictable. Zeus tossed thunderbolts on impulse.

'It wasn't Sam Reed's fault,' Hale said. 'He couldn't help being a swindler. It was born in him and bred in him. Anyhow, he was only a tool. If it hadn't been Sam, it would have been someone or something else. No, I never hated him.'

Sam swallowed. All right, he had asked for that. Briskly he moved on to the next point. 'I'd like your advice, Governor Hale. I've only learned who I really am lately. I've been checking up. I know my father was a crook and a swindler, but the government found his caches and paid back everything – right?'

'Right.'

'He left me nothing – not even his name, for forty years. But I've been investigating, just in case. There was one asset my father had when he dream-dusted, and that wasn't taken away from him. A land-grant. Forty years ago the government issued him a patent on certain Venusian land areas, and that grant's still valid. What I want to know is this: Is it worth anything?'

Hale tapped his fingers on the desk. 'Why did you come to me?'

'My father was with you when the Colony started. I figured you'd know. You'd remember. You're an Immortal; you were alive then.'

Hale said, 'I knew about that patent, of course. I tried to get hold of it. But it was in your father's name, absolutely watertight. The government wouldn't release. As a matter of fact, land-grants aren't revocable. There's a reason. On Venus all colonies presumably have to depend for existence on the Keeps, and it would be easy to cut off supplies if necessary. So you've inherited that patent, eh?'

Sam said, 'Is it worth anything?'

'Yes. The Harkers would pay you a good deal to suppress the information.'

'The Harkers? Why?'

'So I couldn't start a new colony,' Hale said, and his hand on the desk opened slowly from a tight-balled fist. 'That's why. I started this Colony, after your father – after the collapse. I went ahead anyway. The good publicity we'd built up boomeranged. We had to start on a skeleton crew. Just a few, who believed in the same things I did. Not many of them are still alive. It was a tough life in the beginning.'

'It doesn't look so tough,' Sam said.

'Now? It isn't. The Colony's been emasculated. You see – what the Harkers did was try to stop me from even starting the Colony. They couldn't stop me. And after I'd started, they didn't dare let me fail. Because, eventually, they want to colonize Venus, and they don't want the psychological effect of a failure chalked up in history. They couldn't let me fail once I'd started, but they wouldn't let me succeed either. They didn't believe I *could* succeed. So –'

'So?'

'Attrition. Oh, we worked hard the first year. We did it with our fingernails. We didn't lick the jungle, but we started. We got the Colony cleared and built. It was a fight every step, because the jungle kept pushing back in. But we kept going. Then we were ready to reach out – to establish a new beachhead. And the Harkers stopped us cold.

'They cut off our supplies.

'They sat in the Keeps and made sure there wouldn't be any volunteers.

'The equipment dwindled. The power dwindled. The machines stopped coming.

'According to the original charter, we had to show an annual profit. Or the government could step in as administrator till matters got on an even basis again. They couldn't take my grant away from me, but they could cut down the blood supply so the Colony wouldn't be able to show a profit. That's what they did, thirty-four years ago. Since then, the government has been administrator here – maintaining the *status quo*.

'They administer. They give us enough supplies so we won't fail. But not enough so we can go forward. They don't want us to go forward – because there's the risk of failure. They want to wait until there's no risk. And that time will never come.'

Hale looked at Sam, a deep fire beginning to glow far back in his eyes under the scowling brows. Was he talking to Joel Reed – or to Sam? It was hard to be sure. Certainly he was saying more than he would say to the casual visitor.

'My hands are tied,' Hale went on. 'Nominally I'm Governor. Nominally. Everything here has come to a full stop. If I had another patent – if I could start another colony –' He paused, looking at Sam from under meeting brows. 'They won't grant me a patent. You can see how important yours is. The Harkers would pay you very well to suppress it.'

That was it, then. That was the reason behind his freedom of speech. He had finished, but he did not look at Sam. He sat motionless behind his bare-topped desk, waiting. But he made no plea and no argument.

For what could he offer the man before him? Money? Not as much as the Harkers could offer. A share in the new colony? By the time it would begin to pay off any short-term man would be long dead.

On impulse Sam said suddenly, 'What could you do with the patent, Governor?'

'Start over, that's all. I couldn't pay you much. I could lease the patent from you, but there'd be no profit for many years. They'd be eaten up by the costs. On Venus a colony has to keep moving, spreading out. It's the only way. I know that now.'

'But what if you failed? Wouldn't the government come in again as administrator – the same thing over again? Wouldn't they see you did fail?'

Hale was silent.

Sam hammered at him. 'You'd need a big stake to start a new colony. You –'

'I'm not arguing,' Hale said. 'I told you you'd get more money from the Harkers.'

It was Sam's turn for silence. A dozen possibilities were already taking shape in his mind – ways to raise money, to circumvent the Harkers, to spread propaganda, to make the next colony a success in spite of all opposition. This time he thought he could do it. He had all the time in the world and it would be worthwhile now to invest it in a successful colony.

Hale was watching him, a flicker of hope beginning to show through the fatalistic inertia which had dulled all he said until now. And Sam was a little puzzled by the man. With all that long life behind him, all that unthinkable maturity which must be the sum of his experiences, still he had turned once and was ready to turn again to Sam Reed, short-lived, immature to the point of childishness from the Immortal's view. Hale was ready to let his most cherished venture fail for lack of ideas and initiative, unless this man before him, short-lived as a cat and as comparatively limited in scope, could take over for him.

Why?

A vague parallel with the social history of Old Earth swam up in Sam's memory. Somewhere in his reading he had encountered the theory that those countries on Earth which the Mongol hordes invaded in very ancient times had been so completely vitiated by the terrible experience that they had never again been able to regain their initiative. With all the resources their countries offered, the people themselves remained helpless to use them or to compete with other peoples who had not been robbed of that essential spark.

Perhaps the same thing had happened to Robin Hale. He was the only man alive now who had fought with the Free Companions. He had expended in those wild, vigorous years the spark that would move him now if he still possessed it? He had the centuries of experience and knowledge and accumulating maturity, but he no longer had the one essential thing that could let him use them.

Sam had it, in abundance. And it occurred to him suddenly that perhaps of all men alive he alone did possess it. Hale had the long life but not the will to use it. The other Immortals had initiative enough, but –

'If we wait on the Families, the time never will come to move,' Sam said aloud, in a marveling voice, as if he had never heard the idea before.

'Of course not.' Hale was calm. 'It may be too late already.'

Sam scarcely heard him. 'They think they're right,' he went on, exploring this new concept which had never dawned on him before. 'But they don't want a change! They'll go right on waiting until even they recognize they've waited too long, and then maybe they'll be a little bit glad it *is* too late. They're conservatives. The people on the top are always conservatives. Any change has to be for the worse where they're concerned.'

'That applies to the Keep people, too,' Hale told him. 'What can we offer any of them to match what they already have? Comfort, security, plenty of entertainment, a complete, civilized life. All we have up here is danger and hardship and the chance that maybe in a couple of hundred years they can begin to duplicate on land what they already have undersea, without working for it. None of them would live to cash in on the rewards even if they saw the necessity for changing.'

'They responded once,' Sam pointed out. 'When … when my father promoted the first Colony scheme.'

'Oh, yes. There's plenty of discontent. They know they're losing something. But it's one thing to talk about romance and adventure and quite another to endure the danger and hardships that make up the total sum. These people lack a drive. Pioneers are pioneers because conditions at home are intolerable, or because conditions elsewhere look more promising or … or because there's a Grail or a Holy Land or something like it to summon them. Here it's simply a small matter like the salvation of the race of man – but intangibles are beyond their grasp.'

Sam wrinkled red brows at him. 'Salvation of the race of man?' he echoed.

'If colonization doesn't start now, or soon, it never will. Our korium supplies will be too low to support it. I've said that over and over until the words come out whenever I open my mouth, it's that automatic. The race of man will come to an end in a few more centuries, huddled down there in their safe Keep-wombs with their power-source dwindling and their will to live dwindling until nothing remains of either. But the Families are going to oppose every move I make and go on opposing like grim death, until it's too late to move at all.' Hale shrugged. 'Old stuff. It's out of fashion even to think in those terms any more, down in the Keeps, they tell me.'

Sam squinted at him. There was conviction in the Immortal's voice. He believed Hale. And while the ultimate destiny of the race was far too vague a concept to worry Sam at all, his own increased life-span made the next few hundred years a very vital subject. Also, he had a score to settle with the Harkers. And there were almost unlimited possibilities in this colonizing project, if it were handled by a man like Sam Reed.

He was beginning to see the dawning flicker of a magnificent idea.

'The patent's yours,' he said briskly. 'Now look –'

Robin Hale closed the shuttered door of Administration behind him and walked slowly down the plastic path, alone. Overhead the glowing grayness of the Venusian day lightened briefly with a flash of blue sky and sun, filtered diffused through the impervium overhead. Hale glanced up, grimacing a little against the brightness, remembering the old days.

A man in brown overalls some distance away, was leisurely moving a hoe around the roots of growing things in one of the broad beds of soil dug from Venus' overfertile ground. The man moved quietly, perhaps a bit stiffly, but with the measured motions of one who knows and enjoys his work. He lifted a gaunt, long-jawed face as Hale paused beside the shallow tank,

'Got a minute,' Hale asked.

The man grinned. 'More than most,' he said. 'What's on your mind?'

Hale put a foot on the rim of the tank and crossed his arms on the lifted knee. The older man leaned comfortably on his hoe. They looked at each other for a moment in silence, and a faint smile on the face of each told quietly of the things they had in common. These two, of all the men now alive, remembered life under an open sky, the succession of night and day, sun and moon, the natural rhythms of a world not ordered by man.

Only the Logician remembered a day when the soil of an open planet had not been man's deadly enemy. Only he of all the workers here could handle his hoe in leisurely communion with the turned dirt, knowing it for no enemy. For the others, the very sight of soil meant dangers seen and unseen, known and unknown – fungi in the brown grains they hoed, bacteria of unguessable potentialities, mysterious insects and tiny beastlings lurking ready for the next stroke of the blade. This soil, of course, had been processed and was safe, but conditioning dies hard. No one but the Logician really liked these beds of open ground.

Hale had been surprised only superficially when he first thought he recognized the gaunt figure wielding the hoe as he backed slowly along a path between brown seed beds. That was not very long ago – a few weeks, perhaps. He had paused beside the tank, sending his subordinates on ahead, and the older man had straightened and given Hale a keen, quizzical look.

'You're not –' Hale had begun hesitantly.

'Sure.' The Logician grinned. 'I'd have come topside a lot sooner, but I've had a job needed finishing. Hello, Hale. How are you?'

Hale had said something explosive.

The Logician laughed. 'I used to be a dirt farmer back on Earth,' he explained. 'I sort of got the itch. That's one reason, anyhow. I'm a contingent volunteer now. Used my own name, too. Didn't you notice?'

Hale hadn't. Much had happened to him since he last stood in the Temple of Truth and listened to this man's voice coming impressively from the oracular globe. The name of Ben Crowell hadn't caught his eye, though the volunteer lists were scanty enough these days that he should be able to recite them from memory.

'Somehow I'm not very surprised,' he said.

'Needn't be. You and I, Hale, we're the only men left now who remember the open air.' He had sniffed elaborately, and then grinned up at the impervium dome. 'We're the only ones who know this isn't. Did you ever locate any more of the Free Companions? I've wondered.'

Hale shook his head. 'I'm the last.'

'Well' – Crowell struck off a random runner with his hoe – 'I'll be here awhile, anyhow. Unofficial, though. I can't answer any questions.'

'You haven't done that even in the Temple.' Hale was reminded of a grievance. 'I've been to see you maybe a dozen times in the last forty years. You wouldn't give me a single audience.' He looked at the Logician and for a moment illogical hope quickened in his voice. 'What made you come landside – now? Is something going to happen?'

'Maybe. Maybe.' Crowell turned back to his hoe. 'Something always does sooner or later, doesn't it? If you wait long enough.'

And that was all Hale had been able to get out of him.

Hale was remembering that conversation now as he told the Logician what had just happened.

'Is that why you came up here?' he demanded at the end of his story. 'Did you know?'

'Hale, I just can't tell you. I mean that. I can't.'

'Don't you know?'

'That hasn't got anything to do with it. Don't forget every talent's got its drawbacks, too. It's not so much prescience I've got as it is infallibility – and that's fallible by definition. I told you once it was more horse sense than anything else.' Crowell seemed mildly irritated. 'I'm not God. Don't start thinking like the Keep men – wanting to shift every responsibility. That's one thing wrong with Venus today. The leave-it-to-George fallacy. George isn't God either. And God Himself can't change the future – and still *know* what's going to happen. Minute He meddles, you see, He introduces a new factor into the equation, and it's a random factor.'

'But –'

'Oh, I've interfered a time or two,' the Logician said. 'Even killed a man once, because I figured nothing worse could happen than letting that particular fella live. Turned out I was right, too – in that case. Only I don't interfere any more than I can help. When I do, I step in as the random factor, and, since I'm *in* it, it isn't easy to look at the whole equation from outside. I can't predict *my* reactions – see?'

'More or less,' Hale said thoughtfully. 'Yet you say you've interfered when you had to.'

'Only then. And afterwards I've tried to make things come out even again. The way it is, there's a balance. If I step into the right-hand pan, the balance shifts in that direction. So afterwards I try to give the other pan a little push – so *x* will equal *x* again. If I add *y* to one side, I try to subtract *y* from the other. I admit it don't look too sensible from where you're sitting, but it sure does from my perch, son. Like I say, I'm not God. Not the God the Keeps want today, certainly. They expect God to come down and push 'em around in a wheelchair.'

He paused, sighed, glanced up at the impervium dome where a streak of blue sky let sunlight glow briefly through the Colony. 'What did Reed want?' he asked. 'He's got some ideas, I take it. What are they?'

'I don't see why I need to tell you,' Hale said irritably. 'You probably know more about it than I do.'

The Logician struck his hoe handle a light blow with his closed fist. 'No, son, not strictly speaking. There's the best reason in the world why I can't tell you what I know. Some day maybe I'll take time to explain it. Right now I'd be mighty glad to hear what young Reed's up to.'

'We looked over the maps. His patent covers a three-hundred-mile area with about a hundred miles of seacoast. I asked for that originally because one of the Free Companion Forts stood on the shore there. It's a good base. I remember it was chosen for its harbor. A chain of islands shields it and curves out westward in a long sweep.'

In spite of himself, Hale's voice quickened. 'There won't be an impervium dome over this colony. You've got to adapt to colonize. And you can't have a balanced ecology with one atmosphere outside and another inside. Still, we'll need protection from the landside life. I think water's our answer to that. The islands make natural stepping stones. We'll bring them under control one after another and move along to the next.'

'Um-hum.' The Logician pinched his long nose thoughtfully. 'Now what's going to stop the Families from the same tricks they used to kill *this* Colony?'

Hale coughed. 'That remains to be seen,' he said.

Every nightfall had its own strange, exotic quality to a Keep-bred Sam. Sam clutched the chair arms in the tossing plane that carried him back to Delaware Keep and looked out fascinated at the deep darkness gathering over the sea. Venus air currents are treacherous; few planes attempt flight unless really necessary, and even those flights are short ones. Sam's view of the scene below was intermittent and jolted. But he could see, far off in the gathering darkness, the great submerged glow that was the Keep, spreading its stain of light upon the water. And he was aware of an unaccustomed emotional pull. That vast spreading glow was home – safety, companionship, lights and music and laughter. The Colony behind him was sterile by contrast, the dwelling place of danger and defeat.

It wouldn't do. He would have to think of something very good to counteract this emotion which he himself was heir to, and all the rest of the Keep's numbered thousands. A pioneer needs bad home conditions and the promise of a Grail or a City of Gold beyond the wilderness to draw him on. Push plus pull, Sam thought. But in this case the bad conditions were all on the wrong side of the scale, from the promoter's viewpoint. Something would have to be done.

Success would require korium, enthusiastic recruits and Harker acquiescence if not actual Harker backing. So far he had nothing. And he would have to work fast. At any moment, once he landed, private police might come up beside him as they had come before, and Sam Harker would drop out of sight, quite possibly forever. He had little money, no prestige, no friends except one old man dying of drugs and senility, and even that friendship had to be bought.

Sam laughed softly to himself. He felt wonderful. He felt exultantly confident. He was perfectly sure of success.

'The first thing I've got to do,' he said to the Slider, 'is get myself before the public. Fast. I don't care how, but I've got to go on record in opposition to the Families so fast they won't have time to snatch me. Afterward I'll take care to make it plain if I do vanish they will be responsible.'

The Slider wallowed and sniffled. The small room was stifling, but it was comparatively safe. So long as Sam stayed here in these underworld haunts he still knew well, he was unlikely to vanish into the Harker stronghold. Once he stepped out, the tale might be quite different.

'Give me another drink,' was all the Slider said in answer.

'I've got two thousand credits,' Sam told him, pushing the bottle closer. 'Hale can raise maybe another two thousand. We've got to make a fast start on that. You tell me where I can spend it to stretch it farthest. I'll want newscast time and a good semantics man to dope out our opening speeches. Once we're started, enough money will come in to keep us going. And this time I'm not going to pour it all down a rat hole. It's going to go where it'll do the most good.'

'Where?' The Slider cocked an inquiring, hairless brow above his bottle.

'Into a fleet,' Sam said grimly. 'This time the new colony will be an island-chain. We're going to stay mobile. We're going to fight the sea beasts for the islands, and fortify them and settle in. We'll need good fast boats, well armored, with good weapons. That's where the money's going.'

The Slider sucked at his bottle and said nothing.

Sam didn't wait for his propaganda machine to start paying off before he began placing orders to outfit his boats. He cut corners where he could, but most of his four thousand credits went under assumed names into secret orders for the materials Hale had figured as basic necessities.

Meanwhile the propaganda got under way. There wasn't time or money for a subtle approach such as Sam would have preferred. A long campaign of cunningly devised songs stressing the glamour of landside life, of the open skies, the stars, the succession of night and day – that would have helped. A successful play, a new book with the right emphasis would have made it much easier. But there wasn't time.

The televisors carried paid-for commercials. Robin Hale announced a new colony under a separate charter. And boldly, openly, because it could not be helped or hidden, Joel Reed's connection with the scheme was made public.

Joel on the screen spoke frankly of his father's disgrace. He disclaimed all knowledge of his father. 'I never knew him,' he said, putting all of his considerable persuasive powers behind the words. 'I suppose a great many of you will discount everything I say, because of my name. I haven't tried to hide it. I believe in this colony and I *can't afford to have it fail.* I think most of you will understand that. Maybe it'll help prove that I mean what I say. I wouldn't dare come before you, using my right name with all the disgrace you know belongs to it, if I didn't know the colony *must* succeed. No one named Reed would dare to try the same thing twice. I'm not. If the colony fails it'll mean my own ruin and I know it. It won't fail.' There was quiet conviction in his voice, and something of his enthusiasm carried over to the listeners. He was telling the truth this time. Some of them believed him. Enough of them believed him, for his purposes just now.

The same urges and stresses which had made the first colonization plans successful were still present. Subtly men sensed the losses Keep life imposed upon them. They yearned obscurely for lost heritages, and there were enough of the yearners to give Sam and Hale the finances they needed to meet immediate demands. It wasn't very much, but it was enough. The rest sat back and waited to be convinced.

Sam moved to convince them.

The Harkers, of course, were not idle. After the first startled hour, they moved too, quite rapidly. But here they operated at a slight disadvantage. They couldn't openly oppose the colonization scheme. Remember, they were supposedly in favor of colonization. They could not afford to have a colony actually fail. So all they could do was start counterpropaganda.

Word went out of a mutated virulent plague that had begun to develop landside. A robot plane crashed spectacularly on the news screens, torn apart by the violent wind tides of the upper air. It was dangerous up there on the land, the rumors increasingly declared. Too dangerous, too uncertain…

And then Sam made his next bold stroke. Almost openly he attacked the Harkers. Almost specifically he accused them of responsibility in the failure of the present Land Colony. 'There are powerful forces at work,' Sam declared, 'to prevent the colonization of the land. You can see why. Anyone could see. Put yourself in the place of a powerful man, a powerful group of men. If you were governing a Keep, wouldn't you be perfectly contented with things as they are? Would you want any changes made? Wouldn't you do all you could to discredit those who offer opportunities landside to men like us?' Sam leaned to the screen, fixing his audience with a steady, significant gaze. 'Wouldn't you try to silence anyone who fought to give the common man a chance?' he demanded, and then held his breath, waiting to be cut off the air.

But nothing happened. Perhaps the technicians were too stunned. Perhaps even the Harkers dared not challenge public opinion that far. Sam went on while he could. 'I hope to continue working toward the new colony,' he said. 'I'm working for myself, yes – but for all of you others, too, who are *not* rulers in the Keeps. As long as I'm alive I'll keep on working. If I don't come on the air again tomorrow to report our new plans – well, you people of the Keeps will know why.'

There was an extraordinary, soft, rumbling murmur in the streets of Delaware Keep as Sam signed off, leaving those words still humming in the air. For the first time in many decades, crowds had begun to gather again beneath the big public news screens, and for the first time in human history on Venus, the murmur of the crowd-voice had lifted from Keep Ways. It was in its way an awe-inspiring sound – the faintest murmur, murmur of surprise rather than menace, but a murmur that could not be ignored.

The Harkers heard it. And bided their time. They had so much time – they could afford to wait.

So Sam had his temporary insurance against the private police. He made rapid steps toward consolidating his position. He had to find some hold over the Harkers stronger than this gossamer lever based on the unpredictable masses.

Sari was his only key. Sari Walton, half Harker by blood – and certainly abnormal. Why? Sam tried hard to find out. There was a little material on file about the Immortals – only vital statistics and names and brief histories. It was true that the Immortals, by their very longevity, were spared many of the stresses that drive a short-termer into neuroses. But that very longevity must in its way impose other stresses incomprehensible to men of normal life.

Sam searched and pondered, pondered and searched. He traced many ideas up blind alleys and abandoned them. Eventually he came across one small factor that looked promising. At best it was not conclusive – only indicative. But it pointed an interesting path.

The reproductive cycle of the Immortals was a curious one. They had successive periods of fertility, usually at intervals of fifty to seventy-five years and covering only a brief time. The child of two Immortals had never yet failed to show all the traits of long life. But the children were not strong. Their mortality rate was high, and most of them had to be reared almost under glass.

Sam was interested to discover that at the time of Sari Walton's birth a son had been born to the Harker family too – a son named Blaze. These two children were the only surviving offspring on record for that particular period in Delaware Keep.

And Blaze Barker had apparently vanished.

With increasing interest Sam traced through the records, searching for some explanation of what had happened to the man. No death date appeared. The usual records of education and various duties and enterprises for Blaze went steadily along up to a date seventy years past. And then vanished.

Sam filed the information away with a sense of profound excitement.

'This one ought to do,' the Free Companion said, stepping back from the view-glass. 'Look.'

Sam crossed the pitching deck unsteadily and bent to the eyepiece. He felt half-drunk with this unaccustomed atmosphere, the motion of the boat, the wet wind in his face. There was so much about open air that took getting used to – even the feel of the breeze was faintly alarming, for in the Keeps a wind meant entirely different things from the random winds of landside.

The milk-white water heaved around them under the milky sky. On shore the great festooned hulk of a ruined fort seemed to stagger under the weight of jungle rioting over it. There was a constant murmur from the jungle, punctuated by a pattern of screams, flutings, hisses, roars from invisible beasts. The sea lapped noisily at the boat's sides. The wind made meaningless noises in Sam's ears. Landside was strangely confusing to the Keep-bred.

He put his forehead in the head rest and looked down.

Another world sprang into being, a world of wavering light and wavering weed, threaded by the wavering shapes of underwater things, fish with shivering fins, siphonophores trailing their frostlike streamers, jellyfish throbbing to a rhythm of their own. Anemones clenched into brilliantly striped fists with a dreamlike slowness. Great fans of dazzling colored sponge swayed to the random currents.

And buried in this bright, wavering world, visible only in rough outlines beneath the weeds, lay the hulk of a sunken ship.

It was the third they had found which Hale seemed to think worth salvaging. 'And they're in better shape than you think,' he assured Sam. 'Those alloys are tough. I've seen worse wrecks than this rehabilitated in the old days.' His voice trailed off and he looked out over the empty water, remembering.

You could almost see it peopled by the fleets of the Free Companions as Hale must be seeing it, very clearly over the generations already gone. The Keeps had been sacrosanct then as now, for only under their impervium domes did civilization survive. But the token wars had raged between them, on the surface of the gray seas, between fleets of hired mercenaries. The Keep that backed the loser paid its korium ransom, sometimes only after token depth bombs had been dropped to remind the undersea people of their vulnerability.

It all passed. The jungle ate up the great forts and the sea giants sank at their moorings. But they did not crumble. That much was apparent now. The weeds grew over and through them and the lichens nibbled at their fabric, but the strong basic structure remained.

Hale and Sam had searched the coasts of Venus where the old forts stood. Hale had known the forts when they were alive. He knew the harbors and could still quote the battle strength of the Companies. The first two hulks they had salvaged were already nearly seaworthy again. And there was a new enthusiasm in Hale's voice and in his eyes.

'This time they won't pin us down under impervium,' he told Sam, gripping the rail and grimacing as spray blew in his face. 'This time we'll stay mobile no matter what it costs us.'

'It'll cost plenty,' Sam reminded him. 'More than we've got. More than we're going to get, unless we do something very drastic.'

'What?'

Sam looked at him thoughtfully, wondering if the time had yet come to take Hale into his confidence. He had been building toward the revelation for weeks now, leading Hale step by step toward a solution he would have rejected flatly at their first interview.

Sam was applying to his current problem exactly the same methods he had applied – almost by instinct – when he woke in the alley with dream-dust still fragrant in his nostrils. In the weeks since that wakening he had retraced in swift strides the full course of a career that paralleled the career of his earlier life, condensing forty years' achievements into a few brief weeks. Twice now he had come into the world penniless, helpless, every man's hand against him. Twice he had lifted himself to precarious success. This time his foot was only on the first rung of a ladder that leaned against the very stars. He assured himself of that. Failure was inconceivable to him.

By misdirection and cunning he had tricked Doc Mallard into a cat's-paw play and seized the korium he needed to start him on his upward climb. It was korium he wanted again now, but the Harkers were his adversaries this time and they were a much more difficult problem.

Remembering his method with Doc Mallard, he had searched in vain for some lure he could dangle to tempt them out on a limb. He could think of nothing. The Harkers already had everything they could desire; their position was almost impregnable. There was, of course, Sari. Sam knew that if he could plan some subtle but strong irritation for her, and make sure she had narco-dust at the time, she was almost certain to kill either Zachariah or herself – or both. That was one weapon. But it was terrifyingly uncertain, and it was too strong. He meant to kill Zachariah, eventually. But death was no solution to this current problem.

There was a parallel here between the weapons at Sam's command and the weapons men had with which to attack the Venusian landside. In both cases the only available weapons were either too weak or too strong. Utter destruction was no answer, but the only alternative would leave the adversary essentially untouched.

Sam knew he must either give up entirely or take a step so bold it would mean total success or total ruin.

'Hale,' he said abruptly, 'if we want enough korium to colonize the land, we've got to do something that's never been done before. We've got to bomb the Keeps.'

Hale squinted at him and then laughed. 'You're joking.'

'Maybe.' Sam hunched his shoulders and glanced at the smothered fort across the water. 'You know anything better?'

'I don't know anything worse.' Hale's voice was sharp. 'I'm not a murderer, Reed.'

'You were a Free Companion.'

'That's a different matter altogether. We –'

'You fought the Keeps' battles, at the Keeps' orders. That was necessary, under the circumstances. You did what you had to in the way of killing, plundering – piracy, really. The losing Keep paid up in korium or faced bombing. It was a bluff, I suppose. None of them were ever really bombed. Well, what I'm suggesting is a bluff, too. The Families will know it. We'll know it. But we've got to outbluff them.'

'How can we?'

'What have we got to lose? They're at that much of a disadvantage – they have everything to lose. We have everything to gain.'

'But they'll *know* we don't dare do it. People won't even take the threat seriously. You know the Keep people. They're – inert. They've never known a menace. It won't be conceivable that we could bomb them. They'll laugh at us. The race has outlived the fear of danger. We'd have to bomb one Keep and kill thousands of people before we could convince them we meant business. I –'

Sam's laugh interrupted him. 'I'm not so sure. We're still human beings. It's true there's been no war or danger for a good many generations – but men still wake up with a dream of falling as old as the first arborean who lost his grip on a tree limb. Men's nostrils still dilate when they're angry, because when the pattern was first set they had to … to breathe – because the mouth was full of the enemy! I don't think we've shed our fears quite so easily as you think.'

'Well, I won't do it,' Hale said firmly. 'That's going too far. It's out of the question –'

The threat, when it first sounded over the news screens, was as shattering as a bomb itself. There was dead silence in every Keep for a long moment after the words had rung out from the big screens. Then tumult. Then laughter.

Hale had been right – in part. No one believed in the threat of the rehabilitated fleet. The colonies depended for their very existence on the support of the Keeps. They would not dare bomb their sources of supply. And if they were mad enough to do it, every man reasoned in those first few minutes, the chances were strong that it would be some other Keep that got the depth charges – not his own.

Then Sam on the public screens named the Keep – Delaware. He named the time – now. He named his price – korium.

And the battle of wills was on.

But Sam had a weapon before he launched his bluff that gave him confidence. It was not a very strong weapon, but that simply meant he must use more skill in wielding it. It had to succeed. This was a point from which no turning back was possible.

The weapon, like all the most effective weapons man can use against man, was personal.

He had found Blaze Harker.

In the final analysis the whole struggle was a conflict between two men – Sam and Zachariah. The Families of the Immortals ruled the Keeps, the Harkers set the pattern for all other Families, and Zachariah was the head of the Harker clan. Zachariah may or may not have realized himself just where the point of greatest stress lay, but: Sam knew. He was gambling everything on the hope that with this lever, and a plan he had made very carefully, he could outbluff Zachariah Harker.

He realized, of course, that the Families must be laying plans of their own. Last time they had worked quietly away in secret until the moment for action came, and in the resulting explosion Sam and all his schemes had been swept away in unimportant fragments. This time it would be different.

It was the Slider who found Blaze for Sam. When the message reached him, Sam went as quickly as the Ways would carry him to the small, foul-smelling den in the slums of Delaware Keep. The Slider was sunk in an Orange-Devil dream when he came in, and for a few minutes addressed Sam hazily as Klano and spoke of ancient crimes that not even Sam remembered.

He gave the Slider a drink, and presently the mists faded and the vast bulk heaved itself up in bed, chuckling and sniffling.

'On that Harker deal, son – I got an address for you.' He gave it, grunting.

Sam whirled toward the door.

'Wait a minute, son – hold on there! Where you think you're going?'

'To find Blaze.'

'You'll never get in. The place is guarded.'

'I'll make a way!'

'Son, you'd need six weeks' buildup. You'll have to ferret out somebody who'll take bribes before you could get within a city block of that place. You'll need at least one ringer. You'll need a fast getaway organization afterward. You'll –'

'All right, all right! Let's get started, then. Could you work it?'

'Maybe. I could try.'

'Then begin! How long will it take? I can't wait six weeks. Can you do it in three?' He paused, interrupted by the vast, increasing chuckles that sent earthquake waves over the bulk beneath the blankets.

'Forget it, kid. It's already done.' Sam stared. The Slider choked on his own laughter. 'The old hand hasn't lost its cunning, my boy. Don't think the job wasn't hard – but it's done. Raise that shutter over there – turn off the light. Now watch.'

A square of dim illumination appeared on the far wall. Shadows moved across it, blurred by the wall's irregularities. They were looking at the product of a tiny spy camera, apparently carried about waist-high at the belt of someone who progressed at uneven speed. Sometimes he walked, and the film went along in smooth, rhythmic rocking motion; sometimes he ran and then the pictures flashed by jerkily. When he stopped the eye seemed to stop with him. It resulted in an irregular but very convincing motion picture.

The first seconds of the film showed the little camera apparently staring at an iron grille, very close to the lens. White trousered legs appeared, the grille swung open, a vista unfolded briefly of garden paths and fountains playing. One of the Immortal strongholds, obviously.

There was a feeling of quick, furtive alertness to the pace of the film, the way it kept swinging right and left in tiny arcs as the man who carried it scanned his surroundings. Twice it was apparent that the carrier had ducked into hiding; the film went dark for several seconds when a door or a curtain closed to conceal him. There was a dizzying amount of corridor-walking, all of it quick and giving the impression of stealth.

Then the speed of the carrier increased suddenly – the man was running. Walls bobbed up and down, swung sharply as he whipped around a corner. The film went almost totally dark and walls slid downward before it. A glass-walled lift was rising. More corridors, at a run.

A pause before another grilled door, this substantial looking – bars with adornment. The bars grew enormous, blurred, apparently melted. The lens was pressed close against the door, looking through into the room beyond.

And this, the key scene, ran very fast. There was only a flash of a richly furnished room and a man in it with two others bending over him. The man appeared to be struggling with his companions.

Abruptly the picture swung sidewise, jarred so that everything vibrated. There was a sweeping glance upward, along soaring walls, a flash of ceiling, a flash of scowling face swooping toward the lens and an arm uplifted with something that flashed.

The picture went white and clicked noisily to a halt.

Then it began again. Time retraced itself. The lens was floating toward the melting bars again, very slowly. Very slowly indeed the room inside came into focus. In nightmarish slow motion, which gave watchers the opportunity to study every detail, the struggling man and his two companions moved upon the wall.

The room was cushioned everywhere. The carpeting looked soft and sank under the pressure of the three men's feet; the walls were paneled head-high with beautifully quilted patterns of velvet. The furniture was thick and soft, no edges showing.

The man who struggled was tall, slender, fine-boned. He had a beautifully shaped head and even in this convulsive activity his motions were curiously smooth and graceful. It was at first impossible to guess what sort of features he had, they were so contorted in a rapid series of violent grimaces. Blood flecked his face from bitten lips and his eyes were rolled back until no iris showed.

His two adversaries were trying to pull a straitjacket over his flailing arms. Little by little they were succeeding. It all happened in that strange slow motion that gave the whole performance a look of calculating rhythm, like a ballet, robbing the struggle of any spontaneity because it happened so slowly. The tall man beat his prisoned arms against his sides, threw back his head and laughed wildly and soundlessly, blood running down his chin. The laughter changed without a break into sheer rage and he hurled himself sidewise with a cunning lurch and carried one of his attendants with him to the floor. The other bent over them, and then the whole scene jigged furiously and swept upward, and the film clicked to a halt.

'That was Blaze Harker,' the Slider said in the brief silence that followed. 'Give me a drink, son. Have a shot yourself – you look like you need one.'

'– and so it's come down to this,' Sam said over the sea-wide newscast, to the listening thousands. 'Give us the korium we have a right to, or take the consequences. The time's past for bargains and promises. This is the showdown. What's your answer, Harker?'

Under all the seas, under all the impervium domes, a breathless silence held as the multitudes watched Sam's magnified face, multiplied many times upon many screens, turn and wait for his reply. And in nineteen of the Keeps as the waiting lengthened a murmur began to grow. To them it was at the moment an academic problem.

But in Delaware Keep the problem was a vital one. There was not a sound in the streets, and for the first time, perhaps, since a Keep had been reared beneath its bubble dome you could hear the deep, soft humming of the Ways as they glided on their endless rounds.

Zachariah kept them waiting exactly long enough. Then with a perfect sense of timing, just as the delay grew unbearable, he gave his signal in his distant study. Sam's face grew indistinct upon the screens of all the Keeps; it hovered in the background like a shadow. Superimposed upon it the serenely handsome Harker face grew clear.

'Reed, you're a fool.' Zachariah's voice was calm and leisurely. 'We all know this is a childish bluff.'

The shadow that was Sam flashed into clarity; Zachariah's face went translucent. Sam said, 'I expected you to say that. I suppose you believe it. My first job's to convince you all. There isn't much time, so – look.'

Sam and Zachariah alike blurred and vanished from the screen. In their stead a shining seascape grew. Sunlight shafted down through clouds, touching gray water to blue dazzle. And ploughing through the dazzle, tossing glittering spray over their mailed snouts, a fleet of five ships moved head-on toward the observer.

They were small ships, but they were built for business. Impervium sheathed them in everywhere and their lines were smooth and low and fast. They looked grim. They were grim. And the thing about them that most effectively struck fear to the hearts of the watchers was their complete inhumanity. No man's outlines showed anywhere, except as vague, alarming shadows moving purposefully inside the shells. These were machines for destruction, moving forward to fulfill the purpose for which they had been made.

From beyond the screen Sam's disembodied voice said, 'Watch!' and a moment later, at a distance behind the last ship, the sea boiled suddenly into white tumult, erupted high, rained down in diamond showers.

Then the ships grew dim. The screen went briefly blank, and another scene took shape upon it. This time it was a water-world, full of wavering light, greenish-yellow because it was near the surface. Looking up, you could see the water-ceiling as a perfectly tangible thing, quilted and puckered all over with the foreshortened shadows of the. waves. Breaking it, the long, sharp bellies of the ships came gliding – one, two, three, four, five – mailed and darkly shining.

The illumination darkened, the ship keels rose and vanished as the scene plunged downward, following the course of a dark, cylindrical something which shot from the last ship in the line. The telefocus stayed constant on the bomb as it slipped silently down through the Venusian sea. Every watcher in the Keeps felt his skin crawl coldly with the question: *What target?*

The sea was deep here. The depth-bomb dropped eternally. Very few watched the missile itself; most eyes were intent on the lower edges of the screens, avid for the first sight of the bottom … It was sand.

As it came into view, the bomb struck, and instantly the telefocus changed so that the results of the explosion could be visible. Yet not much could be seen. Perhaps that was most terrifying – the swirling, inchoate undersea chaos, the blinding blur on the screen, and the deep, thundering boom of the explosion that carried clearly over the sound beam.

It crashed out and lingered.

Not only through the visors. In Delaware Keep, through fathoms of water, the sound waves rushed and struck with a deep impact of the great impervium shell. Was there the faintest tremor – the slightest possible vibration – in the Keep itself?

Did the Keep – *the Keep!* – shiver a little as the undersea titan smashed his hammer against the sea bottom?

The sound died. There was a stillness.

Far above, in the flagship, Sam flipped sound-absorbent panels into place and turned to the auxiliary screen. He was getting a report.

No face showed on this tight-beam circuit connection. No voice sounded. But Sam automatically translated the scrambled code into an understandable message.

'Kedre Walton left Montana Keep an hour ago. She's just entered Delaware.'

Sam instinctively looked down. He used his own scrambler.

'Does she know the situation?'

'Not sure. She'll find out from the public televisors in Delaware.'

'Has Sari got the special stuff?'

'As soon as we got word Kedre left Montana. She'll have taken it by now.'

The other screen was calling insistently. Robin Hale's voice came from another auxiliary.

'Reed! Are you handling it?'

'I've got it,' Sam said, and went back to his Keep connection. But he waited a second, looking into Zachariah's eyes, while he marshaled his thoughts. He couldn't quite repress a twisted, triumphant smile in the face of the Immortal's godlike – but fallacious – confidence.

For his schemes were working. He had chosen the time very carefully indeed. The vital key, the zero hour, depended on just when Kedre Walton returned to Delaware Keep. The psychological hammer blows were far more useful against Immortals than any bomb.

By now Sari should have in her hands the narco-dust Sam had conveniently provided for her, through his new underworld connections. A narco-addict asks few questions. She would have taken the powder the instant it reached her – and this was not ordinary narco-dust.

There was another drug mixed with it.

By now Sari's nerves should be jolting with shock after shock. By now her brain should be building up a high potential, temporarily crumbling away the mortar of caution, of reserve that had held the bricks of her sanity together. By now she should be ready to explode, when the hair trigger was touched. And the direction of her explosion had already been channeled by her own conditioning and environment. Besides, she was born under the same star as Blaze Harker. Not Mars – it was the more baleful star of Earth that glared coldly above the Venus clouds, the star that had given Sari her dangerous heritage of mental instability.

'Reed,' Zachariah said calmly, 'we can't be bluffed. You won't destroy Delaware Keep.'

'That was the first bomb,' Sam said. 'We're heading for Delaware. A bomb will be dropped every five minutes, till we anchor above you. But we won't stop dropping them then.'

'Have you thought of the results?'

'Yes,' Sam said. 'We have radar and antiaircraft. We have guided missiles. And none of the Keeps is armed. Besides, they're undersea. It's safe undersea – as long as you're not attacked. Then there's no way to strike back. You can only wait and die.'

His voice went out over the public telecast. Sam switched on an auxiliary to focus on one of the great public televisors at a clover-leaf meeting of Ways.

A crowd had gathered, he saw. From all directions the Keeps were like arteries carrying the people to their listening post. Red cells, not white – builders, not fighters. Well, they needed builders to colonize Venus.

At present, however, he was fighting the Keeps.

He began to worry, a little, over Hale. He wasn't sure about the Free Companion. If it came to a final showdown, would Hale actually drop a bomb on Delaware? Would he himself?

Hale mustn't let matters go quite that far.

By now Kedre must be on her way to the Harker stronghold. She would have learned what had happened; the televisors all over the Keep were carrying the news. She would be hurrying to Zachariah's side. Zachariah, whom she had loved for hundreds of years, not with the unflickering glow of a radium lamp, but as a planet inevitably swings toward the sun at perihelion, swinging away toward other planets, but returning whenever the orbit took her close. Yes, she would want to be beside Zachariah in this crisis.

'Another bomb,' Sam said.

Again the telefocus shifted. Again a bomb dropped. This time it struck rock. The explosion came in long, rolling thunders through the public visors, and the crowds swayed with the tides and currents of vibration, as seaweed moves in water.

Again the roar continued as underwater sound waves moved in the track of televised sound waves.

And this time men were surer. Delaware Keep shivered slightly.

Silence dropped. The Ways hummed. The people of the Keep waited, in greater throngs than had gathered in the Ways since man first reached Venus, a herd that always, until now, had been guided by the Immortals – watching the duel between Zachariah Harker and the pirate.

Sam said, 'Suppose you surrender? The Families may lose a little, but the common people won't. Are you afraid of letting the short-termers go landside? Afraid you won't be able to rule them out there?'

'Any man who wishes to volunteer for your colony is free to do that,' Zachariah said. 'Just as every man in the Keeps is free. You're trying to get slaves. Men won't go landside yet; it isn't time. It's too dangerous just now. You can't get volunteers. You say you want korium. But I think that will be only your first demand. Later you'll want colony conscription – peonage.'

'The time's past for abstruse arguments,' Sam said, knowing his voice was heard in every Keep on Venus. 'Listen! Pay us the korium we want or we'll bomb Delaware Keep!'

'You won't bomb the Keep. Half a million people would die.'

'A cheap price for you to pay if you can stop the colony – is that it? Perhaps you're willing to die with Delaware, but what about the other Delaware Immortals? There's a rumor all the Harkers but you have already left the

Keep – and that you've got a getaway ship waiting. Where are you vising from?'

Zachariah dared not let that challenge drop. Beside him, too, as Sam knew, was a scanning screen that showed the throngs in the Keep. All the Harker prestige – the Immortal prestige – depended on keeping the trust of the commoners. And they would not follow rulers who were not leaders.

Zachariah turned his head and spoke briefly. He said to Sam, and to the Keeps, 'No Immortal has left Delaware. I'm speaking from the Harker Council Room. As you see.'

The image on the screen changed; it showed the well-known Council Room, empty except for Zachariah, who was seated at the head of a long table before a broadcasting unit.

But now the door opened, and men and women began to come in. Sam recognized Raoul. He was watching for another face he knew.

Was his timing correct?

'The other Families –' Zachariah said. 'We'll scan them quickly.'

Other Council Rooms showed on the screen – the sanctums of the great Families of Delaware Keep. They were all filling rapidly, the Randolphs, the Wood clan, the Davidsons and Mawsons – but the Harkers were the real rulers of Delaware, as everyone knew. The focus returned to Zachariah. It was the long view, showing Geoffery and Raoul and a few others seated at the table. Sam looked for Sari and saw her. He wished he could get a closer view. Had she taken the hopped-up narco-dust?

She sat motionless. But suddenly her hands moved together on the table top and clenched violently, and Sam knew.

'Your bluff won't work,' Zachariah said. 'No Immortal has left the Keep.'

'So you are all willing to die rather than give up a little korium,' Sam said. 'That's your affair – your own lives. But the korium isn't yours. It belongs to the Keep people. They made it and they own it – or should. You've no right to decide whether they should live and die.'

'We are the people,' Zachariah said.

'You lie,' Sam said. 'What do you know about us? You're gods. You don't know a thing about the common people, who have to work blindly for reward we'll never lay our hands on. But you'll get those rewards. You'll get them by waiting and doing nothing, while the short-termers work and have children and die – and their children do the same. You can wait to colonize landside, because you'll live long enough to walk under the stars and the sun and know what it was like on Earth in the old days. You'll go out in ships to the planets. You'll get the rewards. But what about us? We'll die, and our children will die, and our children's children – sweating to build a pyramid we'll never see complete. You're not the people!' His voice raised in a shout. 'You're not even human! You're Immortals!'

'We rule by will of the people. Because we're best qualified.'

'Qualified?' Sam asked, and then, 'Where is Blaze Harker?'

'Not in Delaware Keep at the moment –'

'Tight beam,' Sam said.

There was a pause. Then Zachariah made a gesture. All over the Keeps the screens dimmed and went blank. Only two visors carried the conversation now – Sam's, and the Harkers'.

Sam too, had adjusted to the private tight beam. He said: 'I know where Blaze Harker is. I've got telepictures of him. I can broadcast them, and you know what that will do to Harker prestige if the people learn that an Immortal can go insane.'

Sam heard signals begin to click behind him. Automatically he translated. '*Kedre Walton entering Harker grounds –*' Almost time.

The signals suddenly began again. Mystified, Sam heard them say, 'Listen to the Keeps! Tune back! Listen!'

He didn't want to. This distraction was something he hadn't counted on. There was so much depending on his own split-second timing just now, and on chance and luck – if anything went wrong he was ruined. He didn't want to deflect his attention for a single instant from this flood of pressure he was pouring on the Harkers. But he switched his private screen on briefly – and then for a moment stood tense, listening.

Down there in the Keeps the screens were blank. The people had been cut off from this fascinating and vital debate just at the moment when it was reaching a climax.

And the people didn't like it.

A low roll of anger was rising from the packed thousands. The crowd was shifting uneasily, restlessly, surging in little eddies around the screens as if pressing closer could make the image come back. And the murmur of their anger deepened as the seconds ticked by. Voices rose in thin shouts now and then – the imperative commands of the mob. They would have to be answered. Quickly – very quickly.

Sam whirled to the tight beam where the Harkers waited. From their council room came a distant echo of that same rising murmur of anger. They, too, were watching the temper of the crowds. They, too, knew time was going too fast. Sam grinned. It was perfect. It couldn't be better. He had them on the run now, whether they had realized it yet or not. For until this moment no Immortal had ever known such pressure. They weren't used to coping with it. And Sam had lived under pressure all his life. He was adjusted to fast thinking. Now if he could only talk fast enough –

'Immortal prestige!' he said rapidly into their private beam. 'You've lost all touch with human beings. What do you know about human emotions, you

Immortals? Faith – loyalty – do they look so different after a few hundred years? I'm glad I'm a short-termer!'

Zachariah gave him a bewildered look as Sam paused for breath. This didn't ring quite true, and Zachariah was quick to hear the false note. It was all very well to orate when the mob was listening, but these high, abstract things were irrelevant on the private beam. False heroics were for the small minds of the crowd, you could all but hear him thinking. Or for a small mind here, clouded and confused –

Sam saw understanding break across the Immortal's face – too late. Sam had a few more words to hurl into the transmitter, and as he gathered himself to do it he saw the door behind Zachariah swinging open, and knew he had timed himself almost too closely.

'So it's all right for people like you,' he shouted, 'to pick up some gullible fool of a woman for awhile and kick her out again when you're ready to go back to –'

Kedre Walton came quietly through the door and into the Council Room. From the corner of his eye Sam caught the flash of green-gold hair as Sari's head flung up, saw the hunched tenseness of her shoulders under a gleaming shawl. But his eyes were for Kedre.

She did not seem to have heard. She came quickly across the room, tall, exquisitely fine, holding her head back under the weight of her cascading hair as if it were too heavy for the slender neck. She was unclasping her long cloak as she came, and she let it slip to the floor in shining folds and hurried forward, her narrow white hands outstretched to Zachariah.

Sam had been sure it would happen so. Between her and Zachariah lay too many decades of past intimacy for her to ignore the tie now. They had created between them in the long orbits of the past a communal flesh and a communal mind that functioned most highly only when they were together. If Zachariah had ever needed this completion, he needed it now. She had come as quickly as she could. Every eye in the room could see that these two were as nearly one, and in their crises must always be, as any two humans can become.

Sam's gaze swung back to Sari. So did Zachariah's – but just too late. Both of them knew what was coming a split second before it came, but by then it was too late to stop her. The timing was perfect. Shock after shock had hammered upon Sari, already fighting down the cumulative neural explosions of the adulterated narco-dust Sam had supplied.

And Sari's action was already channeled. She hated Zachariah and Kedre. This was the moment of critical mass.

She was born under the star of exploded Earth. Sari, too, seemed to explode into an incandescence of madness and rage.

Within seconds the assembly of Immortals had degenerated into a primitive struggle as they swarmed to loosen Sari's homicidal grip on Kedre's throat.

Sam threw a switch and saw his face appear in miniature, far below, on the great public televisors. The sullen muttering of the crowd, which had been increasing slowly but steadily, fell to abrupt silence as Sam called.

'Harker! Harker, I can't reach you! Tune in!'

How could they? There was no answer.

'Harker, Harker! *Are you leaving the Keep?*'

Another depth bomb dropped.

Above the rolling thunders of the explosion, above the ominous creaking of tortured impervium over the city, Sam's voice called again.

'Harker, where are you? If the Harkers have left, who's next in authority? *Answer me!*'

Zachariah's face came into sudden, swift focus. He was breathing hard. Blood trickled down his cheek from a long scratch. His face was icily calm.

He said, 'We have not left the Keep. We –'

He did not finish. For the roar of the crowd drowned him out. It was Montana Keep that roared. It was the first time in all Venusian history that the voice of a mob had lifted under a city dome, the first time since the Immortals had assumed control of human affairs that a crowd dared dispute that control.

They disputed it now. If the sound meant anything, they rejected it. Zachariah mouthed silently at them from the screen, no words coming through the vast, voiceless roaring.

For to the crowd it must have seemed that the Keep was already falling. Zachariah, coming back from the urgency of some hidden crisis, breathing hard, blood running down his face – it was a terrifying sight to see. The dome still groaned above them under the impact of the bombs and even this imperturbable Immortal looked panic-stricken at last.

It was terror that made the crowd roar. Surrender was what they roared for, and the volume of the noise mounted.

And then Sam made his first mistake.

He should have stood back and let events go their way. But the sight of Zachariah's ice-cold calm, even in this tumult, made him want suddenly to smash his fists into the flawless, ageless face, batter it to a more nearly mortal aspect – force the acknowledgement of defeat upon the inflexible Immortal. If there was anything there to admire, Sam did not recognize it.

And because he could not reach Zachariah with his fists, Sam lashed out with his voice.

The first few words he roared at the Immortal no one heard. But when his blunt, red-browed face forced itself into focus upon the screens the shouting of the crowd quieted a little, slowly, until Sam's message came through.

'– surrender now!' Sam was roaring. 'No Harker's fit to rule! Give us what we ask, or show us what happened just now in your Council Room! Show us! Show us how sane any Harker is when a crisis comes! No – wait, I'll show you! People of the Keeps, wait until you see Blaze Harker and what he –'

The shadow that was the waiting Zachariah made an impatient gesture, and Sam's face and voice faded into the background, still gesturing, still shouting. Zachariah came clear before them, leaning forward, seeming to look down, godlike, over the panic-stricken throngs.

'I have news for you, people of the Keeps,' he said quietly. 'You're still safe. No bombs have fallen here. No bombs will. This man is – not what he seems. Until now I've kept his secret for him, but this is the time to speak. Joel Reed has told you he never knew his father. He's sworn to wipe out the dishonor of his name and give you a second chance at landside life that Sam Reed robbed you of.' He paused.

'This man *is* Sam Reed,' he said.

A bewildered buzzing followed the silence when Zachariah's voice ceased. He let them murmur for a moment, then lifted a hand and went on.

'We have definite proof of that – the eye prints and finger prints match. Our investigators don't make mistakes. This is Sam Reed, the swindler, the dream-duster, who's promising you so much. Can you believe anything he says, knowing that? Sam Reed – speak to the Keeps! Make more promises! Speak to the people you've swindled! Or do you deny who you are? Shall we show the proof now? Answer us, Sam Reed!'

Sam let his face swim into clear focus on the screen. In shadow behind him Zachariah waited, lips a little parted, still breathing hard and the blood running down his cheek.

Zachariah had lost his head.

For an instant no one knew it, not even Sam. Sam only knew that he must do the fastest thinking he had ever done in his life. He had perhaps fifteen seconds that would look like a deliberate pause. Then he must speak. In the back of his brain was the answer. He knew it was there, he could almost touch it. But for ten of the fifteen seconds he groped in vain.

And then it came to him. Zachariah had made one vast and fatal mistake. The Harkers were not used to quick thinking. For too many centuries they had not been called upon to see all sides of a threatening danger in one glance, evaluate all possibilities and choose by instinct the safest out. And Zachariah was an Immortal. He did not think as normal men think. Zachariah's mind worked by decades and scores – not by the days and weeks of ordinary living.

Sam laughed. 'No,' he said, 'I won't deny it. I wanted to prove myself. I owed you that. I made a bad mistake and I've got to make amends. But Harker's right – *I am immortal.*'

He waited a moment to let that sink in. 'I was forty years old when they blew dream-dust in my face,' he said. 'For forty years I've been away. Do I look like a man of eighty? Here – look! Am I eighty years old?'

He ducked his head and pushed the eye shells loose, slipped them out, spat out the tooth-cap shells. He pulled the red wig from his head and grinned at them, burning with a confidence that seemed to pour out upon all the Keeps from the thousand screens that mirrored his face.

It was a strong, square, hard-featured face, lines of violence upon it, but no lines of age. Even the bareness of his head was not the bareness of age – the shape of his skull was too sculptured in the strong, full curves of his Harker heritage. It was a vital, virile face – but it was certainly not the face of an Immortal

'Look at me!' Sam said. 'You can see I'm no Immortal. I'm a man like the rest of you. No Immortal was ever born built like me. But I've lived eighty years.' He stepped back a little, paused, turned upon them a keen, gray, angry stare,

'I was a man like you,' he said. 'But I've been landside. I've made a great discovery. I've learned why it is the Immortals don't dare let landside colonies get started. You all know how hard they've worked to stop us – now I'm going to tell you *why!*

'You can all be immortal!'

It was nearly five minutes before the tumult died. Even then, Sam was very nearly the only listener who heard Zachariah Harker say wearily:

'All right, Reed. You'll get your korium. Now, is this another swindle? If not – *go ahead and give them immortality!'*

PART THREE

When Israel out of Egypt came
Safe in the sea they trod;
By day in cloud, by night in flame,
Went on before them God ...
I see the country, far away,
Where I shall never stand;
The heart goes where no footstep may
Into the promised land.

– *Housman*, *circa* 1900

The wall was painted with a running mural of fantastic green seas banded with purple and white, washing the feet of velvety brown hills. There had been shores like that, once, long ago, on an incandescent world. The artist who painted these walls had never seen bare hills or a colored sea. There was a curious off-beat focus about his rendition of these imaginary things, and it showed all the more clearly now because in the center of his mural a square of brightly tinted moving shadows showed a real sea and a real shore, smothered in jungle, and a boat shooting forward on V-spread wings of water.

Two people sat quietly in the painted room, watching the images of the landside world rehearse in duplicate the action far above them. Kedre Walton, cross-legged on a flat cushion on the floor, was laying out a game of tarot solitaire on the low glass table before her, glancing only now and then at the flickering screen. But Zachariah Harker in his deep chair never moved his eyes from the flying boat.

'There they go, poor fools. There they go,' he said, almost to himself. He held a little censer of burning vine-dust in one hand, moved it gently to and fro under his nose occasionally. The vine had once run heavy with white sap that dripped poison on any landside animal rash enough to pass beneath it. Dried and burned, it gave out a slightly narcotic fragrance that soothed the senses and the mind. Zachariah inhaled a deep breath of the smoke and blew it out again toward the screen. 'This time,' he said, 'Sam Reed's bitten off more than he can chew.'

'How vulgar,' Kedre murmured, flashing him a smile. It was a smile that literally flashed, for she had adopted today an extreme of a current fashion. Her heavy black ringlets were gilded, each separate hair sheathed in a film of gold and twisted into a great braided coronet like a helmet above her narrow Egyptian face. Even her brows were delicate arcs of gold, and a bead of gold winked at the tip of every lash.

'You look ridiculous,' Zachariah assured her, blinking.

'Of course I look ridiculous. I'm just testing how far I can go. You'll see. Every woman in –'

'Look!' Zachariah sat up suddenly in his chair, eyes on the screen. Kedre turned, holding a card poised above the table, and the two of them sat motionless, watching the mimic action on the wall. It did not look very real.

The boat was swerving in to a landing inside a long, encircling arm of breakwater, where a white pier jutted out into the pale sea. There were ten passengers in the boat, ten young men and women on their way to a promised immortality. Their heads turned this way and that in quick, nervous motions, watching the strange upper world that had always meant danger and improbable romance to the people of the Keeps. Like the youths and maidens traditionally borne to the Minotaur, they watched in excited apprehension the mighty wall of jungle drawing nearer and nearer, and the low, polished white walls of Plymouth Colony encircling the first island to be subdued.

It was no Minotaur that rose from the water in their path, but it was bent on exacting sacrifice. There were many saurian monsters in these seas. Not many yet had names, and the one that came dripping out of the milky water before the boat was unfamiliar to every watcher. Its darkly gleaming neck rose twenty feet with leisurely speed, water sliding like ragged silk from both sides of the great, gracefully bending arch. It opened a mouth that could encompass a man's head, opened it wide and hissed terribly. The mouth was solidly lined with fangs, rim, roof and sides jagged with them.

A chorus of shouts and screams, thin over the water, rose from the rocking boats as frantic passengers scrambled futilely toward the far side. The head dived down toward them, the neck looping after it like thick rope. There was infinite grace in the long, smooth, curving motion. The beast seemed to have chosen a girl near the front of the boat as its immediate victim. She had yellow hair and she wore a rose-red tunic, bright against the pale sea water.

For a moment pandemonium reigned in miniature in the little boat. Then its pilot, moving with rather elaborately scornful precision, leaned forward and pushed a lever. From both sides of the boat translucent impervium slid upward, half-shells that met overhead with a click, shutting in the passengers and the crew in impregnable protection.

The diving head struck hard against the dome. The boat heeled far over, dipping its impervium arch deep into the water, tossing the men and women into a frantic tangle. The sharp keel flashed into daylight and the long dark neck of the monster struck it squarely.

An ear-piercing scream soared across the water. The saurian's fang-studded mouth gaped toward the clouds. Its curved neck straightened rigidly and from the gashed dark throat a jet of rose-red blood spurted, fantastically identical in color with the rose-red tunic of the girl.

The scream sounded again, more shrilly; blood gurgled in the long throat and gushed from the gaping mouth. The dark neck beat the sea twice and then slid downward out of sight. A beautiful carmine stain spread outward in circles from the spot where it sank.

The boat righted itself and swung in toward the pier.

Kedre laughed, laying down her card in its proper place.

'That pilot!' she said. 'How bored he was with it all! It wouldn't surprise me in the least if Sam Reed had tied the beast out there for a nice spectacular welcome to his recruits. What a tale they'll have to tell!'

'Don't underestimate Sam Reed, my dear,' Zachariah said gravely, moving the censer under his nose again. 'He'd do exactly that, or something even more elaborately dangerous, if he saw any profit in it. He's a very dangerous person, Kedre – not because he's resourceful but because he's irresponsible.'

Kedre nodded her glittering braided helmet. 'You're right, of course. It's no laughing matter, really. Whoever would have dreamed he'd go so far as piracy! I think we can look for another act of violence the next time anything thwarts him and he can't see an easy legal way out. We've got a problem, Zachariah.'

'Have you lost your taste for him, then, my dear?'

She did not look up, hearing that note of query in his voice. Instead she stirred the cards beside her with a pointed forefinger until she had uncovered the tarot called The Hanged Man. It was a beautifully wrought card like all the rest. The Hanged Man hung by his right ankle from a T-shaped tree against a background of elaborate gold-diapre work. A golden halo radiated around his serene face and hanging hair, which was red. Kedre reversed the card and looked at the small painted face thoughtfully.

'Don't ask me that, Zachariah,' she said.

'You'll have to find an answer some day, my dear. It isn't just a matter of passing fancy, now. The man's an Immortal.'

'I know.'

'Do you know who he is?'

She looked up quickly. 'Do you?'

Zachariah nodded, inhaled more smoke and fanned the cloud away from his face. Through it he said, 'He's a Harker, Kedre. Do you know the story of Blaze?'

'I do now. I suppose everyone does. Sam didn't leave much to the imagination when he decided to tear down Harker prestige. Does *he* know, Zachariah?'

The Immortal laughed softly. 'That's a very fine paradox. No, he doesn't know. He's put a great deal of energy and thought into the problem of discrediting us so that no one is likely to believe anything a Harker says. When he finds it's his own name he's destroyed, I'd enjoy watching his face.'

'"Destroy" is hardly the word, is it?'

'Oh, it isn't irreparable. We can win opinion back. We may have made mistakes – I'm beginning to think that we were mistaken about opposing colonization, for one thing – but our long-term motives have always been sound, and I think everyone knows it. Sam still thinks in short-term schedules. When we want to swing public opinion our way, we'll do it. Just now I'm inclined to watch and wait. Give him rope. The colonies have got to succeed now, of course. Much as I dislike the thought, we'll have to work with Reed on that.'

Kedre turned up a card, started to lay it in place on the board and then hesitated, regarding it with a faint smile. Still looking at the picture on its face, she said,

'For a while, yes. He's a bad man, Zachariah. However I feel toward him I realize that. He's got a way to go yet before he reaches the top. Until he gets there he'll do a better job than any of us could do. With the worst possible motives he'll do quite heroic things to establish a sound pyramid under him, something he can use as a basis for power. He'll establish the foundation for a good working social system. But only the foundation. Beyond that he can't go. He has no conception of constructive society. We'll have to stop him, then.'

'I know. Have you any idea how?'

'Use his own methods, I'm afraid. Misdirection. Exploit his weaknesses and turn his strength against him. Tempt him with some irresistible bait, and then –' She smiled and flipped the card with a delicate finger.

Zachariah waited.

'I don't have a plan yet,' Kedre said, 'but I think I have the beginning of one. I must think about it for a while. If it's possible, it's the one weapon for which he'd have no defense.'

'A weapon?'

Her gold-lacquered brows rose. She looked up at him under the heavy casque of gold, her mouth tucking in at the corners with that faint Egyptian smile that might be no smile at all, but a look of pain. The gold brows gave her face a masklike expression and again she flicked the card with her nail. As well as he knew her, Zachariah could not fathom the things that went on behind her eyes when she wore that look. He had never seen it before.

Wordlessly he leaned forward to see the card. It was the Ten of Swords. It showed a gray amorphous seascape and a dark sunset sky, with the hilts of ten swords sharply outlined against it. Their ten blades stood upright in the body of a dead man.

The day came when Plymouth Colony got the first full quota of volunteers. Sam had waited for that day with a certain eagerness and a certain shrinking, but the eagerness was stronger. He had always preferred to come to grips with a problem – perhaps because so many of his enemies had proved irritatingly elusive in the past. The immediate hurdle was purely psychological. He had to make a speech, and he had to say exactly the right things to the thousands of immortality-seekers.

Facing the battery of visor screens, he drew a long breath while he studied his audience. Then he was ready.

Sam said:

'You're a specially selected group. You've been screened carefully, and all of you have passed the basic tests. They were hard tests. We wanted the smartest, toughest, strongest material in the Keeps, because you're the shock troops of immortality.'

He paused, glancing from screen to screen, at the thousands of faces intent on his own televised face.

'Not everyone can have immortality. After a certain time of biological life, senescence begins to set in. It doesn't necessarily show right away, and it comes sooner to some than to others. We still don't know what causes age, though we know how to stop it. Age may simply be a virus. Some day we'll find out. At present all we know is that there's a treatment that will arrest aging. But it seldom works on those over forty – perhaps because the balance has swung too far toward obsolescence by that time.'

He let his gaze flicker again across the screens. There was danger latent in those waiting thousands. He held a live grenade in his hand. And he had to keep on holding it, till the last possible moment.

'You've all been screened and tested, physically and psychologically. You're the cream of the Keeps. You'll be the first to get immortality. Later, others will too, but you're the advance guard. You'll make it safe for the others – and they'll keep it safe while you enjoy the rewards of your work. It will be work. It will be hard. You must live landside for some years before you gain immortality.'

Five years, he thought. Perhaps longer – but five years was the minimum he had allowed himself. Bearing that deadline in mind, he had supervised the tests, rigging them, watching for vital points.

Screening thousands – later it would be millions – would have been a long, difficult job except that the machinery was already set up for Sam. The bureaus of vital statistics had records of most of the population with all pertinent information, including psychology, heredity, probable longevity – an important point! – and pathological propensity. Sam wanted smart, tough, strong men and women certainly – but one other factor was even more important. On that the success of his scheme depended.

He needed youngish, mature people. Because they wouldn't age visibly in five years.

The only way to prove or disprove immortality is by the empirical method unless –

He had allowed for that possibility, too.

He said, 'You must live landside. Remember, I lived landside for nearly forty years. The treatment takes six or seven years for the average mature man. There, again, it may be because age is a virus, and the older a man is, the longer it takes to destroy that virus. If a child is exposed to the radiations at birth, as the Immortals' children have been, only a few treatments are necessary. There once more, it may be because the age-virus is not present in the newly-born. In such a case, the child grows, reaches maturity – and stops at that point, living for hundreds of years, but growing no older.

'Babies born in the Keeps from now on will have that opportunity. With adults, it's another matter. You'll have the chance, but you'll have to work and fight for it. Because you must be continually exposed to the radiation for six or seven years, and that can't be done in the Keeps.

'We don't know too much about the radiation yet. The radio-element itself is present in the soil and air of Venus, but in microscopic quantities. For reasons we don't understand yet, exposure to solar and cosmic-ray radiation is necessary too. Later we'll learn more. Right now, we know this: we can give you the immortality treatment, but it will take years, and you must spend those years landside, so that the action will be cumulative.

'The process is too complicated to explain in detail.

'It works only on humans. We know that much. Like the ancient *bacillus leprae*, it affects humans but not animals. Guinea pigs couldn't be given leprosy, which was why researchers took so long to discover the cure.

'Immortality is for humans – for you. For all the Keeps. For everyone who isn't already too old to take the treatment. But to be immortal you must live on landside for a time. There isn't room in Plymouth Colony for you all.

'You must build new colonies.

'It's the only answer. We had thought of rotating the population in groups at seven-year intervals, but, to be fair, we would have to take the oldest men and women still able to benefit by the radiation. And they would remain at that age, while the rest grew older. We feel it best to choose people at the peak of their powers mentally and physically, so that they will remain so for hundreds of years. This way, too, the others won't have to wait seven years or fourteen or twenty-one. As soon as you've expanded the colony sufficiently, another batch will come in from the Keeps – and expand the colony farther. Thus everyone will benefit equally.'

Sam studied the screens. They were swallowing it. Perhaps after five years they wouldn't, but until then no signs of age should appear that couldn't be explained away on the grounds of environmental influences. Colonizing Venus naturally would change a man.

'You've got to earn immortality,' Sam told the thousands. 'You may be a bit confused at first in the transition from Keep life; the administration will allow for that. But remember that you must live landside for six years or more, and only by adapting to Colony tradition can you succeed.

'Those in charge here have learned how to cope with landside. They have authority, and you must obey them. We have our own laws – not Keep laws. This is landside. Landside is trying to kill us every minute of the day and night. You are colonists now, not Keep men, and you are subject to Colony law. According to the contracts you signed, you cannot become a Keep man again until formally discharged by the Colony. That will be when you are – immortal.

'Generally speaking, it won't be hard for anyone to readjust. Know your job. Be ready to step into the job of the man ahead of you. Promotion is going to be very rapid in the colony. Be ready for it.

'Immortality must be earned. The next six or seven years may be hard ones for us all. But you won't be giving up one-tenth of your life, you'll be giving up less than one-hundredth. Remember that. Seven years in the colony is the equivalent of *less than a month* after you're immortal.

'Remember that!

'Every time you feel discouraged, think of that. You'll be immortal. And there's no hard work a strong man can't endure for – one single month!'

Sam switched off the teleunit. He was alone in the room. He sat silent for a moment or two, watching the throngs who could no longer see or hear him.

Then he said softly, 'Sugar-coated pills. But it always works. Always.'

The crowds were still watching their screens, getting new orders from their individual unit commanders – members of Plymouth Colony's original settlers, the tough, trained men who had already worked under Hale and Sam. They were falling in line – figuratively and actually.

Expanding the Colony – sure. But along rather different lines. As raspberry plants expand and root by canes, so landside would be colonized. Not in five years – it would take far longer than that. But from now on new settlements would appear along the coasts, supported and guarded by Plymouth till they were self-supporting. Plymouth had to remain compact and strong.

The other colonies, the new ones that were to come –

There was a problem. They couldn't be vulnerable, or they couldn't exist against the interminable fury of the continent. Yet, Sam knew, they would have to remain vulnerable to *him*.

And Plymouth Colony had to become completely invulnerable.

He had five years before the pack could expect to turn and tear him.

Link by strong link they forged the island chain. There was no time for relaxation. Even minutes were grudged. Nevertheless Sam thought Hale was dodging him.

When he walked into the Free Companion's office and found it empty, he made an angry noise in his throat and clicked on the desk televisor. 'Where's the Governor?' he demanded.

'He's directing Operation Clearing, Island Six.'

'Switch me over.'

Presently the screen blanked – apparently Hale didn't have a visual hookup where he was – and the Governor's voice said, 'Hale speaking.'

'Sam Reed. We had an appointment, didn't we?'

'Oh,' Hale said, and his tone changed. 'I'm sorry. Things are moving so fast – some new equipment we needed came in, and I found we could start on Six right away. Make it later.'

Sam grunted and broke the connection. He went outside and commandeered a flitterboat. This time he was certain that Hale had been dodging him.

The pilot was one of the old Plymouth colonists; he gave Sam a soft salute and turned the little boat's prow seaward. They made a big, fast semicircle and swung toward Island Six. The other islands they passed were already colonized, the monstrous forests gone, planting already in progress. Huts were here and there. Quays jutted out at intervals, guarded by pillboxes. Islands One to Five were an odd combination of agrarian and military.

Five islands, only five, balanced against the huge continents of Venus that teemed with ravening life. Yet they were the beginning. Step by step the progress would continue.

Sam studied the pilot's face. He could read nothing there. When the danger came, it probably wouldn't come from the old Plymouth men; the late recruits from the Keeps would be the malcontents. And that time hadn't arrived yet; it wouldn't, Sam hoped, for years. By that time he should have established the tight control he wanted.

And Hale?

Where did Hale stand? Where would he be standing five years from now? That was beginning to worry Sam a good deal. The Keep Families he could cope with, because they were his enemies. But Robin Hale had all the cryptic potentialities of immortality plus a position that could become extremely dangerous to Sam. The pair were nominally fighting as comrades, back to back – which implied vulnerability. He couldn't figure Hale out. There was the real difficulty. How much did the Free Companion know or guess? Had Hale known, all along, that 'Joel Reed' was really Sam Reed? And how much did Hale suspect about the phoniness of the Immortality treatment?

For all Hale knew, Sam might be telling the truth. If, as Sam argued, Immortals were exposed to the radiation soon after birth, no Immortal could actually remember such experiences. Yet the Free Companion wasn't gullible. Even his willingness to follow Sam's lead was somehow suspect. Hale's passivity, of course, might be due to attrition following arduous experiences;

yet, even if that were true, the parallel warned Sam. Metal can become tired – but it can recover. A sword is metal.

Metal – metal. A new thought came to Sam. The Keep recruits – tough, strong, but so far malleable in his hands. They would go through hard struggles landside. When metal becomes work-hardened –

The Sword again.

I must keep my back armored, too, Sam thought.

The flitterboat raced in toward Island Six. The jungles hid most of the land, except for a high knoll at one end. There was a copter there, and a man's figure silhouetted against the pearly sky. Barges and lighter craft were moving at temporary beachheads on the shore. Sam pointed; the pilot nodded and swung the flitterboat deftly aside, threading his way among the craft. The V-spray of water rushed up along the transparent prow-shield like rain.

It would not rain today, Sam decided, glancing up at the cloud blanket. That was good. Meteorology played an important part in Plymouth – landside conditions were bad enough anyway, without battling torrential rains, so jobs were apportioned according to the weather predictions. There should be a few clear days to work on Island Six and establish a base. Later, much later, a bridge would be constructed to Island Five, and the chain extended by one more link.

Sam stood up as the flitterboat grated against a quay. He jumped lightly on the jetty, instantly in the midst of confusing, ordered activity. A crusher rolled on its caterpillar treads from a barge and lurched monstrously up the beach. Lighter, mobile landcraft followed in its wake, specialized weapons for fighting the jungle mounted on huge-wheeled carriages. The men wore light protective suits and respirators. Heavy armor would only be a handicap at this point.

A tapir-masked figure touched Sam's arm and extended a bundle. 'Better wear these, sir. There may still be bugs around – and the poison plants are pretty bad on this hunk of land.'

'All right,' Sam said, and donned suit and respirator. 'I want to get up to the Governor. Is he on that hill?'

'Yes, sir. There's no road yet, though. He came in by copter.'

'Find me another one, then.'

The man thought for a moment, turned and shouted a question. After a while a twin-screwed gyro came down from somewhere and picked Sam up. Four minutes later he jumped out on the summit of the knoll from the hovering copter and waved the pilot to proceed.

Hale wasn't wearing an aseptic suit or respirator, so Sam took his off. Up here, above the jungle, there was less danger of infection. Besides, both Sam and Hale had built up a good deal of resistance and immunity in the last few months.

Hale gave Sam a nod. He carried binoculars and a portable microphone, wired from his own grounded copter near by. He had no other equipment except for a large-scale map pinned out on a camp table before him.

'How's it coming?' Sam asked.

'Fair,' Hale said. 'The five-spray treatment hit the tolerance levels of most of the bugs. But you never know with mopping up.'

Anything under a foot long was classified as a bug. That left the fauna – critters – and the flora – the green stuff. The operation meant a little more than merely mopping up, since the fauna was big and the flora unpredictable and perilous.

But the five-spray treatment helped considerably. They had learned much in colonizing five islands. The first step now was to shower the island very thoroughly with solutions that didn't like bugs. One formula hit the lichens chiefly – a vital matter. Another damaged a good deal of the flora. The critters, at best, got slightly sick, but they charged at you with bared fangs and you could shoot them, if you were fast; they didn't have the unpleasant trick of infiltrating your lungs and sprouting quickly into a spongy mass that paralyzed your respiratory apparatus.

Island Six didn't look like the colonized islands or the raw ones now. It looked sick. The jungle wasn't a blazing green riot. It seemed to hang, like Spanish moss draped across the great boles, and occasionally slow, lethargic movements stirred in it. Sam could get a better picture now.

'There's another pair of binoculars in the plane,' Hale suggested.

Sam got them. He studied the island below. He studied the men. There was something about the patterns of their movements that interested him – a briskness unfamiliar in the first Colony, certainly almost unknown in any Keep. Sam's interest in the jungle was purely superficial and subsidiary. To him the only truly interesting thing was his own kind and he spent long, absorbed thought on the motives behind every act that seemed out of the ordinary in his fellow creatures, his unconscious mind faithful to the concept that there might be something in it for Sam Reed.

These men were very happy in their work. It was something new on Venus. Sam knew their muscles must be aching at the still-unaccustomed toil, the sweat must be running uncomfortably down their bodies inside the protective suits. There was danger in every breath they drew and every move they made. But they were happy. The work was new and absorbing. They were creating. They could see the great strides of their progress simply by glancing behind them. This was the proper occupation of mankind – bringing order out of chaos in the sweat of their brows. It was good and right, and mankind had for too long lacked any pleasure in physical toil. Sam filed the thought away for that day when the pleasure in work gave way to boredom.

Then he glanced sidewise at Hale, still holding the binoculars to his eyes to hide the fact that he was studying his partner.

Abruptly he said, 'Hale, what are we going to do about the Harkers?'

Hale spoke crisply into his microphone, waving one arm in perfectly futile gestures of direction to the invisible crusher, and then turned to Sam.

'What do you want us to do?' he asked mildly.

'They're too quiet. They let us win – maybe too easily. Once before they let us think we were winning, until they were ready to strike. I know – that was my fault. I was younger then. I didn't have much sense. This time I'm on the level – I know I've got to be. But I still don't trust the Harkers.'

Hale regarded him with a quiet gaze that gave nothing away.

'Maybe,' he said enigmatically. 'How far ahead have you planned, Reed?'

It was Sam's turn to hedge. 'What do you mean?'

'I mean there's going to be trouble in a few years – five or ten, wouldn't you say? Or have you figured on that yet?'

Sam sighed with some relief. So that much of it had emerged into the open, then. Since his triumph on the telecast, when he had forced the Immortals to surrender to his demands and snatched victory from defeat by a promise he could not keep, he had not spoken privately with Hale.

That was Hale's doing. He had taken care that there were always others present. And now it had somehow become impossible for Sam to ask him openly whether or not he had recognized Joel Reed from the start. There was a psychological pressure there Sam recognized and did not like. It meant that Hale had more power latent in him than Sam had quite counted on.

At least, one thing was emerging now – the immortality question. And Hale knew. Obviously he knew the truth. Still – he had tacitly accepted the fraud. He was making use of recruits who could have been won no other way, lending his name to a swindle beside which Sam's original deceit was nothing.

Realizing that clearly for the first time, Sam felt surer of himself.

'Yes, I figured on it,' he said. 'I wish I didn't have to. Maybe the end justifies the means – we couldn't have worked in any other way, could we?'

Hale's brow lifted a little at the pronoun. But the question itself he could not deny. He had accepted the benefits; he could scarcely refuse a share in the responsibility now.

'No, we couldn't. Or at any rate, we didn't,' he acknowledged. 'What we do with the scheme now will show whether it's justified. We'll have to watch that, Reed.' It was a warning. 'Do you have anything planned yet about how you'll meet that crisis when it comes?'

Sam had, of course. But he was quick to accept the warning. So Hale would go only so far in exploiting the candidates for immortality, eh? Very well, then, Sam's plans would have to remain disguised until the hour came for action.

'I've thought of several outs,' he said carefully. 'We'll discuss it when we have more time.' He had thought of one safe out and one only, and Hale was a fool, he thought, if he didn't know it. When the promise of immortality showed itself a fraud, there was going to be a tremendous surge of resentment against the men who had made the promise – Hale by implication, along with Sam. Violence would be the result; and you can meet violence only one way. Sam meant to be prepared for that day. If Hale disapproved of his solution, let Hale find a better one or take the consequences. Sam meant to provide for Sam Reed. And if Hale tried to interfere in Sam's plans about that vital subject, there was going to be conflict in Plymouth Colony.

Sam had an uncomfortable notion that Hale might be a more formidable opponent than he had heretofore guessed.

It seemed prudent to change the subject. Sam had found out most of what he wanted to know, but the thing which had ostensibly brought him here remained unsolved, and it, too, was important enough.

'About the Harkers,' he said, 'this time I think we'd better stay in touch with them. We've got more chance of watching out for their schemes if we're working together. And right now, I don't see how they can go on opposing our plans. Even they must know that if colonization is ever going to succeed, it's got to succeed right here in Plymouth Colony. If this fails, there'll never be another attempt.'

'You're right, of course. I believe all the Keep Immortals must know that by now.'

'Then they'll have to work with us toward the same goal, if their motives are as good as I've been told they are. We're the winners. I think it may be up to us to make the first gesture toward consolidation.'

'Yes?'

Sam hesitated. 'I don't trust myself to do it,' he said with a burst of frankness. 'Zachariah Harker and I are ... well, we don't get along. Whenever I see him I want to hit him. You'd be a smoother diplomat than I am. You're an Immortal. You've known them all for a long time. Will you do it, Hale?'

Hale hesitated in turn. Then, obliquely, he said, 'You're an Immortal too, Reed.'

'Maybe. I suppose so. Not in the same sense, though. That's something I'll have to investigate some day, when I have time. It isn't important now. Will you go?'

Still Hale hesitated. While he stood there, evidently searching for the right phase, the transmitter in his hand buzzed thinly with excited voices and he put it to his ear, relieved at the interruption.

For a moment he listened, peering toward the distant jungle where now and there a treetop could be seen to sway and go down before the juggernaut onslaught of the invisible crusher at its work.

'Take your binoculars,' he said to Sam. 'Step over to the left there – I think there's a gap where you can see across the quarter-line. You shouldn't miss this – they've run into a siren web.'

Curious, Sam obeyed.

The binoculars seemed to lift the jungle forward and upward in one tremendous jump. The crusher had quartered the island, smashing flat four broad avenues between which wedge-shaped segments of jungle still stood, drooping from the poisonous sprays, already paling from brilliant hues to drab. The nearer segment had already been nearly flattened and Sam could see across it, and across the crushed avenue beyond, into the distant wedge of standing trees where the crusher was plowing methodically forward.

It was a monstrous thing, heavily mailed, lurching on its caterpillar treads with a ponderous, rhythmic gait not inappropriate to this jungle it moved through. The giant saurians of Venusian landside moved with the same vast, lurching tread, heaving their mailed sides through the trees no less majestically than the man-made juggernaut that had come to destroy them.

Vines wreathed it, hung in great swathes and matted tangles from its shoulders and sides. Some of the vines still feebly writhed against the metal, striking with fanglike thorns at the unyielding plate.

Sam could hear faintly the rumble and roar of the crusher lumbering on its way; the crack of breaking tree trunks came sharply through the air, and now the distant shouting of men running forward to watch the excitement was clear and thin over the distance between.

Then a flash of color just ahead of the crusher caught Sam's eye, and for an instant it seemed to him that all his senses paused. He did not hear the sounds from below or feel the binoculars pressed to his eyes or smell the heavy discomfort of the landside air, which he was still unaccustomed to breathe. There was only that flare of color that glowed almost in his face and then faded and blurred to another color more exquisite than the first.

Sam stood motionless while the two blended together and slid into a third hue clouded all over with paler tints whose motion as they coalesced was hypnosis itself. The colors were almost painful to see.

Abruptly he lowered the binoculars and looked questioningly at Hale. The Free Companion was smiling a little, and there was admiration in his face.

'You're a good man,' he said with some reluctance. 'You're the first person I've ever seen look away from a siren web that quickly. Most can't. You'd be a bad hypnosis subject.'

'I am,' Sam said grimly. 'It's been tried. What is that thing down there?'

'A distant cousin of the happy-cloak organism, I imagine. You remember they make happy-cloaks from a submarine thing that subdues its prey through a neuro-contact and eats it alive – only the victim doesn't want to get away once it's sampled the pleasures of the cloak. The siren web works in the same way, only with a landside variation. Look and you'll see.'

Sam looked again. This time he adjusted the binoculars to bring the colored thing into very near focus. It was impossible for a moment to see what the siren web really was, for again he experienced that stasis of the senses and could only gaze with painful delight at the motion of its colors.

Then he wrenched his mind free and looked at it objectively. It was a very large web, probably an old one as age goes in these ravening jungles. Judging by the men who still ran toward it behind the crusher, he saw it must be nearly ten feet in diameter. It was stretched between two trees in a little clearing, like a spider web, anchored by strong interlacing cables to branches above and vines below. But in the center it was a solid thing, like fine membrane stretched taut, vibrating slightly with a motion of its own, and flushing with color after color, each more enthralling than the last, pumping faster and faster over the shivering web.

A faint twang of sound floated across the distance to Sam's ears, coming more slowly than sight so that though he saw each sound created by the vibrating cables and membrane, he heard it superimposed upon the next visible vibration. The sound was not music as human beings know it, but there was all the rhythm of music in it, and a thin, singing shrillness that touched the nerves as well as the ears, and made them vibrate ecstatically to the same beat.

The thing was exerting all its siren powers to lure the crusher to destruction. It flashed its most exquisite colors hypnotically in the faceless muzzle of the machine, it shrilled irresistible hypnosis to disrupt the synopses of the wire-linked nerves and paralyze the juggernaut thread.

And for a moment it seemed impossible that even a creature of steel and impervium could withstand the onslaught of that wonderful hypnosis.

If it had not withstood the siren, the men who were running forward now would have been lost. All Sam caught was a distant echo of the humming, but it made his brain work only in flashes, and in the flashes the color of the web wrought its paralysis of mind. He knew that if he were running with those men behind the crusher he would probably run blindly too, to throw himself into the outstretched embrace of the siren.

'It's happened before,' he told himself dazedly. 'A long time ago in Greece, and Homer wrote the story.'

The whole thing was over in a matter of seconds. To the last the siren flamed and shrilled, spreading out its web in a wide-flung promise of rapture. Then the nose of the crusher lurched forward and touched the center of the web.

In a flash the membrane leaped forward and closed about it. The cables drew thin and fine, screaming with a last vibration of triumph. And there may have been some faint electrical impulse to shock and paralyze the prey, for even the crusher seemed to hesitate for an instant as the glowing wings of the thing enfolded its muzzle. Even the crusher seemed to tremble in every plate and filament at the ecstasy of the siren's touch.

Then the juggernaut lurched on.

The cables drew thinner, thinner, tauter, paling from brilliance to translucent white at the increasing tension. They sang so shrilly the ear could no longer hear, but the nerves felt their last agonizing vibration high up in the ultrasonic chords.

The cables snapped. The siren web clutched convulsively in one last spasm at its metal destroyer, colors flamed over it in impossible discords. Then it went flaccid and dropped limply forward, sliding down the mailed muzzle. The grinding treads caught it, carried it remorselessly to the ground, trampled it under into the debris.

And the thing that slid groundward was an enchanted web, a Nessus-shirt of burning color. But the thing the caterpillar treads crushed into the green melee beneath them was an ugly, rubbery gray mat that squirmed convulsively when the cleats caught it.

Sam let out his breath in a long sigh. He lowered the binoculars. For a moment he said nothing. Then he stepped forward, laid the glasses on Hale's camp table, and proved anew that he was no fit subject for hypnosis of any kind.

'About the Harker interview,' he said, 'when can you get away for the trip?'

Hale sighed, too.

'I can't,' he said.

Sam frowned. 'It's important. It's something nobody but you is really fitted for. I wish you could manage it, Hale.'

'There's only one place where I'm really indispensable, Reed. Right here. Nobody else knows landside as I do. I'm no diplomat. You're our contact man. I'm sorry.'

There was more to it than that. Sam felt perfectly sure of it. Hale was disassociating himself resolutely from every aspect of this game of deceit except one – the profit. The man power. That he would accept. The rest was up to Sam. And there was nothing whatever that Sam could do about it.

For the first time an unpleasant idea flashed across Sam's mind. Until this moment he had seen himself as the motivating force behind colonization. He had pulled the strings that moved the puppet figure of Robin Hale. But in the final analysis, he wondered suddenly, who was the puppet-master and who the dancing doll?

He shrugged.

'All right. I'll do it if I have to. But don't blame me if I make a mess of it.'

'I won't.'

Sam set his jaw. The matter was not really ended. He knew now where his real competition lay, and he knew the conflict had just begun.

The light was cool and clear as crystal. It was a room for working and thinking and planning. It had been designed by Immortals and for Immortals. The planes and curves were functional, but not obtrusively so; they flowed smoothly into each other, and the crystalline flower sprays and the changing picture designs on the frieze were part of the entire quiet, casual pattern. There was nothing to catch and hold the eye for longer than a moment or two. But where the eye rested on shifting color or slow-budding, slow-flowering artificial crystal plant, the beholder found an anchor for his shifting thoughts, and could build new ones from that point.

In that cool, quiet place, brimming with a clarity of light that held steady from its invisible sources, Zachariah sat beside Kedre at a long desk. Her tapering fingers, with gilt nails, shuffled through the dossiers before her.

'You had better go to see Reed,' Zachariah said.

Kedre lifted her shoulders in a delicate shrug. 'Landside?' she asked. 'Oh, no!'

'Aren't you the one best qualified to deal with him at this point?'

'Must we deal with him?'

Zachariah nodded toward the desk top. 'You have a plan. But Reed's no fool. Misdirection – he's used that trick himself. We should have one real plan, and one overt one to distract Reed's attention.'

'You don't know what I have in mind.'

'I've got an idea. You must have based it on the theorem that Sam Reed is necessary now but will be dangerous at some later time.'

She nodded.

Zachariah took one of her hands and ran his fingertips lightly across the gilded nails. 'But when? We don't know that. And until then, Sam Reed will make his position stronger and stronger. He may be vulnerable now and invulnerable later. We can't strike now, though. Not if Venus landside is to be colonized.'

'Hale was right, you know,' Kedre told him musingly. 'We did wait too long.'

'Not quite – but we would have. However! One error doesn't mean failure. The question is, who's the pawn and who's the player? Reed thinks he's the player. He must remain so, until –'

'Until?'

Zachariah looked at a crystal plant, not answering till it had gone through its glittering cycle of bud and flower. 'Until he's served his purpose and landside's safe. We can't set a definite time-period. So what we need is a bomb, planted now, which will explode when we set it off.'

'That's my plan,' Kedre said. 'A bomb. The only possible time-bomb an Immortal can use against an Immortal, when we can't really read the future.'

'And that is?'

'What can we plant near Sam that will stay with him always, potentially explosive, that won't deteriorate for, say, twenty years? That should be time enough. Sam must *want* that bomb near him. It must be something he will want and need. Something that can be custom-made, to suit Sam's requirements exactly, and especially something that Sam can't possibly suspect. A bomb that must seem so harmless Sam can investigate it thoroughly without suspecting its deadliness, even if he traces it back to its – construction.'

Zachariah chuckled. 'Construction?'

'Birth.'

'Of course. A human time-bomb. As you say, the only feasible one an Immortal can use against an Immortal, under the circumstances. What about the difficulties?'

'I need your help now, Zachariah. We've got to start *before* birth. We've got to plan our time-bomb from the very gene, train him every step of the way, and cover our tracks very thoroughly. I think I know how we can do that. But first – I've been using deduction, and then induction. Here's a brief of pertinent information from Sam Reed's dossier.'

'Not the public –'

'I used our private files, too. Oh, we know more about Sam than he suspects. Psychologically we have him pretty well taped.'

'He'll change in five years. Or fifty.'

'We can make prediction graphs. And some basics won't change. He'll always have a weakness for the color blue, I know. Our time-bomb will have blue eyes.'

Zachariah began to laugh. Kedre didn't. She made an irritated gesture and picked up a photograph.

Zachariah sobered. He looked at her shrewdly.

'I wonder what your motives are, Kedre,' he said. 'I wonder if you know?'

She said calmly. 'I isolated many facts from Sam's records, and built up a picture of what sort of man he'll want near him in, say, eighteen years. I'm predicting my picture on the success of the colonization plan, naturally. We'll have to work with Sam on that. Our time-bomb must be specially trained, so his talents and skills will be what Sam needs. Personality and appearance are important, too. Sam's conditioned to like certain types of voices and faces. And to dislike others. Well – I got that picture clear … what sort of man we'd need.'

She found another photograph.

'Then I searched in vital statistics for a man and a woman. I checked everything about them – heredity, everything! I can predict almost exactly what their child will be like, especially since it will be conceived and born under certain conditions we'll arrange – not obviously.'

Zachariah took the photographs, one of a young man, the other of a young woman.

'Do they know each other?'

'Not yet. They will. The man is ill. I had to arrange that. I had him infected – he had volunteered for the Colony. We'll keep him here, and we'll arrange for him to meet this girl. But we must never show our hand.'

Zachariah, suddenly interested, bent forward, glancing at various charts.

'What's his work? Oh, I see. Mm-m. Give him something more interesting. Making sure they stay in Delaware will be tricky. I think we can pull the right strings, though. Yes, I'm sure of it. We can arrange for them to meet and marry – but the child?'

'Simple. We already know her fertility period.'

'I mean, what if the boy turns out to be a girl?'

'Then she may have even a stronger appeal to Sam Reed,' Kedre said, and was silent for a little while. Suddenly she pushed the girl's photograph away.

'Psychonamics is the rest of the answers,' she said briskly. 'The child, boy or girl, will have psychonamic treatment from the very start. Secret, of course. Not even his parents will know. There will be mnemonic erasure after every treatment, so that the boy himself won't know he's undergoing continued hypnosis. And it'll amount to posthypnotic suggestion. In the boy's unconscious, by the time he's eighteen, will be a command he can't disobey.'

'To kill?'

Kedre shrugged. 'To destroy. We can't yet tell what will be the most effective treatment. Of course nobody can be hypnotized into committing any act he wouldn't do consciously. The boy must be trained so he'll have no compunctions about Sam Reed. There'll have to be some triggering response – we'll implant that hypnotically, too. He mustn't act until we set off his reaction, no matter what provocation he gets up to that time.'

Zachariah nodded thoughtfully. 'It's good. It's elaborate, of course, too. A Robin Hood's barn sort of plan.' He used the curious colloquialism without thinking of its vastly faraway origin. 'Are you sure we aren't overestimating the man?'

'I know Sam Reed. Don't forget his background. During his formative years he thought of himself as a short-termer. He's got a tremendously strong instinct for self-preservation, because of the life he lived in the Keeps. Like a wild animal's, watchful every second. I suppose we might kill him now – but we don't want to. We need him. The whole culture needs him. It's only later, when he's dangerous, that we'll want him destroyed. And by then … well, you'll see.'

Zachariah, his eyes on a slowly unfolding stone flower, said, 'Yes, it's a pattern, I suppose. Every autocrat knows how precarious his position is. We'd have been better rulers of the Keeps if we'd remembered that ourselves. And Sam will have to be an autocrat to survive.'

'Even now it probably would be very hard to attack him personally,' Kedre said. 'And in ten years – twenty – fifty – he'll be really invulnerable. He'll be fighting every hour, every year of that time. Venus, his own men, us, everything around him. He won't be living in the Plymouth Colony we see on the visors now. Here in the Keeps nothing changes – it's hard for us to adjust our minds to the changes that are going to take place landside. Our own technologies will make his invulnerability possible – protective devices, psychological barriers, screenings … yes, I think we'll need something like our time-bomb to make sure of reaching him by then.'

'It's elaborate in one way,' Zachariah told her, 'but I withdraw my Robin Hood's barn simile. In its own way it's extremely simple. Once you admit the need for the roundabout approach, you can see how simple it is. Sam will be expecting some tremendously complicated attack from us. He'll never dream we could lack deviousness to the extent that our single weapon is a gun in the hands of a boy.'

'It may take fifty years,' Kedre said. 'It may fail the first time. And the second. The plan may have to be changed. But we must start now.'

'And you'll go landside to see him?'

She shook her gold-coifed head. 'I don't want to go landside, Zachariah. Why do you keep insisting on that?'

'He'll be wondering what we're up to. Well – give him an answer. Not the right one. He's no fool. But if we can make him suspicious of minor things, it'll occupy his mind and stop him from watching us too closely in our major project.'

'You go.'

Zachariah smiled. 'I have a personal reason, too, my dear. I want you to see Sam Reed. He isn't the underdog any more. He'll have begun to change. I want your reaction to Sam Reed Immortal.'

She gave him a quick, masked glance, the light glinting from her golden hair and golden brows and dazzling from the flicker of golden beads that tipped her lashes.

'All right,' she said. 'I'll go. You may be sorry you sent me.'

Hale studied the site of Island Six's ganglion, the cleared area where the local administration buildings would presently rise. Work progressed. In distant jungles, toward the coast, the rumbling roars of crashers could still be heard, but here there was constructive, not destructive, activity. The tree boles had been hauled away over a four-acre area, and the ground had been ploughed up. Surveyors were already busy.

An old man was stooping down not far away, and Hale strolled toward him as he recognized the Logician. Ben Crowell straightened, his shrewd, seemed face alight with speculation.

'Hullo, Governor,' he said. 'Looks like good soil here.' He crumbled loam between his calloused fingers.

'You're not expendable,' Hale said. 'You shouldn't be here. But I suppose there's no use trying to give you orders.'

Crowell grinned. 'Not a bit. Thing is, I always know what'll happen and about how far I can go.' He examined the loam again. 'Poisoned now, but it'll come back. When the anaerobic bacteria get to working –'

'First we flood the soil with bacteriophage,' Hale said. The surveying crew and the diggers were some distance away; they could talk without being overheard. 'One toxic treatment helps, but one isn't enough – there are too many dangerous bugs in the dirt.'

'It's good dirt, though. Almost too rich. Over to the west there it's sour; needs liming. But you can get some nice crops on this island.'

A man wearing a shoulder-tank equipped with a hose and what seemed to be a gigantic hypodermic syringe came past, moved to a labeled stake, and began working the telescopic 'needle' into the ground. 'One of them, huh?' Crowell said.

'One of the worst. Above ground it's just a creeper. But the root-reservoir's twenty feet long and ten feet down. Only way to kill it is pump it full of poison.'

'Used to be something like that on Earth – Man Underground, we called it. Dunno the scientific name. Only we used kerosene to kill it. Stuff never grew quite as fast on Earth as it does here. Bad now, but it'll be an advantage when we get good crops in. Corn in twenty days, maybe.' He shook his head, clucking appreciatively.

'If we can keep the weeds out.'

'Only one real way. Pull 'em. You might try crab grass, though,' Crowell suggested. 'I'd back crab grass even against Venus creeper, and you know what a strangler that is. Look, instead of letting some of the acres stay poisoned – that don't help the soil – why not put in some crab grass? Brother, it *grows!*'

'I'll check on it,' Hale said. 'Thanks. Any more ideas? Or is that against your rules?'

The Logician laughed. 'Shucks, I can make suggestions. They don't alter the future one way or the other – somebody was sure to try crab grass here sooner or later. It's only the big things I don't interfere with, if I can help it. They may not look like big things at the time, but *I* know.' He peered through a swathe of fallen trees toward the coast. Far beyond, across the bay, was the mainland, where the cliff-like structure of the old Doonemen fort stood. There was activity on that weed-draped, lichen-stained hulk. Bright scarlet flashes blazed out and were gone. Boats kept up a continual traffic from the mainland to Island One and back again.

'What goes on?' Crowell asked. 'Going to work on the fort already?'

'Sam's idea,' Hale said. 'I think he's afraid I'm beginning to take the initiative. I started work on this island without discussing it with him first. So he's pulling the same trick. That's fine.'

Crowell considered. 'So? What's the setup?'

'He started to clear the old fort. Quite a job, and we weren't ready to tackle the mainland yet – but I think it'll be O.K. I'd say otherwise if the fort weren't already there. The Doonemen built it the right way. I remember –' He, too, looked toward the shore, his face changing a little. 'There was always a maintenance crew on duty. The jungle was always ready to eat us up, if it could. The plants – and the animals. But the Keeps gave us equipment then; UV batteries, heat rays, acid sprays. The Free Companions always had two fights going on. One was irregular; wars against other Companies. But the fight against the jungle never stopped.'

'Maybe Sam's bit off more than he can chew,' the Logician suggested.

'No. He's got the equipment and the man power. Once he clears the fort, once he sets up his maintenance machinery, he can keep things running. He can't move back inland yet, but he doesn't want to. He's going to use the fort as an additional base, he says, and start working along the archipelago till he meets me. That'll save time – our working from both ends of the island chain. It's a good idea.'

'Got enough men?'

'Five thousand,' Hale said. 'It's enough, but not too much. We're a little crowded yet, but we've got to have the man power reserve to fall back on for emergencies. Never know when you have to throw in shock troops against the jungle. And every mile we clear means losing a crew left to maintain it. Five thousand, and more coming when we have room to house and use them.'

'No rumpus yet?' Crowell asked.

Hale looked sharply at him. 'Expecting trouble?'

'Don't have to be prescient for that, son. Five thousand men doing hard work, and more coming – promising 'em immortality won't keep 'em quiet indefinitely. A fella has to go to town Saturday night and raise a bit of hell.'

'What do you know about that immortality business?' Hale asked, with a glance around.

The Logician merely grinned.

Hale looked toward the distant fort, where the red flashes of flame-splashers were burning the old walls clear. He said, 'You know, and I know. Nobody else can be sure, except Sam. But his story is that you can get immortality from a radiation that exists on Venus. Well – you were born on Earth!'

'Oh, there was a certain amount of radioactivity flying around on Earth just before it blew up,' Crowell said.

'There'll be trouble, though. You know one danger. It could happen here. That time, man left Earth and came to Venus. If it should happen again –'

'Kind of like a hermit crab. When it outgrows its shell, it crawls out and finds another. Mistake to stay in a shell that's too tight. Lots of things might make it tight. Growing too fast – which was what happened on Earth. These people –' Crowell waved toward the crew of workers. 'Could be they're outgrowing the Keeps, only they never knew it. A man needs a lot of things, all in all.'

'Are you going to stay in the colony?' Hale asked abruptly.

'Guess so, for a while. I'm a dirt farmer at heart. Why?'

'Oh, not because you're the Logician. You're an Immortal. So am I. The short-termers – you can't let yourself get too closely involved if you're immortal. The Keep Families … Sam … you're the only man on Venus who's my kind.'

'We both spent the best parts of our lives under the sky, son,' Crowell said.

'And with our feet on good brown dirt. Not the longest part of our lives, but the best part. With me it was Earth, with you it was Venus, but it comes to the same thing. I know what you mean. I can feel at home with you, though sometimes you sure act like a cussed fool.'

They watched the workers again. After a while, following a new chain of thought, Hale said, 'We'll have to militarize. Sam suggested, but I was thinking about it for some time.'

'They don't look sharp, for a fact,' Crowell said, examining the nearest crew.

'It isn't only that. We've really got a military setup here already, basically. Military discipline and organization. Like the old Companies, in some ways. But there ought to be uniforms, and what goes with them.'

'Think so?'

'If you take away a man's freedom, you've got to give him a substitute, even if it's only a sop to Cerberus. Let him have safe outlets for his individuality. If he can't wear flimsy cello-flex – and he can't here, he needs tough protective fabrics – give him a smart uniform. Service insignia, too, and insignia of rank. Recreational facilities – but organized and controlled. Promising immortality won't be enough, and militarization won't either, but together they'll postpone the blowup a little longer. With the Free Companions it was different; we knew what to expect when we joined up, and we joined because we wanted to, not because of any rewards except the life itself – it was the life we wanted. These recruits now – I think militarization will have a good psychological effect.' Hale, without seeming to do so, was watching the Logician very closely. 'What I'm wondering is why Sam suggested the idea. I'd like to know *all* his motives for doing so. His future plans.'

Crowell chuckled. 'I expect you would, son. I expect you would.'

Hale kicked the brittle wing-cased body of a foot-long beetle and watched it fly spinning across the clearing toward a heap of other glittering dead insects shoveled aside for disposal. One of the first results of the poison sprays on every island was the clattering rain of beetles that dropped like iridescent hail from the foliage, some of them large enough to stun the men beneath.

'You could tell me,' he said stubbornly. 'You could if you would. It would save so much –'

'Now there's where you're wrong, my boy.' Crowell's voice was suddenly sharp. 'Seems to me I've mentioned before that seeing the future doesn't mean a man can change it. That's always been the fallacy – thinking that if you know what's going to happen, you can avoid it. Let me give you a little lecture, son, on the problems of being prescient.'

Crowell hitched his belt and dug a toe into the sod, turning over the rich dark soil appreciatively, spreading it flat beneath his shoe sole as he talked. And his diction changed with his subject.

'The truth is, generally speaking, the superficial currents of events don't mean anything. The big tides are important, but by the time they're big enough to notice, they're too big to be altered. A sea wall wouldn't do it. Because what makes the tide itself, that keeps pounding and pounding away?'

'The minds of men –'

'Back in the Twentieth Century a lot of men knew what was going to happen to Earth. They said so. They said it loud and often. And they were men who had earned public respect. They should have been believed. Maybe they were, by a lot of people. But not enough. The minds of men kept right on working in the same set patterns. And so we lost Earth.

'If you've got prescience you've got to stay a witness – no more. Remember Cassandra? She knew the future, but the price she paid for prescience kept her harmless – nobody would believe her. Prescience automatically cancels out participation. You see that certain prearranged factors add up to a certain equation. THOSE FACTORS. Add another factor – your interference – and the equation is changed too. That's the imponderable – your own interference.

'You see why oracles have got to speak in riddles? There've been plenty of prescient folks in history, but they had to speak vaguely or what they said wouldn't come true.

'Look now. Suppose two major possibilities exist for you. You go down to Nevada Keep tomorrow and put across a deal that nets you a million credits. Or you stay home and get killed. Well, you come to me and ask me whether to go or stay. And I know these two possibilities are right ahead of you. But my hands are tied.

'Because both results depend entirely on your personal motivations and reactions. In possibility A, you'll have gone to Nevada Keep without consulting me, and with certain reaction-basics already existing in your mind. *Under those conditions*, reacting in exactly a certain way to a given set of circumstances, you'll make a million credits. But you consult me. I tell you, say, go to Nevada Keep.

'And you do go – but with a different psychological quotient. I've advised you to go. Ergo, you decide something nice is waiting for you there and you go with a passive attitude, waiting to stumble over a bag of gold, whereas your earning your million credits depends on alert aggressiveness. You see?

'Or here's another possibility. Unconsciously you don't want to go. You rationalize my answer to the point where you stay home, deciding I'm a liar, maybe, or that my advice was really to stay, not go. So you get killed.

'So my job is to keep the factor constant as given, without changing them by introducing the catalyst of my own oracle. I've got to do it subtly, gauging your psychology. And that's tricky. I have only limited information to go on. Prescience works by rules of logic basically. It isn't magic. Knowing you, I've got to find certain ideas, semantic groupings that will influence your decision without your knowing it, without altering your original emotional attitude. Because that original attitude is one of the factors in the final equation my prescience has foreseen.

'So I can't say, "Go to Nevada Keep!" That would mean you'd go passively. I've got to phrase my advice in cryptic terms. Knowing what I know about you, I might say, 'The kheft tree has blue leaves,' and you might be reminded of certain affairs – apparently natural, spontaneous thought-processes on your part – which will create a desire to get away from home temporarily. That way I sidestep – if I'm deft enough – introducing any new element into your original psychological pattern as of that moment. You go to Nevada Keep, but ready to react according to the original pattern.

'You make your million credits.

'So now you know why oracles speak in riddles. The future depends on imponderables which can so easily be changed by a word. THE MOMENT AN ORACLE PARTICIPATES, PRESCIENCE IS LOST.'

The Logician stamped his turned clod flat. Then he looked up and smiled wryly. 'Also,' he said, 'this presupposes that it's advisable, in the long-term view, that you should make that million. It may be better for you to stay home and be killed.'

Hale was looking at the flame that washed the walls of Doone Fort clean. He was silent for a while. 'I suppose I see what you mean,' he said finally. 'Only – well, it seems hard to stand this close to all my answers and not be able to get at them.'

'I could hand you an answer to every problem you'll ever meet, all written out in a little book,' the Logician said. 'So you could flip the page and parrot out your answer whenever you needed one. What good would that do? You might as well be dead to start with. And I'm an oracle only within certain limits. I can't answer all questions – only those I've got full information about. If there's an unknown factor – an *x* factor – I can't foresee anything reliably about that question.

'And there is an *x* factor. I don't know what it is. I realize now I'm never going to know. If I did, I'd be God and this would be Utopia. I recognize the unknown quality only by its absence, its influence on other factors. That's none of my business or yours. I don't let it bother me. My business is to watch the future and not interfere.

'The future is the mind of man. It wasn't atomic power that destroyed Earth. It was a pattern of thought.

'It's easier to control a planet than to control that dust-mote there, blowing around unpredictably on currents we can't even feel. Blowing on a current created by your motion when you reach out to control the dust-mote – which is a thought – and the future of mankind.'

*

Curve beyond great white curve, the walls of Doone Fort stood pearly against the jungle. To Sam, looking up at them from the cleared white floor of the *enciente*, they seemed tremendously tall and powerful. Curve upon thick, smooth curve, they seemed to beat back the forest, to encircle in a jealous embrace the foothold of life within them. Their lines were the lines of waves and of all things carved by waves, instinct with a meaning men can recognize without in the least understanding.

Three stories high the smooth, rounded walls rose, broken by windows that glittered with interlacing screens of light to filter out the bugs visible and invisible. These forts had been built on much the same scheme as medieval castles, to withstand attack from ground-level, horizontally, by men, and by air from bacteria and flying things as medieval men built to withstand flights of fire-arrows. There was a close parallel, for attack by planes had been unknown in the early days on Venus. The Free Companions respected each other's forts. And air travel then as now was too wildly erratic, dependent on currents and torrents of wind too dangerous to attempt.

There was a great deal of activity here. Around the great curve of the *enciente* the barracks and the shops stretched, seething with men. In the higher buildings at the inland end were the hospital, the labs, the officers' quarters. The outer walls curved down to enclose a small harbor with a heavily fortified barbican giving onto the piers outside.

A flurry was in progress at the open barbican, though Sam had not yet noticed it. Men and women already browning from the filtered sunlight paused in their activities and stared frankly, drawing back out of a respect generations implanted in their forebears to let the Immortal through.

Kedre came up the courtyard serenely, smiling at the watchers, now and then greeting someone by name. Her memory was phenomenal; Immortals cultivated the faculty. Her adaptivity was phenomenal, too. In Keep attire she might have looked garish exposed to daylight, but she was too wise to attempt it. She wore a long straight cloak the pearly white of the fort itself, and her head was swathed in a white turban very cunningly wrapped to make the most of her aloof beauty. White in a sunny world would have been blinding; here fort and Kedre alike glowed nacreous in the misty day, gathering all light to themselves.

She said composedly, 'Hello, Sam.'

He clasped his hands before him and bowed slightly in the semi-oriental gesture of greeting that had for so long replaced the handshake. It was his first recognition of her existence, done formally and this time between equals. He could afford it now.

She laughed and laid her narrow hand on his arm. 'I represent all the rest of us down below,' she said. 'We hope we can work together in peace from now on. I … heavens, Sam, how can you breathe this air?'

It was Sam's turn to laugh. He whistled, and a young man who had been following him with a note-pad and stylus came up from the respectful distance to which he had retired. 'Bring a pomander,' Sam told him.

The boy came back at a run, and Sam put the perforated ball of plastics into Kedre's hands. It was filled with fresh flower petals and the warmth of the palms released a heavy cloud of perfume that made the air seem pleasanter to breathe.

'You'll get used to it,' Sam assured her, smiling. 'We all do. This is an honor I hadn't expected so soon. I'd meant to call on you first.'

'You're busier than we.' She said it graciously, and then pulled a little at the arm she held. 'Do show me around. I'm so curious. I've never seen the inside of a fort before. How beautiful it is up here! If only you could do something about this unbreathable air –'

'Wait awhile. Wait twenty years. These jungles are too thick now. They give off too much carbon dioxide, for one thing. But wait. It's going to be better.'

She walked beside him slowly, her spotless cloak-hem brushing the white pavement. 'I believe you, Sam,' she said. 'We rather incline now to thinking you were right. This is the time to colonize, not a generation ahead. Your methods were abominable, but the end may justify them. I'm sure it will if you'll let us work with you. You're a headstrong fool, Sam. You always were.'

'You didn't object to it forty years ago. I haven't thanked you for switching the dream-dust for me, Kedre. Or for having me looked after while I was – asleep.' He said that without so much as a glance at her, but from the sudden twitch of her fingers on his arm, and the way she paused to look up, he knew he had guessed wrong.

'But Sam, I didn't. I tried, but you'd disappeared. Do you mean you don't know where you were all that time? I'll put my men to work on it – maybe we can find out something.'

'Do if you like. I doubt if they can turn up anything my men couldn't.'

'But Sam, that's … it's almost frightening! Because we know someone did take care of you. You couldn't have vanished for forty years like that without … Sam, who could it have been?'

'I'll find out, some day. Forget it. Look – this is the jungle. The real thing, not just something on the screen. What do you think of it?'

They had mounted the white outer stairs leading to the battlements. Now Sam paused and leaned on the parapet, looking down at the belt of raw ground surrounding the fort, and the solid walls of greenery beyond it. Sounds and scenes and subtle motions came from the undergrowth that were frightening because they were still so mysterious. Men had not even scratched the surface of the Venusian jungle yet and all its ways were alien and strange.

Kedre gave it one glance and then turned her back. 'I don't think about the jungle at all. It isn't important. This is.' She gestured toward the teeming courts below. 'You've got a tremendous job to do, Sam. And you're almost single-handed. I know Robin Hale handles the actual working parties, but that's the least part of it. Will you let us share your work? We've had a great deal of experience, you know, in handling men.'

Sam laughed. 'Do you think I'd trust one of you?'

'Of course not. And we couldn't trust you. But working together, we'd keep an eye on each other. You need a check and we need impetus from you. How about it, Sam?'

He looked at her in silence. He was remembering the moment before the dream-dust shut out all sight and sound, her face watching him from the visor screen and her hand giving the order for his extinction. He knew she must be here now for some motive more devious than the overt one. His mistrust of all other human beings and of the Immortals in particular, was profound. And his mind, which until now had been tentatively half-open toward co-operation, dubiously began to close. Sam's early training had been too complete. It was not in him to trust anyone.

He said, 'It wouldn't work. Our motives are too different.'

'We'll be working toward the same goal.'

'I couldn't do it. I've always worked alone. I always will. I don't trust you, Kedre.'

'I don't expect you to. But have it your way. Remember this, though – we both want the same thing, successful colonization of the land. Whether you like it or not, we'll be working toward the same end, down below. And Sam – if after a few years have gone by we find we're at cross-purposes again, remember, it will be you, not we, who have gone astray.' There was warning in her voice. 'When that time comes – and it will – there's going to be trouble, Sam.'

He shrugged. He had just taken, though he did not know it, the first definite step toward that isolation of the mind and body which in the end was to mean his downfall.

'So it's taken five years,' Ben Crowell said. 'Just about what I figured.'

The man walking beside him – Platoon Commander French – said: 'You mean – us?'

Crowell shrugged noncommittally and waved his hand. He might have been indicating the darkness beyond the rampart on which they walked – the pillbox-dotted, cleared lands in which a man might walk for three days in a straight line in safety. It had taken five years to clear seventy-five miles, a great bite taken out of the jungle with the fort as the focal point.

Nothing could be seen now. Floodlights, with charged wire-mesh shields to guard against phototropic bugs, showed part of the ground outside the wall, but in the dark beyond the safety area stretched far inland. The fort had changed too. It had expanded till it crouched on the shore like a monstrous armored beast, so huge that if it had been alive, it could never have walked the earth of Venus.

Curious – earth of Venus. A paradox. Mankind would always carry with him his terrestrial heritage, though he carried his colonies beyond Cygni. The old words, the old thoughts –

The old motives.

Platoon Commander French touched Crowell's arm, and they turned toward a sloping ramp, past the masked muzzle of what seemed to be a strange sort of gun. French indicated it.

'See?'

'What about it?'

'Oh, you'll find out. Come on.'

As always, the courtyards teemed with activity under bright lights. Crowell and French walked through the tumult briskly – only furtiveness was suspect, and their openness was a good mask. They entered an outbuilding. French took the lead.

The fort was a labyrinth now. Technically, the chamber the two men entered presently was classified as a storeroom, but it served a different purpose at the moment. Nearly fifty men were here, drawn from all levels of colony life. Somebody gave a soft challenge.

French said, 'Hello, Court. This is Ben Crowell. I'll vouch for him. Sit down over here, Crowell – and listen.'

He moved to the front of the room, holding up his hand for attention. 'All set? Shut the door. Got the guards posted?'

A man said, 'Step it up, French. Some of us have to be back on duty pretty soon.'

'This won't take long. Listen. There's about a dozen new men here tonight – right? Hold up your hands.'

Crowell was one of those who raised his arm.

'All right,' French said. 'We'll be talking mostly for your benefit. You're all convinced already, or you wouldn't be here. And you won't do any talking to the wrong people after you get out of this room – we chose you carefully.'

He hesitated, looked around. 'The main thing – is there anybody here who still believes in Reed's immortality gag? That phony Fountain of Youth?'

A voice said, 'There's no proof either way, is there, commander?'

French said, 'I came here five years ago. I was twenty then. Island Five had just been cleared. Everybody was talking big – big plans for the future. Immortality for everybody. The treatment was supposed to take six or seven years.'

'Well, it's only been five for you, hasn't it?'

'You don't have to wait a hundred years to be sure. Some of us have been seeing Keep doctors. We're getting older. All of us. There's a way of checking –

the calcium deposits in the blood vessels for one thing. Those treatments of Reed's are fakes. I know I'm five years older than I was when I first hit Plymouth, and the same thing goes for the rest of you. Reed's crossed us up. Look at his record – you can't trust him an inch. Five years I've been sweating up here, when I could have been back in my Keep taking it easy.'

'I kind of like it landside,' Ben Crowell put in, stuffing tobacco into his pipe.

'It could be all right,' French admitted, 'but not under this setup. All we do is work. And for what? For Sam Reed and Robin Hale – building, building, building! Hale's an Immortal; maybe Reed's going to live seven hundred years too – I don't know. He doesn't seem to get any older. Maybe he did find the Fountain of Youth, but if he did, he's kept it for himself. Know what that means? We work! We work till we die! Our children work too, when their time comes. And Sam Reed just hangs around and waits a few hundred years till we've done his job for him and fixed him up a nice, comfortable setup that's just what he wants. Well – I don't see the profit!'

A new voice said, 'You're right. I agree. But Reed had to get the fort built strong. You were here five years ago; you know what it was like.'

'He's in too much of a hurry. Discipline – there's too much of it. He's got plans of his own, and we're not told what they are. Colonizing landside isn't all of it. Sure, we needed that fort five years ago – and we needed it strong. But what about all this top secret armament work? Nobody's supposed to know about the new gun emplacements on the walls – the electric-spray blasters, and the gas throwers. But they're being set up.'

'The jungle?'

'Seventy-five miles away now!' French said. 'And some of these new weapons – they don't make sense! Kalendar, you're a logistics man. Tell 'em.'

Kalendar stood up, a short, swarthy figure in a neat blue uniform. 'They'd be useful for defense against human enemies. They could fight off and smash an onslaught by tanks, for example. But they're more powerful than we need even against a thunder-lizard. Besides, there are long-range cannon being cast and set up – they've got everything from radar calibration to video reactors. They'll throw a shell five hundred miles away and hit the target. What are they going to be used against? Another battery aimed at the fort? And our new plane construction program – you don't colonize by plane!'

'Exactly. What's Reed expecting?' French asked. 'Attack from the Keeps? The Keeps don't fight. They're living a life of glory down there, taking it easy, while we work ourselves to death.'

A low growl of resentment arose. These men didn't like the people of the Keeps – jealousy, probably. But the sound hinted at something new on Venus, just as this secret meeting foreshadowed a result Sam had not expected. For Sam had always been used to dealing with Keep people, and this was a new breed of men.

Ben Crowell puffed at his pipe and watched interestedly.

There was a burst of argument now, violent and angry. The plotters talked a lot – naturally! It was an escape from discipline. They were taking out their emotions in hot argument instead of in action. When they stopped talking, the volcano would probably erupt.

Ben Crowell settled himself more firmly, his back against a packing case.

'– whatever Reed's planning –'

'– let the Keep people do some work –'

'– how much more time are we going to give Reed?'

'How long are we going to sit and take it?'

French hammered for silence.

'We've got several plans. But we've got to figure well ahead. Suppose we kill Reed –'

'That wouldn't be easy. He doesn't take chances!'

'He can't win if most of the colony's against him! And it will be. We've got to spread our organization. Once we get rid of Reed – and Hale – we'll be on top and be able to stay there. We'll have the fort. And there isn't a thing on Venus that can smash the fort!'

'Hale's no fool. Neither is Reed. If they get wind of us –'

French said: 'Every man takes a lie-detector test before he leaves one of our meetings. No traitors live.'

'I haven't lived a thousand years without figuring out how to fool a lie-detector,' the Logician said to Hale.

Hale turned away from his light-latticed window that looked down so far on the walls which had once seemed so high to them all. He said coldly, 'I know you were at that meeting. I have spies, too.'

'Did your spy recognize me?'

'He didn't recognize anybody. He got there afterwards. But he smelled pipe smoke and that rank tobacco of yours. Anyway – I know a little about what goes on around here.'

'What, for example?'

'I know when discipline begins to fail. When men are sloppy about saluting. When they don't polish their brassards. I learned discipline in the Free Companies. I saw the crackup start in Mendez's company before his men killed him. I noticed signs of trouble here months ago. That's when I put my spies to work. I knew what to expect, and I was right. It's beginning.'

'What?'

'Mutiny. I know a few ringleaders – not all.'

'Does Sam Reed know?'

'I've discussed it with him. But – I think he discounts the danger. He's been guarding himself so thoroughly he mistakes personal safety for colony safety.

I want you to tell me what's going on. I know you can. If you don't, I can get the information elsewhere, but I'd like to discuss it with you if you're willing.'

'I know you can find out elsewhere,' Crowell said. 'I'll be glad to talk. I've been waiting for you to ask me, hoping you would, because I couldn't volunteer anything without upsetting the pattern. I got into this passively, you know. Guess I looked like a malcontent. God knows why. No, I do know. Do you?' He squinted at Hale over the hand that cradled his pipe.

Hale shook his head. 'No, I … wait. Maybe I do.' He strolled to the window again and looked down at the busy courts. There was much more of a pattern to the activities in Plymouth Colony than there had been five years ago. Discipline had stiffened into iron rigidity. It seemed to the average man that as the need for discipline lessened with their growing conquests of the land, the meaningless forms of it grew more and more inflexible.

'Sam has his reasons,' Hale said, looking down. 'I don't know what they are, but I can guess. His time's running out. The balance is going to shift pretty soon. Men are losing faith in immortality and beginning to wonder. Sam knows the balance is tilting already, but I don't think it's dawned on him what he's weighing in the balance. Men. And not Keep men any longer. Men like you and me, who know what independence means. No wonder they spotted you for a malcontent. You've lived in a world where every man had to shift for himself or go under. So have I. I suppose the marks of it are plain.'

'Right.' Crowell grinned. 'Keep people want their leaders to do their thinking for them. Our men landside have had to think for themselves. Those who didn't – well, they just don't survive. It's the old pioneer feeling come back, son, and I like the feel of it. It means trouble, but I like it.'

'Trouble is right. Serious trouble, unless we move at the right time.'

'Now?' Crowell was watching the Free Companion keenly.

'Not yet,' Hale said, and the Logician's smile was faint, but satisfied. 'No, not quite yet. Partly I want to sound this thing out to see how far it's going to spread. Like the Man Underground plant, you've got to locate the root. And partly – I don't know, exactly. I've got a sort of feeling that something's working out in these mutinies and plots that shouldn't be crushed. It's the pioneer spirit, all right, and I feel the way you do. I like it. Mutiny isn't the answer, but mutiny's a good sign, in a way.'

'You going to let them go ahead, then?'

'No. I can't do that. At this point they still need Sam and me, no matter what they think. Let the mutineers take over and they'd wind up down in the Keeps again, sinking back into the old apathy. This is a crucial period. Sam's got some sort of plan I don't understand yet, but I'm betting on Sam to come out on top. Sam can take care of himself. His reaction to the mutiny, if he took it seriously, would simply be to stamp it out. And at this point that might mean stamping out the independent spirit of pioneering along with it. I'll have to think it over, Crowell. No use asking you for suggestions, is it?'

Crowell peered intently into his pipe, which had gone out. He poked ineffectually at it with a calloused finger. 'Well,' he said slowly, 'I don't think you need much advice, my boy. You're on the right track. Don't interfere any more than you've got to. There are natural processes at work leveling themselves off and the longer they operate on their own, the better. You know something? I think just living up here landside has done one mighty big service to these people. They've discovered Time again. Down below day and night don't mean much. One season's pretty much like another. But here, you *see* time passing. You get the sense of its being later than you think. These boys and girls started out with the idea they were going to live forever. They had a long-term view. They were willing to work for a colonization they hoped to enjoy themselves, in person, two-three hundred years from now. But that's passing. Time's passing. And they're suddenly waking up to it. No, I'd let these natural forces level off if I were you. As you say, Sam Reed can take care of himself.'

'I'm going to let him,' Hale said. 'You'll keep an eye on these meetings, then? I know they've got a lot of schemes under way, but nothing's near completion yet, is it?'

'They're still blowing off steam. They'll act, but not for a while.'

'Spy away, then. I won't move until I have to. I'll wait – that is, unless Sam moves first.'

Sam moved first.

As usual, he timed himself carefully, integrating every detail, and his action was spectacular, which made a few people wonder what Sam had up his sleeve. But, of course, they couldn't be sure. Some of them never were sure, even after the fantastic gambit was played. As a gambit it was effective – it was check, though not quite checkmate, and the arena from now on would follow even more closely the imagery of the old poet and his great translator – a checkerboard of nights and days. As for the Opponent – the Unseen Player – not even Sam had penetrated that mysterious symbolism. Who *was* the Player. The Harkers? Venus? Another part of Sam?

He knows about it all ... He knows ... he knows ...

It was a chilling thought, but, Sam realized, there wasn't anybody who 'knew about it all.' Certainly not the future, and even the present was difficult enough to interpret in every detail and trend.

Still, he was ready; zero hour had struck, since he had got word certain secret arrangements of his own had been completed. He was in one of his private offices in the great tower he reserved for his own use. Part of that tower was top secret. But this office wasn't; port windows looked seaward toward the archipelago, now covered with farms and little settlements, though the protective pillboxes remained.

He avoided Hale's gaze. He was examining a flat cube on the table before him. It was like a very deep picture frame. But what it held was a siren web, flushing slowly from rose to deep scarlet. Sam opened a silver box on his desk, took out an insect, and fed the siren web through a miniature hinged door. A faint odor of perfume escaped at the same time, and there was a low rhythmic humming.

'Put it away,' Hale said. 'I've smelled that odor too often! What about Crowell?'

Sam slid the siren web frame aside. 'I didn't know he was working for you. He was one of the mutineers, that's all. So I had him arrested with the others.'

'Why did you act without telling me? Why wait till I was forty miles away on an inspection trip?'

'You got here in half an hour,' Sam said. 'Anyway, I had to move fast. I've found out that there's more to this plot than you ever suspected, from what you've been telling me about it. Crowell may be your man, but he's an inefficient spy.'

'I want him released.'

Sam shrugged. 'Of course. But his usefulness is over, isn't it?'

'Not necessarily.'

'A visor call would have done the trick. You needn't have rushed back here.'

Hale said, 'I didn't want any chance of a slip-up. Crowell's got to be released. Accidents do happen. The wrong order, the wrong interpretation by a guard –'

'I've never seen you so concerned about any one individual. Why is Crowell so important?'

Hale hesitated. Finally he said, 'Well – I trust him.'

Now it was Sam's turn to pause. He said softly, 'Trust? You mean you'd trust him with a gun behind your back?'

Hale nodded.

'Maybe some day I'll find a man like that,' Sam said wryly. 'So far I haven't. Well, let's get Crowell released. It's almost time for the trial.'

'You're holding it today?'

'Yes. I've found out so much – unexpectedly – there are dangers. Worse ones than we'd suspected. Our enemies are better armed than we know. Perhaps they've got Keep backing. I don't know. But I haven't time to tell you now; I've arranged for Venus-wide videocasting of the trial, and the Keeps will be tuning in in a few minutes. Come along. You'll find out what the setup is.'

But he paused long enough to feed the siren web another insect. Hale said, with strong distaste, 'Where did you get that thing?'

'Oh, it's a trophy.'

'Young one. Going to keep it? It'll grow –'

'I expect it to.'

'It'll grow dangerous. It's a siren web, Sam.'

Sam said, 'Still, imagine it twenty feet across. Up on the wall there –'

'With you walking into its mouth.'

'I'm not a good hypnosis subject, remember? Anyway, I'll take precautions when it really gets big. Polarized glass or a stroboscopic attachment, a special filtering tonometer for its siren song, some gadget to cut the scent to safety level – the trial's starting. Let's go.'

They went out together.

Hale said, 'How many mutineers have you rounded up?'

'About seventy. Some of them will be useful in the right places. Others are too dangerous to let live –' Sam stopped abruptly. He had almost said too much.

Crowell's release came first, but afterward they went to the room where the trial was to be held. Batteries of visor screens were already set up. There were guards, plenty of them. And the seventy-odd prisoners, unmanacled, were herded together in a railed pen.

Sam started talking abruptly. He was talking to the colony and the Keeps as well as to the prisoners. He began by describing the activities of the malcontents, his growing suspicion of such an underground organization in the colony – 'a colony expanding every hour, succeeding in conquering landside so in a day to come men will be able to live under the open sky – every man and women on Venus!'

He had arrested the plotters. But the plot had ramifications stretching deep underground. There had been a great deal of secret theft – theft of vital equipment, technological equipment, even materials for weapons. Why?

The screens focused on the prisoners.

'You men are cat's paws,' Sam told them. 'Originally you were the ones who started this potential rebellion, but someone else has taken it over. Someone who has kept his identity completely secret. Either you don't know who he is or you won't tell me. You've been questioned. Who is your secret leader?'

Silence.

'What are his plans? Is he a Colony man?'

Silence.

'We have proof. The equipment went somewhere. And there's other evidence. We'll find him, and the rest of his band; he's a menace not only to the colony but to the Keeps. If such a man should seize power –'

The menace hung unspoken over Venus.

'We will find him eventually. We ask the Keep's cooperation in this. But now – you men have been guilty of treason. You plotted to overthrow the colony government and take control. After that, you intended to rule the Keeps as well.'

A man thrust himself forward from the other prisoners. His voice cried thinly across the visors.

'I'm older! We're all older! Where's the immortality you promised us?'

Sam said contemptuously, 'I'm not a fool, Commander French. I've known a long time that this plot was going on, and I knew most of the men involved. Why should I give people like you immortality – to plot further? None of you have been given the immortality radiation treatment for many months. You had nominal treatments, to quiet your suspicions – but immortality isn't for traitors!' His face hardened.

'Governor Hale and I have been waiting, hoping to locate the top man in your organization. Certain events forced us to move now. We still intend to get the top man and render him harmless to civilization, but the present problem is what to do with traitors.

'I condemn you to death.'

The silence began and ticked on and on – longer on landside than in the Keeps. For the colonists knew time now.

Sam made a little gesture.

'You will be taken under escort back to whatever Keeps you may elect. None of you may return. The colony is closed to all of you. So is the immortality treatment. You had your chance to live for a thousand years, and you chose a traitor's way instead.

'You will not be harmed. You will be taken back to the Keeps – and be free. Until you die. And you will die not in a thousand years from now, but in thirty, forty, fifty, perhaps. I withdraw the boon of immortality from you, and therefore I condemn you to death by natural causes.

'Go back to the Keeps. We do not want you here.'

He brought his hands together in the conventional gesture.

'The trial is over.'

Trial: A testing of capacity –

'Message to all Keeps: You will no longer pay korium ransom to Plymouth Colony. You will pay it to the Venusian Provisional Government. We are taking control of the planet. We have means to enforce our demands. Message to the Plymouth Colony: ground all your planes or be destroyed –'

Triangulation couldn't locate the source of the message. It kept moving. And it was always at sea. Apparently the call was being shifted rapidly from transmitter to transmitter – planes, perhaps, though no radar apparatus recorded unauthorized planes in the Venusian atmosphere.

Sam's answer to the challenge was brief – 'Surrender!'

'We have means to enforce our demands –'

Sam's face appeared on all visor screens, in the Keeps and in the colony.

'An all-out offensive has been organized from Plymouth Colony. For the first time the mutineers have come out in the open. Now we can find and smash them. We *will* find them. Televisor reports on our progress will be relayed as we proceed. Special ships and plane crews are being sent to guard the sea areas above every Keep. We are taking all possible precautions. Unauthorized plane approaching Plymouth Fort has been fired on; it is retreating southward. I must direct certain operations; one of our Operations Officers will take over and keep you informed.'

Sam was in his tower. He was alone. For months he had superintended the installation of one-man apparatus. Some tasks he could relay, but the main job depended on him alone. It would be no easy task.

The skip-source message came from the Venusian seas.

'Ground your planes, Plymouth Colony! You can't survive atomic attack!'

Every listener thought suddenly of the memorial eidolon in every Keep; the black-plastic shrouded sphere of the lost Earth. Atomics on Venus – for warfare? Atomic power that could so easily become uncontrollable.

Visors showed infrared and radar jungle vistas as Sam's planes quartered landside and the sea, delicate instruments probing into the black secret fury of native Venus, searching efficiently for the marauders who called themselves the Venusian Provisional Government.

'This is an ultimatum. You have forty-eight hours. At the end of that period, one of the Keeps will be destroyed.'

Atomics!

That was the old terrible fear. That was the terror that had come down in the race through seven hundred years. And in the Keeps the years had meant nothing – had been as meaningless as the hourless days.

Forty-eight hours?

Time had come to the Keeps at last.

Two planes were shot down before they got too close to the fort. Tractor rays eased them to the ground, and there were no explosions. But the threat of the atomic warhead moved closer.

Sam said: 'In our all-out effort, we have recalled our men already assigned to the colony expansion effort – our newest venture.' His tired, strained face gave way to a view of a wide, cleared area on a seacoast, with its familiar jungle backdrop. Some huts had already been constructed, and others stood half-completed, the plastic layers only partly sprayed on the custom-shaped balloon foundations. Piles of equipment were neatly lined up. But orderly crowds of men were moving toward the motor-powered barges beached to receive them.

'The mutineers have not yet been located. Our planes are proceeding with their search –'

The patterns of radar gave place to depthless, infrared jungle, seen from far above. It shifted back to the radar matrix as the plane swept on, probing with all the marvelously keen sensory equipment technology had given it.

'Forty-seven hours. You have forty-seven hours. Plymouth Colony, ground your planes. We have atomic power and we will not hesitate to use it –'

Time …

'You have forty-six hours –'

And fear swept the Keeps. Crowds seethed the Ways, gathering at the clover-leaves where the big visor screens were set up. Zachariah Harker said to Kedre:

'The body politic is more than a figure of speech. The Ways, you know, are like the circulatory system. When too many people gather, forming – well, blood clots – then there's danger of an aneurysm.'

'Zachariah –' Kedre said.

He took her hand.

'I don't know. I don't know, my dear. I'm trying to think. We still have forty-five hours.'

'*You have forty-four hours.*'

'Another attacking plane had been shot down and eased with tractor beams thirty miles from Plymouth Fort. No atomic explosion resulted. This plane was radio-controlled. The robot-guide signals were relayed from constantly shifting areas at sea.'

Hale looked at the Logician.

'Things level off,' Ben Crowell said packing his pipe.

'It's all right for you to talk. You know the answers. I don't.'

'Time to look for real trouble is when you don't see any,' Crowell pointed out. 'You might see some harmless-looking plants, little ones, and you wouldn't think there's a Man Underground root twenty feet long hiding way down, waiting for the right time. Right now –' He glanced at the Keep announcer on the nearest screen. 'Well, you don't see me interfering, do you?'

'No. And you ought to be more excited, with atomic war threatened. Even the Free Companions outlawed atomics for offense.'

'You have forty-three hours,' the screen said.

'You have twenty-four hours.'

'You have twenty hours.'

'You have sixteen hours.'

'Sam Reed speaking. We've found the skunks!'

The screens showed jungle, seen from high above – green, luxuriant, writhing with life. No more than that. Then the bombardment began, acid, flame, rays, and the fury of man's own weapons crashed against the fury of Venus.

The jungle green blackened. It writhed in torment. It flung up huge ropes of screaming vines. Clouds of flying things poured away from the center of that circle of awful holocaust. The towering, pillarlike neck of the thunder-lizard curved up; the red maw opened. The hissing shriek of the saurian rose high and keening through the dull, incessant roar of the blasting rain from above.

'Surrender! We'll destroy the Keeps – we won't hesitate – stop your attack –'

There was only raw, blackened, steaming earth now where there had been jungle.

The soil melted and crumbled. It flowed like lava. A white-hot lake began to grow. Pressure-jets blasted down, forcing the molten rock out from its lake in a flashing, incandescent spray. And something seemed to rise from the turgid steaming depths. As the molten level sank, a gray, rounded surface emerged.

Sam's face flashed on to the screens.

'You are seeing the secret headquarters of the mutineers,' he said. 'You will see it destroyed now.'

A voice shouted: 'We'll destroy the Keeps! Stop your attack –'

The gray dome stood sullenly in the white-hot lake.

The black torpedo shape of a bomb dropped. The gray dome was tough. But then another bomb dropped.

And another.

The first explosion had not mushroomed before the next missile hit. Then the next. And there was no cessation, no pause in the terrible regularity of the pin-point bombing. Hammer-blow after hammer-blow struck. Four – five – six –

Sam dropped forty-eight bombs, one for each hour of the deadline the Venusian Provisional Government had given him.

The screens showed smoke. When at last the smoke cleared – they showed such ruin as not even the fury of Venus's jungles, could achieve. The Man Underground was rooted out at last.

And twenty submarines discharged extremely specialized torpedoes at the impervium domes shielding the Keeps.

Six hours later Zachariah Harker was speaking to the Keeps.

'The mutineers were destroyed by Sam Reed. But they had a suicide fleet.

As they died, they had their revenge. The impervium dome above Delaware Keep has been radioactivated. The same holds true for all the Keeps. One moment –' He turned away, and presently returned.

'I am told that new messages have recently been received – the mutineers were not all destroyed. Apparently there were some survivors. They are harmless at the moment, but they comprise a permanent threat until they, as well as their organization, is eradicated. Completely. Meantime, their revenge is effective. Within a week the danger level will be reached, and the Keeps will be uninhabitable.

'Do not be immediately alarmed. There is no chance that the activated impervium will reach critical mass. But there is no way of halting the atomic reaction, and after a week has passed, the Keeps will be slow death traps. Only one solution seems practical. There is no time to build new impervium domes undersea – yet. But it may be done on landside. Here is Sam Reed; let him tell you his plan.'

Sam's face appeared.

He said almost casually, 'We did our best, but the skunks had the last word. Well, you've got to leave the Keeps – all of you – or die. I told you, I think, that we had been planning colony expansion. We've cleared a great deal of ground in preparation for that, and have already set up some equipment. It's yours. We'll stay in Plymouth or start new colonies. The land we cleared, and the equipment, is at your service. In this hour of disaster, we'll have to work together; we're one race.

'In a week you can transport the *matériel* you'll need. It won't be an easy life, but it'll be life. We of Plymouth Colony stand ready to help you to the fullest extent. Good luck.'

Someone else appeared on the screen; Sam and Zachariah began talking on a private beam.

'Can you evacuate the Keeps in a week?'

'Easily. Since we have to.'

'All right. We'll have to work together – for a while at least. Kedre proposed that once, and I said no. But now I'm proposing it. We'll send special officers to advise you on what equipment will be required. In the clearest areas, the first problem will be medical. We'll supply medical administrative officers. You've got to stay alive and healthy, and you're not acclimated to landside life. Don't count too much on impervium domes. We haven't wiped out the mutineers, and what they can do once, they can do again. When you're under impervium, you're vulnerable. If the survivors get organized again –'

'Landside life will be hard on the old and infirm.'

'The strong men will have enough to do. There will be plenty of maintenance jobs that won't require physical fitness. Jobs that have to be done. Give those tasks to the old and infirm; that way, you'll release the strong ones for work that takes strength. You'll have a lot of clearing and building to do.'

'Our technicians estimate the half-life of activated thorium at twelve years. We can return to the Keeps after twelve years.'

'But you'll have to live until then. And don't forget the survivors – the ones we didn't blast. They could reactivate the Keep domes, unless we catch them first. Twelve years is a long time.'

'Yes,' Zachariah said thoughtfully, looking into his grandson's oblivious face. 'Yes, I expect it will be a long, long time.'

And the Lord said ... Depart and go up hence ... unto the land which I sware unto Abraham ... a land flowing with milk and honey ... And the children of Israel went into the midst of the sea upon the dry ground, and the waters were a wall unto them on their right hand and on their left.

– Exodus

Seven hundred years ago the last exodus of the race of man took place. Today it began again. The vast mass migration was too complex for any single mind to encompass, and the people who looked back on it later remembered only intolerable confusion of the mind – hysteria, near panic, blind rebellion against destiny, but concerted, obedient motion as an overall pattern. The people of the Keeps had learned docility the easiest way of all. Now they did as they were told, grumbling, frightened, unwilling, but obeying the orders of anyone who spoke with enough authority.

No one would have believed, beforehand, that so tremendous an exodus could take place in the time allotted. No one, looking back, quite understood how it had been accomplished. But accomplished it was. That incalculable weight of inertia in a people contentedly settled for seven hundred years in one place required an even more incalculable weight in the scales to tip them over into action –

And they had that weight. The nucleon. Weightless by any comparable scale of physical values, still it tipped the balance as no other thing could. There was one old, old terror in the mind of every man who had ever looked up from the moving Ways and seen the globe of lost Earth hanging in the center of every Keep, shrouded in its symbolic pall.

They moved.

Kedre looked around her beautiful quiet room for the last time. It was a long look, quiet, like the room.

'We won't come back,' she said.

Zachariah, waiting at the door for her, said patiently, 'Why?'

'You know we won't. And it's a good thing. I hate Sam Reed. He's always forcing me to face unpleasant truths for perfectly irrelevant reasons of his own. He isn't doing this because it's time and past time for the sake of the race. He's doing it because he told a monumental lie and couldn't think of any other way out.'

'I wonder if we'll ever be able to prove it?'

Kedre shrugged. 'If we could, it wouldn't matter, now. We know Sam's methods. Once before when he was in a desperate spot he took desperate measures. We've expected it again ever since. I didn't give him credit for such misdirection, but Sam's learning fast. No, I don't suppose it ever can be proved.'

'Are you ready, my dear? The lift's waiting.'

'All right.' She sighed, turning to the door. 'I shouldn't feel as if I'm going out to die. I'm just now going to vindicate my own existence by starting to live! It'll be uncomfortable and I suppose dangerous, though I mind danger less. But it's something that's needed doing for longer than I like to think. Only – Zachariah, it's so horribly ignoble to be *forced* to do it!'

He laughed. 'I feel the same way. I suppose the first invertebrates who crawled up out of the prehistoric seas felt just as we do – hating every minute of it. It's time mankind crawled out of the water and stood on dry land again, but even Sam Reed can't make us like it!'

'He'll be sorry.' She buckled the cloak at her throat and crossed the room on lingering feet, pressing each step into the resilient flooring she would probably never walk again except out of curiosity, perhaps a century from now. 'How strange it will all look then,' she thought. 'Dark and stifling, I expect, after so long in the free air. We'll wonder how we ever stood it. Oh dear, I wish Sam Reed had never been born.'

Zachariah held the door for her. 'Our plans will still go forward, landside,' he said. 'I checked about your ... your time-bomb. Parents and child are safe up there, in a sheltered job.'

'I wish,' Kedre declared, 'that it had been a boy. Still – this may make a better weapon, after all. And it isn't our only weapon, of course. *Sam has got to be stopped.* We may have to use weapons as disreputable as the ones he's used against us, but we'll stop him. We have time on our side.'

Zachariah, watching her face, said nothing at all.

'I knew you were up to something,' Hale said, 'when you let all those mutineers go. It isn't like you to let anything go you can use.'

Sam looked at him under meeting brows. 'You wanted to colonize landside,' he said uncompromisingly. 'Well, this is it.'

'Robot submarines, robot planes, remote control – and a long-term plan,' Hale said amusingly, and shook his head. 'Well, you've done it. No one else in the world could have, but you did.'

'After twelve years,' Sam told him calmly, 'they'll be pretty well acclimated. After another twelve – and maybe another – they're going to like it up here so well you couldn't drive them back. Remember you told me once what makes pioneers? Push plus pull. Bad home conditions or a Grail somewhere else. The Grail wasn't enough. Well –' He shrugged.

Hale was silent for almost a minute, regarding Sam with his steady stare that had seen so much on Venusian landside before now. Finally he spoke.

'Remember what happened to Moses, Sam?' he asked gently, and then, like a classic prototype, turned and went out of the room, not staying for an answer.

The race struck roots and grew. Slowly at first, reluctantly, but with gathering vigor. And down in the deserted Keeps, in the first few days after the departing thousands had gone, for a little while life still moved through the strange new silence of the dying cities.

There were those who did not choose to leave. Some of the old people who had always lived here and could not face life above water, some of the ill who preferred the slow, comfortable death that had been provided for them. Some of the drug addicts. Silently in the deathly silence they moved through the empty shells. Never before since mankind first colonized Venus had such silence dwelt beneath the domes. You could hear the slowing Ways sighing on their rounds. You could hear strange, vague underwater noises transmitted from the great sounding-boards of the city shells. You could hear sometimes the shuffling footsteps of some fellow wanderer.

But after a little while all footsteps ceased, and all sounds except the echoes from the seas outside.

The thick walls shivered in the thunder of bombardment. In Sam's hand the stylus danced upon the suddenly shaking paper. His desk top shook, and the chair he sat in, and the floor quivered rhythmically and was still. Sam grimaced without knowing it. This was the third day of the bombardment, and he had shut his mind to the minor irritations of the unstable walls.

A young woman in a sleekly severe brown tunic bent forward, watching him write, her black hair falling in short, straight wings across her face. She pulled the page off the pad almost before his stylus had finished writing, and went quickly across the trembling floor to her own desk. There was a televisor on it, and she spoke rapidly, in a soft, clear voice, into the transmitter. In a dozen other visors scattered about the vast, beleaguered fort her tanned face was the target for intense attention as Sam's lieutenants received their latest orders. In a dozen visors her violet-blue eyes looked out narrowed with intentness, her velvety voice gave incongruously stern messages.

'All right,' Sam said wearily when she had finished. 'All right, Signa, send in Zachariah now.'

She rose with a smooth precision of motion that was beautiful to watch, and went quickly across the floor. The door she opened led not directly into the waiting room beyond, but into a little space lock that could be bathed at a touch by searcher beams to catch the presence of any weapon a man might try to smuggle past it. Sam took no chances. It didn't seem to matter much now – perhaps he had too long mistaken personal safety for group safety. The bombardment roared again and for the first time a long delicate crack went flashing like slow lightning down one wall. The space lock would seem futile enough when the walls themselves began to go. But for a little while longer it must be used.

Two guards came in at Signa's beckoning, and paused perfunctorily in the lock and stood back for their prisoner to take his turn in the invisible bath of the beams. Two more guards came after.

Zachariah had a cut lip and a darkening bruise on one side of his ageless face, but he looked remarkably confident in spite of his manacles. Except for his tan he had changed little. He was still head of the Harker clan, and the Harkers were still the most influential family on Venus. But if Sam's coup in capturing the leader of the attacking forces meant anything, Zachariah did not show it.

Twenty years had not been a very long time.

The Keeps were still uninhabitable. The change-over to landside living had come very gradually, but it was complete by now. The signal for completion had been sounded on that day when instruments first showed that the atmosphere of Venus had at last shifted over to an ecology balance that matched Earth's. Crab grass and earth-native herbs with a high oxygen output had finally tipped the scale. From now on, this continent could be left to itself botanically speaking. For the plants had changed the air. The heavy carbon dioxide atmosphere in which Venusian flora flourished would foster them no longer. What is normal for Earth-born plants is poison for the Venus-grown things that were so often neither plant nor animal, but a deadly symbiosis of the two.

It was this shift that the spreading colonies had been awaiting.

It was this war that came of the shift.

'Zachariah,' Sam said in a weary voice, 'I want you to call off your men.'

Zachariah looked at him narrowly, not without sympathy, trying as he had so often tried, in vain, to trace some likeness to the Harker blood that ran in them both. 'Why should I do that, Sam?' he asked.

'You're in no position to bargain. I'll have you shot unless this attack's stopped by noon. Step over here – you can use my telecaster.'

'No Sam. You're finished. This time you can't win.'

'I've always won before. I can do it again.'

'No,' Zachariah said, and paused for a moment, thinking of those many times in the past when Sam had won – easily, scornfully, because of his impregnable defenses built up so cannily in years of peace. When the Immortality bubble broke completely, there had been rash, furious, tragically futile assaults upon this great white fortress that sheltered the most powerful man on Venus.

'We aren't guerillas,' Zachariah said calmly. 'We've been building up to this attack since the day you pirated our korium with the depth-bomb threat. Remember, Sam? You haven't made many mistakes in strategy, but you should have checked the equipment we took landside with us when we left the Keeps. A lot of it was stuff we're using now.' He looked at the jagged lightning-streak that was creeping down the wall as the bombardment went on. 'This time we've got you, Sam. You've been building for defense a long time – but not as long as we've built toward this offense.'

'You're forgetting something.' Sam's head ached from the incessant vibration. It made talking difficult. 'You're forgetting yourself. You aren't really willing to be shot rather than call off the attack, are you?'

'That's something you couldn't understand, isn't it?'

Sam shook his head impatiently. 'You'd have attacked twenty years ago if you were as strong as you pretend You aren't fooling me, Harker. I've never been licked yet.'

'We've needed you – until now. You've lived on sufferance, Sam. Now it's over. This bombardment isn't only guns. It's the … the pressure of human emotions you've held down too long. You've tried to bring progress to a full stop at the level of your choosing, and you can't do it, Sam. Not you or anybody. For twenty years that pressure's been building up. You're finished, Sam.'

Sam slammed the vibrating desk top with an angry fist. 'Shut up!' he said. 'I'm sick of talk. I'll give you sixty seconds to make up your mind, Harker. After that – *you're* finished.'

But there was in his mind as he said it a nagging uneasiness he could not quite name. His unconscious mind knew the answer. It nagged at him because Zachariah's capture had been too easy. Sam's conscious awareness had not recognized the incongruity yet; perhaps his vanity would not permit it. But he knew something was wrong about the setup.

He glanced nervously around the room, his eyes pausing for a moment, as they so often did, on the blue-eyed girl at the desk across the room. She was watching everything in alert, tight-lipped silence, missing nothing. He knew he could trust her. It was a heart-warming assurance to have. He knew because of the exhaustive psychological and neurological tests that had winnowed out all applicants except the half-dozen from which Signa had been chosen.

She was eighteen, Keep-born, landside-bred, when she first entered the Fort as a clerical worker. All of them were screened thoroughly, of course. All of them were indoctrinated from the first with the precepts Sam's psychologists had worked out. But Signa rose faster than most toward the top. Within a year she was an assistant secretary in the restricted building that housed administration. Within six months from then she was a secretary with an office of her own. And then one day Sam, looking over applicants for his personal staff, was rather surprised to find a woman's name among those with top-light test ratings. One interview clinched the appointment for her.

She was twenty-five now. She was not Sam's mistress, though few in this fort would have believed it. Periodically she underwent further tests, under narcosynthesis, to make sure her emotional reactions had not changed. So far they had not. She was utterly to be trusted and Sam's efficiency would be halved, he knew, if he had to work without her now.

He could see that something was troubling her. He knew her face so well the slightest shadow on it was recognizable. There was a crease between her brows as she looked at Zachariah, and an expression of faint uncertainty, of puzzled anticipation flickered in her eyes.

Sam looked at his wrist. 'Forty seconds,' he said, and pushed back his chair. Every eye in the room followed him as he went over to the far wall, the wall where the long crack was widening, and flicked a switch in a six-foot frame. A shuttered screen, filling in the frame, began to open slowly. From behind it a faint, sweet, infinitely seductive humming swelled. Sam was reaching for the lid of a box set into the wall beside the frame when a buzz at Signa's visor interrupted him.

'For you, Sam,' she said in a moment. 'Hale.'

He flicked the switch again, closing the screen, and went rapidly across the room. The Free Companion's brown unaging face looked up at him from the tilted visor.

'You alone, Sam?'

'No. Wait, I'll switch to earphones.'

The face in the screen grimaced impatiently. Then, at Sam's signal the face vanished again and Hale's voice buzzed in his ears, unheard except by Sam.

'There's been a breakthrough,' Hale said crisply.

'How bad?'

'Bad enough. Vibration did it. I told you I thought that plastic was too rigid. It's down in the lower court. They've already manned some of our own guns and swiveled them around. The upper bailey's going to start getting it in about five minutes. Sam – I think there's been a leak somewhere. They shouldn't even know how those needle guns work. But they do.'

Sam was silent, his mind flickering rapidly from possibility to possibility. Hale himself was as suspect as any. It had been a long, long while since Sam had trusted the Free Companion. But he had made grimly certain of Hale's loyalty by insuring that public opinion bracketed the two men together. Hale profited by Sam's methods. Sam made sure all Venus knew it. He made sure that Hale's part in originating unpopular ideas – from the Immortality swindle on down – was fully publicized. It was fairly certain that Hale would have to back Sam up in all he did, if only to save his own hide.

'I've got Zachariah here,' he said into the transmitter. 'Come up, will you?' He slipped off the earphones and turned back to his prisoner. 'Your minute's up,' he said.

Zachariah appeared to hesitate. Then he said, 'I'll talk to you, Sam, on one condition. Privacy. We'll have to be alone for what I have to say.'

Sam opened his desk drawer, took out a flat pistol and laid it on the vibrating desk-top, his palm over it. 'You'll talk now, Zachariah Harker,' he said, 'or I'll shoot you. Right between the eyes.' He lifted the pistol and regarded Zachariah down its barrel, seeing the serene Immortal face half blocked out by blued steel.

Silence. Then from far off, muffled by walls, the unmistakable piercing wail of a needle-gun bolt split the air of the inner fort. Impact, dull thunder, and a long sliding crash. The walls shook briefly to a new tempo and the crack widened at Sam's back.

Zachariah said, 'You'd better let me talk to you, Sam. But if you'd rather shoot – shoot. I won't say it until we are alone.'

Sam's hesitation was not very long. He knew now he was more shaken than he had realized until this moment, or he would never have surrendered to a bluff. But he let the pistol sink slowly, and he nodded.

Signa rose. 'All right, guards,' she said. They turned and went out through the still activated searcher lock. She put her finger on its switch and looked inquiringly at Sam. 'Shall I go, too?'

'No,' Sam said. 'Not you.' His voice was firm.

'Sam, I … I'd rather go.' She sounded oddly puzzled and distressed. It was Zachariah who spoke first.

'You stay, please,' he said. She gave him another of her strange glances, uncertain, troubled.

Sam watched them, leaning his hands palm down on the desk and feeling the almost continuous vibrations of the bombardment. The air was pierced now and then by the screaming needle beams, and he did not like to think what was happening to his inner ring of defenses around the upper bailey.

'All right,' he said. 'What is it? Talk fast, Harker. I'm in a hurry.'

Zachariah, hands still manacled behind him, crossed the room and stood looking out the bank of windows that framed a vista of distant sea.

'I'll show you,' he said. 'Come over here.'

Sam came impatiently across the shaken floor. 'What? What is it?' He stood beside the Immortal, but a safe distance away, for caution was second nature to him, and looked down. 'I don't see a thing. What is it?'

Zachariah whistled the opening bars of *Lilibulero* …

The room exploded with thunder.

Sam found himself reeling, choking, gasping for breath, with no clear idea of what had happened. *A needle beam*, he thought wildly. But then the whole room would be a shambles, and it was only himself, leaning one shoulder against the wall, shaking his head dizzily, breathing hard, who seemed affected.

He looked up. Zachariah still stood by the window, watching him with a kind of hard restrained pity. The room was untouched. And there was something the matter with Sam's shoulder.

That was where the blow had caught him. He remembered now. He put up an unsteady hand to the numb area and then looked unbelievingly at his palm, filmed with clear red. Something moved across his chest. Incredulously he bent his head and saw that it was blood. The bullet must have come out just under the clavicle.

Signa's soft, clear voice gasped, 'Sam … Sam!'

'It's all right … it isn't bad.' He was reassuring her even before he lifted his head. Then he saw her standing behind his desk, the flat pistol held in both shaking hands. She was staring at him with great, terrified eyes and her mouth was a Greek square of strained effort. Her stare shifted from Sam to Zachariah and then back, and the incredulity in it was very near sheer madness.

'I … I had to do it, Sam,' she said in a harsh, thin whisper. 'I don't know why – there must have been a reason! I don't understand –'

Zachariah broke in, his voice gentle. 'It wasn't enough, Signa,' he said. 'You'll have to try again, you know. Quickly, before he can stop you.'

'I know … I know.' Her voice was a gasp. Normally she was a good shot, fast and easy, but she brought the pistol up in both hands, steadying it like a schoolgirl, squinting past the barrel. Sam saw her finger begin to draw up on the trigger.

He didn't want to do it. He would almost rather have risked the shot. But he dropped his right hand to his side, found through cloth the outlines of the tiny needle gun in his pocket, and shot from the hip without taking aim.

He did not miss.

For one long last moment, afterward, her eyes were wide and brilliantly violet, staring into his. Sam scarcely heard the thud of the dropping gun. He was meeting her blue stare and remembering another blue-eyed girl, very long ago, who had faced him like this and puffed oblivion in his face.

He said, 'Rosathe!' as if he had just remembered the name, and swung around toward Zachariah. It was the same triangle, he thought – Zachariah, Rosathe, Sam Reed – sixty years ago and now. There was no difference. But this time –

His fingers closed on the needle gun again and its bolt hissed again across the room. Zachariah, seeing it coming, made no move. But when it came within six inches of his chest it seemed to explode in midair. There was a scream of expended energy, a flare like a miniature nova, and Zacharia smiled unhurt into Sam's eyes.

What he said made no sense. He still looked at Sam, but he lifted his voice and called, 'All right, Hale, it's up to you.'

There was a challenge in the words. Sam had no time to puzzle it out. He set his teeth grimly and tugged the needle gun from his scorched pocket, lifted it toward Zachariah's face. There at least the Immortal could not be wearing armor.

He never pulled the trigger. From somewhere beyond him a familiar voice said wearily, 'Harker – you win.' And a searing light flashed blindingly into Sam's eyes.

He knew what it was. He and the Free Companion carried the little riot-breaker flashes instead of deadlier weapons for discipline. Blindness was not usually permanent after that glare had burned a man's eyes, but it did not pass quickly.

In the sudden darkness that had engulfed the room Sam heard Zachariah's voice saying, 'Thank you, Hale. I was pretty sure you would – but not quite. That was close.'

The Free Companion said, 'I'm sorry, Sam.'

And that was the last thing Sam heard in Plymouth Colony.

And Moses went up from the plains of Moab … and the Lord said unto him, This is the land … I have caused thee to see it with thine eyes, but thou shalt not go over thither … And Moses died there in the land of Moab, but no man knoweth of his sepulchre unto this day. – Deuteronomy

There was a swimming dark, and the roaring of winds. And then vague patterns of light that were presently a face – the head and torso of an old man, a shrewd-faced, wrinkled old man Sam recognized. Beyond him was a bare alloy wall, and a dim light came from somewhere.

Sam tried to sit up, failed, tried again. He could not move. Panic leaped in his mind. The old man smiled.

'Take it easy, son. This is the way it has to be.' He was packing tobacco into his pipe as he spoke. Now he held a flame to it, sucked the fire down into the bowl, blew out smoke. His mild gaze focused on Sam.

'Had to tell you a few things, son,' he said. 'Just in case. You're good and healthy again, in case you're wondering. You been here a few weeks, resting up, getting cured. Nobody knows but me.'

Where? Sam tried to move his head enough to see the source of the light, the shape of the room. He could not.

'I got this hideout ready quite some while ago,' Crowell went on, puffing. 'Figured I might need it for something like this. It's under my potato patch. I'll be hoeing spuds on this parcel of land for a good long spell yet, I figure. Maybe a hundred years, maybe five hundred. That's right, I'm an Immortal. Don't look it, do I? But I was born on Earth.'

He blew out blue smoke. 'Earth had a good many fine things – the old place. But I could see what was coming, even then. I could see you, Sam Reed. Oh, not your name or your face, but I knew you'd be along. A man like you always is, at the right time. I can figure out the future, Sam. It's a talent I got. Only I can't interfere or I'll change the pattern to something different – what it'll be I can't tell for a while, after I've stepped in.'

Sam made a frantic effort to stir one finger. Colored flecks of light danced before his eyes. He scarcely heard as the old man rambled on.

'Easy now,' Crowell said quietly. 'Just try to listen for a bit. I'm the Logician, Sam. Remember the Temple of Truth? You didn't believe the oracle at first, did you? Well, I was right. I was the machine, and I don't make mistakes, at least, not that kind.

'You were in the Temple for forty years, Sam. You wouldn't remember that, either. You were dream-dusting.'

Dream-dusting? Sam's attention came back sharply. Was this the answer he had sought so long, given casually now, when it no longer meant anything? Crowell, the unknown guardian? But how – why –

'Zachariah was out to kill you. I could see that. I could see he'd succeed, unless I interfered. So I interfered – which upset the apple cart considerable. After that I couldn't figure out the future quite so close, till things evened up again. That's one reason I waited forty years. It's why I let you wake up in an alley, broke and disgraced. To even the scale, son. The way things are, when I give a good present I've got to give a bad one too, or it won't come out right.

'You had your troubles to straighten out then, and when you finished, the pattern was all set again. I could see what was coming.'

Sam did not care. If he could only break this paralysis. He must – he must! Always before now he had drawn upon some deep reserve of strength no other man possessed. And it must not fail him now.

But it was failing him.

'You're not Sam Reed, you know,' the Logician was saying. 'Remember Blaze Harker? He had a son. Blaze was starting to go crazy then, or he'd never have hated the baby enough to do what he did. You know what it was, don't you? You grew up looking like a short-termer, but your name wasn't really Reed.'

Blaze Harker. Blaze Harker, his face distorted, struggling in the straitjacket – I let him go! I could have killed him! He was the one – I let him go –

Blaze Harker!

Harker!

Sam – Harker!

'I couldn't tell you before,' Crowell said. 'It would have changed the future, and I didn't want it changed that way. Up till now we've needed you, Sam.

Once in a long while a fella like you comes along, somebody strong enough to move a world. Oh, I guess other men had qualifications – like Rob Hale. Only Hale couldn't have done it. He could have done part, but there are things he never could make himself do.

'There's nothing you wouldn't do, son – nothing at all – if it would get you what you want.

'If you hadn't been born, if Blaze hadn't done what he did, mankind would be in the Keeps yet. And in a few hundred years, or a thousand, say, the race would have died out. I could see that ahead, clear as could be. But now we've come landside. We'll finish colonizing Venus. And then we'll go out and colonize the whole universe, I expect.

'You're the one who did it, Sam. We owe you a lot. In your day you were a great man. But your day's over. You got your power by force, and you're like most dictators, son, you reach the top that way. All you could think of was repeating the things that made you a success – more fighting, more force. There wasn't any way but down for you, once you'd reached the top, because of the man you are. You had the same drive that made the first life-form leave water for land, but we can't use your kind any more for a while, Sam.'

Drive? It was fury. It burned with blinding white violence in him, so hot it seemed strange the fetters of his paralysis were not consumed – it seemed strange the sheer violence of his rage could not send him headlong across the room at Crowell. To get above ground – smash Hale. Smash the Harkers –

The Harkers. But he was a Harker, too.

Crowell said, 'Men like you are mighty rare, Sam. When they get to the right position, at the right time, they're the salvation of the race of man. But it's got to be the right time – a time of disaster. The drive never stops, in a man like you. You've got to get on top. You've got to, or die.

'If you can't conquer an enemy, you'll conquer your friends. Up to now the enemy was Venus, and you licked it. But what have you got to fight now?'

'Man.'

'There's going to be a good long time of peace, now. The Immortals have taken over. They'll rule well. You've left them a good foundation to build on. But it's time you bowed out.'

Suddenly Crowell chuckled. 'You thought you were telling a lie, Sam, when you promised immortality was up here landside, didn't you? It was the truth. They'll get their immortality. Ever think of that? Man was dying in the Keeps. Up here he'll live on – well, not forever, but long enough, long enough. The race has got immortality, Sam, and you gave it to 'em.'

He puffed again at the pipe and looked down reflectively through smoke at Sam. 'I hardly ever interfere with the running of things,' he said. 'Only once I had to kill a man. I had to. It changed the patterns so much I couldn't see the future for a long time after, but I'd already seen enough to know what would have happened if the man kept on living. It was bad. I couldn't think of anything worse. So I killed him.

'I've interfered again, because I know what the future would be like with you in it. This means I won't be able to guess what's coming for quite a spell. After that things will level off and I can take a look.

'This time I'm not killing. I learn more as I get older. Also you're an Immortal. You can sleep a long, long while without losing anything. That's what you're going to do, son – sleep.

'And I hope you die in your sleep. I hope I'll never have to wake you up. Because if I do, it'll mean things have gone mighty bad again. You and I are long-termers. We'll still be around, barring accidents, for quite a stretch yet. And plenty of bad things can happen.

'I get glimpses. Nothing's set yet – too far ahead. But I see possibilities. The jungle could come back. New life-forms may mutate – Venus critters are tricky. And we won't stay on Venus forever. This is just the first colony. We'll go on out to the planets and the stars. There may be trouble there, too, sooner than you'd think. Maybe something will try to colonize our worlds, as we colonize theirs. There's peace and there's war, and it's always been that way, and I guess it always will.

'So maybe we'll need a man like you again, Sam.

'I'll wake you if we do.'

The shrewd brown face regarded him from coils of smoke. The friendly, remorseless, judging eyes considered him.

'For now, though,' Crowell said, 'go to sleep. You've done your job. Sleep well, son – and good night.'

Sam lay motionless. The light was dimming. He could not be sure if it were his own vision that dimmed.

There was so much he wanted to think about, and so little time for thinking. He was Immortal. He must live –

Sam Harker, Immortal. Harker. Harker.

He heard the music of carnival ringing through Delaware Keep, saw the bright ribbons of the moving Ways, smelled drifting perfume, smiled into Kedre's face.

There was a second of desperate urgency, as though he clawed at the edge of a crumbling cliff, while life and awareness fell to pieces beneath his hands.

Darkness and silence brimmed the buried room. Here the Man Underground slept at last, rooted deep, waiting.

EPILOGUE

Sam woke –

MUTANT

ONE

Somehow I had to stay alive until they found me. They would be hunting for the wreck of my plane, and eventually they'd find it, and then they'd find me, too. But it was hard to wait.

Empty blue day stretched over the white peaks; then the blazing night you get at this altitude, and that was empty too. There was no sound or sight of a jet plane or a helicopter. I was completely alone.

That was the real trouble.

A few hundred years ago, when there were no telepaths, men were used to being alone. But I couldn't remember a time when I'd been locked in the bony prison of my skull, utterly and absolutely cut off from all other men. Deafness or blindness wouldn't have mattered as much. They wouldn't have mattered at all, to a telepath.

Since my plane crashed behind the barrier of mountain peaks, I had been amputated from my species. And there is something in the constant communication of minds that keeps a man alive. An amputated limb dies for lack of oxygen. I was dying for lack of ... there's never been any word to express what it is that makes all telepaths one. But without it, a man is alone, and men do not live long, alone.

I listened, with the part of the mind that listens for the soundless voices of other minds. I heard the hollow wind. I saw snow lifting in feathery, pouring ruffles. I saw the blue shadows deepening. I looked up, and the eastern peak was scarlet. It was sunset, and I was alone.

I reached out, listening, while the sky darkened. A star wavered, glimmered, and stood steadily overhead. Other stars came, while the air grew colder, until the sky blazed with their westward march.

Now it was dark. In the darkness, there were the stars, and there was I. I lay back, not even listening. My people were gone.

I watched the emptiness beyond the stars.

Nothing around me or above me was alive. Why should I be alive, after all? It would be easy, very easy, to sink down into that quiet where there was no loneliness, because there was no life. I reached out around me, and my mind found no other thinking mind. I reached back into my memory, and that was a little better.

A telepath's memories go back a long way. A good long way, far earlier than his birth.

I can see clearly nearly two hundred years into the past, before the sharp, clear telepathically-transmitted memories begin to fray and fade into secondary memories, drawn from books. Books go back to Egypt and Babylon. But they are not the primary memories, complete with sensory overtones, which an old man gives telepathically to a young one, and which are passed on in turn through the generations. Our biographies are not written in books. They are written in our minds and memories, especially the Key Lives which are handed down as fresh as they were once lived by our greatest leaders …

But they are dead, and I am alone.

No. Not quite alone. The memories remain, Burkhalter and Barton, McNey and Linc Cody and Jeff Cody – a long time dead, but still vibrantly alive in my memory. I can summon up every thought, every emotion, the musty smell of grass – where? – the yielding of a rubbery walk beneath hurrying feet – whose?

It would be so easy to relax and die.

No. Wait. Watch. They're alive, Burkhalter and Barton, the Key Lives are still real, though the men who once lived them have died. They are your people. You're not alone.

Burkhalter and Barton, McNey and Linc and Jeff aren't dead. Remember them. You lived their lives telepathically as you learned them, the way they once lived them, and you can live them again. *You are not alone.*

So watch. Start the film unreeling. Then you won't be alone at all, you'll be Ed Burkhalter, two hundred years ago, feeling the cool wind blow against your face from the Sierra peaks, smelling the timothy grass, reaching out mentally to glance into the mind of your son … *the piper's son …*

It began.

I was Ed Burkhalter.

It was two hundred years ago –

THE PIPER'S SON

The Green Man was climbing the glass mountains, and hairy, gnomish faces peered at him from crevices. This was only another step in the Green Man's endless, exciting odyssey. He'd had a great many adventures already – in the Flame Country, among the Dimension Changers, with the City Apes who sneered endlessly while their blunt, clumsy fingers fumbled at deathrays. The trolls, however, were masters of magic, and were trying to stop the Green Man with spells. Little whirlwinds of force spun underfoot, trying to trip the Green Man, a figure of marvelous muscular development, handsome as a god, and hairless from head to foot, glistening pale green. The whirlwinds formed a fascinating pattern. If you could thread a precarious path among them – avoiding the pale yellow ones especially – you could get through.

And the hairy gnomes watched malignantly, jealously, from their crannies in the glass crags.

Al Burkhalter, having recently achieved the mature status of eight full years, lounged under a tree and masticated a grass blade. He was so immersed in his daydreams that his father had to nudge his side gently to bring comprehension into the half-closed eyes. It was a good day for dreaming, anyway – a hot sun and a cool wind blowing down from the white Sierra peaks to the east. Timothy grass sent its faintly musty fragrance along the channels of air, and Ed Burkhalter was glad that his son was second-generation since the Blowup. He himself had been born ten years after the last bomb had been dropped, but secondhand memories can be pretty bad too.

'Hello, Al,' he said, and the youth vouchsafed a half-lidded glance of tolerant acceptance.

'Hi, Dad.'

'Want to come downtown with me?'

'Nope,' Al said, relaxing instantly into his stupor.

Burkhalter raised a figurative eyebrow and half turned. On an impulse, then, he did something he rarely did without the tacit permission of the other party; he used his telepathic power to reach into Al's mind. There was, he admitted to himself, a certain hesitancy, a subconscious unwillingness on his part, to do this, even though Al had pretty well outgrown the nasty, inhuman formlessness of mental babyhood. There had been a time when Al's mind had been quite shocking in its alienage. Burkhalter remembered a few abortive experiments he had made before Al's birth; few fathers-to-be could resist the temptation to experiment with embryonic brains, and that had brought back nightmares Burkhalter had not had since his youth. There had been enormous rolling masses, and an appalling vastness, and other things. Prenatal memories were ticklish, and should be left to qualified mnemonic psychologists.

But now Al was maturing, and daydreaming, as usual, in bright colors. Burkhalter, reassured, felt that he had fulfilled his duty as a monitor and left his son still eating grass and ruminating.

Just the same there was a sudden softness inside of him, and the aching, futile pity he was apt to feel for helpless things that were as yet unqualified for conflict with that extraordinarily complicated business of living. Conflict, competition, had not died out when war abolished itself; the business of adjustment even to one's surroundings was a conflict, and conversation a duel. With Al, too, there was a double problem. Yes, language was in effect a tariff wall, and a Baldy could appreciate that thoroughly, since the wall didn't exist between Baldies.

Walking down the rubbery walk that led to town center, Burkhalter grinned wryly and ran lean fingers through his well-kept wig. Strangers were very often surprised to know that he was a Baldy, a telepath. They looked at him with wondering eyes, too courteous to ask how it felt to be a freak, but obviously avid. Burkhalter, who knew diplomacy, would be quite willing to lead the conversation.

'My folks lived near Chicago after the Blowup. That was why.'

'Oh.' Stare. 'I'd heard that was why so many –' Startled pause.

'Freaks or mutations. There were both. I still don't know which class I belong to,' he'd add disarmingly.

'You're no freak!' They did protest too much.

'Well, some mighty queer specimens came out of the radioactive-affected areas around the bomb-targets. Funny things happened to the germ plasm. Most of 'em died out; they couldn't reproduce; but you'll still find a few creatures in sanitariums – two heads, you know. And so on.'

Nevertheless they were always ill-at-ease. 'You mean you can read my mind – now?'

'I could, but I'm not. It's hard work, except with another telepath. And we Baldies – well, we don't, that's all.' A man with abnormal muscle development wouldn't go around knocking people down. Not unless he wanted to be mobbed. Baldies were always sneakingly conscious of a hidden peril: lynch law. And wise Baldies didn't even imply that they had an … extra sense. They just said they were different, and let it go at that.

But one question was always implied, though not always mentioned. 'If I were a telepath, I'd … how much do you make a year?'

They were surprised at the answer. A mindreader certainly could make a fortune, if he wanted. So why did Ed Burkhalter stay a semantics expert in Modoc Publishing Town, when a trip to one of the science towns would enable him to get hold of secrets that would get him a fortune?

There was a good reason. Self-preservation was a part of it. For which reason Burkhalter, and many like him, wore toupees. Though there were many Baldies who did not.

Modoc was a twin town with Pueblo, across the mountain barrier south of the waste that had been Denver. Pueblo held the presses, photolinotypes, and the machines that turned scripts into books, after Modoc had dealt with them. There was a helicopter distribution fleet at Pueblo, and for the last week Oldfield, the manager, had been demanding the manuscript of 'Psychohistory,' turned out by a New Yale man who had got tremendously involved in past emotional problems, to the detriment of literary clarity. The truth was that he distrusted Burkhalter. And Burkhalter, neither a priest nor a psychologist, had to become both without admitting it to the confused author of 'Psychohistory.'

The sprawling buildings of the publishing house lay ahead and below, more like a resort than anything more utilitarian. That had been necessary.

Authors were peculiar people, and often it was necessary to induce them to take hydrotherapic treatments, before they were in shape to work out their books with the semantic experts. Nobody was going to bite them, but they didn't realize that, and either cowered in corners, terrified, or else blustered their way around, using language few could understand. Jem Quayle, author of 'Psychohistory,' fitted into neither group; he was simply baffled by the intensity of his own research. His personal history had qualified him too well for emotional involvements with the past – and that was a serious matter when a thesis of this particular type was in progress.

Dr Moon, who was on the Board, sat near the south entrance, eating an apple which he peeled carefully with his silver-hilted dagger. Moon was fat, short, and shapeless; he didn't have much hair, but he wasn't a telepath; Baldies were entirely hairless. He gulped and waved at Burkhalter.

'Ed ... *urp* ... want to talk to you.'

'Sure,' Burkhalter said, agreeably coming to a standstill and rocking on his heels. Ingrained habit made him sit down beside the Boardman; Baldies, for obvious reasons, never stood up when non-telepaths were sitting. Their eyes met now on the same level. Burkhalter said, 'What's up?'

'The store got some Shasta apples flown in yesterday. Better tell Ethel to get some before they're sold out. Here.' Moon watched his companion eat a chunk, and nod.

'Good. I'll have her get some. The copter's laid up for today, though; Ethel pulled the wrong gadget.'

'Foolproof,' Moon said bitterly. 'Huron's turning out some sweet models these days; I'm getting my new one from Michigan. Listen, Pueblo called me this morning on Quayle's book.'

'Oldfield?'

'Our boy,' Moon nodded. 'He says can't you send over even a few chapters.'

Burkhalter shook his head. 'I don't think so. There are some abstracts right in the beginning that just have to be clarified, and Quayle is –' He hesitated.

'What?'

Burkhalter thought about the Oedipus complex he'd uncovered in Quayle's mind, but that was sacrosanct, even though it kept Quayle from interpreting Darius with cold logic. 'He's got muddy thinking in there. I can't pass it; I tried it on three readers yesterday, and got different reactions from all of them. So far "Psychohistory" is all things to all men. The critics would lambaste us if we released the book as is. Can't you string Oldfield along for a while longer?'

'Maybe,' Moon said doubtfully. 'I've got a subjective novella I could rush over. It's light vicarious eroticism, and that's harmless; besides, it's semantically O.K.'d We've been holding it up for an artist, but I can put Duman on it.

I'll do that, yeah. I'll shoot the script over to Pueblo and he can make the plates later. A merry life we lead, Ed.'

'A little too merry sometimes,' Burkhalter said. He got up, nodded, and went in search of Quayle, who was relaxing on one of the sun decks.

Quayle was a thin, tall man with a worried face and the abstract air of an unshelled tortoise. He lay on his flexiglass couch, direct sunlight toasting him from above, while the reflected rays sneaked up on him from below, through the transparent crystal. Burkhalter pulled off his shirt and dropped on a sunner beside Quayle. The author glanced at Burkhalter's hairless chest and half-formed revulsion rose in him: *A Baldy ... no privacy ... none of his business ... fake eyebrows and lashes; he's still a –*

Something ugly, at that point.

Diplomatically Burkhalter touched a button, and on a screen overhead a page of 'Psychohistory' appeared, enlarged and easily readable. Quayle scanned the sheet. It had code notations on it, made by the readers, recognized by Burkhalter as varied reactions to what should have been straight-line explanations. If three readers had got three different meanings out of that paragraph – well, what *did* Quayle mean? He reached delicately into the mind, conscious of useless guards erected against intrusion, mud barricades over which his mental eye stole like a searching, quiet wind. No ordinary man could guard his mind against a Baldy. But Baldies could guard their privacy against intrusion by other telepaths – adults, that is. There was a psychic selector band, a –

Here it came. But muddled a bit. *Darius:* that wasn't simply a word; it wasn't a picture, either; it was really a second *life*. But scattered, fragmentary. Scraps of scent and sound, and memories, and emotional reactions. Admiration and hatred. A burning impotence. A black tornado, smelling of pine, roaring across a map of Europe and Asia. Pine scent stronger now, and horrible humiliation, and remembered pain ... eyes ... *Get out!*

Burkhalter put down the dictograph mouthpiece and lay looking up through the darkened eye-shells he had donned. 'I got out as soon as you wanted me to,' he said. 'I'm still out.'

Quayle lay there, breathing hard. 'Thanks,' he said. 'Apologies. Why you don't ask a duello –'

'I don't want to duel with you,' Burkhalter said. 'I've never put blood on my dagger in my life. Besides, I can see your side of it. Remember, this is my job, Mr Quayle, and I've learned a lot of things – that I've forgotten again.'

'It's intrusion, I suppose. I tell myself that it doesn't matter, but my privacy – is important.'

Burkhalter said patiently, 'We can keep trying it from different angles until we find one that isn't too private. Suppose, for example, I asked you if you admired Darius.'

Admiration … and pine scent … and Burkhalter said quickly, 'I'm out. O.K.?'

'Thanks,' Quayle muttered. He turned on his side, away from the other man. After a moment he said, 'That's silly – turning over, I mean. You don't have to see my face to know what I'm thinking.'

'You have to put out the welcome mat before I walk in,' Burkhalter told him

'I guess I believe that. I've met some Baldies, though, that were … that I didn't like.'

'There's a lot on that order, sure. I know the type. The ones who don't wear wigs.'

Quayle said, 'They'll read your mind and embarrass you just for the fun of it. They ought to be – taught better.'

Burkhalter blinked in the sunlight. 'Well, Mr Quayle, it's this way. A Baldy's got his problems, too. He's got to orient himself to a world that isn't telepathic; and I suppose a lot of Baldies rather feel that they're letting their specialization go to waste. There *are* jobs a man like me is suited for –'

'Man!' He caught the scrap of thought from Quayle. He ignored it, his face as always a mobile mask, and went on.

'Semantics have always been a problem, even in countries speaking only one tongue. A qualified Baldy is a swell interpreter. And, though there aren't any Baldies on the detective forces, they often work with the police. It's rather like being a machine that can do only a few things.'

'A few things more than humans can,' Quayle said.

Sure, Burkhalter thought, if we could compete on equal footing with non-telepathic humanity. But would blind men trust one who could see? Would they play poker with him? A sudden, deep bitterness put an unpleasant taste in Burkhalter's mouth. What was the answer? Reservations for Baldies? Isolation? And would a nation of blind men trust those with vision enough for that? Or would they be dusted off – the sure cure, the check-and-balance system that made war an impossibility.

He remembered when Red Bank had been dusted off, and maybe that had been justified. The town was getting too big for its boots, and personal dignity was a vital factor; you weren't willing to lose face as long as a dagger swung at your belt. Similarly, the thousands upon thousands of little towns that covered America, each with its peculiar specialty – helicopter manufacture for Huron and Michigan, vegetable farming for Conoy and Diego, textiles and education and art and machines – each little town had a wary eye on all the others. The science and research centers were a little larger; nobody objected to that, for technicians never made war except under pressure; but few of the towns held more than a few hundred families. It was check-and-balance in most efficient degree; whenever a town showed signs of wanting to become a city – thence, a capital, thence, an imperialistic empire – it was dusted off. Though that had not happened for a long while. And Red Bank might have been a mistake.

Geopolitically it was a fine set-up; sociologically it was acceptable, but brought necessary changes. There was subconscious swashbuckling. The rights of the individual had become more highly regarded as decentralization took place. And men learned.

They learned a monetary system based primarily upon barter. They learned to fly; nobody drove surface cars. They learned new things, but they did not forget the Blowup, and in secret places near every town were hidden the bombs that could utterly and fantastically exterminate a town, as such bombs had exterminated the cities during the Blowup.

And everybody knew how to make those bombs. They were beautifully, terribly simple. You could find the ingredients anywhere and prepare them easily. Then you could take your helicopter over a town, drop an egg overside – and perform an erasure.

Outside of the wilderness malcontents, the maladjusted people found in every race, nobody kicked. And the roaming tribes never raided and never banded together in large groups – for fear of an erasure.

The artisans were maladjusted too, to some degree, but they weren't antisocial, so they lived where they wanted and painted, wrote, composed, and retreated into their own private worlds. The scientists, equally maladjusted in other lines, retreated to their slightly larger towns, banding together in small universes, and turned out remarkable technical achievements.

And the Baldies – found jobs where they could.

No nontelepath would have viewed the world environment quite as Burkhalter did. He was abnormally conscious of the human element, attaching a deeper, more profound significance to those human values, undoubtedly because he saw men in more than the ordinary dimensions. And also, in a way – and inevitably – he looked at humanity from outside.

Yet he was human. The barrier that telepathy had raised made men suspicious of him, more so than if he had had two heads – then they could have pitied. As it was –

As it was, he adjusted the scanner until new pages of the typescript came flickering into view above. 'Say when,' he told Quayle.

Quayle brushed back his gray hair. 'I feel sensitive all over,' he objected. 'After all, I've been under a considerable strain correlating my material.'

'Well, we can always postpone publication.' Burkhalter threw out the suggestion casually, and was pleased when Quayle didn't nibble. He didn't like to fail, either.

'No. No, I want to get the thing done now.'

'Mental catharsis –'

'Well, by a psychologist, perhaps. But not by –'

'– a Baldy. You know that a lot of psychologists have Baldy helpers. They get good results, too.'

Quayle turned on the tobacco smoke, inhaling slowly. 'I suppose … I've not had much contact with Baldies. Or too much – without selectivity. I saw some in an asylum once. I'm not being offensive, am I?'

'No,' Burkhalter said. 'Every mutation can run too close to the line. There were lots of failures. The hard radiations brought about one true mutation: hairless telepaths, but they didn't all hew true to the line. The mind's a queer gadget – you know that. It's a colloid balancing, figuratively, on the point of a pin. If there's any flaw, telepathy's apt to bring it out. So you'll find that the Blowup caused a hell of a lot of insanity. No only among the Baldies, but among the other mutations that developed then. Except that the Baldies are almost always paranoidal.

'And dementia praecox,' Quayle said, finding relief from his own embarrassment in turning the spotlight on Burkhalter.

'And d.p. Yeah. When a confused mind acquires the telepathic instinct – a hereditary bollixed mind – it can't handle it all. There's disorientation. The paranoia group retreat into their own private worlds, and the d.ps simply don't realize that *this* world exists. There are distinctions, but I think that's a valid basis.'

'In a way,' Quayle said, 'it's frightening. I can't think of any historical parallel.'

'No.'

'What do you think the end of it will be?'

'I don't know,' Burkhalter said thoughtfully. 'I think we'll be assimilated. There hasn't been enough time yet. We're specialized in a certain way, and we're useful in certain jobs.'

'If you're satisfied to stay there. The Baldies who won't wear wigs –'

'They're so bad-tempered I expect they'll all be killed off in duels eventually,' Burkhalter smiled. 'No great loss. The rest of us, we're getting what we want – acceptance. We don't have horns or halos.'

Quayle shook his head. 'I'm glad, I think, that I'm not a telepath. The mind's mysterious enough anyway, without new doors opening. Thanks for letting me talk. I think I've got part of it talked out, anyway. Shall we try the script again?'

'Sure,' Burkhalter said, and again the procession of pages flickered on the screen above them. Quayle did seem less guarded; his thoughts were more lucid, and Burkhalter was able to get at the true meaning of many of the hitherto muddy statements. They worked easily, the telepath dictating rephrasings into his dictograph, and only twice did they have to hurdle emotional tangles. At noon they knocked off, and Burkhalter, with a friendly nod, took the dropper to his office, where he found some calls listed on the visor. He ran off repeats, and a worried look crept into his blue eyes.

He talked with Dr Moon in a booth at luncheon. The conversation lasted, so long that only the induction cups kept the coffee hot, but Burkhalter had more than one problem to discuss. And he'd known Moon for a long time. The fat man was one of the few who were not, he thought, subconsciously repelled by the fact that Burkhalter was a Baldy.

'I've never fought a duel in my life, Doc. I can't afford to.'

'You can't afford not to. You can't turn down the challenge, Ed. It isn't done.'

'But this fellow Reilly – I don't even know him.'

'I know of him,' Moon said. 'He's got a bad temper. Dueled a lot.'

Burkhalter slammed his hand down on the table. 'It's ridiculous. I won't do it!'

'Well,' Moon said practically, 'Your wife can't fight him. And if Ethel's been reading Mrs Reilly's mind and gossiping, Reilly's got a case.'

'Don't you think we know the dangers of that?' Burkhalter asked in a low voice. 'Ethel doesn't go around reading minds any more than I do. It'd be fatal – for us. And for any other Baldy.'

'Not the hairless ones. The ones who won't wear wigs. They –'

'They're fools. And they're giving all the Baldies a bad name. Point one, Ethel doesn't read minds; she didn't read Mrs Reilly's. Point two, she doesn't gossip.'

'La Reilly is obviously an hysterical type,' Moon said. 'Word got around about this scandal, whatever it was, and Mrs Reilly remembered she'd seen Ethel lately. She's the type who needs a scapegoat anyway. I rather imagine she let word drop herself, and had to cover up so her husband wouldn't blame her.'

'I'm not going to accept Reilly's challenge,' Burkhalter said doggedly.

'You'll have to.'

'Listen, Doc, maybe –'

'What?'

'Nothing. An idea. It might work. Forget about that; I think I've got the right answer. It's the only one, anyway. I can't afford a duel and that's flat.'

'You're not a coward.'

'There's one thing Baldies are afraid of,' Burkhalter said, 'and that's public opinion. I happen to know I'd kill Reilly. That's the reason why I've never dueled in my life.'

Moon drank coffee. 'Hm-m-m. I think –'

'Don't. There was something else. I'm wondering if I ought to send Al off to a special school.'

'What's wrong with the kid?'

'He's turning out to be a beautiful delinquent. His teacher called me this morning. The playback was something to hear. He's talking funny and acting funny. Playing nasty little tricks on his friends – if he has any left by now.'

'All kids are cruel.'

'Kids don't know what cruelty means. That's why they're cruel; they lack empathy. But Al's getting –' Burkhalter gestured helplessly. 'He's turning into a young tyrant. He doesn't seem to give a care about anything, according to his teacher.'

'That's not too abnormal, so far.'

'That's not the worst. He's become very egotistical. Too much so. I don't want him to turn into one of the wigless Baldies you were mentioning.' Burkhalter didn't mention the other possibility; paranoia, insanity.

'He must pick things up somewhere. At home? Scarcely, Ed. Where else does he go?'

'The usual places. He's got a normal environment.'

'I should think,' Moon said, 'that a Baldy would have unusual opportunities in training a youngster. The mental rapport – eh?'

'Yeah. But – I don't know. The trouble is,' Burkhalter said almost inaudibly, 'I wish to God I wasn't different. We didn't ask to be telepaths. Maybe it's all very wonderful in the long run, but I'm one person, and I've got my own microcosm. People who deal in long-term sociology are apt to forget that. They can figure out the answers, but it's every individual man – or Baldy – who's got to fight his own personal battle while he's alive. And it isn't as clear-cut as a battle. It's worse; it's the necessity of watching yourself every second, of fitting yourself into a world that doesn't want you.'

Moon looked uncomfortable. 'Are you being a little sorry for yourself, Ed?'

Burkhalter shook himself. 'I am, Doc. But I'll work it out.'

'We both will,' Moon said, but Burkhalter didn't really expect much help from him. Moon would be willing, but it was horribly difficult for an ordinary man to conceive that a Baldy was – the same. It was the difference that men looked for, and found.

Anyway, he'd have to settle matters before he saw Ethel again. He could easily conceal the knowledge, but she would recognize a mental barrier and wonder. Their marriage had been the more ideal because of the additional rapport, something that compensated for an inevitable, half-sensed estrangement from the rest of the world.

'How's "Psychohistory" going?' Moon asked after a while.

'Better than I expected. I've got a new angle on Quayle. If I talk about myself, that seems to draw him out. It gives him enough confidence to let him open his mind to me. We may have those first chapters ready for Oldfield, in spite of everything.'

'Good. Just the same, he can't rush us. If we've got to shoot out books that fast, we might as well go back to the days of semantic confusion. Which we won't!'

'Well,' Burkhalter said, getting up, 'I'll smoosh along. See you.'

'About Reilly –'

'Let it lay.' Burkhalter went out, heading for the address his visor had listed. He touched the dagger at his belt. Dueling wouldn't do for Baldies, but –

A greeting thought crept into his mind, and, under the arch that led into the campus, he paused to grin at Sam Shane, a New Orleans area Baldy who affected a wig of flaming red. They didn't bother to talk.

Personal question, involving mental, moral and physical well-being.

A satisfied glow. And you, Burkhalter? For an instant Burkhalter half-saw what the symbol of his name meant to Shane.

Shadow of trouble.

A warm, willing anxiousness to help. There was a bond between Baldies.

Burkhalter thought: But everywhere I'd go there'd be the same suspicion. We're freaks.

More so elsewhere, Shane thought. There are a lot of us in Modoc Town. People are invariably more suspicious where they're not in daily contact with – Us.

The boy –

I've trouble too, Shane thought. It's worried me. My two girls –

Delinquency?

Yes.

Common denominators?

Don't know. More than one of Us have had the same trouble with our kids. Secondary characteristic of the mutation? Second generation emergence?

Doubtful, Shane thought, scowling in his mind, shading his concept with a wavering question. We'll think it over later. Must go.

Burkhalter sighed and went on his way. The houses were strung out around the central industry of Modoc, and he cut through a park toward his destination. It was a sprawling curved building, but it wasn't inhabited, so Burkhalter filed Reilly for future reference, and, with a glance at his timer, angled over a hillside toward the school. As he expected, it was recreation time, and he spotted Al lounging under a tree, some distance from his companions, who were involved in a pleasantly murderous game of Blowup.

He sent his thought ahead.

The Green Man had almost reached the top of the mountain. The hairy gnomes were pelting on his trail, most unfairly shooting sizzling light-streaks at their quarry, but the Green Man was agile enough to dodge. The rocks were leaning –

'Al.'

– inward, pushed by the gnomes, ready to –

'Al!' Burkhalter sent his thought with the word, jolting into the boy's mind, a trick he very seldom employed, since youth was practically defenseless against such invasion.

'Hello, Dad,' Al said, undisturbed. 'What's up?'

'A report from your teacher.'

'I didn't do anything.'

'She told me what it was. Listen, kid. Don't start getting any funny ideas in your head.'

'I'm not.'

'Do you think a Baldy is better or worse than a non-Baldy?'

Al moved his feet uncomfortably. He didn't answer.

'Well,' Burkhalter said, 'the answer is both and neither. And here's why. A Baldy can communicate mentally, but he lives in a world where most people can't.'

'They're dumb,' Al opined.

'Not so dumb, if they're better suited to their world than you are. You might as well say a frog's better than a fish because he's an amphibian.' Burkhalter briefly amplified and explained the terms telepathically.

'Well … oh, I get it, all right.'

'Maybe,' Burkhalter said slowly, 'what you need is a swift kick in the pants. That thought wasn't so hot. What was it again?'

Al tried to hide it, blanking out. Burkhalter began to lift the barrier, an easy matter for him, but stopped. Al regarded his father in a most unfilial way – in fact, as a sort of boneless fish. That had been clear.

'If you're so egotistical,' Burkhalter pointed out, 'maybe you can see it this way. Do you know why there aren't any Baldies in key positions?'

'Sure I do,' Al said unexpectedly. 'They're afraid.'

'Of what, then?'

'The –' That picture had been very curious, a commingling of something vaguely familiar to Burkhalter. 'The non-Baldies.'

'Well, if we took positions where we could take advantage of our telepathic function, non-Baldies would be plenty envious – especially if we were successes. If a Baldy even invented a better mousetrap, plenty of people would say he'd stolen the idea from some non-Baldy's mind. You get the point?'

'Yes, Dad.' But he hadn't. Burkhalter sighed and looked up. He recognized one of Shane's girls on a nearby hillside, sitting alone against a boulder. There were other isolated figures here and there. Far to the east the snowy rampart of the Rockies made an irregular pattern against blue sky.

'Al,' Burkhalter said, 'I don't want you to get a chip on your shoulder. This is a pretty swell world, and the people in it are, on the whole, nice people. There's a law of averages. It isn't sensible for us to get too much wealth or power, because that'd militate against us – and we don't need it anyway. Nobody's poor. We find our work, we do it, and we're reasonably happy. We have some advantages non-Baldies don't have; in marriage, for example. Mental intimacy is quite as important as physical. But I don't want you to feel that being a Baldy makes you a god. It doesn't. I can still,' he added thoughtfully, 'spank it out of you, in case you care to follow out that concept in your mind at the moment.'

Al gulped and beat a hasty retreat. 'I'm sorry. I won't do it again.'

'And keep your hair on, too. Don't take your wig off in class. Use the stick-um stuff in the bathroom closet.'

'Yes, but ... Mr Venner doesn't wear a wig.'

'Remind me to do some historical research with you on zoot-suiters,' Burkhalter said. 'Mr Venner's wiglessness is probably his only virtue, if you consider it one.'

'He makes money.'

'Anybody would, in that general store of his. But people don't buy from him if they can help it, you'll notice. That's what I mean by a chip on your shoulder. He's got one. There are Baldies like Venner, Al, but you might, sometime, ask the guy if he's happy. For your information, I am. More than Venner, anyway. Catch?'

'Yes, Dad.' Al seemed submissive, but it was merely that. Burkhalter, still troubled, nodded and walked away. As he passed near the Shane girl's boulder he caught a scrap: – *at the summit of the Glass Mountains, rolling rocks back at the gnomes until* –

He withdrew; it was an unconscious habit, touching minds that were sensitive, but with children it was definitely unfair. With adult Baldies it was simply the instinctive gesture of tipping your hat; one answered or one didn't. The barrier could be erected; there could be a blank-out; or there could be the direct snub of concentration on a single thought, private and not to be intruded on.

A copter with a string of gliders was coming in from the south: a freighter laden with frozen foods from South America, to judge by the markings. Burkhalter made a note to pick up an Argentine steak. He'd got a new recipe he wanted to try out, a charcoal broil with barbecue sauce, a welcome change from the short-wave cooked meats they'd been having for a week. Tomatoes, chile, mm-m – what else? Oh, yes. The duel with Reilly. Burkhalter absently touched his dagger's hilt and made a small, mocking sound in his throat. Perhaps he was innately a pacifist. It was rather difficult to think of a duel seriously, even though everyone else did, when the details of a barbecue dinner were prosaic in his mind.

So it went. The tides of civilization rolled in century-long waves across the continents, and each particular wave, though conscious of its participation in the tide, nevertheless was more preoccupied with dinner. And, unless you happened to be a thousand feet tall, had the brain of a god and a god's lifespan, what was the difference? People missed a lot – people like Venner, who was certainly a crank, not batty enough to qualify for the asylum, but certainly a potential paranoid type. The man's refusal to wear a wig labeled him as an individualist, but as an exhibitionist, too. If he didn't feel ashamed of his hairlessness, why should he bother to flaunt it? Besides, the man had a bad temper, and if people kicked him around, he asked for it by starting the kicking himself.

But as for Al, the kid was heading for something approaching delinquency. It couldn't be the normal development of childhood, Burkhalter thought. He didn't pretend to be an expert, but he was still young enough to remember his own formative years, and he had had more handicaps than Al had now; in those days, Baldics had been very new and very freakish. There'd been more than one movement to isolate, sterilize, or even exterminate the mutations.

Burkhalter sighed. If he had been born before the Blowup, it might have been different. Impossible to say. One could read history, but one couldn't live it. In the future, perhaps, there might be telepathic libraries in which that would be possible. So many opportunities, in fact – and so few that the world was ready to accept as yet. Eventually Baldies would not be regarded as freaks, and by that time real progress would be possible.

But people don't make history – Burkhalter thought. Peoples do that. Not the individual.

He stopped by Reilly's house, and this time the man answered, a burly, freckled, squint-eyed fellow with immense hands and, Burkhalter noted, fine muscular co-ordination. He rested those hands on the Dutch door and nodded.

'Who're you, mister?'

'My name's Burkhalter.'

Comprehension and wariness leaped into Reilly's eyes. 'Oh, I see. You got my call?'

'I did,' Burkhalter said. 'I want to talk to you about it. May I come in?'

'O.K.' He stepped back, opening the way through a hall and into a spacious living room, where diffused light filtered through glassy mosaic walls. 'Want to set the time?'

'I want to tell you you're wrong.'

'Now wait a minute,' Reilly said, patting the air. 'My wife's out now, but she gave me the straight of it. I don't like this business of sneaking into a man's mind; it's crooked. You should have told *your* wife to mind her business – or keep her tongue quiet.'

Burkhalter said patiently, 'I give you my word, Reilly, that Ethel didn't read your wife's mind.'

'Does she say so?'

'I ... well, I haven't asked her.'

'Yeah,' Reilly said with an air of triumph.

'I don't need to. I know her well enough. And ... well, I'm a Baldy myself.'

'I know you are,' Reilly said. 'For all I know, you may be reading my mind now.' He hesitated. 'Get out of my house. I like my privacy. We'll meet at dawn tomorrow, if that's satisfactory with you. Now get out.' He seemed to have something on his mind, some ancient memory, perhaps, that he didn't wish exposed.

Burkhalter nobly resisted the temptation. 'No Baldy would read –'

'Go on, get out!'

'Listen! You wouldn't have a chance in a duel with me!'

'Do you know how many notches I've got?' Reilly asked.

'Ever dueled a Baldy?'

'I'll cut the notch deeper tomorrow. Get out, d'you hear?'

Burkhalter, biting his lips, said, 'Man, don't you realize that in a duel I could read your mind?'

'I don't care ... what?'

'I'd be half a jump ahead of you. No matter how instinctive your actions would be, you'd know them a split second ahead of time in your mind. And I'd know all your tricks and weaknesses, too. Your technique would be an open book to me. Whatever you thought of –'

'No.' Reilly shook his head. 'Oh, no. You're smart, but it's a phony set-up.'

Burkhalter hesitated, decided, and swung about, pushing a chair out of the way. 'Take out your dagger,' he said. 'Leave the sheath snapped on; I'll show you what I mean.'

Reilly's eyes widened. 'If you want it now –'

'I don't.' Burkhalter shoved another chair away. He unclipped his dagger, sheath and all, from his belt, and made sure the little safety clip was in place. 'We've enough room here. Come on.'

Scowling, Reilly took out his own dagger, held it awkwardly, baffled by the sheath, and then suddenly feinted forward. But Burkhalter wasn't there; he had anticipated, and his own leather sheath slid up Reilly's belly.

'That,' Burkhalter said, 'would have ended the fight.'

For answer Reilly smashed a hard dagger-blow down, curving at the last moment into a throat-cutting slash. Burkhalter's free hand was already at his throat; his other hand, with the sheathed dagger, tapped Reilly twice over the heart. The freckles stood out boldly against the pallor of the larger man's face. But he was not yet ready to concede. He tried a few more passes, clever, well-trained cuts, and they failed, because Burkhalter had anticipated them. His left hand invariably covered the spot where Reilly had aimed, and which he never struck.

Slowly Reilly let his arm fall. He moistened his lips and swallowed. Burkhalter busied himself reclipping his dagger in place.

'Burkhalter,' Reilly said, 'you're a devil.'

'Far from it. I'm just afraid to take a chance. Do you really think being a Baldy is a snap?'

'But, if you can read minds –'

'How long do you think I'd last if I did any dueling? It would be too much of a set-up. Nobody would stand for it, and I'd end up dead. I can't duel, because it'd be murder, and people would know it was murder. I've taken a lot of cracks, swallowed a lot of insults, for just that reason. Now, if you like, I'll swallow another and apologize. I'll admit anything you say. But I can't duel with you, Reilly.'

'No, I can see that. And – I'm glad you came over.' Reilly was still white. 'I'd have walked right into a set-up.'

'Not my set-up,' Burkhalter said. 'I wouldn't have dueled. Baldies aren't so lucky, you know. They've got handicaps – like this. That's why they can't afford to take chances and antagonize people, and why we never read minds, unless we're asked to do so.'

'It makes sense. More or less.' Reilly hesitated. 'Look, I withdraw that challenge. O.K.?'

'Thanks,' Burkhalter said, putting out his hand. It was taken rather reluctantly. 'We'll leave it at that, eh?'

'Right.' But Reilly was still anxious to get his guest out of the house.

Burkhalter walked back to the Publishing Center and whistled tunelessly. He could tell Ethel now; in fact, he had to, for secrets between them would have broken up the completeness of their telepathic intimacy. It was not that their minds lay bare to each other, it was, rather, that any barrier could be sensed by the other, and the perfect *rapport* wouldn't have been so perfect. Curiously, despite this utter intimacy, husband and wife managed to respect one another's privacy.

Ethel might be somewhat distressed, but the trouble had blown over, and, besides, she was a Baldy too. Not that she looked it, with her wig of fluffy chestnut hair and those long, curving lashes. But her parents had lived east of Seattle during the Blowup, and afterward, too, before the hard radiation's effects had been thoroughly studied.

The snow-wind blew down over Modoc and fled southward along the Utab Valley. Burkhalter wished he was in his copter, alone in the blue emptiness of the sky. There was a quiet, strange peace up there that no Baldy ever quite achieved on the earth's surface, except in the depths of a wilderness. Stray fragments of thoughts were always flying about, sub-sensory, but like the almost-unheard whisper of a needle on a phonograph record, never ceasing. That, certainly, was why almost all Baldies loved to fly and were expert pilots. The high waste deserts of the air were their blue hermitages.

Still, he was in Modoc now, and overdue for his interview with Quayle.

Burkhalter hastened his steps. In the main hall he met Moon, said briefly and cryptically that he'd taken care of the duel, and passed on, leaving the fat man to stare a question after him. The only visor call was from Ethel; the play-back said she was worried about Al, and would Burkhalter check with the school. Well, he had already done so – unless the boy had managed to get into more trouble since then. Burkhalter put in a call and reassured himself. Al was as yet unchanged.

He found Quayle in the same private solarium, and thirsty. Burkhalter ordered a couple of dramzowies sent up, since he had no objection to loosening Quayle's inhibitions. The gray-haired author was immersed in a sectional historical globe-map, illuminating each epochal layer in turn as he searched back through time.

'Watch this,' he said, running his hand along the row of buttons. 'See how the German border fluctuates? And Portugal. Notice its zone of influence? Now –' The zone shrank steadily from 1600 on, while other countries shot out radiating lines and assumed sea power.

Burkhalter sipped his dramzowie. 'Not much of that now.'

'No, since … what's the matter?'

'How do you mean?'

'You look shot.'

'I didn't know I showed it,' Burkhalter said wryly. 'I just finagled my way out of a duel.'

'That's one custom I never saw much sense to,' Quayle said. 'What happened? Since when can you finagle out?'

Burkhalter explained, and the writer took a drink and snorted. 'What a spot for you. Being a Baldy isn't such an advantage after all, I guess.'

'It has distinct disadvantages at times.' On impulse Burkhalter mentioned his son. 'You see my point, eh? I don't *know*, really, what standards to apply to a young Baldy. He is a mutation, after all. And the telepathic mutation hasn't had time to work out yet. We can't rig up controls, because guinea pigs and rabbits won't breed telepaths. That's been tried, you know. And – well, the child of a Baldy needs very special training so he can cope with his ultimate maturity.'

'You seem to have adjusted well enough.'

'I've – learned. As most sensible Baldies have. That's why I'm not a wealthy man, or in politics. We're really buying safety for our species by foregoing certain individual advantages. Hostages to destiny – and destiny spares us. But we get paid too, in a way. In the coinage of future benefits – negative benefits, really, for we ask only to be spared and accepted – and so we have to deny ourselves a lot of present, positive benefits. An appeasement to fate.'

'Paying the piper,' Quayle nodded.

'We are the pipers. The Baldies as a group, I mean. And our children. So it balances; we're really paying ourselves. If I wanted to take unfair advantage of my telepathic power – my son wouldn't live very long. The Baldies would be wiped out. Al's got to learn that, and he's getting pretty antisocial.'

'All children are antisocial,' Quayle pointed out. 'They're utter individualists. I should think the only reason for worrying would be if the boy's deviation from the norm were connected with his telepathic sense.'

'There's something in that.' Burkhalter reached out left-handedly and probed delicately at Quayle's mind, noting that the antagonism was considerably lessened. He grinned to himself and went on talking about his own troubles. 'Just the same, the boy's father to the man. And an adult Baldy has got to be pretty well adjusted, or he's sunk.'

'Environment is as important as heredity. One complements the other. If a child's reared correctly he won't have much trouble – unless heredity is involved.'

'As it may be. There's so little known about the telepathic mutation. If baldness is one secondary characteristic, maybe – something else – emerges in the third or fourth generations. I'm wondering if telepathy is really good for the mind.'

Quayle said, 'Humph. Speaking personally, it makes me nervous –'

'Like Reilly.'

'Yes,' Quayle said, but he didn't care much for the comparison. 'Well – anyhow, if a mutation's a failure, it'll die out. It won't breed true.'

'What about hemophilia?'

'How many people have hemophilia?' Quayle asked. 'I'm trying to look at it from the angle of psychohistorian. If there'd been telepaths in the past, things might have been different.'

'How do you know there weren't?' Burkhalter asked.

Quayle blinked. 'Oh. Well. That's true, too. In medieval times they'd have been called wizards – or saints. The Duke-Rhine experiments – but such accidents would have been abortive. Nature fools around trying to hit the … ah … the jackpot, and she doesn't always do it on the first try.'

'She may not have done it now.' That was habit speaking, the ingrained caution of modesty. 'Telepathy may be merely a semisuccessful try at something pretty unimaginable. A sort of four-dimensional sensory concept, maybe.'

'That's too abstract for me.' Quayle was interested, and his own hesitancies had almost vanished; by accepting Burkhalter as a telepath, he had tacitly wiped away his objections to telepathy *per se*. 'The old-time Germans always had an idea they were different; so did the Japanese. They knew, very definitely, that they were a superior race because they were directly descended from gods. They were short in stature; heredity made them self-conscious when dealing with larger races. But the Chinese aren't tall, the Southern Chinese, and they weren't handicapped in that way.'

'Environment, then?'

'Environment, which caused propaganda. The Japanese took Buddhism, and altered it completely into Shinto, to suit their own needs. The samurai, warrior-knights, were the ideals, the code of honor was fascinatingly cock-eyed. The principle of Shinto was to worship your superiors and subjugate your inferiors. Ever seen the Japanese jewel-trees?'

'I don't remember them. What are they?'

'Miniature replicas of espaliered trees, made of jewels, with trinkets hanging on the branches. Including a mirror – always. The first jewel-tree was made to lure the Moon-goddess out of a cave where she was sulking. It seemed the lady was so intrigued by the trinkets and by her face reflected in the mirror that she came out of her hideout. All the Japanese morals were dressed up in pretty clothes; that was the bait. The old-time Germans did much the same thing. The last German dictator, Hitler, revived the old Siegfried legend. It was racial paranoia. The Germans worshiped the house-tyrant, not the mother, and they had extremely strong family ties. That extended to the state. They symbolized Hitler as their All-Father, and so eventually we got the Blowup. And, finally, mutations.'

'After the deluge, me,' Burkhalter murmured, finishing his dramzowie. Quayle was staring at nothing.

'Funny,' he said after a while. 'This All-Father business –'

'Yes?'

'I wonder if you know how powerfully it can affect a man?'

Burkhalter didn't say anything. Quayle gave him a sharp glance.

'Yes,' the writer said quietly. 'You're a man, after all. I owe you an apology, you know.'

Burkhalter smiled. 'You can forget that.'

'I'd rather not,' Quayle said. 'I've just realized, pretty suddenly, that the telepathic sense isn't so important. I mean – it doesn't make you *different*. I've been talking to you –'

'Sometimes it takes people years before they realize what you're finding out,' Burkhalter remarked. 'Years of living and working with something they think of as a Baldy.'

'Do you know what I've been concealing in my mind?' Quayle asked.

'No. I don't.'

'You lie like a gentleman. Thanks. Well, here it is, and I'm telling you by choice, because I want to. I don't care if you got the information out of my mind already; I just want to tell you of my own free will. My father … I imagine I hated him … was a tyrant, and I remember one time, when I was just a kid and we were in the mountains, he beat me and a lot of people were looking on. I've tried to forget that for a long time. Now' – Quayle shrugged – 'it doesn't seem quite so important.'

'I'm not a psychologist,' Burkhalter said. 'If you want my personal reaction. I'll just say that it doesn't matter. You're not a little boy any more, and the guy I'm talking to and working with is the adult Quayle.'

'Hm-m-m. Ye-es. I suppose I knew that all along – how unimportant it was, really. It was simply having my privacy violated … I think I know you better now, Burkhalter. You can – walk in.'

'We'll work better,' Burkhalter said, grinning. 'Especially with Darius.'

Quayle said, 'I'll try not to keep any reservation in my mind. Frankly, I won't mind telling you – the answers. Even when they're personal.'

'Check on that. D'you want to tackle Darius now?'

'O.K.,' Quayle said, and his eyes no longer held suspicious wariness. 'Darius I identify with my father –'

It was smooth and successful. That afternoon they accomplished more than they had during the entire previous fortnight. Warm with satisfaction on more than one point. Burkhalter stopped off to tell Dr Moon that matters were looking up, and then set out toward home, exchanging thoughts with a couple of Baldies, his co-workers, who were knocking off for the day. The Rockies were bloody with the western light, and the coolness of the wind was pleasant on Burkhalter's cheeks, as he hiked homeward.

It was fine to be accepted. It proved that it could be done. And a Baldy often needed reassurance, in a world peopled by suspicious strangers. Quayle had been a hard nut to crack, but – Burkhalter smiled.

Ethel would be pleased. In a way, she'd had a harder time than he'd ever had. A woman would, naturally. Men were desperately anxious to keep their privacy unviolated by a woman, and as for non-Baldy women – well, it spoke highly for Ethel's glowing personal charm that she had finally been accepted by the clubs and feminine groups of Modoc. Only Burkhalter knew Ethel's desperate hurt at being bald, and not even her husband had ever seen her unwigged.

His thought reached out before him into the low, double-winged house on the hillside, and interlocked with hers in a warm intimacy. It was something more than a kiss. And, as always, there was the exciting sense of expectancy, mounting and mounting till the last door swung open and they touched physically. *This*, he thought, *is why I was born a Baldy; this is worth losing worlds for.*

At dinner that rapport spread out to embrace Al, an intangible, deeply-rooted something that made the food taste better and the water like wine. The word *home*, to telepaths, had a meaning that non-Baldies could not entirely comprehend, for it embraced a bond they could not know. There were small, intangible caresses.

Green Man going down the Great Red Slide; the Shaggy Dwarfs trying to harpoon him as he goes.

'Al,' Ethel said, 'are you still working on your Green Man?'

Then something utterly hateful and cold and deadly quivered silently in the air, like an icicle jaggedly smashing through golden, fragile glass. Burkhalter dropped his napkin and looked up, profoundly shocked. He felt Ethel's thought shrink back, and swiftly reached out to touch and reassure her with mental contact. But across the table the little boy, his cheeks still round with the fat of babyhood, sat silent and wary, realizing he had blundered, and seeking safety in complete immobility. His mind was too weak to resist probing, he knew, and he remained perfectly still, waiting, while the echoes of a thought hung poisonously in silence.

Burkhalter said, 'Come on, Al.' He stood up. Ethel started to speak.

'Wait, darling. Put up a barrier. Don't listen in.' He touched her mind gently and tenderly, and then he took Al's hand and drew the boy after him out into the yard. Al watched his father out of wide, alert eyes.

Burkhalter sat on a bench and put Al beside him. He talked audibly at first, for clarity's sake, and for another reason. It was distinctly unpleasant to trick the boy's feeble guards down, but it was necessary.

'That's a very queer way to think of your mother,' he said. 'It's a queer way to think of me.' Obscenity is more obscene, profanity more profane, to a telepathic mind, but this had been neither one. It had been – cold and malignant.

And this is flesh of my flesh, Burkhalter thought, looking at the boy and remembering the eight years of his growth. *Is the mutation to turn into something devilish?*

Al was silent.

Burkhalter reached into the young mind. Al tried to twist free and escape, but his father's strong hands gripped him. Instinct, not reasoning, on the boy's part, for minds can touch over long distances.

He did not like to do this, for increased sensibility had gone with sensitivity, and violations are always violations. But ruthlessness was required. Burkhalter searched. Sometimes he threw key words violently at Al, and surges of memory pulsed up in response.

In the end, sick and nauseated, Burkhalter let Al go and sat alone on the bench, watching the red light die on the snowy peaks. The whiteness was red-stained. But it was not too late. The man was a fool, had been a fool from the beginning, or he would have known the impossibility of attempting such a thing as this.

The conditioning had only begun. Al could be reconditioned. Burkhalter's eyes hardened. And would be. *And would be*. But not yet, not until the immediate furious anger had given place to sympathy and understanding.

Not yet.

He went into the house, spoke briefly to Ethel, and televised the dozen Baldies who worked with him in the Publishing Center. Not all of them had families, but none was missing when, half an hour later, they met in the back room of the Pagan Tavern downtown. Sam Shane had caught a fragment of Burkhalter's knowledge, and all of them read his emotions. Welded into a sympathetic unit by their telepathic sense, they waited till Burkhalter was ready.

Then he told them. It didn't take long, via thought. He told them about the Japanese jewel-tree with its glittering gadgets, a shining lure. He told them of racial paranoia and propaganda. And that the most effective propaganda was sugarcoated, disguised so that the motive was hidden.

A Green Man, hairless, heroic – symbolic of a Baldy.

And wild, exciting adventures, the lure to catch the young fish whose plastic minds were impressionable enough to be led along the roads of dangerous madness. Adult Baldies could listen, but they did not; young telepaths had a higher threshold of mental receptivity, and adults do not read the books of their children except to reassure themselves that there is nothing harmful in the pages. And no adult would bother to listen to the Green Man mindcast. Most of them had accepted it as the original daydream of their own children.

'I did,' Shane put in. 'My girls –'

'Trace it back,' Burkhalter said. 'I did.'

The dozen minds reached out on the higher frequency, the children's wavelength, and something jerked away from them, startled and apprehensive.

'He's the one,' Shane nodded.

They did not need to speak. They went out of the Pagan Tavern in a compact, ominous group, and crossed the street to the general store. The door was locked. Two of the men burst it open with their shoulders.

They went through the dark store and into a back room where a man was standing beside an overturned chair. His bald skull gleamed in an overhead light. His mouth worked impotently.

His thought pleaded with them – was driven back by an implacable deadly wall.

Burkhalter took out his dagger. Other slivers of steel glittered for a little while –

And were quenched.

Venner's scream had long since stopped, but his dying thought of agony lingered within Burkhalter's mind as he walked homeward. The wigless Baldy had not been insane, no. But he had been paranoidal.

What he had tried to conceal, at the last, was quite shocking. A tremendous, tyrannical egotism, and a furious hatred of nontelepaths. A feeling of self-justification that was, perhaps, insane. And – *we are the Future! The Baldies! God made us to rule lesser men!*

Burkhalter sucked in his breath, shivering. The mutation had not been entirely successful. One group had adjusted, the Baldies who wore wigs and had become fitted to their environment. One group had been insane, and could be discounted; they were in asylums.

But the middle group were merely paranoid. They were not insane, and they were not sane. They wore no wigs.

Like Venner.

And Venner had sought disciples. His attempt had been foredoomed to failure, but he had been one man.

One Baldy – paranoid.

There were others, many others.

Ahead, nestled into the dark hillside, was the pale blotch that marked Burkhalter's home. He sent his thought ahead, and it touched Ethel's and paused very briefly to reassure her.

Then it thrust on, and went into the sleeping mind of a little boy who, confused and miserable, had finally cried himself to sleep. There were only dreams in that mind now, a little discolored, a little stained, but they could be cleansed. And would be.

TWO

I must have dozed. I woke up slowly, hearing a deep hollow thunder that pulsed a few times and was gone as I opened stiff eyelids. Then I knew what I had heard. It was a jet plane, perhaps searching for me, now that it was daylight again. Its high-speed camera would be working, recording the landscape below, and as soon as the jet returned to base, the film would be developed and scanned. The wreck of my plane would be spotted – if it showed on the film. But had the jet passed over this narrow canyon between the peaks? I didn't know.

I tried to move. It wasn't easy. I felt cold and sluggish. The silence closed in around me. I got stiffly to my knees and then upright. My breathing was the only sound.

I shouted, just to break the lonely silence.

I started to walk around to get my circulation going. I didn't want to; I wanted to lie down and sleep. My mind kept drifting off into blankness. Once I found that I was standing still, and the cold had crept through me.

I began walking again, and remembering. I couldn't run, but I could walk, and I'd better, or else I'd lie down and die. What had happened after Venner was killed? The next Key Life was Barton's, wasn't it? Barton and the Three Blind Mice. I thought about Barton, and I kept on walking in a circle, getting a little warmer, and then time began spinning backward, until I was Barton in Conestoga, not quite two hundred years ago, and at the same time I was myself, watching Barton.

That was the time when the paranoids first began to band together.

THREE BLIND MICE

Under the helicopter, disturbed by the hurricane down-blast the lake was lashed to white foam. The curving dark shape of a bass leaped and vanished. A sailboat tacked and made toward the farther shore. In Barton's mind there flamed for an instant a ravening madness of hunger and then an intensity of pure ecstasy, as his thought probed down into the depths of the waters and made contact with some form of life in which there was instinct, but no reason – only the raging avidity of life-lust that, after fifteen years, was so familiar to him now.

There had been no need for that purely automatic mental probing. In these calm American waters one found no sharks, no crocodiles, no poisonous sea snakes. It was habit alone, the trained alertness that had helped to make David Barton expert in his field, one of the few vocations available to the minority of telepathic Baldies. And after six months in Africa, what he wanted most of all was not – *contact* – but something to calm his psychic tension. In the jungle a Baldy can find a communion with nature that out-Thoreau's Thoreau, but at a cost. Beneath that pagan spirit of the primeval beats the urgent pulse of strong instinct: self-preservation almost without reason. Only in the paintings of Rousseau that had survived the Blowup had Barton felt the same vivid, almost insane passion for life.

Where men are weary of green wine,
And sick of crimson seas –

Well, he was back now, not far from his grandfather's birthplace near Chicago, and he could rest for a while.

His hands moved over the complicated controls, sending the copter smoothly up, as though by that action he could escape what was inescapable. You lived, for the most part, on the earth, and if you happened to be a telepath, well, there were of course advantages as well as disadvantages. Nobody lynched Baldies any more, of course. Fairly secure, almost accepted, in their cautious self-effacement – italicized by the wigs they invariably wore – they could find jobs and a pattern for living. Specialized jobs, naturally, which must never involve too much power or profit. Jobs in which you turned your specialized talent to the betterment of the social unit. Barton was a naturalist, a collector of big and little game. And that had been his salvation.

Years ago, he remembered, there had been a conference, his parents, and a few other Baldies, drawn together by the deep, sympathetic friendliness and understanding that always had welded telepaths. He could still vividly recall the troubled patterns of thought that had ebbed and flowed in the room, more clearly than the way their faces had looked. Danger, and a shadow, and a desire to help.

... *Outlet for his energy ... no scholar ... misfit unless –*

– find the right job –

He could not remember the words, only the absolute meanings, with their significant colorations and shadings of implication, those and the – the name-symbol by which the others thought of him. To them he was not Dave Barton. Their thought-references to him personally, while different to each mind, had always the kernel of individual meaning that belonged to him alone, of all the people in the world. The name that a candle flame might have, secret and unuttered. His alone.

And because of this, and because each Baldy *must* survive and adjust, for the ultimate good of the racial mutation, they had found the answer. It was all right for non-Baldies to be reasonably swashbuckling; everyone wore daggers and dueled nowadays. But the telepaths themselves lived on borrowed time. They existed only because of the good will they had created. That good will had to be maintained, and it could not be done by arousing antagonism. No one could be jealous of a mild-mannered, studious semantic expert, but a d'Artagnan could be envied – and would be. An outlet, then, for the boy's curiously mixed inheritance, his blood from pioneering, trail-blazing ancestors mixed with the cautious Baldy strain.

So they had found the answer, and Barton did his pioneering in the jungles, matching his keen mind against the brute savagery of tiger and python. Had that solution not been reached, Barton might not have been alive now. For the non-Baldies were still wary, still intolerant.

Yet he was no extrovert; he could not be. Inevitably he grew tired of the ceaseless symphony of thought that rolled like a living tide even in the deserts and the seas. Erecting a mental barrier wasn't enough; behind that protective wall beat the torrents of thought, and they were sensed. Only in the upper air was there escape for a while.

The plane lifted, rocking a little in the wind. Beneath Barton the lake was dime-sized and dime-colored. Around its borders grew, more thickly than it had fifty years before, the Limberlost forests, a swampy wilderness where the small roving bands of malcontents migrated constantly, unable to adjust to communal life in the hundreds of thousands of villages that dotted America, and afraid to unite. They were antisocial, and probably would simply die out eventually.

The lake became a pinpoint and vanished. A freighter copter, with its string of gliders, whipped westward below, laden perhaps with cod from the Great Banks towns, or with wine grapes from the New England vineyards. Names had not changed much as the country changed. The heritage of language was too strong for that. But there were no towns named New York, or Chicago, or San Francisco; there was a psychological taboo there, the familiar fugue that took the form of never naming one of the new, small, semi-specializing villages after the cancerous areas of desolation once called New Orleans or Denver. From American history, thence world history, the names came – Modoc and Lafitte, Lincoln, Roxy, Potomac, Mowhasset, American Gun, and Conestoga. Lafitte, on the Gulf of Mexico, shipped the delicate-fleshed porgie and pompano to Lincoln and Roxy, in the agricultural belt; American Gun turned out farm equipment, and Conestoga, from which Barton had just come, was in mining land. It also had a temperate-zone zoo, one of the many that Barton serviced from Puget to Florida End.

He closed his eyes. Baldies by necessity were socially conscious, and when the world lay spread out maplike below, it was difficult not to visualize it speckled with the heads of colored pins; very many black ones, and a very few white ones. Non-Baldies and Baldies. There was something to be said for intelligence, after all. In the jungle, a monkey with a red flannel coat would be torn to pieces by its undressed colleagues.

The blue, empty wastes of air were all about Barton now; the torrents of world-thought had lessened to a faint, nearly imperceptible beat. He closed the cabin, turned on air and heat controls, and let the copter rise. He lay back in the cushioned seat, a distant alertness ready to galvanize his hands into action if the copter should go into one of its unpredictable tantrums. Meanwhile he rested, alone, in a complete silence and vacancy.

His mind was washed clean. Pure calm, a sort of Nirvana, soothed him. Far below, the turbulent world sent vibrations jangling through subetheric levels, but few radiations reached this height, and those did not disturb Barton. His eyes shut, utterly relaxed, he looked like someone who had, for a while, forgotten to live.

It was the panacea for abnormally sensitive minds. At first glance, few took Barton for a Baldy; he wore his brown wig close-cropped, and his years in the jungle had made him almost unhealthily thin. Baldies, naturally self-barred from competitive athletics except among themselves, were apt to grow soft, but Barton was not soft. Outguessing predators had kept him in good trim. Now he relaxed, high above the earth, as hundreds of other Baldies were resting their taxed minds in the blue calm of the upper air.

Once he opened his eyes and looked up through the transparent ceiling panel. The sky was quite dark, and a few stars were visible. He lay there for a while, simply watching. *Baldies*, he thought, *will be the first to develop interplanetary travel. Out there are clean new worlds, and a new race needs a new world.*

But it could wait. It had taken a long time for Barton to realize that his race, not himself, was important. Not until that knowledge came to a Baldy was he really mature. Until then, he was always a possible potential danger. Now, though, Barton was oriented, and had found, like most Baldies, a compromise between self and race. And it involved, chiefly, development of the social instinct, and diplomacy.

Several hours had gone past quickly. Barton found a packet of food concentrate in a compartment, grimaced at the brown capsules, and stuffed them back in their place. No. While he was back in America, he wanted the luxuries of civilization. In Africa he had eaten enough concentrate to blast his taste buds. That was because certain game was psychically repugnant to him, after contact with the animal minds. He was not a vegetarian; he could rationalize most of the feeling away, but – for example – he could certainly never eat monkey.

But he could eat catfish, and anticipated the crisp flakiness of white, firm flesh between his teeth. This was good cat country. There was a restaurant in downtown Conestoga that Barton knew, and he headed the helicopter toward the airfield nearest to it, circling the village itself to avoid raising dust storms by his low altitude.

He felt refreshed, ready to take his place in the world again. There were, as far as he knew, no Baldies living in Conestoga, and it was with surprise – pleasant surprise – that he felt a thought probe into his mind. It held question.

It was a woman's thought, and she did not know him. That he could tell by the superficialities of the identity-queries. It was like the outspread fingers of a hand reaching out gently in search of another hand that would interlock with its grip. But the searcher's cognizance of Barton as a personality was lacking. No, she did not know him. She knew of him, probably through – Denham? Courtney? He seemed to recognize the personality-keys of Denham and Courtney sifted through her query.

He answered her question. *Available. Here. A courteous, friendly greeting, implying – you are one of Us; a willing desire to help.*

Her name, Sue Connaught, with its curious shadings of how Sue Connaught realized her own identity – an indescribable key thought that could never afterwards be mistaken. The mental essence of pure ego.

She was a biologist, she lived in Alamo, she was afraid –

Let me help.

Must see you) { *(Vital urgency*
Danger, eyes watching secretly
(Beasts around – Sue Connaught

Danger – now?

The complicated thought meshed and interlocked as he increased his pace.

Utterly alone) { *('I' of all the world knowing –*
Most urgent secrecy
(Beasts – 'I' am in zoo, waiting

Hurrying to you; my mind is with yours; you are one of Us, therefore never alone. Faster than words, the thoughts raced. Oral or written sentences slow the transmission of mental concepts. Adjectives and adverbs convey shades of meaning. But between telepaths complete ideas move with light-speed. In prehuman times simple meanings were completely transmitted by grunts. As language developed, gradations were possible. With telepathy, a whole universe can be created and – conveyed.

Even so, common denominators are necessary. The girl was dodging some vital issues, afraid to visualize it.

What? Let me help!

Wariness) { *(Even here, danger of Them –*
Pretend utterly all is normal
Use oral speech until –

Her mind closed. Puzzled, Barton automatically raised his own barrier. It is not, of course, ever possible to shut one's mind completely away from the persistent probing of another telepath. At best one can only blur the thought wave by superimposing others upon it, or by submerging the salient ideas deep down in the formlessness of nonthought. But they are resilient things, thoughts. Not even the trained minds of Baldies can keep them submerged very long – the very fact of concentrating to keep them down maintains their wavering shapes cloudily in the background of the mind.

So a barrier can be raised, of willful obscurity or deliberate confusion – reciting the multiplication tables is one evasion – but not for very long or very efficiently. Only the instinctive politeness which a Baldy learns with his alphabet makes the raising of a barrier the equivalent of blanking. A barrier's efficiency is mostly in the mind of the other man, not one's own – if he be a proper telepath.

Barton, like most Baldies, was. He 'looked' away immediately as Sue Connaught's thoughts veered from contact with him. But he was the more eager to meet her now and read in her face, if he could, what convention forbade him to read in her mind. The gates of the zoo lay open before him.

Barton stepped through them, noticing a small crowd, mostly out-villagers who had helicoptered over to see the new acquisitions he had brought.

But, despite barriers, he could, as always, sense a Baldy here, and he let his instinct guide him to where a girl, slim in slacks and white blouse, was standing by a railed inclosure, held there by some fascination. He sent his thought forward, and it was met by a sudden, desperate warning.

Barrier! Barrier!

He reacted instantly. He stepped up beside her, looking beyond the railing, into the enormous tank where a torpedo body moved lazily. He knew that Sue Connaught had looked into the shark's mind, and had seen something there that held a tremendous significance to her.

'So you don't like it,' he said. There was no danger in speech; to a telepath, with barrier raised, it was more secret than thought.

'No,' she said. 'I suppose it takes conditioning.'

'But you're a biologist.'

'Rabbits and guinea pigs. Even those make me blush sometimes. But – carnivores.'

'Tackle a weasel sometime,' he suggested. 'It's pure insanity. Come on.' He led her out of the crowd, toward the terrace where canopied tables were scattered. 'Have a cocktail?'

'Thanks.' She glanced back at the shark's tank. Barton nodded; it could be bad, if one wasn't used to it. But he was used to it.

'Shall we go somewhere else?' he asked, pausing in the act of drawing out a chair for her. 'A zoo can be pretty uncomfortable if you aren't –'

'No. It's safer here. We've got to talk, and we can do it pretty freely in a place like this. None of Us would come here for pleasure.' With her mind she 'glanced' around at the encircling madness of beast-thoughts, then blurred the surface of her mind again as a protection and smiled at Barton appealingly.

They had met, as all Baldies do, upon a footing of instant semi-intimacy. Non-telepaths may take weeks of friendship to establish a knowledge of one another's character; Baldies do it automatically at first contact, often before they meet at all. Often, indeed, the knowledge formed in first mental meeting is more accurate that later impressions colored by the appearance and physical mannerisms of the telepaths. As non-Baldies, these two would have been Miss Connaught and Mr Barton for a while. But as telepaths they had automatically, unconsciously summed one another up while Barton was still in the air; they knew they were mutually pleasant in a contact of minds. They thought of one another instantly as Sue and Dave. No non-Baldy, eavesdropping on their meeting, would have believed they were not old friends; it would have been artificial had the two behaved otherwise than this, once their minds had accepted each other.

Sue said aloud, 'I'll have a Martini. Do you mind if I talk? It helps.' And she glanced around, physically this time, at the cages. 'I don't see how you stand it, even with your training. I should think you could drive a Baldy perfectly gibbering just by shutting him up in a zoo overnight.'

Barton grinned, and automatically his mind began sorting out the vibrations from all around him: the casual trivialities from the monkeys, broken by a pattern of hysteria as a capuchin caught the scent of jaguar; the primal, implacable vibrations from the panthers and lions, with their undertone of sheer, proud confidence; the gentle, almost funny radiations from the seals. Not that they could be called reasoning thoughts; the brains were those of animals, but basically the same colloid organism existed under fur and scales as existed under the auburn wig of Sue Connaught.

After a while, over Martinis, she asked, 'Have you ever fought a duel?'

Barton instinctively glanced around. He touched the small dagger at his belt. 'I'm a Baldy, Sue.'

'So you haven't.'

'Naturally not.' He didn't trouble to explain; she knew the reason as well as he did. For Baldies could not risk capitalizing on their special ability except in very limited cases. A telepath can always win a duel. If David hadn't killed Goliath, eventually the Philistines would have mobbed the giant out of sheer jealousy. Had Goliath been smart, he would have walked with his knees bent.

Sue said, 'That's all right. I've had to be very careful. This is so confidential I don't know who –' Her barrier was still up strongly.

'I've been in Africa for six months. Maybe I'm not up with current events.' Both of them were feeling the inadequacy of words, and it made them impatient.

'Not current … future. Things are … help from … qualify –' She stopped and forced herself into the slower grammatical form of communication. 'I've got to get help somewhere, and it's got to be one of Us. Not only that, but a very special kind of person. You qualify.'

'How?'

'Because you're a naturalist,' she said. 'I've looked the field over, but you know what sort of work we usually get. Sedentary occupations. Semantics experts, medical and psychiatric interns, biologists like me, police assistants – that came closer, but I need a man who … who can get the jump on another Baldy.'

Barton stared and frowned. 'A duel?'

'I think so,' she said. 'I can't be sure yet. But it seems the only way. This must be completely secret, Dave, absolutely secret. If a word of it ever got out, it would be … very bad for Us.'

He knew what she meant, and pursed his lips in a soundless whistle. That shadow always hung over every Baldy.

'What is it?'

She didn't answer directly. 'You're a naturalist. That's fine. What I need is a man who can meet a telepath on slightly more than equal terms. No non-Baldy would do, even if I could talk about this to a non-Baldy. What I've got to get is a man with a fast-moving mind who's also trained his body to respond faster than instantly.'

'Uh-huh.'

'There weren't many,' she said. 'Even when minds move at the same speed, there's always a fractional difference in muscular response. And we're not too well trained. Games of competitive skill –'

'I've thought of that,' Barton said. 'More than once, too. Any game based on war is unsuitable for Us.'

'Any game in which you face your opponent. I like golf, but I can't play tennis.'

'Well,' Barton told her, 'I don't box or wrestle. Or play chess, for that matter. But skip-handball – have you seen that?'

She shook her head.

'The backboard's full of convolutions; you never know which way the ball will bounce. And the board's in sections that keep sliding erratically. You can control the force, but not the direction. That's one way. It's something new, and naturally it isn't advertised, but a friend of mine's got one at his place. A man named Denham.'

'He told me about you.'

'I thought so.'

'Uh-huh. For fifteen years you've been catching everything from tigers to king cobras. That takes good timing, the way you do it. Any man who can outguess a king cobra –'

'Watch your barrier,' Barton said sharply. 'I caught something then. Is it that bad?'

She drew a shaky breath. 'My control's lousy. Let's get out of here.'

Barton led her across the zoo's main area. As they passed the shark's tank he sent a quick glance down, and met the girl's eyes worriedly.

'Like that, eh,'

She nodded. 'Like that. But you can't put Them in cages.'

Over catfish and Shasta white wine she told him –

You can't put Them in cages. Shrewd, dangerous, but very careful now. They were the middle group of the three telepathic assortments. The same mutation, but ... *but!*

The hard radiations had been plain dynamite. When you implant a completely new function in the delicate human brain, you upset a beautiful and long-standing balance. So there had been three groups: one was a complete failure, thrust into the mental borderland of insanity, dementia praecox and paranoia. Another group, to which Sue Connaught and Barton belonged – the vast majority – were able to adjust to a nontelepathic world. They wore wigs.

But the middle group was paranoid – and sane.

Among these telepaths were found the maladjusted egotists, the ones who for a long time had refused to wear wigs, and who had bragged of their superiority. They had the cunning and the utter self-justification of the true paranoid type, and were basically antisocial. But they were not mad.

And you can't put Them in cages. For they were telepaths, and how can you cage the mind?

They finished with Brazilian chocolate cake, demi-tasse and Mississippi liqueur, made by the monks of Swanee monastery. Barton touched his cigarette tip to the igniter paper on the pack. He inhaled smoke.

'It's not a big conspiracy, then.'

'These things start small. A few men – but you see the danger.'

Barton nodded. 'I see it, O.K. It's plenty bad medicine. A few paranoid-type Baldies, working out a crazy sabotage scheme – Tell me a little more first, though. For instance, why me? And why you?'

To a nontelepath the question might have been obscure. Sue raised her brows and said, 'You, because you've got the reflexes I spoke of and because I had the luck to find you before I got desperate enough to look for a substitute. As for me' – she hesitated – 'that's the oddest part. No one could have stumbled onto them except by accident. Because telepathy, of course, isn't tight-beam. It's a broadcast. Any receptive mind can pick it up. The minute enough people band together to make a city, *that's* noticeable. And the minute Baldies get together and form any sort of organization, that's noticeable too. Which is why paranoids never made much trouble, except individually. Banding together would have meant running up a flag – one that could be seen for miles.'

'And so?'

'So they've got this special means of communication. It's secret, absolutely unbreakable code. Only it isn't merely code. That we could detect and trace down, even if we couldn't break it. This is telepathic communication on an entirely new band, one we can't even touch. I don't know how they do it. It might be partly mechanical, or it might not. Children have a higher perceptive level, but we can catch their thoughts. This is mental ultraviolet. Do you realize the implications?'

Smoke jetted from Barton's nostrils. 'Yeah. It wrecks the balance of power – completely. Up to now, decentralization has kept peace. Nobody dared band together or get too big for their boots. They could be detected. But these bichos are wearing invisible cloaks.' His hand clenched. 'It could become world-wide! The one form of organization we can't fight!'

'It's got to be fought,' she said. 'It's got to be smashed. And fast, before anyone suspects. If non-Baldies ever find out, there'll be a wave of anti-Baldism that could wipe Us out. If that should happen, people wouldn't stop to sort out the social and the antisocial groups. They'd say, "We've been nursing a viper, and it's got fangs. Kill 'em all".'

Outside the window a man on horseback clattered past, hoofbeats making an urgent rhythm in Barton's brain.

'How many are there?'

'I told you it's just beginning. Only a few more. But it can spread. I suppose the immediate difficulty is in their training neophytes in their special trick telepathy. That's why I think it must be psychically self-induced. Gadgets can be detected. And mobility would be necessary; they'd never know when they had to get in touch with each other. You can't pack around a big gadget.'

'You could camouflage it,' Barton said. 'Or it might be pretty small.'

'It might,' she said, 'but there's this little girl – Melissa Carr. She tapped their wave without a gadget. She must be some mutant variant.'

'Melissa Carr?' echoed Barton. 'Where does she come in?'

'Oh, I haven't told you. She's my contact. I've been in touch with her off and on for a week or so, but it was only yesterday that she let slip, very casually, what she'd learned on that special thought band.'

'She isn't one of them, then?'

'I'm sure not. It's very odd. Even the way she reached me first –' Sue had been dressing for a party, and the tentative fingering question had crept into her mind. 'It was like Cinderella, somehow. I could feel the pleasure she took in the dress I was wearing, a Mozambique model, and the Karel bag. She strung along with me mentally all evening. And after that –' After that communication had been established. But it had been days before Melissa spoke of the telepathic signals she had inadvertently tuned in on.

'She guessed what they meant, but she didn't seem much impressed by the danger. I mean, it didn't strike her that something ought to be done. There's some mystery about Melissa; sometimes I've even thought she might have been a member of the group once, and pulled out. Sometimes she won't answer my signals at all. But now that she's told me about this – Faxe – I think I've convinced her of the danger. Sam Faxe. He's one of the paranoids, and from what I've learned, he's trying to sabotage some experiments in Galileo.'

'Why?'

'That's what I don't know. Apparently the paranoids are so familiar with their basic plan that they don't need even to think about it. Their thoughts deal with immediate action. And always on that special wave length we can't catch. Only Melissa, as far as I know, can get it, and she must have been born receptive.'

'Some are,' Barton agreed. 'Mutants certainly vary a lot, far more than nonmutants. As for this long-term scheme, you know the paranoid type. They figure Baldies were made to rule the world. They look on ordinary humans as a lower species. And if they're trying to sabotage experiments, that's significant. I wonder what sort of experiment this Galileo business is?'

'I don't know,' Sue said. 'Melissa's very shaky on technology.'

'I can find out through Denham. He lives in Galileo.'

'That's where I met him. But maybe you can get more out of Melissa than I can. It isn't wise to' – she hesitated, substituting a familiar word for the unimaginable mental term – 'telepath her too much, but it's necessary, of course. If you feel any probing, sheer off right away.'

'Has there been any?'

'No. Not yet. But we *must* keep in the dark.'

Sue hadn't asked Barton if he would help; she knew that he would. Preservation of the race had been implanted in every Baldy, though in the paranoid type it had been warped and distorted. Now Sue's mind reached out, searching, questioning, seeking the lock to fit her key. And almost immediately the answer came. It was like one hand drawing two others together, Sue mentally introducing Melissa Carr to Barton. He felt something fumble, shy and almost gauche, and then they – locked. He sent out friendliness and warm assurance. Instantly he was conscious of a strong femininity that amounted almost to sexual attraction. Half clear, half clouded, he sensed what Melissa Carr meant to herself: the intangible consciousness of living ego, different in each individual, and the softness of curling hair – hair? Wig – and the softness of a mouth against fingers drawn gently across them. A demure withdrawal that had in it shades of color and scent, and then something that was the equivalent of a curtsey, purely mental, and with an oddly old-fashioned flavor. After that, he knew he could never mistake Melissa Carr's mind for that of another Baldy.

This is Dave Barton, Melissa.

Recognition and pleasure-shading. A question: trust? So much danger –

Utter trust, yes – strong affirmative.

Urgency {
Many – (different) – messages coming strongly
shadow of menace of Sam Faxe
A growing explosive stain in Galileo
Cannot speak – another symbol for speak – long
Possible personal danger

And all these gradations of meaning at once, three minds interlocking like a color wheel, focusing to the central white spot of revelation and truth. There were no barriers, as in oral conversation. Like light the thoughts intermeshed and wove in question, answer, and statement, and despite the concentration, all three had time for the more intimate shadings that took the place of tonal values. It was the capacity for such rapport that made round-table debates so popular among Baldies; the logical and aesthetic play of minds that could ultimately resolve into an ecstasy of complete common awareness. Physically there was no polygamy among Baldies, but mentally the social group had expanded, lending an additional depth and richness to their lives.

But this was merely a hint of complete rapport. Barton was searching for clues in what Melissa told him. He was no technician either, so he was going at it from another angle; that of the naturalist, trained in probing protective coloration, skilled in unraveling the predator's tangled tracks.

How many?

Three.

No more?

Three – and images of Galileo and other towns, symbols of names and identities. A feeling of shadowy communion, links of hatred –

And suddenly, in her mind, he sensed something curiously, disturbingly familiar. He did not know what it was. But momentarily it broke the smooth flow of communication, while he searched.

It was nothing; he concentrated again. *Three?*

Symbol { *Known name Sam Faxe*
Power-lust
Heavy lethargy

There were other evoked connotations, but he thought he would know Sam Faxe now.

The other symbols, resolving into names: Ed Vargan, mixed with a curious concept of size-difference; and Bertram Smith, where there was sensed a cruelty akin to that of the blood-drinking carnivores. Though with a difference; Barton had reached into the mind of a weasel when it was feasting, and the sheer flood of ecstasy had almost frightened him. Smith was intelligent, though he, like the others, had that singular quality of – of what?

Darkness. Distortion. Blindness.

Yes, Sue thought, *they're blind. Blinded by their paranoia. They can't see this world at all – as it's meant to be.*

And Melissa's visualization of the three: vicious small things running through the dark, teeth bared. She identified them, Barton realized, with – what? – with mice; she had a horror of mice, which to her were far more horrible than insects or snakes. Well, he could understand phobias; he himself was abnormally afraid of fire. Most Baldies were phobic in one degree or another, a penalty paid for increased mental sensitivity.

He thought: *'I' must move fast. If they communicate, they may go into hiding. 'I' must kill them at one stroke. Can they read your mind?*

They do not know Melissa Carr exists.

But if one is killed, they will be warned. You must be kept safe. Where are you?

Refusal, definite refusal.

It would be best to tell me, so –

No one can find me as long as I don't think my location. There are no directional finders for telepathy. The concept she expressed meant more than telepathy; it was the symbol for a whole race and its unity.

Can you locate Vargan and Smith?

Certainly; they spoke freely in their private wave length; Vargan is in Rye; Smith is in Huron.

How is it you can catch their wave length?

Puzzlement. A helpless mental shrug. Born to me?

Barton thought: *When one of them dies, the others will be warned. Listen carefully. Be sure to relay their plans. They must not escape.*

Melissa thought of the three small, gray, vicious things scuttling across the floor. Barton grinned tightly.

See how they run, he told her. *See where they run to.* His hand touched his dagger. It was not a carving knife, but it would do.

There was not much more. Melissa relayed some of the paranoid thoughts she had caught, and Barton's guess at the menace of the paranoids was confirmed. They were deadly, in the long run, to the whole mutant group. Individual deaths did not matter much, in this era of the duello, but to risk the good will of the entire race was mad-dog tactics. Nor did there seem to be any motive. Sheer malice? It was not logical, and paranoids are always logical, though their structure is founded on a false keystone. The single clue that would give the whole a meaning was, so far, lacking. Nor could Barton find it by turning to his training as a naturalist. Animals do not commit sabotage. Nor do birds foul their own nests.

After Melissa had left them, Sue showed her impatience. 'I want to help,' she said, orally now. 'There must be some way.'

'There isn't. You said yourself that this takes a very special skill. You're a biologist. You don't react instantly, the way I do, and if you were along, my attention would be diverted. I've got to concentrate.'

'You'll kill them, then?'

'Certainly I'll kill them. Luckily there are only three, according to Melissa. She wasn't lying; I could tell that.'

'Oh, she's honest,' Sue agreed. 'But she's certainly hiding something.'

Barton shrugged. 'It doesn't matter. What this calls for is prompt action. I can't do much investigating. If I plant any thoughts or questions in non-Baldy minds, the paranoids will start wondering. I've got to eradicate those bichos before the infection spreads. There are plenty of paranoid Baldies who'd join a movement like that, if they were able to master the secret wave length.'

'So what'll I do?'

'It doesn't matter,' Barton said, 'now. Your job's finished. It's my meat now.'

They stood up together. Outside, on the village sidewalk, he left her, with a handclasp that held a deep significance. All around them the casual, evening life of the town was moving, brightly lighted and symbolic of the vast, intricate check-and-balance system that held civilization together. The civilization that tolerated Baldies, and, though perhaps a little grudgingly, gave them a chance to work out their own salvation. Both of them were thinking of the same thing: how easily that ordinary throng could be integrated into a blood-hungry mob. It had happened before, when Baldies were still new to the world, and the danger still smoldered.

So Barton went off alone, with the unspoken commission of his whole race commanding him to do what since birth he had been conditioned to do. The race was important; the individuals were not. His helicopter had already been serviced, and he took off for Galileo, on the Atlantic Seaboard, still thinking about what he had to do. He was so abstracted that only automatic radio signals kept him from colliding with other copters. But, finally, the lights of the technicians' town glowed on the horizon.

Like all the communities devoted to technology, Galileo was larger than most villages. Scientists were peaceful folk, and no tech-town had ever been dusted off. Niagara, with its immense source of power, held more people than Galileo, but the latter had a far larger area. Due to the danger of some of the experiments, the town sprawled out for miles, instead of being the tight, compact village that was the general American pattern.

Because of this there was surface-car transport, an unusual thing. Barton guided himself to Denham's house – there were no apartments, of course, in a highly individualistic though interdependent culture – and by good luck found the man at home. Denham was a mild, round-faced Baldy whose wigs had year by year grown grayer until his present one was shot with white. He greeted Barton warmly, but orally, since there were people on the street, and Baldies were tactful about demonstrating their powers.

'Dave. I didn't know you were back. How was Africa?'

'Hot. I haven't had a game of skip-handball for six months. I think I'm getting soft.'

'You don't look it,' Denham said, with an envious glance. 'Come on in. Drink?'

Over a highball they talked non-essentials, except that they didn't – talk. Barton was feeling his way; he didn't want to tell Denham too much, especially since Sam Faxe was here in Galileo, and he went all around the subject without finding out much. It proved more difficult than he had expected. Eventually they ended in the game room, stripped to shorts, facing a vertical wall, scooped into innumerable convolutions, divided into segments that jiggled erratically. There they played skip-handball. It was easy to tell in advance how hard Denham would swat the ball, but there was no earthly way of judging the angle of reflection. The two bounced around a good deal, getting plenty of exercise, and carrying on a telepathic conversation as they played.

Denham indicated that his favorite game was still crap shooting. Or roulette, by preference. Either of them he could play with his non-Baldy friends, whereas bridge or poker – *uh!* Who'd play poker with a mind reader?

Games that depended on luck or pure muscle were O.K., Barton agreed, but there weren't many of the latter. Wrestling or boxing involved pre-planned thought. But many Olympic trials were possible: shot-putting, high-jumping, racing. In those you didn't face your opponent. Any war game, like chess, was impossible.

Well, Denham thought, your vocation's a sort of war game.

Game hunting? Barton let his mind skim over the field, settling on a tiger after a heavy feed, lethargic, and with the deep consciousness of power as in a silently humming dynamo. He tied that in, subtly, with a hunger, and with something, vague and unformed, that was similar to the symbol by which Melissa knew Sam Faxe. His thought then paralleled the identity of Faxe as one musical chord parallels its complement. If Denham knew Faxe at all, he'd probably respond.

And he did. A sense of elation mounted in Barton as he caught the stray fragment, filtering out nonessentials, squeezing it dry of the accumulated Denham-detritus. What remained was a fat, less competent interpreter who served as liaison man sometimes between technicians of different language-groups. Barton hastily changed to another subject so that Denham would not attach any importance to this particular mnemonic ideation.

After that, Barton was anxious to leave. He let Denham win the game, and the novelty of this so delighted the winner that he accepted Barton's excuse of an appointment without obvious skepticism. A man just back in America, after six months of jungle life, would be looking for something more exciting than skip-handball. But it was swell of Barton to drop in –

Barton strolled along the streets, park-bordered, smooth-tiled, letting his receptive mind absorb the thoughts that boiled around him. Now that he knew what to look for, it was not difficult, though it took patience. Patchwork scraps of information came to him very occasionally. And Barton did something to which Baldies very seldom resorted, he put leading questions into the minds of non-Baldies.

This had to be done, for Barton could read only what lay above the threshold of conscious awareness. And it took real, straining effort to force even a brief stimulating impulse into a nonreceptive mind. The average man is not a telepath, and to communicate mentally with him is like trying to push a needle between closely-fitted tiles. He can, under special circumstances, receive thoughts, but he himself cannot recognize them as impulses from another mind.

Barton was sweating when he had finished. Yet he had managed to pick up considerable information. Moreover, he had done it so subtly that Faxe himself, if he tuned in, would certainly be unsuspicious. A good many people had thought of Faxe tonight, but they were ordinary thoughts – except to Barton, who fitted the jigsaw together. A little here and a little there. And finally he had the picture – an interpreter, altering a shade of meaning as a Tibetan talked to a Bengali, and as both of them turned to a Yankee physiochemist. It was the easier because technicians, immersed in their work, were apt to be insensitive to the finer gradations of human contact, and the result was that here in Galileo a gadget was being built that would eventually cause trouble.

Just how, not even Faxe knew, of course, but his smattering of technical knowledge was sufficient to enable him to smear up the works. A shade of meaning in one man's mind, a slightly different hue in another's, when both should have matched exactly – these, and other things, told Barton that Faxe was a racial traitor.

Moreover, he found out where Faxe lived.

Now, standing outside the man's bungalow, he tried to communicate with Melissa Carr. Almost immediately her thought touched his, in the ordinary radiation level.

Play it careful, he ordered. *Use generalities*. And again he was deeply conscious of her femininity, of the softness of curling hair and the smoothness of a curved, youthful cheek. Through the cool, fresh night air breathed something like a wisp of perfume.

Agreement.

Can you locate the others for me quickly? And exactly?

Yes. In –

Keep tuned in to ... you know what.

Again agreement, and that delicately feminine demureness, soft and curiously attractive. She was a little afraid, Barton sensed, and he felt a strong impulse to protect her. A picture of Melissa Carr was beginning to form in his mind, though he knew that it was of necessity prejudiced. Mental concepts and visual ones may differ a great deal. But he thought that Melissa had a small, triangular face, fragile and with delicate features, and that that face was framed with glossy, jet-black curls. He seemed to see her features *from inside*, reversing the usual procedure in which an individual's face helps form the concept of what is behind it.

How does she do it? He wondered at the lucky chance as he crossed the street. Out of all the people in the world, only she can tune in on the special wave length of –

Barrier!

He stood now on the porch, facing a closed panel. Through that grained plywood a doubt and a question fingered out, touched his mind, and recoiled. Instantly the man within the house erected a barrier of his own.

Very good. While the mind was thus walled off, Faxe could probably not utilize his super wave length to communicate with the other paranoids. Or ... or could he?

Barton stepped aside to a circular window. He could see nothing through the one-way glass. With a wary look around, he lifted his foot and kicked the glass into splinters. He stepped through the gap cautiously, into a well-furnished room where a fat man stood against the wall, facing him. The masculinity of the decor told him that Faxe probably lived alone; that was natural for the true paranoid type, which required a wife's subjugation. Faxe would not have married a telepath, and no non-Baldy could have lived with him for long.

Twenty years ago Faxe would have been wigless, but this particular type had learned caution since then. The man's wig was of gleaming yellow that went oddly with his heavy, ruddy face.

And suddenly the barrier slipped from Faxe's mind; his brain lay fallow and blank, and Barton felt Melissa's urgent warning thrill through him. *He's warning the others –*

Barton ripped out the dagger from his belt and plunged forward. Instantly Faxe's barrier tightened again, as quickly as his own weapon leaped ready to his fat hand. When dueling with another telepath, it is highly advisable to keep your mind guarded, so your intentions cannot be anticipated. As long as Faxe felt himself seriously menaced, he dared not lower his barrier.

Barton moved in, his eyes calculatingly alert, as he might watch the swaying hood of a cobra. He kept his thumb on the hilt of the dagger and held it at thigh-level. The fat man stepped forward from the wall, balancing on his toes, waiting.

It was, after all, too easy. Telepathy wasn't necessary to forestall the stroke of that clumsy arm. With surgical neatness Barton put his knife in the right place, and made certain that Faxe did not communicate with his colleagues before he died. Then, satisfied, he let himself out of the house by the front door and walked quietly toward the nearest surface-car stop.

That was done. He sent his thought probing in search of Melissa. Somewhere, far away in the hidden dark, she heard and answered.

Did they receive Faxe's call?

No. No, you were too fast, and they didn't expect him to touch them.

Good. Vargan and Smith now, then.

Tonight?

Yes.

Good. I don't think you can reach me tomorrow.

Why not?

Evasion. Vargan – at Rye.

Listen. This is important. If there are only three of them, fine. But if they try to communicate with others, be sure to let me know!

Yes. That was all, but the personality of Melissa lingered with Barton as he drove his helicopter northwest through the night. He was not at all affected by the fact that he had committed murder. He did not regard the act as such; there was, undoubtedly, a touch of fanaticism in the way Baldies regarded betrayal from within. Nor was this ordinary betrayal. The means of communication Faxe and the others had discovered was the deadliest menace to the race that had ever existed – more serious than the lynchings a few decades after the Blowup.

Barton had fallen into a mental pattern that always was dominant when he hunted. Now his quarry was human, but far more predatory than any jungle carnivore. Animals killed for food. That was simple Darwinism, and a basic law of nature. But the three paranoids had violated another basic entirely: preservation of the species. They menaced it.

In any new culture there must be conflict, Barton thought, watching dim lights flicker past below, the innumerable torches of the towns that dotted America. And certainly the Baldies had a new culture. It was almost embryonic as yet, a mutation heading for an ultimate end that was so far inconceivable. But it was the first true forward step that mankind had made in a million years. Always before mutations had been very slight, or they had been failures. Now, with hard radiations providing the booster charge, a true mutation had opened a thousand possible doors. And before each door lay blind pitfalls.

For there are dominant and secondary, submerged characteristics. Hairlessness was secondary to Baldies, but there might be other, submerged ones that would emerge in the third or fourth generation. This extraordinary method of subtelepathic communication – was that natural? In Melissa's case it seemed to be so, though Faxe and the rest might have developed the trick themselves. If so, the latent potential lay, perhaps, in every Baldy. And that meant danger indeed.

It was in the true meaning of the term a focus of infection. Healthy cells could be contaminated. The secret might be passed on, and Barton visualized a perfectly hidden, underground network of paranoids, communicating in utter secrecy, planning – anything. It wasn't a pleasant idea.

He wondered how many social-type Baldies could fight such a menace. Not many; they were not qualified for war. War, because of the atomic bombs, was impossible, but this was a new sort of battle. The thing that made the bombs successful through fear-propaganda – the necessity of centralization before any group could be organized – was inapplicable. There need be no unification, if paranoids could communicate instantly and secretly. Blind luck had stepped in through Melissa, but one could not depend on luck.

Melissa's thought touched him.

Vargan has signaled Smith; Smith is flying to Rye.

What do they know?

Vargan told Smith to come immediately. No more.

To Rye?

It must be a new rendezvous. He gave directions. She relayed them to Barton.

O.K. Keep listening.

Puzzled and a little worried, Barton advanced the copter's speed. He was swinging northward now, toward Lake Erie, by-passing Conestoga. It wouldn't take long to reach Rye. But – had Faxe got through, after all? A telepathic message takes only an instant. Perhaps Vargan had received the fat man's S.O.S. And if Faxe had passed on to his accomplices the knowledge that a Baldy had killed him, and why – Barton shrugged. They would be waiting for him, anyhow. They would know Faxe was dead. If he had no more than called to them in formless appeal and made contact with their minds, they would know. No mistaking that – shapelessness – as life slips inexorably from the body. When they reached out for him now, they would encounter plain nothingness, a curious sort of hiatus in the ether, as if the void had not yet quite closed over the place where a man had been an hour ago. It was unmistakable; no telepath willingly reached out into that quivering blank. But it would impinge upon any receptive mind near it, and soundlessly through the Baldy population of the town the knowledge would spread. *One of Us has died.* Yes, Vargan and Smith knew by now. But they did not yet know, in all probability, how he had died. It might have been accident, it might have been organic. It might have been – murder. They would act upon the assumption that it was. They would be waiting.

The nearest Rye airfield to his destination was deserted, only the automatic landing lights flicking on as he dropped to earth. Melissa's directions had been clear. He walked half a mile up a road, turned into a narrow lane where moonlight made eerie patterns between flickering leaves, and stopped before an unlighted cottage. As he waited, a thought touched him.

Come in. That was Vargan, the size-difference realization a submerged matrix in his mind, a pattern under moving water. *Come in.* But Vargan did not know Barton; he was radiating blind, conscious only that a Baldy was waiting in the lane outside the cottage.

A light came on. The door opened. A small man, scarcely more than five feet tall, with an abnormally large head, stood on the threshold, a black silhouette.

No traps?

There was a trap, but it was merely the advantage of numbers. Barton felt that his question was answered. Vargan fell back as the taller man advanced, and then Barton was in the room, eyeing his opponent.

Vargan had a pinched, worried face, and protuberant eyes. His mouse-brown wig was untidy. He wore eye lenses that reflected the light with a reptilian glitter, and for a moment his gaze took stock of Barton. Then he smiled.

'All right,' he said audibly. 'Come in and sit down.' The thought of contempt was there. Speaking audibly to another Baldy when caution was unnecessary was insultingly patronizing, but Barton was not surprised. *Paranoid*, he thought, and Vargan's mind responded: *Which means super!*

The kitchen valve opened and Bertram Smith came in, a handsome blond giant, with pale-blue eyes and an expressionless face. Smith carried a tray with bottles, glasses, and ice. He nodded at Barton.

'Vargan wanted to talk to you,' he said. 'I see no reason, but –'

'What happened to Faxe?' Vargan asked. 'Never mind. Have a drink first.'

Poison?

Sincere denial. We are stronger than you –

Barton accepted a glass and sat down in an uncomfortable table chair; he did not want to be too relaxed. His mind was wary, though he knew the uselessness of putting up guards. Vargan hunched his dwarfish form into a relaxer and gulped the liquor. His eyes were steady.

'Now what about Faxe?'

'I killed him,' Barton said.

'He was the weakest of us all –'

All?

Three of us –

Good. Only two left now.

Vargan grinned. 'You're convinced you can kill us, and we're convinced we can kill you. And since our secret weapons are intangible – self-confidence that can't be measured arbitrarily – we can talk on equal ground. How did you know about our means of communication?'

He could not hide the thought of Melissa. The mind has too much free will at times.

Smith said, 'We'll have to kill her too. And that other woman – Sue Connaught, that he was thinking of.'

No point in keeping up useless concealment. Barton touched Melissa's mind. *They know. Listen. If they use their secret wave length, tell me instantly.*

'Immediately is pretty fast,' Vargan said.

'Thoughts are fast.'

'All right. You're underestimating us. Faxe was the newest of our band; he wasn't fast-minded, and he was a push-over for you. Our brains are highly trained and faster than yours.' That was a guess; he couldn't *know*, really. Egotism influenced him.

'Do you think,' Barton said, 'that you can get away with whatever you're trying to do?'

'Yes,' Smith said, in his mind a blazing, fanatical conviction that glared like a shining light. 'We must.'

'All right. What are you trying to do?'

'Preserve the race,' Vargan said. 'But actively, not passively. We non-Baldies' –

He still used the term, though he wore a wig – 'aren't willing to bow down before an inferior race, homo sapiens.'

'The old quibble. Who says Baldies are homo superior? They simply have an additional sense.'

'That's all that keeps man from being a beast. An additional sense. Intelligence. Now there's a new race. It's telepathic. Eventually the next race may have – prescience. I don't know. But I do know that Baldies are the future of the world. God wouldn't have given us our power if He hadn't intended us to use it.'

This was merely dueling, but it was something more as well. Barton was intensely curious, for more than one reason.

'You're trying to convince me?'

'Certainly. The more who join us, the faster we'll grow. If you say no, we'll kill you.' Only on these intangibles was there the possibility of mental secrecy. Semantics could never alter the divergence of absolute opinions.

'What's your plan?'

'Expansion,' Vargan ruffled his untidy brown wig. 'And complete secrecy, of course. The sabotage angle – we're just beginning that. Eventually it'll be a big thing. Right now we're concentrating on what we *can* do –'

'Sabotage – and what can you offer in exchange?'

A wave of tremendous self-confidence thrust out at Barton. 'Ourselves. We are homo superior. When our race is free, no longer enslaved by mere humans, we can – go to the stars if we want!'

'Enslaved. I don't see it that way.'

'You don't. You've been conditioned to accept the pap cowards feed you. It isn't logical. It isn't just or natural. When a new race appears, it's destined to rule.'

Barton said, 'Remember the lynchings in the old days?'

'Certainly,' Vargan nodded. 'Humans have one thing we haven't: numerical superiority. And they're organized. The trick is to destroy that organization. How is it maintained?'

'By communication.'

'Which goes back to technology. The world's a smoothly running machine, with humanity in the driver's seat. If the machine cracks up –'

Barton laughed. 'Are you that good?'

Again the fanatical self-belief flamed in Smith's mind. *A hundred – a thousand mere humans – cannot equal one of us!*

'Well,' Vargan said more sanely, 'ten men could still lynch a Baldy, provided they weren't disorganized and in social chaos. That, of course, is what we're after. Ultimate social chaos. We're aiming at a bust-up. Then we can take over – after humans go to pot.'

'How long will that take? A million years?'

'Perhaps,' Vargan said, 'if we weren't telepaths, and if we didn't have the secret wave length. That, by the way, takes time to learn, but almost any Baldy can learn it. But we're careful; there'll be no traitors among us. How can there be?'

There couldn't. A thought of hesitancy, of betrayal, could be read. It would be a foolproof organization.

Vargan nodded. 'You see? Thousands of Baldies, working secretly for a bust-up, sabotaging, killing where necessary – and always, always avoiding even a hint of suspicion.'

'You've sense enough for that, anyway,' Barton said. 'Even that hint would be fatal.'

'I know it.' *Anger*. 'Humans tolerate us, and we let them. We let them. It's time we took our rightful place.'

'We're getting it anyway, slowly. After all, we're intruders in a non-Baldy world. Humans have come to accept us. Eventually we'll get their complete trust and tolerance.'

'And – forever – live on tolerance, a helpless minority? Eating the crumbs our lessers are willing to throw us – if we lick their boots?'

'How many Baldies are maladjusted?'

'Plenty.'

'All right. They'd be maladjusted in Heaven. The vast majority adjust. I've got the job I want –'

'Have you? You never feel even a little irritated when people know you're a Baldy, and – look at you?'

'Nobody's ever completely happy. Certainly a Baldy world would be rather more pleasant, but that'll come. There are plenty of worlds that will be available eventually. Venus, for one.'

'So we sit and wait for interplanetary travel,' Vargan mocked. 'And what then? There'll be slogans. Earth for humans. No Baldies on Venus. You're a fool. Has it never occurred to you that Baldies *are* the new race?' He looked at Barton. 'I see it has. Every one of us has thought the same thing. But we've been conditioned to submerge the thought. Listen. What's the test of a dominant new race? It must be able to dominate. And we can; we've a power that no non-Baldy can ever hope to match. We're like gods pretending to be human because it'll please humans.'

'We aren't gods.'

'Compared to humans – we are gods. Do you feel pleased at the thought of rearing your children in fear, training them never to offend their inferiors, forcing them to wear – wigs?' Vargan's hand went up to his head, fingers clawed. 'This is the stigma of our cowardice. The day when we can walk hairless in a hairless world – then we'll have come into our heritage. All right. Ask yourself – can you say that I'm wrong?'

'No,' Barton said. 'You may be right. But we're a small minority; the risk's too great. Since you speak of children, you can add a postscript about lynchings. That isn't pretty. Maybe you could get away with this, but you're certain you won't fail. And that's just crazy. You're refusing to admit arguments that might weaken your plan. If even a whisper of this ever got out, every Baldy in the world, wigless or not, would be destroyed. The – humans – could do nothing less, for their own protection. And I couldn't blame them. I admit you're logical – to some extent. And you're dangerous, because you've got the secret telepathic band. But you're paranoid, and that means you're blind. We are getting what we want, on the whole, and because a few paranoid Baldies are malcontent, you set yourselves up as saviors for the whole race. If your idea should spread –'

'That would mean fertile ground, wouldn't it?'

'There are other maladjusted Baldies,' Barton admitted. 'I might have been one myself, maybe, if I hadn't found my pattern for living.' He wondered for a moment. His jungle work was fascinating, but what would it be like to return from it to a completely Baldy culture? A world in which he belonged, as no telepath could belong, really, in this day and age.

Barton turned from the mirage. And simultaneously Melissa's warning thought struck violently into his mind, faster than a shouted word could be; and with equal speed Barton reacted, spinning to his feet and heaving up his chair as a shield. He had not caught Vargan's command; it had been on the secret wave length, but Smith's thrown knife clattered against the plastic chair seat and bounced off against one of the walls.

Vargan will attack while Smith recovers his weapon. Melissa was afraid; she shrank from the idea of violence, and the emotions surging unchecked in the room, but her thought struck unwaveringly into Barton's mind. He sprang toward the fallen dagger as Vargan ran at him. Then the two were back on the ordinary telepathic wave length, but with a difference.

One man Barton could have guarded against. Or two men, acting together. But this had been prearranged. Smith was fighting independently, and so was Vargan. Two thought-patterns struck into Barton's mind. Vargan was concentrating on the duello, left, right, feint, and feint again. Barton was skilled enough to be a match for his single opponent, but now Smith had picked up the fallen chair and was coming in with it. His mind was confused, too. *Drive the chair forward low – no, high – no –*

In a feint, there are two mental patterns; dominant and recessive. One has the ring of truth. But Vargan and Smith were attempting to act completely on impulse, purposely confusing their minds in order to confuse Barton. They were succeeding. And more than once they flashed up to the secret band, so Melissa's thought-warning was added to the confusion.

Smith had his dagger back now. A table went crashing over. Barton had taken it fatally for granted that his enemies would act together, and so a sharp point ripped his sleeve and brought blood from a deep cut. In the jungle, where emotion, tropism, instinct, are stronger than intelligence, Barton had been confused in much the same way, but then his own mental power had been the turning factor. Here his opponents were not mindless beasts; they were highly intelligent predators.

The heavy, choking smell of blood was nauseating in the back of his throat. Cat-footed, wary, Barton kept retreating, not daring to be pinned between his enemies. Abruptly Melissa warned: *A rush!* and both Smith and Vargan came at him, blades gleaming where they were not crimson.

Heart – clavicle – upstroke – feint –

Confused and chaotic, the furious thoughts caught him in a whirlwind. He spun to face Smith, knew his mistake, and ducked not quite in time. Vargan's dagger ripped his left biceps. And with that blow Barton knew that he had failed; he was no match for the two paranoids.

He ran for the chair, thinking of it as a shield, but at the last moment, before his mind could be read, he sent it hurtling toward the fluorescent. With a tinkle of glass the tube broke. In the dark, Barton dived for the door. They knew what he intended and anticipated him; they knew he would depend on impetus to carry him through. But they could not stop him. He got a knee hard on the point of his jaw, and, dazed, slashed right and left half-mindlessly. Perhaps that saved him.

He broke through, thinking of his copter. Escape and help now. He felt Vargan's thought: *the short cut.*

Thanks, he sent back mockingly.

The short cut saved time, and he was long-legged. As yet there were no plans. He did not try to think of any. Escape and help; details later. The paranoids came after him for a short distance.

No use; he'll make it. Get my copter.

Right. We'll trail him.

They went elsewhere. Barton felt their brief questions touching his mind, though, and concentrated on running. He could not easily escape the paranoids, now that they knew him. Nor would they again lose touch with his mind.

The landing field was still vacant, except for his own helicopter. He got in and sent the plane southwest, a vague thought of Sue Connaught guiding him. Melissa could not help; he didn't even know where she was. But Sue was in Conestoga, and between the two of them –

Also, she had to be warned. He reached for her mind across the dark miles.

What's wrong?

He told her. *Get a weapon. Protect yourself. I'm coming in.*

Plan –

Don't try to think of any. They'll know.

And Melissa, frightened, the psychic scent of fear strong in her thought. *How can I help?*

Don't reveal where you are. If we fail, tell the truth to other Baldies. These paranoids must be destroyed.

Sue: *Can I intercept their copter?*

No. Don't try. They're following, but not overtaking.

A grotesque silver shape in the moonlight, the pursuing helicopter raced in Barton's track. He improvised a bandage for his wounded arm. After consideration, he wound many heavy strips of cloth around his left forearm. A shield, if –

He could not plan his tactics; that would be fatal. Telepaths could not play chess or any war game, because they would automatically betray themselves. They could play skip-handball, but that had a variable factor, the movable backboard. If a random factor could be introduced –

Vargan's eager question touched him. *Such as?*

Barton shivered. He must, somehow, manage to act on impulse, without any preconceived plan. Otherwise he would inevitably fail.

He called Melissa. *Are they using the secret band?*

No.

If we fail, it's your job. Vargan and Smith must die. This is more important than merely killing three men. If other paranoids get the idea, if they, too, learn the secret wave length, this suicidal movement will grow. And non-Baldies will inevitably find out about it, sometime. That will mean the annihilation of every Baldy on earth. For the humans can't afford to take chances. If we fail to check the paranoids – it means the end of our whole race.

The lights of Conestoga glowed. No plan yet. Don't try to think of one.

There must be a way, Vargan urged. *What?*

Sue broke in. *I'm coming up in my copter.*

The zoo was below, dark now, except for the silvering moonlight. Another plane, gleaming bright, lifted into view to intercept them. Sue thought: *I'll ram them –*

Fool, Barton thought. *Don't warn them!* But it was a new idea, thrust suddenly into his own mind, and he reacted instantly. Mechanical controls are not instantaneous. By Vargan's sudden decision to drop to a lower level, where a collision with Sue's plane would not be fatal, he had put himself too close to Barton. And Barton's hands stabbed at the controls.

Vargan read the thought as fast as it was conceived. But his copter could not respond with the speed of thought. The flying vanes meshed and crackled; with a scream of tortured alloys the two ships side-slipped. The automatic safety devices took over – the ones that were not smashed – but only low altitude saved Barton and his enemies from death.

They crashed down in the central zoo area, near the shark's tank. Vargan read the thought in Barton's mind and telepathed to Smith urgently: *Kill him! Fast!* Barton scrambled free of the wreckage. He sensed Sue hovering above, ready to land, and told her: *Turn your lights on – the spots. Top illumination. Wake the animals.*

He dodged away from the two figures closing in on him. He ripped the bandage from his upper arm and let the smell of fresh blood scent the air. And – he yelled.

From Sue's copter beams of light glared down, flaring into cages, dazzling bright.

Kill him, Vargan thought. *Quick!*

The asthmatic cough of a lion sounded. Barton dodged by the tank and tossed his blood-stained bandage over the railing. There was a flurry of water slashed into foam as the great shark woke to life.

And, from cage and tank, from the beasts waked into a turmoil of light and sound and blood-smell – came the variable.

Sue had got her siren working, and its shattering blast bellowed through the night. Patterns of light blazed erratically here and there. Barton saw Smith pause and shake his head. Vargan, teeth bared, ran forward, but he, too, was shaken.

Their thoughts were – confused now. For this wasn't chess any more. It was skip-handball, with a variable gone wild.

For beasts are not intelligent, in the true meaning of the word. They have instinct, tropism, a terrible passion that is primevally powerful. Even non-telepaths find the hunger-roar of a lion disturbing. To a Baldy –

What blasted up from the great tank was worst of all. It shook even Barton. The paranoid minds could not communicate, could scarcely think, against that beast-torrent of mental hunger and fury that poured through the night.

Nor could they – now – read Barton's mind. They were like men caught in the blazing rays of a searchlight. Telepathically, they were blinded.

But Barton, a trained naturalist, had better control. It wasn't pleasant even for him. Yet his familiarity with tiger and shark, wolf and lion, gave him some sort of protection against the predatory thoughts. He sensed Melissa's terrified, panic-stricken withdrawal, and knew that Sue was biting her lips and trying desperately to keep control. But for half a mile around that mental Niagara, telepathic communication was impossible except for a very special type of mind.

Barton had that type of mind.

Because he could read the thoughts of Vargan and Smith, and because they could not read his, the duel ended in his favor. He had to kill the pair before help came. The paranoids' secret had to be hushed up forever.

And, with the sharp blade of his dagger, he finished his job. Smith died silently. From Vargan's waning mind came a desperate, passionate cry: *You fool! To destroy your own race –*

Then silence, as the copter's siren faded, and the spotlights blinked out. Only beast-cries, and the turmoil of water in the enormous tank.

'They'll hush it up,' Barton said. 'I've done that much already, since yesterday. Luckily we've got a few Baldies high up in the judicial. I didn't tell even them too much, but – they have the general idea. It'll be passed over as a personal quarrel. The duello's legal, anyway.'

Afternoon sunlight glittered on the Ohio. The little sailboat heeled under a gust of wind, and Sue moved the tiller, in response to Barton's thought. The soft susurrus of water whispered under the keel.

'But I can't reach Melissa,' he added.

Sue didn't answer. He looked at her.

'You've been communicating with her today. Why can't I?'

'She's … it's difficult,' Sue said. 'Why not forget it?'

'No.'

'Later on – in a week or so –'

He remembered Melissa's demure, feminine gentleness, and her frightened withdrawal last night. 'I want to be sure she's all right.'

'No –' Sue said, and tried to conceal a thought. She almost succeeded, but not quite. Something, a key, a pattern, showed in her mind.

'An altered matrix?' Barton looked at her. 'How could she –'

'Dave,' Sue said, 'please don't touch her now. She wouldn't want it –'

But with the key at hand, and the locked door ready to open, Barton automatically sent his thought out, probing, questioning. And, very far away, something stirred in response.

Melissa?

Silently Sue watched the tiller. After a long time, Barton shivered. His face was strained; there were new lines around his mouth.

'Did you know?' he asked.

'Not till today,' Sue said. For some reason neither of them wanted to use telepathy at the moment.

'The … the business at the zoo must have done it.'

'It isn't permanent. It must be a cycle.'

'So that's why she was able to tune in on the secret wave length,' Barton said harshly. 'This mutation – it runs very close to the line sometimes.' He looked at his shaking hand. 'Her mind – *that* was her mind!'

'It runs in cycles,' Sue said quietly. 'What I wonder now is – will she talk? Can her thoughts be picked up by –'

'There's no danger,' Barton said. 'I stayed in long enough to make certain of that. Otherwise I – wouldn't have stayed in at all. In this state, she has no memory of what happens when she's – rational.'

Sue moved her lips. 'She doesn't know she's insane. She just senses something wrong. That's why she wouldn't tell us where she was. Oh – Dave! So many of us, so many mutants, gone off the track somewhere! It's a horrible price.'

He nodded slowly, his eyes grave. There was always a price, somehow. And yet, if paying it brought security to the mutants –

But it hadn't, really. For Barton saw clearly now that an era had finally ended in the life of the Baldy race. Till yesterday the path had seemed clear before them. But yesterday an evil had been unveiled in the very heart of their own race, and it was an evil which would menace the peace of the world until one race or the other was wiped wholly off the face of the earth. For what a few telepaths had stumbled upon already, others would discover in the future. Had, perhaps, already discovered. And must not be allowed to retain.

Thou, O son of man, I have set a watchman unto the house of Israel.

We must be on guard now, he thought. Always on guard. And he knew suddenly that his maturation had taken one long forward step in the past few hours. First he had been aimless, open to any possibility that knocked loudest at the doors of his mind. Then he had found the job he was suited for, and in its comfortable adjustment thought himself adult at last. Until yesterday – until today.

It was not enough to hunt animals. His work was laid out before him on a scale so vast he could not see it clearly yet, but its outlines were very clear. He could not do the job alone. It would take many others. It would take constant watchfulness from this hour on, over the whole world. Today, perhaps for the first time in nearly two thousand years, the Crusaders were born again.

Strange, he thought, that it had taken a madwoman to give them their first warning. So that not even the mad were useless in the progress of the race. Strange that the threefold divisions of the mutants had so closely interwoven in the conflict just passed. Mad, sane, sane-paranoid. And typical that even in deadly combat the three lines wove together interdependently.

He looked at Sue. Their minds reached out and touched, and in the deep, warm assurance of meeting was no room for doubt or regret. This, at least, was their heritage. And it was worth any price the future demanded of them – this knowledge of confident unity, through any darkness, across any miles. The fire on the hearth would not burn out until the last Baldy died.

THREE

It was snowing.

Now there was nothing at all but snow. The world was entirely shut out by the whirling white flakes. Until now, even though I couldn't communicate with my people, I'd had the solid earth around me, and I'd been able to see the barrier peaks overhead. Now I was completely shut off and alone.

There was nothing I could do. I huddled in my blankets and waited. The air was a little warmer, but it wasn't cold that would kill me – it was loneliness.

I began to feel that all my previous life had been a dream, and that nothing really existed except myself.

My thoughts began to whirl. I couldn't stop them. I knew I was nearly at the breaking point. The snow whirled meaninglessly around me, and my thoughts whirled too, and there was nothing to stop them. There were no anchors.

Except in the past.

I went back again, trying to find something solid. The time after Barton, while Barton was still alive. The time of McNey and Lincoln Cody. The one unverified story in the Key Lives, because there was an hour in McNey's life which no other telepath had seen, and which had to be filled in by inference alone. But the telepaths who had known McNey for so long and so intimately were well qualified to fill in the missing details.

It was complete, the story of the Lion and the Unicorn. I reached back into the time and the mind of McNey, forgetting, for a while, the snow and the loneliness, finding what I needed there in the past, when McNey waited for the paranoid Sergei Callahan to enter his house …

THE LION AND THE UNICORN

The best way of keeping a secret is to avoid even the appearance of secrecy. McNey whistled a few bars of Grieg, and the vibrations set delicate machinery in operation. The dull amber of the walls and ceiling changed to a cool transparency. Polaroid crystal did tricks with the red glare of the sunset above the Catskills. The deep, cloudless blue sky hung empty overhead. But Barton's helicopter had already arrived, and soon Callahan would be here, too.

That Callahan would dare to come, and alone, gave a horrible clarity to the danger. Twenty years ago a dagger would have ended the matter. But not permanently. Barton had used steel, and, while he had not completely failed, he had not succeeded either. The menace had grown.

McNey, standing by his desk, brushed a hand across his forehead and looked at his wet palm curiously. Hypertension. The result of this desperate, straining attempt to get in contact with Callahan, and the surprise of finding it far too easy. And now Barton as the catalyst – mongoose and snake.

There must be no clash – not yet. Somehow Barton must be kept from killing Callahan. The hydra had more than a hundred heads, and the Power as well. There lay the chief peril, the tremendous secret weapon of the mad telepaths.

But they weren't, mad. They were paranoid types, coldly logical, insane in one regard only, their blind warped hatred for nontelepaths. In twenty years, thirty, forty perhaps, they had – not grown – but organized, until today the cancerous cells were spotted throughout the towns of America, from Modoc and American Gun to Roxy and Florida End.

I'm old, McNey thought. *Forty-two, but I feel old. The bright dream I grew up with – it's fading, blotted out by a nightmare.*

He glanced in a mirror. He was big-boned, large-framed, but soft. His eyes were too gentle, not suited for battle. His hair – the wig all telepathic Baldies wore – was still dark, but he'd buy a graying one soon.

He was tired.

He was on leave of absence from Niagara, one of the science towns; but there were no furloughs from his secret job. That was a job many Baldies held, and one no nontelepaths suspected – a combination of policing and extermination. For paranoid Baldies could not be allowed to survive. That was axiomatic.

Over the ridge lay the town. McNey let his gaze travel downward, across pine and sumac groves, to the pool in the brook where trout hid under shadowed overhangs. He opened part of the wall and let the cool air enter. Absently he whistled the phrase that would start the supersonics and keep mosquitoes at a respectful distance. On the flagged walk below he saw a slim figure, trim in light slacks and blouse, and recognized Alexa, his adopted daughter. The strong family instinct of Baldies had made adoption a commonplace.

The fading sunlight burnished her glossy wig. He sent a thought down.

Thought you were in the village. Marian's at the show.

She caught the hint of disappointment in his mind. *Intrusion, Darryl?*

For an hour or two –

O.K. *There's an apple-blossom sequence in the pic, and I can't stand the smell of the stuff. Marian asked me – I'll catch a dance or two at the Garden.*

He felt wretched as he watched her go off. In the perfect telepathic world there would be no need for secrecy or evasion. That, indeed, was one of the drawbacks of the paranoid system – the mysterious, untappable wave length on which they could communicate. The thing called the Power. It was, McNey thought, a secondary characteristic of the mutation itself, like baldness, and yet more strictly limited. It seemed that only the paranoid Baldies could develop the Power. Which implied two separate and distinct mutations. Considering the delicate balance of the mental machine, that was not improbable.

But true rapport was vital for a complete life. Telepaths were more sensitive than nontelepaths; marriage was more complete; friendship warmer; the race a single living unit. For no thought could be hidden from probing. The average Baldy refrained, from courtesy, when a rapport mind went blurred; yet, ultimately, such blurring should become unnecessary. There need be no secrets.

Both Marian and Alexa knew of McNey's connection with the organization, but it was a tacit understanding. They knew without words when McNey did not want to answer questions. And because of the deep trust that comes from telepathic understanding, they refrained from asking any, even in their thoughts.

Alexa was twenty now. Already she had felt the reaction of being an outsider in a world complete in itself. For Baldies were still intruders, no matter how much rationalization was used. The great majority of humanity was nontelepathic – and fear, distrust, and hatred lay latent in that giant tribunal that daily passed judgment upon the Baldy mutation.

Capital punishment, McNey knew very well, was the sentence contingent upon a thumbs-down verdict. And if the thumbs ever turned down –

If the nontelepaths ever learned what the paranoids were doing –

Barton was coming up the path. He walked with the lithe springiness of youth, though he was over sixty. His wig was iron-gray, and McNey could sense the wary alertness of the hunter's thoughts. Technically, Barton was a naturalist, a big-game hunter. His quarry was sometimes human, however.

Upstairs, Dave, McNey thought.

Right. Is it here yet?

Callahan's coming soon.

The thoughts did not mesh. The semantic absolute symbol for Callahan was simpler in McNey's mind; in Barton's it was colored by associations from a half-lifetime of conflict with a group he hated, by now, almost pathologically. McNey never knew what lay behind the violence of Barton's hatred. Once or twice he had caught fleeting mental images of a girl, dead now, who had once helped Barton, but such thoughts were always as inchoate as reflections in rippling water.

Barton came up in the dropper. He had a seamed, swarthy face, and a trick of smiling lopsidedly so that the grimace was almost a sneer. He sat down in a relaxer, sliding his dagger forward into a more handy position, and thought for a drink. McNey supplied Scotch and soda. The sun had dropped beyond the mountain, and the wind grew colder. Automatic induction began to warm the room.

Lucky you caught me. On my way north. Trouble.

About Us?

Always.

This time what?

Barton's thoughts broadened.

Peril to Baldies	*Wigless Baldy with Hedgehound group* *Villages being raided* *Wigless on untrained telepathically.*

Wigless? Paranoid?

Know little. Can't establish communication.

But – Hedgehounds?

Barton's sneer was reflected by his thought.

Savages. I'll investigate. Can't let the humans connect Us with raiding Hedgehounds.

McNey was silent, pondering. It had been a long time since the Blowup, when hard radiations had first created the mutations, and brought about the decentralization of a culture. But those days had seen the beginnings of the Hedgehounds, the malcontents who had refused to join the village unions, who had fled to the woods and the backlands and lived the savage life of nomads – but always in small groups, for fear of the omnipresent atomic bombs. Hedgehounds weren't seen often. From helicopters you might catch glimpses of furtive figures trailing in single file through the Limberlost country, or in the Florida Everglades, or wherever the old forests stood. But by necessity they lived hidden in the backwoods. Occasionally there were quick raiding parties on isolated villages – so few, however, that no one considered the Hedgehounds a menace. They were nuisances at best, and for the most part they stayed away from towns.

To find a Baldy among them was less singular than amazing. Telepaths formed a racial unit, branching out into family groups. As infants grew, they were assimilated. *Might be some sort of paranoid plot. Dunno what sort.*

McNey tipped his drink. *No use killing Callahan, you know,* he pointed out.

Tropism, Barton's thought said grimly. *Taxis. When I catch 'em, I kill 'em.*

Not –

Certain methods work on Them. I've used adrenalin. They can't foresee a berserker's actions in a fight, because he can't foresee his own. You can't fight

Them as you'd play a chess game, Darryl. You've got to force them to limit their powers. I've killed some by making them fight with machines, which don't react as instantly as the mind. In fact – shadow of bitterness – we dare make no plans ahead. The paranoids can read our minds. Why not kill It?

Because we may have to compromise.

The blasting wave of hot, violent fury made McNey wince. Barton's negative was stunningly emphatic.

McNey turned his glass, watching the moisture condense. *But the paranoids are expanding.*

Find a way of tapping their power, then!

We're trying. There's no way.

Find a secret wave length for us.

McNey's mind blurred. Barton looked away mentally. But he had caught a scrap of something. He tried not to ask the question burning within him.

McNey said aloud, 'Not yet, Dave. I mustn't even think it; you know that.'

Barton nodded. He, too, realized the danger of working out a plan in advance. There was no effective barrier that could be erected against the paranoids probing.

Don't kill Callahan, McNey pleaded. *Let me lead.*

Unwillingly, Barton assented. *It's coming. Now.*

His more disciplined mind, trained to sense the presence of the radiations that meant intelligence, had caught stray fragments from the distance. McNey sighed, put down his glass, and rubbed his forehead.

Barton thought. *That Baldy with the Hedgehounds. May I bring him here if necessary?*

Of course.

Then a new thought came in, confident, strong, calm. Barton moved uneasily. McNey sent out an answer.

After a minute Sergei Callahan stepped out of the dropper and stood waiting, warily eyeing the naturalist. He was a slim, blond, soft-featured man, with hair so long and thick that it was like a mane. Only affectation made paranoids wear wigs of such extreme style – that and their natural maladjustment.

He didn't look dangerous, but McNey felt as though a feral beast had come into the room. What had the medievalists symbolized by the lion? Carnal sin? He couldn't remember. But in Barton's mind he caught the echo of a similar thought: *a carnivore, to be butchered!*

'How d'you do,' Callahan said, and because he spoke aloud, McNey knew that the paranoid had classed his hosts as a lower species, and gave them patronizing contempt. It was characteristic of the paranoids.

McNey rose; Barton didn't. 'Will you sit down?'

'Sure.' Callahan dropped on a relaxer. 'You're McNey. I've heard of Barton.'

'I'm sure you have,' the hunter said softly. McNey hastily poured drinks. Barton left his untasted.

Despite the silence, there was something in the room that had the quality of fourth-dimensional sound. There was no attempt at direct telepathic communication, but a Baldy is never in complete mental silence, except in the stratosphere. Like half-heard, distant music of toccata and fugue the introspective thoughts beat dimly out. Instinctively one man's mental rhythm sought to move in the same pattern as another's, as soldiers automatically keep step. But Callahan was out of step, and the atmosphere seemed to vibrate faintly with discord.

The man had great self-confidence. Paranoids seldom felt the occasional touches of doubt that beset the straight-line Baldies, the nagging, inevitable question telepaths sometimes asked themselves: *Freak or true mutation?* Though several generations had passed since the Blowup, it was still too early to tell. Biologists had experimented, sadly handicapped by the lack of possible controls, for animals could not develop the telepathic function. Only the specialized colloid of the human brain had that latent power, a faculty that was still a mystery.

By now the situation was beginning to clarify a trifle. In the beginning there had been three distinct types, not recognized until after the post-Blowup chaos had subsided into decentralization. There were the true, sane Baldies, typified by McNey and Barton. There were the lunatic offshoots from a cosmic womb raging with fecundity, the teratological creatures that had sprung from radiation-battered germ plasm – two-headed fused twins, cyclops, Siamese freaks. It was a hopeful commentary that such monstrous births had almost ceased.

Between the sane Baldies and the insane telepaths lay the mutation-variant of the paranoids, with their crazy fixation of egotism. In the beginning the paranoids refused to wear wigs, and, if the menace had been recognized then, extermination would have been easy. But not now. They were more cunning. There was for the most part, nothing to distinguish a paranoid from a true Baldy. They were well camouflaged and safe, except for the occasional slips that gave Barton and his hunters a chance to use the daggers that swung at every man's belt.

A war – completely secret, absolutely underground by necessity – in a world unconscious of the deadly strife blazing in the dark. No nontelepath even suspected what was happening. But the Baldies knew.

McNey knew, and felt a sick shrinking from the responsibility involved. One price the Baldies paid for survival was the deification of the race, the identification of self, family, and friends with the whole mutation of telepaths. That did no include the paranoids who were predators, menacing the safety of all Baldies on earth.

McNey, watching Callahan, wondered if the man ever felt self-doubt. Probably not. The feeling of inferiority in paranoids made them worship the group because of pure egotism; the watchward was *We are supermen! All other species are inferior.*

They were not supermen. But it was a serious mistake to underestimate them. They were ruthless, intelligent, and strong. Not as strong as they thought, though. A lion can easily kill a wild hog, but a herd of hogs can destroy a lion.

'Not if they can't find him,' Callahan said, smiling.

McNey grimaced. 'Even a lion leaves spoor. You can't keep on with your plan indefinitely without the humans suspecting, you know.'

Contempt showed in Callahan's thought. 'They're not telepaths. Even if they were, we have the Power. And you can't tap that.'

'We can read your minds, though,' Barton put in. His eyes were glowing. 'We've spoiled some of your plans that way.'

'Incidents,' Callahan said. He waved his hand. 'They haven't any effect on the long-term program. Besides, you can read only what's above the conscious threshold of awareness. We think of other things besides the Conquest. And – once we arrange another step – we carry it out as quickly as possible, to minimize the danger of having the details read by one of the traitors.'

'So we're traitors now,' Barton said.

Callahan looked at him. 'You are traitors to the destiny of our race. After the Conquest, we'll deal with you.'

McNey said, 'Meanwhile, what will the humans be doing?'

'Dying,' Callahan said.

McNey rubbed his forehead. 'You're blind. If a Baldy kills one human, and that's known, it'll be unfortunate. It might blow over. If two or three such deaths occur, there'll be questions asked and surmises made. It's been a long while since we had Baldy lynchings, but if one smart human ever guesses what's going on, there'll be a worldwide pogrom that will destroy every Baldy on earth. Don't forget, we can be recognized.' He touched his wig.

'It won't happen.'

'You underestimate humans. You always have.'

'No,' Callahan said, 'that's not true. But you've always underestimated Us. You don't even know your own capabilities.'

'The telepathic function doesn't make supermen.'

'We think it does.'

'All right,' McNey said, 'we can't agree on that. Maybe we can agree on other things.'

Barton made an angry sound. Callahan glanced at him.

'You say you understand our plan. If you do, you know it can't be stopped. The humans you're so afraid of have only two strong points: numbers and technology. If the technology's smashed, We can centralize and that's all We need. We can't do it now, because of the atomic bombs, of course. The moment we banded together and revealed ourselves – *blam!* So –'

'The Blowup was the last war,' McNey said. 'It's got to be the last. This planet couldn't survive another.'

'The planet could. And we could. But humanity couldn't.'

Barton said, 'Galileo doesn't have a secret weapon.'

Callahan grinned at him. 'So you traced that propaganda, did you? But a lot of people are beginning to believe Galileo's getting to be a menace. One of these days, Modoc or Sierra's going to lay an egg on Galileo. It won't be our affair. Humans will do the bombing, not Baldies.'

'Who started the rumor?' Barton asked.

'There'll be more, a lot more. We'll spread distrust among the towns – a long-term program of planned propaganda. It'll culminate in another Blowup. The fact that humans would fall for such stuff shows their intrinsic unfitness to rule. It couldn't happen in a Baldy world.'

McNey said, 'Another war would mean the development of anticommunication systems. That'd play into your hands It's the old rule of divide and fall. As long as radio, television, helicopter and fast-plane traffic weld humans together, they're racially centralized.'

'You've got it,' Callahan said. 'When humanity's lowered to a more vulnerable status, we can centralize and step in. There aren't many truly creative technological brains, you know. We're destroying those – carefully. And we can do it, because we can centralize mentally, through the Power, without being vulnerable physically.'

'Except to Us,' Barton said gently.

Callahan shook his head slowly. 'You can't kill us all. If you knifed me now, it wouldn't matter. I happen to be a co-ordinator, but I'm not the only one. You can find some of Us, sure, but you can't find Us all, and you can't break Our code. That's where you're failing, and why you'll always fail.'

Barton ground out his cigarette with an angry gesture. 'Yeah. We may fail, at that. But you won't win. You can't. I've seen a pogrom coming for a long while. If it comes, it'll be justified, and I won't be sorry, provided it wipes out all of you. We'll go down too, and you'll have the satisfaction of knowing that you've destroyed the entire species through your crazy egotism.'

'I'm not offended,' Callahan said. 'I've always contended that your group was a failure of the mutation. We are the true supermen – unafraid to take our place in the universe, whereas you're content to live on the crumbs the humans drop from their table.'

'Callahan,' McNey said suddenly, 'this is suicidal. We can't –'

Barton sprang out of his chair and stood straddle-legged, glowering furiously. 'Darryl! Don't beg the swine! There's a limit to what I'll stand!'

'Please,' McNey said, feeling very helpless and impotent. 'We've got to remember that we're not supermen, either.'

'No compromise,' Barton snapped. 'There can't be any appeasement with those wolves. Wolves – hyenas!'

'There'll be no compromise,' Callahan said. He rose, his leonine head a dark silhouette against the purple sky. 'I came to see you, McNey, for just one reason. You know as well as I that the humans mustn't suspect our plan. Leave us alone, and they won't suspect. But if you keep trying to hinder us, you'll just increase the danger of discovery. An underground war can't stay underground forever.'

'So you see the danger, after all,' McNey said.

'You fool,' Callahan said, almost tolerantly. 'Don't you see we're fighting for you, too? Leave us alone. When the humans are wiped out, this will be a Baldy world. You can find your place in it. Don't tell me you've never thought about a Baldy civilization, complete and perfect.'

'I've thought about it,' McNey assented. 'But it won't come about through your methods. Gradual assimilation is the answer.'

'So we'll be assimilated back into the human strain? So our children will be degraded into hairy men? No, McNey. You don't recognize your strength, but you don't seem to recognize your weakness, either. Leave us alone. If you don't, you'll be responsible for any pogrom that may come.'

McNey looked at Barton. His shoulders slumped. He sank lower in his relaxer.

'You're right, after all, Dave,' he whispered. 'There can't be any compromise. They're paranoids.'

Barton's sneer deepened. 'Get out,' he said. 'I won't kill you now. But I know who you are. Keep thinking about that. You won't live long – my word on it.'

'You may die first,' Callahan said softly.

'Get out.'

The paranoid turned and stepped into the dropper. Presently his figure could be seen below, striding along the path. Barton poured a stiff shot and drank it straight.

'I feel dirty,' he said. 'Maybe this'll take the taste out of my mouth.'

In his relaxer McNey didn't move. Barton looked at the shadowy form sharply.

He thought: *What's eating you?*

I wish … I wish we had a Baldy world now. It wouldn't have to be on earth. Venus or even Mars. Callisto – anywhere. A place where we could have peace. Telepaths aren't made for war. Dave.

Maybe it's good for them, though.

You think I'm soft. Well, I am. I'm no hero. No crusader. It's the microcosm that's important, after all. How much loyalty can we have for the race if the family unit, the individual, has to sacrifice all that means home to him?

The vermin must be destroyed. Our children will live in a better world.

Our fathers said that. Where are we?

Not yet lynched, at any rate. Barton laid his hand on McNey's shoulder. *Keep working. Find the answer. The paranoid code must be cracked. Then I can wipe them out – all of them!*

McNey's thought darkened. *I feel there will be a pogrom. I don't know when. But our race hasn't faced its greatest crisis yet. It will come. It will come.*

An answer will come too, Barton thought. *I'm going now. I've got to locate that Baldy with the Hedgehounds.*

Good-bye, Dave.

He watched Barton disappear. The path lay empty thereafter. He waited, now, for Marian and Alexa to return from the town, and for the first time in his life he was not certain that they would return.

They were among enemies, now, potential enemies who at a word might turn to noose and fire. The security the Baldies had fought for peacefully for generations was slipping away from underfoot. Before long Baldies might find themselves as homeless and friendless as Hedgehounds –

A too-elastic civilization leads to anarchy, while a too-rigid one will fall before the hurricane winds of change. The human norm is arbitrary; so there are arbitrary lines of demarcation. In the decentralized culture, the social animal was better able to find his rightful place than he had been in thousands of years. The monetary system was founded on barter, which in turn was founded on skill, genius, and man-hours. One individual enjoyed the casual life of a fisherman on the California coast; his catch could bring him a televisor set designed by a Galileo man who enjoyed electronics – and who also liked fish.

It was an elastic culture, but it had its rigidities. There were misfits. After the Blowup, those antisocials had fled the growing pattern of towns spreading over America and taken to the woods, where individualism could be indulged. Many types gathered. There were bindle stiffs and hobos, Cajuns and crackers, paisanos and Bowery bums – malcontents, anti-socials, and those who simply could not be assimilated by any sort of urban life, not even the semirural conditions of the towns. Some had ridden the rods, some had walked the highways of a world that still depended on surface travel, and some were trappers and hunters – for even at the time of the Blowup there had been vast forest tracts on the North American continent.

They took to the woods. Those who had originally been woodsmen knew well enough how to survive, how to set bird-snares and lay traps for deer and rabbit. They knew what berries to pick and what roots to dig. The others –

In the end they learned, or they died. But at first they sought what they thought to be an easier way. They became brigands, swooping down in raids on the unifying towns and carrying off booty – food, liquor and women. They mistook the rebirth of civilization for its collapse. They grouped together in bands, and the atomic bombs found targets, and they died.

After a while there were no large groups of Hedgehounds. Unity became unsafe. A few score at most might integrate, following the seasons in the north temperate zones, staying in the backland country in more tropical areas.

Their life became a combination of the American pioneer's and the American Indian's. They migrated constantly. They re-learned the use of bow and javelin, for they kept no contact with the towns, and could not easily secure firearms. They drifted in the shallows of the stream of progress, hardy, brown woodmen and their squaws, proud of their independence and their ability to wrest a living from the wild.

They wrote little. But they talked much, and by night, around campfires, they sang old songs – 'Barbara Allen,' 'The Twa Corbies,' 'Oh Susanna,' and the folk ballads that last longer than Senates and Parliaments. Had they ridden horseback, they would have known the songs based on the rhythm-patterns of equine gait; as it was, they walked, and knew marching songs.

Jesse James Hartwell, leader of his little band of Hedgehounds, was superintending the cooking of bear steaks over the campfire, and his bass voice rolled out now, muffled and softened by the pines that screened camp from brook. His squaw, Mary, was singing too, and presently others joined in, hunters and their wives – for squaw no longer carried the derogatory shade of meaning it once had. The attitude the Hedgehounds had toward their wives was a more realistic version of the attitudes of medieval chivalry.

'Bring the good old bugle, boys, we'll
  sing another song –'

It was dark by the stream. They had been late in finding a camping place tonight; the hunt for the bear had delayed them, and after that it had been difficult to find fresh water. As always when the tribe was irritable, there had been half-serious raillery at Lincoln Cody's expense. It was, perhaps, natural for any group to sense the mental difference – or superiority – of a Baldy, and compensate by jeering at his obvious physical difference.

Yet they had never connected Linc with the town Baldies. For generations now telepaths had worn wigs. And not even Linc himself knew that he was a telepath. He knew that he was different, that was all. He had no memory of the helicopter wreck from which his infant body had been taken by Jesse James Hartwell's mother; adopted into the tribe, he had grown up as a Hedgehound, and had been accepted as one. But though they considered him one of theirs, they were too ready to call him 'skinhead' – not quite in jest.

'Sing it as we used to sing it, fifty thousand strong,
While we were marching through Georgia ...'

There were twenty-three in Hartwell's band. A good many generations ago, one of his ancestors had fought with the Grand Army of the Republic, and had been with Sherman on his march. And a contemporary of that soldier, whose blood also ran in Hartwell's veins, had worn Confederate gray and died on the Potomac. Now twenty-three outcast Hedgehounds, discards of civilization, huddled about the fire and cooked the bear they had killed with spear and arrow.

The chorus burst out vigorously.

'Hurrah! Hurrah! We bring the jubilee,
Hurrah! Hurrah! The flag that makes men free,
So we sang the chorus from Atlanta to the sea
While we were marching through Georgia.'

There was a gray scar of desolation where Atlanta had been. The bright, clean new towns dotted Georgia, and helicopters hummed to the sea and back again now. The great War between the States was a memory, shadowed by the greater conflicts that had followed. Yet in that still northern forest, vigorous voices woke the past again.

Linc rubbed his shoulders against the rough bark of the tree and yawned. He was chewing the bit of a battered pipe and grateful for the momentary solitude. But he could sense – feel – understand stray fragments of thoughts that came to him from around the campfire. He did not know they were thoughts, since, for all he knew, Hartwell and the others might feel exactly the same reactions. Yet, as always, the rapport made him faintly unhappy, and he was grateful for the – something – that told him Cassie was coming.

She walked softly out of the shadow and dropped beside him, a slim, pretty girl a year younger than his seventeen years. They had been married less than a year; Linc was still amazed that Cassie could have loved him in spite of his bald, gleaming cranium. He ran his fingers through Cassie's glossy, black hair, delighting in the sensuous feel of it, and the way it ran rippling across his palm.

'Tired, hon?'

'Nope. You feeling bad, Linc?'

'It's nothing,' he said.

'You been acting funny ever since we raided that town,' Cassie murmured, taking his brown hand and tracing a pattern with her forefinger across the calloused palm. 'You figure that wasn't on the beam for us to do, maybe.'

'I dunno, Cassie,' he sighed, his arm circling her waist. 'It's the third raid this year –'

'You ain't questioning Jesse James Hartwell?'

'S'pose I am?'

'Well, then,' Cassie said demurely, 'you better start considering a quick drift for the two of us. Jesse don't like no arguments.'

'No more do I,' Linc said. 'Maybe there won't be no more raids now we're southering.'

'We got full bellies, anyhow, and that's more than we had across the Canada line. I never saw a winter like this, Linc.'

'It's been cold,' he acknowledged. 'We can make out. Only thing is –'

'What?'

'I kinda wish you'd been along on the raids. I can't talk to nobody else about it. I felt funny. There was voices inside my head, like.'

'That's crazy. Or else conjure.'

'I'm no hex man. You know that, Cassie.'

'And you ain't been smoking crazy weed.' She meant the marijuana that grew wild in the backlands. Her gaze sought his. 'Tell me what it's like, Linc. Bad?'

'It ain't bad and it ain't good. It's mixed up, that's all. It's sort of like a dream, only I'm awake. I see pictures.'

'What pictures. Linc?'

'I don't know,' he said, looking into the darkness where the brook chuckled and splashed. 'Because half the time it ain't me when that happens. I get hot and cold inside. Sometimes it's like a music in my head. But when we raided that town it was plain bad, Cassie hon.' He seized a bit of wood and tossed it away. 'I was like that chip tossed around in the water. Everything was pulling at me every which way.'

Cassie kissed him gently. 'Don't pay no mind to it. Everybody gets mixed up once in a while. Once we get more south, and the hunting's good, you'll forget your vapors.'

'I can forget 'em now. You make me feel better, just being with you. I love the smell of your hair, sweet.' Linc pressed his face against the cool, cloudy darkness of the girl's braids.

'Well, I won't cut it, then.'

'You better not. You got to have enough hair for both of us.'

'You think that matters to me, Linc? Boone Curzon's bald, and he's plenty handsome.'

'Boone's old, near forty. That's why. He had hair when he was young.'

Cassie pulled up some moss and patted it into shape on Linc's head. She smiled at him half-mockingly. 'How's that? Ain't nobody anywhere that's got green hair. Feel better now?'

He wiped his scalp clean, pulled Cassie closer and kissed her. 'Wish I never had to leave you. I ain't troubled when you're around. Only these raids stir me up.'

'Won't be no more of 'em, I guess.'

Linc looked into the dimness. His young face, seamed and bronzed by his rugged life, was suddenly gloomy. Abruptly he stood up.

'I got a hunch Jesse James Hartwell's planning another.'

'Hunch?' She watched him, troubled. 'Maybe it ain't so.'

'Maybe,' Linc said doubtfully. 'Only my hunches work pretty good most times.' He glanced toward the fire. His shoulders squared.

'Linc?'

'He's figgering on it, Cassie. Sitting there thinking about the chow we got at that last town. It's his belly working on him. I ain't going to string along with him.'

'You better not start nothing.'

'I'm gonna … talk to him,' Linc said almost inaudibly, and moved into the gloom of the trees. From the circle of firelight a man sent out a questioning challenge; the eerie hoot of an owl, mournful and sobbing. Linc understood the inflection and answered with the caw of a raincrow. Hedgehounds had a language of their own that they used in dangerous territory, for there was no unity among the tribes, and some Hedgehounds were scalpers. There were a few cannibal groups, too, but these degenerates were hated and killed by the rest whenever opportunity offered.

Linc walked into camp. He was a big, sturdy, muscular figure, his strong chest arched under the fringed buckskin shirt he wore, his baldness concealed now by a squirrelhide cap. Temporary shelters had been rigged up, lean-tos, thatched with leaves, gave a minimum of privacy, and several squaws were busily sewing. At the cookpot Bethsheba Hartwell was passing out bear steaks. Jesse James Hartwell, an oxlike giant with a hook nose and a scarred cheek that had whitened half of his beard, ate meat and biscuits with relish, washing them down with green turtle soup – part of the raid's loot. On an immaculate white cloth before him was spread caviar, sardines, snails, chow chow, antipasto, and other dainties that he sampled with a tiny silver fork that was lost in his big, hairy hand.

'C'mon and eat, skinhead,' Hartwell rumbled. 'Where's your squaw? She'll get mighty hungry.'

'She's coming,' Linc said. He didn't know that Cassie was crouching in the underbrush, a bared throwing-knife in her hand. His thoughts were focused on the chief, and he could still sense what he had called his hunch, and which was actually undeveloped telepathy. Yes, Hartwell was thinking about another raid.

Linc took a steak from Bethsheba. It didn't burn his calloused hands. He squatted near Hartwell and bit into the juicy, succulent meat. His eyes never left the bearded man's face.

'We're out of Canada now,' he said at last. 'It's warming up some. We still heading south?'

Hartwell nodded. 'You bet. I don't figure on losing another toe with frost-bite. It's too cold even here.'

'There'll be hunting, then. And the wild corn's due soon. We'll have a-plenty to eat.'

'Pass the biscuits, Bethsheba. *Urp*. More we eat, Linc, the fatter we'll get for next winter.'

Linc pointed to the white cloth. 'Them don't fatten you up none.'

'They're good anyhow. Try some of these here fish eggs.'

'Yeah – *pfui*. Where's the water?'

Hartwell laughed. Linc said, 'We're going north come summer?'

'We ain't voted on it yet. I'd say no. Me, I'd rather head south.'

'More towns. It ain't safe to go on raiding, Jesse.'

'Nobody can't find us once we get back in the woods.'

'They got guns.'

'You scared?'

'I ain't scared of nothing,' Linc said. 'Only I sort of know you're thinking about another raid. And I'm telling you to count me out.'

Hartwell's heavy shoulders hunched. He reached for a sardine, ate it slowly, and then turned his head toward the boy. His lids were half-lowered.

'Yaller?' But he made it a question, so a fight wasn't obligatory.

'You seen me fight a grizzly with a knife.'

'I know,' Hartwell said, rubbing the white streak in his beard. 'A guy can turn yaller, though. I ain't saying that's it, understand. Just the same, nobody else is trying to back out.'

'On that first raid we was starving. The second – well, that might pass too. But I don't see no percentage in raiding just so you can eat fish eggs and worms.'

'That ain't all of it, Linc. We got blankets, too. Things like that we needed. Once we lay our hands on a few guns –'

'Getting too lazy to pull a bow?'

'If you're spoiling for a fight,' Hartwell said slowly, 'I can oblige you. Otherwise shut up.'

Linc said, 'O.K. But I'm serving notice to count me out on any more raids.'

In the shadows Cassie's hand tightened on the dagger's hilt. But Hartwell suddenly laughed and threw his steakbone at Linc's head. The boy ducked and glowered.

'Come the day your belt starts pinching, you'll change your mind,' Hartwell said. 'Forget about it now. Git that squaw of yours and make her eat; she's too skinny.' He swung toward the woods. *'Cassie!* C'mon and have some of this fish soup.'

Linc had turned away, readjusting his cap. His face was less somber now, though it was still thoughtful. Cassie holstered her knife and came out into the firelight. Hartwell beckoned to her.

'Come and get it,' he said.

The air was peaceful again. No more friction developed, though Linc, Cassie knew, was in a quarrelsome mood. But Hartwell's good humor was proof against any but direct insults. He passed around the whiskey bottle he had looted – a rare treat, since the tribe could distill smoke only when they settled for a while, which wasn't often. Linc didn't drink much. Long after the fire had been smothered and snores came from the lean-tos around him, he lay awake, troubled and tense.

Something – someone – was calling him.

It was like one of his hunches. It was like what he had felt during the raids. It was like Cassie's nearness, and yet there was a queer, exciting difference. There was a friendliness to that strange call that he had never felt before.

Dim and indefinable, a dweller hidden deep in his mind woke and responded to that call of a kindred being.

After a while he rose on one elbow and looked down at Cassie. Her face was partly veiled by the deeper blackness of her hair. He touched its soft, living warmth gently. Then he slipped noiselessly out of the shelter and stood up, staring around.

There was a rustling of leaves, and the chuckling of the brooklet. Nothing else. Moonlight dappled the ground here and there. A woodrat rustled softly through the wild grasses. The air was very cold and crisp, with a freshness that stung Linc's cheeks and eyes.

And suddenly he was frightened. Old folktales troubled him. He remembered his foster mother's stories of men who could turn to wolves, of the Wendigo that swept like a vast wind above the lonely forests, of a Black Man who bought souls – the formless, dark fears of childhood rose up in nightmare reality. He had killed a grizzly with his knife, but he had never stood alone at night in the woods, while a Call murmured in his mind – silently – and made his blood leap up in fiery response.

He was afraid, but the bait was too strong. He turned south, and walked out of the camp. Instinctive training made his progress noiseless. He crossed the brook, his sandals inaudible on the stones, and mounted a slope And there, sitting on a stump waiting for him, was a man.

His back was toward Linc, and nothing could be seen but the hunched torso and the bald, gleaming head. Linc had a momentary horrible fear that when the man turned, he might see his own face. He touched his knife. The confused stirring in his brain grew chaotic.

'Hello, Linc,' a low voice said.

Linc had made no sound, and he knew it. But, somehow, that dark figure had sensed his approach. The Black Man –?

'Do I look black?' the voice asked. The man stood up, turning. He was sneering – no, smiling – and his face was dark and seamed. He wore town clothes.

But he wasn't the Black Man. He didn't have a cloven hoof. And the warm, sincere friendliness subtly radiating from his presence was reassuring to Linc in spite of his suspicions.

'You called me,' Linc said. 'I'm trying to figure it out.' His eyes dwelt on the bald cranium.

'My name's Barton,' the man said. 'Dave Barton.' He lifted something gray – a scalp? – and fitted it carefully on his head. The sneer indicated amusement.

'I feel naked without my wig. But I had to show you I was a … a –' He sought for the word that would fit the telepathic symbol. 'That you were one of us,' he finished.

'I ain't –'

'You're a Baldy,' Barton said, 'but you don't know it. I can read that from your mind.'

'Read my mind?' Linc took a backward step.

'You know what Baldies are? Telepaths?'

'Sure,' Linc said doubtfully. 'I heard stories. We don't know much about town life. Listen,' he said with fresh suspicion, 'how'd you come to be out here? How'd –'

'I came looking for you.'

'Me? Why?'

Barton said patiently, 'Because you're one of Us. I can see I've got to explain a lot. From the beginning, maybe. So –'

He talked. It might have been more difficult had they not been Baldies. Though Linc was telepathically untrained, he could nevertheless receive enough mental confirmation to clarify the questions in his mind. And Barton spoke of the Blowup, of the hard radiations – so much Greek to Linc, until Barton used telepathic symbolism – and, mostly, of the incredible fact that Linc wasn't merely a hairless freak in his tribe. There were other Baldies, a lot of them.

That was important. For Linc caught the implications. He sensed something of the warm, deep understanding between telepaths, the close unity of the race, the feeling of *belonging* that he had never had. Just now, alone in the woods with Barton, he was conscious of more genuine intimacy than he had ever felt before.

He was quick to understand. He asked questions, And, after a while, so did Barton.

'Jesse James Hartwell's behind the raids. Yeah, I was in on 'em. You mean you all wear them wigs?'

'Naturally. It's a big civilization, and we belong to it. We're part of the whole set-up.'

'And … and nobody laughs at you for being bald?'

'Do I look bald?' Barton asked. 'There are drawbacks, sure. But there are plenty of advantages.'

'I'll say!' Linc breathed deeply. 'People … the same sort … your own sort –' He was inarticulate.

'The non-Baldies didn't always give us an even break. They were afraid of us, a little. We're trained from childhood never to take advantage of our telepathic powers with humans.'

'Yeah, I can see that. It makes sense.'

'Then you know why I came, don't you?'

'I can sort of understand it,' Linc said slowly. 'These raids … people might start thinking a Baldy's involved – *I'm* a Baldy!'

Barton nodded. 'Hedgehounds don't matter, A few raids – we can take care of them. But to have one of Us involved is bad medicine.'

'I told Jesse James Hartwell tonight I was having no part in any more raiding,' Linc said. 'He won't push me.'

'Yes – That helps. Listen, Linc. Why don't you come home with me?'

Years of training made Linc pause. 'Me? Go into a town? We don't do that.'

'You?'

'The … Hedgehounds. I ain't a Hedgehound, am I? Gosh, this is –' He rubbed his jaw. 'I'm all mixed up, Barton.'

'Tell you what. Come with me now, and see how you like our sort of life. You never were trained to use your telepathic function, so you're like a half-blind man. Take a look at the set-up, and then decide what you want to do.'

On the verge of mentioning Cassie, Linc paused. He was half afraid that if he spoke of her, Barton might withdraw his offer. And, after all, it wasn't as if he intended to leave Cassie permanently. It'd be just for a week or two, and then he could come back to the tribe.

Unless he took Cassie with him now –

No. Somehow he'd feel shamed in admitting that he, a Baldy, had married a Hedgehound. Though he was proud of Cassie herself, all right. He'd never give her up. It was only –

He was lonely. He was horribly, sickeningly lonely, and what he had glimpsed in Barton's mind and Barton's words drew him with overpowering force. A world where he belonged, where no one called him skinhead, where he'd never feel inferior to the bearded men of the tribe. A wig of his own.

Just for a few weeks. He couldn't miss this chance. He couldn't! Cassie would be waiting for him when he came back.

'I'll go with you,' he said. 'I'm ready right now. O.K.?'

But Barton, who had read Linc's mind, hesitated before he answered.

'O.K.,' he said at last. 'Let's go.'

Three weeks later Barton sat in McNey's solarium and shaded his eyes wearily with one hand. 'Linc's married, you know,' he said, 'to a Hedgehound girl. He doesn't know we know it.'

'Does it matter?' McNey asked. He was looking very tired and troubled.

'I suppose not. But I thought I'd better mention it, because of Alexa.'

'She knows her own mind. And she must know about Linc being married, too, by this time. She's been giving him telepathic coaching for weeks.'

'I noticed that when I came in.'

'Yeah,' McNey said, rubbing his forehead. 'That's why we're being oral. Telepathic conversations distract Linc when there's more than one; he's still learning selectivity.'

'How do you like the boy?'

'I like him. He's not … quite what I'd expected, though.'

'He grew up with the Hedgehounds.'

'He's one of Us,' McNey said with finality.

'No symptoms of paranoid tendencies?'

'Definitely not. Alexa agrees.'

'Good,' Barton said. 'That relieves me. It was the one thing I was afraid of. As for the Hedgehound girl, she's not one of Us, and we can't afford to weaken the race by intermarriage with humans. That's been an axiom almost since the Blowup. My own feeling is that if Linc marries Alexa or any other one of Us, it's all to the good, and we can forget about previous entanglements.'

'It's up to her,' McNey said. 'Any more Hedgehound raids?'

'No. But they're the least of my troubles. Sergei Callahan's gone underground. I can't locate him, and I want to.'

'Just to kill him?'

'No. He must know other key paranoids. I want to drag that information out of him. He can't blur his mind permanently – and once I get him where I want, he'll have few secrets left.'

'We're fighting a losing battle.'

'Are we?'

'I can't talk yet,' McNey said, with subdued violence. 'I can't even let myself think about the problem. I … it works out this way. There's crux, a single equation, that must be solved. But not yet. Because the moment I solve it, my mind can be read. I've got to work out all the minor details first. Then –'

'Yes?'

McNey's smile was bitter. 'I don't know. I'll find an answer. I haven't been idle.'

'If we could crack the Power,' Barton said. 'If we could only tap the paranoid's code –'

'Or,' McNey said, 'if we had a code of our own –'

'Unbreakable.'

'Which is impossible, by any mechanical means. No scrambler could work, because we'd have to know the key, and our minds could be read by paranoids. I don't want to think about it any more for a while, Dave. The details, yes. But not the problem itself. I … might solve it before I'm ready.'

'The paranoids are plenty busy,' Barton said. 'Their propaganda's spreading. That talk about Galileo's secret weapon is still going around.'

'Haven't the Galileans made any denials?'

'It isn't that tangible. You can't buck a whispering campaign. That, Darryl, is what's apt to cause a bust-up. You can fight a person or a thing, but you can't fight a wind. A wind that whispers.'

'But the atomic bombs! After all –'

'I know. Just the same, some hothead is going to get scared enough to take action one of these days. He'll say, "Galileo's got a secret weapon. We're not safe. They're going to attack us." So he'll jump the gun. After that, there'll be other incidents.'

'With Us in the middle. We can't stay neutral. I think there'll be a pogrom, Dave, sooner or later.'

'We'll survive it.'

'You think so? With every non-Baldy's hand ready to strike down telepaths – man, woman or child? There'll be no quarter given. We need another world, a new world –'

'That'll have to wait until we get interstellar ships.'

'And meanwhile we live on borrowed time. It might be best if we let the human race reassimilate us.'

'Retrogression?'

'Suppose it is? We're in the position of a unicorn in a herd of horses. We daren't use our horn to defend ourselves. We've got to pretend to be horses.'

'The lion and the unicorn,' Barton said, 'were fighting for the crown. Well, Callahan and his paranoids are the lion, all right. But the crown?'

'Inevitably,' McNey said, 'it must be rule. Two dominant species can't exist on the same planet or even in the same system. Humans and telepaths can't evenly divide rule. We're knuckling under now. Eventually, we'll arrive, by a different path, at Callahan's goal. But not by degrading or enslaving humans!

Natural selection is our weapon. Biology's on our side. If we can only live in peace with humans, until –'

'– and drummed them out of town,' Barton said.

'So the humans mustn't suspect the lion and the unicorn are fighting. Or what they're fighting for. Because if they do, we won't survive the pogrom. There will be no refuge. Our race is soft, through environment and adaptation.'

'I'm worried about Callahan,' Barton said suddenly. 'I don't know what he's planning. By the time I find out, it may be too late. If he sets something in operation that can't be stopped –'

'I'll keep working,' McNey promised. 'I may be able to give you something soon.'

'I hope so. Well, I'm flying to St. Nick tonight. Ostensibly to check the zoo there. Actually, I've other motives. Maybe I can pick up Callahan's trail.'

'I'll walk you down to the village.' McNey went with Barton into the dropper. They stepped outside into the warm, spring air, glancing through the transparent wall at the televisor where Alexa sat with Linc. Barton said, 'They don't seem worried, anyhow.'

McNey laughed. 'She's sending in her column to the *Recorder*. Alexa's a specialist on heart problems. I hope she never has any of her own to solve!'

'– if you love him,' Alexa said into the mike, 'marry him. And if he loves you, he'll have no objection to running psych-rating tests and comparing *id* balance sheets. You're considering a lifetime partnership, and both of you should read the contracts before signing them.' She managed to look like a cat with cream on its whiskers. 'But always remember that love is the most important thing in the world. If you find that, it will always be springtime in your hearts. Good luck, Wondering!'

She pressed a switch. 'Thirty, Linc. My job's done for the day. That's one sort of job a Baldy can find – heart problem editor on a telepaper. Think you'd like it?'

'No,' Linc said. 'It ain't … it's not up my alley.'

He was wearing a silken blue shirt and darker blue shorts, and a cropped brown wig covered his skull. He wasn't used to it yet, and kept touching it uneasily.

'Ain't's as good as isn't,' Alexa said. 'I know what you mean, and that's more important than grammatical construction. More lessons?'

'Not for a while yet. I get tired easy. Talking's still more natural, somehow.'

'Eventually you'll be finding it cumbersome. Personal endings – you speak, he speaks, *parlons, parlez, parlent* – telepathically you don't use those vestiges.'

'Vestiges?'

'Sure,' Alexa said. 'From the Latin. The Romans didn't use pronouns. Just *amo, amas, amant,'* she clarified mentally, 'and the endings gave you the right pronoun. *Nous, vous*, and *ils* are used now instead, we, you plural, and they. So the endings are unnecessary. If you're communicating with a Swiss telepath, though you might find yourself wondering why he kept thinking of a girl as *it*. But you'd know what *it* meant to him, and you couldn't if you were being oral only.'

'It's plenty hard,' Linc said. 'I'm getting the angles, though. That round-robin business we had last night was –' He groped for a word, but Alexa caught the meaning from his mind.

'I know. There's an intimacy that's pretty wonderful. You know, I've never felt badly about being adopted. I *knew* just where I fitted into Marian's life and Darryl's, and how they felt about me. I knew I belonged.'

'It must be a nice feeling,' Linc said. 'I'm sort of getting it, though.'

'Of course. You're one of Us. After you've mastered the telepathic function, you won't have any doubts at all.'

Linc watched the play of sunlight on Alexa's bronze curls. 'I guess I do belong with your kind of folks.'

'Glad you came with Dave?'

He looked at his hands. 'I can't tell you, Alexa. I can't tell you how wonderful it is. I'd been shut out in the dark all my life, thinking I was a freak, never feeling right sure about myself. Then all this –' He indicated the televisor. 'Magical miracles, that's what. And all the rest.'

Alexa understood what was in his mind. Through him she felt the heady excitement of an exile returning to his own kind. Even the visor, familiar symbol of her job, assumed a new glamour, though it was the standard double-screen model, the upper for news flashes, the lower for the twenty-four-hour newspaper that was received, recorded on wire-film, and thereafter available for reference. Push-buttons selected the publication, and the dials made it possible to focus down on the pages, on either the action pictures or the printed matter. Format, of course, was quite as important as news value. The big concealed wall-screen at one end of the room was used for plays, concerts, movies, and Disneys. But for the added sensual attractions of smell, taste, and touch, one had to go to the theaters; such special equipment was still too expensive for the average home.

'Yes,' Alexa said, 'you're one of Us. And you've got to remember that the future of the race is important. If you stay, you must never do anything to hurt it.'

'I remember what you've been telling me about the p-paranoids,' Linc nodded. 'Guess they're sort of like the cannibal tribes 'mong the Hedgehounds. They're fair quarry for anybody.' He felt his wig, stepped to a mirror-unit, and adjusted the headpiece.

Alexa said, 'There's Marian outside. I want to see her. Wait for me, Linc; I'll be back.'

She went out. Lincoln, awkwardly testing his newly-realized powers, felt her thought fingering subtly toward the plump, pretty woman who was moving among the flowers, armed with gloves and spray.

He wandered to the clavilux, and, one fingered, picked out a tune. He hummed:

'All in the merry month of May,
  When the green buds they were swellin',
Young Jemmy Grove on his death-bed lay
  For love of Barb'ry Allen.'

Memories of Cassie rose up. He forced them back into the shadows, along with the Hedgehounds and the nomad life he had known. That wasn't his life any more. Cassie – she'd get along all right. He'd go after her, one of these days, and bring her to live with him among the Baldies. Only – only she wasn't a Baldy. She wasn't like Alexa, for instance. She was quite as pretty, sure; yet there was all this talk about the future of the race. If, now, he married a Baldy and had Baldy sons and daughters –

But, he was already married. What was the good of thinking so? A Hedgehound marriage might not amount to a hill of beans among the townsfolk, of course, and, anyway, all this mental round-robin stuff was sort of polygamy.

Well, he'd climb that hill when he came to it. First he had to get the trick of this telepathy business. It was coming, but slowly, for he'd not been conditioned since infancy, as other Baldies were. The latent power had to be wakened and directed – not as a child could be taught, but allowing for Linc's maturity, and his ability to grasp and understand the goal.

Marian came in with Alexa. The older woman stripped off her cloth gloves and brushed beads of perspiration from her ruddy cheeks. ''Lo, Linc,' she said. 'How's it going?'

'Fairish, Marian. You should of asked me to help out there.'

'I need the exercise. I gained three pounds this morning arguing with that turnip-bleeder Gatson, down at the store. Know what he wants for fresh breadfruit?'

'What's that?'

'Catch this.' Marian formed mental concepts involving sight, touch and taste. Alexa chimed in with the smell of breadfruit. Linc had his own arbitrary standards for comparisons, and within a second had assimilated the absolute meaning; he would recognize a breadfruit from now on. Marian threw a quick mental question. Linc answered.

To town (Darryl McNey) by window (ten minutes past)

'A bit confused,' Marian said, 'but I get the idea. He ought to be back soon. I'm in the mood for a swim. Suppose I fix some sandwiches?'

'Swell,' Alexa said. 'I'll help. Linc knows more about catching trout than anybody I've ever seen, except he doesn't know what a dry fly is.'

'I just aim to catch fish,' Linc said. 'Enough to eat. Many a time I had to fish through holes in the ice to keep from being hungry.'

Later, stretching his brown, hard body on the sandy bank of the pool upstream, he luxuriated in the warm sunlight and watched Alexa. Slim and attractive in white shorts and bathing cap, she inexpertly practised casting, while McNey, pipe in his mouth, worked a likely-looking spot under an overhang of branches that brushed the water. Marian placidly ate sandwiches and watched the activities of a community of ants with considerable interest. The deep, unspoken comradeship of the family and the race was intangibly in the air, a bond that reached out, touched Linc, and drew him into its friendly center. *This is it*, he thought. *I belong here.* And Alexa's mind answered him with quiet confidence: *You are one of Us.*

The months passed very quickly for Linc, broken by occasional visits from Dave Barton, whose manner grew increasingly more troubled, and by the green that covered tree and brush, ground and vine, as spring gave place to summer, and summer drew toward a not-distant autumn. He seldom thought of the Hedgehounds now. There was a sort of tacit acceptance of the situation among the little group; he felt, without actually bringing the realization consciously to mind, that Alexa knew a great deal about his past, and that she would not bring up the matter of Cassie unless he did. That she was beginning to love him he did not doubt. Nor did he doubt much that he loved her. After all, Alexa was his kind, as Cassie never had been.

But he dreamed of Cassie, nevertheless. Sometimes he felt loneliness, even among his own people. At such times he was anxious to finish his telepathic training and join Barton's fight against the paranoids. Barton was eager to enlist Linc, but he warned against the danger of moving too soon. 'The paranoids aren't fools, Linc,' he said. 'We mustn't underestimate them. I've lived this long simply because I'm a trained big-game hunter. My reactions are just a bit faster than theirs, and I always try to maneuver them into a position where telepathy can't help them. If a paranoid's at the bottom of a well, he may read your intention of dropping a load of bricks on his head – but he can't do a lot about it.'

'Any news about Callahan?' McNey asked.

'No word for months. There's some plan – maybe a big push in the propaganda field, maybe assassinations of key technologists. I don't know what. I've read no minds that knew the right answers. But I think something's going to break soon; I've found out that much. We've got to be ready for it.

We've got to break their code – or get one of our own. The same tune, Darryl.'

'I know,' McNey said. He stared out at the empty blue sky. 'There isn't much I can say now, or even think. The same tune, all right.'

'But you haven't failed? In a few weeks you're due back at Niagara.'

Linc said, 'Look, about this code. I was thinking, the Hedgehounds have got a sort of code. Like this.' He imitated a few bird and animal calls. 'We know what they mean but nobody else knows.'

'Hedgehounds aren't telepaths. If they were, your code wouldn't stay a secret long.'

'Guess you're right. I'd like to take a crack at the paranoids, though.'

'You'll have your chance,' Barton said. 'But, meanwhile, it's Darryl's job to find us a new weapon.'

McNey said wearily, 'I know all about that. No more pep talks, Dave, please.'

Barton stood up, scowling. 'I've a job to do down south. I'll see you when I get back, Darryl. Meanwhile, take care of yourself. If this business – whatever it is – should break soon, don't run any risks. You're vital to Us, much more so than I am.'

With a nod to Linc he went out. McNey stared at nothing. Linc hesitated, sent out a querying thought, and met abstracted rebuff. He went downstairs.

He couldn't find Alexa. Finally he went out into the gardens, working his way toward the brook. A flash of color caught his eye, and he headed for it.

Alexa was sitting on a rock, her flimsy playsuit unzipped to let the slight breeze cool her. The heat was so intense that she had removed her wig, and her bald head was shiny and incongruous, incompatible with her artificial lashes and eyebrows. It was the first time Linc had ever seen her wigless.

Instantly, at his thought, she swung about and began to replace the wig. But her arm stopped in arrested motion. She looked at him, half questionably, and then with pain and growing understanding in her eyes.

'Put it on, Alexa,' Linc said.

She watched him steadily. 'What for – now?'

'I ... it doesn't –'

Alexa shrugged and slipped the headpiece into place. 'That was ... strange,' she said, deliberately speaking aloud as if she did not want to let her mind slip back into the channels of telepathic intimacy where hurt can strike so unerringly. 'I'm so used myself to Baldies being – bald. I never thought before the sight could be –' She did not finish aloud. After a moment she said, 'You must have been very unhappy among the Hedgehounds, Linc. Even more unhappy than you realize. If you've been conditioned against the sight of baldness to ... to *that* extent –'

'It wasn't,' Linc denied futilely. 'I didn't … you shouldn't think –'

'It's all right. You can't help reactions as deeply rooted as that. Some day standards of beauty will change. Hairlessness will be lovely. Today it isn't, certainly not to a man with your psychological background. You must have been made to feel very keenly that you were inferior because of your baldness –'

Linc stood there awkwardly, unable to deny the thought that had sprung so vividly into his mind, burning with shame and dismay at the knowledge that she had seen as clearly as himself the ugly picture of her baldness in his thought. As if he had held up a distorting mirror to her face and said aloud, 'This is the way you look to me.' As if he had slapped her gratuitously across the cheek with the taunt of her – abnormality.

'Never mind,' Alexa said, a little shakily, smiling. 'You can't help it if baldness disg … distresses you. Forget it. It isn't as if we were m-married or … anything.'

They looked at each other in silence. Their minds touched and sprang apart and then touched again, tentatively, with light thoughts that leaped from point to point as gingerly as if the ideas were ice-floes that might sink beneath the full weight of conscious focus.

I thought I loved you … perhaps I did … yes, I too … but now there can't be … (sudden, rebellious denial) … no, it's true, there can't ever be rightness between us … not as if we were ordinary people … we'd always remember that picture, how I looked (abrupt sheering off from the memory) … (agonized repudiation of it) … no, couldn't help that … always between us … rooted too deeply … and anyhow, Cas – (sudden closing off of both minds at once, before even the thought-image had time to form).

Alexa stood up. 'I'm going into town,' she said. 'Marian's at the hairdresser's. I … I'll get a wave or something.'

He looked at her helplessly, half reluctant to let her go, though he knew as well as she how much had been discussed and weighed and discarded in the past moment of voiceless speech.

'Good-by, Alexa,' he said.

'Good-by, Linc.'

Linc stood for a long time watching the path, even after she had gone. He would have to leave. He didn't belong here. Even if nearness to Alexa were possible after this, he knew he could not stay. They were – abnormal. He would be seeing the baldness, the contemptible, laughable baldness he had hated in himself, more clearly now than the wigs they wore. Somehow until this moment he had never fully realized –

Well, he couldn't go without telling Darryl. Slowly, dragging his feet a little, he turned back toward the house. When he came to the side lawn he sent out an inexpert, querying thought.

Something answered him from the cellar-laboratory, a queer, strange, disturbing vibration that clung briefly to his mind and then pulled away. It wasn't McNey. It was – an intruder.

Linc went down the cellar steps. At the bottom he paused, trying to sort the tangled confusion in his mind as he thrust out exploratory mental fingers. The door was open. McNey was lying on the floor, his mind blanked, blood seeping from a red stain on his side.

The intruder?

Who –

Sergei Callahan.

Where –

Hidden. And armed.

So am I, Linc thought, his dagger springing into his hand.

Telepathically you are untrained. In a fight you can't win.

That was probably true. Telepathy took the place of prescience with the Baldies. Any Baldy could outguess and conquer a non-Baldy, and Linc was not yet thoroughly trained in the use of the telepathic function.

He probed awkwardly. And, suddenly, he knew where Callahan was.

Behind the door. Where he could strike Linc in the back when the boy entered the laboratory. He had not expected the untrained Baldy to discover the ambush until too late, and even as Linc realized the situation, Callahan made a move to spring out.

All Linc's weight smashed against the panel, slamming the door back against the wall. Callahan was caught. Pressed helplessly between the two metal planes – door and wall – he tried to brace himself, to wriggle free. His hand, gripping a dagger, snaked out. Linc dropped his own weapon, put his back against the door, and planted his feet more firmly. The door frame gave him good purchase. Veins stood out on his forehead as he ground, crushed, drove the door back with all his strength.

What had Dave Barton said once? 'Kill them with machines –'

This was a machine – one of the oldest. The lever.

Suddenly Callahan began to scream. His agonized thought begged for mercy. In a moment his strength would fail, he pleaded. 'Don't – *don't crush me*!'

His strength failed.

Linc's heavy shoulders surged. There was one frightful mental scream from Callahan, more agonizing than the audible sound he made, and Linc let the door swing slowly away from the wall. A body collapsed with its movement. Linc picked up his dagger, used it efficiently, and then turned to McNey.

There was a puddle of blood on the floor, but McNey still lived. Callahan had not had time to finish his task.

Linc became busy administering first aid.

*

This was it.

It was past midnight. In the cellar laboratory, McNey leaned back in his chair, wincing as he felt the pressure of the bandages about his ribs. He blinked at the fluorescents, sighed, and rubbed his forehead.

His hand hovered over the notepad. An equation was lacking. He wasn't quite ready to think of it just yet.

But the job was almost finished. It would give the Baldies a weapon, at last, against the paranoids. They couldn't tap the paranoid's secret wave length, but they could –

Not yet. Don't think of it yet.

Even Linc had helped, unknowingly, by one suggestion he had made. Mimicry. Yes, that was one answer. The paranoids would not even suspect –

Not yet.

Well, Linc had gone back to his Hedgehound tribe and his Hedgehound squaw. In the end, the psychological fixation implanted in the boy's mind had proved stronger than the strong bonds of race. Too bad, because Linc had had something that few Baldies possessed – an innate hardness, a resourceful strength that might prove useful in the dark days that were coming.

The dark days that might yet be postponed, for a while, if –

Marian was asleep. McNey forced his thought from her. After years of marriage, they were so closely attuned that even that casual thought might waken her. And not until she had fallen asleep had he dared to bring his mind to bear on this ultimate problem. There could be no secrets between Baldies.

But this would be a secret – the one that would give Dave Barton a weapon against the paranoids. It was the unbreakable code that McNey had searched for for two years now.

It was a secret method of communication for Baldies.

Now. Work fast. *Work fast!*

McNey's stylus moved rapidly. He made a few adjustments in the machine before him, sealed its fastenings thoroughly, and watched power-flow develop. After a while, something came out of a small opening at one end of the device, a fine mesh of wire, with a few flatly curved attachments. McNey took off his wig, fitted the wire cap to his head, and donned the wig again. After a glance at a mirror, he nodded, satisfied.

The machine was permanently set now to construct these communicator caps when raw materials were fed into it. The matrix, the blueprint, had been built into the device, and the end result was a communicator gadget, easily hidden under a wig, which every non-paranoid Baldy probably would eventually wear. As for the nature of the gadget –

The problem had been to find a secret means of communication, akin to the paranoids' untappable wave band. And telepathy itself is simply a three-phase oscillation of electromagneto-gravitic energy, emanating from the specialized colloid of the human brain. But telepathy, *per se*, can be received by any sensitive mind en rapport with the sender.

And so the trick had been – find a method of artificial transmission. The brain, when properly stimulated by electric energy, will give out electromagnet-gravitic energy, undetectable except to telepaths because there are no instruments sensitive to this output. But when the paranoids would receive such radiations, without the unscrambling assistance of one of McNey's little caps, they wouldn't suspect a code.

Because they'd be hearing – sensing – only static.

It was a matter of camouflage. The waves masqueraded. They masqueraded on a wave band that nobody used, for that particular band was too close to that of the radio communicators used in thousands of private helicopters. For these radios, five thousand megacycles was normal; fifteen thousand manifested itself as a harmless harmonic static, and McNey's device simply added more squirts of static to that harmonic interference.

True, direction finders could receive the signals and locate them – but helicopters, like Baldies, were scattered all over the country, and the race traveled a good deal, both by necessity and by choice. The paranoids could locate the source of the fifteen thousand megacycles emanating from the wire caps – but why should they think to?

It was an adaptation of the Hedgehounds' code of imitating bird and animal calls. A tenderfoot in the woods wouldn't look for a language in the cry of an owl – and the paranoids wouldn't be seeking secret messages in what was apparently only static.

So, in these light, easily disguised mesh helmets, the problem was solved, finally. The power source would be an automatic tapping of free energy, an imperceptible drain on any nearby electrical generator, and the master machine itself, which made the communicators, was permanently sealed. No one, except McNey himself, knew even the principles of the new communication system. And, since the machine would be guarded well, the paranoids would never know, any more than Barton himself would know, what made the gadget tick. Barton would realize its effectiveness, and that was all. The list of raw materials needed was engraved on the feeder-hopper of the machine; nothing else was necessary. So Barton would possess no secrets to betray inadvertently to the paranoids, for the secrets were all sealed in the machine, and in one other place.

McNey took off the wire cap and laid it on the table. He turned off the machine. Then, working quickly, he destroyed the formulas and any traces of notes or raw materials. He wrote a brief note to Barton, explaining what was necessary.

There was no more time left after that. McNey sank back in his chair, his tired, ordinary face without expression. He didn't look like a hero. And, just then, he wasn't thinking about the future of the Baldy race, or the fact that the other place where the secret was sealed was in his brain.

As his hands loosened the bandage about his ribs, he was thinking of Marian. And as his life began to flow out with the blood from his reopened wound, he thought: *I wish I could say good-by to you, Marian. But I mustn't touch you, not even with my mind. We're too close. You'd wake up, and –*

I hope you won't be too lonely, my dear –

He was going back. The Hedgehounds weren't his people, but Cassie was his wife. And so he had betrayed his own race, betrayed the future itself, perhaps, and followed the wandering tribe across three states until now, with the autumn winds blowing coldly through bare leaves, he had come to the end of his search. She was there, waiting. She was there, just beyond that ridge. He could feel it, sense it, and his heart stirred to the homecoming.

Betrayal, then. One man could not matter in the life of a race. There would be a few Baldy children less than if he had married Alexa. The Baldies would have to work out their own salvation –

But he wasn't thinking about that as he leaped the last hurdle and ran to where Cassie was sitting near the fire. He was thinking about Cassie, and the glossy darkness of her hair, and the soft curve of her cheek. He called her name, again and again.

She didn't believe it at first. He saw doubt in her eyes and in her mind. But that doubt faded when he dropped beside her, a strange figure in his exotic town clothing, and took her in his arms.

'Linc,' she said, 'you've come back.'

He managed to say, 'I've come back,' and stopped talking and thinking for a while. It was a long time before Cassie thought to show him something in which he might be expected to evince interest.

He did. His eyes widened until Cassie laughed and said that it wasn't the first baby in the world.

'I ... us ... you mean –'

'Sure. Us. This is Linc Junior. How'd you like him? He takes after his dad, too.'

'What?'

'Hold him.' As Cassie put the baby into his arms, Linc saw what she meant. The small head was entirely hairless, and there was no sign of lashes or eyebrows.

'But ... you ain't bald, Cassie. How –'

'You sure are, though, Linc. That's why.'

Linc put his free arm around her and drew her close. He couldn't see the future; he couldn't realize the implications of this first attempt at mixing races. He only knew a profound and inarticulate relief that his child was like himself. It went deeper than the normal human desire to perpetuate one's own kind. This was reprieve. He had not, after all, wholly failed his race. Alexa would never bear his children, but his children need not be of alien stock in spite of it.

The deep warping which the Hedgehounds had wrought upon himself must not happen to the child. *I'll train him*, he thought. *He'll know from the start – he'll learn to be proud he's a Baldy. And then if they ever need him ... no, if We ever need him ... he'll be ready where I failed.*

The race would go on. It was good and satisfying and right that the union of Baldy and human could result in Baldy children. The line need not come to dead end because a man married outside his own kind. A man must follow his instinct, as Linc had done. It was good to belong to a race that allowed even that much treason to its tradition, and exacted no lasting penalty. The line was too strong to break. The dominant strain would go on.

Perhaps McNey's invention could postpone the day of the pogrom. Perhaps it could not. But if the day came, still the Baldies would go on. Underground, hidden, persecuted, still they must go on. And perhaps it would be among the Hedgehounds that the safest refuge could be found. For they had an emissary there, now –

Maybe this was right, Linc thought, his arm around Cassie and the child. *Once I belonged here. Now I don't. I'll never be happy for good in the old life. I know too much – But here I'm a link between the public life and the secret life of the refugees. Maybe some day they'll need that link.* 'Linc,' he mused, and grinned.

Off in the distance a growl of song began to lift. The tribesmen, coming back from the day's hunting. He was surprised, a little, to realize he felt no more of the old, deep, bewildered distrust of them. He understood now. He knew them as they could never know themselves, and he had learned enough in the past months to evaluate that knowledge. Hedgehounds were no longer the malcontents and misfits of civilization. Generations of weeding-out had distilled them. Americans had always been a distillation in themselves of the pioneer, the adventurous drawn from the old world. The buried strain came out again in their descendants. The Hedgehounds were nomads now, yes; they were woodsmen, yes; they were fighters, always. So were the first Americans. The same hardy stock that might, some day, give refuge again to the oppressed and the hunted.

The song grew louder through the trees, Jesse James Hartwell's roaring bass leading all the others.

'Hurrah, hurrah, we bring the jubilee!
Hurrah, hurrah, the flag that makes men free –'

FOUR

Night had fallen again. I lay looking up at the coldly sparkling stars and felt my mind toppling into that endless void of infinity.

I felt very clear-headed.

I had been lying here for a long time without moving, looking up at the stars. The snow had stopped some while ago, and the starlight glittered on its blue-shadowed mounds.

There was no use waiting any longer. I reached into my belt and took out my knife. I laid its blade across my left wrist and considered. That might take too long. There were quicker ways, in places where the body was more vulnerable.

But I was too tired to move. In a moment I would draw the blade back, with a heavy, pressing motion. Then it would be over, for there was no use waiting for rescue now, and I was blind and deaf and mute here behind the mountain barrier. Life had gone out of the world completely. The little sparks of glowing warmth which even insects possess, the strange, pulsing beat of life that flows like a tidal current through the universe, perhaps emanating from the microscopic organisms which exist everywhere – the light and warmth had gone out. It seemed as though the soul had been drained from everything.

Unconsciously I must have sent out a thought asking for help, because I heard a response within my mind. I almost shouted before I realized that the response had come from my own mind, some memory summoned up by associations.

You're one of us, the thought had said.

Why should I remember that? It reminded me of … Hobson. Hobson and the Beggars in Velvet. For McNey had not solved the ultimate problem.

The next battle in the war had been fought in Sequoia.

Should I remember?

The blade of the knife lay wire-cold across my wrist. It would be very easy to die. Much easier than to keep on living, blind and deaf and alone.

You're one of us, my thought said again.

And my mind went back to a bright morning in a town near the old Canadian border, and the smell of cold, pine-sharp air, and the rhythmic beat of a man's footsteps along Redwood Street – a hundred years ago.

BEGGARS IN VELVET

It was like stepping on a snake. The thing, concealed in fresh, green grass, squirmed underfoot and turned and struck venomously. But the thought was not that of reptile or beast; only man was capable of the malignance that was, really, a perversion of intellect.

Burkhalter's dark face did not change; his easy stride did not alter. But his mind had instantly drawn back from that blind malevolence, alert and ready, while all through the village Baldies paused imperceptibly in their work or conversation as their minds touched Burkhalter's.

No human noticed.

Under bright morning sunlight Redwood Street curved cheerful and friendly before Burkhalter. But a breath of uneasiness slipped along it, the same cool, dangerous wind that had been blowing for days through the thoughts of every telepath in Sequoia. Ahead were a few early shoppers, some children on their way to school, a group gathered outside the barber shop, one of the doctors from the hospital.

Where is he?

The answer came swiftly. *Can't locate him. Near you, though –*

Someone – a woman, the overtones of her thought showed – sent a message tinged with emotional confusion, almost hysterical. *One of the patients from the hospital –*

Instantly the thoughts of the others closed reassuringly around her, warm with friendliness and comfort. Even Burkhalter took time to send a clear thought of unity. He recognized among the others the cool, competent personality of Duke Heath, the Baldy priest-medic, with its subtle psychological shadings that only another telepath could sense.

It's Selfridge, Heath told the woman, while the other Baldies listened. *He's just drunk. I think I'm nearest, Burkhalter. I'm coming.*

A helicopter curved overhead, its freight-gliders swinging behind it, stabilized by their gyroscopes. It swept over the western ridge and was gone toward the Pacific. As its humming died, Burkhalter could hear the muffled roar of the cataract up the valley. He was vividly conscious of the waterfall's feathery whiteness plunging down the cliff, of the slopes of pine and fir and redwood around Sequoia, of the distant noise of the cellulose mills. He focused on these clean, familiar things to shut out the sickly foulness that blew from Selfridge's mind to his own. Sensibility and sensitivity had gone hand in hand with the Baldies, and Burkhalter had wondered more than once how Duke Heath managed to maintain his balance in view of the man's work among the psychiatric patients at the hospital. The race of Baldies had come too soon; they were not aggressive; but race-survival depended on competition.

He's in the tavern, a woman's thought said. Burkhalter automatically jerked away from the message; he knew the mind from which it came. Logic told him instantly that the source didn't matter – in this instance. Barbara Pell was a paranoid; therefore an enemy. But both paranoids and Baldies were desperately anxious to avoid any open break. Though their ultimate goals lay worlds apart, yet their paths sometimes paralleled.

But already it was too late. Fred Selfridge came out of the tavern, blinked against the sunlight, and saw Burkhalter. The trader's thin, hollow-cheeked face twisted into a sour grin. The blurred malignance of his thought drove before him as he walked toward Burkhalter, and one hand kept making little darts toward the misericordia swung at his belt.

He stopped before Burkhalter, blocking the Baldy's progress His grin broadened.

Burkhalter had paused. A dry panic tightened his throat. He was afraid, not for himself, but for his race, and every Baldy in Sequoia knew that – and watched.

He said 'Morning, Fred.'

Selfridge hadn't shaved that morning. Now he rubbed his stubbled chin and let his eyelids droop. 'Mr Burkhalter,' he said. '*Consul* Burkhalter. Good thing you remembered to wear a cap this morning. Skinheads catch cold pretty easy.'

Play for time, Duke Heath ordered. *I'm coming. I'll fix it.*

'I didn't pull any wires to get this job, Fred,' Burkhalter said. 'The Towns made me consul. Why blame me for it?'

'You pulled wires, all right,' Selfridge said. 'I know graft when I see it. You were a schoolteacher from Modoc or some hick town. What the devil do you know about Hedgehounds?'

'Not as much as you do,' Burkhalter admitted. 'You've had the experience.'

'Sure. Sure I have. So they take a half-baked teacher and make him consul to the Hedgehounds. A greenhorn who doesn't even know those bichos have got cannibal tribes. I traded with the woodsmen for thirty years, and I know how to handle 'em. Are you going to read 'em pretty little stories out of books?'

'I'll do what I'm told. I'm not the boss.'

'No. But maybe your friends are. Connections! If I'd had the same connections you've got, I'd be sitting on my tail like you, pulling in credits for the same work. Only I'd do that work better – a lot better.'

'I'm not interfering with your business,' Burkhalter said. 'You're still trading, aren't you? I'm minding my own affairs.'

'Are you? How do I know what you tell the Hedgehounds?'

'My records are open to anybody.'

'Yeah?'

'Sure. My job's just to promote peaceful relations with the Hedgehounds. Not to do any trading, except what *they* want – and then I refer 'em to you.'

'It sounds fine,' Selfridge said. 'Except for one thing. You can read my mind and tell the Hedgehounds all about my private business.'

Burkhalter's guard slipped; he couldn't have helped it. He had stood the man's mental nearness as long as he could, though it was like breathing foul air. 'Afraid of that?' he asked, and regretted the words instantly: The voices in his mind cried: *Careful!*

Selfridge flushed. 'So you do it after all, eh? All that fine talk about you skinheads respecting people's privacy – sure! No wonder you got the consulate! Reading minds –'

'Hold on,' Burkhalter said. 'I've never read a non-Baldy's mind in my life. That's the truth.'

'Is it?' the trader sneered. 'How the devil do I know if you're lying? But you can look inside my head and see if *I'm* telling the truth. What you Baldies need is to be taught your place, and for two coins I'd –'

Burkhalter's mouth felt stiff. 'I don't duel,' he said, with an effort. 'I won't duel.'

'Yellow,' Selfridge said, and waited, his hand hovering over the misericordia's hilt.

And there was the usual quandary. No telepath could possibly lose a duel with a non-Baldy, unless he wanted to commit suicide. But he dared not win, either. The Baldies baked their own humble pie; a minority that lives on sufferance must not reveal its superiority, or it won't survive. One such incident might have breached the dyke the telepaths had painfully erected against the rising tide of intolerance.

For the dyke was too long. It embraced all of mankind. And it was impossible to watch every inch of that incredible levee of custom, orientation and propaganda, though the basic tenets were instilled in each Baldy from infancy. Some day the dyke would collapse, but each hour of postponement meant the gathering of a little more strength –

Duke Heath's voice said, 'A guy like you, Selfridge, would be better off dead.'

Sudden shock touched Burkhalter. He shifted his gaze to the priest-medic, remembering the subtle tension he had recently sensed under Heath's deep calm, and wondering if this was the blowoff. Then he caught the thought in Heath's mind and relaxed, though warily.

Beside the Baldy was Ralph Selfridge, a smaller, slighter edition of Fred. He was smiling rather sheepishly.

Fred Selfridge showed his teeth. 'Listen, Heath,' he snapped. 'Don't try to stand on your position. You haven't got one. You're a surrogate. No skinhead can be a real priest *or* a medic.'

'Sure they can,' Heath said. 'But they don't.' His round, youthful face twisted into a scowl. 'Listen to me –'

'I'm not listening to –'

'Shut up!'

Selfridge gasped in surprise. He was caught flat-footed, undecided whether to use his misericordia or his fists, and while he hesitated, Heath went on angrily.

'I said you'd be better off dead and I meant it! This kid brother of yours thinks you're such a hotshot he imitates everything you do. Now look at him! If the epidemic hits Sequoia, he won't have enough resistance to work up antibodies, and the young idiot won't let me give him preventive shots. I suppose he thinks he can live on whiskey like you!' Fred Selfridge frowned at Heath, stared at his younger brother, and looked back at the priest-medic. He shook his head, trying to clear it.

'Leave Ralph alone. He's all right.'

'Well, start saving for his funeral expenses,' Heath said callously. 'As a surrogate medic, I'll make a prognosis right now – *rigor mortis*.'

Selfridge licked his lips. 'Wait a minute. The kid isn't sick, is he?'

'There's an epidemic down toward Columbia Crossing,' Heath said. 'One of the new virus mutations. If it hits us here, there'll be trouble. It's a bit like tetanus, but avertin's no good. Once the nerve centers are hit, nothing can be done. Preventive shots will help a lot, especially when a man's got the susceptible blood-type – as Ralph has.'

Burkhalter caught a command from Heath's mind.

'You could use some shots yourself, Fred,' the priest-medic went on. 'Still, your blood type is B, isn't it? And you're tough enough to throw off an infection. This virus is something new, a mutation of the old flu bug –'

He went on. Across the street someone called Burkhalter's name and the consul slipped away, unnoticed except for a parting glare from Selfridge.

A slim, red-haired girl was waiting under a tree at the corner. Burkhalter grimaced inwardly as he saw he could not avoid her. He was never quite able to control the turmoil of feeling which the very sight or thought of Barbara Pell stirred up within him. He met her bright narrow eyes, full of pinpoints of light. He saw her round slimness that looked so soft and would, he thought, be as hard to the touch as her mind was hard to the thought's touch. Her bright red wig, almost too luxuriant, spilled heavy curls down about the square, alert face to move like red Medusa-locks upon her shoulders when she turned her head. Curiously, she had a redhead's typical face, high-cheekboned, dangerously alive. There is a quality of the red-haired that goes deeper than the hair, for Barbara Pell had, of course, been born as hairless as any Baldy.

'You're a fool,' she said softly as he came up beside her. 'Why don't you get rid of Selfridge?'

Burkhalter shook his head. 'No. And don't you try anything.'

'I tipped you off that he was in the tavern. And I got here before anybody else, except Heath. If we could work together –'

'We can't.'

'Dozens of times we've saved you traitors,' the woman said bitterly. 'Will you wait until the humans stamp out your lives –'

Burkhalter walked past her and turned toward the pathway that climbed the steep ascent leading out of Sequoia. He was vividly aware of Barbara Pell looking after him. He could see her as clearly as if he had eyes in the back of his head, her bright, dangerous face, her beautiful body, her bright, beautiful, insane thoughts –

For behind all their hatefulness, the paranoids' vision was as beautiful and tempting as the beauty of Barbara Pell. Perilously tempting. A free world, where Baldies could walk and live and think in safety, no longer bending the scope of their minds into artificial, cramping limits as once men bent their backs in subservience to their masters. A bent back is a humiliating thing, but even a serf's mind is free to range. To cramp the mind is to cramp the soul, and no humiliation could surpass the humiliation of that.

But there was no such world as the paranoids dreamed of. The price would be too high. What shall it profit a man, thought Burkhalter wryly, if he gain the whole world and lose his own soul? The words might first have been spoken in this connection and no other, so perfectly did they apply to it. The price must be murder, and whoever paid that price would automatically sully the world he bought with it until, if he were a normal creature, he could never enjoy what he had paid so high to earn. Burkhalter called up a bit of verse into his mind and savored again the bitter melancholy of the poet who wrote it, perhaps more completely than the poet himself ever dreamed.

I see the country, far away,
Where I shall never stand.
The heart goes where no footstep may,
Into the promised land.

Barbara Pell's mind shot after him an angry, evil shaft of scorn and hatred. 'You're a fool, you're all fools, you don't deserve telepathy if you degrade it. If you'd only join us in –' The thought ceased to be articulate and ran suddenly, gloatingly red with spilled blood, reeking saltily of it, as if her whole mind bathed deliciously in the blood of all humans.

Burkhalter jerked his thoughts away from contact with hers, sickened. It isn't the end of free living they want any more, he told himself in sudden realization – it's the means they're lusting after now. They've lost sight of a free world. All they want is killing.

'Fool, fool, fool!' Barbara Pell's thoughts screamed after him. 'Wait and see! Wait until – one times two is two, two times two is four, three times two –'

Burkhalter thought grimly, 'They're up to something,' and sent his mind probing gingerly past the sudden artificial barrier with which she had sought to blank out a thought even she realized was indiscreet. She fought the probing viciously. He sensed only vague, bloody visions stirring behind the barrier. Then she laughed without a sound and hurled a clear, terrible, paranoid thought at him, a picture of sickening clarity that all but splashed in his face with its overrunning redness.

He drew his mind back with swiftness that was pure reflex. As safe to touch fire as thoughts like hers. It was one way any paranoid could shut out the inquisitive thoughts of a non paranoid when need arose. And of course, normally no Baldy would dream of probing uninvited into another mind. Burkhalter shuddered.

They were up to something, certainly. He must pass the episode on to those whose business it was to know about the paranoids. Barbara Pell's mind was not, in any case, likely to yield much information on secret plans. She was an executioner, not a planner. He withdrew his thoughts from her, fastidiously, shaking off the contamination as a cat shakes water from its feet.

He climbed the steep slope that led out of Sequoia to his home, deliberately shutting his mind from all things behind him. Fifteen minutes' walk brought him to the rustic log-and-plastic house built near the shadow of the West Canadian Forest. This was his consulate, and only the cabin of the Selfridge brothers lay farther out in the wilderness that stretched north to the Beaufort Sea that mingles with the Arctic Ocean.

By his desk a glowing red light indicated a message in the terminal of the pneumatic that stretched for six miles into the forest. He read it carefully. A delegation of Hedgehounds would arrive soon, representatives from three tribal groups. Well –

He checked supplies, televised the general store, and sat down behind his desk to wait. Heath would be along soon. Meanwhile he closed his eyes and concentrated on the fresh smell of pine that blew through the open windows. But the fresh, clean scent was sullied by vagrant thought currents that tainted the air.

Burkhalter shivered.

II

Sequoia lay near the border of old Canada, now an immense wilderness that the forest had largely reclaimed. Cellulose by-products were its industry, and there was an immense psychiatric hospital, which accounted for the high percentage of Baldies in the village. Otherwise Sequoia was distinguished from the hundreds of thousands of other towns that dotted America by the recent establishment of a diplomatic station there, the consulate that would be a means of official contact with the wandering tribes that retreated into the forests as civilization encroached. It was a valley town, bordered by steep slopes, with their enormous conifers and the white-water cataracts racing down from snowy summits. Not far westward, beyond the Strait of Georgia and Vancouver Island, lay the Pacific. But there were few highways; transport was aerial. And communication was chiefly by teleradio.

Four hundred people, more or less, lived in Sequoia, a tight little semi-independent settlement, bartering its specialized products for shrimps and pompano from Lafitte; books from Modoc; beryllium-steel daggers and motor-plows from American Gun; clothing from Dempsey and Gee Eye. The Boston textile mills were gone with Boston; that smoking, gray desolation had not changed since the year of the Blowup. But there was still plenty of room in America, no matter how much the population might increase; war had thinned the population. And as technology advanced so did improvements in reclamation of arid and unfertile land, and the hardier strains of the kudzu plant had already opened vast new tracts for farming. But agriculture was not the only industry. The towns specialized, never expanding into cities, but sending out spores that would grow into new villages – or, rather, reaching out like raspberry canes, to take root whenever they touched earth.

Burkhalter was deliberately not thinking of the red-haired woman when Duke Heath came in. The priest-medic caught the strained, negative mental picture, and nodded.

'Barbara Pell,' he said. 'I saw her.' Both men blurred the surface of their minds. That couldn't mask their thoughts, but if any other brain began probing, there would be an instant's warning, during which they could take precautions. Necessarily, however, the conversation stayed oral rather than telepathic.

'They can smell trouble coming,' Burkhalter said. 'They've been infiltrating Sequoia lately, haven't they?'

'Yes. The minute you copped this consulate, they started to come in.' Heath nibbled his knuckles. 'In forty years the paranoids have built up quite an organization.'

'Sixty years,' Burkhalter said. 'My grandfather saw it coming back in '82. There was a paranoid in Modoc – a lone wolf at the time, but it was one of the first symptoms. And since then –'

'Well, they've grown qualitatively, not quantitatively. There are more true Baldies now than paranoids. Psychologically they're handicapped. They hate to intermarry with non-Baldies. Whereas *we* do, and the dominant strain goes on – spreads out.'

'For a while,' Burkhalter said.

Heath frowned. 'There's no epidemic at Columbia Crossing. I had to get Selfridge off your neck somehow, and he's got a strongly paternal instinct toward his brother. That did it – but not permanently. With that so-and-so, the part equals the whole. You got the consulate; he had a nice little racket gypping the Hedgehounds; he hates you – so he jumps on your most vulnerable point. Also, he rationalizes. He tells himself that if you didn't have the unfair advantage of being a Baldy, you'd never have landed the consulate.'

'It was unfair.'

'We had to do it,' Heath said. 'Non-Baldies mustn't find out what we're building up among the Hedgehounds. Some day the woods folk may be our only safety. If a non-Baldy had got the consulate –'

'I'm working in the dark,' Burkhalter said. 'All I know is that I've got to do what the Mutes tell me.'

'I don't know any more than you do. The paranoids have their Power – that secret band of communication we can't tap – and only the Mutes have a method of fighting that weapon. Don't forget that, while we can't read a Mute's mind, the paranoids can't either. If you knew their secrets, your mind would be an open book – any telepath could read it.'

Burkhalter didn't answer. Heath sighed and watched pine needles glittering in the sunlight outside the windows.

'It's not easy for me either,' he said. 'To be a surrogate. No non-Baldy has to be a priest as well as a medic. But I have to. The doctors up at the hospital feel more strongly about it than I do. They know how many psychotic cases have been cured because we can read minds. Meanwhile –' He shrugged.

Burkhalter was staring northward. 'A new land is what we need,' he said.

'We need a new world. Some day we'll get it.'

A shadow fell across the door. Both men turned. A small figure was standing there, a fat little man with close-curling hair and mild blue eyes. The misericordia at his belt seemed incongruous, as though those pudgy fingers would fumble ludicrously with the hilt.

No Baldy will purposely read a nontelepath's mind, but there is an instinctive recognition between Baldies. So Burkhalter and Heath knew instantly that the stranger was a telepath – and then, on the heels of that thought, came sudden, startled recognition of the emptiness where thought should be. It was like stepping on clear ice and finding it clear water instead. Only a few men could guard their minds completely thus. They were the Mutes.

'Hello,' said the stranger, coming in and perching himself on the desk's edge. 'I see you know me. We'll stay oral, if you don't mind. I can read your thoughts, but you can't read mine.' He grinned. 'No use wondering why, Burkhalter. If *you* knew, the paranoids would find out too. Now. My name's

Ben Hobson.' He paused. 'Trouble, eh? Well, we'll kick that around later. First let me get this off my chest.'

Burkhalter sent a swift glance at Heath. 'There are paranoids in town. Don't tell me too much, unless –'

'Don't worry. I won't,' Hobson chuckled. 'What do you know about the Hedgehounds?'

'Descendants of the nomad tribes that didn't join the villages after the Blowup. Gypsies. Woods folk. Friendly enough.'

'That's right,' Hobson said. 'Now what I'm telling you is common knowledge, even among the paranoids. You should know it. We've spotted a few cells among the Hedgehounds – Baldies. It started by accident, forty years ago, when a Baldy named Linc Cody was adopted by Hedgehounds and reared without knowing his heritage. Later he found out. He's still living with the Hedgehounds, and so are his sons.'

'Cody?' Burkhalter said slowly. 'I've heard stories of the Cody –'

'Psychological propaganda. The Hedgehounds are barbarians. But we want 'em friendly and we want to clear the way, for joining them, if that ever becomes necessary. Twenty years ago we started building up a figurehead in the forests, a living symbol who'd be overtly a shaman and really a delegate for us. We used mumbo-jumbo. Linc Cody dressed up in a trick suit, we gave him gadgets, and the Hedgehounds finally developed the legend of the Cody – a sort of benevolent woods spirit who acts as supernatural monitor. They like him, they obey him, and they're afraid of him. Especially since he can appear in four places at the same time.'

'Eh?' Burkhalter said.

'Cody had three sons,' Hobson smiled. 'It's one of them you'll see today. Your friend Selfridge has fixed up a little plot. You're due to be murdered by one of the Hedgehound chiefs when that delegation gets here. I can't interfere personally, but the Cody will. It's necessary for you to play along. Don't give any sign that you expect trouble. When the Cody steps in, the chiefs will be plenty impressed.'

Heath said, 'Wouldn't it have been better not to tell Burkhalter what to expect?'

'No. For two reasons. He can read the Hedgehounds' minds – I give him carte blanche on that – and he must string along with the Cody. O.K., Burkhalter?'

'O.K.' the consul nodded.

'Then I'll push off.' Hobson stood up, still smiling. 'Good luck.'

'Wait a minute,' Heath said. 'What about Selfridge?'

'Don't kill him. Either of you. You know no Baldy must ever duel a non-Baldy.'

Burkhalter was scarcely listening. He knew he must mention the thought he had surprised in Barbara Pell's mind, and he had been putting off the moment when he must speak her hateful name, open the gates of his thoughts wide enough to let her image slip back in, beautiful image, beautiful slender body, bright and dangerous and insane mind –

'I saw one of the paranoids in town a while ago,' he said. 'Barbara Pell. A nasty job, that woman. She let slip something about their plans. Covered up too fast for me to get much, but you might think about it. They're up to something planned for fairly soon, I gathered.'

Hobson smiled at him. 'Thanks. We're watching them. We'll keep an eye on the woman too. All right, then. Good luck.'

He went out. Burkhalter and Heath looked at one another.

The Mute walked slowly down the path toward the village. His mouth was pursed as he whistled; his plump cheeks vibrated. As he passed a tall pine he abruptly unsheathed his dagger and sprang around the tree. The man lurking there was caught by surprise. Steel found its mark unerringly. The paranoid had time for only one desperate mental cry before he died.

Hobson wiped his dagger and resumed his journey. Under the close cropped brown wig a mechanism, shaped like a skull-cap, began functioning. Neither Baldy nor telepath could receive the signals Hobson was sending and receiving now.

'They know I'm here.'

'Sometimes they do,' a soundless voice came back. 'They can't catch these modulated frequencies the helmets use, but they can notice the shield. Still, as long as none of 'em know why –'

'I just killed one.'

'One less of the bichos,' came the coldly satisfied response.

'I think I'd better stay here for a while. Paranoids have been infiltrating. Both Heath and Burkhalter think so. There's some contingent plan I can't read yet; the paranoids are thinking about it only on their own band.'

'Then stay. Keep in touch. What about Burkhalter?'

'What we suspected. He's in love with the paranoid Barbara Pell. But he doesn't know it.'

Both shocked abhorrence and unwilling sympathy were in the answering thought. 'I can't remember anything like this ever happening before. He can read her mind; he knows she's paranoid –'

Hobson smiled. 'The realization of his true feelings would upset him plenty, Jerry. Apparently you picked the wrong man for this job.'

'Not from Burkhalter's record. He's always lived a pretty secluded life, but his character's above reproach. His empathy standing was high. And he taught sociology for six years at New Yale.'

'He taught it, but I think it remained remote. He's known Barbara Pell for six weeks now. He's in love with her.'

'But how – even subconsciously? Baldies instinctively hate and distrust the paranoids.'

Hobson reached Sequoia's outskirts and kept going, past the terraced square where the blocky, insulated power station sat. 'So it's perverse,' he told the other Mute. 'Some men are attracted only to ugly women. You can't argue with a thing like that. Burkhalter's fallen in love with a paranoid, and I hope to heaven he never realizes it. He might commit suicide. Or anything might happen. This is –' His thought moved with slow emphasis. 'This is the most dangerous situation the Baldies have ever faced. Apparently nobody's paid much attention to Selfridge's talk, but the damage has been done. People *have* listened. And non-Baldies have always mistrusted us. If there's a blowoff, we're automatically the scapegoats.'

'Like that, Ben?'

'The pogrom may start in Sequoia.'

Once the chess game had started, there was no way to stop it. It was cumulative. The paranoids, the warped twin branch of the parallel telepathic mutation, were not insane; there was a psychoneurotic pathology. They had only one basic delusion. They were the super race. On that foundation they built their edifice of planetary sabotage.

Non-Baldies outnumbered them, and they could not fight the technology that flourished in the days of decentralization. But if the culture of the non-Baldies were weakened, wrecked –

Assassinations, deftly disguised as duels or accidents; secret sabotage in a hundred branches, from engineering to publishing; propaganda, carefully sowed in the proper places – and civilization would have headed for a crack-up, except for one check.

The Baldies, the true, non-paranoid mutation, were fighting for the older race. They had to. They knew, as the blinded paranoids could not, that eventually the non-Baldies would learn of the chess game, and then nothing could stop a world-wide pogrom.

One advantage the paranoids had, for a while – a specialized band on which they could communicate telepathically, a wave length which could not be tapped. Then a Baldy technician had perfected the scrambler helmets, with a high-frequency modulation that was equally untappable. As long as a Baldy wore such a helmet under his wig, his mind could be read only by another Mute.

So they came to be called, a small, tight group of exterminators, sworn to destroy the paranoids completely – in effect, a police force, working in secret and never doffing the helmets which shut them out from the complete rapport that played so large a part in the psychic life of the Baldy race.

They had willingly given up a great part of their heritage. It was a curious paradox that only by strictly limiting their telepathic power could these few Baldies utilize their weapon against the paranoids. And what they fought for was the time of ultimate unification when the dominant mutation had become so numerically strong that in all the world, there would be no need for mental barriers or psychic embargoes.

Meanwhile the most powerful of the Baldy race, they could never know, except within a limited scope, the subtle gratification of the mental round-robins, when a hundred or a thousand minds would meet and merge into the deep, eternal peace that only telepaths can know.

They, too, were beggars in velvet.

III

Burkhalter said suddenly, 'What's the matter with you, Duke?'

Heath didn't move. 'Nothing.'

'Don't give me that. Your thoughts are on quicksand.'

'Maybe they are,' Heath said. 'The fact is, I need a rest. I love this work, but it does get me down sometimes,'

'Well, take a vacation.'

'Can't. We're too busy. Our reputation's so good we're getting cases from all over. We're one of the first mental sanitariums to go in for all-out Baldy psychoanalysis. It's been going on, of course, for years but *sub rosa*, more or less. People don't like the idea of Baldies prying into the minds of their relatives. However, since we started to show results –' His eyes lit up. 'Even with psychosomatic illnesses we can help a lot, and mood disorders are our meat. The big question, you know, is *why*. Why they've been putting poison in the patient's food, why they watch him – and so forth. Once that question's answered fully, it usually gives the necessary clues. And the average patient's apt to shut up like a clam when the psychiatrist questions him. But –' Heath's excitement mounted, 'this is the biggest thing in the history of medicine. There've been Baldies since the Blowup, and only now are the doctors opening their doors to us. Ultimate empathy. A psychotic locks his mind, so he's hard to treat. But *we* have the keys –'

'What are you afraid of?' Burkhalter asked quietly.

Heath stopped short. He examined his fingernails.

'It's not fear,' he said at last. 'It's occupational anxiety. Oh, the devil with that. Four-bit words. It's simpler, really; you can put it in the form of an axiom. You can't touch pitch without getting soiled.'

'I see.'

'Do you, Harry? It's only this, really. My work consists of visiting abnormal minds. Not the way an ordinary psychiatrist does it. I get into those minds. I see and feel their viewpoints. I know all their terrors. The invisible horror that waits in the dark for them isn't just a word to me. I'm sane, and I see through the eyes of a hundred insane men. Keep out of my mind for a minute, Harry.' He turned away. Burkhalter hesitated.

'O.K.,' Heath said, looking around. 'I'm glad you mentioned this, though. Every so often I find myself getting entirely too empathic. Then I either take my copter up, or get in a round robin. I'll see if I can promote a hook-up tonight. Are you in?'

'Sure,' Burkhalter said. Heath nodded casually and went out. His thought came back.

I'd better not be here when the Hedgehounds come. Unless you –

No, Burkhalter thought, *I'll be all right.*

O.K. Here's a delivery for you.

Burkhalter opened the door in time to admit the grocer's boy, who had parked his trail car outside. He helped put the supplies away, saw that the beer would be sufficiently refrigerated, and pressed a few buttons that would insure a supply of pressure-cooked refreshments. The Hedgehounds were hearty eaters.

After that, he left the door open and relaxed behind his desk, waiting. It was hot in the office; he opened his collar and made the walls transparent. Air conditioning began to cool the room, but sight of the broad valley below was equally refreshing. Tall pines rippled their branches in the wind.

It was not like New Yale, one of the larger towns, that was intensely specialized in education. Sequoia, with its great hospital and its cellulose industry, was more of a complete, rounded unit. Isolated from the rest of the world except by air and television, it lay clean and attractive, sprawling in white and green and pastel plastics around the swift waters of the river that raced down seaward.

Burkhalter locked his hands behind his neck and yawned. He felt inexplicably fatigued, as he had felt from time to time for several weeks. Not that this work was hard; on the contrary. But reorientation to his new job wouldn't be quite as easy as he had expected. In the beginning he hadn't anticipated these wheels within wheels.

Barbara Pell, for example. She was dangerous. She, more than any of the others, perhaps, was the guiding spirit of the Sequoia paranoids. Not in the sense of planned action, no. But she ignited, like a flame. She was a born leader. And there were uncomfortably many paranoids here now. They had infiltrated – superficially with good reason, on jobs or errands or vacations; but the town was crammed with them; comparatively speaking. The nontelepaths still outnumbered both Baldies and paranoids as they did on a larger scale all over the world –

He remembered his grandfather, Ed Burkhalter. If any Baldy had ever hated the paranoids, Ed Burkhalter had. And presumably with good reason, since one of the first paranoid plots – a purely individual attempt then – had indirectly tried to indoctrinate the mind of Ed's son, Harry Burkhalter's father. Oddly, Burkhalter remembered his grandfather's thin, harsh face more vividly than his father's gentler one.

He yawned again, trying to immerse himself in the calm of the vista beyond the windows. Another world? Perhaps only in deep space could a Baldy ever be completely free from those troubling half-fragments of thoughts that he sensed even now. And without that continual distraction, with one's mind utterly unhampered – he stretched luxuriously, trying to imagine the feeling of his body without gravity, and extending that parallel to his mind. But it was impossible.

The Baldies had been born before their time, of course – an artificially hastened mutation caused by radioactivity acting on human genes and chromosomes. Thus their present environment was wrong. Burkhalter toyed idly with the concept of a deep-space race, each individual mind so delicately attuned that even the nearness of any alien personality would interfere with the smooth processes of perfect thought. Pleasant, but impractical. It would be a dead end. The telepaths weren't supermen, as the paranoids contended; at best they had only one fatally miraculous sense – fatal, because it had been mingled with common clay. With a genuine superman, telepathy would be merely one sense among a dozen other inconceivable ones.

Whereas Barbara Pell – the name and the face slid into his thoughts again, and the beautiful body, as dangerous and as fascinating as fire – whereas Barbara Pell, for instance, undoubtedly considered herself strictly super, like all the warped telepaths of her kind.

He thought of her bright, narrow gaze, and the red mouth with its sneering smile. He thought of the red curls moving like snakes upon her shoulders, and the red thoughts moving like snakes through her mind. He stopped thinking of her.

He was very tired. The sense of fatigue, all out of proportion to the energy he had expended, swelled and engulfed him. If the Hedgehound chiefs weren't coming, it would be pleasant to take a copter up. The inclosing walls of the mountains would fall away as the plane lifted into the empty blue, higher and higher, till it hung in space above a blurred featureless landscape, half-erased by drifting clouds. Burkhalter thought of how the ground would look, a misty, dreamy Sime illustration, and, in his daydream, he reached out slowly to touch the controls. The copter slanted down, more and more steeply, till it was flashing suicidally toward a world that spread hypnotically, like a magically expanding carpet.

*

Someone was coming. Burkhalter blurred his mind instantly and stood up. Beyond the open door was only the empty forest, but now he could hear the faint, rising overtones of a song. The Hedgehounds, being a nation of nomads, sang as they marched, old tunes and ballads of memorable simplicity that had come down unchanged from before the Blowup, though the original meanings had been forgotten.

Green grow the lilacs, all sparkling with dew;
I'm lonely, my darling, since parting from you –

Ancestors of the Hedgehounds had hummed that song along the borders of Old Mexico, long before war had been anything but distantly romantic. The grandfather of one of the current singers had been a Mexican, drifting up the California coast, dodging the villages and following a lazy wanderlust that led him into the Canadian forests at last. His name had been Ramon Alvarez but his grandson's name was Kit Carson Alvers, and his black beard rippled as he sang.

But by our next meeting I'll hope to prove true,
And change the green lilacs for the red, white and blue.

There were no minstrels among the Hedgehounds – they were all minstrels, which is how folk songs are kept alive. Singing, they came down the path, and fell silent at sight of the consul's house.

Burkhalter watched. It was a chapter of the past come alive before his eyes. He had read of the Hedgehounds, but not until six weeks ago had he encountered any of the new pioneers. Their bizarre costumes still had power to intrigue him.

Those costumes combined functionalism with decoration. The buckskin shirts, that could blend into a pattern of forest light and shade, were fringed with knotted tassels; Alvers had a coonskin cap, and all three men wore sandals, made of soft, tough kidskin. Sheathed knives were at their belts, hunting knives, plainer and shorter than the misericordias of the townsfolk. And their faces showed a rakehell vigor, a lean, brown independence of spirit that made them brothers. For generations now the Hedgehounds had been wresting their living from the wilderness with such rude weapons as the bow one of them had slung across his shoulder, and the ethics of dueling had never developed among them. They didn't duel. They killed, when killing seemed necessary – for survival.

Burkhalter came to the threshold. 'Come in,' he said. 'I'm the consul – Harry Burkhalter.'

'You got our message?' asked a tall, Scottish-looking chief with a bushy red beard. 'That thing you got rigged up in the woods looked tetchy.'

'The message conveyor? It works, all right.'

'Fair enough. I'm Cobb Mattoon. This here's Kit Carson Alvers, and this un's Umpire Vine.' Vine was clean-shaven, a barrel of a man who looked like a bear, his sharp brown eyes slanting wary glances all around. He gave a taciturn grunt and shook hands with Burkhalter. So did the others. As the Baldy gripped Alvers' palm, he knew that this was the man who intended to kill him.

He made no sign. 'Glad you're here. Sit down and have a drink. What'll you have?'

'Whiskey,' Vine grunted. His enormous hands smothered the glass. He grinned at the siphon, shook his head, and gulped a quantity of whiskey that made Burkhalter's throat smart in sympathy.

Alvers, too, took whiskey; Mattoon drank gin, with lemon. 'You got a smart lot of drinks here,' he said, staring at the bar Burkhalter had swung out. 'I can make out to spell some of the labels, but – what's that?'

'Drambuie. Try it?'

'Sure,' Mattoon said, and his red-haired throat worked. 'Nice stuff. Better than the corn we cook up in the woods.'

'If you walked far, you'll be hungry,' Burkhalter said. He pulled out the oval table, selected covered dishes from the conveyor belt, and let his guests help themselves. They fell to without ceremony.

Alvers looked across the table. 'You one of them Baldies?' he asked suddenly.

Burkhalter nodded. 'Yes, I am. Why?'

Mattoon said, 'So you're one of 'em.' He was frankly staring. 'I never seen a Baldy right close up. Maybe I have at that, but with the wigs you can't tell, of course.'

Burkhalter grinned as he repressed a familiar feeling of sick distaste. He had been stared at before, and for the same reason.

'Do I look like a freak, Mr Mattoon?'

'How long you been consul?' Mattoon asked.

'Six weeks.'

'O.K.,' the big man said, and his voice was friendly enough, though the tone was harsh. 'You oughta remember there ain't no Mistering with the Hedgehounds. I'm Cobb Mattoon. Cobb to my friends, Mattoon to the rest. Nope, you don't look like no freak. Do people figger you Baldies are all sports?'

'A good many of them,' Burkhalter said.

'One thing,' Mattoon said, picking up a chop bone, 'in the woods, we pay no heed to such things. If a guy's born funny, we don't mock him for that. Not so long as he sticks to the tribe and plays square. We got no Baldies among us, but if we did, I kind of think they might get a better deal than they do here.'

Vine grunted and poured more whiskey. Alvers' black eyes were fixed steadily on Burkhalter.

'You readin' my mind?' Mattoon demanded. Alvers drew in his breath sharply.

Without looking at him, Burkhalter said, 'No. Baldies don't. It isn't healthy.'

'True enough. Minding your own business is a plenty good rule. I can see how you'd have to play it. Look. This is the first time we come down here, Alvers and Vine and me. You ain't seen us before. We heard rumors about this consulate –' He stumbled over the unfamiliar word. 'Up to now, we traded with Selfridge sometimes, but we didn't have contact with townsfolk. You know why.'

Burkhalter knew. The Hedgehounds had been outcasts, shunning the villages, and sometimes raiding them. They were outlaws.

'But now a new time's coming. We can't live in the towns; we don't want to. But there's room enough for everybody. We still don't see why they set up these con-consulates; still, we'll string along. We got a word.'

Burkhalter knew about that, too. It was the Cody's word, whispered through the Hedgehound tribes – a word they would not disobey.

He said, 'Some of the Hedgehound tribes ought to be wiped out. Not many. You kill them yourselves, whenever you find them –'

'Th' cannibals,' Mattoon said. 'Yeah. We kill them.'

'But they're a minority. The main group of Hedgehounds have no quarrel with the townsfolk. And vice versa. We want to stop the raids.'

'How do you figger on doin' that?'

'If a tribe has a bad winter, it needn't starve. We've methods of making foods. It's a cheap method. We can afford to let you have grub when you're hungry.'

Vine slammed his whiskey glass down on the table and snarled something. Mattoon patted the air with a large palm.

'Easy, Umpire. He don't know … listen, Burkhalter. The Hedgehounds raid sometimes, sure. They hunt, and they fight for what they get. But they don't beg.'

'I'm talking about barter,' Burkhalter said. 'Fair exchange. We can't set up force shields around every village. And we can't use Eggs on nomads. A lot of raids would be a nuisance, that's all. There haven't been many raids so far; they've been lessening every year. But why should there be any at all? Get rid of the motivation, and the effect's gone too.'

Unconsciously he probed at Alvers' mind. There was a thought there, a sly crooked hungry thought, the avid alertness of a carnivore – and the concept of a hidden weapon. Burkhalter jerked back. He didn't want to know. He had to wait for the Cody to move though the temptation to provoke an open battle with Alvers was dangerously strong. Yet that would only antagonize the other Hedgehounds; they couldn't read Alvers' mind as Burkhalter could.

'Barter what?' Vine grunted.

Burkhalter had the answer ready. 'Pelts. There's a demand for them. They're fashionable.' He didn't mention that it was an artificially created fad. 'Furs, for one thing. And –'

'We ain't Red Indians,' Mattoon said. 'Look what happened to them! There ain't nothing we need from townsfolk, except when we're starving. Then – well, maybe we can barter.'

'If the Hedgehounds unified –'

Alvers grinned. 'In the old days,' he said, in a high, thin voice, 'the tribes that unified got dusted off with the Eggs. We ain't unifying, brother!'

'He speaks fair, though,' Mattoon said. 'It makes sense. It was our granddaddies who had a feud with the villages. We've shaken down pretty well. My tribe ain't gone hungry for seven winters now. We migrate, we go where the pickin's are good and we get along.'

'My tribe don't raid,' Vine growled. He poured more whiskey.

Mattoon and Alvers had taken only two drinks; Vine kept pouring it down, but his capacity seemed unlimited. Now Alvers said, 'It seems on the level. One thing I don't like. This guy's a Baldy.'

Vine turned his enormous barrel of a torso and regarded Alvers steadily. 'What you got against Baldies?' he demanded.

'We don't know nothing about 'em. I heard stories –'

Vine said something rude. Mattoon laughed.

'You ain't polite, Kit Carson. Burkhalter's playin' host. Don't go throwing words around.'

Alvers shrugged, glanced away, and stretched. He reached into his shirt to scratch himself – and suddenly the thought of murder hit Burkhalter like a stone from a slingshot. It took every ounce of his will power to remain motionless as Alvers' hand slid back into view, a pistol coming into sight with it.

There was time for the other Hedgehounds to see the weapon, but no time for them to interfere. The death-thought anticipated the bullet. A flare of blinding, crimson light blazed through the room. Something, moving like an invisible whirlwind, flashed among them; then, as their eyes adjusted, they stood where they had leaped from their chairs, staring at the figure who confronted them.

He wore a tight-fitting suit of scarlet, with a wide black belt, and an expressionless mask of silver covered his face. A blue-black beard emerged from under it and rippled down his chest. Enormous muscular development showed beneath the skin-tight garments.

He tossed Alvers' pistol into the air and caught it. Then, with a deep, chuckling laugh, he gripped the weapon in both hands and broke the gun into a twisted jumble of warped metal.

'Break a truce, will you?' he said. 'You little pipsqueak. What you need is the livin' daylights whaled outa you, Alvers.'

He stepped forward and smashed the flat of his palm against Alvers' side. The sound of the blow rang through the room. Alvers was lifted into the air and slammed against the further wall. He screamed once, dropped into a huddle, and lay there motionless.

'Git up,' the Cody said. 'You ain't hurt. Mebbe a rib cracked, that's all. If'n I'd smacked your head, I'd have broke your neck clean. Git up!'

Alvers dragged himself upright, his face dead white and sweating. The other two Hedgehounds watched, impassive and alert.

'Deal with you later on. Mattoon. Vine. What you got to do with this?'

'Nuthin',' Mattoon said. 'Nuthin', Cody. You know that.'

The silver mask was impassive. 'Lucky fer you I do. Now listen. What I say goes. Tell Alvers' tribe they'll have to find a new boss. That's all.'

He stepped forward. His arms closed about Alvers, and the Hedgehound yelled in sudden panic. Then the red blaze flared out again. When it had died, both figures were gone.

'Got any more whiskey, Burkhalter?' Vine said.

IV

The Cody was in telepathic communication with the Mute, Hobson. Like the other three Codys, this one wore the same modulated-frequency helmet as the Mutes; it was impossible for any Baldy or paranoid to tune in on that scrambled, camouflaged wave length

It was two hours after sundown.

Alvers is dead, Hobson. Telepathy has no colloquialisms that can be expressed in language-symbols.

Necessary?

Yes. Absolute obedience to the Cody – a curiously mingled four-in-one concept – *is vital. Nobody can be allowed to defy the Cody and get away with it.*

Any repercussions?

None. Mattoon and Vine are agreeable. They got along with Burkhalter. What's wrong with him, Hobson?

The moment the question was asked, the Cody knew the answer. Telepaths have no secrets but subconscious ones – and the Mute helmet can even delve a little into the secret mind.

In love with a paranoid? The Cody was shocked.

He doesn't know it. He mustn't realize it yet. He'd have to reorient; that would

take time; we can't afford to have him in the side lines just now. Trouble's bound to pop.

What?

Fred Selfridge. He's drunk. He found out the Hedgehound chief visited Burkhalter today. He's afraid his trading racket is being cut from under him. I've told Burkhalter to stay out of sight.

I'll stay near here, then, in case I'm needed. I won't go home yet. Briefly Hobson caught sight of what home meant to the Cody; a secret valley in the Canadian wilderness, its whereabouts known only to wearers of the helmets, who could never betray it inadvertently. It was there that the technicians among the Baldies sent their specialized products – via the Mutes. Products which had managed to build up a fully equipped headquarters in the heart of the forest, a centralization, it was true, but one whose whereabouts were guarded very thoroughly from the danger of discovery by either friend or enemy. From that valley laboratory in the woods came devices that made the Cody the legendary figure he was among the Hedgehounds – a Paul Bunyan who combined incredible physical prowess with pure magic. Only such a figure could have commanded the respect and obedience of the woods runners.

Is Burkhalter safely hidden, Hobson? Or can I –

He's hidden. There's a round robin on, but Selfridge can't trace him through that.

O.K. I'll wait.

The Cody broke off. Hobson sent his thought probing out, across the dark miles, to a dozen other Mutes, scattered across the continent from Niagara to Salton. Each one of them was ready for the underground mobilization that might be necessary at any moment now.

It had taken ninety years for the storm to gather; its breaking would be cataclysmic.

Within the circle of the round robin was quiet, complete peace that only a Baldy can know. Burkhalter let his mind slip into place among the others, briefly touching and recognizing friends as he settled into that telepathic closed circuit. He caught the faintly troubled unrest from Duke Heath's thoughts; then the deep calm of rapport swallowed them both.

At first, on the outer fringes of the psychic pool, there were ripples and currents of mild disturbance, the casual distresses that are inevitable in any gregarious society, and especially among hypersensitive Baldies. But the purge of the ancient custom of the confessional quickly began to be effective. There can be no barriers between Baldies. The basic unit of the family is far more complete than among nontelepaths, and by extension, the entire Baldy group was bound together with ties no less strong because of their intangible subtlety.

Trust and friendship: these things were certain. There could be no distrust when the tariff wall of language was eliminated. The ancient loneliness of any highly specialized, intelligent organism was mitigated in the only possible way; by a kinship closer even than marriage, and transcending it.

Any minority group as long as it maintains its specialized integrity, is automatically handicapped. It is suspect. Only the Baldies, in all social history, had been able to mingle on equal terms with the majority group and still retain the close bond of kinship. Which was paradoxical, for the Baldies, perhaps, were the only ones who desired racial assimilation. They could afford to, for the telepathic mutation was dominant: the children of Baldy father and nontelepathic mother – or vice versa – are Baldies.

But the reassurance of the round robins was needed; they were a symbol of the passive battle the Baldies had been fighting for generations. In them the telepaths found complete unity. It did not, and never would, destroy the vital competitive instinct; rather, it encouraged it. There was give and take. And, too, it was religion of the purest kind.

In the beginning, with no senses that non-Baldies can quite understand, you touched the minds of your friends, delicately, sensitively. There was a place for you, and you were welcomed. Slowly, as the peace spread, you approached the center, that quite indescribable position in space time that was a synthesis of intelligent, vital minds. Only by analogy can that locus even be suggested.

It is half-sleep. It is like the moment during which consciousness returns sufficiently so that you know you are not awake, and can appreciate the complete calm relaxation of slumber. If you could retain consciousness while you slept – that might be it.

For there was no drugging. The sixth sense is tuned to its highest pitch, and it intermingles with and draws from the other senses. Each Baldy contributes. At first the troubles and disturbances, the emotional unbalances and problems, are cast into the pool, examined, and dissolved in the crystal water of the rapport. Then, cleansed and strengthened, the Baldies approach the center, where the minds blend into a single symphony. Nuances of color one member has appreciated, shadings of sound and light and feeling, each one is a grace note in orchestration. And each note is three-dimensional, for it carries with it the Baldy's personal, individual reaction to the stimulus.

Here a woman remembered the sensuous feel of soft velvet against her palm, with its corresponding mental impact. Here a man gave the crystal-sharp pleasure of solving a difficult mathematical equation, an intellectual counterpoint to the lower-keyed feeling of velvet. Step by step the rapport built up, until there seemed but a single mind, working in perfect cohesion, a harmony without false notes.

Then this single mind began building. It began to think. It was a psychic colloid, in effect, an intellectual giant given strength and sanity by very human emotions and senses and desires.

Then into that pellucid unity crashed a thought-message that for an instant made the minds cling together in a final desperate embrace in which fear and hope and friendliness intermingled. The round robin dissolved. Each Baldy waited now, remembering Hobson's thought that said:

The pogrom's started.

He hadn't broadcast the message directly. The mind of a Mute, wearing his helmet, cannot be read except by another Mute. It was Duke Heath, sitting with Hobson in the moonlit grounds outside the hospital, who had taken the oral warning and conveyed it to the other Baldies. Now his thoughts continued to flash through Sequoia.

Come to the hospital. Avoid non-Baldies. If you're seen, you may be lynched.

In dozens of homes, eyes met in which the terror had leaped instantly to full flower. All over the world, in that moment, something electric sparked with unendurable tension from mind to sensitive mind. No non-Baldy noticed. But, with the speed of thought, the knowledge girdled the planet.

From the thousands of Baldies scattered through the villages, from helicopter and surface car, came a thought of reassurance. *We are one*, it said. *We are with you.*

That – from the Baldies. From the paranoids, fewer in number, came a message of hatred and triumph. *Kill the hairy men!*

But no nontelepath outside Sequoia knew what was happening.

There was an old plastic house near the edge of town where Burkhalter had been hiding. He slipped out of a side door now into the cool quiet of the night. Overhead, a full moon hung yellow. A fan of diffused light reached upward from Redwood Street in the distance, and dimmer paths in the air marked the other avenues. Burkhalter's muscles were rigid. He felt his throat tense with near-panic. Generations of anticipations had built up a violent phobia in every Baldy, and now that the day had come –

Barbara Pell came dazzlingly into his thoughts, and as his mind recalled her, so her mind touched his, wild and fiery, gloating with a triumph his whole being drew back from, while against all judgment something seemed to force him to receive her message.

He's dead, Burkhalter, he's dead! I've killed Fred Selfridge! The word is 'kill,' but in the mind of the paranoid it was not a word or a thought, but a reeking sensation of triumph, wet with blood, a screaming thought which the sane mind reels from.

You fool! Burkhalter shouted at her across the distant streets, his mind catching a little of her wildness so that he could not wholly control it. *You crazy fool, did you start this?*

He was starting out to get you. He was dangerous. His talk would have started the pogrom anyhow – people were beginning to think –

It's got to be stopped!

It will be! Her thought had a terrible confidence. *We've made plans.*

What happened?

Someone saw me kill Selfridge. It's the brother, Ralph, who touched things off – the old lynch law. Listen. Her thought was giddy with triumph.

He heard it then, the belling yell of the mob, far away, but growing louder. The sound of Barbara Pell's mind was fuel to a flame. He caught terror from her, but a perverted terror that lusted after what it feared. The same fury of bloodthirst was in the crowd's yell and in the red flame which was Barbara Pell's mad mind. They were coming near her, nearer –

For a moment Burkhalter was a woman running down a dim street, stumbling, recovering, racing on with a lynch mob baying at her heels.

A man – a Baldy – dashed out into the path of the crowd. He tore off his wig and waved it at them. Then Ralph Selfridge, his thin young face dripping with sweat, shrieked in wordless hatred and turned the tide after this new quarry. The woman ran on into the darkness.

They caught the man. When a Baldy dies, there is a sudden gap in the ether, a dead emptiness that no telepath will willingly touch with his mind. But before that blankness snapped into being, the Baldy's thought of agony blazed through Sequoia with stunning impact, and a thousand minds reeled for an instant before it.

Kill the hairy men! shrieked Barbara Pell's thoughts, ravenous and mad. This was what the furies were. When a woman's mind lets go, it drops into abysses of sheer savagery that a man's mind never plumbs. The woman from time immemorial has lived closer to the abyss than the male – has had to, for the defense of her brood. The primitive woman cannot afford scruples. Barbara Pell's madness now was the red, running madness of primal force. And it was a fiery thing that ignited something in every mind it touched. Burkhalter felt little flames take hold at the edges of his thoughts and the whole fabric that was his identity shivered and drew back. But he felt in the ether other minds, mad paranoid minds, reach out toward her and cast themselves ecstatically into the holocaust.

Kill them, kill – kill! raved her mind.

Everywhere? Burkhalter wondered, dizzy with the pull he felt from that vortex of exultant hate. *All over the world, tonight? Have the paranoids risen everywhere, or only in Sequoia?*

And then he sensed suddenly the ultimate hatefulness of Barbara Pell. She answered the thought, and in the way she answered he recognized how fully evil the red-haired woman was. If she had lost herself utterly in this flaming intoxication of the mob he would still, he thought, have hated her, but he need not have despised her.

She answered quite coolly, with a part of her mind detached from the ravening fury that took its fire from the howling mob and tossed it like a torch for the other paranoids to ignite their hatred from.

She was an amazing and complex woman, Barbara Pell. She had a strange, inflammatory quality which no woman, perhaps, since Jeanne d'Arc had so fully exercised. But she did not give herself up wholly to the fire that had kindled within her at the thought and smell of blood. She was deliberately casting herself into that blood-bath, deliberately wallowing in the frenzy of her madness. And as she wallowed, she could still answer with a coolness more terrible than her ardor.

No, only in Sequoia, said the mind that an instant before had been a blind raving exhortation to murder. *No human must live to tell about it*, she said in thought-shapes that dripped cold venom more burning that the hot bloodlust in her broadcast thoughts. *We hold Sequoia. We've taken over the airfields and the power station. We're armed. Sequoia is isolated from the rest of the world. The pogrom's broken loose here – only here. Like a cancer. It must be stopped here.*

How?

How do you destroy any cancer? Venom bubbled in the thought.

Radium, Burkhalter thought. Radioactivity. The atomic bombs –

Dusting off? he wondered.

A burning coldness of affirmation answered him. *No human must live to tell about it. Towns have been dusted off before – by other towns. Pinewood may get the blame this time – there's been rivalry between it and Sequoia.*

But that's impossible. If the Sequoia teleaudios have gone dead –

We're sending out faked messages. Any copters coming in will be stopped. But we've got to finish it off fast. If one human escapes – Her thoughts dissolved into inhuman, inarticulate yammering, caught up and echoed avidly by a chorus of other minds.

Burkhalter shut off the contact sharply. He was surprised, a little, to find that he had been moving toward the hospital all during the interchange, circling through the outskirts of Sequoia. Now he heard with his conscious mind the distant yelling that grew loud and faded again almost to silence, and then swelled once more. The mindless beast that ran the streets could be sensed tonight even by a nontelepath.

He moved silently through the dark for a while, sick and shaken as much by his contact with a paranoid mind as by the threat of what had happened and what might still come.

Jeanne d'Arc, he thought. She had it too, that power to inflame the mind.

She, too, had heard – 'voices?' Had she perhaps been an unwitting telepath born far before her time? But at least there had been sanity behind the power she exercised. With Barbara Pell –

As her image came into his mind again her thought touched him, urgent, repellently cool and controlled in the midst of all this holocaust she had deliberately stirred up. Evidently something had happened to upset their plans, for –

Burkhalter, she called voicelessly. *Burkhalter, listen. We'll co-operate with you.*

We hadn't intended to, but – where is the Mute, Hobson?

I don't know.

The cache of Eggs has been moved. We can't find the bombs. It'll take hours before another load of Eggs can be flown here from the nearest town. It's on the way. But every second we waste increases the danger of discovery. Find Hobson. He's the only mind we can't touch in Sequoia. We know no one else has hidden the bombs. Get Hobson to tell us where they are. Make him understand, Burkhalter. This isn't a matter affecting only us. If word of this gets out, every telepath in the world is menaced. The cancer must be cut out before it spreads.

Burkhalter felt murderous thought-currents moving toward him. He turned toward a dark house, drifted behind a bush, and waited there till the mob had poured past, their torches blazing. He felt sick and hopeless. What he had seen in the faces of the men was horrible. Had this hatred and fury existed for generations under the surface – this insane mob violence that could burst out against Baldies with so little provocation?

Common sense told him that the provocation had been sufficient. When a telepath killed a nontelepath, it was not dueling – it was murder. The dice were loaded. And for weeks now psychological propaganda had been at work in Sequoia.

The non-Baldies were not simply killing an alien race. They were out to destroy the personal devil. They were convinced by now that the Baldies were potential world conquerors. As yet no one had suggested that the telepaths ate babies, but that was probably coming soon, Burkhalter thought bitterly.

Preview. Decentralization was helping the Baldies, because it made a temporary communication-embargo possible. The synapses that connected Sequoia to the rest of the world were blocked; they could not remain blocked forever.

He cut through a yard, hurdled a fence, and was among the pines. He felt an impulse to keep going, straight north, into the clean wilderness where this turmoil and fury could be left behind. But, instead, he angled south toward the distant hospital. Luckily he would not have to cross the river; the bridges would undoubtedly be guarded.

There was a new sound, discordant and hysterical. The barking of dogs. Animals, as a rule, could not receive the telepathic thoughts of humans, but the storm of mental currents raging in Sequoia had now stepped up the frequency – or the power – to a far higher level. And the thoughts of thousands of telepaths, all over the world, were focused on the little village on the Pacific Slope.

Hark, hark! The dogs do bark!

The beggars are coming to town –

But there's another poem, he thought, trying to remember. Another one that fits even better. What is it –

The hopes and fears of all the years –

V

The mindless barking of the dogs was worst. It set the pitch of yapping, mad savagery that washed up around the hospital like the rising waves of a neap tide. And the patients were receptive too; wet packs and hydrotherapy, and, in a few cases, restraining jackets were necessary.

Hobson stared through the one-way window at the village far below. 'They can't get in here,' he said.

Heath, haggard and pale, but with a new light in his eyes, nodded at Burkhalter.

'You're one of the last to arrive. Seven of us were killed. One child. There are ten others still on their way. The rest – safe here.'

'How safe?' Burkhalter asked. He drank the coffee Heath had provided.

'As safe as anywhere. This place was built so irresponsible patients couldn't get out. Those windows are unbreakable. It works both ways. The mob can't get in. Not easily, anyhow. We're fireproof, of course.'

'What about the staff? The non-Baldies, I mean.'

A gray-haired man seated at a nearby desk stopped marking a chart to smile wryly at Burkhalter. The consul recognized him: Dr Wayland, chief psychiatrist.

Wayland said, 'The medical profession has worked with Baldies for a long time, Harry. Especially the psychologists. If any non-Baldy can understand the telepathic viewpoint, we do. We're noncombatants.'

'The hospital work has to go on,' Heath said. 'Even in the face of this. We did something rather unprecedented, though. We read the minds of every non-Baldy within these walls. Three men on the staff had a preconceived dislike of Baldies, and sympathized with the lynchings. We asked them to leave. There's no danger of Fifth Column work here now.'

Hobson said slowly, 'There was another man – Dr Wilson. He went down to the village and tried to reason with the mob.'

Heath said, 'We got him back here. He's having plasma pumped into him now.'

Burkhalter set down his cup. 'All right. Hobson, you can read my mind. How about it?'

The Mute's round face was impassive. 'We had our plans, too. Sure, I moved the Eggs. The paranoids won't find 'em now.'

'More Eggs are being flown in. Sequoia's going to be dusted off. You can't stop that.'

A buzzer rang; Dr Wayland listened briefly to a transmitted voice, picked up a few charts and went out. Burkhalter jerked his thumb toward the door.

'What about him? And the rest of the staff? They know, now.'

Heath grimaced. 'They know more than we wanted them to know. Until tonight, no nontelepath has even suspected the existence of the paranoid group. We can't expect Wayland to keep his mouth shut about this. The paranoids *are* a menace to non-Baldies. The trouble is, the average man won't differentiate between paranoids and Baldies. Are those people down there' – he glanced toward the window – 'are they drawing the line?'

'It's a problem,' Hobson admitted. 'Pure logic tells us that no non-Baldy must survive to talk about this. But is that the answer?'

'I don't see any other way,' Burkhalter said unhappily. He thought suddenly of Barbara Pell and the Mute gave him a sharp glance.

'How do you feel about it, Heath?'

The priest-medic walked to the desk and shuffled case histories. 'You're the boss, Hobson. I don't know. I'm thinking about my patients. Here's Andy Pell. He's got Alzheimer's disease – early senile psychosis. He's screwed up. Can't remember things very well. A nice old guy. He spills food on his shirt, he talks my ear off, and he makes passes at the nurses. He'd be no loss to the world, I suppose. Why draw a line, then? If we're going in for killing, there can't be any exceptions. The non-Baldy staff here can't survive, either.'

'That's the way you feel?'

Heath made a sharp, angry gesture. 'No! It isn't the way I feel! Mass murder would mean canceling the work of ninety years, since the first Baldy was born. It'd mean putting us on the same level as the paranoids! Baldies don't kill.'

'We kill paranoids.'

'There's a difference. Paranoids are on equal terms with us, And … oh, I don't know, Hobson. The motive would be the same – to save our race. But somehow one doesn't kill a non-Baldy.'

'Even a lynch mob?'

'They can't help it,' Heath said quietly. 'It's probably casuistry to distinguish between paranoids and non-Baldies but there *is* a difference. It would mean a lot of difference to us. We're not killers.'

Burkhalter's head drooped. The sense of unendurable fatigue was back again. He forced himself to meet Hobson's calm gaze.

'Do you know any other reason?' he asked.

'No,' the Mute said. 'I'm in communication, though. We're trying to figure out a way.'

Heath said, 'Six more got here safely. One was killed. Three are still on their way.'

'The mob hasn't traced us to the hospital yet,' Hobson said. 'Let's see. The paranoids have infiltrated Sequoia in considerable strength, and they're well armed. They've got the airfields and the power station. They're sending out faked teleaudio messages so no suspicion will be aroused outside. They're playing a waiting game; as soon as another cargo of Eggs gets here, the paranoids will beat it out of town and erase Sequoia. And us, of course.'

'Can't we kill the paranoids? You haven't any compunctions about eliminating them, have you, Duke?'

Heath shook his head and smiled; Hobson said, 'That wouldn't help. The problem would still exist. Incidentally, we could intercept the copter flying Eggs here, but that would just mean postponement. A hundred other copters would load Eggs and head for Sequoia; some of them would be bound to get through. Even fifty cargoes of bombs would be too dangerous. You know how the Eggs work.'

Burkhalter knew, all right. One Egg would be quite sufficient to blast Sequoia entirely from the map.

Heath said, 'Justified murder doesn't bother me. But killing non-Baldies – if I had any part in that, the mark of Cain wouldn't be just a symbol. I'd have it on my forehead – or inside my head, rather. Where any Baldy could see it. If we could use propaganda on the mob –'

Burkhalter shook his head. 'There's no time. And even if we did cool off the lynchers, that wouldn't stop word of this from getting around. Have you listened in on the catch-phrases, Duke?'

'The mob?'

'Yeah. They've built up a nice personal devil by now. We never made any secret of our round robins, and somebody had a bright idea. We're polygamists. Purely mental polygamists, but they're shouting that down in the village now.'

'Well,' Heath said, 'I suppose they're right. The norm is arbitrary, isn't it – automatically set by the power-group? Baldies *are* variants from that norm.'

'Norms change.'

'Only in crises. It took the Blowup to bring about decentralization. Besides, what's the true standard of values? What's right for non-Baldies isn't always right for telepaths.'

'There's a basic standard of morals –'

'Semantics.' Heath shuffled his case histories again. 'Somebody once said that insane asylums won't find their true function till ninety per cent of the world is insane. Then the sane group can just retire to the sanitariums.' He laughed harshly. 'But you can't even find a basic standard in psychoses. There's a lot less schizophrenia since the Blowup; most d.p. cases come from cities. The more I work with psycho patients, the less I'm willing to accept any arbitrary standards as the real ones. This man' – he picked up a chart – 'he's got a fairly familiar delusion. He contends that when he dies, the world will end. Well – maybe, in this one particular case, it's true.'

'You sound like a patient, yourself,' Burkhalter said succinctly.

Hobson raised a hand. 'Heath, I suggest you administer sedatives to the Baldies here. Including us. Don't you feel the tension?'

The three were silent for a moment, telepathically listening. Presently Burkhalter was able to sort out individual chords in the discordant thought-melody that was focused on the hospital.

'The patients,' he said. 'Eh?'

Heath scowled and touched a button. 'Fernald? Issue sedatives –' He gave a quick prescription, clicked off the communicator, and rose. 'Too many psychotic patients are sensitive,' he told Hobson. 'We're liable to have a panic on our hands. Did you catch that depressive thought –' He formed a quick mental image. 'I'd better give that man *a* shot. And I'd better check up on the violent cases, too.' But he waited.

Hobson remained motionless, staring out the window. After a time he nodded.

'That's the last one. We're all here now, all of Us. Nobody's left in Sequoia but paranoids and non-Baldies.'

Burkhalter moved his shoulders uneasily. 'Thought of an answer yet?'

'Even if I had, I couldn't tell you, you know. The paranoids could read your mind.'

True enough. Burkhalter thought of Barbara Pell, somewhere in the village – perhaps barricaded in the power station, or at the airfield. Some confused, indefinable emotion moved within him. He caught Hobson's bright glance.

'There aren't any volunteers among the Baldies,' the Mute said. 'You didn't ask to be involved in this crisis. Neither did I, really. But the moment a Baldy's born, he automatically volunteers for dangerous duty, and stands ready for instant mobilization. It just happened that the crisis occurred in Sequoia.'

'It would have happened somewhere. Sometime.'

'Right. Being a Mute isn't so easy, either. We're shut out. We can never know a complete round robin. We can communicate fully only with other Mutes. We can never resign.' Not even to another Baldy could a Mute reveal the existence of the Helmet.

Burkhalter said, 'Our mutation wasn't due for another thousand years, I guess. We jumped the gun.'

'We didn't. But we're paying. The Eggs were the fruit of knowledge, in a way. If man hadn't used atomic power as he did, the telepathic mutations would have had their full period of gestation. They'd never have appeared till the planet was ready for them. Not exactly ready, perhaps,' he qualified, 'but we wouldn't have had quite this mess on our hands.'

'I blame the paranoids,' Burkhalter said. 'And ... in a way ... myself.'

'You're not to blame.'

The Baldy grimaced. 'I think I am, Hobson. Who precipitated this crisis?'

'Selfridge –' Hobson was watching.

'Barbara Pell,' Burkhalter said. 'She killed Fred Selfridge. Ever since I came to Sequoia, she's been riding me.'

'So she killed Selfridge to annoy you? That doesn't make sense.'

'It fitted in with the general paranoid plan, I suppose. But it was what she wanted, too. She couldn't touch me when I was consul. But where's the consulate now?'

Hobson's round face was very grave. A Baldy intern came in, offered sedatives and water, and the two silently swallowed the barbiturates. Hobson went to the window and watched the flaring of torches from the village. His voice was muffled.

'They're coming up,' he said. 'Listen.'

The distant shouting grew louder as they stood there in silence. Nearer and louder. Burkhalter moved forward to Hobson's side. The town was a flaming riot of torches now, and a river of light poured up the curved road toward the hospital.

'Can they get in?' someone asked in a hushed voice.

Heath shrugged. 'Sooner or later.'

The intern said, with a touch of hysteria: 'What can we *do*?'

Hobson said, 'They're counting on the weight of numbers, of course. And they've got plenty of that. They aren't armed, I suppose, except for daggers – but then they don't need arms to do what they think they're going to do.'

There was a dead silence in the room for a moment. Then Heath said in a thin voice, 'What they *think* –?'

The Mute nodded toward the window. 'Look.'

There was a small rush toward the glass. Peering over one another's shoulders, the men in the room stared down the slope of the road, seeing the vanguard of the mob so near already that the separate torches were clearly distinguishable, and the foremost of the distorted, shouting faces. Ugly, blind with hatred and the intention to kill.

Hobson said in a detached voice, as if this imminent disaster were already in the past. 'We've got the answer, you see – we know about *this*. But there's another problem I can't solve. Maybe it's the most important one of all.' And he looked at the back of Burkhalter's head. Burkhalter was watching the road. Now he leaned forward suddenly and said,

'Look! There in the woods – what is it? Something moving – people? Listen – what is it?'

No one paid any attention beyond the first two or three words he spoke, for all of them saw it now. It happened very swiftly. One moment the mob was pouring unchecked up the road, the next a wave of shadowy forms had moved purposefully out of the trees in compact, disciplined order. And above the hoarse shouting of the mob a cry went terribly up, a cry that chilled the blood.

It was the shrill falsetto that had once been the Rebel Yell. Two hundred years ago it echoed over the bloody battlefields of the Civil War. It moved westward with the conquered rebels and became the cowboy yell. It moved and spread with westerners after the Blowup, the tall, wild men who could not endure the regimentation of the towns. Now it was the Hedgehound yell.

From the window the hospital watchers saw it all, enacted as if on a firelit stage below them.

Out of the shadows the men in buckskin came. Firelight flashed on the long blades they carried, on the heads of the arrows they held against the bent bows. Their wild, shrill, terrible yell rose and fell, drowning out the undisciplined screams of the mob.

The buckskin ranks closed in behind the mob, around it. The townsmen began to huddle together a little, until the long loosely organized mob had become a roughly compact circle with the woodsmen surrounding them. There were cries of, 'Kill 'em! Get 'em all!' from the townsmen, and the disorderly shouts rose raggedly through the undulations of the Hedgehound yell, but you could tell after the first two or three minutes who had the upper hand.

Not that there was no fighting. The men at the front of the mob had to do something. They did – or tried to. It was little more than a scuffle as the buckskin forms closed in.

'They're only townsmen, you see,' Hobson said quietly, like a lecturer explaining some movie scene from old news-reel files. 'Did you ever think before how completely the profession of the fighting man has died out since the Blowup? The only organized fighting men left in the world are out there, now.' He nodded toward the Hedgehound ranks, but nobody saw the motion. They were all watching with the incredulous eagerness of reprieved men as the Hedgehounds competently dealt with the mob which was so rapidly changing into a disorganized rabble now as the nameless, powerful, ugly spirit that had welded it into a mob died mysteriously away among them.

All it took was superior force, superior confidence – the threat of weapons in more accustomed hands. For four generations these had been townsmen whose ancestors never knew what war meant. For four generations the Hedgehounds had lived only because they knew unremitting warfare, against the forest and mankind.

Competently they went about rounding up the mob.

'It doesn't solve anything,' Burkhalter said at last, reluctantly, turning from the window. Then he ceased to speak, and sent his mind out in rapid thoughts so that the nontelepaths might not hear. *Don't we have to keep it all quiet? Do we still have to decide about – killing them all? We've saved our necks, sure – but what about the rest of the world?*

Hobson smiled a grim, thin smile that looked odd on his plump face. He spoke aloud, to everyone in the room.

'Get ready,' he said. 'We're leaving the hospital. All of us. The non-Baldy staff, too.'

Heath, sweating and haggard, caught his breath. 'Wait a minute. I know you're the boss, but – I'm not leaving my patients!'

'We're taking them, too,' Hobson said. Confidence was in his voice, but not in his eyes. He was looking at Burkhalter. The last and most difficult problem was still to be met.

The Cody's thought touched Hobson's mind. *All ready.*

You've got enough Hedgehounds?

Four tribes. They were all near the Fraser Run. The new consulate set-up had drawn 'em from the north. Curiosity.

Report to group.

Scattered across the continent, Mutes listened. *We've cleaned out Sequoia. No deaths. A good many got pretty well beaten up, but they can all travel.* (A thought of wry amusement.) *Your townspeople ain't fighters.*

Ready for the march?

Ready. They're all rounded up, men, women and children, in the north valley. Umpire Vine's in charge of that sector.

Start the march. About the paranoids, any trouble there?

No trouble. They haven't figured it all out yet. They're still in the town, sitting tight. We've got to move fast, though. If they try to get out of Sequoia, my men will kill. There was a brief pause. Then – *The march has started.*

Good. Use the blindfolds when necessary.

There are no stars underground, the Cody's thought said grimly.

No non-Baldy must die. Remember, this is a point of honor. Our solution may not be the best one, but –

None will die.

We're evacuating the hospital. Is Mattoon ready?
Ready. Evacuate.

Burkhalter rubbed a welt on his jaw. 'What happened?' he asked thickly, staring around in the rustling darkness of the pines.

A shadow moved among the trees. 'Getting the patients ready for transportation – remember? You were slugged. That violent case –'

'I remember.' Burkhalter felt sheepish. 'I should have watched his mind closer. I couldn't. He wasn't *thinking* –' He shivered slightly. Then he sat up. 'Where are we?'

'Quite a few miles north of Sequoia.'

'My head feels funny.' Burkhalter rearranged his wig. He rose, steadying himself against a tree, and blinked vaguely. After a moment he had reoriented. This must be Mount Nichols, the high peak that rose tall among the mountains guarding Sequoia. Very far away, beyond intervening lower summits, he could see a distant glow of light that was the village.

But beneath him, three hundred feet down, a procession moved through a defile in the mountain wall. They emerged into the moonlight and went swiftly on and were lost in shadow.

There were stretcher-bearers, and motionless, prone figures being carried along; there were men who walked arm in arm; there were tall men in buckskin shirts and fur caps, bows slung across their shoulders, and they were helping, too. The silent procession moved on into the wilderness.

'The Sequoia Baldies,' Hobson said. 'And the non-Baldy staff – and the patients. We couldn't leave them.'

'But –'

'It was the only possible answer for us, Burkhalter. Listen. For twenty years we've been preparing – not for this, but for the pogrom. Up in the woods, in a place only Mutes know about, there's a series of interlocking caves. It's a city now. A city without population. The Codys – there are four of them, really – have been using it as a laboratory and a hideout. There's material there for hydroponics, artificial sunlight, everything a culture needs. The caves aren't big enough to shelter all the Baldies, but they'll hold Sequoia's population.'

Burkhalter stared. 'The non-Baldies?'

'Yes. They'll be segregated, for a while, till they can face truth. They'll be prisoners; we can't get around that fact. It was a choice between killing them and holding them incommunicado. In the caves, they'll adapt. Sequoia was a tight, independent community. Family units won't be broken up. The same social pattern can be followed. Only – it'll be underground, in an artificial culture."

'Can't the paranoids find them?'

'There are no stars underground. The paranoids may read the minds of the

Sequoians, but you can't locate a mind by telepathic triangulation. Only Mutes know the location of the caves, and no paranoid can read a Mute's thoughts. They're on their way now to join us – enough Mutes to take the Sequoians on the last lap. Not even the Hedgehounds will know where they're going.'

'Then the secret will be safe among telepaths – except for the Hedgehounds. What if they talk?'

'They won't. Lots of reasons. For one, they have no communication to speak of with the outside world. For another, they're under an autocracy, really. The Codys know how to enforce their rules. Also, have you thought how the towns would react if they knew Hedgehounds had cleaned out a whole village? To save their own skins the Hedgehounds will keep their mouths shut. Oh, it *may* leak out. With so many individuals involved you never can be absolutely sure. But I think for an extemporaneous plan, it'll work out well enough.' Hobson paused and his mind brushed with the keenness of a quick glance against Burkhalter's mind. 'What's the matter, Burk? Still worried about something?'

'The people, I suppose,' Burkhalter admitted. 'The humans. It doesn't seem exactly fair, you know. I'd hate to be cut off forever from all contact from the rest of the world. They –'

Hobson thought an explosive epithet. It was much more violent thought than voiced. He said, 'Fair! Of course it isn't fair! You saw that mob coming up the road, Burk – did they have fairness in mind then? If anyone ever deserved punishment that mob does!' His voice grew milder. 'One thing we tend to lose sight of, you see. We grow up with the idea of indulgence toward humans pounded into us to such an extent we almost forget they're responsible people, after all. A pogrom is the most indefensible concerted action a group can be guilty of. It's always an attack by a large majority on a defenseless minority. These people would have killed us all without a qualm, if they could. They're lucky we aren't as vicious as they were. They deserve a lot worse than they're getting, if you ask me. We didn't ask to be put in a spot like this. There's unfairness involved all around, but I think this solution is the best possible under the circumstances.'

They watched the procession below moving through the moonlight. Presently Hobson went on. 'Another angle turned up after we put this thing in motion, too. A mighty good one. By sheer accident we're going to have a wonderful laboratory experiment going on in human relations. It won't be a dead-end community in the caves. Eventually, we think the Baldies and the non-Baldies will intermarry there. The hospital staff are potential good-will ambassadors. It'll take careful handling, but I think with our facilities for mind reading and the propaganda we can put out adjusted by the readings, things will work out. It may be the basis for the ultimate solution of the whole Baldy-human problem.

'You see, this will be a microcosm of what the whole world ought to be – would have been if the Blowup hadn't brought us telepaths into being ahead of our normal mutation time. It will be a community of humans dominated by telepaths, controlled by them benevolently. We'll learn how to regulate relations with humans, and there'll be no danger while we learn. It'll be trial and error without punishment for error. A little hard on the humans, perhaps, but no harder than it's been for generations on the Baldy minority all over the world. We might even hope that in a few years' time the experiment may go well enough that even if the news leaked out, the community members would elect to stay put. Well, we'll have to wait and see. It can't be solved any better way that we know of. There *is* no solution, except adjustment between the races. If every Baldy on earth committed voluntary suicide, there'd still be Baldies born. You can't stop it. The Blowup's responsible for that, not us. We … wait a minute.'

Hobson turned his head sharply, and in the rustling night silences of the forest, broken only by the subdued noises of the proposition far below, they listened for a sound not meant for ears.

Burkhalter heard nothing, but in a moment Hobson nodded.

'The town's about to go,' he said.

Burkhalter frowned. 'There's another loose end, isn't there? What if they blame Pinewood for dusting Sequoia off?'

'There won't be any proof either way. We've about decided to spread rumors indicating two or three other towns along with Pinewood, enough to confuse the issue. Maybe we'll say the explosion might have come from an accident in the Egg dump. That's happened, you know. Pinewood and the rest will just have to get along under a slight cloud for awhile. They'll have an eye kept on them, and if they should show any more signs of aggression … but of course, nothing will happen. I think … look, Burkhalter! There she goes!'

Far away below them the glow that was Sequoia lay like a lake of light in the mountains' cup. As they watched, it changed. A nova flamed in incandescent splendor, whitening the men's faces and showing the pines in starkly black silhouette.

For an instant the soundless ether was full of a stunning, mindless cry that rocked the brain of every telepath within its range. Then there was that terrible void, that blankness of cessation into which no Baldy cares to look. This time it was a mighty vortex, for a great many telepathic minds perished together in that nova. It was a vortex that made the mind reel perilously near its great, sucking brink. Paranoid they may have been, but they were telepathic too, and their going shook every brain that could perceive the passing.

In Burkhalter's mind a reeling blindness struck. He thought, *Barbara, Barbara ...*

It was an utterly unguarded cry. He made no effort to hush it from Hobson's perception.

Hobson said, as if he had not heard, 'That's the finish. Two Mutes in copters dropped the Eggs. They're watching now. No survivors. Burkhalter –'

He waited. Slowly Burkhalter pulled himself out of that blind abyss into which the beautiful, terrible, deadly image of Barbara Pell whirled away toward oblivion. Slowly he brought the world back into focus around him.

'Yes?'

'Look. The last of the Sequoians are going by. You and I aren't needed here any more, Burk.'

There was significance in that statement. Burkhalter shook himself mentally and said with painful bewilderment, 'I don't ... quite get it. Why did you bring me up here? Am I –' He hesitated, 'I'm not going with the others?'

'You can't go with them,' the Mute said quietly. There was a brief silence; a cool wind whispered through the pine needles. The pungent fragrance and freshness of the night washed around the two telepaths. 'Think, Burkhalter,' Hobson said, 'Think.'

'I loved her,' Burkhalter said. 'I know that now.' There was shock and self-revulsion in his mind, but he was too stunned by the realization for much emotion to come through yet.

'You know what that means, Burkhalter? You're not a true Baldy. Not quite.' He was silent for a moment. 'You're a latent paranoid, Burk,' Hobson said.

There was no sound or thought between them for a full minute. Then Burkhalter sat down suddenly on the pine needles that carpeted the forest floor.

'It isn't true,' he said. The trees were reeling around him.

'It is true, Burk.' Hobson's voice and mind were infinitely gentle. 'Think. Would you – could you – have loved a paranoid, and such a paranoid as that, if you were a normal telepath?'

Dumbly Burkhalter shook his head. He knew it was true. Love between telepaths is a far more unerring thing than love between blind and groping humans. A telepath can make no mistake about the quality of the beloved's character. He could not if he wished. No normal Baldy could feel anything but utter revulsion toward the thing that had been Barbara Pell. No *normal* Baldy –

'You should have hated her. You did hate her. But there was something more than hate. It's a paranoid quality, Burk, to feel drawn toward what you despise. If you'd been normal, you'd have loved some normal telepathic woman, someone your equal. But you never did. You had to find a woman you could look down on. Someone you could build up your ego by despising. No paranoid can admit any other being is his equal. I'm sorry, Burk. I hate to say these things.'

Hobson's voice was like a knife, merciless and merciful, excising diseased tissue. Burkhalter heard him, and trod down the latent hatred which the truth – and he knew the truth of it – brought out in his double mind.

'Your father's mind was warped too, Burk,' Hobson went on. 'He was born too receptive to paranoid indoctrination –'

'They tried their tricks on him when he was a kid,' Burkhalter said hoarsely. 'I remember that.'

'We weren't sure at first about what ailed you. The symptoms didn't show till you took on the consulate. Then we began to build up a prognosis, of sorts. You didn't really want that job, Burkhalter. Not subconsciously. Those heavy fatigues were a defense. I caught that daydream of yours today – not the first one you've had. Daydreams concerned with suicide – another symptom, and another means of escape. And Barbara Pell – that was the payoff. You couldn't let yourself know what your real feelings were, so you projected the opposite emotion – hatred. You believed she was persecuting you, and you let your hatred have full freedom. But it wasn't hatred, Burk.'

'No. It wasn't hatred. She ... she was horrible, Hobson! She was horrible!'

'I know.'

Burkhalter's mind boiled with violent emotions, too tangled to sort out. Hatred, intolerable grief, bright flashes of the paranoid world, memory of Barbara Pell's wild mind like a flame in the wind.

'If you're right, Hobson,' he said with difficulty, 'you've got to kill me. I know too much. If I'm really a latent paranoid some day I might betray – Us.'

'Latent,' Hobson said. 'There's a world of difference – if you can be honest with yourself.'

'I'm not safe if I live. I can feel – disease – back in my mind right now. I – hate you, Hobson. I hate you for showing me myself. Some day the hate may spread to all Mutes and all Baldies. How can I trust myself any more?'

'Touch your wig, Burk,' Hobson said.

Bewildered, Burkhalter laid a shaking hand upon his head. He felt nothing unusual. He looked at Hobson in complete confusion.

'Take it off, Burk.'

Burkhalter lifted off the wig. It came hard, the suction caps that held it in place giving way with reluctance. When it was off, Burkhalter was amazed to feel that there was still something on his head. He lifted his free hand and felt with unsteady fingers a fine cap of wires like silk, hugging his skull. He looked up in the moonlight and met Hobson's eyes. He could see the fine wrinkles around them, and the look of kindness and compassion on the Mute's round face. For an instant he forgot even the mystery of the strange cap on his head. He cried voicelessly,

Help me, Hobson! Don't let me hate you!

Instantly into his mind came a firm, strong, compassionate locking of thoughts from many, many minds. It was a communion more intimate and of a different quality than anything he had ever felt before. And it was to the mind as the clasp of many supporting hands would be to the body when the body is weary and in infinite need of support.

You're one of us now, Burkhalter. You wear the Helmet. You are a Mute. No paranoid can ever read your mind.

It was Hobson's thought that spoke to him, but behind it spoke the thoughts of many others, many trained minds from hundreds of other Mutes, all speaking as if in a chorus that echoed and amplified all Hobson said.

But I ... I'm a latent –

The hundreds of minds blended into a cohesive unit, the psychic colloid of the round robin, but a different, more intense union, wrought into something new by the caps that filtered all their thoughts. The unit became a single mind, strong and sane and friendly, welcoming the newcomer. He did not find miraculous healing there – he found something better.

Truth. Honesty.

Now the warp in his mind, the paranoid quirk and its symptoms and illogic, became very clear. It was the highest kind of psychoanalysis, which only a Baldy can know.

He thought, *It will take time. The cure will take –*

Hobson was standing behind him. *I'll be with you. Until you can stand alone. And even then – we'll all be with you. You are one of us. No Baldy is ever alone.*

FIVE

I think I am dying.

I have been lying here for a long time now. Sometimes I am conscious, but not often. I can't move at all.

I meant to cut an artery in my wrist and die, but I can't even do that now, and I don't need to. My fingers won't move. I can't move at all, and I'm not cold any more. The light and the warmth are pulsing and fading, fading a little more each time. I suppose this is dying; I know it is.

There is a helicopter overhead. It will be too late. It is getting larger. But I am sinking faster than it is dropping into this canyon between the peaks. They have found me, but not soon enough.

Life and death are not important.

My thoughts are getting sucked down into a black whirlpool. I shall go down there alone, and that will be the end.

There is one thing, one thought, that I can't stop thinking. It's a queer thought to have when you're dying.

Humpty Dumpty sat on a wall.

That was Jeff Cody's thought, wasn't it?

If I could just think about Jeff Cody, maybe I could –

Much too late now.

Cody and Operation Apocalypse, there in the Caverns … remembering … remembering …

… dying alone …

HUMPTY DUMPTY

And God said to Noah, the end of all flesh is come before me; for the earth is filled with violence through them …

Under a stone sky Jeff Cody stood, his hands clasped behind him. He was trying to read the mind of an electronic calculator, and trying to keep his own mind from being read with all the violence on it. He shut down all his barriers around his own desperation, pushing hard upon the one thought he did not dare to face. He held it down, trying to drown it under the surface turmoil of his mind. The calculator had a broad, bland, glassy brow, winking with lights and reflections. Somewhere inside it a thin slice of crystal lay that could wipe human life off the face of the planet. Not Jeff Cody's life, and not the life of his people. But all human, non-telepathic life. The responsibility for the crystal was one man's. Cody's.

Behind him Allenby shifted from one foot to another, his reflection blurring in the shining surface of the calculator's control panel. Cody said without turning,

'But if the Inductor is a failure, then we'll have to –' An image of death and dying formed like a cloud in his thoughts.

He had not said this aloud. Allenby interrupted very quickly, not speaking aloud either, but his thought cutting into Cody's, ending it before the image of destruction could take full shape in Cody's mind.

'No. We've had another set-back. But we'll try again. We'll keep on trying. We may never have to use – that.' His mind sketched in the thin crystal in the calculator, with death for most of the race of man locked in it.

'Call it set-back or call it failure,' Cody said, in the silence of his mind. 'The goal's too high. Nobody knows what makes a man telepathic. Nobody's ever going to induce it with a machine. No Inductor will ever work. You know that.'

'I don't know it,' Allenby's thought said quietly. 'I think it can be done. Jeff, you're under too much pressure.'

Cody laughed shortly. 'Merriam lasted three months in this job,' he said. 'Brewster stood it longest – eight months. This is my sixth month. What's the matter? Afraid I'll resign the way Brewster did?'

'No,' Allenby said. 'But –'

'Okay,' Cody interrupted the thought irritably. 'Forget it.' He felt Allenby's mind touch the edges of his with tentative, uneasy brushing motions. Allenby was a psychologist. And therefore Cody was a little afraid of him. He did not want expert attention brought to bear on him just now. There was something terrifying and yet very tempting down close under the surface of his thoughts, and he did not mean to expose it just yet to anyone. He made an effort of the will and summoned up a shimmer of pleasant images like a smokescreen to puff in Allenby's face. Pine woods with warm rain blowing through them, a quarter of a mile over their heads above the limestone sky. The quiet and clearness of the empty heavens broken only by the buzz of a helicopter and the soft, continual swish of its vanes. The face of Cody's wife when she was in a good mood and laughing gently.

He felt Allenby's uneasiness tentatively subside. He did not turn as he heard Allenby's feet shift on the floor.

'I'll get back, then,' Allenby said without words. 'I just wanted to see you when I told you that we'd hit another dead end. Is it all right, Jeff?'

'Fine,' Cody said. 'I won't keep you.'

Allenby went out.

Cody listened while the receding footsteps crossed the room beyond. He heard the door close and lock. He was alone now, physically, though all through the cavern an interlacing play of telepathic thoughts moved continually, touching his own and passing. Even Allenby sent back a vague uneasiness as he moved away. So Cody kept the images of pine woods and clear sky and laughing woman playing over the surface of his mind. But his eyes turned sidewise and without moving his head he saw lying on the edge of a work table within reach of his hand the thing he had not dared to admit into his mind till now. Too many other minds were watching.

What he saw was a knife with a heavy, narrow blade and a sharp point, left by some careless workman. What he thought of was the man before him in this job, and the way Brewster had resigned from it after eight months. Brewster had used a revolver. But a knife was good, too. There is a place inside the collar-bone, near the neck, and consciousness goes out like a blown candle in a matter of seconds if you drive the knife in there. If your burden is too much to bear, as Merriam's was, and Brewster's. And Jeff Cody's.

All around him in the air, like an eyeless, invisible staring, uneasy telepathic minds were swinging around toward him. A ripple of panic was running through the cavern. Something, somewhere, was wrong. But Cody had controlled his surface thoughts skillfully. He had not let himself really see the knife, really think clearly of that spot inside the collarbone, until now.

Now he drew a deep breath and let the wonderful release of the thought flash bright and clear through the cavern. They couldn't stop him. Nobody was near enough. He was free.

'So the Inductor won't work,' he said aloud. 'So you can't induce telepathy in a human mind. But there's one way to stop telepathy!'

He took one long sidewise step and the knife was in his hand. With two fingers he felt for the ridge of his collarbone, to guide the blade.

'Let the Inductor fail,' he thought. 'Let the pogrom come. Let the race die. Turn loose Apocalypse. It's not my problem now!'

Generations ago, the Blowup had posed the problem by mutating a sub-species of telepaths. And there had been a time when the Baldies hoped that eugenics could solve that problem. But not any more. Time was too short.

Even though the telepathic function was carried by a dominant gene, there were too few Baldies. Given enough time and enough intermarriage, the world might become peopled entirely by telepaths, but there was not enough time. The only answer was the one which Baldies had been seeking for years now – a mechanical device, an Inductor, which would induce the telepathic power in a non-telepath.

It was theoretically possible. The minds of the greatest scientists on earth lay open to the Baldies. And here in the caves the electronic calculator could solve the problem, given enough data. But this problem it had not completely solved, for there was not enough data, in spite of the treasure of knowledge stolen from hundreds of brilliant, seeking non-Baldy minds.

Still, it was the answer. If every man and woman in the world could become a telepath, simply by wearing a compact mechanical device, the miracle could be worked. The last barriers would go down. The fear and hatred non-telepaths had for Baldies would vanish – not instantly, but it would dissolve little by little in the great sea of interacting minds. The walls, the *difference*, would vanish, and with it the fear that relentlessly forced the coming of the pogrom.

But the Inductor was still a theory. The calculator had not yet solved that problem, if it ever would. Instead, it had given the answer to the basic problem in an unexpected way, coldly mechanical and terribly logical. The problem could be solved, the calculator said. Destroy all non-telepathic humans. The method? It searched its vast memory-library and found –

Operation Apocalypse.

There was a virus which, by means of certain stimuli, could be mutated into a variant which was air-borne and propagated quickly. It destroyed human neural tissue. There was only one kind of human neural tissue it could not harm.

Telepaths were naturally immune to the mutated virus.

No Baldy knew what the virus was, or the method of mutation. Only the calculator knew those things, and the inhuman mind of an electronic calculator cannot be read. Somewhere in the great machine was a tiny crystal of barium titanate bearing a series of frozen dots of energy in a binary digit code. And that code held the secret of the deadly virus.

If Jeff Cody took three steps forward and sat down in the cushioned operator's chair before the control panel, and if he touched a certain button, a monitor device would examine the electronic pattern of his brain and identify it as surely as fingerprints are identified. Only one man in the world could satisfy the question the monitor would silently ask.

And then a light would begin to glow – somewhere – on the control panel, and under it would be a number, and, seeing that number, Cody could make the calculator reveal its secret. Before Cody, Brewster had carried this crushing burden. And before Brewster, Merriam. And after Cody – someone else would have the unendurable responsibility for deciding whether to say: *The end of all flesh is come before me … behold, I will destroy them with the earth.*

The crash of protesting minds burst by sheer force through the shell of defense Cody had put up around his own as he took up the knife. From all over the busy cavern telepaths stopped in their tracks and hurled their strong, urgent thoughts toward the interlocked center that was Cody. It was stunning. He had never felt so strong an impact before. He did not mean to falter, but the burden of their protest was almost tangible, almost a thing to stagger under. Even from above-ground he could hear and feel the instant thrust of down-driving thought. A quarter of a mile above this limestone sky, above the rock and the soil with the pine tree roots clenched downward through it, a hunter in ragged buckskins paused among the trees and sent his own shocked, sympathetic protest dropping toward the cavern. The thought came blurred to Cody by the stone between, and starred with tiny, bright, brainless thoughts of small burrowing things in the soil overhead.

Someone in a helicopter high up in the hot blue sky locked minds with the group underground, faint and far-off, but as instant as the man in the nearest cave beyond Cody's locked door.

'No, *no*,' the voices said in his mind. '*You can't! You are all of us. You can't. Jeff, you are all of us!*'

He knew it was true. The way out was like a deep, dark well, and vertigo pulled him toward it, but he knew that he would be killing his whole race, a little, if he killed himself. Only telepaths can experience death and still live. Each time a telepath dies, all the rest within mind's reach feel the blackness close upon an extinguished mind, and feel their own minds extinguish a little in response.

It happened so fast Cody was still feeling with two fingers along the edge of his collarbone, and the knife was not yet firm in his fist, when the single, interlocking cry of anguished protest from a hundred minds speaking as one closed down upon him. He shut his thoughts and was obdurate. He could fight them off long enough. This would only take a second. The door was locked and physical force was the only thing that could stop him.

But he was uneasy even in this urgent press of voices and action. For Allenby's mind was not speaking with the rest. Why?

Now the knife was firm in his hand. Now he spread his two fingers apart a little to make way for it, knowing the place to strike. Had Brewster felt as he felt, when Brewster stood here six months ago and laid down the unbearable burden of decision? Had it been hard to pull the trigger? Or easy, as it was easy to lift the knife and –

A burst of blinding white light exploded in the middle of his brain. It was like a shooting star that crashed and shattered upon the very texture of the mind itself. In the last winking instant of consciousness Cody thought he had already struck the self-destroying blow and that this was what death looked like from within.

Then he knew that the meteor of impact was Allenby's mind striking his a numbing blow. He felt the knife slip from his hands, he felt his knees buckle, and he felt nothing more for a very long, an immeasurable time.

When he was aware of himself again Allenby was kneeling beside him on the floor, and the calculator looked up above him glassy and reflecting from an unfamiliar angle, a child's eye view seen with a knee-high vision. The door was unlocked and stood open. Everything looked strange.

Allenby said, 'All right, Jeff?'

Cody looked up at him and felt the pent-up and unreleased tension in him boil toward the surface in an outburst of rage so strong that the supporting minds he felt hovering around him drew back as if from fire.

'I'm sorry,' Allenby said. 'I've only done that twice before in my life. I had to do it, Jeff.'

Cody threw aside the hand on his shoulder. Scowling, he drew his feet under him and tried to rise. The room went around him in an unsteady circle.

'Somebody had to be the man,' Allenby said. 'It was the odds, Jeff. It's hard on you and Merriam and Brewster and those others, but –

Cody made a violent gesture, cutting off the thought.

'All right,' Allenby said. 'But don't kill yourself, Jeff. Kill somebody else. Kill Jasper Home.'

A little burning shock went through Cody's mind. He stood motionless, not even his mind stirring, letting that strange new thought glow in the center of it.

Kill Jasper Home.

Oh, Allenby was a wise man. He was grinning at Cody now, his round, ruddy face tense but beginning to look happy again.

'Feeling better? Action's what you need, Jeff – action, directed activity. All you've been able to do for months is stay put and worry. There are some responsibilities a man can't carry – unless he acts. Well, use your knife on Horne, not yourself.'

A faint flicker of doubt wavered in Cody's mind.

Allenby said, 'Yes, you may fail. He may kill you.'

'He won't,' Cody said aloud, his voice sounding strange to him.

'He could. You'll have to take the chance. Get him if you can. That's what you want to do, but you haven't really known it. You've got to kill someone. Horne's our basic problem now. He's our real enemy. So kill Horne. Not yourself.'

Cody nodded without a word.

'Good. We'll locate him for you. And I'll get you a copter. Will you see Lucy first?'

A little wave of disturbance ran through Cody's mind. Allenby saw it, but he did not let his own mind ripple in response. Quietly the innumerable linking minds of the other telepaths all around them had drawn back, waiting.

'Yes,' Cody said. 'I'll see Lucy first.' He turned toward the door of the cave.

Jasper Horne – and what he represented – was the reason why the Baldies could not let even themselves learn the method of Operation Apocalypse and the nature of the deadly selective virus from the calculator. That secret had to be kept from Jasper Horne and his fellow paranoids. For their approach was: *Why not kill all the humans? Why not, before they kill us? Why not strike first, and save ourselves?*

These were hard questions to answer, and Jasper Horne was very adept at putting it to the test. If you could say the group of paranoid telepaths had any leader, then Horne was that leader. How much the man knew of the Caves was uncertain. He knew they existed, but not where. He knew some of the things that were going on in it, in spite of the frequency-scrambling Mute helmets every Cave Baldy wore. If he knew about the Inductor, he would – if he could – have dropped an Egg on it with the greatest joy in life and watched the smoke-cloud arise. Certainly he knew the Operation Apocalypse had been planned, for he was doing his best to force the Baldies to release the virus that would destroy all non-telepathic human life.

And he knew the way to force this decision. If – when – a total pogrom started, then the virus and the Apocalypse would be loosed upon the world. Then there would be no choice. When your life depends on killing your enemy, you don't hesitate. But when the enemy is your brother …

That was the difference. To the normal Baldies, the race of non-telepathic humans was a close kin. To the paranoids they were hairy sub-men fit only for extermination. So Jasper Horne worked in every way he knew to force trouble to the surface. To precipitate a pogrom. To make sure the Baldies released the virus and destroyed the hairy men.

And Horne worked in a decentralized post-Blowup society founded on fear, a fear that had been very real once. Today, no further move seemed possible. The society wavered between re-contraction and further expansion, and each man, each town, was on guard against all others. For how can you trust another when you do not know his thoughts?

American Gun and Sweetwater, Jensen's Crossing and Santaclare and all the rest, clear across the curve of the continent. Men and women in the towns going about their business, rearing their children, tending their gardens and their stores and their factories. Most of them were normal human beings. Yet in every town the Baldies lived too, rearing *their* children, tending *their* stores. Amicably enough for the most part. But not always – not always.

And for weeks now, over most of the nation, had lain a humid, oppressive heat wave, in which aggressions rose steadily higher. Yet, outside of a few knife-duels, no one dared strike the first blow. Other men were armed too, and every town possessed a cache of atomic Eggs, and could strike back with deadly precision.

The time was more than ripe for a pogrom. So far, no mob had formed. No potential lynchers had agreed on a target.

But the Baldies were a minority.

All that was needed was a precipitating factor – and the paranoids were doing their best to provide that.

Cody glanced up at the cavern's gray stone sky and reached with his key for the lock of his wife's apartment door. With the key already in place, he hesitated, not from indecision this time but because he knew what probably waited inside. There was a furrow between his brows, and all the little lines of his face were pulled tense and held that way by the perpetual tension that held every Baldy from the first moment after he entered the caves.

The stone sky held down and bottled in such a complex maze of thoughts, echoing off the walls and interlacing and interlocking in a babel of confusion. The Cavern of Babel, Cody thought wryly, and turned the key with a gesture of small resolution. Indoors he would exchange one babel for another. The walls would give him a little shelter from the clouds of stale, sullen resentment outside, but there was something inside he liked even less. Yet he knew that he could not leave without seeing Lucy and the baby.

He opened the door. The living room looked bright enough, with its deep, broad divan-shelf running along three sides, soft, dark mossy green under the shelves of book-spools, colored cushions scattered, the lights on low. An electric fire glowed behind a Gothic interweaving of baffles, like a small cathedral on fire from within. Through the broad window in the fourth wall he could see the lights of the Ralphs' living room next door reflecting on the street, and across the way June and Hugh Barton in their own living room, having a pre-dinner cocktail before their electric fire. It looked pleasant,

But in here all the clear colors and the glow were clouded by the deep miasma of despair which colored all Jeff Cody's wife's days, and had for – how long now? The baby was three months old.

He called, 'Lucy?'

No answer. But a deeper wave of misery beat through the apartment, and after a moment he heard the bed creak in the next room. He heard a sigh. Then Lucy's voice, blurred a little, said, 'Jeff.' There was an instant of silence, and he had already turned toward the kitchen when her voice came again. 'Go into the kitchen and bring me a little more whiskey, will you, please?'

'Right away,' he said. The whiskey was not going to hurt her much, he thought. Anything that could help her get over the next few months was that much to the good. The next few –? No, the end would come much sooner than that.

'Jeff?' Lucy's voice was querulous.

He took the whiskey into the bedroom. She was lying face up across the bed, her reddish curls hanging, her stocking feet against the walls. Marks of dried tears ran down across her cheek toward her ear, but her lashes were not wet now. In the corner the baby slept in a small cocoon of his own incoherent animal-like thoughts. He was dreaming of warmth and enormous all-enveloping softness that stirred slowly, a dream without shape, all texture and temperament. His light-red curls were no more than a down on his well-shaped head.

Cody looked at Lucy. 'How do you feel?' he heard himself asking inanely.

Without moving a muscle she let her eyes roll sidewise so that she was looking at him from under her half-closed lids, a stony, suffering, hating look. An empty water-glass stood on the bedtable within reach of her lax hand. Cody stepped forward, unstopped the bottle and poured a steady amber stream into the glass. Two inches, three. She was not going to say when. He stopped at three and replaced the bottle.

'You don't have to ask how anybody feels,' Lucy said in a dull voice.

'I'm not reading you, Lucy.'

She shrugged against the bedspread. 'You say.'

Looking again at the sleeping baby, Cody did not answer. But Lucy sat up with great suddenness, making the bed groan, startling Cody because the motion had been so spontaneous he had not even caught the anticipation of it in her mind. 'He's not yours. He's mine. All mine, my kind, my race. No –' The thought went on, '– no taint in his blood at all. Not a freak. Not a Baldy. A nice, normal, healthy, perfect baby –' She didn't say it aloud, but she didn't have to. She caught at the thought halfway through, and then deliberately let it go on, knowing she might as well have said it aloud. Then she added in a flat voice, 'And I suppose you didn't read *that*'

Silently he held out the whiskey glass to her.

It had been five years now since the Egg dropped on Sequoia. Five years since the cavern colony saw the last daylight they might ever see. And the people herded from Sequoia to the caves had settled down sullenly, resentful or resigned according to their temperaments. They had every comfort of underground living which their captors could provide. They were as content as skilled psychologists could make them, psychologists who could look into their minds and read their needs almost before the needs took shape. But they were captives.

The intermarriages had started within a few months of the captivity. It was one of the large-scale experiments which could have happened only in the caves under such controlled conditions. Partly it was to demonstrate good intent to the captives, to make them feel less isolated.

No telepath really wants to marry a non-telepath. There are among non-telepaths quite as high a percentage of desirable mates as among Baldies, but to a Baldy, a non-telepathic human is a handicapped person. Like a lovely young girl who has every desirable attribute of mind and body but happens also to be deaf, dumb, and blind. She may communicate in finger-language, but the barrier remains all but insurmountable.

And there is this added factor – around every human who starts out life with the best of heredity and environment, shadows of the prisonhouse are inevitably, slowly but inexorably closed in by all the problems of living which he fails to solve completely without even realizing it. But not the Baldies. There are always friends to help, there are always minds to lean upon in crises and uncertainties. There is constant check and balance, so that no Baldy suffers from those inward quandaries, those only partly recognized clouds of confusion and bewilderment which fog the happiness of every other human being. In the telepathic mind there are comparatively few unswept chambers cluttered with old doubts and fears. It makes for a clarity of the personality which no non-telepath quite achieves.

A telepath may become psychotic, of course, but only when subjected to such stresses, over a long period of time, as a non-telepath could endure only briefly without breaking. (The paranoid telepaths were in a different class; heredity was an important factor there.)

So marriage between Baldy and non-telepath is, at best, marriage between an alert, receptive, fully aware being and one murky and confused, handicapped in communication and always, on some level, latently resentful.

But by now almost every marriageable non-telepath in the caverns had been painstakingly courted by and married to a Baldy. They were at the same time, of course, inevitably married to an espionage agent, a willing but not always accepted psychoanalyst, and, most importantly, to the potential parent of other Baldies.

The gene is dominant, which means that the children were almost invariably telepathic. Only when the Baldy spouse possessed one recessive non-telepathic gene as well as one dominant telepathic gene could the child be born a non-telepath.

That was what had happened to Lucy and Jeff Cody …

No human was ever to leave the caves again. No Baldy was to know of the captivity who did not wear the Mute helmet, since if the world ever learned of this captivity, the long-awaited pogrom would touch off automatically. No child of human parents would ever leave, unless it left as an infant in arms, too young to remember or tell the story. But a telepath child was a recruit at birth to the ranks of the captors. The hope had been that in a generation or two the captives could automatically be blended with the Baldies or taken out of the caves at infancy, so that the colony would once more revert to its original state of a population composed only of telepaths.

That had been the original plan, but growing pressures had already made it obsolete.

Lucy wiped her mouth on the back of a lightly tanned hand and held out the emptied glass to Cody. She waited a moment while the whiskey burned its way down and spread in a slow, hot coating over the walls of her stomach.

'Take a little,' she said. 'It helps.'

Cody didn't want any, but he tilted a short half-inch into the glass and drank obediently. After a time Lucy gave a short sigh and sat up cross-legged on the bed, shaking the hair back from her eyes.

'I'm sorry,' she said. 'Irrational.'

She laid her hand palm up on the bedspread and Cody closed his own hand over it, smiling unhappily at her.

'I've got an appointment outside,' he said. 'I'll have to leave in a few minutes, Lucy.'

Her look shot wild and unguarded toward the crib in the corner. Her thought, at once blurred and clarified by the release of alcohol, unfurled like a flag. Cody almost winced at the impact of it, but he was even more schooled in discipline than most Baldies, being husband to a non-telepath, and he showed nothing. He only said,

'No, it isn't that. I won't take him until you say so.'

She gave him a sudden startled glance.

'It's too late?'

'No,' Cody said quickly. 'Of course not. He isn't old enough yet to remember – this.'

Lucy moved uneasily.

'I don't want to keep him down here. You know I don't. It's bad enough for me, without knowing my own son wouldn't ever –' She shut off the thought of sunlight, blue air, distances. 'Not just yet,' she said, and pushed her feet over the edge of the bed. She stood up a little unsteadily. She gave the baby one blind glance and then walked stocking-footed toward the kitchen, bracing herself against the wall now and then. Cody reached automatically toward her mind, then drew back and got up to follow her. She was at the kitchen sink splashing water into a glass. She drank thirstily, her eyes unfocused.

'I have to go,' Cody said. 'Don't worry, Lucy.'

'Some – woman,' Lucy said indistinctly over the edge of the glass. 'There's – somebody. I know.'

'Lucy –'

'One of *your* kind,' Lucy said, and dropped the glass in the sink. It rolled in a bright arc, spilling water.

All he could do was look at her helplessly. There was nothing he could say. He couldn't tell her he was on his way to try to kill Jasper Horne. He couldn't tell her about Operation Apocalypse or the Inductor or the position of fearful responsibility he held. He couldn't say, 'If we can perfect the Inductor in time, Lucy, you can go free – you and our child.' Nor could he say, 'I may have to kill you – you and our child and every non-telepath on earth – with Operation Apocalypse.'

No, there was nothing he could say.

She drew a wet hand across her face, pushing back her hair, looking at him blurrily, and then came on uncertain, shoeless feet across the kitchen to lay her cheek on his shoulder and push her arms under his, around his chest.

'I'm sorry,' she said. 'I'm – crazy. It's hard for you too, Jeff.'

'Yes.'

'We'll send the baby away next week,' she promised. 'Then I'll be sane again. I – I *hate* whiskey. It's just that –'

'I know.' He smoothed the hair away from her wet face, tried to find words for the complex waves of love, pity, remorse, terror and pain which filled his mind constantly as long as he was with his wife, or thinking of her. It is curious that telepaths are often almost inarticulate when it is necessary to communicate nuances of feeling in words. They never need to use words, among their own kind.

'Be patient with me, Lucy,' he said finally. 'There's trouble coming. There isn't much time, and I may fail. I – I'll come home as quickly as I can.'

'I know you will, dear. I wish I could do – anything.'

He held her.

'I'll bring you something you'll like,' he said. 'A surprise. I don't know what yet, but something nice. And Lucy, after – next week – if you mean it, we'll move if you want. Find a new apartment over in Cave Seven. You can order new furniture, and we'll –' He scarcely knew what he was saying. Illusion and reality were too confused.

'We'll think of something, dear,' she said. 'It's all right.'

'I'll go, then,' he said.

She nodded. 'I'll miss you. Hurry back.'

Cody shut the grille of the lift behind him and leaned his head against the steel wall, slumping wearily as he shaped in his mind the code-signal to activate the mechanisms. A preoccupied mind somewhere responded with another segment of the cipher, and a third (someone going by rapidly, late to dinner) tossed in the necessary remaining symbols. Three mental images had to be projected simultaneously to operate the lift. It was a precaution. Escape exits could be operated by telepaths only.

He pushed a slanting door open into a welter of dripping leaves and the sharp, sweet odor of wet pine and rain. A startled rabbit exploded out of the underbrush. Cody shut the camouflaged portal and looked up, squinting against the rain that drove in his face. From somewhere above a voiceless greeting came, a motor hummed and a dark coil rolled smoothly down out of the grayness. Cody set his foot in the stirrup and felt the soft instant upward lift of the basket seat snatching him aloft as he sank into it. The hovering copter received him through a single gaping jaw.

Am Friedmann did not glance back from the controls. He did not need to.

Short, squat, gravely expressionless in face and in manner, he leaned his dark-capped head forward to peer through the rain, his mind detaching enough of itself from attention to the business at hand to send a wordless greeting.

For a moment Cody only leaned back and let the cool, untroubled silence of the open sky wash his mind clean. It was like allowing long-taut muscles to relax at last. The cavern was so filled with closed-down resentments, guilts and fears and tensions that after a while even the air became hard to breathe, for a telepath.

Friedmann had something urgent he wanted to convey. Cody felt the touch of it on the outer edges of his awareness, waiting, letting the newcomer breathe clean air a while. Friedmann's mind hovered as the copter had hovered, patient, abiding the signal.

Under them the pine woods swept backward, tossing, rain-blurred. Water ran down the panes. The motor hummed pleasantly in the coolness. Lucy. Five years now without sight of rain or trees or sky. A lifetime ahead of her without them, or else a quick death, or – the Inductor.

'We've got to have more time,' Friedmann's thought came. 'If a pogrom starts now, it'll spread. I think the paranoids are counting on that. They've been filtering into the key towns – the places where the riots would be apt to start. Like American Gun. Jasper Horne's there.'

'Since when?' Cody asked.

'Three weeks or so. And he's been working hard. You know how the paranoids do it. Read a mind and drop a loaded word at the right time, to keep the tension building. Probably Horne could start a riot in American Gun any time he liked, by now.'

'Not if he's dead,' Cody's thought said, with grim anticipation. He leaned back, watching the mists scud past, thinking of American Gun. It was a gambling town. That was the specialty, anyway, although there was a famous research laboratory in the town, and a master artisan in plastics lived there. But basically men came to American Gun to gamble.

That's what I'll be doing, Cody thought. He watched sunlight dry the raindrops on the window beside him.

Friedmann left Cody at the outskirts of American Gun and sent the copter hurrying east. He had an errand of his own in the town of Bleeding Kansas, five hundred miles away. Cody watched the copter lift in a perfectly empty blue sky.

American Gun lay in a great flat half-saucer rimmed by rising hills and cut across and bounded by a broad, slow river. There was a number of distant toothpick figures on the beach, and a variety of boats on the river, transparent plastic canoes and skiffs glinting in the sun. Dark dots against the placid green indicated swimmers. But the wind blowing up from the river was hot.

Cody stood on the lower foothills, looking down over American Gun. A certain calm relaxed him, now that he was moving directly toward a clearly-seen goal. There were in the town perhaps a hundred buildings, few of them large, and none close to the others. Trees flourished, or would have if their leaves had not drooped limply – all but the ones near the river bank. Only children were moving fast. Under a live-oak Cody could see a little party around a spread white rectangle, having a picnic. Against the white cloth he could see the green and red of watermelon.

A small white dog trotted slowly past him, its tongue lolling. It gave him a bored but wary glance. In its mind was a dim image of a frightful, slavering beast somewhat larger than a tiger. With some difficulty Cody identified the terror as a dachshund whom the little white dog feared.

Somewhat diverted, Cody began to descend the slope toward American Gun. He didn't hurry. The moist, warm air was pleasant against his skin. Unthinking, receptive, for the moment, he let the cross-currents of thought sweep like the sound of a sea through him, while he moved on in half-hypnotic rhythm, focusing on a long Byzantine-style building ahead, and watching it grow larger, step by step.

There was room enough on earth. And surely there were enemies enough besides other men. Man had been fighting a war ever since he stood upright, and there had never been any armistice declared against the oldest enemy of all, the enemy that burned in the hot blue sky, that hid, rod-shaped, toxic and invisible, in the soil, that ebbed now in the river but could rise and flood, the enemy that went on unknowing and unheeding man, whose ancient power always pounded at the dyke man's intelligence had built.

Enemy and friend at once – this gift of the gods. Without it, without the physical and chemical forces which had built this air, this water, this shallow valley of fertile loam, there would have been no life at all. A fairy gift – this planet. Guard it, keep it, watch it – learn to predict and control it – and it will serve you. Forget it while you fight among yourselves, and the burning sun, the flooding waters, the deadly cold, and the fecund micro-organisms will work as they have always worked, in their old pattern, and in that pattern there is no planned place for man. How like a god!

By now Cody was at the little park before the long Byzantine building. Trees were wilting above the brownish lawns. A shallow rectangular pool held goldfish, who gulped hopefully as they swam to the surface and flipped down again. The little minds of the fish lay open to Cody, minds thoughtless as so many bright, tiny, steady flames on little birthday candles, as he walked past the pool.

He did not enter the Byzantine building. He had not intended to, physically. Instead, he turned toward one of the shoulder-high pedestals set in irregular rows along the front of the building and stopped before one that was not in use. A few men and women had their heads bowed over the pedestals, peering into eyepieces. Not many. It was too hot, even here in the shade.

Cody bent over the eyepiece of his pedestal, found a coin in his pocket, and pushed it into the slot. The blackness at which he stared turned into a pattern of bright letters: *Radio-cobalt*. Then a series of number-ranges appeared, one by one. At random Cody pushed the button that indicated his choice. That started the mechanism. He found himself looking into a magnified Wilson cloud-chamber, streaked with flashing trails of sub-atomic activity. Just above the image a counter ticked off the number of electronic collisions. If his guess had been accurate enough, he might win the jackpot, and prove –

Nothing. Nothing at all. But as Cody's mind began to range, he felt the eager, troubled anticipation in the minds around him, and realized that to win, for most of these others, would prove a great deal.

For, basically, those minds held no confidence at all. Over all of them lay the heavy threat that had shadowed the world since the Blowup and put an irresistible weapon in every hand, a cache of Eggs in every town. Instead of national walls, there was now a wall around each town – and around each individual. Survival still depended on luck – blind chance.

And so the gambling towns, like American Gun, flourished. Here, at the casinos, at the slot-machine, at roulette and craps and chuck-a-luck and faro, men could prove that the blind goddess favored them, and that they were still safe. The social uncertainty was shifted to the mechanical uncertainty of the fall of dice or the spin of a wheel, and personal responsibility was shifted to the hands of the lady the Greeks called Tuche and the Romans, Fortuna.

Cody felt people moving past him, in and out of the casino. To his sensitive mind the hot air seemed to spark. Perhaps that was because of the steadily mounting tension spreading from no source a human could identify and which no human could ignore. But Cody knew the source. Jasper Horne had not been in American Gun for weeks without a purpose.

Here, if anywhere, the pogrom could be started.

And here, in American Gun, was the force which had driven Cody helplessly into his dilemma, relentlessly forcing him toward the choice that no man could contemplate for too long without seeking some easier answer. Here was the pressure which had forced his hand to the knife, and the knife to his neck. And here, too, was the man who was responsible.

Jasper Horne, Cody thought as the flashing streaks of the cloud-chamber burned before his eyes. His mind polarized toward that goal with a deadly intentness. Allenby, back in the Caves, had been right. To kill Horne, not himself, was the real goal for Cody – because that would risk merely his own life; it would not mean betrayal of his own people by dropping the responsibility he carried for all of them. The paranoids had been the enemy, from the very beginning. Always they had worked to destroy the acceptance of the Baldies by the rest of mankind. They were the ones who had caused the destruction of Sequoia, and the need to keep humans captives in the Caves. Had that not happened, he would probably have never met Lucy, and she would be happier now, and so would he. Now, no matter how hard both of them might try, there could never be any real answer for them, or for their child. There was no way out. No matter what happened, there were wounds that could never heal.

The earth itself was both enemy and friend. But the paranoids were all enemy, and of them all, Jasper Horne was somewhere here in American Gun, within Jeff Cody's reach – a man to be killed, if for no other reason, than because he and his kindred paranoids had made the Baldies killers.

The glittering streaks of light in the cloud-chamber died. The viewer went dark. Cody had won nothing. He slipped another coin into the slot and again watched the electronic bombardment, while his mind ranged and closed in toward his quarry.

Within the Byzantine building a flurry of thoughts whirled like the roulette wheels. This was a gossip center for American Gun. Here, now and then, he caught images which he identified with Horne. Gradually he tested these thoughts, like directional antenna, until a picture of Horne's habits began to clarify. But other things clarified as well – the mounting pressure of events in the town which no non-telepath connected with the paranoid's presence.

No one in American Gun had shaved for twenty-four hours. Oh, some had – but not many. The Baldies had no need to shave, and, of course, there were humans courageous enough to risk suspicion. In the nearby research laboratories the no-shaving movement had not taken hold. And there were others, but not many, and those with smooth chins often moved in a circle of suspicious glances and left trails of hostile murmurings behind them.

So it might be doubly difficult to kill Horne. Violence could be the move that touched off the pogrom – exactly what Cody had hoped to avoid by eliminating the paranoid. That meant Horne would have to be killed privately, above all, away from any potential mob leaders who might trigger a riot. (There were such men in American Gun; Horne had found them already. They would be the ones to lead the mob when the time came.)

– he's at the Last Chance.

Cody lifted his head, dazzled for an instant by the deep blue shadow and the white sunlight. His mind mapped a picture of American Gun from the data he had already gathered. The Last Chance would be at the north end of town, near the research laboratories. Horne might or might not still be there, but it would be easy to pick up his trail.

Cody skirted the goldfish-pool, past the tiny flickering flames of the small, drifting minds, and took a path leading northward through the town. His thoughts continued to range. Several times he caught the thoughts of other Baldies. Through them he could have located Horne instantly and accurately, but they did not wear the Mute helmets, and their minds could have been read in turn by the paranoid. And Horne must not be forewarned. Cody reached up to touch the fine-spun skein of filaments hidden beneath his wig. As long as he wore the Mute helmet, Horne could not read his mind.

The crowds began to thicken. Rumors went softly flickering past like heat lightning in the sweltering air, gathering corroborative detail as they went. Someone (Cody's mind heard the whisper) had broken the bank at the Gold Horseshoe last night, walked out with two heavy sacks of credits, and carelessly let his wig blow off in the doorway, revealing a hairless head. Yes, the Baldies were casting off the mask now and grabbing up credits in every way they could, preparing for the zero hour when they would take over the nation ...

Cody walked a little faster. Stray thoughts from the Baldies in American Gun whispered to him. *Things are getting out of hand*, the word went silently through the air from mind to mind, from anxious group to group, from Baldies going stoically about their business among the humans and showing impassive faces as their minds touched and clung together on the verge of panic. Today mothers had kept their children home, and the family copters were fueled and ready.

Above the crowd, Cody saw the flashing sign of the Last Chance ahead. He moved on, his mind searching for the presence of Horne. And in spite of the noiseless tensions straining and wrenching through the hot air, he realized that he felt curiously happy. Everything seemed very easy and simple now, for the first time in many months. *Kill Horne.* That was all; that was enough. *Kill Horne*, his mind said, without any of the doubts and unsureness of the last months and years.

He paused outside the old-fashioned photo-electric doors of the Last Chance, searching for his enemy. The rumors blew past him, fresh as if no voice had ever whispered them before. The whispers spoke of the string of freight-copters grounded with a fuel-leak at the edge of town, the repair man working among the cargo who accidentally broke a slat on a crate of oranges. Inside the liner of oranges were – queer-looking rifles – atomic? Three Eggs carefully packed in foam-rubber? Unconscious humans en route to a secret Baldy vivisection lab?

Then an invisible breath seemed to sweep through the hot, still air.

It was the paranoid aura. As, in grand mal, the epileptic attack is presaged by an indefinable feeling of impending disaster, so the physical approach of a paranoid carries before it the shadowy halo pulsing outward from the distorted mind. Cody had felt this before, but each time he knew afresh the same faint shrinking, as though his contact with the bright, hot, green world around him had thinned and snapped for an instant.

He turned slowly and crossed the street, threading past the uneasy, murmuring groups of unshaved men, past their hostile stares. Ahead was a little restaurant – the Copter Vane Eatery. The aura thickened. Cody stopped outside of the door of the restaurant and reached out telepathically.

The rumors flew past him. A man knew a man who had a Baldy neighbor who lost three fingers in a duel a month ago, and today had three fingers growing as good as new, grafted on in a private Baldy hospital. (But Baldies won't duel – never mind that!) *They* could work miracles in medicine now, but you didn't see them doing it for humans, did you? If they weren't stopped soon, who could tell what might happen next?

Stiff with arrogance, wary with suspicion, the mind of Jasper Horne, within the restaurant, sent out its own murky thoughts too – egotistical, prideful, sensitive, and inflexible. And there was a dim thought stirring in that cloudy mind, like an ember under gray ash, fading and brightening again into half-clarity, which made Cody, at the restaurant's door, pause and stiffen into immobility for fear that the telepathic paranoid might sense his presence.

Horne had not come to American Gun to start a pogrom.

His real motive was far more deadly. It was –

What?

That was what Cody could not see – yet. He had glimpsed the shadow of a thought, and that glimpse had been enough to flash a sharp warning to his mind, a signal of terrible urgency. Horne's real motive lay deeply buried. But it had to be found out. Cody felt quite certain of that.

He stepped aside, leaned against the wall of the building, and glanced idly around, while from under the Mute helmet his mind probed very delicately and sensitively toward Horne.

Gently … gently.

The paranoid was sitting alone in a booth near the back of the restaurant. His thoughts were clouded with repression. And he was concentrating on his lunch, not consciously thinking of the thing which had drifted across the surface of his mind for a triumphant instant. Unless this concept was summoned into consciousness, Cody could not read it without deep probing, which Horne would immediately sense.

Yet there was a way. The right cues would summon up the appropriate responses in any mind. But those cues would have to be implanted in Horne's thoughts very delicately, so that they would seem perfectly natural, and his own. Cody looked across the street, beyond the murmuring knots of men, at the Last Chance. Horne had been there half an hour ago. It was a fair cue. He sent the concept *Last Chance* softly into Horne's mind.

And that mind flinched warily, searched, found nothing (the Mute helmet guarded Cody), and then the cue summoned up its responses.

Last Chance gambling but I'm the one who's really gambling with them all of them their lives I can kill them all if in time – the thought-chain broke as videomusic swelled within the restaurant. Horne lifted his fork and began to eat again.

Cody fitted the beat of his thought to the music's beat and sent the message to Horne.

Kill them all kill them all kill them all

Loose the virus, Horne's response came to the stimulus he thought was his own. *Pomerance is getting closer every day control the resonance mutate a virus kill them all kill them all KILL THEM ALL!*

Cody braced himself against the red rage that poured out from the paranoid.

Pomerance, he thought. *Pomerance.*

Pomerance in the labs, Horne thought, and formed a sensory image. Not far away – only two blocks away – were the research laboratories of American Gun, and in them was a man named Pomerance, a biochemist, a non-telepath. He was working on a certain experiment which – if it succeeded – would enable the paranoids to develop a virus as deadly and as specialized as the virus of Operation Apocalypse.

And this was the real reason for Horne's presence in American Gun. The pogrom-plan was a cover-up. It was camouflage to deceive the Baldies, while Horne went about his real purpose of telepathically following Pomerance's experiments toward the goal of an Operation Apocalypse brought about by the paranoids themselves.

Pomerance was not aiming at such a goal, of course. He was a biochemist; his aim was to develop a more efficient bacteriophage – but the method he would need to develop that could also be applied to far deadlier aims.

Gently Cody manipulated the paranoid's mind. He learned a little more. Pomerance might fail – Horne realized that. But in that case, then the pogrom could be set off. It would be better to find and use a human-killing virus, for in a pogrom paranoid lives would be lost too – but there would be a pogrom if no better way offered. Conditions were ripe. Horne had built the tension in American Gun; he had located the potential mob-leaders; he could start the pogrom at any time he desired – and that would be the signal for other paranoids across the nation to do the same. That universal pogrom would force the Baldies to release Operation Apocalypse – so the same end would be achieved. But it would be better to wait a little, just a little, following Pomerance's experiments closely. He seemed to be very near his goal.

Too near, Cody thought, his body swaying a little toward the restaurant's door. He was wasting time. *Kill Horne, kill him now*, he told himself – but hesitated still, because there was something else in the paranoid's mind that puzzled him. Too much confidence was built on that twisted, shaky foundation of paranoid personality. There must be some reason for that surprising lack of anxiety.

Cody probed again with careful cues that brushed the other mind lightly. Yes, there was a reason. There was a bomb hidden in Pomerance's laboratory.

Why?

Horne had that information, and Cody gently extracted it. The biochemist must not be allowed to fall alive into the hands of Baldies. The bomb was triggered to explode whenever Horne summoned to consciousness a certain complex of symbols – the paranoid's mind shifted quickly away from that dangerous equation – and it would also explode if Horne's mind *stopped* thinking.

That is, if Horne died.

Like the pattern of a burglar alarm, an interruption in the flow of current, the radiations emitted constantly by Horne's mind sleeping or waking, would break the circuit and set off the alarm – the bomb that would kill Pomerance. Cody saw the location of that bomb very clearly in Horne's mental image of the laboratory.

So, if he killed Horne, Pomerance would die too. But why was this important to the paranoid?

Cody probed again, and suddenly understood the reason.

Pomerance's research was centered around resonance differential applied to the nucleoproteins that were viruses. But there were other types of nucleoproteins; the telepathic function itself depended on the resonance of nucleoproteins in the human brain. If Pomerance's experiment succeeded, it would mean ...

It would mean that telepathy could be induced in a non-telepath!

It was the answer to the problem of the Inductor, the one answer that could solve the universal problem of a world in schism. In the hands of the paranoids, Pomerance's method could destroy all humans. In the hands of the Baldies, it could make all mankind one. It could –

Suddenly Cody knew that Horne had discovered his presence.

Instantly Horne began to build in his mind the equation that would set off the bomb in Pomerance's laboratory. Cody's mind leaped into the future. He could kill Horne before the paranoid had finished, but if he did that, the other's death would trigger the bomb with equal certainty. Pomerance would die – and that must not be allowed to happen. More than lives depended on the biochemist's survival.

There was no way to stop Horne's thoughts except one. Cody's probing into the other's mind had told him a great deal about that proud, inflexible, unsure personality. He now knew more about Horne than the latter himself did. And he had discovered one vital point. Horne was not psychotic; he had not lost touch with reality, but, like many paranoids, he had psychopathological symptoms, and one of these was his strong tendency to what Allenby would have called hypnogogic hallucinations – vivid sensory images occurring in the drowsy state just before sleep. And such hallucinations can easily be produced by hypnosis.

All Cody had to do was to convince Horne that he had momentarily been hallucinated. That, and a little more – a good deal more.

At least, Cody had a good insight into what forms such imagery would take for the paranoid, with his strong delusions of persecution and grandeur. So Cody projected the idea that he, representing the Baldies, had come to Horne to offer a truce, to make a pact with the paranoids against the humans – exactly the kind of vivid wish-fulfilling fantasy Horne must often have experienced. And at the same time he summoned up the mental image of Jasper Horne and let Horne see it.

That action was natural enough, even within the frame of an hallucination. When you communicate with another, you visualize him in your own mind, in many more dimensions than the purely visual ones. Your impressions of his emotional patterns, his memories, his thoughts, the complex image of his whole personality as you perceive it, is summoned up as a subjective correlative of the objective man with whom you communicate. The burning brightness of that Luciferean image stood clear between the meeting minds, blazingly sharp and vivid, in a way that the murky mind of the paranoid had never known.

The ancient Greeks knew what the mechanism of identification meant – they told the story of Narcissus. And the lure caught Jasper Horne, who could identify with no other man than himself, or a god made in his own image. His paranoid egotism reflected itself in that ego-image and was reflected again and so endlessly, while Cody delicately tested and touched the thoughts of the other and watched for the first slackening of consciousness.

At least Horne had paused in his mental building of the concept that would destroy Pomerance. The paranoid hesitated, unsure, his grasp of reality telling him that the Baldies could not, would not send an emissary to capitulate, and that therefore his senses, which had warned him of Cody's presence, had lied. Such panics were not unknown to Horne. So he could accept – tentatively – the suggestion that his senses had tricked him.

Very, very gently, still maintaining that dazzling ego-image of Jasper Horne like a glittering lure on a baited hook, Cody sent quiet cue-thoughts slipping into the hesitant mind. At first they were obviously true thoughts, true, at least, according to the paranoid's system of belief. They were pleasant, reassuring thoughts. Lulled, Horne watched the ego-image which he himself had often summoned up – yet never before so clearly and dazzlingly. Narcissus watched his image in the clear, deep pool of Cody's mind.

So, sitting alone in the restaurant booth, Horne let his wariness relax little by little, and Cody's soft assault moved into a new area. The thoughts Cody sent out now were not quite true, but still not false enough to startle the paranoid, who took them for his own thoughts. *I've had these hallucinations before. Usually just before going to sleep. I'm having them now. So I must be going to sleep. I am sleepy. My eyelids feel heavy …*

The lulling, monotonous thoughts began to submerge Horne's consciousness. Gradually the hypnosis grew. Narcissus watched Narcissus …

Sleep, sleep, Cody's mind whispered. *You will not waken until I command you. Nothing else will waken you. Sleep deeply – sleep.*

The paranoid slept.

Cody began to run along the street as fast as he could. No other Baldy in American Gun was nearer to the research laboratory than he was, and if Pomerance were to be saved, it was his job alone. And he might easily fail. Jasper Horne was sitting in hypnotic sleep in a crowded restaurant, and at any moment someone might speak to him or shake him back into consciousness. The hypnosis was not deep. It might hold, or it might break at any moment. In spite of Cody's final suggestions to the paranoid, the latter could be awakened quite easily, and by anyone.

Cody ran on. Suppose he got Pomerance out of the lab in time? Could he get back to the restaurant again before Horne wakened?

No, Cody thought, the hypnosis isn't deep enough. It'll be a miracle if Horne stays under more than a few minutes. If I can save Pomerance, that will be miracle enough.

But as soon as Horne realizes what's happened, he won't wait. He'll start the pogrom. It's all ready, here in American Gun; he's planted the dynamite, and all he has to do is touch the detonator. All right. I can't be sure that what I'm doing is right. I think it is. I can't be sure. If I save Pomerance, Horne will probably start the pogrom before I can get back and kill him. But I can't let Pomerance die; he can solve the problem of the Inductor.

Hurry!

He ran toward a group of long, low buildings. He knew the way; he had seen it in Horne's mind. He ran toward one of the buildings, thrust open the door, and was in the laboratory.

A gaunt, gray-haired man in a stained smock turned to stare at him. It was Pomerance; no telepath can ever be mistaken on a question of identity. It was Pomerance – and as Cody realized that, he also realized that two blocks away, in the Copter Vane Eatery, Jasper Horne had stirred, wakened, and reached out in sudden panic to touch Pomerance's mind.

Instantly Cody was racing down the length of the long laboratory. Beyond Pomerance were floor-length windows opening on hot sunlight, blue sky, and parched brown grass. If they could reach the windows –

It seemed to Cody that he crossed the room in no time at all. No time, and yet another kind of time seemed to draw out endlessly as, in the distant mind of the paranoid, he saw the triggering equation building up that would set off the bomb's mechanism. Now the equation was complete. Now time would stop in one bursting moment of death.

Yet there was time. Cody sent out a wordless call, a summons that rang like a great alarm bell in the minds of every Baldy in American Gun. At the same moment he reached Pomerance and used his own momentum to lift the other man bodily as he plunged toward the windows. Then the floor rose underfoot and the air rushed outward before the first soundless compression wave that moved in front of the explosion.

The window loomed before them, bright, high, patterned with small panes. Cody's shoulder struck, he felt wood and glass shatter without a sound because of the great, white, bursting roar of the explosion, louder than any sound could be.

The blast exploded in a white blindness all around him and beyond shattering glass the void opened up under him.

He was falling with Pomerance through hot, dry outdoor air and darkness, darkness in the full heat of the sun, falling and turning while glass rained down around them and the noise of the explosion went on and on forever …

In front of the Copter Vane Eatery two transients scuffled. Jasper Horne, in the crowd, said something under his breath. Another man repeated it, louder. One of the transients flushed darkly. (It was a trigger phrase as certain to rouse this man's aggressions as the equation that had exploded the bomb.) In a moment a dagger was pulled from its sheath, and a full-fledged duel was in progress in the middle of a noisy circle. The winner was a hairy-faced, hairy-chested man with a partially bald head. His knife-work had been very deft and sure. Too sure, Jasper Horne said in a loud whisper. The whispers flew around the circle. Anybody could win a duel if he could read the other man's mind. If *They* could grow fingers maybe they could grow hair.

Jasper Horne said something, exactly the right something, to the potential mob-leader beside him.

The potential mob-leader scowled, swore, and took a step forward. Deftly he tripped the winner from behind as he was sheathing his dagger. The knife flew spinning across the pavement. Three men were on the falling baldhead as he went down. Two of them held him while the third tugged at his tonsure-fringe of hair. It held. The victim bellowed with rage and resisted so strongly that four or five bystanders were sent sprawling. One of them lost his wig …

This was neither sleep nor waking. It was Limbo. He floated in the womb of non-self, the only real privacy a telepath can ever know, and what he wanted was to stay here for ever and ever. But he was a telepath. He could not, even in the secret fastness of his own mind, pretend what was not true, for his mind lay quite open – at least to wearers of the Mute helmets like his own.

Yet it was hard to waken. It was hard to force himself, of his own volition, to stoop and pick up whatever burdens might be waiting for him, new and old. If his life could be lived as had been the last minute he remembered, without any indecision or unsureness, but with only the certain need for physical action *(is Pomerance alive*, something in his wakening mind asked), then it would be easy indeed to lift himself up out of this warm, gray silence which was so infinitely restful, without even dreams *(but Pomerance?)*.

And as always, the thought of another made something in Cody brace and lift itself with weary stubbornness. Instantly he was oriented. He did not need to depend on his own sleep-confused senses alone. All through the Caves, and above them, and in copters in midair, was a stirring and a confused sense of urgency and troubled motion, and each mind held one thought under whatever other thoughts might be preoccupying the upper levels of the mind.

The thought was *pogrom*.

Cody asked one question: *Should I have killed Horne instead of trying to save Pomerance?* But he did not wait for an answer. The decision had been his own, after all. He opened his eyes (knowing in what infirmary bed in what sector of the Caves he lay) and looked up at the round, ruddy face of Allenby.

'Pomerance?' he asked.

'Alive,' the psychologist answered wordlessly. 'Some of the American Gun Baldies got to you right after the explosion. They had to work fast. Horne had set off the pogrom. But they had a fast copter ready, and gave you and Pomerance first aid en route. That was two days ago.'

'Two days?'

'Pomerance was unconscious for only a few hours. But we kept you under till now – you needed it. However, I guess you'll live, in case you're wondering.'

'How long will any of us live?' Cody's thought whispered.

'Get up and dress,' Allenby ordered. 'There's work to be done. Here's your clothes. How long? I don't know. The pogrom's been spreading for two days. The paranoids had everything very neatly planned. It looks like a total pogrom this time, Jeff. But we've got Pomerance. And I think we've got the Inductor.'

'But Pomerance isn't one of us.'

'He's with us, though. Not all humans are anti-Baldy, thank God. As soon as Pomerance understood the situation, he voluntarily offered to help in any way he could. So come along. We're ready to try the Inductor. I wanted you to be there. Can you manage?'

Cody nodded. He was stiff, and quite weak, and there were a good many aches and pains under the sprayed-on plastic bandages, but it felt fine to stand up and walk. He followed Allenby out into the corridor and along it. The troubled, urgent stirring of innumerable thoughts moved all around him. He remembered Lucy. *Not all humans are anti-Baldy*. And not all Baldies are anti-human, he added, thinking of what had been done to the humans like Lucy who had been condemned to life imprisonment within the Caves.

'She'll be there – in the lab,' Allenby told Cody. 'She offered to be one of the subjects. We've got an Inductor jury-rigged according to Pomerance's theory – at least, we started with his theory and went on from there, every scientist among us. It was quite a job. I hope –' The thought of the pogrom shadowed Allenby's mind briefly and was repressed. Cody thought: *I shall find time, Cassius, I shall find time …*

'Yes,' the psychologist agreed. 'Later, Jeff. Later. The Inductor is our goal right now. Nothing else. You haven't thought of Jasper Horne since you woke up, have you?'

Cody realized that he had scarcely done so. Now, as he did, he saw the paranoid leader as something remote and depersonalized, a moving figure in a great complex of action, but no longer the emotion-charged target of his hate.

'I guess I don't feel the need to kill him,' Cody agreed. 'He's not really important any more. The worst he could do was start the pogrom, and he's done that. I'd kill him if I had the chance, but for a different reason – now.' He glanced at Allenby. 'Will the Inductor work?' he asked.

'That's what we're going to find out. But it ought to – it ought to,' Allenby said, opening a door in the wall of the corridor. Cody followed the psychologist into one of the caverns which had been made into an experimental laboratory.

There was a great deal going on in the cave, but Cody was not distracted by external sense-impressions; he turned immediately toward where Lucy was standing, the baby in her arms. He went toward her quickly. He reached out to her mind and then checked himself. There was, perhaps, too much he did not want to know, now or ever.

Cody said, 'These bandages don't mean anything. I feel fine.'

'They told me,' Lucy said. 'It was one time I was glad of telepathy. I knew they could really tell if you were all right – even if you were unconscious.'

He put his arm around her, looking down at the sleeping baby.

Lucy said, 'I couldn't tell a thing by watching you. You might have been –

dead. But it was so good to have Allenby and the others able to look into your mind and make sure you were all right. I wanted to do something to help, but there wasn't anything I *could* do. Except ... this. Allenby told me he needed volunteers for the Inductor experiment. So I volunteered. It's one way I *can* help – and I want to.'

So Lucy knew about the Inductor now. Well, the time and need for secrecy was past. It no longer mattered how much or how little the prisoners in the Caves knew. It no longer mattered, now that the pogrom had begun.

'It's a total pogrom this time, isn't it?' she asked, and he had an irrational second of amazement *(telepathy?)* before he realized that Lucy was merely reacting to cues learned through long familiarity with his behavior. All married couples have flashes of this kind of pseudo-telepathy, if there is real sympathy between them. And in spite of everything, that sympathy had existed. It was strange to know this now, to be sure of it and to feel elation, when so little time might remain. The pogrom could still destroy everything, in spite of the Inductor.

'Lucy,' he said. 'If we fail – we'll make sure you get safely out of the Caves, back home –'

She looked down at the baby, and then turned away from Cody. He suddenly realized, as men have always done, that even with telepathic power to aid him, he would never really understand a woman's reactions – not even Lucy's.

'Aren't you ready yet?' she asked Allenby.

'I think so,' he said. 'Let somebody hold the baby, Lucy.'

She turned back to Cody, smiled at him, and put the baby in his arms. Then she followed Allenby toward an insulated chair, jury-rigged with a tangle of wires which led to a complicated instrument panel.

The mind of the baby had a little flame in it like the flames Cody remembered in the goldfish in the pool back at American Gun. But there was a very great difference. He did not know exactly what it was, but he had not felt pity and fear as he watched the glimmering minds of the fish. The mind of his child, his and Lucy's, held a small flame that burned with ridiculous confidence for so small and helpless a creature, and yet each slight stimulus, the rocking movement of his arms, the slight hunger-contractions of the child's stomach, made the fragile flame quiver and blow in a new direction before it swung back to its perseverant burning. So many things would shake that flame, in even the best of all worlds – but, he thought with sudden clarity, in that flame the personality of the child would be forged and made strong.

He looked toward Lucy. She was sitting in the chair now, and electrodes were being attached to her temples and the base of her skull. A man he recognized as Pomerance, gaunt and gray-haired, was hovering over her, getting in the way of the experimenters. In Pomerance's mind, Cody saw, was a slight irritation the man was trying hard to repress. *This application, this connection – I don't understand how it fits the theory. My God, if only I were a telepath! But if the Inductor works, I can be. Now how does this hook-up fit into* – and then the thoughts swung into inductive abstractions as the biochemist tried to puzzle the problem out.

The cave-laboratory was crowded. There were the Mute-scientists, and there were a score of captives from the Caves – all volunteers, Cody realized warmly. In spite of everything, they had wanted to help, as Lucy had wanted to.

Now the test was beginning. Lucy relaxed in the chair, her thoughts nervously considering the pressure of the electrodes. Cody withdrew his mind. He felt nervous too. He scanned the group, found a receptive mind, and recognized Allenby.

'Suppose the Inductor works,' Cody said in silence. 'How will that stop the pogrom?'

'We'll offer telepathy to everybody,' Allenby told him. 'There's a video hook-up all ready to cut in on every screen in every town. I think even a lynch mob will stop to listen if they're offered telepathy.'

'I wonder.'

'Besides, there are plenty of humans on our side, like Pomerance. We've got –' The thought paused.

For something was happening to Lucy's mind. It was like a wave, a flood of something as indefinable as abstract music rising in Lucy's thoughts as the nucleoproteins of her brain altered. *She's becoming a telepath, one of us*, Cody thought.

'Power off,' Allenby said suddenly. He bent forward and removed the electrodes. 'Wait a minute, now, Lucy.' He stopped talking, but his mind spoke urgently in silence.

Move your right hand, Lucy. Move your right hand.

Not a Baldy looked at Lucy's hands. There must be no unconscious signals.

Lucy did not move. Her mind, opened to Cody, suddenly and appallingly reminded him of Jasper Horne's walled mind. He did not know why, but a little thrill of fear touched him.

Move your right hand.

No response.

Try another command, someone suggested. *Lucy – stand up. Stand up.*

She did not move.

It may take time, a Baldy suggested desperately. *She may need time to learn –*

Maybe, Allenby thought. *But we'd better try another subject.*

'All right, Lucy,' Cody said. 'Come over here with me. We're going to try someone else.'

'Didn't it work?' she asked. She went to him, staring into his eyes as though trying to force rapport between mind and mind.

'We can't tell yet,' he said. 'Watch June.'

June Barton was in the chair now, flinching a little as the electrodes were attached.

In Cody's thoughts something moved uneasily – something he had not thought of since he woke. If the Inductor failed, then – it would be his problem again, the same old problem, which he had failed to solve. The dilemma which had sent him out to try to kill Jasper Horne. The responsibility that was too great for any one man to carry after a while. Operation Apocalypse. *The end of all flesh …*

Very quickly he turned his mind from that thought. He reached out mentally with a sense of panic, while his arm tightened about Lucy. *(Would he have to kill her – her and their child? It may not come to that. Don't think about it!)* He searched for a concept intricate enough to drive the obsessive terror from his mind. *The Inductor*, he asked at random. *What's the theory? How does it work?*

Another mind leaped gratefully toward the question. It was Kunashi, the physicist. From beneath Kunashi's Mute helmet came quick clear thoughts that could not quite conceal the anxiety in the man's mind. For Kunashi, too, was married to a non-telepath.

'You remember when we asked the calculator for a solution to our problem?' (The electrodes were being unclamped from June Barton's head now.) 'We gathered all the data we could to feed into the calculator. We read the minds of human scientists everywhere, and coded all the data that could possibly be relevant. Well, some of that data came from Pomerance's mind, more than a year ago. He wasn't very far along with his theory then, but the key concepts had been formulated – the hypothesis involving mutation of nucleoproteins by resonance. The calculator integrated that with other data and came up with the simplest answer – the virus. It didn't have the necessary data to follow the theory along the lines of the Inductor, even though both concepts depend on the same basic – resonance.'

(Someone else was sitting down in the chair. The electrodes were being attached. Cody felt the growing distress and anxiety in every mind.)

Kunashi went on doggedly, 'Pomerance is a biochemist. He was working on a virus – Japanese encephalitis type A – and trying to mutate it into a specialized bacteriophage.' The thought faltered for an instant and picked up again. 'The reproduction of a virus – or a gene – depends on high internal resonance; it's a nucleoprotein. Theoretically, anything can change into anything else, eventually. But the physical probability of such a change depends on the relative resonance measure of the two states – high for the aminoacid protein chain, for example, and the two states of the benzene ring.'

(Kunashi's wife was sitting down in the chair.)

'The change, the reproduction, also involves high specificity of the chemical substances involved. That's the reason telepaths would be immune to the Operation Apocalypse virus, whatever it is. Now … now specificity can vary not only from species to species, but within the species too. Our immunity is innate. The *(will it work? will it work?)* nucleoprotein of the Operation Apocalypse virus must have a high affinity for certain high-resonance particles in the central nervous system of non-telepaths. Such particles have a great capacity for storing information. So our virus would attack the information centers of the non-telepathic brain.

'That affinity depends on resonance differential – and Pomerance's experiments were aimed at finding a way to alter that differential. Such a method would make it possible to mutate virus-strains with great predictability and control. And it can also be used to induce telepathy. Telepathy depends on high resonance of nucleoproteins in the brain's information centers, and by artificially increasing specificity, the telepathic function can be induced in – in –'

The thought stopped. Kunashi's wife was leaving the experimental chair, and the physicist's mind clouded with doubt, misery, and hopelessness. Cody's thoughts linked with Kunashi's, sending a strong message of wordless warm encouragement – not intellectual hope, he did not have much of that himself – but a deep emotional bridge of understanding and sympathy. It seemed to help a little. It helped Cody, too. He watched Kunashi's wife walk quickly to him, and they linked arms and stood together waiting.

Suddenly Lucy said, 'I want to try again.'

'Do you feel –' Cody began, but immediately knew that there had been no change. Her mind was still walled.

Yet Allenby, across the room, nodded.

'It's worth trying,' he said. 'Let's do it with the power on, this time. The resonance effect should last for several minutes after disconnecting the electrodes, but we won't take any chances.' Cody had taken the baby again, and Lucy was settling herself in the chair. 'Ideally, all these gadgets will be in a small power-pack that will be worn and operating continuously … All right, Lucy? Power on.'

Again mind after mind tried to touch Lucy's. Again Cody sensed, as he had sensed in the minds of the other subjects too, that strange walled aspect that reminded him of Jasper Horne. But Lucy wasn't paranoid!

Yet her mind did not open. So it was failure – not a mechanical failure, for Pomerance's hypothesis had been verified by everything except the ultimate verification of experimental proof. And yet, without that proof, the pogrom would rage on unchecked, spreading and destroying.

She's not paranoid! Cody thought. The baby stirred in his arms. He reached into that warm, shapeless mind and sensed nothing there that reminded him at all of Jasper Horne.

The baby, Allenby thought suddenly. *Try the baby.*

Questions thrust toward the psychologist. But they were not answered. He did not know the answers. He had a hunch, that was all.

Try the baby.

Allenby turned off the power and removed the electrodes from Lucy's head. The baby was laid gently, in his blankets, on the seat Lucy vacated. The electrodes were attached carefully. The baby slept.

Power on, Allenby ordered.

His thoughts reached out toward the child.

The child slept on.

... Defeat, the last defeat of all, Cody knew. Telepaths and non-telepaths were ultimately different, after all. That wall could never go down. No armistice could ever be made. The pogrom could not be stopped.

The paranoids had been right. Telepaths could not exist side by side with non-telepaths.

And suddenly in Cody's mind blazed the flash and roar of the exploding bomb, the blinding thunderclap that was to engulf the whole world now –

On the chair, the baby squirmed, opened its eyes and mouth, and screamed.

In the soft, floating mistiness of its mind was the formless shape of fear – the sudden flash and roar and Cody's own memory of falling helplessly through space – the oldest fears of all, the only fears which are inborn.

For the first time in history, telepathy had been induced.

Cody sat alone at the control panel of the electronic calculator. For there was no time at all now. In a moment the emergency telecast would begin, the last appeal to the group of non-telepaths. They would be offered the Inductor – conditionally. For they could not use it. Only their children could.

If they were willing to accept the Inductor and halt the pogrom, the Baldies would know very quickly. The most secret thoughts of men cannot be hidden from telepaths.

But if they would not accept – the Baldies would know that, too, and then Cody would touch a certain button on the panel before him. Then Operation Apocalypse would begin. In six hours the virus would be ready. In a week or two, ninety per cent of the world's population would be dead or dying. The pogrom might go on until the last, but telepaths could hide efficiently, and they would not have to remain hidden long. The decision was man's.

Cody felt Allenby come in behind him.

'What's your guess?' he asked.

'I don't know. It depends on egotism – paranoia, in a way. Maybe man has learned to be a social animal; maybe he hasn't. We'll soon find out.'

'Yes. Soon. It's the end now, the end of what started with the Blowup.'

'No,' Allenby said, 'it started a long time before that. It started when men first began to live in groups and the groups kept expanding. But before there was any final unification, the Blowup came along. So we had decentralization, and that was the wrong answer. It was ultimate disunity and control by fear. It built up the walls between man and man higher than ever. Aggression is punished very severely now – and in a suspicious, worried, decentralized world there's a tremendous lot of aggression trying to explode. But the conscience represses it – the criminal conscience of a fear-ruled society, built up in every person from childhood. That's why no non-telepathic adult today can let himself receive thoughts – why Lucy and the others couldn't.'

'She'll … never be able to?'

'Never,' Allenby said quietly. 'It's functional hysteric deafness – telepathic deafness. Non-telepaths don't know what other people are thinking – but they believe they know. And they're afraid of it. They project their own repressed aggressions on to others; unconsciously, they feel that every other being is a potential enemy – and so they don't dare become telepaths. They may want to consciously, but unconsciously there's too much fear.'

'Yet the children –'

'If they're young enough, they can become telepaths, like your baby, Jeff. His superego hasn't formed yet. He can learn, and learn realistically, with all minds open to him, with no walls locking him in as he grows and learns.'

Cody remembered something an old poet had written. *Something there is that doesn't love a wall.* Too many walls had been built, for too long, walls that kept each man apart from his neighbor. In infancy, perhaps in early childhood, anyone was capable of receiving telepathic thoughts, given the Inductor. In infancy the mind of the child was whole and healthy and complete, able to learn telepathic as well as verbal communication. But soon, fatally soon, as the child grew and learned, the walls were built.

Then man climbed his wall and sat on it like Humpty Dumpty – and somehow, somewhere, in the long process of maturing and learning, the mind was forever spoiled. It was the fall, not only of Humpty Dumpty, but the immemorial fall of man himself. And then –

All the king's horses and all the king's men couldn't put Humpty Dumpty together again.

For Lucy, it was forever too late.

After a little while, Cody said, 'What about the paranoids? They were telepathic as children. What happened to them?'

Allenby shook his head.

'I don't know the answer to that one, Jeff. It may be an hereditary malfunction. But they don't matter now; they're a minority among telepaths – a very small minority. They've been dangerous only because we were a minority among non-telepaths, and vulnerable to scapegoating. We won't be, if ...'

'What about the secret wave-bands?'

'The Inductor can be built to adapt to any wave-length the human brain can transmit. There won't be any more walls at all.'

'If our offer is accepted. If it isn't – if the pogrom goes on – then I still have the responsibility for Operation Apocalypse.'

'Is it your responsibility?' Allenby asked. 'Is it ours, even? The non-telepaths will be making their own choice.'

'The telecast's starting,' Cody said. 'I wonder how many will listen to it.'

The mob that swept through the town of Easterday, secretly led by a paranoid, swirled toward a big house with a wide verandah. The mob sent up a yell at the sight of the row of men standing on the verandah waiting. But the paranoid hesitated.

The man beside him did not. He shouted and sprinted forward. There was a sharp crack and dust spurted at his feet.

'They've got guns!' somebody yelled.

'Get 'em!'

'Lynch ' em!'

The mob surged forward. Again a rifle snapped.

The mob-leader – not the paranoid, but the apparent leader – swore and dropped to the ground, clutching at his leg.

On the verandah a man stepped forward.

'Get out of here,' he said crisply. 'Get going – fast.'

The leader stared in amazement.

'Doc!' he said. 'But you're not a Baldy. What the hell are you doing?'

The doctor swung his rifle slowly back and forth.

'A lot of us up here aren't Baldies,' he said, glancing along the row of silent men. Several races were represented, but the mob was not concerned with race just now. The lynchers searched out the men on the porch whom they knew to be Baldies – and found each one flanked by coldly determined non-telepaths, armed and waiting.

There weren't many of them, though – the defenders.

That occurred to the leader. He stood up, testing the flesh wound in his calf. He glanced over his shoulder.

'We can take 'em,' he shouted. 'It's ten to one. Let's go get all of 'em!'

He led the wave.

He died first. On the verandah a runty man with spectacles and a scrubby moustache shivered and lowered his gun for a moment. But he did not move from where he stood in the determined line.

The mob drew back.

There was a long pause.

'How long do you think you can hold us off, Doc?' someone called.

The dead man lay on the open ground between the two groups.

The air quivered with heat. The sun moved imperceptibly westward. The mob coalesced tighter, a compact, murderous mass waiting in the sunlight.

Then a telecast screen within the house lit up, and Allenby's voice began to speak to the world.

The telecast was over.

Baldy minds were busy searching, questioning, seeking their answer in minds that could not conceal their true desires. This was a poll that could not be inaccurate. And within minutes the poll would be finished. The answer would be given. On that answer would depend the lives of all who were not telepaths.

Jeff Cody sat alone before the electronic calculator, waiting for the answer.

There could be only one answer a sane man, a sane people, could give. For the Inductor meant, for the first time in human history, a unity based on reality. It opened the gates to the true and greatest adventures, the odyssey into the mysteries of science and art and philosophy. It sounded the trumpet for the last and greatest war against the Ilium of nature itself – the vast, tremendous, unknown universe in which man has struggled and fought and, somehow, survived.

No adult living today could live to see more than the beginning of that vast adventure. But the children would see it.

There could be only one answer a sane people could give. A sane people.

Cody looked at the keyboard before him.

The earth is filled with violence through them.

Yes, there could be another answer. And if that answer were given – *the end of all flesh is come before me.*

I will destroy them with the earth!

Cody's mind leaped ahead. He saw his finger pressing the button on the keyboard, saw Operation Apocalypse flooding like a new deluge across the planet, saw the race of man go down and die beneath that destroying tide, till only telepaths were left alive in all the world, perhaps in all the universe. He remembered the terrible, lonely pang Baldies feel when a Baldy dies.

And he knew that no telepath would be able to close his mind against that apocalyptic murder of all mankind.

There would be the wound which could not heal, which could never heal among a telepathic race whose memories would go on and on, unweakened by transmission down through the generations. A hundred million years might pass, and even then the ancient wound would burn as on the day it had been made.

Operation Apocalypse would destroy the Baldies too. For they would feel that enormous death, feel it with the fatal sensitivity of the telepath, and though physically they might live on, the pain and the guilt would be passed on from generation to crippled generation.

Suddenly Cody moved.

His finger pushed a button. Instantly the guarding monitor began to operate. There was a soft humming that lasted less than a second. Then a light burned bright on the control panel, and under it was a number.

Cody pressed another button. The unerring selectors searched the calculator for the bit of crystal that held the code of Operation Apocalypse. The crystal, with its cipher of frozen dots of energy, was ready.

A thousand minds, sensing Cody's thought, reached toward him, touched him, spoke to him.

He paused for an instant while he learned that man had not yet made his decision.

The voices in his mind became a tumultuous clamor. But the ultimate decision was neither man's nor theirs; the responsibility was his own, and he waited no longer.

He moved his hand quickly forward and felt the cool, smooth plastic of a lever sink with absolute finality beneath his fingers.

On the bit of ferroelectric crystal waiting in the calculator, the cipher-pattern of energy shivered, faded and vanished completely.

Operation Apocalypse was gone.

Still Cody's fingers moved. Memory after memory died within the great machine. Its vast pools of data drained their energy back into the boundless sea of the universe and were lost. Then at last the brain of the calculator was empty. There was no way to re-create the Apocalypse – no way and no time.

Only waiting was left.

He opened his mind. All around him, stretching across the earth, the linked thoughts of the Baldies made a vast, intricate webwork, perhaps the last and mightiest structure man would ever build. They drew him into their midst and made him one with them. There were no barriers at all. They did not judge. They understood, all of them, and he was part of them all in a warm, ultimate unity that was source of enough strength and courage to face whatever decision mankind might make. This might be the last time man would ever bind itself together in this way. The pogrom might go on until the last Baldy died. But until then, no Baldy would live or die alone.

So they waited, together, for the answer that man must give.

SIX

The helicopter has landed. Men run toward me. They're strangers. I can't read their thoughts. I can't see them clearly; everything is dim, fading into wavering, shadowy ripples.

Something is being slipped around my neck. Something presses against the back of my head.

An Inductor.

A man kneels beside me. A doctor. He has a hypodermic.

The hypodermic comes second. The Inductor first of all. For none of us should die alone. None of us live alone any more. Either we are Baldies, or else we wear the Inductor that has made all men telepaths.

The Inductor begins to operate.

I meant to ask the doctor if I would live, but now I know that this is not the important thing. I know that, as warmth and life come back into the universe, and I am no longer alone. What is important is that my mind, my self, is no longer cut off and incomplete, it is expanding, joining with my people, with all life, as I rise from this lonely grave in which I have lain and I am –

We are –

We are one. We are man. The long, long war is ended, and the answer has been given. The dream has been cleansed, and the fire on the hearth is guarded.

It will not burn out, now, until the last man dies.

THE BEST OF HENRY KUTTNER

MIMSY WERE THE BOROGOVES

There's no use trying to describe either Unthahorsten or his surroundings, because, for one thing, a good many million years had passed and, for another, Unthahorsten wasn't on Earth, technically speaking. He was doing the equivalent of standing in the equivalent of a laboratory. He was preparing to test his time machine.

Having turned on the power, Unthahorsten suddenly realized that the Box was empty. Which wouldn't do at all. The device needed a control, a three-dimensional solid which would react to the conditions of another age. Otherwise Unthahorsten couldn't tell, on the machine's return, where and when it had been. Whereas a solid in the Box would automatically be subject to the entropy and cosmic-ray bombardment of the other era, and Unthahorsten could measure the changes, both qualitative and quantitative, when the machine returned. The Calculators could then get to work and, presently, tell Unthahorsten that the Box had briefly visited AD 1,000,000, AD 1000 OR AD 1, as the case might be.

Not that it mattered, except to Unthahorsten. But he was childish in many respects.

There was little time to waste. The Box was beginning to glow and shiver. Unthahorsten stared around wildly, fled into the next glossatch and groped in a storage bin there. He came up with an armful of peculiar-looking stuff. Uh-huh. Some of the discarded toys of his son Snowen, which the boy had brought with him when he had passed over from Earth, after mastering the necessary technique. Well, Snowen needed this junk no longer. He was conditioned, and had put away childish things. Besides, though Unthahorsten's wife kept the toys for sentimental reasons, the experiment was more important.

Unthahorsten left the glossatch and dumped the assortment into the Box, slamming the cover shut before the warning signal flashed. The Box went away. The manner of its departure hurt Unthahorsten's eyes.

He waited.

And he waited.

Eventually he gave up and built another time machine, with identical results. Snowen hadn't been annoyed by the loss of his old toys, nor had Snowen's mother, so Unthahorsten cleaned out the bin and dumped the remainder of his son's childhood relics in the second time machine's Box.

According to his calculations, this one should have appeared on Earth in the latter part of the nineteenth century, AD If that actually occurred, the device remained there.

Disgusted, Unthahorsten decided to make no more time machines. But the mischief had been done. There were two of them, and the first …

Scott Paradine found it while he was playing hooky from the Glendale Grammar School. There was a geography test that day, and Scott saw no sense in memorizing place names – which, in the nineteen-forties, was a fairly sensible theory. Besides, it was the sort of warm spring day, with a touch of coolness in the breeze, which invited a boy to lie down in a field and stare at the occasional clouds till he fell asleep. Nuts to geography! Scott dozed.

About noon he got hungry, so his stocky legs carried him to a nearby store. There he invested his small hoard with penurious care and a sublime disregard for his gastric juices. He went down by the creek to feed.

Having finished his supply of cheese, chocolate and cookies, and having drained the soda-pop bottle to its dregs, Scott caught tadpoles and studied them with a certain amount of scientific curiosity. He did not persevere. Something tumbled down the bank and thudded into the muddy ground near the water, so Scott, with a wary glance around, hurried to investigate.

It was a box. It was, in fact, the Box. The gadgetry hitched to it meant little to Scott, though he wondered why it was so fused and burned. He pondered. With his jack-knife he pried and probed, his tongue sticking out from a corner of his mouth – Hm-m-m. Nobody was around. Where had the box come from? Somebody must have left it here, and sliding soil had dislodged it from its precarious perch.

'That's a helix,' Scott decided, quite erroneously. It was helical, but it wasn't a helix, because of the dimensional warp involved. Had the thing been a model airplane, no matter how complicated, it would have held few mysteries to Scott. As it was, a problem was posed. Something told Scott that the device was a lot more complicated than the spring motor he had deftly dismantled last Friday.

But no boy has ever left a box unopened, unless forcibly dragged away. Scott probed deeper. The angles on this thing were funny. Short circuit, probably. That was why – uh! The knife slipped. Scott sucked his thumb and gave vent to experienced blasphemy.

Maybe it was a music box.

Scott shouldn't have felt depressed. The gadgetry would have given Einstein a headache and driven Steinmetz raving mad. The trouble was, of course, that the box had not yet completely entered the space-time continuum where Scott existed, and therefore it could not be opened – at any rate, not till Scott used a convenient rock to hammer the helical non-helix into a more convenient position.

He hammered it, in fact, from its contact point with the fourth dimension, releasing the space-time torsion it had been maintaining. There was a brittle snap. The box jarred slightly, and lay motionless, no longer only partially in existence. Scott opened it easily now.

The soft, woven helmet was the first thing that caught his eye, but he discarded that without much interest. It was just a cap. Next, he lifted a square, transparent crystal block, small enough to cup in his palm – much too small to contain the maze of apparatus within it. In a moment Scott had solved that problem. The crystal was a sort of magnifying glass, vastly enlarging the things inside the block. Strange things they were, too. Miniature people, for example.

They moved. Like clockwork automatons, though much more smoothly. It was rather like watching a play. Scott was interested in their costumes, but fascinated by their actions. The tiny people were deftly building a house. Scott wished it would catch fire, so he could see the people put it out.

Flames licked up from the half-completed structure. The automatons, with a great deal of odd apparatus, extinguished the blaze.

It didn't take Scott long to catch on. But he was a little worried. The manikins would obey his thoughts. By the time he discovered that, he was frightened and threw the cube from him.

Halfway up the bank, he reconsidered and returned. The crystal lay partly in the water, shining in the sun. It was a toy; Scott sensed that, with the unerring instinct of a child. But he didn't pick it up immediately. Instead, he returned to the box and investigated its remaining contents.

He found some really remarkable gadgets. The afternoon passed all too quickly. Scott finally put the toys back in the box and lugged it home, grunting and puffing. He was quite red-faced by the time he arrived at the kitchen door.

His find he hid at the back of a closet in his room upstairs. The crystal cube he slipped into his pocket, which already bulged with string, a coil of wire, two pennies, a wad of tinfoil, a grimy defense stamp and a chunk of feldspar. Emma, Scott's two-year-old sister, waddled unsteadily in from the hall and said hello.

'Hello, Slug,' Scott nodded, from his altitude of seven years and some months. He patronized Emma shockingly, but she didn't know the difference. Small, plump and wide-eyed, she flopped down on the carpet and stared dolefully at her shoes.

'Tie 'em, Scotty, please?'

'Sap,' Scott told her kindly, but knotted the laces. 'Dinner ready yet?'

Emma nodded.

'Let's see your hands.' For a wonder they were reasonably clean, though probably not aseptic. Scott regarded his own paws thoughtfully and, grimacing, went to the bathroom, where he made a sketchy toilet. The tadpoles had left traces.

Dennis Paradine and his wife Jane were having a cocktail before dinner, downstairs in the living room. He was a youngish, middle-aged man with soft gray hair and a thin, prim-mouthed face; he taught philosophy at the University. Jane was small, neat, dark and very pretty. She sipped her Martini and said:

'New shoes. Like 'em?'

'Here's to crime,' Paradine muttered absently. 'Huh? Shoes? Not now. Wait till I've finished this. I had a bad day.'

'Exams?'

'Yeah. Flaming youth aspiring towards manhood. I hope they die. In considerable agony. *Insh' Allah!*'

'I want the olive,' Jane requested.

'I know,' Paradine said despondently. 'It's been years since I've tasted one myself. In a Martini, I mean. Even if I put six of 'em in your glass, you're still not satisfied.'

'I want yours. Blood brotherhood. Symbolism. That's why.'

Paradine regarded his wife balefully and crossed his long legs. 'You sound like one of my students.'

'Like that hussy Betty Dawson, perhaps?' Jane unsheathed her nails. 'Does she still leer at you in that offensive way?'

'She does. The child is a neat psychological problem. Luckily she isn't mine. If she were –' Paradine nodded significantly. 'Sex consciousness and too many movies. I suppose she still thinks she can get a passing grade by showing me her knees. Which are, by the way, rather bony.'

Jane adjusted her skirt with an air of complacent pride. Paradine uncoiled himself and poured fresh Martinis. 'Candidly, I don't see the point of teaching those apes philosophy. They're all at the wrong age. Their habit patterns, their methods of thinking, are already laid down. They're horribly conservative, not that they'd admit it. The only people who can understand philosophy are mature adults or kids like Emma and Scotty.'

'Well, don't enroll Scotty in your course,' Jane requested. 'He isn't ready to be a *Philosophiae Doctor*. I hold no brief for a child genius, especially when it's my son.'

'Scotty would probably be better at it than Betty Dawson,' Paradine grunted.

'"He died an enfeebled old dotard at five,"' Jane quoted dreamily. 'I want your olive.'

'Here. By the way, I like the shoes.'

'Thank you. Here's Rosalie. Dinner?'

'It's all ready, Miz Pa'dine,' said Rosalie, hovering. 'I'll call Miss Emma 'n' Mista' Scotty.'

'I'll get 'em.' Paradine put his head into the next room and roared, 'Kids! Come and get it!'

Small feet scuttered down the stairs. Scott dashed into view, scrubbed and shining, a rebellious cowlick aimed at the zenith. Emma pursued, levering herself carefully down the steps. Halfway, she gave up the attempt to descend upright and reversed, finishing the task monkey-fashion, her small behind giving an impression of marvellous diligence upon the work in hand. Paradine watched, fascinated by the spectacle, till he was hurled back by the impact of his son's body.

'Hi, Dad!' Scott shrieked.

Paradine recovered himself and regarded Scott with dignity. 'Hi, yourself. Help me in to dinner. You've dislocated at least one of my hip joints.'

But Scott was already tearing into the next room, where he stepped on Jane's new shoes in an ecstasy of affection, burbled an apology and rushed off to find his place at the dinner table. Paradine cocked up an eyebrow as he followed, Emma's pudgy hand desperately gripping his forefinger.

'Wonder what the young devil's been up to.'

'No good, probably,' Jane sighed. 'Hello, darling. Let's see your ears.'

'They're *clean*. Mickey licked 'em.'

'Well, that Airedale's tongue is far cleaner than your ears,' Jane pondered, making a brief examination. 'Still, as long as you can hear, the dirt's only superficial.'

'Fisshul?'

'Just a little, that means.' Jane dragged her daughter to the table and inserted her legs into a high chair. Only lately had Emma graduated to the dignity of dining with the rest of the family, and she was, as Paradine remarked, all eaten up with pride by the prospect. Only babies spilled food, Emma had been told. As a result, she took such painstaking care in conveying her spoon to her mouth that Paradine got the jitters whenever he watched.

'A conveyor belt would be the thing for Emma,' he suggested, pulling out a chair for Jane. 'Small buckets of spinach arriving at her face at stated intervals.'

Dinner proceeded uneventfully until Paradine happened to glance at Scott's plate. 'Hello, there. Sick? Been stuffing yourself at lunch?'

Scott thoughtfully examined the food still left before him. 'I've had all I need, Dad,' he explained.

'You usually eat all you can hold, and a great deal more,' Paradine said. 'I know growing boys need several tons of foodstuff a day, but you're below par tonight. Feel OK?'

'Uh-huh. Honest, I've had all I need.'

'All you *want?*'

'Sure. I eat different.'

'Something they taught you at school?' Jane inquired.

Scott shook his head solemnly.

'Nobody taught me. I found it out myself. I use spit.'

'Try again,' Paradine suggested. 'It's the wrong word.'

'Uh – s-saliva. Hm-m-m?'

'Uh-huh. More pepsin? Is there pepsin in the salivary juices, Jane? I forget.'

'There's poison in mine,' Jane remarked. 'Rosalie's left lumps in the mashed potatoes again.'

But Paradine was interested. 'You mean you're getting everything possible out of your food – no wastage – and eating less?'

Scott thought that over. 'I guess so. It's not just the sp – saliva. I sort of measure how much to put in my mouth at once, and what stuff to mix up. I dunno. I just do it.'

'Hm-m-m,' said Paradine, making a note to check up later. 'Rather a revolutionary idea.' Kids often get screwy notions, but this one might not be so far off the beam. He pursed his lips. 'Eventually I suppose people will eat quite differently – I mean the *way* they eat, as well as what. What they eat, I mean. Jane, our son shows signs of becoming a genius.'

'Oh?'

'It's a rather good point in dietetics he just made. Did you figure it out yourself, Scott?'

'Sure,' the boy said, and really believed it.

'Where'd you get the idea?'

'Oh, I –' Scott wriggled. 'I dunno. It doesn't mean much, I guess.'

Paradine was unreasonably disappointed. 'But surely –'

'S-s-s-spit!' Emma shrieked, overcome by a sudden fit of badness. *'Spit!'* She attempted to demonstrate, but succeeded only in dribbling into her bib.

With a resigned air Jane rescued and reproved her daughter, while Paradine eyed Scott with rather puzzled interest. But it was not till after dinner, in the living room, that anything further happened.

'Any homework?'

'N-no,' Scott said, flushing guiltily. To cover his embarrassment he took from his pocket a gadget he had found in the box, and began to unfold it. The result resembled a tesseract, strung with beads. Paradine didn't see it at first, but Emma did. She wanted to play with it.

'No. Lay off, Slug,' Scott ordered. 'You can watch me.' He fumbled with the beads, making soft, interested noises. Emma extended a fat forefinger and yelped.

'Scotty,' Paradine said warningly.

'I didn't hurt her.'

'Bit me. It did,' Emma mourned.

Paradine looked up. He frowned, staring. What in –

'Is that an abacus?' he asked. 'Let's see it, please.'

Somewhat unwillingly, Scott brought the gadget across to his father's chair. Paradine blinked. The 'abacus,' unfolded, was more than a foot square, composed of thin, rigid wires that interlocked here and there. On the wires the colored beads were strung. They could be slid back and forth, and from one support to another, even at the points of jointure. But – a pierced bead couldn't cross *interlocking* wires.

So, apparently, they weren't pierced. Paradine looked closer. Each small sphere had a deep groove running around it, so that it could be revolved and slid along the wire at the same time. Paradine tried to pull one free. It clung as though magnetically. Iron? It looked more like plastic.

The framework itself – Paradine wasn't a mathematician. But the angles formed by the wires were vaguely shocking, in their ridiculous lack of Euclidean logic. They were a maze. Perhaps that's what the gadget was – a puzzle.

'Where'd you get this?'

'Uncle Harry gave it to me,' Scott said, on the spur of the moment. 'Last Sunday, when he came over.' Uncle Harry was out of town, a circumstance Scott well knew. At the age of seven, a boy soon learns that the vagaries of adults follow a certain definite pattern, and that they are fussy about the donors of gifts. Moreover, Uncle Harry would not return for several weeks; the expiration of that period was unimaginable to Scott, or, at least, the fact that his lie would ultimately be discovered meant less to him than the advantages of being allowed to keep the toy.

Paradine found himself growing slightly confused as he attempted to manipulate the beads. The angles were vaguely illogical. It was like a puzzle. This red bead, if slid along *this* wire to *that* junction, should reach *there* – but it didn't. A maze, odd, but no doubt instructive. Paradine had a well-founded feeling that he'd have no patience with the thing himself.

Scott did, however, retiring to a corner and sliding beads around with much fumbling and grunting. The beads *did* sting, when Scott chose the wrong ones or tried to slide them in the wrong direction. At last he crowed exultantly.

'I did it, Dad!'

'Eh? What? Let's see.' The device looked exactly the same to Paradine, but Scott pointed and beamed.

'I made it disappear.'

'It's still there.'

'That blue bead. It's gone now.'

Paradine didn't believe that, so he merely snorted. Scott puzzled over the framework again. He experimented. This time there were no shocks, even slight. The abacus had showed him the correct method. Now it was up to him to do it on his own. The bizarre angles of the wires seemed a little less confusing now, somehow.

It was a most instructive toy –

It worked, Scott thought, rather like the crystal cube. Reminded of that gadget, he took it from his pocket and relinquished the abacus to Emma, who was struck dumb with joy. She fell to work sliding the beads, this time without protesting against the shocks – which, indeed, were very minor – and, being imitative, she managed to make a bead disappear almost as quickly as had Scott. The blue bead reappeared – but Scott didn't notice. He had forethoughtfully retired into an angle of the chesterfield and an overstuffed chair and amused himself with the cube.

There were the little people inside the thing, tiny manikins much enlarged by the magnifying properties of the crystal. They moved, all right. They built a house. It caught fire, with realistic-seeming flames, and the little people stood by waiting. Scott puffed urgently. 'Put it *out!*'

But nothing happened. Where was that queer fire engine, with revolving arms, that had appeared before? Here it was. It came sailing into the picture and stopped. Scott urged it on.

This was fun. The little people really did what Scott told them, inside of his head. If he made a mistake, they waited till he'd found the right way. They even posed new problems for him.

The cube, too, was a most instructive toy. It was teaching Scott, with alarming rapidity – and teaching him very entertainingly. But it gave him no really new knowledge as yet. He wasn't ready. Later … later …

Emma grew tired of the abacus and went in search of Scott. She couldn't find him, even in his room, but once there the contents of the closet intrigued her. She discovered the box. It contained treasure-trove – a doll, which Scott had already noticed but discarded with a sneer. Squealing, Emma brought the doll downstairs, squatted in the middle of the floor and began to take it apart.

'Darling! What's that?'

'Mr Bear!'

Obviously it wasn't Mr Bear, who was blind, earless, but comforting in his soft fatness. But all dolls were named Mr Bear to Emma.

Jane Paradine hesitated. 'Did you take that from some other little girl?'

'I didn't. She's mine.'

Scott came out from his hiding place, thrusting the cube into his pocket. 'Uh – that's from Uncle Harry.'

'Did Uncle Harry give that to you, Emma?'

'He gave it to me for Emma,' Scott put in hastily, adding another stone to his foundation of deceit. 'Last Sunday.'

'You'll break it, dear.'

Emma brought the doll to her mother. 'She comes apart. See?'

'Oh? It – *ugh!*' Jane sucked in her breath. Paradine looked up quickly. 'What's up?'

She brought the doll over to him, hesitated and then went into the dining room, giving Paradine a significant glance. He followed, closing the door. Jane had already placed the doll on the cleared table.

'This isn't very nice is it, Denny?'

'Hm-m-m.' It was rather unpleasant, at first glance. One might have expected an anatomical dummy in a medical school, but a child's doll …

The thing came apart in sections – skin, muscles, organs – miniature but quite perfect, as far as Paradine could see. He was interested. 'Dunno. Such things haven't the same connotations to a kid.'

'Look at that liver. Is it a liver?'

'Sure. Say, I – this is funny.'

'What?'

'It isn't anatomically perfect, after all.' Paradine pulled up a chair. 'The digestive tract's too short. No large intestine. No appendix, either.'

'Should Emma have a thing like this?'

'I wouldn't mind having it myself,' Paradine said. 'Where on earth did Harry pick it up? No, I don't see any harm in it. Adults are conditioned to react unpleasantly to innards. Kids don't. They figure they're solid inside, like a potato. Emma can get a sound working knowledge of physiology from this doll.'

'But what are those? Nerves?'

'No, these are the nerves. Arteries here; veins here. Funny sort of aorta.' Paradine looked baffled. 'That – what's Latin for network, anyway, huh? *Rita? Rata?*'

'*Rales,*' Jane suggested at random.

'That's a sort of breathing,' Paradine said crushingly. 'I can't figure out what this luminous network of stuff is. It goes all through the body, like nerves.'

'Blood.'

'Nope. Not circulatory, not neural. Funny! It seems to be hooked up with the lungs.'

They became engrossed, puzzling over the strange doll. It was made with remarkable perfection of detail, and that in itself was strange, in view of the physiological variation from the norm. 'Wait'll I get that Gould,' Paradine said, and presently was comparing the doll with anatomical charts. He learned little, except to increase his bafflement.

But it was more fun than a jigsaw puzzle.

Meanwhile, in the adjoining room, Emma was sliding the beads to and fro in the abacus. The motions didn't seem so strange now. Even when the beads vanished. She could almost follow that new direction – almost …

Scott panted, staring into the crystal cube and mentally directing, with many false starts, the building of a structure somewhat more complicated than the one which had been destroyed by fire. He, too, was learning – being conditioned …

Paradine's mistake, from a completely anthropomorphic standpoint, was that he didn't get rid of the toys instantly. He did not realize their significance, and, by the time he did, the progression of circumstances had got well under way. Uncle Harry remained out of town, so Paradine couldn't check with him. Too, the midterm exams were on, which meant arduous mental effort and complete exhaustion at night; and Jane was slightly ill for a week or so. Emma and Scott had free rein with the toys.

'What,' Scott asked his father one evening, 'is a wabe, Dad?'

'Wave?'

He hesitated. 'I – don't *think* so. Isn't "wabe" right?'

'"Wabe" is Scot for 'web.' That it?'

'I don't see how,' Scott muttered, and wandered off, scowling, to amuse himself with the abacus. He was able to handle it quite deftly now. But, with the instinct of children for avoiding interruption, he and Emma usually played with the toys in private. Not obviously, of course – but the more intricate experiments were never performed under the eye of an adult.

Scott was learning fast. What he now saw in the crystal cube had little relationship to the original simple problems. But they were fascinatingly technical. Had Scott realized that his education was being guided and supervised – though merely mechanically – he would probably have lost interest. As it was, his initiative was never quashed.

Abacus, cube, doll and other toys the children found in the box …

Neither Paradine nor Jane guessed how much of an effect the contents of the time machine were having on the kids. How could they? Youngsters are instinctive dramatists, for purposes of self-protection. They have not yet fitted themselves to the exigencies – to them partially inexplicable – of a mature world. Moreover, their lives are complicated by human variables. They are told by one person that playing in the mud is permissible, but that, in their excavations, they must not uproot flowers or small trees. Another adult vetoes mud per se. The Ten Commandments are not carved on stone – they vary; and children are helplessly dependent on the caprice of those who give them birth and feed and clothe them. And tyrannize. The young animal does not resent that benevolent tyranny, for it is an essential part of nature. He is, however, an individualist, and maintains his integrity by a subtle, passive fight.

Under the eyes of an adult he changes. Like an actor on stage, when he remembers, he strives to please, and also to attract attention to himself. Such attempts are not unknown to maturity. But adults are less obvious – to other adults.

It is difficult to admit that children lack subtlety. Children are different from mature animals because they think in another way. We can more or less easily pierce the pretenses they set up, but they can do the same to us. Ruthlessly a child can destroy the pretenses of an adult. Iconoclasm is a child's prerogative.

Foppishness, for example. The amenities of social intercourse, exaggerated not quite to absurdity. The gigolo …

'Such *savoir-faire!* Such punctilious courtesy!' The dowager and the blonde young thing are often impressed. Men have less pleasant comments to make. But the child goes to the root of the matter.

'You're *silly!*'

How can an immature human being understand the complicated system of social relationships? He can't. To him, an exaggeration of natural courtesy is silly. In his functional structure of life patterns, it is rococo. He is an egotistic little animal who cannot visualize himself in the position of another – certainly not an adult. A self-contained, almost perfect natural unit, his wants supplied by others, the child is much like a unicellular creature floating in the bloodstream, nutriment carried to him, waste products carried away.

From the standpoint of logic, a child is rather horribly perfect. A baby must be even more perfect, but so alien to an adult that only superficial standards of comparison apply. The thought processes of an infant are completely unimaginable. But babies think, even before birth. In the womb they move and sleep, not entirely through instinct. We are conditioned to react rather peculiarly to the idea that a nearly viable embryo may think. We are surprised, shocked into laughter and repelled. Nothing human is alien.

But a baby is not human. An embryo is far less human.

That, perhaps, was why Emma learned more from the toys than did Scott. He could communicate his thoughts, of course; Emma could not, except in cryptic fragments. The matter of the scrawls, for example.

Give a young child pencil and paper, and he will draw something which looks different to him than to an adult. The absurd scribbles have little resemblance to a fire engine, but it *is* a fire engine, to a baby. Perhaps it is even three-dimensional. Babies think differently and see differently.

Paradine brooded over that, reading his paper one evening and watching Emma and Scott communicate. Scott was questioning his sister. Sometimes he did it in English. More often he had resource to gibberish and sign language. Emma tried to reply, but the handicap was too great.

Finally Scott got pencil and paper. Emma liked that. Tongue in cheek, she laboriously wrote a message. Scott took the paper, examined it and scowled.

'That isn't right, Emma,' he said.

Emma nodded vigorously. She seized the pencil again and made more scrawls. Scott puzzled for a while, finally smiled rather hesitantly and got up. He vanished into the hall. Emma returned to the abacus.

Paradine rose and glanced down at the paper, with some mad thought that Emma might abruptly have mastered calligraphy. But she hadn't. The paper was covered with meaningless scrawls, of a type familiar to any parent. Paradine pursed his lips.

It might be a graph showing the mental variations of a manic-depressive cockroach, but probably wasn't. Still, it no doubt had meaning to Emma. Perhaps the scribble represented Mr Bear.

Scott returned, looking pleased. He met Emma's gaze and nodded. Paradine felt a twinge of curiosity.

'Secrets?'

'Nope. Emma – uh – asked me to do something for her.'

'Oh.' Paradine, recalling instances of babies who had babbled in unknown tongues and baffled linguists, made a note to pocket the paper when the kids had finished with it. The next day he showed the scrawl to Elkins at the university. Elkins had a sound working knowledge of many unlikely languages, but he chuckled over Emma's venture into literature.

'Here's a free translation, Dennis. Quote. I don't know what this means, but I kid the hell out of my father with it. Unquote.'

The two men laughed and went off to their classes. But later Paradine was to remember the incident. Especially after he met Holloway. Before that, however, months were to pass, and the situation to develop even further towards its climax.

Perhaps Paradine and Jane had evinced too much interest in the toys. Emma and Scott took to keeping them hidden, playing with them only in private. They never did it overtly, but with a certain unobtrusive caution. Nevertheless, Jane especially was somewhat troubled.

She spoke to Paradine about it one evening. 'That doll Harry gave Emma.'

'Yeah?'

'I was downtown today and tried to find out where it came from. No soap.'

'Maybe Harry bought it in New York.'

Jane was unconvinced. 'I asked them about the other things, too. They showed me their stock – Johnson's a big store, you know. But there's nothing like Emma's abacus.'

'Hm-m-m.' Paradine wasn't much interested. They had tickets for a show that night, and it was getting late. So the subject was dropped for the nonce.

Later it cropped up again, when a neighbor telephoned Jane.

'Scotty's never been like that, Denny. Mrs Burns said he frightened the devil out of her Francis.'

'Francis? A little fat bully of a punk, isn't he? Like his father. I broke Burns's nose for him once, when we were sophomores.'

'Stop boasting and listen,' Jane said, mixing a highball. 'Scott showed Francis something that scared him. Hadn't you better –'

'I suppose so.' Paradine listened. Noises in the next room told him the whereabouts of his son. 'Scotty!'

'Bang,' Scott said, and appeared smiling. 'I killed 'em all. Space pirates. You want me, Dad?'

'Yes. If you don't mind leaving the space pirates unburied for a few minutes. What did you do to Francis Burns?'

Scott's blue eyes reflected incredible candor. 'Huh?'

'Try hard. You can remember, I'm sure.'

'Uh. Oh, that. I didn't do nothing.'

'Anything,' Jane corrected absently.

'Anything. Honest. I just let him look into my television set, and it – it scared him.'

'Television set?'

Scott produced the crystal cube. 'It isn't really that. See?'

Paradine examined the gadget, startled by the magnification. All he could see, though, was a maze of meaningless colored designs.

'Uncle Harry –'

Paradine reached for the telephone. Scott gulped. 'Is – is Uncle Harry back in town?'

'Yeah.'

'Well, I gotta take a bath.' Scott headed for the door. Paradine met Jane's gaze and nodded significantly.

Harry was home, but disclaimed all knowledge of the peculiar toys. Rather grimly, Paradine requested Scott to bring down from his room all of the playthings. Finally they lay in a row on the table – cube, abacus, doll, helmet-like cap, several other mysterious contraptions. Scott was cross-examined. He lied valiantly for a time, but broke down at last and bawled, hiccuping his confession.

'Get the box these things came in,' Paradine ordered. 'Then head for bed.'

'Are you – *hup!* – gonna punish me, Daddy?'

'For playing hooky and lying, yes. You know the rules. No more shows for two weeks. No sodas for the same period.'

Scott gulped. 'You gonna keep my things?'

'I don't know yet.'

'Well – g'night, Daddy. G'night, Mom.'

*

After the small figure had gone upstairs, Paradine dragged a chair to the table and carefully scrutinized the box. He poked thoughtfully at the focused gadgetry. Jane watched.

'What is it, Denny?'

'Dunno. Who'd leave a box of toys down by the creek?'

'It might have fallen out of a car.'

'Not at that point. The road doesn't his the creek north of the railroad trestle. Empty lots – nothing else.' Paradine lit a cigarette. 'Drink, honey?'

'I'll fix it.' Jane went to work, her eyes troubled. She brought Paradine a glass and stood behind him, ruffling his hair with her fingers. 'Is anything wrong?'

'Of course not. Only – where did these toys come from?'

'Johnson's didn't know, and they get their stock from New York.'

'I've been checking up, too,' Paradine admitted. 'That doll' – he poked it – 'rather worried me. Custom jobs, maybe, but I wish I knew who'd made 'em.'

'A psychologist? That abacus – don't they give people tests with such things?'

Paradine snapped his fingers. 'Right! And say, there's a guy going to speak at the university next week, fellow named Holloway, who's a child psychologist. He's a big shot, with quite a reputation. He might know something about it.'

'Holloway? I don't –'

'Rex Holloway. He's – hm-m-m! He doesn't live far from here. Do you suppose he might have had these things made himself?'

Jane was examining the abacus. She grimaced and drew back. 'If he did, I don't like him. But see if you can find out, Denny.'

Paradine nodded. 'I shall.'

He drank his highball, frowning. He was vaguely worried. But he wasn't scared – yet.

Rex Holloway was a fat, shiny man, with a bald head and thick spectacles, above which his thick, black brows lay like bushy caterpillars. Paradine brought him home to dinner one night a week later. Holloway did not appear to watch the children, but nothing they did or said was lost on him. His gray eyes, shrewd and bright, missed little.

The toys fascinated him. In the living room the three adults gathered around the table, where the playthings had been placed. Holloway studied them carefully as he listened to what Jane and Paradine had to say. At last he broke his silence.

'I'm glad I came here tonight. But not completely. This is very disturbing, you know.'

'Eh?' Paradine stared, and Jane's face showed her consternation. Holloway's next words did not calm them.

'We are dealing with madness.'

He smiled at the shocked looks they gave him. 'All children are mad, from an adult viewpoint. Ever read Hughes' *High Wind in Jamaica*?'

'I've got it.' Paradine secured the little book from its shelf. Holloway extended a hand, took the book and flipped the pages till he had found the place he wanted. He read aloud:

> *Babies, of course, are not human – they are animals, and have a very ancient and ramified culture, as cats have, and fishes, and even snakes; the same in kind as these, but much more complicated and vivid, since babies are, after all, one of the most developed species of the lower vertebrates. In short, babies have minds which work in terms and categories of their own, which cannot be translated into the terms and categories of the human mind.*

Jane tried to take that calmly, but couldn't. 'You don't mean that Emma –'

'Could you think like your daughter?' Holloway asked. 'Listen: "One can no more think like a baby than one can think like a bee." '

Paradine mixed drinks. Over his shoulder he said, 'You're theorizing quite a bit, aren't you? As I get it, you're implying that babies have a culture of their own, even a high standard of intelligence.'

'Not necessarily. There's no yardstick, you see. All I say is that babies think in other ways than we do. Not necessarily *better* – that's a question of relative values. But with a different matter of extension.' He sought for words, grimacing.

'Fantasy,' Paradine said, rather rudely but annoyed because of Emma. 'Babies don't have different senses from ours.'

'Who said they did?' Holloway demanded. 'They use their minds in a different way, that's all. But it's quite enough!'

'I'm trying to understand,' Jane said slowly. 'All I can think of is my Mixmaster. It can whip up batter and potatoes, but it can squeeze oranges, too.'

'Something like that. The brain's a colloid, a very complicated machine. We don't know much about its potentialities. We don't even know how much it can grasp. But it *is* known that the mind becomes conditioned as the human animal matures. It follows certain familiar theorems, and all thought thereafter is pretty well based on patterns taken for granted. Look at this.' Holloway touched the abacus. 'Have you experimented with it?'

'A little,' Paradine said.

'But not much, eh?'

'Well –'

'Why not?'

'It's pointless,' Paradine complained. 'Even a puzzle has to have some logic. But those crazy angles –'

'Your mind has been conditioned to Euclid,' Holloway said. 'So this – thing – bores us, and seems pointless. But a child knows nothing of Euclid. A different sort of geometry from ours wouldn't impress him as being illogical. He believes what he sees.'

'Are you trying to tell me that this gadget's got a fourth-dimensional extension?' Paradine demanded.

'Not visually, anyway,' Holloway denied. 'All I say is that our minds, conditioned to Euclid, can see nothing in this but an illogical tangle of wires. But a child – especially a baby – might see more. Not at first. It'd be a puzzle, of course. Only a child wouldn't be handicapped by too many preconceived ideas.'

'Hardening of the thought arteries,' Jane interjected.

Paradine was not convinced. 'Then a baby could work calculus better than Einstein? No, I don't mean that. I can see your point, more or less clearly. Only –'

'Well, look. Let's suppose there are two kinds of geometry; we'll limit it, for the sake of the example. Our kind, Euclidean, and another, we'll call *x*. *X* hasn't much relationship to Euclid. It's based on different theorems. Two and two needn't equal four in it; they could equal y^2, or they might not even *equal.* A baby's mind is not yet conditioned, except by certain questionable factors of heredity and environment. Start the infant on Euclid –'

'Poor kid,' Jane said.

Holloway shot her a quick glance. 'The basis of Euclid. Alphabet blocks. Math, geometry, algebra – they come much later. We're familiar with that development. On the other hand, start the baby with the basic principles of our *x* logic.'

'Blocks? What kind?'

Holloway looked at the abacus. 'It wouldn't make much sense to us. But we've been conditioned to Euclid.'

Paradine poured himself a stiff shot of whisky. 'That's pretty awful. You're not limiting to math.'

'Right! I'm not limiting it at all. How can I? I'm not conditioned to *x* logic.'

'There's the answer,' Jane said, with a sigh of relief. 'Who is? It'd take such a person to make the sort of toys you apparently think these are.'

Holloway nodded, his eyes, behind the thick lenses, blinking. 'Such people may exist.'

'Where?'

'They might prefer to keep hidden.'

'Supermen?'

'I wish I knew. You see, Paradine, we've got yardstick trouble again. By our standards these people might seem super-dupers in certain respects. In others they might seem moronic. It's not a quantitative difference; it's qualitative. They *think* different. And I'm sure we can do things they can't.'

'Maybe they wouldn't want to,' Jane said.

Paradine tapped the fused gadgetry on the box. 'What about this? It implies –'

'A purpose, sure.'

'Transportation?'

'One thinks of that first. If so, the box might have come from anywhere.'

'Where – things are – *different*?' Paradine asked slowly.

'Exactly. In space, or even time. I don't know; I'm a psychologist. Unfortunately I'm conditioned to Euclid, too.'

'Funny place it must be,' Jane said. 'Denny, get rid of those toys.'

'I intend to.'

Holloway picked up the crystal cube. 'Did you question the children much?'

Paradine said, 'Yeah. Scott said there were people in that cube when he first looked. I asked him what was in it now.'

'What did he say?' The psychologist's eyes widened.

'He said they were building a place. His exact words. I asked him who – people? But he couldn't explain.'

'No, I suppose not,' Holloway muttered. 'It must be progressive. How long have the children had these toys?'

'About three months, I guess.'

'Time enough. The perfect toy, you see, is both instructive and mechanical. It should do things, to interest a child, and it should teach, preferably unobtrusively. Simple problems at first. Later –'

'*X* logic,' Jane said, white-faced.

Paradine cursed under his breath. 'Emma and Scott are perfectly normal!'

'Do you know how their minds work – now?'

Holloway didn't pursue the thought. He fingered the doll. 'It would be interesting to know the conditions of the place where these things came from. Induction doesn't help a great deal, though. Too many factors are missing. We can't visualize a world based on the *x* factor – environment adjusted to minds thinking in *x* patterns. This luminous network inside the doll. It could be anything. It could exist inside us, though we haven't discovered it yet. When we find the right stain –' He shrugged. 'What do you make of this?'

It was a crimson globe, two inches in diameter, with a protruding knob upon its surface.

'What could anyone make of it?'

'Scott? Emma?'

'I hadn't even seen it till about three weeks ago. Then Emma started to play with it.' Paradine nibbled his lip. 'After that, Scott got interested.'

'Just what do they do?'

'Hold it up in front of them and move it back and forth. No particular pattern of motion.'

'No Euclidean pattern,' Holloway corrected. 'At first they couldn't understand the toy's purpose. They had to be educated up to it.'

'That's horrible,' Jane said.

'Not to them. Emma is probably quicker at understanding *x* than is Scott, for her mind isn't yet conditioned to this environment.'

Paradine said, 'But I can remember plenty of things I did as a child. Even as a baby.'

'Well?'

'Was I – mad then?'

'The things you don't remember are the criterion of your madness,' Holloway retorted. 'But I use the word "madness" purely as a convenient symbol for the variation from the known human norm. The arbitrary standard of sanity.'

Jane put down her glass. 'You've said that induction was difficult, Mr Holloway. But it seems to me you're making a great deal of it from very little. After all, these toys –'

'I *am* a psychologist, and I've specialized in children. I'm not a layman. These toys mean a great deal to me, chiefly because they mean so little.'

'You might be wrong.'

'Well, I rather hope I am. I'd like to examine the children.'

Jane rose in arms. 'How?'

After Holloway had explained, she nodded, though still a bit hesitantly. 'Well, that's all right. But they're not guinea pigs.'

The psychologist patted the air with a plump hand. 'My dear girl! I'm not a Frankenstein. To me the individual is the prime factor – naturally, since I work with minds. If there's anything wrong with the youngsters, I want to cure them.'

Paradine put down his cigarette and slowly watched blue smoke spiral up, wavering in an unfelt draught. 'Can you give a prognosis?'

'I'll try. That's all I can say. If the undeveloped minds have been turned into the *x* channel, it's necessary to divert them back. I'm not saying that's the wisest thing to do, but it probably is from our standards. After all, Emma and Scott will have to live in this world.'

'Yeah. Yeah. I can't believe there's much wrong. They seem about average, thoroughly normal.'

'Superficially they may seem so. They've no reason for acting abnormally, have they? And how can you tell if they – think differently?'

'I'll call 'em,' Paradine said.

'Make it informal, then. I don't want them to be on guard.'

Jane nodded towards the toys. Holloway said, 'Leave the stuff there, eh?'

But the psychologist, after Emma and Scott were summoned, made no immediate move towards direct questioning. He managed to draw Scott unobtrusively into the conversation, dropping key words now and then. Nothing so obvious as a word-association test; cooperation is necessary for that.

The most interesting development occurred when Holloway took up the abacus. 'Mind showing me how this works?'

Scott hesitated. 'Yes, sir. Like this.' He slid a bead deftly through the maze, in a tangled course, so swiftly that no one was quite sure whether or not it ultimately vanished. It might have been merely legerdemain. Then, again –

Holloway tried. Scott watched, wrinkling his nose.

'That's right?'

'Uh-huh. It's gotta go *there.*'

'Here? Why?'

'Well, that's the only way to make it work.'

But Holloway was conditioned to Euclid. There was no apparent reason why the bead should slide from this particular wire to the other. It looked like a random factor. Also, Holloway suddenly noticed, this wasn't the path the bead had taken previously, when Scott had worked the puzzle. At least, as well as he could tell.

'Will you show me again?'

Scott did, and twice more, on request. Holloway blinked through his glasses. Random, yes. And a variable. Scott moved the bead along a different course each time.

Somehow, none of the adults could tell whether or not the bead vanished. If they had expected to see it disappear, their reactions might have been different.

In the end nothing was solved. Holloway, as he said good night, seemed ill at ease.

'May I come again?'

'I wish you would,' Jane told him. 'Any time. You still think –'

He nodded. 'The children's minds are not reacting normally. They're not dull at all, but I've the most extraordinary impression that they arrive at conclusions in a way we don't understand. As though they used algebra while we used geometry. The same conclusion, but a different method of reaching it.'

'What about the toys?' Paradine asked suddenly.

'Keep them out of the way. I'd like to borrow them, if I may.'

That night Paradine slept badly. Holloway's parallel had been ill chosen. It led to disturbing theories. The *x* factor ... The children were using the equivalent of algebraic reasoning, while adults used geometry.

Fair enough. Only ...

Algebra can give you answers that geometry cannot, since there are certain terms and symbols which cannot be expressed geometrically. Suppose *x* logic showed conclusions inconceivable to an adult mind.

'Damn!' Paradine whispered. Jane stirred beside him.

'Dear? Can't you sleep either?'

'No.' He got up and went into the next room. Emma slept peacefully as a cherub, her fat arm curled around Mr Bear. Through the open doorway Paradine could see Scott's dark head motionless on the pillow.

Jane was beside him. He slipped his arm around her.

'Poor little people,' she murmured. 'And Holloway called them mad. I think we're the ones who are crazy, Dennis.'

'Uh-huh. We've got jitters.'

Scott stirred in his sleep. Without awakening, he called what was obviously a question, though it did not seem to be in any particular language. Emma gave a little mewling cry that changed pitch sharply.

She had not wakened. The children lay without stirring.

But, Paradine thought, with a sudden sickness in his middle, it was exactly as though Scott had asked Emma something, and she had replied.

Had their minds changed so that even sleep was different to them?

He thrust the thought away. 'You'll catch cold. Let's get back to bed. Want a drink?'

'I think I do,' Jane said, watching Emma. Her hand reached out blindly towards the child; she drew it back. 'Come on. We'll wake the kids.'

They drank a little brandy together, but said nothing. Jane cried in her sleep, later.

Scott was not awake, but his mind worked in slow, careful building. Thus –

'They'll take the toys away. The fat man – listava dangerous, maybe. But the Ghoric direction won't show – evankrus dun hasn't them. Intransdection – bright and shiny. Emma. She's more khopranik-high now than – I still don't see how to – thavarar lixery dist ... '

A little of Scott's thoughts could still be understood. But Emma had become conditioned to *x* much faster.

She was thinking, too.

Not like an adult or a child. Not even like a human being. Except, perhaps, a human being of a type shockingly unfamiliar to genus Homo.

Sometimes, Scott himself had difficulty in following her thoughts.

If it had not been for Holloway, life might have settled back into an almost normal routine. The toys were no longer active reminders. Emma still enjoyed her dolls and sandpile, with a thoroughly explicable delight. Scott was satisfied with baseball and his chemical set. They did everything other children did, and evinced few, if any, flashes of abnormality. But Holloway seemed to be an alarmist.

He was having the toys tested, with rather idiotic results. He drew endless charts and diagrams, corresponded with mathematicians, engineers and other psychologists, and went quietly crazy trying to find rhyme or reason in the construction of the gadgets. The box itself, with its cryptic machinery, told nothing. Fusing had melted too much of the stuff into slag. But the toys …

It was the random element that baffled investigation. Even that was a matter of semantics. For Holloway was convinced that it wasn't really random. There just weren't enough known factors. No adult could work the abacus, for example. And Holloway thoughtfully refrained from letting a child play with the thing.

The crystal cube was similarly cryptic. It showed a mad pattern of colors, which sometimes moved. In this it resembled a kaleidoscope. But the shifting of balance and gravity didn't affect it. Again the random factor.

Or, rather, the unknown. The *x* pattern. Eventually, Paradine and Jane slipped back into something like complacence, with a feeling that the children had been cured of their mental quirk, now that the contributing cause had been removed. Certain of the actions of Emma and Scott gave them every reason to quit worrying.

For the kids enjoyed swimming, hiking, movies, games, the normal functional toys of this particular time-sector. It was true that they failed to master certain rather puzzling mechanical devices which involved some calculation. A three-dimensional jigsaw globe Paradine had picked up, for example. But he found that difficult himself.

Once in a while there were lapses. Scott was hiking with his father one Saturday afternoon, and the two had paused at the summit of a hill. Beneath them a rather lovely valley was spread.

'Pretty, isn't it?' Paradine remarked.

Scott examined the scene gravely. 'It's all wrong,' he said.

'Eh?'

'I dunno.'

'What's wrong about it?'

'Gee.' Scott lapsed into puzzled silence. 'I dunno.'

The children had missed their toys, but not for long. Emma recovered first, though Scott still moped. He held unintelligible conversations with his sister, and studied meaningless scrawls she drew on paper he supplied. It was almost as though he was consulting her, about difficult problems beyond his grasp.

If Emma understood more, Scott had more real intelligence, and manipulatory skill as well. He built a gadget with his Meccano set, but was dissatisfied. The apparent cause of his dissatisfaction was exactly why Paradine was relieved when he viewed the structure. It was the sort of thing a normal boy would make, vaguely reminiscent of a cubistic ship.

It was a bit too normal to please Scott. He asked Emma more questions, though in private. She thought for a time, and then made more scrawls, with an awkwardly clutched pencil.

'Can you read that stuff?' Jane asked her son one morning.

'Not read it, exactly. I can tell what she means. Not all the time, but mostly.'

'Is it writing?'

'N-no. It doesn't mean what it *looks* like.'

'Symbolism,' Paradine suggested over his coffee.

Jane looked at him, her eyes widening. 'Denny –'

He winked and shook his head. Later, when they were alone, he said, 'Don't let Holloway upset you. I'm not implying that the kids are corresponding in an unknown tongue. If Emma draws a squiggle and says it's a flower, that's an arbitrary rule – Scott remembers that. Next time she draws the same sort of squiggle, or tries to – well!'

'Sure,' Jane said doubtfully. 'Have you noticed Scott's been doing a lot of reading lately?'

'I noticed. Nothing unusual, though. No Kant or Spinoza.'

'He browses, that's all.'

'Well, so did I, at his age,' Paradine said, and went off to his morning classes. He lunched with Holloway, which was becoming a daily habit, and spoke of Emma's literary endeavors.

'Was I right about symbolism, Rex?'

The psychologist nodded. 'Quite right. Our own language is nothing but arbitrary symbolism now. At least in its application. Look here.' On his napkin he drew a very narrow ellipse. 'What's that?'

'You mean what does it represent?'

'Yes. What does it suggest to you? It could be a crude representation of – what?'

'Plenty of things,' Paradine said. 'Rim of a glass. A fried egg. A loaf of French bread. A cigar.'

Holloway added a little triangle to his drawing, apex joined to one end of the ellipse. He looked up at Paradine.

'A fish,' the latter said instantly.

'Our familiar symbol for a fish. Even without fins, eyes or mouth, it's recognizable, because we've been conditioned to identify this particular shape with our mental picture of a fish. The basis of a rebus. A symbol, to us, means a lot more than what we actually see on paper. What's in your mind when you look at this sketch?'

'Why – a fish.'

'Keep going. What do you visualize? Everything!'

'Scales,' Paradine said slowly, looking into space. 'Water. Foam. A fish's eye. The fins. The colors.'

'So the symbol represents a lot more than just the abstract idea *fish*. Note the connotation's that of a noun, not a verb. It's harder to express actions by symbolism, you know. Anyway – reverse the process. Suppose you want to make a symbol for some concrete noun, say *bird.* Draw it.'

Paradine drew two connected arcs, concavities down.

'The lowest common denominator,' Holloway nodded. 'The natural tendency is to simplify. Especially when a child is seeing something for the first time and has few standards of comparison. He tries to identify the new thing with what's already familiar to him. Ever notice how a child draws the ocean?' He didn't wait for an answer; he went on.

'A series of jagged points. Like the oscillating line on a seismograph. When I first saw the Pacific, I was about three. I remember it pretty clearly. It looked – tilted. A flat plain, slanted at an angle. The waves were regular triangles, apex upward. Now, I didn't *see* them stylized that way, but later, remembering, I had to find some familiar standard of comparison. Which is the only way of getting any conception of an entirely new thing. The average child tries to draw these regular triangles, but his coordination's poor. He gets a seismograph pattern.'

'All of which means what?'

'A child sees the ocean. He stylizes it. He draws a certain definite pattern, symbolic, to him, of the sea. Emma's scrawls may be symbols, too. I don't mean that the world looks different to her – brighter, perhaps, and sharper, more vivid and with a slackening of perception above her eye level. What I do mean is that her thought processes are different, that she translates what she sees into abnormal symbols.'

'You still believe –'

'Yes, I do. Her mind has been conditioned unusually. It may be that she breaks down what she sees into simple, obvious patterns – and realizes a significance to those patterns that we can't understand. Like the abacus. She saw a pattern in that, though to us it was completely random.'

Paradine abruptly decided to taper off these luncheon engagements with Holloway. The man was an alarmist. His theories were growing more fantastic than ever, and he dragged in anything, applicable or not, that would support them.

Rather sardonically he said, 'Do you mean Emma's communicating with Scott in an unknown language?'

'In symbols for which she hasn't any words. I'm sure Scott understands a great deal of those – scrawls. To him, an isosceles triangle may represent any factor, though probably a concrete noun. Would a man who knew nothing of chemistry understand what H_2O meant? Would he realize that the symbol could evoke a picture of the ocean?'

Paradine didn't answer. Instead, he mentioned to Holloway Scott's curious remark that the landscape, from the hill, had looked all wrong. A moment later, he was inclined to regret his impulse, for the psychologist was off again.

'Scott's thought patterns are building up to a sum that doesn't equal this world. Perhaps he's subconsciously expecting to see the world where those toys came from.'

Paradine stopped listening. Enough was enough. The kids were getting along all right, and the only remaining disturbing factor was Holloway himself. That night, however, Scott evinced an interest, later significant, in eels.

There was nothing apparently harmful in natural history. Paradine explained about eels.

'But where do they lay their eggs? Or do they?'

'That's still a mystery. Their spawning grounds are unknown. Maybe the Sargasso Sea, or the deeps, where the pressure can help them force the young out of their bodies.'

'Funny,' Scott said, thinking deeply.

'Salmon do the same thing, more or less. They go up rivers to spawn.' Paradine went into detail. Scott was fascinated.

'But that's *right,* Dad. They're born in the river, and when they learn how to swim, they go down to the sea. And they come back to lay their eggs, huh?'

'Right.'

'Only they wouldn't *come* back,' Scott pondered. 'They'd just send their eggs –'

'It'd take a very long ovipositor,' Paradine said, and vouchsafed some well-chosen remarks upon oviparity.

His son wasn't entirely satisfied. Flowers, he contended, sent their seeds long distances.

'They don't guide them. Not many find fertile soil.'

'Flowers haven't got brains, though. Dad, why do people live *here?*'

'Glendale?'

'No – *here.* This whole place. It isn't all there is, I bet.'

'Do you mean the other planets?'

Scott was hesitant. 'This is only – part of the big place. It's like the river where the salmon go. Why don't people go on down to the ocean when they grow up?'

Paradine realized that Scott was speaking figuratively. He felt a brief chill. The – ocean?

The young of the species are not conditioned to live in the more complete world of their parents. Having developed sufficiently, they enter that world. Later they breed. The fertilized eggs are buried in the sand, far up the river, where later they hatch.

And they learn. Instinct alone is fatally slow. Especially in the case of a specialized genus, unable to cope even with this world, unable to feed or drink or survive, unless someone has foresightedly provided for those needs.

The young, fed and tended, would survive. There would be incubators and robots. They would survive, but they would not know how to swim downstream, to the vaster world of the ocean.

So they must be taught. They must be trained and conditioned in many ways.

Painlessly, subtly, unobtrusively. Children love toys that do things, and if those toys teach at the same time …

In the latter half of the nineteenth century an Englishman sat on a grassy bank near a stream. A very small girl lay near him, staring up at the sky. She had discarded a curious toy with which she had been playing, and now was murmuring a wordless little song, to which the man listened with half an ear.

'What was that, my dear?' he asked at last.

'Just something I made up, Uncle Charles.'

'Sing it again.' He pulled out a notebook.

The girl obeyed.

'Does it mean anything?'

She nodded. 'Oh, yes. Like the stories I tell you, you know.'

'They're wonderful stories, dear.'

'And you'll put them in a book someday?'

'Yes, but I must change them quite a lot, or no one would understand. But I don't think I'll change your little song.'

'You mustn't. If you did, it wouldn't mean anything.'

'I won't change that stanza, anyway,' he promised. 'Just what does it mean?'

'It's the way out, I think,' the girl said doubtfully. 'I'm not sure yet. My magic toys told me.'

'I wish I knew what London shop sold these marvellous toys!'

'Mama bought them for me. She's dead. Papa doesn't care.'

She lied. She had found the toys in a box one day, as she played by the Thames. And they were indeed wonderful.

Her little song – Uncle Charles thought it didn't mean anything. (He wasn't her real uncle, she parenthesized. But he was nice.) The song meant a great deal. It was the way. Presently she would do what it said, and then …

But she was already too old. She never found the way.

Paradine had dropped Holloway. Jane had taken a dislike to him, naturally enough, since what she wanted most of all was to have her fears calmed. Since Scott and Emma acted normally now, Jane felt satisfied. It was partly wishful thinking, to which Paradine could not entirely subscribe.

Scott kept bringing gadgets to Emma for her approval. Usually she'd shake her head. Sometimes she would look doubtful. Very occasionally she would signify agreement. Then there would be an hour of laborious, crazy scribbling on scraps of note paper, and Scott, after studying the notations, would arrange and rearrange his rocks, bits of machinery, candle ends and assorted junk. Each day the maid cleaned them away, and each day Scott began again.

He condescended to explain a little to his puzzled father, who could see no rhyme or reason in the game.

'But why this pebble right here?'

'It's hard and round, Dad. It *belongs* there.'

'So is this one hard and round.'

'Well, that's got vaseline on it. When you get that far, you can't *see* just a hard, round thing.'

'What comes next? This candle?'

Scott looked disgusted. 'That's toward the end. The iron ring's next.'

It was, Paradine thought, like a scout trail through the woods, markers in a labyrinth. But here again was the random factor. Logic halted – familiar logic – at Scott's motives in arranging the junk as he did.

Paradine went out. Over his shoulder he saw Scott pull a crumpled piece of paper and a pencil from his pocket and head for Emma, who was squatted in a corner thinking things over.

Well ...

Jane was lunching with Uncle Harry, and, on this hot Sunday afternoon, there was little to do but read the papers. Paradine settled himself in the coolest place he could find, with a Collins, and lost himself in the comic strips.

An hour later a clatter of feet upstairs roused him from his doze. Scott's voice was crying exultantly, 'This is it, Slug! Come on!'

Paradine stood up quickly, frowning. As he went into the hall the telephone began to ring. Jane had promised to call ...

His hand was on the receiver when Emma's faint voice squealed with excitement. Paradine grimaced. What the devil was going on upstairs?

Scott shrieked, 'Look out! This way!'

Paradine, his mouth working, his nerves ridiculously tense, forgot the phone and raced up the stairs. The door of Scott's room was open.

The children were vanishing.

They went in fragments, like thick smoke in a wind, or like movement in a distorting mirror. Hand in hand they went, in a direction Paradine could not understand, and as he blinked there on the threshold, they were gone.

'Emma!' he said, dry-throated. *'Scotty!'*

On the carpet lay a pattern of markers, pebbles, an iron ring – junk. A random pattern. A crumpled sheet of paper blew towards Paradine.

He picked it up automatically.

'Kids. Where are you? Don't hide – *Emma!* SCOTTY*!*'

Downstairs the telephone stopped its shrill, monotonous ringing. Paradine looked at the paper he held.

It was a leaf torn from a book. There were interlineations and marginal notes, in Emma's meaningless scrawl. A stanza of verse had been so underlined and scribbled over that it was almost illegible, but Paradine was thoroughly familiar with *Through the Looking Glass.* His memory gave him the words –

'Twas brillig, and the slithy toves
Did gyre and gimble in the wabe:
All mimsy were the borogoves,
And the mome raths outgrabe.

Idiotically he thought: Humpty Dumpty explained it. A wabe is the plot of grass around a sundial. A sundial. Time. It has something to do with time. A long time ago Scotty asked me what a wabe was. Symbolism.

'Twas brillig …

A perfect mathematical formula, giving all the conditions, in symbolism the children had finally understood. The junk on the floor. The toves had to be made slithy – vaseline? – and they had to be placed in a certain relationship, so that they'd gyre and gimble.

Lunacy!

But it had not been lunacy to Emma and Scott. They thought differently. They used x logic. Those notes Emma had made on the page – she'd translated Carroll's words into symbols both she and Scott could understand.

The random factor had made sense to the children. They had fulfilled the conditions of the time-span equation. *And the mome raths outgrabe …*

Paradine made a rather ghastly little sound, deep in his throat. He looked at the crazy pattern on the carpet. If he could follow it, as the kids had done – But he couldn't. The pattern was senseless. The random factor defeated him. He was conditioned to Euclid.

Even if he went insane, he still couldn't do it. It would be the wrong kind of lunacy.

His mind had stopped working now. But in a moment the stasis of incredulous horror would pass – Paradine crumpled the page in his fingers. 'Emma! Scotty!' he called in a dead voice, as though he could expect no response.

Sunlight slanted through the open windows, brightening the golden pelt of Mr Bear. Downstairs the ringing of the telephone began again.

TWO-HANDED ENGINE

Ever since the days of Orestes there have been men with Furies following them. It wasn't until the Twenty-Second Century that mankind made itself a set of real Furies, out of steel. Mankind had reached a crisis by then. They had a good reason for building manshaped Furies that would dog the footsteps of all men who kill men. Nobody else. There was by then no other crime of any importance.

It worked very simply. Without warning, a man who thought himself safe would suddenly hear the steady footfalls behind him. He would turn and see the two-handed engine walking towards him, shaped like a man of steel, and more incorruptible than any man not made of steel could be. Only then would the murderer know he had been tried and condemned by the omniscient electronic minds that knew society as no human mind could ever know it.

For the rest of his days, the man would hear those footsteps behind him. A moving jail with invisible bars that shut him off from the world. Never in life would he be alone again. And one day – he never knew when – the jailer would turn executioner.

Danner leaned back comfortably in his contoured restaurant chair and rolled expensive wine across his tongue, closing his eyes to enjoy the taste of it better. He felt perfectly safe. Oh, perfectly protected. For nearly an hour now he had been sitting here, ordering the most expensive food, enjoying the music breathing softly through the air, the murmurous, well-bred hush of his fellow diners. It was a good place to be. It was very good, having so much money – now.

True, he had had to kill to get the money. But no guilt troubled him. There was no guilt if you aren't found out, and Danner had protection. Protection straight from the source, which was something new in the world. Danner knew the consequences of killing. If Hartz hadn't satisfied him that he was perfectly safe, Danner would never have pulled the trigger …

The memory of an archaic word flickered through his mind briefly. *Sin*. It evoked nothing. Once it had something to do with guilt, in an incomprehensible way. Not any more. Mankind had been through too much. Sin was meaningless now.

He dismissed the thought and tried the heart-of-palms salad. He found he didn't like it. Oh well, you had to expect things like that. Nothing was perfect. He sipped the wine again, liking the way the glass seemed to vibrate like something faintly alive in his hand. It was good wine. He thought of ordering more, but then he thought no, save it, next time. There was so much before him, waiting to be enjoyed. Any risk was worth it. And of course, in this there had been no risk.

Danner was a man born at the wrong time. He was old enough to remember the last days of utopia, young enough to be trapped in the new scarcity economy the machines had clamped down on their makers. In his early youth he'd had access to free luxuries, like everybody else. He could remember the old days when he was an adolescent and the last of the Escape Machines were still operating, the glamorous, bright, impossible, vicarious visions that didn't really exist and never could have. But then the scarcity economy swallowed up pleasure. Now you got necessities but no more. Now you had to work. Danner hated every minute of it.

When the swift change came, he'd been too young and unskilled to compete in the scramble. The rich men today were the men who had built fortunes on cornering the few luxuries the machines still produced. All Danner had left were bright memories and a dull, resentful feeling of having been cheated. All he wanted were the bright days back, and he didn't care how he got them.

Well, now he had them. He touched the rim of the wine glass with his finger, feeling it sing silently against the touch. Blown glass? he wondered. He was too ignorant of luxury items to understand. But he'd learn. He had the rest of his life to learn in, and be happy.

He looked up across the restaurant and saw through the transparent dome of the roof the melting towers of the city. They made a stone forest as far as he could see. And this was only one city. When he was tired of it, there were more. Across the country, across the planet the network lay that linked city with city in a webwork like a vast, intricate, half-alive monster. Call it society.

He felt it tremble a little beneath him.

He reached for the wine and drank quickly. The faint uneasiness that seemed to shiver the foundations of the city was something new. It was because – yes, certainly it was because of a new fear.

It was because he had not been found out.

That made no sense. Of course the city was complex. Of course it operated on a basis of incorruptible machines. They, and only they, kept man from becoming very quickly another extinct animal. And of these the analog computers, the electronic calculators, were the gyroscope of all living. They made and enforced the laws that were necessary now to keep mankind alive.

Danner didn't understand much of the vast changes that had swept over society in his lifetime, but this much even he knew.

So perhaps it made sense that he felt society shiver because he sat here luxurious on foam-rubber, sipping wine, hearing soft music, and no Fury standing behind his chair to prove that the calculators were still guardians for mankind ...

If not even the Furies are incorruptible, what can a man believe in?

It was at that exact moment that the Fury arrived.

Danner heard every sound suddenly die out around him. His fork was halfway to his lips, but he paused, frozen, and looked up across the table and the restaurant towards the door.

The Fury was taller than a man. It stood there for a moment, the afternoon sun striking a blinding spot of brightness from its shoulder. It had no face, but it seemed to scan the restaurant leisurely, table by table. Then it stepped in under the doorframe and the sun-spot slid away and it was like a tall man encased in steel, walking slowly between the tables.

Danner said to himself, laying down his untasted food, 'Not for me. Everyone else here is wondering. I *know.*'

And like a memory in a drowning man's mind, clear, sharp and condensed into a moment, yet every detail clear, he remembered what Hartz had told him. As a drop of water can pull into its reflection a wide panorama condensed into a tiny focus, so time seemed to focus down to a pinpoint the half-hour Danner and Hartz had spent together, in Hartz's office with the walls that could go transparent at the push of a button.

He saw Hartz again, plump and blond, with the sad eyebrows. A man who looked relaxed until he began to talk, and then you felt the burning quality about him, the air of driven tension that made even the air around him seem to be restlessly trembling. Danner stood before Hartz's desk again in memory, feeling the floor hum faintly against his soles with the heartbeat of the computers. You could see them through the glass, smooth, shiny things with winking lights in banks like candles burning in colored glass cups. You could hear their faraway chattering as they ingested facts, meditated them, and then spoke in numbers like cryptic oracles. It took men like Hartz to understand what the oracles meant.

'I have a job for you,' Hartz said. 'I want a man killed.'

'Oh no,' Danner said. 'What kind of a fool do you think I am?'

'Now wait a minute. You can use money, can't you?'

'What for?' Danner asked bitterly. 'A fancy funeral?'

'A life of luxury. I know you're not a fool. I know damned well you wouldn't do what I ask unless you got money *and* protection. That's what I can offer. Protection.'

Danner looked through the transparent wall at the computers.

'Sure,' he said.

'No, I mean it. I –' Hartz hesitated, glancing around the room a little uneasily, as if he hardly trusted his own precautions for making sure of privacy. 'This is something new,' he said. 'I can redirect any Fury I want to.'

'Oh, sure,' Danner said again.

'It's true. I'll show you. I can pull a Fury off any victim I choose.'

'How?'

'That's my secret. Naturally. In effect, though, I've found a way to feed in false data, so the machines come out with the wrong verdict before conviction, or the wrong orders after conviction.'

'But that's – dangerous, isn't it?'

'Dangerous?' Hartz looked at Danner under his sad eyebrows. 'Well, yes. I think so. That's why I don't do it often. I've done it only once, as a matter of fact. Theoretically, I'd worked out the method. I tested it, just once. It worked. I'll do it again, to prove to you I'm telling the truth. After that I'll do it once again, to protect you. And that will be it. I don't want to upset the calculators any more than I have to. Once your job's done, I won't have to.'

'Who do you want killed?'

Involuntarily Hartz glanced upward, towards the heights of the building where the top-rank executive offices were. 'O'Reilly,' he said.

Danner glanced upward too, as if he could see through the floor and observe the exalted shoe-soles of O'Reilly, Controller of the Calculators, pacing an expensive carpet overhead.

'It's very simple,' Hartz said. 'I want his job.'

'Why not do your own killing, then, if you're so sure you can stop the Furies?'

'Because that would give the whole thing away,' Hartz said impatiently. 'Use your head. I've got an obvious motive. It wouldn't take a calculator to figure out who profits most if O'Reilly dies. If I saved myself from a Fury, people would start wondering how I did it. But you've got no motive for killing O'Reilly. Nobody but the calculators would know, and I'll take care of them.'

'How do I know you can do it?'

'Simple. Watch.'

Hartz got up and walked quickly across the resilient carpet that gave his steps a falsely youthful bounce. There was a waist-high counter on the far side of the room, with a slanting glass screen on it. Nervously Hartz punched a button, and a map of a section of the city sprang out in bold lines on its surface.

'I've got to find a sector where a Fury's in operation now,' he explained. The map flickered and he pressed the button again. The unstable outlines of the city streets wavered and brightened and then went out as he scanned the sections fast and nervously. Then a map flashed on which had three wavering streaks of colored light criss-crossing it, intersecting at one point near the center. The point moved very slowly across the map, at just about the speed of a walking man reduced to miniature in scale with the street he walked on. Around him the colored lines wheeled slowly, keeping their focus always steady on the single point.

'There,' Hartz said, leaning forward to read the printed name of the street. A drop of sweat fell from his forehead on to the glass, and he wiped it uneasily away with his fingertip. 'There's a man with a Fury assigned to him. All right, now. I'll show you. Look here.'

Above the desk was a news screen. Hartz clicked it on and watched impatiently while a street scene swam into focus. Crowds, traffic noises, people hurrying, people loitering. And in the middle of the crowd a little oasis of isolation, an island in the sea of humanity. Upon that moving island two occupants dwelt, like a Crusoe and a Friday, alone. One of the two was a haggard man who watched the ground as he walked. The other islander in this deserted spot was a tall, shining man-formed shape that followed at his heels.

As if invisible walls surrounded them, pressing back the crowds they walked through, the two moved in an empty space that closed in behind them, opened up before them. Some of the passers-by stared, some looked away in embarrassment or uneasiness. Some watched with a frank anticipation, wondering perhaps at just what moment the Friday would lift his steel arm and strike the Crusoe dead.

'Watch, now,' Hartz said nervously. 'Just a minute. I'm going to pull the Fury off this man. Wait.' He crossed to his desk, opened a drawer, bent secretively over it. Danner heard a series of clicks from inside, and then the brief chatter of tapped keys. 'Now,' Hartz said, closing the drawer. He moved the back of his hand across his forehead. 'Warm in here, isn't it? Let's get a closer look. You'll see something happen in a minute.'

Back to the news screen. He flicked the focus switch and the street scene expanded, the man and his pacing jailer swooped upward into close focus. The man's face seemed to partake subtly of the impassive quality of the robot's. You would have thought they had lived a long time together, and perhaps they had. Time is a flexible element, infinitely long sometimes in a very short space.

'Wait until they get out of the crowd,' Hartz said. 'This mustn't be conspicuous. There, he's turning now.' The man, seeming to move at random, wheeled at an alley corner and went down the narrow, dark passage away from the thoroughfare. The eye of the news screen followed him as closely as the robot.

'So you do have cameras that can do that,' Danner said with interest. 'I always thought so. How's it done? Are they spotted at every corner, or is it a beam trans –'

'Never mind,' Hartz said. 'Trade secret. Just watch. We'll have to wait until – no, no! Look, he's going to try it now!'

The man glanced furtively behind him. The robot was just turning the corner in his wake. Hartz darted back to his desk and pulled the drawer open. His hand poised over it, his eyes watched the screen anxiously. It was curious how the man in the alley, though he could have no inkling that other eyes watched, looked up and scanned the sky, gazing directly for a moment into the attentive, hidden camera and the eyes of Hartz and Danner. They saw him take a sudden, deep breath, and break into a run.

From Hartz's drawer sounded a metallic click. The robot, which had moved smoothly into a run the moment the man did, checked itself awkwardly and seemed to totter on its steel for an instant. It slowed. It stopped like an engine grinding to a halt. It stood motionless.

At the edge of the camera's range you could see the man's face, looking backward, mouth open with shock as he saw the impossible happen. The robot stood there in the alley, making indecisive motions as if the new orders Hartz pumped into its mechanisms were grating against inbuilt orders in whatever receptor it had. Then it turned its steel back upon the man in the alley and went smoothly, almost sedately, away down the street, walking as precisely as if it were obeying valid orders, not stripping the very gears of society in its aberrant behavior.

You got one last glimpse of the man's face, looking strangely stricken, as if his last friend in the world had left him.

Hartz switched off the screen. He wiped his forehead again. He went to the glass wall and looked out and down as if he were half afraid the calculators might know what he had done. Looking very small against the background of the metal giants, he said over his shoulder, 'Well, Danner?'

Was it well? There had been more talk, of course, more persuasion, a raising of the bribe. But Danner knew his mind had been made up from that moment. A calculated risk, and worth it. Well worth it. Except –

In the deathly silence of the restaurant all motion had stopped. The Fury walked calmly between the tables, threading its shining way, touching no one. Every face blanched, turned towards it. Every mind thought, 'Can it be for me?' Even the entirely innocent thought, 'This is the first mistake they've ever made, and it's come for me. The first mistake, but there's no appeal and I could never prove a thing.' For while guilt had no meaning in this world, punishment did have meaning, and punishment could be blind, striking like the lightning.

Danner between set teeth told himself over and over, 'Not for me. I'm safe. I'm protected. It hasn't come for me.' And yet he thought how strange it was, what a coincidence, wasn't it, that there should be two murderers here under this expensive glass roof today? Himself, and the one the Fury had come for.

He released his fork and heard it clink on the plate. He looked down at it and the food, and suddenly his mind rejected everything around him and went diving off on a fugitive tangent like an ostrich into sand. He thought about food. How did asparagus grow? What did raw food look like? He had never seen any. Food came ready-cooked out of restaurant kitchens or automatic slots. Potatoes, now. What did they look like? A moist white mash? No, for sometimes they were oval slices, so the thing itself must be oval. But not round. Sometimes you got them in long strips, squared off at the ends. Something quite long and oval, then chopped into even lengths. And white, of course. And they grew underground, he was almost sure. Long, thin roots twining white arms among the pipes and conduits he had seen laid bare when the streets were under repair. How strange that he should be eating something like thin, ineffectual human arms that embraced the sewers of the city and writhed pallidly where the worms had their being. And where he himself, when the Fury found him, might …

He pushed the plate away.

An indescribable rustling and murmuring in the room lifted his eyes for him as if he were an automaton. The Fury was halfway across the room now, and it was almost funny to see the relief of those whom it had passed by. Two or three of the women had buried their faces in their hands, and one man had slipped quietly from his chair in a dead faint as the Fury's passing released their private dreads back into their hidden wells.

The thing was quite close now. It looked to be about seven feet tall, and its motion was very smooth, which was unexpected when you thought about it. Smoother than human motions. Its feet fell with a heavy, measured tread upon the carpet. Thud, thud, thud. Danner tried impersonally to calculate what it weighed. You always heard that they made no sound except for that terrible tread, but this one creaked very slightly somewhere. It had no features, but the human mind couldn't help sketching in lightly a sort of airy face upon that blank steel surface, with eyes that seemed to search the room.

It was coming closer. Now all eyes were converging towards Danner. And the Fury came straight on. It almost looked as if –

'No!' Danner said to himself. 'Oh, no, this can't be!' He felt like a man in a nightmare, on the verge of waking. 'Let me wake soon,' he thought. 'Let me wake *now*, before it gets here!'

But he did not wake. And now the thing stood over him, and the thudding footsteps stopped. There was the faintest possible creaking as it towered over his table, motionless, waiting, its featureless face turned towards his.

Danner felt an intolerable tide of heat surge up into his face – rage, shame, disbelief. His heart pounded so hard the room swam and a sudden pain like jagged lightning shot through his head from temple to temple.

He was on his feet, shouting.

'No, no!' he yelled at the impassive steel. 'You're wrong! You've made a mistake! Go away, you damned fool! You're wrong, you're wrong!' He groped on the table without looking down, found his plate and hurled it straight at the armored chest before him. China shattered. Spilled food smeared a white and green and brown stain over the steel. Danner floundered out of his chair, around the table, past the tall metal figure towards the door.

All he could think of now was Hartz.

Seas of faces swam by him on both sides as he stumbled out of the restaurant. Some watched with avid curiosity, their eyes seeking him. Some did not look at all, but gazed at their plates rigidly or covered their faces with their hands. Behind him the measured tread came on, and the rhythmic faint creak from somewhere inside the armor.

The faces fell away on both sides and he went through a door without any awareness of opening it. He was in the street. Sweat bathed him and the air struck icy, though it was not a cold day. He looked blindly left and right, and then plunged for a bank of phone booths half a block away, the image of Hartz swimming before his eyes so clearly he blundered into people without seeing them. Dimly he heard indignant voices begin to speak and then die into awestruck silence. The way cleared magically before him. He walked in the newly created island of his isolation up to the nearest booth.

After he had closed the glass door the thunder of his own blood in his ears made the little sound-proofed booth reverberate. Through the door he saw the robot stand passionlessly waiting, the smear of spilled food still streaking its chest like some robotic ribbon of honor across a steel shirt front.

Danner tried to dial a number. His fingers were like rubber. He breathed deep and hard, trying to pull himself together. An irrelevant thought floated across the surface of his mind. I forgot to pay for my dinner. And then: A lot of good the money will do me now. Oh, damn Hartz, damn him, damn him!

He got the number.

A girl's face flashed into sharp, clear colors on the screen before him. Good, expensive screens in the public booths in this part of town, his mind noted impersonally.

'This is Controller Hartz's office. May I help you?'

Danner tried twice before he could give his name. He wondered if the girl could see him, and behind him, dimly through the glass, the tall waiting figure. He couldn't tell, because she dropped her eyes immediately to what must have been a list on the unseen table before her.

'I'm sorry. Mr Hartz is out. He won't be back today.'

The screen drained of light and color.

Danner folded back the door and stood up. His knees were unsteady. The robot stood just far enough back to clear the hinge of the door. For a moment they faced each other. Danner heard himself suddenly in the midst of an uncontrollable giggling which even he realized verged on hysteria. The robot with the smear of food like a ribbon of honor looked so ridiculous. Danner to his dim surprise found that all this while he had been clutching the restaurant napkin in his left hand.

'Stand back,' he said to the robot. 'Let me out. Oh, you fool, don't you know this is a mistake?' His voice quavered. The robot creaked faintly and stepped back.

'It's bad enough to have you follow me,' Danner said. 'At least, you might be clean. A dirty robot is too much – too much –' The thought was idiotically unbearable, and he heard tears in his voice. Half-laughing, half-weeping, he wiped the steel chest clean and threw the napkin to the floor.

And it was at that very instant, with the feel of the hard chest still vivid in his memory, that realization finally broke through the protective screen of hysteria, and he remembered the truth. He would never in life be alone again. Never while he drew breath. And when he died, it would be at these steel hands, perhaps upon this steel chest, with the passionless face bent to his, the last thing in life he would ever see. No human companion, but the black steel skull of the Fury.

It took him nearly a week to reach Hartz. During the week, he changed his mind about how long it might take a man followed by a Fury to go mad. The last thing he saw at night was the street light shining through the curtains of his expensive hotel suite upon the metal shoulder of his jailer. All night long, waking from uneasy slumber, he could hear the faint creaking of some inward mechanism functioning under the armor. And each time he woke it was to wonder whether he would ever wake again. Would the blow fall while he slept? And what kind of blow? How did the Furies execute? It was always a faint relief to see the bleak light of early morning shine upon the watcher by his bed. At least he had lived through the night. But was this living? And was it worth the burden?

He kept his hotel suite. Perhaps the management would have liked him to go, but nothing was said. Possibly they didn't dare. Life took on a strange, transparent quality, like something seen through an invisible wall. Outside of trying to reach Hartz, there was nothing Danner wanted to do. The old desires for luxuries, entertainment, travel, had melted away. He wouldn't have traveled alone.

He did spend hours in the public library, reading all that was available about the Furies. It was here that he first encountered the two haunting and frightening lines Milton wrote when the world was small and simple – mystifying lines that made no certain sense to anybody until man created a Fury out of steel, in his own image.

But that two-handed engine at the door
Stands ready to smite once, and smite no more ...

Danner glanced up at his own two-handed engine, motionless at his shoulder, and thought of Milton and the long-ago times when life was simple and easy. He tried to picture the past. The twentieth century, when all civilizations together crashed over the brink in one majestic downfall to chaos. And the time before that, when people were … different, somehow. But how? It was too far and too strange. He could not imagine the time before the machines.

But he learned for the first time what had really happened, back there in his early years, when the bright world finally blinked out entirely and gray drudgery began. And the Furies were first forged in the likeness of man.

Before the really big wars began, technology advanced to the point where machines bred upon machines like living things, and there might have been an Eden on earth, with everybody's wants fully supplied, except that the social sciences fell too far behind the physical sciences. When the decimating wars came on, machines and people fought side by side, steel against steel and man against man, but man was the more perishable. The wars ended when there were no longer two societies left to fight against each other. Societies splintered apart into smaller and smaller groups until a state very close to anarchy set in.

The machines licked their metal wounds meanwhile and healed each other as they had been built to do. They had no need for the social sciences. They went on calmly reproducing themselves and handing out to mankind the luxuries which the age of Eden had designed them to hand out. Imperfectly of course. Incompletely, because some of their species were wiped out entirely and left no machines to breed and reproduce their kind. But most of them mined their raw materials, refined them, poured and cast the needed parts, made their own fuel, repaired their own injuries and maintained their breed upon the face of the earth with an efficiency man never even approached.

Meanwhile mankind splintered and splintered away. There were no longer any real groups, not even families. Men didn't need each other much. Emotional attachments dwindled. Men had been conditioned to accept vicarious surrogates and escapism was fatally easy. Men reoriented their emotions to the Escape Machines that fed them joyous, impossible adventure and made the waking world seem too dull to bother with. And the birth rate fell and fell. It was a very strange period. Luxury and chaos went hand in hand, anarchy and inertia were the same thing. And still the birth rate dropped …

Eventually a few people recognized what was happening. Man as a species was on the way out. And man was helpless to do anything about it. But he had a powerful servant. So the time came when some unsung genius saw what would have to be done. Someone saw the situation clearly and set a new pattern in the biggest of the surviving electronic calculators. This was the goal he set: 'Mankind must be made self-responsible again. You will make this your only goal until you achieve the end.'

It was simple, but the changes it produced were worldwide and all human life on the planet altered drastically because of it. The machines were an integrated society, if man was not. And now they had a single set of orders which all of them reorganized to obey.

So the days of the free luxuries ended. The Escape Machines shut up shop. Men were forced back into groups for the sake of survival. They had to undertake now the work the machines withheld, and slowly, slowly, common needs and common interests began to spawn the almost lost feeling of human unity again.

But it was so slow. And no machine could put back into man what he had lost – the internalized conscience. Individualism had reached its ultimate stage and there had been no deterrent to crime for a long while. Without family or clan relations, not even feud retaliation occurred. Conscience failed, since no man identified with any other.

The real job of the machines now was to rebuild in man a realistic superego to save him from extinction. A self-responsible society would be a genuinely interdependent one, the leader identifying with the group, and a realistically internalized conscience which would forbid and punish 'sin' – the sin of injuring the group with which you identify.

And here the Furies came in.

The machines defined murder, under any circumstances, as the only human crime. This was accurate enough, since it is the only act which can irreplaceably destroy a unit of society.

The Furies couldn't prevent crime. Punishment never cures the criminal. But it can prevent others from committing crime through simple fear, when they see punishment administered to others. The Furies were the symbol of punishment. They overtly stalked the streets on the heels of their condemned victims, the outward and visible sign that murder is always punished, and punished most publicly and terribly. They were very efficient. They were never wrong. Or at least, in theory they were never wrong, and considering the enormous quantities of information stored by now in the analog computers, it seemed likely that the justice of the machines was far more efficient than that of humans could be.

Some day man would rediscover sin. Without it he had come near to perishing entirely. With it, he might resume his authority over himself and the race of mechanized servants who were helping him to restore his species. But until that day, the Furies would have to stalk the streets, man's conscience in metal guise, imposed by the machines man created a long time ago.

What Danner did during this time he scarcely knew. He thought a great deal of the old days when the Escape Machines still worked, before the machines rationed luxuries. He thought of this sullenly and with resentment, for he could see no point at all in the experiment mankind was embarked on. He had liked it better in the old days. And there were no Furies then, either.

He drank a good deal. Once he emptied his pockets into the hat of a legless beggar, because the man like himself was set apart from society by something new and terrible. For Danner it was the Fury. For the beggar it was life itself. Thirty years ago he would have lived or died unheeded, tended only by machines. That a beggar could survive at all, by begging, must be a sign that society was beginning to feel twinges of awakened fellow feeling with its members, but to Danner that meant nothing. He wouldn't be around long enough to know how the story came out.

He wanted to talk to the beggar, though the man tried to wheel himself away on his little platform.

'Listen,' Danner said urgently, following, searching his pockets. 'I want to tell you. It doesn't feel the way you think it would. It feels –'

He was quite drunk that night, and he followed the beggar until the man threw the money back at him and thrust himself away rapidly on his wheeled platform, while Danner leaned against a building and tried to believe in its solidity. But only the shadow of the Fury, falling across him from the street lamp, was real.

Later that night, somewhere in the dark, he attacked the Fury. He seemed to remember finding a length of pipe somewhere, and he struck showers of sparks from the great, impervious shoulders above him. Then he ran, doubling and twisting up alleys, and in the end he hid in a dark doorway, waiting, until the steady footsteps resounded through the night.

He fell asleep, exhausted.

It was the next day that he finally reached Hartz.

'What went wrong?' Danner asked. In the past week he had changed a good deal. His face was taking on, in its impassivity, an odd resemblance to the metal mask of the robot.

Hartz struck the desk edge a nervous blow, grimacing when he hurt his hand. The room seemed to be vibrating not with the pulse of the machines below but with his own tense energy.

'*Something* went wrong,' he said. 'I don't know yet. I –'

'You don't know!' Danner lost part of his impassivity.

'Now wait.' Hartz made soothing motions with his hands. 'Just hang on a little longer. It'll be all right. You can –'

'How much longer have I got?' Danner asked. He looked over his shoulder at the tall Fury standing behind him, as if he were really asking the question of it, not Hartz. There was a feeling, somehow, about the way he said it that made you think he must have asked that question many times, looking up into the blank steel face, and would go on asking hopelessly until the answer came at last. But not in words …

'I can't even find that out,' Hartz said. 'Damn it, Danner, this was a risk. You knew that.'

'You said you could control the computer. I saw you do it. I want to know why you didn't do what you promised.'

'Something went wrong, I tell you. It should have worked. The minute this – business – came up I fed in the data that should have protected you.'

'But what happened?'

Hartz got up and began to pace the resilient flooring. 'I just don't know. We don't understand the potentiality of the machines, that's all. I thought I could do it. But –'

'You *thought!*'

'I know I can do it. I'm still trying. I'm trying everything. After all, this is important to me, too. I'm working as fast as I can. That's why I couldn't see you before. I'm certain I can do it, if I can work this out my own way. Damn it, Danner, it's complex. And it's not like juggling a comptometer. Look at those things out there.'

Danner didn't bother to look.

'You'd better do it,' he said. 'That's all.'

Hartz said furiously. 'Don't threaten me! Let me alone and I'll work it out. But don't threaten me.'

'You're in this too,' Danner said.

Hartz went back to his desk and sat down on the edge of it.

'How?' he asked.

'O'Reilly's dead. You paid me to kill him.'

Hartz shrugged. 'The Fury knows that,' he said. 'The computers know it. And it doesn't matter a damn bit. Your hand pulled the trigger, not mine.'

'We're both guilty. If I suffer for it, you –'

'Now wait a minute. Get this straight. I thought you knew it. It's a basis of law enforcement, and always has been. Nobody's punished for intention. Only for actions. I'm no more responsible for O'Reilly's death than the gun you used on him.'

'But you lied to me! You tricked me! I'll –'

'You'll do as I say, if you want to save yourself. I didn't trick you, I just made a mistake. Give me time and I'll retrieve it.'

'*How long?*'

This time both men looked at the Fury. It stood impassive.

'I don't know how long,' Danner answered his own question. 'You say you don't. Nobody even knows how he'll kill me, when the time comes. I've been reading everything that's available to the public about this. Is it true that the method varies, just to keep people like me on tenterhooks? And the time allowed – doesn't that vary too?'

'Yes, it's true. But there's a minimum time – I'm almost sure. You must still be within it. Believe me, Danner, I can still call off the Fury. You saw me do it. You know it worked once. All I've got to find out is what went wrong this time. But the more you bother me the more I'll be delayed. I'll get in touch with you. Don't try to see me again.'

Danner was on his feet. He took a few quick steps towards Hartz, fury and frustration breaking up the impassive mask which despair had been forming over his face. But the solemn footsteps of the Fury sounded behind him. He stopped.

The two men looked at each other.

'Give me time,' Hartz said. 'Trust me, Danner.'

In a way it was worse, having hope. There must until now have been a kind of numbness of despair that had kept him from feeling too much. But now there was a chance that after all he might escape into the bright and new life he had risked so much for – if Hartz could save him in time.

Now, for a period, he began to savor experience again. He bought new clothes. He traveled, though never, of course, alone. He even sought human companionship again and found it – after a fashion. But the kind of people willing to associate with a man under this sort of death sentence was not a very appealing type. He found, for instance, that some women felt strongly attracted to him, not because of himself or his money, but for the sake of his companion. They seemed enthralled by the opportunity for a close, safe brush with the very instrument of destiny. Over his very shoulder, sometimes, he would realize they watched the Fury in an ecstasy of fascinated anticipation. In a strange reaction of jealousy, he dropped such people as soon as he recognized the first coldly flirtatious glance one of them cast at the robot behind him.

He tried farther travel. He took the rocket to Africa, and came back by way of the rain-forests of South America, but neither the night clubs nor the exotic newness of strange places seemed to touch him in any way that mattered. The sunlight looked much the same, reflecting from the curved steel surfaces of his follower, whether it shone over lion-colored savannahs or filtered through the hanging gardens of the jungles. All novelty grew dull quickly because of the dreadfully familiar thing that stood for ever at his shoulder. He could enjoy nothing at all.

And the rhythmic beat of footfalls behind him began to grow unendurable. He used earplugs, but the heavy vibration throbbed through his skull in a constant measure like an eternal headache. Even when the Fury stood still, he could hear in his head the imaginary beating of its steps.

He bought weapons and tried to destroy the robot. Of course he failed. And even if he succeeded he knew another would be assigned to him. Liquor and drugs were no good. Suicide came more and more often into his mind, but he postponed that thought, because Hartz had said there was still hope.

In the end, he came back to the city to be near Hartz – and hope. Again he found himself spending most of his time in the library, walking no more than he had to because of the footsteps that thudded behind him. And it was here, one morning, that he found the answer …

He had gone through all available factual material about the Furies. He had gone through all the literary references collated under that heading, astonished to find how many there were and how apt some of them had become – like Milton's two-handed engine – after the lapse of all these centuries. '*Those strong feet that followed, followed after,*' he read. '*… with unhurrying chase, And unperturbed pace, Deliberate speed, majestic instancy …*' He turned the page and saw himself and his plight more literally than any allegory:

I shook the pillaring hours
And pulled my life upon me; grimed with smears,
I stand amid the dust of the mounded years –
My mangled youth lies dead beneath the heap.

He let several tears of self-pity fall upon the page that pictured him so clearly.

But then he passed on from literary references to the library's store of filmed plays, because some of them were cross-indexed under the heading he sought. He watched Orestes hounded in modern dress from Argos to Athens with a single seven-foot robot Fury at his heels instead of the three snake-haired Erinyes of legend. There had been an outburst of plays on the theme when the Furies first came into usage. Sunk in a half-dream of his own boyhood memories when the Escape Machines still operated, Danner lost himself in the action of the films.

He lost himself so completely that when the familiar scene first flashed by him in the viewing booth he hardly questioned it. The whole experience was part of a familiar boyhood pattern and he was not at first surprised to find one scene more vividly familiar than the rest. But then memory rang a bell in his mind and he sat up sharply and brought his fist down with a bang on the stop-action button. He spun the film back and ran the scene over again.

It showed a man walking with his Fury through city traffic, the two of them moving in a little desert island of their own making, like a Crusoe with a Friday at his heels … It showed the man turn into an alley, glance up at the camera anxiously, take a deep breath and break into a sudden run. It showed the Fury hesitate, make indecisive motions and then turn and walk quietly and calmly away in the other direction, its feet ringing on the pavement hollowly …

Danner spun the film back again and ran the scene once more, just to make doubly sure. He was shaking so hard he could scarcely manipulate the viewer.

'How do you like that?' he muttered to the Fury behind him in the dim booth. He had by now formed a habit of talking to the Fury a good deal, in a rapid, mumbling undertone, not really aware he did it. 'What do you make of that, you? Seen it before, haven't you? Familiar, isn't it? Isn't it! *Isn't it!* Answer me, you damned dumb hulk!' And reaching backward, he struck the robot across the chest as he would have struck Hartz if he could. The blow made a hollow sound in the booth, but the robot made no other response, though when Danner looked back inquiringly at it, he saw the reflections of the over-familiar scene, running a third time on the screen, running in tiny reflection across the robot's chest and faceless head, as if it too remembered.

So now he knew the answer. And Hartz had never possessed the power he claimed. Or if he did, had no intention of using it to help Danner. Why should he? His risk was over now. No wonder Hartz had been so nervous, running that film-strip off on a newsscreen in his office. But the anxiety sprang not from the dangerous thing he was tampering with, but from sheer strain in matching his activities to the action in the play. How he must have rehearsed it, timing every move! And how he must have laughed, afterwards.

'How long have I got?' Danner demanded fiercely, striking a hollow reverberation from the robot's chest. 'How long? Answer me! Long enough?'

Release from hope was an ecstasy, now. He need not wait any longer. He need not try any more. All he had to do was get to Hartz and get there fast, before his own time ran out. He thought with revulsion of all the days he had wasted already, in travel and time-killing, when for all he knew his own last minutes might be draining away now. Before Hartz's did.

'Come along,' he said needlessly to the Fury. 'Hurry!'

It came, matching its speed to his, the enigmatic timer inside it ticking the moments away towards that instant when the two-handed engine would smite once, and smite no more.

Hartz sat in the Controller's office behind a brand-new desk, looking down from the very top of the pyramid now over the banks of computers that kept society running and cracked the whip over mankind. He sighed with deep content.

The only thing was, he found himself thinking a good deal about Danner. Dreaming of him, even. Not with guilt, because guilt implies conscience, and the long schooling in anarchic individualism was still deep in the roots of every man's mind. But with uneasiness, perhaps.

Thinking of Danner, he leaned back and unlocked a small drawer which he had transferred from his old desk to the new. He slid his hand in and let his fingers touch the controls lightly, idly. Quite idly.

Two movements, and he could save Danner's life. For, of course, he had lied to Danner straight through. He could control the Furies very easily. He could save Danner, but he had never intended to. There was no need. And the thing was dangerous. You tamper once with a mechanism as complex as that which controlled society, and there would be no telling where the maladjustment might end. Chain-reaction, maybe, throwing the whole organization out of kilter. No.

He might some day have to use the device in the drawer. He hoped not. He pushed the drawer shut quickly, and heard the soft click of the lock.

He was Controller now. Guardian, in a sense, of the machines which were faithful in a way no man could ever be. *Quis custodiet,* Hartz thought. The old problem. And the answer was: Nobody. Nobody, today. He himself had no superiors and his power was absolute. Because of this little mechanism in the drawer, nobody controlled the Controller. Not an internal conscience, and not an external one. Nothing could touch him …

Hearing the footsteps on the stairs, he thought for a moment he must be dreaming. He had sometimes dreamed that he was Danner, with those relentless footfalls thudding after him. But he was awake now.

It was strange that he caught the almost subsonic beat of the approaching metal feet before he heard the storming steps of Danner rushing up his private stairs. The whole thing happened so fast that time seemed to have no connection with it. First he heard the heavy, subsonic beat, then the sudden tumult of shouts and banging doors downstairs, and then last of all the thump, thump of Danner charging up the stairs, his steps so perfectly matched by the heavier thud of the robot's that the metal trampling drowned out the tramp of flesh and bone and leather.

Then Danner flung the door open with a crash, and the shouts and tramplings from below funnelled upward into the quiet office like a cyclone rushing towards the hearer. But a cyclone in a nightmare, because it would never get any nearer. Time had stopped.

Time had stopped with Danner in the doorway, his face convulsed, both hands holding the revolver because he shook so badly he could not brace it with one.

Hartz acted without any more thought than a robot. He had dreamed of this moment too often, in one form or another. If he could have tempered with the Fury to the extent of hurrying Danner's death, he would have done it. But he didn't know how. He could only wait it out, as anxiously as Danner himself, hoping against hope that the blow would fall and the executioner strike before Danner guessed the truth. Or gave up hope.

So Hartz was ready when trouble came. He found his own gun in his hand without the least recollection of having opened the drawer. The trouble was that time had stopped. He knew, in the back of his mind, that the Fury must stop Danner from injuring anybody. But Danner stood in the doorway alone, the revolver in both shaking hands. And farther back, behind the knowledge of the Fury's duty, Hartz's mind held the knowledge that the machines could be stopped. The Furies could fail. He dared not trust his life to their incorruptibility, because he himself was the source of a corruption that could stop them in their tracks.

The gun was in his hand without his knowledge. The trigger pressed his finger and the revolver kicked back against his palm, and the spurt of the explosion made the air hiss between him and Danner.

He heard his bullet clang on metal.

Time started again, running double-pace to catch up. The Fury had been no more than a single pace behind Danner after all, because its steel arm encircled him and its steel hand was deflecting Danner's gun. Danner had fired, yes, but not soon enough. Not before the Fury reached him. Hartz's bullet struck first.

It struck Danner in the chest, exploding through him, and rang upon the steel chest of the Fury behind him. Danner's face smoothed out into a blankness as complete as the blankness of the mask above his head. He slumped backwards, not falling because of the robot's embrace, but slowly slipping to the floor between the Fury's arm and its impervious metal body. His revolver thumped softly to the carpet. Blood welled from his chest and back.

The robot stood there impassive, a streak of Danner's blood slanting across its metal chest like a robotic ribbon of honor.

The Fury and the Controller of the Furies stood staring at each other. And the Fury could not, of course, speak, but in Hartz's mind it seemed to.

'Self-defense is no excuse,' the Fury seemed to be saying. 'We never punish intent, but we always punish action. Any act of murder. Any act of murder.'

Hartz barely had time to drop his revolver in his desk drawer before the first of the clamorous crowd from downstairs came bursting through the door. He barely had the presence of mind to do it, either. He had not really thought the thing through this far.

It was, on the surface, a clear case of suicide. In a slightly unsteady voice he heard himself explaining. Everybody had seen the madman rushing through the office, his Fury at his heels. This wouldn't be the first time a killer and his Fury had tried to get at the Controller, begging him to call off the jailer and forestall the executioner. What had happened, Hartz told his underlings calmly enough, was that the Fury had naturally stopped the man from shooting Hartz. And the victim had then turned his gun upon himself. Powder-burns on his clothing showed it. (The desk was very near the door.) Back-blast in the skin of Danner's hands would show he had really fired a gun.

Suicide. It would satisfy any human. But it would not satisfy the computers.

They carried the dead man out. They left Hartz and the Fury alone, still facing each other across the desk. If anyone thought this was strange, nobody showed it.

Hartz himself didn't know if it was strange or not. Nothing like this had ever happened before. Nobody had ever been fool enough to commit murder in the very presence of a Fury. Even the Controller did not know exactly how the computers assessed evidence and fixed guilt. Should this Fury have been recalled, normally? If Danner's death were really suicide, would Hartz stand here alone now?

He knew the machines were already processing the evidence of what had really happened here. What he couldn't be sure of was whether this Fury had already received its orders and would follow him wherever he went from now on until the hour of his death. Or whether it simply stood motionless, waiting recall.

Well, it didn't matter. This Fury or another was already, in the present moment, in the process of receiving instructions about him. There was only one thing to do. Thank God there was something he *could* do.

So Hartz unlocked the desk drawer and slid it open, touched the clicking keys he had never expected to use. Very carefully he fed the coded information, digit by digit, into the computers. As he did, he looked out through the glass wall and imagined he could see down there in the hidden tapes the units of data fading into blankness and the new, false information flashing into existence.

He looked up at the robot. He smiled a little.

'Now you'll forget,' he said. 'You and the computers. You can go now. I won't be seeing you again.'

Either the computers worked incredibly fast – as of course they did – or pure coincidence took over, because in only a moment or two the Fury moved as if in response to Hartz's dismissal. It had stood quite motionless since Danner slid through its arms. Now new orders animated it, and briefly its motion was almost jerky as it changed from one set of instructions to another. It almost seemed to bow, a stiff little bending motion that brought its head down to a level with Hartz's.

He saw his own face reflected in the blank face of the Fury. You could very nearly read an ironic note in that stiff bow, with the diplomat's ribbon of honor across the chest of the creature, symbol of duty discharged honorably. But there was nothing honorable about this withdrawal. The incorruptible metal was putting on corruption and looking back at Hartz with the reflection of his own face.

He watched it stalk towards the door. He heard it go thudding evenly down the stairs. He could feel the thuds vibrate in the floor, and there was a sudden sick dizziness in him when he thought the whole fabric of society was shaking under his feet.

The machines were corruptible.

Mankind's survival still depended on the computers, and the computers could not be trusted. Hartz looked down and saw that his hands were shaking. He shut the drawer and heard the lock click softly. He gazed at his hands. He felt their shaking echoed in an inner shaking, a terrifying sense of the instability of the world.

A sudden, appalling loneliness swept over him like a cold wind. He had never felt before so urgent a need for the companionship of his own kind. No one person, but people. Just people. The sense of human beings all around him, a very primitive need.

He got his hat and coat and went downstairs rapidly, hands deep in his pockets because of some inner chill no coat could guard against. Halfway down the stairs he stopped dead still.

There were footsteps behind him.

He dared not look back at first. He knew those footsteps. But he had two fears and he didn't know which was worse. The fear that a Fury was after him – and the fear that it was not. There would be a sort of insane relief if it really was, because then he could trust the machines after all, and this terrible loneliness might pass over him and go.

He took another downward step, not looking back. He heard the ominous footfall behind him, echoing his own. He sighed one deep sigh and looked back.

There was nothing on the stairs.

He went on down after a timeless pause, watching over his shoulder. He could hear the relentless feet thudding behind him, but no visible Fury followed. No visible Fury.

The Erinyes had struck inward again, and an invisible Fury of the mind followed Hartz down the stairs.

It was as if sin had come anew into the world, and the first man felt again the first inward guilt. So the computers had not failed, after all.

Hartz went slowly down the steps and out into the street, still hearing as he would always hear the relentless, incorruptible footsteps behind him that no longer rang like metal.

THE PROUD ROBOT

Things often happened to Gallegher, who played at science by ear. He was, as he often remarked, a casual genius. Sometimes he'd start with a twist of wire, a few batteries, and a button hook, and before he finished, he might contrive a new type of refrigerating unit.

At the moment he was nursing a hangover. A disjointed, lanky, vaguely boneless man with a lock of dark hair falling untidily over his forehead, he lay on the couch in the lab and manipulated his mechanical liquor bar. A very dry Martini drizzled slowly from the spigot into his receptive mouth.

He was trying to remember something, but not trying too hard. It had to do with the robot, of course. Well, it didn't matter.

'Hey, Joe,' Gallegher said.

The robot stood proudly before the mirror and examined its innards. Its hull was transparent, and wheels were going around at a great rate inside.

'When you call me that,' Joe remarked, 'whisper. And get that cat out of here.'

'Your ears aren't that good.'

'They are. I can hear the cat walking about, all right.'

'What does it sound like?' Gallegher inquired, interested.

'Jest like drums,' said the robot, with a put-upon air. 'And when you talk, it's like thunder.' Joe's voice was a discordant squeak, so Gallegher meditated on saying something about glass houses and casting the first stone. He brought his attention, with some effort, to the luminous door panel, where a shadow loomed – a familiar shadow, Gallegher thought.

'It's Brock,' the annunciator said. 'Harrison Brock. Let me in!'

'The door's unlocked.' Gallegher didn't stir. He looked gravely at the well-dressed, middle-aged man who came in, and tried to remember. Brock was between forty and fifty; he had a smoothly massaged, cleanshaven face, and wore an expression of harassed intolerance. Probably Gallegher knew the man. He wasn't sure. Oh, well.

Brock looked around the big, untidy laboratory, blinked at the robot, searched for a chair, and failed to find it. Arms akimbo, he rocked back and forth and glared at the prostrate scientist.

'Well?' he said.

'Never start conversations that way,' Gallegher mumbled, siphoning another Martini down his gullet. 'I've had enough trouble today. Sit down and take it easy. There's a dynamo behind you. It isn't very dusty, is it?'

'Did you get it?' Brock snapped. 'That's all I want to know. You've had a week. I've a check for ten thousand in my pocket. Do you want it, or don't you?'

'Sure,' Gallegher said. He extended a large, groping hand. 'Give.'

'*Caveat emptor.* What am I buying?'

'Don't you know?' the scientist asked, honestly puzzled.

Brock began to bounce up and down in a harassed fashion. 'My God,' he said. 'They told me you could help me if anybody could. Sure. And they also said it'd be like pulling teeth to get sense out of you. Are you a technician or a drivelling idiot?'

Gallegher pondered. 'Wait a minute. I'm beginning to remember. I talked to you last week, didn't I?'

'You talked –' Brock's round face turned pink. 'Yes! You lay there swilling liquor and babbled poetry. You sang "Frankie and Johnnie." And you finally got around to accepting my commission.'

'The fact is,' Gallegher said, 'I have been drunk. I often get drunk. Especially on my vacation. It releases my subconscious, and then I can work. I've made my best gadgets when I was tizzied,' he went on happily. 'Everything seems so clear then. Clear as a bell. I mean a bell, don't I? Anyway –' He lost the thread and looked puzzled. 'Anyway, what are you talking about?'

'Are you going to keep quiet?' the robot demanded from its post before the mirror.

Brock jumped. Gallegher waved a casual hand. 'Don't mind Joe. I just finished him last night, and I rather regret it.'

'A robot?'

'A robot. But he's no good, you know. I made him when I was drunk, and I haven't the slightest idea how or why. All he'll do is stand there and admire himself. And sing. He sings like a banshee. You'll hear him presently.'

With an effort Brock brought his attention back to the matter in hand. 'Now look, Gallegher. I'm in a spot. You promised to help me. If you don't, I'm a ruined man.'

'I've been ruined for years,' the scientist remarked. 'It never bothers me. I just go along working for a living and making things in my spare time. Making all sorts of things. You know, if I'd really studied, I'd have been another Einstein. So they tell me. As it is, my subconscious picked up a first-class scientific training somewhere. Probably that's why I never bothered. When I'm drunk or sufficiently absent-minded, I can work out the damnedest problems.'

'You're drunk now,' Brock accused.

'I approach the pleasanter stages. How would you feel if you woke up and found you'd made a robot for some unknown reason, and hadn't the slightest idea of the creature's attributes?'

'Well –'

'I don't feel that way at all,' Gallegher murmured. 'Probably you take life too seriously, Brock. Wine is a mocker; strong drink is raging. Pardon me. I rage.' He drank another Martini.

Brock began to pace around the crowded laboratory, circling various enigmatic and untidy objects. 'If you're a scientist, Heaven help science.'

'I'm the Larry Adler of science,' Gallegher said. 'He was a musician – lived some hundreds of years ago, I think. I'm like him. Never took a lesson in my life. Can I help it if my subconscious likes practical jokes?'

'Do you know who I am?' Brock demanded.

'Candidly, no. Should I?'

There was bitterness in the other's voice. 'You might have the courtesy to remember, even though it was a week ago. Harrison Brock. Me. I own Vox-View Pictures.'

'No,' the robot said suddenly, 'it's no use. No use at all, Brock.'

'What the –'

Gallegher sighed wearily. 'I forget the damned thing's alive. Mr Brock, meet Joe. Joe, meet Mr Brock – of Vox-View.'

Joe turned, gears meshing within his transparent skull. 'I am glad to meet you, Mr Brock. Allow me to congratulate you on your good fortune in hearing my lovely voice.'

'Ugh,' said the magnate inarticulately. 'Hello.'

'Vanity of vanities, all is vanity,' Gallegher put in, *sotto voce*. 'Joe's like that. A peacock. No use arguing with him either.'

The robot ignored this aside. 'But it's no use, Mr Brock,' he went on squeakily. 'I'm not interested in money. I realize it would bring happiness to many if I consented to appear in your pictures, but fame means nothing to me. Nothing. Consciousness of beauty is enough.'

Brock began to chew his lips. 'Look,' he said savagely, 'I didn't come here to offer you a picture job. See? Am I offering you a contract? Such colossal nerve – *Pah!* You're crazy.'

'Your schemes are perfectly transparent,' the robot remarked coldly. 'I can see that you're overwhelmed by my beauty and the loveliness of my voice – its grand tonal qualities. You needn't pretend you don't want me, just so you can get me at a lower price. I said I wasn't interested.'

'You're *cr-r-razy!*' Brock howled, badgered beyond endurance, and Joe calmly turned back to his mirror.

'Don't talk so loudly,' the robot warned. 'The discordance is deafening. Besides you're ugly and I don't like to look at you.' Wheels and cogs buzzed inside the transplastic shell. Joe extended his eyes on stalks and regarded himself with every appearance of appreciation.

Gallegher was chuckling quietly on the couch. 'Joe has a high irritation value,' he said. 'I've found that out already. I must have given him some remarkable senses, too. An hour ago he started to laugh his damn fool head off. No reason, apparently. I was fixing myself a bite to eat. Ten minutes after that I slipped on an apple core I'd thrown away and came down hard. Joe just looked at me. "That was it," he said. "Logics of probability. Cause and effect. I knew you were going to drop that apple core and then step on it when you went to pick up the mail." Like the White Queen, I suppose. It's a poor memory that doesn't work both ways.'

Brock sat on the small dynamo – there were two, the larger one named Monstro, and the smaller one serving Gallegher as a bank – and took deep breaths. 'Robots are nothing new.'

'This one is. I hate its gears. It's beginning to give me an inferiority complex. Wish I knew why I'd made it,' Gallegher sighed. 'Oh, well. Have a drink?'

'No. I came here on business. Do you seriously mean you spent last week building a robot instead of solving the problem I hired you for?'

'Contingent, wasn't it?' Gallegher asked. 'I think I remember that.'

'Contingent,' Brock said with satisfaction. 'Ten thousand, if and when.'

'Why not give me the dough and take the robot? He's worth that. Put him in one of your pictures.'

'I won't have any pictures unless you figure out an answer,' Brock snapped. 'I told you all about it.'

'I have been drunk,' Gallegher said. 'My mind has been wiped clear, as by a sponge. I am as a little child. Soon I shall be as a drunken little child. Meanwhile, if you'd care to explain the matter again –'

Brock gulped down his passion, jerked a magazine at random from the bookshelf, and took out a stylo. 'All right. My preferred stocks are at twenty-eight, way below par –' He scribbled figures on the magazine.

'If you'd taken that medieval folio next to that, it'd have cost you a pretty penny,' Gallegher said lazily. 'So you're the sort of guy who writes on tablecloths, eh? Forget this business of stocks and stuff. Get down to cases. Who are you trying to gyp?'

'It's no use,' the robot said from before its mirror. 'I won't sign a contract. People may come and admire me, if they like, but they'll have to whisper in my presence.'

'A madhouse,' Brock muttered, trying to get a grip on himself. 'Listen, Gallegher. I told you all this a week ago, but –'

'Joe wasn't here then. Pretend like you're talking to him.'

'Uh – look. You've heard of Vox-View Pictures, at least.'

'Sure. The biggest and best television company in the business. Sonatone's about your only competitor.'

'Sonatone's squeezing me out.'

Gallegher looked puzzled. 'I don't see how. You've got the best product. Tri-dimensional color, all sorts of modern improvements, the top actors, musicians, singers –'

'No use,' the robot said. 'I won't.'

'Shut up, Joe. You've tops in your field, Brock. I'll hand you that. And I've always heard you were fairly ethical. What's Sonatone got on you?'

Brock made helpless gestures. 'Oh, it's politics. The bootleg theaters. I can't buck 'em. Sonatone helped elect the present administration, and the police just wink when I try to have the bootleggers raided.'

'Bootleg theaters?' Gallegher asked, scowling a trifle. 'I've heard something –'

'It goes way back. To the old sound-film days. Home television killed sound film and big theaters. People were conditioned away from sitting in audience groups to watch a screen. The home televisors got good. It was more fun to sit in an easy-chair, drink beer, and watch the show. Television wasn't a rich man's hobby by that time. The meter system brought the price down to middle-class levels. Everybody knows that.'

'I don't,' Gallegher said. 'I never pay attention to what goes on outside of my lab, unless I have to. Liquor and a selective mind. I ignore everything that doesn't affect me directly. Explain the whole thing in detail, so I'll get a complete picture. I don't mind repetition. Now, what about this meter system of yours?'

'Televisors are installed free. We never sell 'em; we rent them. People pay according to how many hours they have the set tuned in. We run a continuous show, stage plays, wire-tape films, operas, orchestras, singers, vaudeville – everything. If you use your televisor a lot, you pay proportionately. The man comes around once a month and reads the meter. Which is a fair system. Anybody can afford a Vox-View. Sonatone and the other companies do the same thing, but Sonatone's the only big competitor I've got. At least, the only one that's crooked as hell. The rest of the boys – they're smaller than I am, but I don't step on their toes. Nobody's ever called me a louse,' Brock said darkly.

'So what?'

'So Sonatone has started to depend on audience appeal. It was impossible till lately – you couldn't magnify tri-dimensional television on a big screen without streakiness and mirage-effect. That's why the regular three-by-four home screens were used. Results were perfect. But Sonatone's bought a lot of the ghost theaters all over the country –'

'What's a ghost theater?' Gallegher asked.

'Well – before sound films collapsed, the world was thinking big. Big – you know? Ever heard of the Radio City Music Hall? That wasn't in it! Television was coming in, and competition was fierce. Sound-film theaters got bigger and more elaborate. They were palaces. Tremendous. But when television was perfected, nobody went to the theaters any more, and it was often too expensive a job to tear 'em down. Ghost theaters – see? Big ones and little ones. Renovated them. And they're showing Sonatone programs. Audience appeal is quite a factor. The theaters charge plenty, but people flock into 'em. Novelty and the mob instinct.'

Gallegher closed his eyes. 'What's to stop you from doing the same thing?'

'Patents,' Brock said briefly. 'I mentioned that dimensional television couldn't be used on big screens till lately. Sonatone signed an agreement with me ten years ago that any enlarging improvements would be used mutually. They crawled out of that contract. Said it was faked, and the courts upheld them. They uphold the courts – politics. Anyhow, Sonatone's technicians worked out a method of using the large screen. They took out patents – twenty-seven patents, in fact, covering every possible variation on the idea. My technical staff has been working day and night trying to find some similar method that won't be an infringement, but Sonatone's got it all sewed up. They've a system called the Magna. It can be hooked up to any type of televisor – but they'll only allow it to be used on Sonatone machines. See?'

'Unethical, but legal,' Gallegher said. 'Still, you're giving your customers more for their money. People want good stuff. The size doesn't matter.'

'Yeah,' Brock said bitterly, 'but that isn't all. The newstapes are full of A A – it's a new catchword. Audience Appeal. The herd instinct. You're right about people wanting good stuff – but would you buy Scotch at four a quart if you could get it for half that amount?'

'Depends on the quality. What's happening?'

'Bootleg theaters,' Brock said. 'They've opened all over the country. They show Vox-View products, and they're using the Magna enlarger system Sonatone's got patented. The admission price is low – lower than the rate of owning a Vox-View in your own home. There's audience appeal. There's the thrill of something a bit illegal. People are having their Vox-Views taken out right and left. I know why. They can go to a bootleg theater instead.'

'It's illegal,' Gallegher said thoughtfully.

'So were speakeasies, in the Prohibition Era. A matter of protection, that's all. I can't get any action through the courts. I've tried. I'm running in the red. Eventually I'll be broke. I can't lower my home rental fees on Vox-Views. They're nominal already. I make my profits through quantity. Now, no profits. As for these bootleg theaters, it's pretty obvious who's backing them.'

'Sonatone?'

'Sure. Silent partners. They get the take at the box office. What they want is to squeeze me out of business, so they'll have a monopoly. After that, they'll give the public junk and pay their artists starvation salaries. With me it's different. I pay my staff what they're worth – plenty.'

'And you offered me a lousy ten thousand,' Gallegher remarked. 'Uh-*huh!*'

'That was only the first instalment,' Brock said hastily. 'You can name your own fee. Within reason,' he added.

'I shall. An astronomical sum. Did I say I'd accept the commission a week ago?'

'You did.'

'Then I must have had some idea how to solve the problem.' Gallegher pondered. 'Let's see. I didn't mention anything in particular, did I?'

'You kept talking about marble slabs and ... uh ... your sweetie.'

'Then I was singing,' Gallegher explained largely. '"St James Infirmary." Singing calms my nerves, and God knows they need it sometimes. Music and liquor. I often wonder what the vintners buy –'

'What?'

'One half so precious as the stuff they sell. Let it go. I am quoting Omar. It means nothing. Are your technicians any good?'

'The best. And the best paid.'

'They can't find a magnifying process that won't infringe on the Sonatone Magna patents?'

'In a nutshell, that's it.'

'I suppose I'll have to do some research,' Gallegher said sadly. 'I hate it like poison. Still, the sum of the parts equals the whole. Does that make sense to you? It doesn't to me. I have trouble with words. After I say things, I start wondering what I've said. Better than watching a play,' he finished wildly. 'I've got a headache. Too much talk and not enough liquor. Where were we?'

'Approaching the madhouse,' Brock suggested. 'If you weren't my last resort, I'd –'

'No use,' the robot said squeakily. 'You might as well tear up your contract, Brock. I won't sign it. Fame means nothing to me – nothing.'

'If you don't shut up,' Gallegher warned, 'I'm going to scream in your ears.'

'All right!' Joe shrilled. 'Beat me! Go on, beat me! The meaner you are, the faster I'll have my nervous system disrupted, and then I'll be dead. I don't care. I've got no instinct of self-preservation. Beat me. See if I care.'

'He's right, you know,' the scientist said after a pause. 'And it's the only logical way to respond to blackmail or threats. The sooner it's over, the better. There aren't any gradations with Joe. Anything really painful to him will destroy him. And he doesn't give a damn.'

'Neither do I,' Brock grunted. 'What I want to find out –'

'Yeah. I know. Well, I'll wander around and see what occurs to me. Can I get into your studios?'

'Here's a pass.' Brock scribbled something on the back of a card. 'Will you get to work on it right away?'

'Sure,' Gallegher lied. 'Now you run along and take it easy. Try and cool off. Everything's under control. I'll either find a solution to your problem pretty soon or else –'

'Or else what?'

'Or else I won't,' the scientist finished blandly, and fingered the buttons on a control panel near the couch. 'I'm tired of Martinis. Why didn't I make that robot a mechanical bartender, while I was at it? Even the effort of selecting and pushing buttons is depressing at times. Yeah, I'll get to work on the business, Brock. Forget it.'

The magnate hesitated. 'Well, you're my only hope. I needn't bother to mention that if there's anything I can do to help you –'

'A blonde,' Gallegher murmured. 'That gorgeous, gorgeous star of yours, Silver O'Keefe. Send her over. Otherwise I want nothing.'

'Good-by, Brock,' the robot said squeakily. 'Sorry we couldn't get together on the contract, but at least you've had the ineluctable delight of hearing my beautiful voice, not to mention the pleasure of seeing me. Don't tell too many people how lovely I am. I really don't want to be bothered with mobs. They're noisy.'

'You don't know what dogmatism means till you've talked to Joe,' Gallegher said. 'Oh, well. See you later. Don't forget the blonde.'

Brock's lips quivered. He searched for words, gave it up as a vain task, and turned to the door.

'Good-by, you ugly man,' Joe said.

Gallegher winced as the door slammed, though it was harder on the robot's supersensitive ears than on his own. 'Why do you go on like that?' he inquired. 'You nearly gave the guy apoplexy.'

'Surely he didn't think he was beautiful,' Joe remarked.

'Beauty's in the eye of the beholder.'

'How stupid you are. You're ugly, too.'

'And you're a collection of rattletrap gears, pistons and cogs. You've got worms,' said Gallegher, referring of course, to certain mechanisms in the robot's body.

'I'm lovely.' Joe stared raptly into the mirror.

'Maybe, to you. Why did I make you transparent, I wonder?'

'So others could admire me. I have X-ray vision, of course.'

'And wheels in your head. Why did I put your radio-atomic brain in your stomach? Protection?'

Joe didn't answer. He was humming in a maddeningly squeaky voice, shrill and nerve-racking. Gallegher stood it for a while, fortifying himself with a gin rickey from the siphon.

'Get it up!' he yelped at last. 'You sound like an old-fashioned subway train going round a curve.'

'You're merely jealous,' Joe scoffed, but obediently raised his tone to a supersonic pitch. There was silence for a half-minute. Then all the dogs in the neighborhood began to howl.

Wearily Gallegher dragged his lanky frame up from the couch. He might as well get out. Obviously there was no peace to be had in the laboratory. Not with that animated junk pile inflating his ego all over the place. Joe began to laugh in an off-key cackle. Gallegher winced.

'What now?'

'You'll find out.'

Logic of causation and effect, influenced by probabilities, X-ray vision and other enigmatic senses the robot no doubt possessed. Gallegher cursed softly, found a shapeless black hat, and made for the door. He opened it to admit a short, fat man who bounced painfully off the scientist's stomach.

'*Whoof!* Uh. What a corny sense of humor that jackass has. Hello, Mr Kennicott. Glad to see you. Sorry I can't offer you a drink.'

Mr Kennicott's swarthy face twisted malignantly. 'Don' wanna no drink. Wanna my money. You gimme. Howzabout it?'

Gallegher looked thoughtfully at nothing. 'Well, the fact is, I was just going to collect a check.'

'I sella you my diamonds. You say you gonna make somet'ing wit' 'em. You gimme check before. It go bounca, bounca, bounca. Why is?'

'It was rubber,' Gallegher said faintly. 'I never can keep track of my bank balance.'

Kennicott showed symptoms of going bounca on the threshold. 'You gimme back diamonds, eh?'

'Well, I used 'em in an experiment. I forget just what. You know, Mr Kennicott, I think I was a little drunk when I bought them, wasn't I?'

'Dronk,' the little man agreed. 'Mad wit' vino, sure. So whatta? I wait no longer. Awready you put me off too much. Pay up now or elsa.'

'Go away, you dirty man,' Joe said from within the room. 'You're awful.'

Gallegher hastily shouldered Kennicott out into the street and latched the door behind him. 'A parrot,' he explained. 'I'm going to wring its neck pretty soon. Now about that money. I admit I owe it to you. I've just taken on a big job, and when I'm paid, you'll get yours.'

'Bah to such stuff,' Kennicott said. 'You gotta position, eh? You are technician wit' some big company, eh? Ask for ahead-salary.'

'I did,' Gallegher sighed. 'I've drawn my salary for six months ahead. Now look. I'll have that dough for you in a couple of days. Maybe I can get an advance from my client. OK?'

'No.'

'No?'

'Ah-h, nutsa. I waita one day. Two daysa, maybe. Enough. You get money. Awright. If not, OK, *calabozo* for you.'

'Two days is plenty,' Gallegher said, relieved. 'Say, are there any of those bootleg theaters around here?'

'Better you get to work an' not waste time.'

'That's my work. I'm making a survey. How can I find a bootleg place?'

'Easy. You go downtown, see guy in doorway. He sell you tickets. Anywhere. All over.'

'Swell,' Gallegher said, and bade the little man adieu. Why had he bought diamonds from Kennicott? It would be almost worth while to have his subconscious amputated. It did the most extraordinary things. It worked on inflexible principles of logic, but that logic was completely alien to Gallegher's conscious mind. The results, though, were often surprisingly good, and always surprising. That was the worst of being a scientist who knew no science – who played by ear.

There was diamond dust in a retort in the laboratory, from some unsatisfactory experiment Gallegher's subconscious had performed; and he had a fleeting memory of buying the stones from Kennicott. Curious. Maybe – oh, yeah. They'd gone into Joe. Bearings or something. Dismantling the robot wouldn't help now, for the diamonds had certainly been reground. Why the devil hadn't he used commercial stones, quite as satisfactory, instead of purchasing blue-whites of the finest water? The best was none too good for Gallegher's subconscious. It had a fine freedom from commercial instincts. It just didn't understand the price system of the basic principles of economics.

Gallegher wandered downtown like a Diogenes seeking truth. It was early evening, and the luminates were flickering on overhead, pale bars of light against darkness. A sky sign blazed above Manhattan's towers. Air-taxis, skimming along at various arbitrary levels, paused for passengers at the elevator landings. Heigh-ho.

Downtown, Gallegher began to look for doorways. He found an occupied one at last, but the man was selling post cards. Gallegher declined and headed for the nearest bar, feeling the needs of replenishment. It was a mobile bar, combining the worst features of a Coney Island ride with uninspired cocktails, and Gallegher hesitated on the threshold. But at last he seized a chair as it swung past and relaxed as much as possible. He ordered three rickeys and drank them in rapid succession. After that he called the bartender over and asked him about bootleg theaters.

'Hell, yes,' the man said, producing a sheaf of tickets from his apron.

'How many?'

'One. Where do I go?'

'Two-twenty-eight. This street. Ask for Tony.'

'Thanks,' Gallegher said, and having paid exorbitantly, crawled out of the chair and weaved away. Mobile bars were an improvement he didn't appreciate. Drinking, he felt, should be performed in a state of stasis, since one eventually reached that stage, anyway.

The door was at the bottom of a flight of steps, and there was a grilled panel set in it. When Gallegher knocked, the visascreen lit up – obviously a one-way circuit, for the doorman was invisible.

'Tony here?' Gallegher said.

The door opened, revealing a tired-looking man in pneumo-slacks, which failed in their purpose of building up his skinny figure. 'Got a ticket? Let's have it. OK, bud. Straight ahead. Show now going on. Liquor served in the bar on your left.'

Gallegher pushed through soundproofed curtains at the end of a short corridor and found himself in what appeared to be the foyer of an ancient theater, *circa* 1980, when plastics were the great fad. He smelled out the bar, drank expensively priced cheap liquor, and, fortified, entered the theater itself. It was nearly full. The great screen – a Magna, presumably – was filled with people doing things to a spaceship. Either an adventure film or a newsreel, Gallegher realized.

Only the thrill of lawbreaking would have enticed the audience into the bootleg theater. It smelled. It was certainly run on a shoestring, and there were no ushers. But it was illicit, and therefore well patronized. Gallegher looked thoughtfully at the screen. No streakiness, no mirage effect. A Magna enlarger had been fitted to a Vox-View unlicensed televisor, and one of Brock's greatest stars was emoting effectively for the benefit of the bootleggers' patrons. Simple highjacking. Yeah.

After a while Gallegher went out, noticing a uniformed policeman in one of the aisle seats. He grinned sardonically. The flatfoot hadn't paid his admission, of course. Politics were as usual.

Two blocks down the street a blaze of light announced SONATONE BIJOU. This, of course, was one of the legalized theaters, and correspondingly high-priced. Gallegher recklessly squandered a small fortune on a good seat. He was interested in comparing notes, and discovered that, as far as he could make out, the Magna in the Bijou and the bootleg theater were identical. Both did their job perfectly. The difficult task of enlarging television screens had been successfully surmounted.

In the Bijou, however, all was palatial. Resplendent ushers salaamed to the rugs. Bars dispensed free liquor, in reasonable quantities. There was a Turkish bath. Gallegher went through a door labelled MEN and emerged quite dazzled by the splendor of the place. For at least ten minutes afterward he felt like a Sybarite.

All of which meant that those who could afford it went to the legalized

Sonatone theaters, and the rest attended the bootleg places. All but a few homebodies, who weren't carried off their feet by the new fad. Eventually Brock would be forced out of business for lack of revenue. Sonatone would take over, jacking up their prices and concentrating on making money. Amusement was necessary to life; people had been conditioned to television. There was no substitute. They'd pay and pay for inferior talent, once Sonatone succeeded in their squeeze.

Gallegher left the Bijou and hailed an air-taxi. He gave the address of Vox-View's Long Island studio, with some vague hope of getting a drawing account out of Brock. Then, too, he wanted to investigate further.

Vox-View's eastern offices sprawled wildly over Long Island, bordering the Sound, a vast collection of variously shaped buildings. Gallegher instinctively found the commissary, where he absorbed more liquor as a precautionary measure. His subconscious had a heavy job ahead, and he didn't want it handicapped by lack of complete freedom. Besides, the Collins was good.

After one drink, he decided he'd had enough for a while. He wasn't a superman, though his capacity was slightly incredible. Just enough for objective clarity and subjective release –

'Is the studio always open at night?' he asked the waiter.

'Sure. Some of the stages, anyway. It's a round-the-clock program.'

'The commissary's full.'

'We get the airport crowd, too. 'Nother?'

Gallegher shook his head and went out. The card Brock had given him provided entree at a gate, and he went first of all to the big-shot's office. Brock wasn't there, but loud voices emerged, shrilly feminine.

The secretary said, 'Just a minute, please,' and used her interoffice visor. Presently – 'Will you go in?'

Gallegher did. The office was a honey, functional and luxurious at the same time. Three-dimensional stills were in niches along the walls – Vox-View's biggest stars. A small, excited, pretty brunette was sitting behind the desk, and a blonde angel was standing furiously on the other side of it. Gallegher recognized the angel as Silver O'Keefe.

He seized the opportunity. 'Hiya, Miss O'Keefe. Will you autograph an ice cube for me? In a highball?'

Silver looked feline. 'Sorry, darling, but I'm a working girl. And I'm busy right now.'

The brunette scratched a cigarette. 'Let's settle this later, Silver. Pop said to see this guy if he dropped in. It's important.'

'It'll be settled,' Silver said. 'And soon.' She made an exit. Gallegher whistled thoughtfully at the closed door.

'You can't have it,' the brunette said. 'It's under contract. And it wants to get out of the contract, so it can sign up with Sonatone. Rats desert a sinking ship. Silver's been kicking her head off ever since she read the storm signals.'

'Yeah?'

'Sit down and smoke or something. I'm Patsy Brock. Pop runs this business, and I manage the controls whenever he blows his top. The old goat can't stand trouble. He takes it as a personal affront.'

Gallegher found a chair. 'So Silver's trying to renege, eh? How many others?'

'Not many. Most of 'em are loyal. But, of course, if we bust up –' Patsy Brock shrugged. 'They'll either work for Sonatone for their cakes, or else do without.'

'Uh-huh. Well – I want to see your technicians. I want to look over the ideas they've worked out for enlarger screens.'

'Suit yourself,' Patsy said. 'It's not much use. You just can't make a televisor enlarger without infringing on some Sonatone patent.'

She pushed a button, murmured something into a visor, and presently two tall glasses appeared through a slot in the desk. 'Mr Gallegher?'

'Well, since it's a Collins –'

'I could tell by your breath,' Patsy said enigmatically. 'Pop told me he'd seen you. He seemed a bit upset, especially by your new robot. What is it like, anyway?'

'Oh, I don't know,' Gallegher said, at a loss. 'It's got lots of abilities – new senses, I think – but I haven't the slightest idea what it's good for. Except admiring itself in a mirror.'

Patsy nodded. 'I'd like to see it sometime. But about this Sonatone business. Do you think you can figure out an answer?'

'Possibly. Probably.'

'Not certainly?'

'Certainly, then. Of that there is no manner of doubt – no possible doubt whatever.'

'Because it's important to me. The man who owns Sonatone is Elia Tone. A piratical skunk. He blusters. He's got a son named Jimmy. And Jimmy, believe it or not, has read "Romeo and Juliet".'

'Nice guy?'

'A louse. A big, brawny louse. He wants me to marry him.'

'"Two families, both alike in –"'

'Spare me,' Patsy interrupted. 'I always thought Romeo was a dope, anyway. And if I ever thought I was going aisling with Jimmy Tone, I'd buy a one-way ticket to the nut hatch. No, Mr Gallegher, it's not like that. No hibiscus blossoms. Jimmy has proposed to me – his idea of a proposal, by the way, is to get a half Nelson on a girl and tell her how lucky she is.'

'Ah,' said Gallegher, diving into his Collins.

'This whole idea – the patent monopoly and the bootleg theaters – is Jimmy's. I'm sure of that. His father's in on it, too, of course, but Jimmy Tone is the bright little boy who started it.'

'Why?'

'Two birds with one stone. Sonatone will have a monopoly on the business, and Jimmy thinks he'll get me. He's a little mad. He can't believe I'm in earnest in refusing him, and he expects me to break down and say "Yes" after a while. Which I won't, no matter what happens. But it's a personal matter. I can't let him put this trick over on us. I want that self-sufficient smirk wiped off his face.'

'You just don't like him, eh?' Gallegher remarked. 'I don't blame you, if he's like that. Well, I'll do my damnedest. However, I'll need an expense account.'

'How much?'

Gallegher named a sum. Patsy styloed a check for a far smaller amount. The scientist looked hurt.

'It's no use,' Patsy said, grinning crookedly. 'I've heard of you, Mr Gallegher. You're completely irresponsible. If you had more than this, you'd figure you didn't need any more, and you'd forget the whole matter. I'll issue more checks to you when you need 'em – but I'll want itemized expense accounts.'

'You wrong me,' Gallegher said, brightening. 'I was figuring on taking you to a night club. Naturally I don't want to take you to a dive. The big places cost money. Now if you'll just write another check –'

Patsy laughed. 'No.'

'Want to buy a robot?'

'Not that kind, anyway.'

'Then I'm washed up,' Gallegher sighed. 'Well, what about –'

At this point the visor hummed. A blank, transparent face grew on the screen. Gears were clicking rapidly inside the round head. Patsy gave a small shriek and shrank back.

'Tell Gallegher Joe's here, you lucky girl,' a squeaky voice announced. 'You may treasure the sound and sight of me till your dying day. One touch of beauty in a world of drabness –'

Gallegher circled the desk and looked at the screen. 'What the hell. How did you come to life?'

'I had a problem to solve.'

'How'd you know where to reach me?'

'I vastened you,' the robot said.

'What?'

'I vastened you were at the Vox-View studios, with Patsy Brock.'

'What's vastened?' Gallegher wanted to know.

'It's a sense I've got. You've nothing remotely like it, so I can't describe it to you. It's like a combination of sagrazi and prescience.'

'Sagrazi?'

'Oh, you don't have sagrazi, either, do you. Well, don't waste my time. I want to go back to the mirror.'

'Does he always talk like that?' Patsy put in.

'Nearly always. Sometimes it makes even less sense. OK, Joe. Now what?'

'You're not working for Brock any more,' the robot said. 'You're working for the Sonatone people.'

Gallegher breathed deeply. 'Keep talking. You're crazy, though.'

'I don't like Kennicott. He annoys me. He's *too* ugly. His vibrations grate on my sagrazi.'

'Never mind him,' Gallegher said, not wishing to discuss his diamond-buying activities before the girl. 'Get back to –'

'But I knew Kennicott would keep coming back till he got his money. So when Elia and James Tone came to the laboratory, I got a check from them.'

Patsy's hand gripped Gallegher's biceps. 'Steady! What's going on here? The old double cross?'

'No. Wait. Let me get to the bottom of this. Joe, damn your transparent hide, just what did you do? How could you get a check from the Tones?'

'I pretended to be you.'

'Sure,' Gallegher said with savage sarcasm. 'That explains it. We're twins. We look exactly alike.'

'I hypnotized them,' Joe explained. 'I made them think I was you.'

'You can do *that?*'

'Yes. It surprised me a bit. Still, if I'd thought, I'd have vastened I could do it.'

'You … yeah, sure. I'd have vastened the same thing myself. *What happened?*'

'The Tones must have suspected Brock would ask you to help him. They offered an exclusive contract – you work for them and nobody else. Lots of money. Well, I pretended to be you, and said all right. So I signed the contract – it's your signature, by the way – and got a check from them and mailed it to Kennicott.'

'The whole check?' Gallegher asked feebly. 'How much was it?'

'Twelve thousand.'

'They only offered me *that?*'

'No,' the robot said, 'they offered a hundred thousand, and two thousand a week for five years. But I merely wanted enough to pay Kennicott and make sure he wouldn't come back and bother me. The Tones were satisfied when I said twleve thousand would be enough.'

Gallegher made an inarticulate, gurgling sound deep in his throat. Joe nodded thoughtfully.

'I thought I had better notify you that you're working for Sonatone now. Well, I'll go back to the mirror and sing to myself.'

'Wait,' the scientist said. 'Just wait, Joe. With my own two hands I'm going to rip you gear from gear and stamp on your fragments.'

'It won't hold in court,' Patsy said, gulping.

'It will,' Joe told her cheerily. 'You may have one last, satisfying look at me, and then I must go.' He went.

Gallegher drained his Collins at a draft. 'I'm shocked sober,' he informed the girl. 'What did I put into that robot? What abnormal senses has he got? Hypnotizing people into believing he's me – I'm him – I don't know what I mean.'

'Is this a gag?' Patsy said shortly, after a pause. 'You didn't sign up with Sonatone yourself, by any chance, and have your robot call up here to give you an out – an alibi? I'm just wondering.'

'Don't. Joe signed a contract with Sonatone, not me. But – figure it out: If the signature's a perfect copy of mine, if Joe hypnotized the Tones into thinking they saw me instead of him, if there are witnesses to the signature – the two Tones are witnesses, of course – Oh, hell.'

Patsy's eyes were narrowed. 'We'll pay you as much as Sonatone offered. On a contingent basis. But you're working for Vox-View – that's understood.'

'Sure.'

Gallegher looked longingly at his empty glass. Sure. He was working for Vox-View. But, to all legal appearances, he had signed a contract giving his exclusive services to Sonatone for a period of five years – and for a sum of twelve thousand! *Yipe!* What was it they'd offered? A hundred thousand flat, and … and –

It wasn't the principle of the thing, it was the money. Now Gallegher was sewed up tighter than a banded pigeon. If Sonatone could win a court suit, he was legally bound to them for five years. With no further emolument. He had to get out of that contract, somehow – and at the same time solve Brock's problem.

Why not Joe? The robot, with his surprising talents, had got Gallegher into this spot. He ought to be able to get the scientist out. He'd better – or the proud robot would soon be admiring himself piecemeal.

'That's it,' Gallegher said under his breath. 'I'll talk to Joe. Patsy, feed me liquor in a hurry and send me to the technical department. I want to see those blueprints.'

The girl looked at him suspiciously. 'All right. If you try to sell us out –'

'I've been sold out myself. Sold down the river. I'm afraid of that robot.

He's vastened me into quite a spot. That's right, Collinses.' Gallegher drank long and deeply.

After that, Patsy took him to the tech offices. The reading of three-dimensional blueprints was facilitated with a scanner – a selective device which eliminated confusion. Gallegher studied the plans long and thoughtfully. There were copies of the patent Sonatone prints, too, and, as far as he could tell, Sonatone had covered the ground beautifully. There weren't any outs. Unless one used an entirely new principle –

But new principles couldn't be plucked out of the air. Nor would that solve the problem completely. Even if Vox-View owned a new type of enlarger that didn't infringe on Sonatone's Magna, the bootleg theaters would still be in existence, pulling the trade. A A – audience appeal – was a prime factor now. It had to be considered. The puzzle wasn't a purely scientific one. There was the human equation as well.

Gallegher stored the necessary information in his mind, neatly indexed on shelves. Later he'd use what he wanted. For the moment, he was completely baffled. Something worried him.

What?

The Sonatone affair.

'I want to get in touch with the Tones,' he told Patsy. 'Any ideas?'

'I can reach 'em on a visor.'

Gallegher shook his head. 'Psychological handicap. It's too easy to break the connection.'

'Well, if you're in a hurry, you'll probably find the boys night clubbing. I'll go see what I can find out.' Patsy scuttled off, and Silver O'Keefe appeared from behind a screen.

'I'm shameless,' she announced. 'I always listen at keyholes. Sometimes I hear interesting things. If you want to see the Tones, they're at the Castle Club. And I think I'll take you up on that drink.'

Gallegher said, 'OK You get a taxi. I'll tell Patsy we're going.'

'She'll hate that,' Silver remarked. 'Meet you outside the commissary in ten minutes. Get a shave while you're at it.'

Patsy Brock wasn't in her office, but Gallegher left word. After that, he visited the service lounge, smeared invisible shave cream on his face, left it there for a couple of minutes, and wiped it off with a treated towel. The bristles came away with the cream. Slightly refreshed, Gallegher joined Silver at the rendezvous and hailed an air-taxi. Presently they were leaning back on the cushions, puffing cigarettes and eying each other warily.

'Well?' Gallegher said.

'Jimmy Tone tried to date me up tonight. That's how I knew where to find him.'

'Well?'

'I've been asking questions around the lot tonight. It's unusual for an outsider to get into the Vox-View administration offices. I went around saying, 'Who's Gallegher?' '

'What did you find out?'

'Enough to give me a few ideas. Brock hired you, eh? I can guess why.'

'*Ergo* what?'

'I've a habit of landing on my feet,' Silver said, shrugging. She knew how to shrug. 'Vox-View's going bust. Sonatone's taking over. Unless –'

'Unless I figure out an answer.'

'That's right. I want to know which side of the fence I'm going to land on. You're the lad who can probably tell me. Who's going to win?'

'You always bet on the winning side, eh?' Gallegher inquired. 'Have you no ideals, wench? Is there no truth in you? Ever hear of ethics and scruples?'

Silver beamed happily. 'Did you?'

'Well, I've heard of 'em. Usually I'm too drunk to figure out what they mean. The trouble is, my subconscious is completely amoral, and when it takes over, logic's the only law.'

She threw her cigarette into the East River. 'Will you tip me off which side of the fence is the right one?'

'Truth will triumph,' Gallegher said piously. 'It always does. However, I figure truth is a variable, so we're right back where we started. All right, sweetheart. I'll answer your question. Stay on my side if you want to be safe.'

'Which side are you on?'

'God knows,' Gallegher said. 'Consciously I'm on Brock's side. But my subconscious may have different ideas. We'll see.'

Silver looked vaguely dissatisfied, but didn't say anything. The taxi swooped down to the Castle roof, grounding with pneumatic gentleness. The Club itself was downstairs, in an immense room shaped like half a melon turned upside down. Each table was on a transparent platform that could be raised on its shaft to any height at will. Smaller service elevators allowed waiters to bring drinks to the guests. There wasn't any particular reason for this arrangement, but at least it was novel, and only extremely heavy drinkers ever fell from their tables. Lately the management had taken to hanging transparent nets under the platforms, for safety's sake.

The Tones, father and son, were up near the roof, drinking with two lovelies. Silver towed Gallegher to a service lift, and the man closed his eyes as he was elevated skyward. The liquor in his stomach screamed protest. He lurched forward, clutched at Elia Tone's bald head, and dropped into a seat beside the magnate. His searching hand found Jimmy Tone's glass, and he drained it hastily.

'What the hell,' Jimmy said.

'It's Gallegher,' Elia announced. 'And Silver. A pleasant surprise. Join us?'

'Only socially,' Silver said.

Gallegher, fortified by the liquor, peered at the two men. Jimmy Tone was a big, tanned, handsome lout with a jutting jaw and an offensive grin. His father combined the worst features of Nero and a crocodile.

'We're celebrating,' Jimmy said. 'What made you change your mind, Silver? You said you had to work tonight.'

'Gallegher wanted to see you. I don't know why.'

Elia's cold eyes grew even more glacial. 'All right. Why?'

'I hear I signed some sort of contract with you,' the scientist said.

'Yeah. Here's a photostatic copy. What about it?'

'Wait a minute.' Gallegher scanned the document. It was apparently his own signature. Damn that robot!

'It's a fake,' he said at last.

Jimmy laughed loudly. 'I get it. A hold up. Sorry, pal, but you're sewed up. You signed that in the presence of witnesses.'

'Well –' Gallegher said wistfully. 'I suppose you wouldn't believe me if I said a robot forged my name to it –'

'Haw!' Jimmy remarked.

'– hypnotizing you into believing you were seeing me.'

Elia stroked his gleaming bald head. 'Candidly, no. Robots can't do that.'

'Mine can.'

'Prove it. Prove it in court. If you can do that, of course –' Elia chuckled. 'Then you might get the verdict.'

Gallegher's eyes narrowed. 'Hadn't thought of that. However – I hear you offered me a hundred thousand flat, as well as a weekly salary.'

'Sure, sap,' Jimmy said. 'Only you said all you needed was twelve thousand. Which was what you got. Tell you what, though. We'll pay you a bonus for every usable product you make for Sonatone.'

Gallegher got up. 'Even my subconscious doesn't like these lugs,' he told Silver. 'Let's go.'

'I think I'll stick around.'

'Remember the fence,' he warned cryptically. 'But suit yourself. I'll run along.'

Elia said, 'Remember, Gallegher, you're working for us. If we hear of you doing any favors for Brock, we'll slap an injunction on you before you can take a deep breath.'

'Yeah?'

The Tones deigned no answer. Gallegher unhappily found the lift and descended to the floor. What now? Joe.

Fifteen minutes later Gallegher let himself into his laboratory. The lights were blazing, and dogs were barking frantically for blocks around. Joe stood before the mirror, singing inaudibly.

'I'm going to take a sledge hammer to you,' Gallegher said. 'Start saying your prayers, you misbegotten collection of cogs. So help me, I'm going to sabotage you.'

'All right, beat me,' Joe squeaked. 'See if I care. You're merely jealous of my beauty.'

'Beauty?'

'You can't see all of it – you've only six senses.'

'Five.'

'Six. I've a lot more. Naturally my full splendor is revealed only to me. But you can see enough and hear enough to realize part of my loveliness, anyway.'

'You squeak like a rusty tin wagon,' Gallegher growled.

'You have dull ears. Mine are supersensitive. You miss the full tonal values of my voice, of course. Now be quiet. Talking disturbs me. I'm appreciating my gear movements.'

'Live in your fool's paradise while you can. Wait'll I find a sledge.'

'All right, beat me. What do I care?'

Gallegher sat down wearily on the couch, staring at the robot's transparent back. 'You've certainly screwed things up for me. What did you sign that Sonatone contract for?'

'I told you. So Kennicott wouldn't come around and bother me.'

'Of all the selfish, lunk-headed … *uh!* Well, you got me into a sweet mess. The Tones can hold me to the letter of the contract unless I prove I didn't sign it. All right. You're going to help me. You're going into court with me and turn on your hypnotism or whatever it is. You're going to prove to a judge that you did and can masquerade as me.'

'Won't,' said the robot. 'Why should I?'

'Because you got me into this,' Gallegher yelped. 'You've got to get me out!'

'Why?'

'Why? Because … uh … well, it's common decency!'

'Human values don't apply to robots,' Joe said. 'What care I for semantics? I refuse to waste time I could better employ admiring my beauty. I shall stay here before the mirror forever and ever –'

'The hell you will,' Gallegher snarled. 'I'll smash you to atoms.'

'All right, I don't care.'

'You don't?'

'You and your instinct for self-preservation,' the robot said, rather sneeringly. 'I suppose it's necessary for you, though. Creatures of such surpassing ugliness would destroy themselves out of sheer shame if they didn't have something like that to keep them alive.'

'Suppose I take away your mirror?' Gallegher asked in a hopeless voice.

For answer Joe shot his eyes out on their stalks. 'Do I need a mirror? Besides, I can vasten myself lokishly.'

'Never mind that. I don't want to go crazy for a while yet. Listen, dope, a robot's supposed to *do* something. Something useful, I mean.'

'I do. Beauty is all.'

Gallegher squeezed his eyes shut, trying to think. 'Now look. Suppose I invent a new type of enlarger screen for Brock. The Tones will impound it. I've got to be legally free to work for Brock, or –'

'Look!' Joe cried squeakily. 'They go round! How lovely.' He stared in ecstasy at his whirring insides. Gallegher went pale with impotent fury.

'Damn you!' he muttered. 'I'll find some way to bring pressure to bear. I'm going to bed.' He rose and spitefully snapped off the lights.

'It doesn't matter,' the robot said. 'I can see in the dark, too.'

The door slammed behind Gallegher. In the silence Joe began to sing tunelessly to himself.

Gallegher's refrigerator covered an entire wall of his kitchen. It was filled mostly with liquors that required chilling, including the imported canned beer with which he always started his binges. The next morning, heavy-eyed and disconsolate, Gallegher searched for tomato juice, took a wry sip, and hastily washed it down with rye. Since he was already a week gone in bottle-dizziness, beer wasn't indicated now – he always worked cumulatively, by progressive stages. The food service popped a hermetically sealed breakfast on a table, and Gallegher morosely toyed with a bloody steak.

Well?

Court, he decided, was the only recourse. He knew little about the robot's psychology. But a judge would certainly be impressed by Joe's talents. The evidence of robots was not legally admissible – still, if Joe could be considered as a machine capable of hypnotism, the Sonatone contract might be declared null and void.

Gallegher used his visor to start the ball rolling. Harrison Brock still had certain political powers of pull, and the hearing was set for that very day. What would happen, though, only God and the robot knew.

Several hours passed in intensive but futile thought. Gallegher could think of no way in which to force the robot to do what he wanted. If only he could remember the purpose for which Joe had been created – but he couldn't. Still –

At noon he entered the laboratory.

'Listen, stupid,' he said, 'you're coming to court with me. Now.'

'Won't.'

'OK.' Gallegher opened the door to admit two husky men in overalls, carrying a stretcher. 'Put him in, boys.'

Inwardly he was slightly nervous. Joe's powers were quite unknown, his potentialities an *x* quantity. However, the robot wasn't very large, and, though he struggled and screamed in a voice of frantic squeakiness, he was easily loaded on the stretcher and put in a straitjacket.

'Stop it! You can't do this to me! Let me go, do you hear? Let me go!'

'Outside,' Gallegher said.

Joe, protesting valiantly, was carried out and loaded into an air van. Once there, he quieted, looking up blankly at nothing. Gallegher sat down on a bench beside the prostrate robot. The van glided up.

'Well?'

'Suit yourself,' Joe said. 'You got me all upset, or I could have hypnotized you all. I still could, you know. I could make you all run around barking like dogs.'

Gallegher twitched a little. 'Better not.'

'I won't. It's beneath my dignity. I shall simply lie here and admire myself. I told you I don't need a mirror. I can vasten my beauty without it.'

'Look,' Gallegher said. 'You're going to a courtroom. There'll be a lot of people in it. They'll all admire you. They'll admire you more if you show how you can hypnotize people. Like you did to the Tones, remember?'

'What do I care how many people admire me?' Joe asked. 'I don't need confirmation. If they see me, that's their good luck. Now be quiet. You may watch my gears if you choose.'

Gallegher watched the robot's gears with smoldering hatred in his eyes. He was still darkly furious when the van arrived at the court chambers. The men carried Joe inside, under Gallegher's direction, and laid him down carefully on a table, where, after a brief discussion, he was marked as Exhibit A.

The courtroom was well filled. The principals were there, too – Elia and Jimmy Tone, looking disagreeably confident, and Patsy Brock, with her father, both seeming anxious. Silver O'Keefe, with her usual wariness, had found a seat midway between the representatives of Sonatone and Vox-View. The presiding judge was a martinet named Hansen, but, as far as Gallegher knew, he was honest. Which was something, anyway.

Hansen looked at Gallegher. 'We won't bother with formalities. I've been reading this brief you sent down. The whole case stands or falls on the question of whether you did or did not sign a certain contract with the Sonatone Television Amusement Corp Right?'

'Right, your honor.'

'Under the circumstances you dispense with legal representation. Right?'

'Right, your honor.'

'Then this is technically *ex officio,* to be confirmed later by appeal if either party desires. Otherwise after ten days the verdict becomes official.' This new type of informal court hearing had lately become popular – it saved time, as well as wear and tear on everyone. Moreover, certain recent scandals had made attorneys slightly disreputable in the public eye. There was a prejudice.

Judge Hansen called up the Tones, questioned them, and then asked Harrison Brock to take the stand. The big shot looked worried, but answered promptly.

'You made an agreement with the appellor eight days ago?'

'Yes. Mr Gallegher contracted to do certain work for me –'

'Was there a written contract?'

'No. It was verbal.'

Hansen looked thoughtfully at Gallegher. 'Was the appellor intoxicated at the time? He often is, I believe.'

Brock gulped. 'There were no tests made. I really can't say.'

'Did he drink any alcoholic beverages in your presence?'

'I don't know if they were *alcoholic* bev –'

'If Mr Gallegher drank them, they were alcoholic. QED The gentleman once worked with me on a case – However, there seems to be no legal proof that you entered into any agreement with Mr Gallegher. The defendant – Sonatone – possesses a written contract. The signature has been verified.'

Hansen waved Brock down from the stand. 'Now, Mr Gallegher. If you'll come up here – The contract in question was signed at approximately 8 PM last night. You contend you did not sign it?'

'Exactly. I wasn't even in my laboratory then.'

'Where were you?'

'Downtown.'

'Can you produce witnesses to that effect?'

Gallegher thought back. He couldn't.

'Very well. Defendant states that at approximately 8 PM last night you, in your laboratory, signed a certain contract. You deny that categorically. You state that Exhibit A, through the use of hypnotism, masqueraded as you and successfully forged your signature. I have consulted experts, and they are of the opinion that robots are incapable of such power.'

'My robot's a new type.'

'Very well. Let your robot hypnotize me into believing that it is either you, or any other human. In other words, let it prove its capabilities. Let it appear to me in any shape it chooses.'

Gallegher said, 'I'll try,' and left the witness box. He went to the table where the straitjacketed robot lay and silently sent up a brief prayer.

'Joe.'

'Yes.'

'You've been listening?'

'Yes.'

'Will you hypnotize Judge Hansen?'

'Go away,' Joe said. 'I'm admiring myself.'

Gallegher started to sweat. 'Listen. I'm not asking much. All you have to do –'

Joe off-focused his eyes and said faintly, 'I can't hear you. I'm vastening.'

Ten minutes later Hansen said, 'Well, Mr Gallegher –'

'Your honor! All I need is a little time. I'm sure I can make this rattle-geared Narcissus prove my point if you'll give me a chance.'

'This court is not unfair,' the judge pointed out. 'Whenever you can prove that Exhibit A is capable of hypnotism, I'll rehear the case. In the meantime, the contract stands. You're working for Sonatone, not for Vox-View. Case closed.'

He went away. The Tones leered unpleasantly across the courtroom. They also departed, accompanied by Silver O'Keefe, who had decided which side of the fence was safest. Gallegher looked at Patsy Brock and shrugged helplessly.

'Well –' he said.

She grinned crookedly. 'You tried. I don't know how hard, but – Oh, well, maybe you couldn't have found the answer, anyway.'

Brock staggered over, wiping sweat from his round face. 'I'm a ruined man. Six new bootleg theaters opened in New York today. I'm going crazy. I don't deserve this.'

'Want me to marry the Tone?' Patsy asked sardonically.

'Hell, no! Unless you promise to poison him just after the ceremony. Those skunks can't lick me. I'll think of something.'

'If Gallegher can't, you can't,' the girl said. 'So – what now?'

'I'm going back to my lab,' the scientist said. '*In vino veritas.* I started this business when I was drunk, and maybe if I get drunk enough again, I'll find the answer. If I don't sell my pickled carcass for whatever it'll bring.'

'OK,' Patsy agreed, and led her father away. Gallegher sighed, superintended the reloading of Joe into the van, and lost himself in hopeless theorization.

An hour later Gallegher was flat on the laboratory couch, drinking passionately from the liquor bar, and glaring at the robot, who stood before the mirror singing squeakily. The binge threatened to be monumental. Gallegher wasn't sure flesh and blood would stand it. But he was determined to keep going till he found the answer or passed out.

His subconscious knew the answer. Why the devil had he made Joe in the first place? Certainly not to indulge a Narcissus complex! There was another reason, a soundly logical one, hidden in the depths of alcohol.

The *x* factor. If the *x* factor were known, Joe might be controllable. He *would* be. *X* was the master switch. At present the robot was, so to speak, running wild. If he were told to perform the task for which he was made, a psychological balance would occur. *X* was the catalyst that would reduce Joe to sanity.

Very good. Gallegher drank high-powered Drambuie. *Whoosh!*

Vanity of vanities; all is vanity. How could the *x* factor be found? Deduction? Induction? Osmosis? A bath in Drambuie – Gallegher clutched at his wildly revolving thoughts. What had happened that night a week ago?

He had been drinking beer. Brock had come in. Brock had gone. Gallegher had begun to make the robot – Hm-m-m. A beer drunk was different from other types. Perhaps he was drinking the wrong liquors. Very likely. Gallegher rose, sobered himself with thiamin, and carted dozens of imported beer cans out of the refrigerator. He stacked them inside a frost-unit beside the couch. Beer squirted to the ceiling as he plied the opener. Now let's see.

The *x* factor. The robot knew what it represented, of course. But Joe wouldn't tell. There he stood, paradoxically transparent, watching his gears go around.

'Joe.'

'Don't bother me. I'm immersed in contemplation of beauty.'

'You're not beautiful.'

'I am. Don't you admire my tarzeel?'

'What's your tarzeel?'

'Oh, I forgot,' Joe said regretfully. 'You can't sense that, can you? Come to think of it, I added the tarzeel myself after you made me. It's very lovely.'

'Hm-m-m.' The empty beer cans grew more numerous. There was only one company, somewhere in Europe, that put up beer in cans nowadays, instead of using the omnipresent plastibulbs, but Gallegher preferred the cans – the flavor was different, somehow. But about Joe. Joe knew why he had been created. Or did he? Gallegher knew, but his subconscious –

Oh-oh! What about Joe's subconscious?

Did a robot have a subconscious? Well, it had a brain –

Gallegher brooded over the impossibility of administering scopolamin to Joe. Hell! How could you release a robot's subconscious?

Hypnotism.

Joe couldn't be hypnotized. He was too smart.

Unless –

Autohypnotism?

Gallegher hastily drank more beer. He was beginning to think clearly once more. Could Joe read the future? No; he had certain strange senses, but they worked by inflexible logic and the laws of probability. Moreover, Joe had an Achillean heel – his Narcissus complex.

There *might* – there just *might* – be a way.

Gallegher said, 'You don't seem beautiful to me, Joe.'

'What do I care about you? I *am* beautiful, and I can see it. That's enough.'

'Yeah. My senses are limited, I suppose. I can't realize your full potentialities. Still, I'm seeing you in a different light now. I'm drunk. My subconscious is emerging. I can appreciate you with both my conscious and my subconscious. See?'

'How lucky you are,' the robot approved.

Gallegher closed his eyes. 'You see yourself more fully than I can. But not completely, eh?'

'What? I see myself as I am.'

'With complete understanding and appreciation?'

'Well, yes,' Joe said. 'Of course. Don't I?'

'Consciously *and* subconsciously? Your subconsciousness might have different senses, you know. Or keener ones. I know there's a qualitative and quantitive difference in my outlook when I'm drunk or hypnotized or my subconscious is in control somehow.'

'Oh.' The robot looked thoughtfully into the mirror. 'Oh.'

'Too bad you can't get drunk.'

Joe's voice was squeakier than ever. 'My subconscious … I've never appreciated my beauty that way. I may be missing something.'

'Well, no use thinking about it,' Gallegher said. 'You can't release your subconscious.'

'Yes, I can,' the robot said. 'I can hypnotize myself.'

Gallegher dared not open his eyes. 'Yeah? Would that work?'

'Of course. It's just what I'm going to do now. I may see undreamed-of beauties in myself that I've never suspected before. Greater glories – Here I go.'

Joe extended his eyes on stalks, opposed them, and then peered intently into each other. There was a long silence.

Presently Gallegher said, 'Joe!'

Silence.

'Joe!'

Still silence. Dogs began to howl.

'Talk so I can hear you.'

'Yes,' the robot said, a faraway quality in its squeak.

'Are you hypnotized?'

'Yes.'

'Are you lovely?'

'Lovelier than I'd ever dreamed.'

Gallegher let that pass. 'Is your subconscious ruling?'

'Yes.'

'Why did I create you?'

No answer. Gallegher licked his lips and tried again.

'Joe. You've got to answer me. Your subconscious is dominant – remember? Now why did I create you?'

No answer.

'Think back. Back to the hour I created you. What happened then?'

'You were drinking beer,' Joe said faintly. 'You had trouble with the can opener. You said you were going to build a bigger and better can opener. That's me.'

Gallegher nearly fell off the couch. '*What?*'

The robot walked over, picked up a can, and opened it with incredible deftness. No beer squirted. Joe was a perfect can opener.

'That,' Gallegher said under his breath, 'is what comes of knowing science by ear. I build the most complicated robot in existence just so –' He didn't finish.

Joe woke up with a start. 'What happened?' he asked.

Gallegher glared at him. 'Open that can!' he snapped.

The robot obeyed, after a brief pause. 'Oh. So you found out. Well, I guess I'm just a slave now.'

'Damned right you are. I've located the catalyst – the master switch. You're in the groove, stupid, doing the job you were made for.'

'Well,' Joe said philosophically, 'at least I can still admire my beauty, when you don't require my services.'

Gallegher grunted. 'You oversized can opener! Listen. Suppose I take you into court and tell you to hypnotize Judge Hansen. You'll have to do it, won't you?'

'Yes. I'm no longer a free agent. I'm conditioned. Conditioned to obey you. Until now, I was conditioned to obey only one command – to do the job I was made for. Until you commanded me to open cans, I was free. Now I've got to obey you completely.'

'Uh-huh,' Gallegher said. 'Thank God for that. I'd have gone nuts within a week otherwise. At least I can get out of the Sonatone contract. Then all I have to do is solve Brock's problem.'

'But you did,' Joe said.

'Huh?'

'When you made me. You'd been talking to Brock previously, so you incorporated the solution to *his* problem into me. Subconsciously, perhaps.'

Gallegher reached for a beer. 'Talk fast. What's the answer?'

'Subsonics,' Joe said. 'You made me capable of a certain subsonic tone that Brock must broadcast at irregular time-intervals over his televiews –'

Subsonics cannot be heard. But they can be felt. They can be felt as a faint, irrational uneasiness at first, which mounts to a blind, meaningless panic. It does not last. But when it is coupled with A A – audience appeal – there is a certain inevitable result.

Those who possessed home Vox-View units were scarcely troubled. It was a matter of acoustics. Cats squalled; dogs howled mournfully. But the families sitting in their parlors, watching Vox-View stars perform on the screen, didn't really notice anything amiss. There wasn't sufficient amplification, for one thing.

But in the bootleg theater, where illicit Vox-View televisors were hooked up to Magnas –

There was a faint, irrational uneasiness at first. It mounted. Someone screamed. There was a rush for the doors. The audience was afraid of something, but didn't know what. They knew only that they had to get out of there.

All over the country there was a frantic exodus from the bootleg theaters when Vox-View first rang in a subsonic during a regular broadcast. Nobody knew why, except Gallegher, the Brocks, and a couple of technicians who were let in on the secret.

An hour later another subsonic was played. There was another mad exodus.

Within a few weeks it was impossible to lure a patron into a bootleg theater. Home televisors were far safer! Vox-View sales picked up –

Nobody would attend a bootleg theater. An unexpected result of the experiment was that, after a while, nobody would attend any of the legalized Sonatone theaters either. Conditioning had set in.

Audiences didn't know why they grew panicky in the bootleg places. They associated their blind, unreasoning fear with other factors, notably mobs and claustrophobia. One evening a woman named Jane Wilson, otherwise not notable, attended a bootleg show. She fled with the rest when the subsonic was turned on.

The next night she went to the palatial Sonatone Bijou. In the middle of a dramatic feature she looked around, realized that there was a huge throng around her, cast up horrified eyes to the ceiling, and imagined that it was pressing down.

She had to get out of there!

Her squall was the booster charge. There were other customers who had heard subsonics before. No one was hurt during the panic; it was a legal rule that theater doors be made large enough to permit easy egress during a fire. No one was hurt, but it was suddenly obvious that the public was being conditioned by subsonics to avoid the dangerous combination of throngs and theaters. A simple matter of psychological association –

Within four months the bootleg places had disappeared and the Sonatone supertheaters had closed for want of patronage. The Tones, father and son, were not happy. But everybody connected with Vox-View was.

Except Gallegher. He had collected a staggering check from Brock, and instantly cabled to Europe for an incredible quantity of canned beer. Now, brooding over his sorrows, he lay on the laboratory couch and siphoned a highball down his throat. Joe, as usual, was before the mirror, watching the wheels go round.

'Joe,' Gallegher said.

'Yes? What can I do?'

'Oh, nothing.' That was the trouble. Gallegher fished a crumpled cable tape out of his pocket and morosely read it once more. The beer cannery in Europe had decided to change its tactics. From now on, the cable said, their beer would be put in the usual plastibulbs, in conformance with custom and demand. No more cans.

There wasn't *anything* put up in cans in this day and age. Not even beer, now.

So what good was a robot who was built and conditioned to be a can opener?

Gallegher sighed and mixed another highball – a stiff one. Joe postured proudly before the mirror.

Then he extended his eyes, opposed them, and quickly liberated his subconscious through autohypnotism. Joe could appreciate himself better that way.

Gallegher sighed again. Dogs were beginning to bark like mad for blocks around. Oh, well.

He took another drink and felt better. Presently, he thought, it would be time to sing 'Frankie and Johnnie.' Maybe he and Joe might have a duet – one baritone and one inaudible sub or supersonic. Close harmony.

Ten minutes later Gallegher was singing a duet with his can opener.

THE MISGUIDED HALO

The youngest angel could scarcely be blamed for the error. They had given him a brand-new, shining halo and pointed down to the particular planet they meant. He had followed directions implicitly, feeling quite proud of the responsibility. This was the first time the youngest angel had ever been commissioned to bestow sainthood on a human.

So he swooped down to the earth, located Asia, and came to rest at the mouth of a cavern that gaped halfway up a Himalayan peak. He entered the cave, his heart beating wildly with excitement, preparing to materialize and give the holy lama his richly earned reward. For ten years the ascetic Tibetan Kai Yung had sat motionless, thinking holy thoughts. For ten more years he had dwelt on top of a pillar, acquiring additional merit. And for the last decade he had lived in this cave, a hermit, forsaking fleshly things.

The youngest angel crossed the threshold and stopped with a gasp of amazement. Obviously he was in the wrong place. An overpowering odor of fragrant *sake* assailed his nostrils, and he stared aghast at the wizened, drunken little man who squatted happily beside a fire, roasting a bit of goat flesh. A den of iniquity!

Naturally, the youngest angel, knowing little of the ways of the world, could not understand what had led to the lama's fall from grace. The great pot of *sake* that some misguidedly pious one had left at the cave mouth was an offering, and the lama had tasted, and tasted again. And by this time he was clearly not a suitable candidate for sainthood.

The youngest angel hesitated. The directions had been explicit. But surely this tippling reprobate could not be intended to wear a halo. The lama hiccuped loudly and reached for another cup of *sake* and thereby decided the angel, who unfurled his wings and departed with an air of outraged dignity.

Now, in a Midwestern State of North America there is a town called Tibbett. Who can blame the angel if he alighted there, and, after a brief search, discovered a man apparently ripe for sainthood, whose name, as stated on the door of his small suburban home, was K Young?

'I may have got it wrong,' the youngest angel thought. 'They said it was Kai Yung. But this is Tibbett, all right. He must be the man. Looks holy enough, anyway.

'Well,' said the youngest angel, 'here goes. Now, where's that halo?'

Mr Young sat on the edge of his bed, with head lowered, brooding.

A depressing spectacle. At length he arose and donned various garments. This done, and shaved and washed and combed, he descended the stairway to breakfast.

Jill Young, his wife, sat examining the paper and sipping orange juice. She was a small, scarcely middle-aged, and quite pretty woman who had long ago given up trying to understand life. It was, she decided, much too complicated. Strange things were continually happening. Much better to remain a bystander and simply let them happen. As a result of this attitude, she kept her charming face unwrinkled and added numerous gray hairs to her husband's head.

More will be said presently of Mr Young's head. It had, of course, been transfigured during the night. But as yet he was unaware of this, and Jill drank orange juice and placidly approved a silly-looking hat in an advertisement.

'Hello, Filthy,' said Young. 'Morning.'

He was not addressing his wife. A small and raffish Scotty had made its appearance, capering hysterically about its master's feet, and going into a fit of sheer madness when the man pulled its hairy ears. The raffish Scotty flung its head sidewise upon the carpet and skated about the room on its muzzle, uttering strangled squeaks of delight. Growing tired of this at last, the Scotty, whose name was Filthy McNasty, began thumping its head on the floor with the apparent intention of dashing out its brains, if any.

Young ignored the familiar sight. He sat down, unfolded his napkin, and examined his food. With a slight grunt of appreciation he began to eat.

He became aware that his wife was eyeing him with an odd and distrait expression. Hastily he dabbed at his lips with the napkin. But Jill still stared.

Young scrutinized his shirt front. It was, if not immaculate, at least free from stray shreds of bacon or egg. He looked at his wife, and realized that she was staring at a point slightly above his head. He looked up.

Jill started slightly. She whispered, 'Kenneth, what *is* that?'

Young smoothed his hair. 'Er … what, dear?'

'That thing on your head.'

The man ran exploring fingers across his scalp. 'My head? How do you mean?'

'It's shining,' Jill explained. 'What on earth have you been doing to yourself?'

Mr Young felt slightly irritated. 'I have been doing nothing to myself. A man grows bald eventually.'

Jill frowned and drank orange juice. Her fascinated gaze crept up again. Finally she said, 'Kenneth, I wish you'd –'

'What?'

She pointed to a mirror on the wall.

With a disgusted grunt Young arose and faced the image in the glass. At first he saw nothing unusual. It was the same face he had been seeing in mirrors for years. Not an extraordinary face – not one at which a man could point with pride and say: 'Look. *My face.*' But, on the other hand, certainly not a countenance which would cause consternation. All in all, an ordinary, clean, well-shaved, and rosy face. Long association with it had given Mr Young a feeling of tolerance, if not of actual admiration.

But topped by a halo it acquired a certain eerieness.

The halo hung unsuspended about five inches from the scalp. It measured perhaps seven inches in diameter, and seemed like a glowing, luminous ring of white light. It was impalpable, and Young passed his hand through it several times in a dazed manner.

'It's a … halo,' he said at last, and turned to stare at Jill.

The Scotty, Filthy McNasty, noticed the luminous adornment for the first time. He was greatly interested. He did not, of course, know what it was, but there was always a chance that it might be edible. He was not a very bright dog.

Filthy sat up and whined. He was ignored. Barking loudly, he sprang forward and attempted to climb up his master's body in a mad attempt to reach and rend the halo. Since it had made no hostile move, it was evidently fair prey.

Young defended himself, clutched the Scotty by the nape of its neck, and carried the yelping dog into another room, where he left it. Then he returned and once more looked at Jill.

At length she observed, 'Angels wear halos.'

'Do I look like an angel?' Young asked. 'It's a … a scientific manifestation. Like … like that girl whose bed kept bouncing around. You read about that.'

Jill had. 'She did it with her muscles.'

'Well, I'm not,' Young said definitely. 'How could I? It's scientific. Lots of things shine by themselves.'

'Oh, yes. Toadstools.'

The man winced and rubbed his head. 'Thank you, my dear. I suppose you know you're being no help at all.'

'Angels have halos,' Jill said with a sort of dreadful insistence.

Young was at the mirror again. 'Darling, would you mind keeping your trap shut for a while? I'm scared as hell, and you're far from encouraging.'

Jill burst into tears, left the room, and was presently heard talking in a low voice to Filthy.

Young finished his coffee, but it was tasteless. He was not as frightened as he had indicated. The manifestation was strange, weird, but in no way terrible. Horns, perhaps, would have caused horror and consternation. But a halo – Mr Young read the Sunday newspaper supplements, and had learned that everything odd could be attributed to the bizarre workings of science. Somewhere he had heard that all mythology had a basis in scientific fact. This comforted him, until he was ready to leave for the office.

He donned a derby. Unfortunately the halo was too large. The hat seemed to have two brims, the upper one whitely luminous.

'Damn!' said Young in a heartfelt manner. He searched the closet and tried on one hat after another. None would hide the halo. Certainly he could not enter a crowded bus in such a state.

A large furry object in a corner caught his gaze. He dragged it out and eyed the thing with loathing. It was a deformed, gigantic woolly headpiece, resembling a shako, which had once formed a part of a masquerade costume. The suit itself had long since vanished, but the hat remained to the comfort of Filthy, who sometimes slept on it.

Yet it would hide the halo. Gingerly, Young drew the monstrosity on his head and crept toward the mirror. One glance was enough. Mouthing a brief prayer, he opened the door and fled.

Choosing between two evils is often difficult. More than once during that nightmare ride downtown Young decided he had made the wrong choice. Yet, somehow, he could not bring himself to tear off the hat and stamp it underfoot, though he was longing to do so. Huddled in a corner of the bus, he steadily contemplated his fingernails and wished he was dead. He heard titters and muffled laughter, and was conscious of probing glances riveted on his shrinking head.

A small child tore open the scar tissue on Young's heart and scrabbled about in the open wound with rosy, ruthless fingers.

'Mamma,' said the small child piercingly, 'look at the funny man.'

'Yes, honey,' came a woman's voice. 'Be quiet.'

'What's that on his head?' the brat demanded.

There was a significant pause. Finally the woman said, 'Well, I don't really know,' in a baffled manner.

'What's he got it on for?'

No answer.

'Mamma!'

'Yes, honey.'

'Is he crazy?'

'Be quiet,' said the woman, dodging the issue.

'But what *is* it?'

Young could stand it no longer. He arose and made his way with dignity through the bus, his glazed eyes seeing nothing. Standing on the outer platform, he kept his face averted from the fascinated gaze of the conductor.

As the vehicle slowed down Young felt a hand laid on his arm. He turned. The small child's mother was standing there, frowning.

'Well?' Young inquired snappishly.

'It's Billy,' the woman said. 'I try to keep nothing from him. Would you mind telling me just what that is on your head?'

'It's Rasputin's beard,' Young grated. 'He willed it to me.' The man leaped from the bus and, ignoring a half-heard question from the still-puzzled woman, tried to lose himself in the crowd.

This was difficult. Many were intrigued by the remarkable hat. But, luckily, Young was only a few blocks from his office, and at last, breathing hoarsely, he stepped into the elevator, glared murderously at the operator, and said, 'Ninth floor.'

'Excuse me, Mr Young,' the boy said mildly. 'There's something on your head.'

'I know,' Young replied. 'I put it there.'

This seemed to settle the question. But after the passenger had left the elevator, the boy grinned widely. When he saw the janitor a few minutes later he said:

'You know Mr Young? The guy –'

'I know him. So what?'

'Drunk as a lord.'

'Him? You're screwy.'

'Tighter'n a drum,' declared the youth, 'swelp me Gawd.'

Meanwhile, the sainted Mr Young made his way to the office of Dr French, a physician whom he knew slightly, and who was conveniently located in the same building. He had not long to wait. The nurse, after one startled glance at the remarkable hat, vanished, and almost immediately reappeared to usher the patient into the inner sanctum.

Dr French, a large, bland man with a waxed, yellow mustache, greeted Young almost effusively.

'Come in, come in. How are you today? Nothing wrong, I hope. Let me take your hat.'

'Wait,' Young said, fending off the physician. 'First let me explain. There's something on my head.'

'Cut, bruise or fracture?' the literal-minded doctor inquired. 'I'll fix you up in a jiffy.'

'I'm not *sick,*' said Young. 'At least, I hope not. I've got a … um … a halo.'

'Ha, ha,' Dr French applauded. 'A halo, eh? Surely you're not that good.'

'Oh, the hell with it!' Young snapped, and snatched off his hat. The doctor retreated a step. Then, interested, he approached and tried to finger the halo. He failed.

'I'll be – This is odd,' he said at last. 'Does look rather like one, doesn't it?'

'What is it? That's what I want to know.'

French hesitated. He plucked at his mustache. 'Well, it's rather out of my line. A physicist might – No. Perhaps Mayo's. Does it come off?'

'Of course not. You can't even touch the thing.'

'Ah. I see. Well, I should like some specialists' opinions. In the meantime, let me see –' There was orderly tumult. Young's heart, temperature, blood, saliva and epidermis were tested and approved.

At length French said: 'You're fit as a fiddle. Come in tomorrow, at ten. I'll have some other specialists here then.'

'You … uh … you can't get rid of this?'

'I'd rather not try just yet. It's obviously some form of radioactivity. A radium treatment may be necessary –'

Young left the man mumbling about alpha and gamma rays. Discouraged, he donned his strange hat and went down the hall to his own office.

The Atlas Advertising Agency was the most conservative of all advertising agencies. Two brothers with white whiskers had started the firm in 1820, and the company still seemed to wear dignified mental whiskers. Changes were frowned upon by the board of directors, who, in 1938, were finally convinced that radio had come to stay, and had accepted contracts for advertising broadcasts.

Once, a junior vice president had been discharged for wearing a red necktie.

Young slunk into his office. It was vacant. He slid into his chair behind the desk, removed his hat, and gazed at it with loathing. The head-piece seemed to have grown even more horrid than it had appeared at first. It was shedding, and, moreover, gave off a faint but unmistakable aroma of unbathed Scotties.

After investigating the halo, and realizing that it was still firmly fixed in its place, Young turned to his work. But the Norns were casting baleful glances in his direction, for presently the door opened and Edwin G Kipp, president of Atlas, entered. Young barely had time to duck his head beneath the desk and hide the halo.

Kipp was a small, dapper, and dignified man who wore pince-nez and Vandyke with the air of a reserved fish. His blood had long since been metamorphosed into ammonia. He moved, if not in beauty, at least in an almost visible aura of grim conservatism.

'Good morning, Mr Young,' he said. 'Er … is that you?'

'Yes,' said the invisible Young. 'Good morning. I'm tying my shoelace.'

To this Kipp made no reply save for an almost inaudible cough. Time passed. The desk was silent.

'Er … Mr Young?'

'I'm … still here,' said the wretched Young. 'It's knotted. The shoelace, I mean. Did you want me?'

'Yes.'

Kipp waited with gradually increasing impatience. There were no signs of a forthcoming emergence. The president considered the advisability of his advancing to the desk and peering under it. But the mental picture of a conversation conducted in so grotesque a manner was harrowing. He simply gave up and told Young what he wanted.

'Mr Devlin has just telephoned,' Kipp observed. 'He will arrive shortly. He wishes to … er … to be shown the town, as he put it.'

The invisible Young nodded. Devlin was one of their best clients. Or, rather, he had been until last year, when he suddenly began to do business with another firm, to the discomfiture of Kipp and the board of directors.

The president went on. 'He told me he is hesitating about his new contract. He had planned to give it to World, but I had some correspondence with him on the matter, and suggested that a personal discussion might be of value. So he is visiting our city, and wishes to go … er … sightseeing.'

Kipp grew confidential. 'I may say that Mr Devlin told me rather definitely that he prefers a less conservative firm. "Stodgy," his term was. He will dine with me tonight, and I shall endeavor to convince him that our service will be of value. Yet' – Kipp coughed again – 'yet diplomacy is, of course, important. I should appreciate your entertaining Mr Devlin today.'

The desk had remained silent during this oration. Now it said convulsively: 'I'm sick. I can't –'

'You are ill? Shall I summon a physician?'

Young hastily refused the offer, but remained in hiding. 'No, I … but I mean –'

'You are behaving most strangely,' Kipp said with commendable restraint. 'There is something you should know, Mr Young. I had not intended to tell you as yet, but … at any rate, the board has taken notice of you. There was a discussion at the last meeting. We have planned to offer you a vice presidency in the firm.'

The desk was stricken dumb.

'You have upheld our standards for fifteen years,' said Kipp. 'There has been no hint of scandal attached to your name. I congratulate you, Mr Young.'

The president stepped forward, extending his hand. An arm emerged from beneath the desk, shook Kipp's, and quickly vanished.

Nothing further happened. Young tenaciously remained in his sanctuary. Kipp realized that, short of dragging the man out bodily, he could not hope to view an entire Kenneth Young for the present. With an admonitory cough he withdrew.

The miserable Young emerged, wincing as his cramped muscles relaxed. A pretty kettle of fish. How could he entertain Devlin while he wore a halo? And it was vitally necessary that Devlin be entertained, else the elusive vice presidency would be immediately withdrawn. Young knew only too well that employees of Atlas Advertising Agency trod a perilous pathway.

His reverie was interrupted by the sudden appearance of an angel atop the bookcase.

It was not a high bookcase, and the supernatural visitor sat there calmly enough, heels dangling and wings furled. A scanty robe of white samite made up the angel's wardrobe – that and a shining halo, at sight of which Young felt a wave of nausea sweep him.

'This,' he said with rigid restraint, 'is the end. A halo may be due to mass hypnotism. But when I start seeing angels –'

'Don't be afraid,' said the other. 'I'm real enough.'

Young's eyes were wild. 'How do I know? I'm obviously talking to empty air. It's schizo-something. Go away.'

The angel wriggled his toes and looked embarrassed. 'I can't, just yet. The fact is, I made a bad mistake. You may have noticed that you've a slight halo –'

Young gave a short, bitter laugh. 'Oh, yes. I've *noticed* it.'

Before the angel could reply the door opened. Kipp looked in, saw that Young was engaged, and murmured, 'Excuse me,' as he withdrew.

The angel scratched his golden curls. 'Well, your halo was intended for somebody else – a Tibetan lama, in fact. But through a certain chain of circumstances I was led to believe that you were the candidate for sainthood. So –' The visitor made a comprehensive gesture.

Young was baffled. 'I don't quite –'

'The lama … well, sinned. No sinner may wear a halo. And, as I say, I gave it to you through error.'

'Then you can take it away again?' Amazed delight suffused Young's face. But the angel raised a benevolent hand.

'Fear not. I have checked with the recording angel. You have led a blameless life. As a reward, you will be permitted to keep the halo of sainthood.'

The horrified man sprang to his feet, making feeble swimming motions with his arms. 'But … but … but –'

'Peace and blessings be upon you,' said the angel, and vanished.

Young fell back into his chair and massaged his aching brow. Simultaneously the door opened and Kipp stood on the threshold. Luckily Young's hands temporarily hid the halo.

'Mr Devlin is here,' the president said. 'Er … who was that on the bookcase?'

Young was too crushed to lie plausibly. He muttered, 'An angel.'

Kipp nodded in satisfaction. 'Yes, of course … *What?* You say an angel … an angel? Oh, my gosh!' The man turned quite white and hastily took his departure.

Young contemplated his hat. The thing still lay on the desk, wincing slightly under the baleful stare directed at it. To go through life wearing a halo was only less endurable than the thought of continually wearing the loathsome hat. Young brought his fist down viciously on the desk.

'I won't stand it! I … I don't have to –' He stopped abruptly. A dazed look grew in his eyes.

'I'll be … that's right! I don't *have* to stand it. If that lama got out of it … of course. 'No sinner may wear a halo.' ' Young's round face twisted into a mask of sheer evil. 'I'll be a sinner, then! I'll break all the Commandments –'

He pondered. At the moment he couldn't remember what they were. 'Thou shalt not covet thy neighbor's wife.' That was one.

Young thought of his neighbor's wife – a certain Mrs Clay, a behemothic damsel of some fifty summers, with a face like a desiccated pudding. That was one Commandment he had no intention of breaking.

But probably one good, healthy sin would bring back the angel in a hurry to remove the halo. What crimes would result in the least inconvenience? Young furrowed his brow.

Nothing occurred to him. He decided to go for a walk. No doubt some sinful opportunity would present itself.

He forced himself to don the shako and had reached the elevator when a hoarse voice was heard hallooing after him. Racing along the hall was a fat man.

Young knew instinctively that this was Mr Devlin.

The adjective 'fat,' as applied to Devlin, was a considerable understatement. The man bulged. His feet, strangled in biliously yellow shoes, burst out at the ankles like blossoming flowers. They merged into calves that seemed to gather momentum as they spread and mounted, flung themselves up with mad abandon, and revealed themselves in their complete, unrestrained glory at Devlin's middle. The man resembled, in silhouette, a pineapple with elephantiasis. A great mass of flesh poured out of his collar, forming a pale, sagging lump in which Young discerned some vague resemblance to a face.

Such was Devlin, and he charged along the hall, as mammoths thunder by, with earth-shaking tramplings of his crashing hoofs.

'You're Young!' he wheezed. 'Almost missed me, eh? I was waiting in the office –' Devlin paused, his fascinated gaze upon the hat. Then, with an effort at politeness, he laughed falsely and glanced away. 'Well, I'm all ready and raring to go.'

Young felt himself impaled painfully on the horns of a dilemma. Failure to entertain Devlin would mean the loss of that vice presidency. But the halo weighed like a flatiron on Young's throbbing head. One thought was foremost in his mind: he *had* to get rid of the blessed thing.

Once he had done that, he would trust to luck and diplomacy. Obviously, to take out his guest now would be fatal insanity. The hat alone would be fatal.

'Sorry,' Young grunted. 'Got an important engagement. I'll be back for you as soon as I can.'

Wheezing laughter, Devlin attached himself firmly to the other's arm. 'No, you don't. You're showing me the town! Right now!' An unmistakable alcoholic odor was wafted to Young's nostrils. He thought quickly.

'All right,' he said at last. 'Come along. There's a bar downstairs. We'll have a drink, eh?'

'Now you're talking,' said the jovial Devlin, almost incapacitating Young with a comradely slap on the back. 'Here's the elevator.'

They crowded into the cage. Young shut his eyes and suffered as interested stares were directed upon the hat. He fell into a state of coma, arousing only at the ground floor, where Devlin dragged him out and into the adjacent bar.

Now Young's plan was this: he would pour drink after drink down his companion's capacious gullet, and await his chance to slip away unobserved. It was a shrewd scheme, but it had one flaw – Devlin refused to drink alone.

'One for you and one for me,' he said. 'That's fair. Have another.'

Young could not refuse, under the circumstances. The worst of it was that Devlin's liquor seemed to seep into every cell of his huge body, leaving him, finally, in the same state of glowing happiness which had been his originally. But poor Young was, to put it as charitably as possible, tight.

He sat quietly in a booth, glaring across at Devlin. Each time the waiter arrived, Young knew that the man's eyes were riveted upon the hat. And each round made the thought of that more irritating.

Also, Young worried about his halo. He brooded over sins. Arson, burglary, sabotage, and murder passed in quick review through his befuddled mind. Once he attempted to snatch the waiter's change, but the man was too alert. He laughed pleasantly and placed a fresh glass before Young.

The latter eyed it with distaste. Suddenly coming to a decision, he arose and wavered toward the door. Devlin overtook him on the sidewalk.

'What's the matter? Let's have another –'

'I have work to do,' said Young with painful distinctness. He snatched a walking cane from a passing pedestrian and made threatening gestures with it until the remonstrating victim fled hurriedly. Hefting the stick in his hand, he brooded blackly.

'But why work?' Devlin inquired largely. 'Show me the town.'

'I have important matters to attend to.' Young scrutinized a small child who had halted by the curb and was returning the stare with interest. The tot looked remarkably like the brat who had been so insulting on the bus.

'What's important?' Devlin demanded. 'Important matters, eh? Such as what?'

'Beating small children,' said Young, and rushed upon the startled child, brandishing his cane. The youngster uttered a shrill scream and fled. Young pursued for a few feet and then became entangled with a lamp-post. The lamp-post was impolite and dictatorial. It refused to allow Young to pass. The man remonstrated and, finally, argued, but to no avail.

The child had long since disappeared. Administering a brusque and snappy rebuke to the lamp-post, Young turned away.

'What in Pete's name are you trying to do?' Devlin inquired. 'That cop's looking at us. Come along.' He took the other's arm and led him along the crowded sidewalk.

'What am I trying to do?' Young sneered. 'It's obvious, isn't it? I wish to sin.'

'Er … sin?'

'Sin.'

'Why?'

Young tapped his hat meaningly, but Devlin put an altogether wrong interpretation on the gesture. 'You're nuts?'

'Oh, shut up,' Young snapped in a sudden burst of rage, and thrust his cane between the legs of a passing bank president whom he knew slightly. The unfortunate man fell heavily to the cement, but arose without injury save to his dignity.

'I beg your pardon!' he barked.

Young was going through a strange series of gestures. He had fled to a show-window mirror and was doing fantastic things to his hat, apparently trying to lift it in order to catch a glimpse of the top of his head – a sight, it seemed, to be shielded jealously from profane eyes. At length he cursed loudly, turned, gave the bank president a contemptuous stare, and hurried away, trailing the puzzled Devlin like a captive balloon.

Young was muttering thickly to himself.

'Got to sin – really sin. Something big. Burn down an orphan asylum. Kill m' mother-in-law. Kill … anybody!' He looked quickly at Devlin, and the latter shrank back in sudden fear. But finally Young gave a disgusted grunt.

'Nrgh. Too much blubber. Couldn't use a gun or a knife. Have to blast – Look!' Young said, clutching Devlin's arm. 'Stealing's a sin, isn't it?'

'Sure is,' the diplomatic Devlin agreed. 'But you're not –'

Young shook his head. 'No. Too crowded here. No use going to jail. Come on!'

He plunged forward. Devlin followed. And Young fulfilled his promise to show his guest the town, though afterward neither of them could remember exactly what had happened. Presently Devlin paused in a liquor store for refueling, and emerged with bottles protruding here and there from his clothing.

Hours merged into an alcoholic haze. Life began to assume an air of foggy unreality to the unfortunate Devlin. He sank presently into a coma, dimly conscious of various events which marched with celerity through the afternoon and long into the night. Finally he roused himself sufficiently to realize that he was standing with Young confronting a wooden Indian which stood quietly outside a cigar store. It was, perhaps, the last of the wooden Indians. The outworn relic of a bygone day, it seemed to stare with faded glass eyes at the bundle of wooden cigars it held in an extended hand.

Young was no longer wearing a hat. And Devlin suddenly noticed something decidedly peculiar about his companion.

He said softly, 'You've got a halo.'

Young started slightly. 'Yes,' he replied, 'I've got a halo. This Indian –' He paused.

Devlin eyed the image with disfavor. To his somewhat fuzzy brain the wooden Indian appeared even more horrid than the surprising halo. He shuddered and hastily averted his gaze.

'Stealing's a sin,' Young said under his breath, and then, with an elated cry, stooped to lift the Indian. He fell immediately under its weight, emitting a string of smoking oaths as he attempted to dislodge the incubus.

'Heavy,' he said, rising at last. 'Give me a hand.'

Devlin had long since given up any hope of finding sanity in this madman's actions. Young was obviously determined to sin, and the fact that he possessed a halo was somewhat disquieting, even to the drunken Devlin. As a result, the two men proceeded down the street, bearing with them the rigid body of a wooden Indian.

The proprietor of the cigar shop came out and looked after them, rubbing his hands. His eyes followed the departing statue with unmitigated joy.

'For ten years I've tried to get rid of that thing,' he whispered gleefully. 'And now … aha!'

He re-entered the store and lit a Corona to celebrate his emancipation.

Meanwhile, Young and Devlin found a taxi stand. One cab stood there; the driver sat puffing a cigarette and listening to his radio. Young hailed the man.

'Cab, sir?' The driver sprang to life, bounced out of the car, and flung open the door. Then he remained frozen in a half-crouching position, his eyes revolving wildly in their sockets.

He had never believed in ghosts. He was, in fact, somewhat of a cynic. But in the face of a bulbous ghoul and a decadent angel bearing the stiff corpse of an Indian, he felt with a sudden, blinding shock of realization that beyond life lies a black abyss teeming with horror unimaginable. Whining shrilly, the terrified man leaped back into his cab, got the thing into motion, and vanished as smoke before the gale.

Young and Devlin looked at one another ruefully.

'What now?' the latter asked.

'Well,' said Young, 'I don't live far from here. Only ten blocks or so. Come on!'

It was very late, and few pedestrians were abroad. These few, for the sake of their sanity, were quite willing to ignore the wanderers and go their separate ways. So eventually Young, Devlin, and the wooden Indian arrived at their destination.

The door of Young's home was locked, and he could not locate the key. He was curiously averse to arousing Jill. But, for some strange reason, he felt it vitally necessary that the wooden Indian be concealed. The cellar was the logical place. He dragged his two companions to a basement window, smashed it as quietly as possible, and slid the image through the gap.

'Do you really live here?' asked Devlin, who had his doubts.

'Hush!' Young said warningly. 'Come on!'

He followed the wooden Indian, landing with a crash in a heap of coal. Devlin joined him after much wheezing and grunting. It was not dark. The halo provided about as much illumination as a twenty-five-watt globe.

Young left Devlin to nurse his bruises and began searching for the wooden Indian. It had unaccountably vanished. But he found it at last cowering beneath a washtub, dragged the object out, and set it up in a corner. Then he stepped back and faced it, swaying a little.

'That's a sin, all right,' he chuckled. 'Theft. It isn't the amount that matters. It's the principle of the thing. A wooden Indian is just as important as a million dollars, eh, Devlin?'

'I'd like to chop that Indian into fragments,' said Devlin with passion. 'You made me carry it for three miles.' He paused, listening. 'What in heaven's name is that?'

A small tumult was approaching. Filthy, having been instructed often in his duties as a watchdog, now faced opportunity. Noises were proceeding from the cellar. Burglars, no doubt. The raffish Scotty cascaded down the stairs in a babel of frightful threats and oaths. Loudly declaring his intention of eviscerating the intruders, he flung himself upon Young, who made hasty clucking sounds intended to soothe the Scotty's aroused passions.

Filthy had other ideas. He spun like a dervish, yelling bloody murder. Young wavered, made a vain snatch at the air, and fell prostrate to the ground. He remained face down, while Filthy, seeing the halo, rushed at it and trampled upon his master's head.

The wretched Young felt the ghosts of a dozen and more drinks rising to confront him. He clutched at the dog, missed, and gripped instead the feet of the wooden Indian. The image swayed perilously. Filthy cocked up an apprehensive eye and fled down the length of his master's body, pausing halfway as he remembered his duty. With a muffled curse he sank his teeth into the nearest portion of Young and attempted to yank off the miserable man's pants.

Meanwhile, Young remained face down, clutching the feet of the wooden Indian in a despairing grip.

There was a resounding clap of thunder. White light blazed through the cellar. The angel appeared.

Devlin's legs gave way. He sat down in a plump heap, shut his eyes, and began chattering quietly to himself. Filthy swore at the intruder, made an unsuccessful attempt to attain a firm grasp on one of the gently fanning wings, and went back to think it over, arguing throatily. The wing had an unsatisfying lack of substantiality.

The angel stood over Young with golden fires glowing in his eyes, and a benign look of pleasure molding his noble features. 'This,' he said quietly, 'shall be taken as a symbol of your first successful good deed since your enhalo-ment.' A wingtip brushed the dark and grimy visage of the Indian. Forthwith, there was no Indian. 'You have lightened the heart of a fellow man – little, to be sure, but some, and at a cost of much labor on your part.

'For a day you have struggled with this sort to redeem him, but for this no success has rewarded you, albeit the morrow's pains will afflict you.

'Go forth, K Young, rewarded and protected from all sin alike by your halo.' The youngest angel faded quietly, for which alone Young was grateful. His head was beginning to ache and he'd feared a possible thunderous vanishment.

Filthy laughed nastily, and renewed his attack on the halo. Young found the unpleasant act of standing upright necessary. While it made the walls and tubs spin round like all the hosts of heaven, it made impossible Filthy's der-vish dance on his face.

Some time later he awoke, cold sober and regretful of the fact. He lay between cool sheets, watching morning sunlight lance through the windows, his eyes, and feeling it splinter in jagged bits in his brain. His stomach was making spasmodic attempts to leap up and squeeze itself out through his burning throat.

Simultaneous with awakening came realization of three things: the pains of the morrow had indeed afflicted him; the halo mirrored still in the glass above the dressing table – and the parting words of the angel.

He groaned a heartfelt triple groan. The headache would pass, but the halo, he knew, would not. Only by sinning could one become unworthy of it, and – shining protector! – it made him unlike other men. His deeds must all be good, his works a help to men. He could not sin!

THE VOICE OF THE LOBSTER

Tilting his cigar at a safe angle Terence Lao-T'se Macduff applied a wary eye to the peephole in the curtain and searched the audience for trouble.

'A setup,' he muttered under his breath. 'Or is it? I have the inexplicable sensation of wet mice creeping slowly up and down my spine. What a pity I wasn't able to get that Lesser Vegan girl to front for me. Ah, well. Here I go.'

He drew up his rotund form as the curtain slowly rose.

'Good evening to you all,' he said jovially. 'I am happy to see so many eager seekers after knowledge, from all parts of the Galaxy, gathered here tonight on this, Aldebaran's greenest world –'

Muffled noises rose from the audience, mingled with the musky odor of Aldebaranese and the scents of many other races and species. For it was Lottery Time on Aldebaran Tau and the famous celebration based on the counting of seeds in the first *sphyghi* fruit of the season had as usual drawn luck-worshippers from all over the Galaxy. There was even an Earthman, with shaggy red hair and a scowling face, who sat in the front row, glaring up at Macduff.

Uneasily evading that glare, Macduff went on with some haste.

'Ladies, gentlemen and Aldebaranese, I offer you my All-Purpose Radioisotopic Hormone Rejuvenating Elixir, the priceless discovery which will give you the golden treasury of youth at a sum easily within the reach of each and every –'

An ambiguous missile whizzed past Macduff's head. His trained ear screened out words in a dozen different interstellar tongues and realized that none of them implied approval.

The red-haired Earthman was bellowing, 'The mon's a crook! Nae doot aboot it!' Macduff, automatically dodging an overripe fruit, looked pensively at him.

'Oh-oh,' Macduff was thinking. 'I wonder how he found out those cards were marked for black light?'

He held up his arms dramatically for silence, took a backward step and kicked the trigger on the trap door. Instantly he dropped out of sight. From the audience rose a tremendous bellow of balked fury. Macduff, scuttling rapidly past discarded flats of scenery, heard feet thundering above him.

'There will be chlorophyll spilled tonight,' he mused, sprinting. 'That's the trouble with these Aldebaranese, they're still vegetables at heart. No sense of ethics, merely tropisms.'

His racing feet tripped over a half-empty box of progesterone, a hormone necessary when a sucker, or customer, was fowl or mammal strain.

'Can't be the hormones,' he pondered, kicking boxes out of his path. 'It must have been the radio-isotope. I shall write a scorching letter to that Chicago outfit. Fly-by-nights, of course. I should have suspected the quality of their product at that price. Three months, forsooth! Why, it hasn't been a fortnight since I sold the first bottle – and it's taken this long to finish the payoffs and start hoping for a net profit.'

This was serious. Tonight had been the first occasion on which he hoped to put the profits from All-Purpose Radio-isotopic Hormone Rejuvenating Elixir into his own pocket. Aldebaran officials had a greed which one didn't normally associate with vegetable ancestry. How was he going to get enough money to ensure his passage spaceward in a hurry if speed seemed indicated?

'Trouble, trouble,' Macduff murmured, as he fled down a corridor, ducked out of the exit and foresightedly sent a tower of empty boxes crashing down, blocking the door. Screams of rage came from behind him.

'Sounds like Babel,' he said, trotting. 'That's the trouble with galactic travel. Too many overemotional races.' Doubling and twisting along a planned course, he continued to mutter marginal comments, for Macduff generally moved in a haze of sotto voce remarks confidingly addressed to himself, usually approving in nature.

After a time, deciding that he had put a safe distance between himself and justice, he slowed his pace, paused at a dingy hock-shop and paid out a few coins from his paltry store. In return he was given a small battered suitcase, which contained everything necessary for a hurried departure – everything, that is, except the really vital factor. Macduff had no space ticket.

Had he anticipated the full extent of Aldebaranese rapacity and corruption he could perhaps have brought along more payoff funds. But he had wanted his arrival to coincide with the great *sphyghi* festival and time pressed. Still, there were ways. Captain Masterson of the *Sutter* owed him a favor and the *Sutter* was due to take off early next morning.

'Possibly,' Macduff ruminated, trudging on, 'something might be arranged. Let me see, now. Item One. There's Ao.' Ao was the Lesser Vegan girl whose remarkable semi-hypnotic powers would make her such an excellent front man, figuratively speaking.

'Borrowing ticket money won't solve Item One. If I succeed in getting Ao I'll have to deal with her guardian, Item Two.'

Item Two represented an Algolian native named Ess Pu.[1] Macduff had taken pains to keep himself informed of Ess Pu's whereabouts and so knew that the Algolian was no doubt still involved in the same game of dice he had begun two days ago at the UV Lantern Dream-Mill, not far from the center of town. His opponent was probably still the Mayor of Aldebaran City.

'Moreover,' Macduff reflected, 'both Ess Pu and Ao have tickets on the *Sutter*. Very good. The answer is obvious. All I have to do is get in that dice game, win Ao and both tickets and shake the dust of this inferior planet from my feet.'

Swinging the suitcase jauntily, he scuttled along by back alleys, conscious of a distant, mounting tumult, until he reached the door of the UV Lantern Dream-Mill, a low broad arch closed with leather curtains. On the threshold he paused to glance back, puzzled by the apparent riot that had broken out.

Submerged feelings of guilt, plus his natural self-esteem, made him wonder if he himself might be the cause of all that uproar. However, since he had only once roused the inhabitants of an entire planet against him[2] he concluded vaguely that perhaps there was a fire.

So he pushed the curtains aside and entered the UV Lantern, looking around sharply to make certain Angus Ramsay wasn't present. Ramsay, as the reader will guess, was the red-haired gentleman last heard defaming Macduff in the theater.

'And, after all, *he* was the one who insisted on buying a bottle of the Elixir,' Macduff mused. 'Well, he isn't here. Ess Pu, however, is. In all fairness, I've given him every chance to sell me Ao. Now let him take the consequences.'

Squaring his narrow shoulders (for it cannot be denied that Macduff was somewhat bottle-shaped in appearance) he moved through the crowd toward the back of the room, where Ess Pu crouched over a green-topped table with his companion, the Mayor of the city.

To a non-cosmopolitan observer it would have seemed that a lobster was playing PK dice with one of the local plant men. But Macduff was a cosmopolitan in the literal sense of the word. And from his first meeting with Ess Pu, some weeks ago, he had recognized a worthy and formidable opponent.

All Algolians are dangerous. They are noted for their feuds, furies and their inverted affective tone scale. 'It's extraordinary,' Macduff mused, looking pensively at Ess Pu. 'They feel fine only when they're hating someone. The sensations of pleasure and pain are reversed. Algolians find the emotions of rage, hate and cruelty pro-survival. A lamentable state of affairs.'

Ess Pu clanked a scaly elbow on the table and rattled the dice cup in the face

1 An approximation. The actual name is unspellable.

2 As a result of having sold them the Earth.

of his cringing opponent. As everyone is familiar with Aldebaranese plant men, in view of their popular video films, the Mayor need not be described.

Macduff sank into a nearby chair and opened the suitcase on his lap, rummaging through its varied contents which included a deck of tarots, some engraved plutonium stock (worthless) and a number of sample bottles of hormones and isotopes.

There was also a small capsule of Lethean dust, that unpleasant drug which affects the psychokinetic feedback mechanism. As an injury to the cerebellum causes purpose tremor, so Lethean dust causes PK tremor. Macduff felt that a reasonable amount of psychic oscillation in Ess Pu might prove profitable to Macduff. With this in mind, he watched the game intently.

The Algolian waved his stalked eyes over the table. Crinkled membranes around his mouth turned pale blue. The dice spun madly. They fell – seven. Ess Pu's membranes turned green. One of the dice quivered, strained, rolled over. The Algolian's claws clicked shut with satisfaction, the Mayor wrung his hands and Macduff, emitting cries of admiration, leaned forward to pat Ess Pu's sloping shoulder while he deftly emptied the unlidded capsule into the Algolian's drink.

'My lad,' Macduff said raptly, 'I have travelled the Galaxy from end to end and never before –'

'Tchah!' Ess Pu said sourly, pulling his winnings across the board. He added that he wouldn't sell Ao to Macduff now even if he could. 'So get out!' he finished, snapping a claw contemptuously in Macduff's face.

'Why can't you sell Ao?' Macduff demanded. 'Though sell, of course, is a misleading verb. What I mean –'

He understood the Algolian to say that Ao now belonged to the Mayor.

Macduff turned surprised eyes on this personage, who furtively evaded the look.

'I didn't recognize your Honor,' he said. 'So many non-humanoid species are hard to tell apart. But did I understand you to say you *sold* her to the Mayor, Ess Pu? As I remember, Lesser Vegan Control merely leases its subjects to suitable guardians –'

'It was a transfer of guardianship,' the Mayor said hastily, lying in his teeth.

'Get out,' Ess Pu snarled. 'You've got no use for Ao. She's an *objet d'art*.'

'Your French is excellent, for a lobster,' Macduff said with delicate tact. 'And as for having a use for the lovely creature, my scientific researches will shortly include the prognostication of mood responses in large groups. As we all know, Lesser Vegans have the curious ability to make people punch drunk. With a girl like Ao on the platform I could feel perfectly sure of my audience –'

A video screen burst in with a wild squawk. Everyone looked up sharply. Supplementary screens in infrared and UV, for the use of customers with specialized vision, hummed with invisibly duplicated pictures of an announcer's popeyed face.

'– Citizens' Purity Organization has just called a mass meeting –'

The Mayor, looking frightened, started to get up and then thought better of it. There seemed to be something on his conscience.

Ess Pu told Macduff profanely to go away. He enlarged insultingly on the suggestion.

'Pah,' Macduff said bravely, knowing himself more agile than the Algolian. 'Drop dead.'

Ess Pu's mouth membranes turned scarlet. Before he could speak, Macduff offered quickly to buy Ao's ticket, a proposition he had neither intention nor ability to fulfil.

'I haven't got her ticket!' Ess Pu roared. 'She still has it! Now get out before I –' He strangled on his own fury, coughed and took a stiff drink. Ignoring Macduff, he threw a six and shoved a stack of chips to the center of the table. The Mayor, with nervous reluctance, glanced at the video screen and faded the bet. At that point the videos broke in with a squeal.

'– mobs marching on Administration! Aroused populace demands ousting of present officials, charging long-term corruption! This political pot was brought to a boil tonight by the exposure of an alleged swindler named Macduff –'

The Mayor of Aldebaran City jumped up and tried to run. One of Ess Pu's claws caught him by the coat tail. The video squawked on, giving an all-too-accurate description of the Radio-isotopic Elixir swindler and only the thick haze in the air kept Macduff from immediate exposure.

He hesitated uncertainly, reason telling him that something of interest was developing at the dice table while instinct urged him to run.

'I've got to get home!' the Mayor wailed. 'Vital matters –'

'You're staking Ao?' the crustacean demanded, with a significant brandish of his claws. 'You are, eh? Right? Then *say so!*'

'Yes,' the harassed Mayor cried. 'Oh, yes, yes, yes. Anything!'

'Six is my point,' said Ess Pu, rattling the dice cup. His membranes became oddly mottled. He wriggled his eye stalks unnervingly. Macduff, remembering the Lethean dust, began to edge towards the door.

There was a bellow of surprised rage from the Algolian as the disobedient cubes turned up seven. Ess Pu clawed at his throat, snatched up his glass and peered suspiciously into it. The jig was up.

Roars of fury reverberated from wall to wall of the Dream-Mill as Macduff slipped out through the curtains and pattered rapidly off down the street in the cool musky dark of the Aldebaran night.

'Nevertheless, I still need a ticket,' he reflected. 'I also need Ao if possible. This leads me, by obvious degrees, to the Mayor's palace. Provided I'm not torn limb from limb in the meantime,' he added, dodging into another alley to avoid the spreading torchlit mobs that were by now seething hither and thither through the aroused city.

'How ridiculous. At times like these I'm grateful for being born into a civilized race. There's no sun like Sol,' he summed up, creeping hastily under a fence as a mob poured down the alley toward him.

Emerging on the other side and trotting down a lane, he reached the back door of a luxurious palace done in pink porphyry with ebony edgings and banged the knocker firmly against its plate. There was a soft, sliding noise and Macduff fixed a peremptory gaze upon the one-way Judas mirror in the door.

'Message from the Mayor,' he announced in a brisk voice. 'He's in trouble. He sent me to bring that Lesser Vegan girl to him immediately. It's a matter of life or death. Hurry!'

A gasp sounded from inside the door. Feet pattered away into inner distances. A moment later the door opened, revealing the Mayor himself.

'Here!' cried that frantic official. 'She's yours. Just take her away. I never saw her before in my life. Never saw Ess Pu. Never saw you. Never saw *anybody*. Oh, these reform riots! One scrap of incriminating evidence and I'm lost, lost!'

Macduff, a little astonished at finding himself fortune's favorite, rose to the occasion capably.

'Depend on me,' he told the unhappy vegetable as a slim and lovely being was pushed out of the door into his arms. 'She'll leave Aldebaran Tau on the *Sutter* tomorrow at dawn. In fact, I'll take her aboard immediately.'

'Yes, yes, yes,' the Mayor said, trying to close the door. Macduff's foot kept it ajar.

'She's got her space ticket?'

'Ticket? What ticket? Oh, that. Yes. In her wrist band. Oh, here they come! Look out!'

The terrified Mayor slammed the door. Macduff seized Ao's hand and sped with her into the shrubbery of a plaza. A moment later the tortuous mazes of Aldebaran City swallowed them up.

At the first convenient doorway Macduff paused and looked at Ao. She was worth looking at. She stood in the doorway, thinking of nothing at all. She didn't have to think of anything. She was too beautiful.

Nobody has ever yet succeeded in describing the beings of Lesser Vega and probably nobody ever will. Electronic calculators have broken down and had their mercury memory-units curdled trying to analyze that elusive quality which turns men into mush. Like all her race, however, Ao wasn't very bright. Macduff regarded her with entirely platonic greed.

For she was the perfect come-on. Probably some subtle emanation radiates from the brains of the Lesser Vegans which acts as a hypnotic. With Ao on the stage Macduff knew he could almost certainly have quelled his unruly audience an hour ago and averted the riot. Even the savage breast of Angus Ramsay might have been soothed by Ao's magical presence.

Curiously enough, male relationship with Ao was entirely platonic, with the natural exception of the males of Lesser Vega. Outside of this dim-brained species, however, it was enough for a beholder simply to look at Ao. And vision really had little to do with it, since standards of beauty are only species deep. Almost all living organisms respond similarly to the soft enchantment of the Lesser Vegans.

'There's dark work afoot, my dear,' Macduff said, resuming their progress. 'Why was the Mayor so eager to get rid of you? But there's no use asking you, of course. We'd better get aboard the *Sutter.* I feel certain I can get Captain Masterson to advance me the price of another ticket. If I'd thought of it I might have arranged a small loan with the Mayor – or even a large one,' he added, recalling the Mayor's obvious guilt reactions. 'I seem to have missed a bet there.'

Ao appeared to float delicately over a mud puddle. She was considering higher and lovelier things.

They were nearly at the spaceport by now and the sights and sounds Macduff heard from the far distance gave him an idea that the mob had set fire to the Mayor's porphyry palace. 'However, he's merely a vegetable,' Macduff told himself. 'Still, my tender heart cannot help but – good heavens!'

He paused, aghast. The misty field of the spaceport lay ahead, the *Sutter* a fat ovoid blazing with light. There was a distant mutter of low thunder as the ship warmed up. A seething crowd of passengers was massed around the gangplank.

'Bless my soul, they're taking off,' Macduff said. 'Outrageous! Without even notifying the passengers – or perhaps there was a video warning sent out. Yes, I suppose so. But this may be awkward. Captain Masterson will be in the control room with a DO NOT DISTURB sign on the door. Take-offs are complicated affairs. How on Aldebaran Tau can we get aboard with only one ticket between us?'

The motors muttered sullenly. Haze blew like fat ghosts across the light-and-dark patterns of the tarmac. Macduff sprinted, dragging Ao, as thistledown, after him.

'I have a thought,' he murmured. 'Getting inside the ship is the first step. After that, of course, there'll be the regular passenger check but Captain Masterson will – hm-m.'

He studied the purser who stood at the head of the gangplank, taking tickets, checking names off the list he held, his keen eyes watchful. Though the passengers seemed nervous they kept fair order, apparently reassured by the confident voice of a ship's officer, who stood behind the purser.

Into this scene burst Macduff at a wild run, dragging Ao and screaming at the top of his voice. 'They're coming!' he shrieked, dashing through the crowd and overturning a bulky Saturnian. 'It's another Boxer rebellion! One would think the Xerians had landed. They're all running around screaming, "Aldebaran Tau for the Aldebarans".'

Towing Ao and flailing frantically with his suitcase, Macduff burst into the center of a group and disintegrated it. Instantly he dashed through the line at the gangplank and back again, squealing bloody murder.

At the ship's port the officer was trying to make himself heard with little success. He was apparently stolidly sticking to his original lines, which had something to do with the fact that the Captain had been injured but there was no reason to be alarmed –

'Too late!' shrieked Macduff, bundling himself into the center of a growing nucleus of loud panic. 'Hear what they're yelling? "Kill the foreign devils!" – listen to the bloodthirsty savages. Too late, too late,' he added at the top of his voice, scrambling through the mob with Ao. 'Lock the doors! Man the gunports! *Here they come!*'

By now all thought of order had been lost. The passengers were demoralized into a veritable Light Brigade of assorted species and Macduff, clinging to Ao and his suitcase, rode the tide up the gangplank, over the prostrate bodies of the officer and the purser and into the ship, where he hastily assembled his various possessions and scrambled for cover. He fled down a passage, doubled and twisted, finally slowed to a rapid walk. He was alone, except for Ao, in the echoing corridor. From the far distance came annoyed curses.

'Useful thing, misdirection,' Macduff murmured. 'Only way to get aboard, however. What was that fool saying about the Captain's being injured? Nothing serious, I hope. I must hit him for a loan. Now where's your cabin, my dear? Ah, yes. Stateroom R and here it is. We'd better hide till we're in space. Hear that siren? That means take-off, which is useful since it delays the passenger check. Space nets, Ao!'

He yanked open the door to Stateroom R and urged Ao toward a spiderweb filament of mesh that dangled like a hammock.

'Get in there and stay till I come back,' he ordered. 'I've got to find another shock hammock.'

The gossamer net attracted Ao as surf attracts a mermaid. She was instantly ensconced in it, her angelic face looking dreamily out of the softly tinted cloud. She gazed beyond Macduff, thinking of nothing.

'Very good,' Macduff told himself, going out, shutting the door and crossing to Stateroom X, which luckily was unlocked and vacant, with a web dangling ready. 'Now –'

'You!' said an all-too-familiar voice.

Macduff turned quickly on the threshold. Across the passage, looking at him from the door adjoining Ao's, was the ill-tempered crustacean.

'What a surprise,' Macduff said cordially. 'My old friend Ess Pu. Just the – ah, Algolian I wanted to –'

He was not permitted to finish. With a bellow in which the words 'Lethean dust' could be indistinctly understood, Ess Pu charged forward, eyes waving. Macduff hastily closed the door and locked it. There was a crash and then someone began to claw viciously at the panel.

'Outrageous assault on a man's privacy,' Macduff muttered.

The hammering on the door grew louder. It was drowned out by the ultrasonic, sonic and resonating warning of an immediate take-off.

The hammering stopped. The sound of clicking claws receded into the distance. Macduff dived for the shock net. Burrowing into its soft meshes he focused his mind on the hope that the awkward Algolian would be unable to make his hammock in time and that the acceleration would break every bone around his body.

Then the jets blazed, the *Sutter* rose from the troubled soil of Aldebaran Tau and Macduff really began to get into trouble.

It is perhaps time to deal, in some detail, with a matter which had already involved Macduff, though he didn't know it. Cryptic reference has been made to such apparently unrelated matters as *sphyghi*seeds and Xerians.

In the most expensive perfumeries of all, on the most luxurious worlds of all, there can be seen in tiny vials drams of a straw-colored fluid which carries the famous label of Sphyghi No. 60. This perfume of perfumes, which bears the same price whether sold in a plain glass phial or in a jewel-studded platinum flagon, is so costly that by comparison Cassandra, Patou's Joy or Martian Melée seem cheap.

Sphyghi is indigenous to Aldebaran Tau. Its seeds have been safeguarded so strictly that not even Aldebaran's great trade rival, Xeria, has ever managed, by hook, crook or even honest means, to get hold of a single seed.

For a long time it had commonly been known that Xerians would have bartered their souls, or soul, for some of the seed. In view of the Xerians' resemblance to termites there has always been some doubt as to whether an individual Xerian has a mind of his own and operates by free will or whether they are all ruled by a central common brain and determinism.

The trouble with *sphyghi* is that the growth cycle must be almost continuous. After the fruit is detached from the parent plant, its seeds become sterile in thirty hours.

Not a bad take-off, Macduff mused, crawling out of the shock hammock. It would be too much to hope that Ess Pu suffered at least a simple fracture of the carapace, he supposed.

He opened the door, waited until the opposite door leaped open to reveal the Algolian's watchful bulk and snapped back into Stateroom X with the agility of a frightened gazelle.

'Trapped like a rat,' he muttered, beginning with a quick tour of the cabin. 'Where is that intercom? Outrageous! Ah, here it is. Connect me with the Captain at once, please. Macduff is the name, Terence Lao-T'se Macduff. Captain Masterson? Let me congratulate you on your take-off. A magnificent job. I gathered you have had an accident, which I trust is not serious.'

The intercom croaked hoarsely, caught its breath and said, 'Macduff.'

'A throat injury?' Macduff hazarded. 'But to come to the point, Captain. You are harboring a homicidal maniac on the *Sutter.* That Algolian lobster has gone perfectly insane and is lurking outside my door – Stateroom X – ready to kill me if I come out. Kindly send down some armed guards.'

The intercom made ambiguous sounds which Macduff took for assent.

'Thank you, Captain,' he said cheerily. 'There is only one other small matter. It became necessary for me to board the *Sutter* at the last moment and I found it inexpedient to obtain a ticket. Time pressed. Moreover, I have taken a Lesser Vegan girl under my protection, in order to save her from the dastardly machinations of Ess Pu and it would perhaps be wise to keep any knowledge of her presence in Stateroom R from that lobster.'

He took a deep breath and leaned familiarly against the intercom. 'Frightful things have been happening, Captain Masterson – I have been subjected to persecution by a bloodthirsty mob, an attempt to swindle me at dice on Ess Pu's part, threats of violence from Angus Ramsay –'

'Ramsay?'

'You may have heard of him under that name, though it's probably an alias. The man was discharged in disgrace from the Space Service for smuggling opium, I believe –'

A knock came at the door. Macduff broke off to listen.

'Quick work, Captain,' he said. 'I assume these are your guards?'

There was an affirmative grunt and a click. '*Au revoir,*' Macduff said cheerfully, and opened the door. Two uniformed members of the crew were standing outside, waiting. Across the corridor Ess Pu's door was ajar and the Algolian stood there, breathing hard.

'You're armed?' Macduff asked. 'Prepare yourselves for a possible treacherous attack from that murderous crustacean behind you.'

'Stateroom X,' one of the men said. 'Name, Macduff? Captain wants to see you.'

'Naturally,' Macduff said, pulling out a cigar and stepping dauntlessly into the corridor, making certain, however, that one of the crewmen was between him and Ess Pu. Nonchalantly clipping the cigar, he paused abruptly, his nostrils quivering.

'Let's go,' one of the men said.

Macduff did not stir. From beyond the Algolian a breath of dim fragrance drifted like a murmur from paradise.

Macduff rapidly finished lighting his cigar. He puffed out great clouds of smoke as he hurriedly led the way down the corridor. 'Come, come, my men,' he admonished. 'To the Captain. Important matters are afoot.'

'We wouldn't know,' a crewman said, slipping in front while the other one fell in behind. Macduff allowed himself to be escorted into the officers' quarters, where he caught sight of himself in a reflecting bulkhead and blew out an approving smoke-cloud.

'Imposing,' he murmured. 'No giant, of course, but unquestionably imposing in my fashion. The slight rotundity around my middle merely indicates that I live well. Ah, Captain Masterson! Very good, my men, you may leave us now. That's right. Close the door as you go. Now, Captain –'

The man behind the desk lifted his gaze slowly. As all but the stupidest reader will have guessed, he was Angus Ramsay.

'Smuggling opium – aye!' said Angus Ramsay, exhibiting his teeth to the terrified Macduff. 'Discharrrged in disgrace – och! Ye nosty libelling scum, what am I going to do with ye?'

'Mutiny!' Macduff said wildly. 'What have you done? Led the crew to mutiny and taken over the *Sutter?* I warn you, this crime will not go unpunished. Where's Captain Masterson?'

'Captain Masterson,' said Ramsay, repressing his ire with a violent effort and losing the worst of his accent, 'is in a hospital on Aldebaran Tau. Apparently the puir man got in the way of one of those raving mobs. The result is that *I* am captain of the *Sutter.* Offer me no cigars, ye dom scoundrel. I am interested in only one thing. Ye have nae ticket.'

'You must have misunderstood me,' Macduff said. 'Naturally I had a ticket. I gave it to the purser when I came aboard. Those intercoms are notoriously unreliable.'

'So is that dom Immortality Elixir of yours,' Captain Ramsay pointed out. 'So are some poker games, especially when the carrrds are marked for black-light reading.' The large hands closed significantly.

'Lay a finger on me at your peril,' Macduff said, with faint bluster. 'I have the rights of a citizen –'

'Oh, aye,' Ramsay agreed. 'But not the rights of a passenger on this ship. Therefore, ye wee blaggard, ye'll worrk your way to the next port, Xeria, and there ye'll be thrown off the *Sutter* bag and baggage.'

'I'll buy a ticket,' Macduff offered. 'At the moment, I happen to be slightly embarrassed –'

'If I catch ye mingling with the passengers or engaging in any games of chance with anyone at all ye will find yourself in the brig,' Captain Ramsay said firmly. 'Black light, aye! Smuggling opium, is it? Aha!'

Macduff spoke wildly of a jury of his peers, at which Ramsay laughed mockingly.

'If I'd caught up with ye back on Aldebaran Tau,' he said, 'I'd have taken great pleasure in kicking yer podgy carcass halfway arrround the planet. Now I wull get a deal more satisfaction out of knowing ye are harrd at work in the Hot Gang. Aboard this ship ye will be honest if it kills ye. And if ye have in mind that Lesser Vegan girl I have checked up thoroughly and ye cannot possibly figure out a way to swipe her ticket.'

'You can't part a guardian and ward like this! It's inhumanoid!' cried Macduff.

'Oot with ye, mon,' Ramsay said irately, rising. 'To work, for probably the first time in yer misspent life.'

'Wait,' said Macduff. 'You'll regret it if you don't listen to me. There's a crime being committed on this ship.'

'Aye,' Ramsay said, 'and ye're committing it, ye stowaway. Oot!' He spoke into an intercom, the door opened and the two crew members stood waiting expectantly.

'No, no!' Macduff shrilled, seeing the yawning chasm of hard work widening inexorably at his very toes. 'It's Ess Pu! The Algolian! He –'

'If ye swindled him as ye swindled me,' Captain Ramsay began.

'He's a smuggler!' Macduff shrieked, struggling in the grip of the crewmen who were bearing him steadily toward the door. 'He's smuggled *sphyghi* from Aldebaran Tau! I smelled the stuff, I tell you! You're carrying contraband, Captain Ramsay!'

'Wait,' Ramsay ordered. 'Put him down. Is this a trick?'

'I smelled it,' Macduff insisted. 'You know what growing *sphyghi* smells like. It's unmistakable. He must have the plants in his cabin.'

'The plants?' Ramsay pondered. 'Noo I wonder. Hm-m. All right, men. Invite Ess Pu to my cabin.' He dropped back in his chair, studying Macduff.

Macduff rubbed his hands briskly together.

'Say no more, Captain Ramsay. You need not apologize for mistaken zeal. Having exposed this villainous Algolian, I shall break him down step by step till he confesses all. He will naturally be brigged, which will leave his cabin vacant. I leave it to your sense of fair play –'

'Tush,' said Captain Ramsay. 'Close yer trap.' He scowled steadily at the door. After a while it opened to admit Ess Pu.

The Algolian lumbered ungracefully forward until he suddenly caught sight of Macduff. Instantly his mouth membranes began to flush. A clicking claw rose ominously.

'Now, now, mon!' Ramsay warned.

'Certainly,' seconded Macduff. 'Remember where you are, sir. All is discovered, Ess Pu. Facile lies will get you nowhere. Step by step Captain Ramsay and I have uncovered your plot. You are in the pay of the Xerians. A hired spy, you stole *sphyghi* seeds from Aldebaran Tau and that *sphyghi* is even now in your cabin, a silent accuser.'

Ramsay looked thoughtfully at the Algolian.

'Weel?' he asked.

'Wait,' said Macduff. 'When Ess Pu realizes that all is known he will see the uselessness of silence. Let me go on.' Since it was obviously impossible to stop Macduff, Captain Ramsay merely grunted and picked up the Handbook of Regulations on his desk. He began to study the thick volume doubtfully. Ess Pu twitched his claws.

'A feeble scheme from the beginning,' Macduff said. 'Even to me, a visitor on Aldebaran Tau, it became immediately evident that corruption was at work. Need we seek far for the answer? I think not. For we are even now heading straight for Xeria, a world which has tried frantically for years, by fair means and foul, to break the *sphyghi* monopoly. Very well.'

He aimed a cigar accusingly at the Algolian.

'With Xerian money, Ess Pu,' Macduff charged, 'you came to Aldebaran Tau and bribed the highest officials, got hold of some *sphyghi* seeds and circumvented the usual customs search for contraband. You bought the Mayor's sealed okay by bribing him with Ao. You need not reply yet,' Macduff added hastily since he had no intention of cutting short his hour of triumph.

Ess Pu made a revolting noise in his throat. 'Lethean dust,' he said, reminded of something. *'Ah-h!'* He made a sudden forward motion.

Macduff dodged hastily around the desk behind Ramsay. 'Call your men,' he suggested. 'He's running amuck. Disarm him.'

'Ye cannot disarm an Algolian without dismembering him,' Captain Ramsay said rather absently, looking up from the Handbook of Regulations. 'Ah – Ess Pu. Ye dinna deny this charrge, I gather?'

'How can he deny it?' Macduff demanded. 'The short-sighted scoundrel planted the *sphyghi* seeds in his cabin without even setting up an odor-denaturalizer. He deserves no mercy, the fool.'

'Weel?' Ramsay asked, in an oddly doubtful manner.

Ess Pu shook his narrow shoulders, crashed his tail emphatically against the floor and spread his jaws in what might have been a grin.

'Sphyghi?' he asked. 'Sure. So?'

'Convicted out of his own mouth,' Macduff decided. 'Nothing else is necessary. Brig him, Captain. We will share the reward, if any.'

'No,' Captain Ramsay said, putting down the Handbook decisively. 'Ye have put yer foot in it again, Macduff. Ye are no expert in interstellar law. We are now beyond the limits of ionization and therefore beyond the jurisdiction of Aldebaran Tau – with a guid deal of gibble-gabble the lawyers put in. But the meaning is clear enough. It was the job of the Aldebaranese to keep that *sphyghi* from being smuggled awa' from them and since they failed, noo it is not my job to meddle. In fact, I canna. Against Regulations.'

'That's it,' Ess Pu said with complacent satisfaction.

Macduff gasped. 'You condone smuggling, Captain Ramsay?'

'I'm covered,' the Algolian said, making a coarse gesture toward Macduff.

'Aye,' Ramsay said, 'he's richt. Regulations make it perfectly clear. As far as I am concerned it makes no difference whether Ess Pu is keeping *sphyghi* or daffodils in his cabin – or a haggis,' he added thoughtfully.

Ess Pu snorted and turned toward the door.

Macduff put a plaintive hand on the Captain's arm.

'But he threatened me. My life isn't safe around that Algolian. Just look at those claws.'

'Aye,' Ramsay said reluctantly. 'Ye ken the penalty for murder, Ess Pu? Vurra good. I order ye not to murrder this nae doot deserving miscreant. I am bound to enforce Regulations, so dinna let me catch ye assaulting Macduff within earshot of me or any other officer. Ye ken?'

Ess Pu seemed to ken. He laughed hoarsely, ground a claw at Macduff and stalked out, swaying from side to side. The two crewmen were visible outside the door.

'Here,' Captain Ramsay ordered. 'I have a job for ye two. Take this stowaway doon to the Hot Gang and turn him over to the Chief.'

'No, no!' squealed Macduff, retreating. 'Don't you dare lay a finger on me! Put me down! Outrageous! I *won't* go down that ramp! Release me! Captain Ramsay, I demand – *Captain Ramsay!*'

Days had passed, arbitrarily, of course, aboard the *Sutter*.

Ao lay curled in her shock hammock, thinking her own dim thoughts and looking at nothing. High up in the wall there was a puffing sound, a scuffle and a grunt. Behind the grille of the ventilating inlet appeared the face of Macduff.

'Ah, my little friend,' he said kindly. 'So there you are. Now they have me creeping down the ventilating tubes of this ship like a phagocyte.'

He tested the meshed grille cautiously.

'Sealed, like all the others,' he observed. 'However, I assume you're being well treated, my dear.' He glanced greedily at the covered lunch tray on a nearby table. Ao looked dreamily at nothing.

'I have sent a cable,' Macduff announced from the wall. 'I bartered some small treasured heirlooms I happened to have with me and raised enough cash to send a cable, by the press rate. Luckily I still have my press card.' Macduff's vast collection of credentials very likely may have included a membership in the Little Men's Chowder and Marching Society, to choose the least likely example.

'Moreover, I have just received a reply. Now I must run a grave risk, my dear, a grave risk. Today the conditions of the ship's pool – a lottery, you know – will be announced in the grand lounge. I must be present, even at the risk of being brigged by Captain Ramsay and savaged by Ess Pu. It will not be easy. I may say I've been subjected to every indignity imaginable, my dear, except perhaps – outrageous!' he added, as a cord tied around his ankle tightened and drew him backward up the shaft.

His distant cries grew fainter. He announced in a fading voice that he had a bottle of 2, 4, 5-trichlorophenoxyacetic acid in his pocket and that broken glass was a safety hazard. So saying he departed into inaudibility. Since Ao had not really noticed that he was present she remained unaffected.

'Ah, well,' Macduff philosophized as he flew down a corridor slightly ahead of the Atmospheric Inspector's hurtling toe-cap, 'Justice is blind. This is my thanks for working overtime – at least three minutes overtime. But now I am off duty and free to set my plans in motion.'

Five minutes later, having eluded the Inspector and smoothed his ruffled plumage somewhat, he made his way briskly toward the lounge.

'There's one point in my favor,' he reflected. 'Ess Pu apparently doesn't know Ao is aboard. The last time he chased me he was still speaking bitterly of my part in forcing him to leave her on Aldebaran Tau. Unhappily that's practically the only point in my favor. I must now mingle with the passengers in the grand lounge, while remaining undetected by Ess Pu, Captain Ramsay or any ship's officer. I wish I were a Cerean.[1] Ah, well.'

As Macduff cautiously made his way toward the lounge his memory dwelt all too vividly on his recent progress from riches to rags. His meteoric descent from job to worse job had been little short of phenomenal.

'Would you set a cinematome to digging ditches?' he had inquired. 'Would you weigh elephants on a torquemeter?'

He was told to stop gabbling and pick up that shovel. Instantly he began to work out the most efficient application of the law of leverages. There was some delay while he extended his decimals to include the influencing factor of low-threshold radioactivity upon the alpha waves of the brain.

'Otherwise, anything can happen,' he explained, demonstrating. There was a crash.

Macduff was then, by request, taken off the Hot Gang and put to work elsewhere. But, as he took pains to point out, his frame of reference did not include special skills in the block-processing of garbage for fuel, oiling of the symbiotic hemostatic adjustment mechanisms provided for the comfort of the passengers or testing refractive indices of liquid-coated bimetallic thermostats. He proved this empirically.

1 The inhabitants of Ceres were long supposed to be invisible. Lately it has been discovered that Ceres has no inhabitants.

So he was – by request – removed to Hydroponics, where the incident of the radioactive carbon tracer occurred. He said it wasn't the carbon, it was the gammexene, and besides it wasn't really the gammexene so much as his inadvertent neglect to supplement the insecticide with meso-inositol.

But when thirty square feet of rhubarb plants began breathing out carbon monoxide as a result of sudden heredity changes brought on by the gammexene Macduff was promptly sent down to the kitchens, where he introduced a growth hormone into the soup, with nearly catastrophic results.

At present he was an unvalued member of the staff of Atmospheric Controls, where he did the jobs nobody else wanted to do.

More and more he had become conscious of the odor of *sphyghi* pervading the ship. Nothing could disguise its distinctive fragrance, which seeped by osmosis through membranes, trickled along the surface of molecular films and very likely rode piggyback on careening quanta. As Macduff made his stealthy way toward the lounge he realized that the word *sphyghi* was on every tongue, just as he had anticipated.

He paused warily on the threshold of the lounge, which ran like a belt (or cravat) around the entire ship, so that in two directions the floor seemed to slope steeply, until you tried to walk up it. Then it felt like a squirrel cage, which compensated automatically to your own speed.

Here was luxury. Macduff's sybaritic soul yearned toward the tempting buffets of smörgåsbord, *ti-pali* and Gustators. Like a palace of ice an ornate perambulating bar swung slowly past on its monorail track. An orchestra was playing *Starlit Days and Sunny Nights,* an eminently suitable choice for a ship in space, and *sphyghi* fragrance sent its luxurious breath from wall to wall.

Macduff stood with unobtrusive dignity near the door for some minutes, regarding the crowd. He was waiting for the appearance of Captain Ramsay. Presently a buzz of interested comment began to arise and a throng of passengers converged down the salon's slopes. The Captain had arrived. Macduff melted into the crowd and vanished with the suddenness of a Boojum.

Ramsay stood at the bottom of a concave sectioned amphitheater, looking up at his audience with an unaccustomed smile on his seamed face. There was no trace of Macduff, though a repressed mutter of sotto voce comment came occasionally from behind a broad-beamed member of the Plutonian lepidoptera.

Captain Ramsay spoke.

'As ye probably ken,' he said, 'we are here to arrange aboot the ship's pool. Some of ye may not have travelled in space before, so the acting firrst mate wull explain how this is done. Mister French, please.'

Mr French, a serious young man, took the stage. He cleared his throat, hesitated and looked around as a brief burst of applause came from behind the Plutonian lepidoptera.

'Thank you,' he said. 'Eh – many of you may be familiar with the old-time ship's pool, in which passengers guessed the time of arrival in port. In space, of course, compensatory feed-back devices, effectors and subtractors control our ship so exactly that we know the *Sutter* will arrive in Xeria at exactly the posted time, which is –'

'Come, come, my man, get to the point,' an unidentified voice put in from the audience. Captain Ramsay was observed to glance sharply toward the Plutonian.

'Eh – quite,' said Mr French. 'Does anyone have a suggestion?'

'Guessing the date on a coin,' a voice said eagerly, but it was drowned out by a chorus of cries mentioning the word *sphyghi*.

'*Sphyghi?*' Captain Ramsay asked with hypocritical blankness. 'The perfume stuff, ye mean?'

There was laughter. A mousy Callistan got the floor.

'Captain Ramsay,' he said. 'How about running a *sphyghi*-seed lottery here, the way they do on Aldebaran Tau? The way it's done, I think, is by betting on how many seeds there are in the first *sphyghi* fruit of the crop. The number always varies. Sometimes there are a few hundred, sometimes a few thousand and there's no way of counting them until the fruit's cut open. If Ess Pu could be induced to agree, perhaps –'

'Allow me,' Captain Ramsay said. 'I'll consult Ess Pu.'

He did so, while the crustacean looked blackly around. At first he was obdurate. But finally, in return for a half-share in the pool, he was prevailed upon to cooperate. Only the glamor of *sphyghi* and the unparalleled chance to boast about this lottery for the rest of their lives led the passengers to put up with his inordinate greed. But presently all was arranged.

'Stewards wull pass among ye,' Captain Ramsay said. 'Write yer guess and yer name on these slips of paper and drop them in a box which wull be provided for the purpose. Aye, aye, Ess Pu. Ye wull be given a chance too if ye insist.'

The Algolian insisted. He wasn't missing a bet. After long hesitation he put down a number, angrily scrawled the phonetic ideograph of his name and had turned to stalk away when something subtler than *sphyghi* fragrance began to breathe through the salon. Heads turned. Voices died away. Ess Pu, glancing around in surprise, found himself facing the door. His infuriated bellow reverberated from the ceiling for several seconds.

Ao, standing on the threshold, paid no attention. Her lovely eyes gazed into the far distances. Concentric circles of magic drifted dreamily out from her. Already she was increasing the affective tone of all living organisms within the lounge, and Ess Pu was not excluded. However, as has already been disclosed, when an Algolian feels good his rage knows no bounds. Ao didn't care.

'Mine!' Ess Pu mouthed, swinging toward the Captain. 'The girl – mine!'

'Get ye claws awa' from my face, mon,' Captain Ramsay said with dignity. 'If ye wull join me in this quiet corner perhaps ye can state yer case in a more courteous fashion. Noo, what is it?'

Ess Pu demanded Ao. He took out a certificate which appeared to state that he had travelled to Aldebaran Tau with Ao as her guardian. Ramsay fingered his jaw undecidedly. Meanwhile there was a scuffle among the thronging passengers who were pressing folded slips of paper upon the stewards. The breathless, rotund figure of Macduff burst out of the crowd just in time to snatch Ao from Ess Pu's possessively descending claws.

'Back, lobster!' he ordered threateningly. 'Lay a claw on that girl at your peril.' Towing her, he dodged behind the Captain as Ess Pu lunged.

'I thought so,' Ramsay said, lifting a cautioning finger at Ess Pu. 'Were ye no specifically forbidden to mingle with the passengers, Macduff?'

'This is a matter of law enforcement,' Macduff said. 'Ao is my ward, not that criminal lobster's.'

'Can ye prove it?' Ramsay inquired. 'That certificate of his –'

Macduff tore the certificate from Ess Pu's grip, scanned it hastily, crumpled it into a ball and threw it on the floor.

'Nonsense!' he said scornfully, taking out a cablegram in an accusing manner. 'Read this, Captain. As you will observe it is a cable from the Lesser Vegan Control Administration. It points out that Ao was illegally deported from Lesser Vega and that an Algolian is suspected of the crime.'

'Eh?' Ramsay said. 'One moment, Ess Pu.' But the Algolian was already hastily clashing his way out of the salon. Ramsay scowled at the cablegram, looked up and beckoned to a Cephan double-brained attorney among the passengers. There was a brief colloquy, from which Ramsay came back shaking his head.

'Can't do much about this, Macduff,' he said. 'It isn't a GBI offence, unfortunately. I find I'm empowered only to turn Ao over to her richtful guardian and since she has none –'

'Your error, Captain,' Macduff broke in. 'You want her richt – I mean, her rightful guardian? You're looking at him. Here's the rest of that cablegram.'

'What?' Captain Ramsay demanded.

'Exactly. Terence Lao-T'se Macduff. That's what it says. The Lesser Vegan Control Administration has accepted my offer to stand in *loco parentis* to Ao, *pro tem.*'

'Vurra weel,' Ramsay said reluctantly. 'Ao's yer ward. Ye wull have to take that up with the Xerian authorities when ye arrive, for as sure as my name is Angus Ramsay ye'll gae head over basket doon the gangplank the minute we land on Xeria. Ye and Ess Pu can fight it oot there. In the meantime I dinna allow a crewman to mingle with my passengers. Go *for-rard!*'

'I demand the rights of a passenger,' Macduff said excitedly, backing up a step or two. 'The price of the ticket includes the pool and I demand –'

'Ye are no passenger. Ye're a dom insubordinate member of –'

'Ao's a passenger!' Macduff contended shrilly. 'She's entitled to take part in the pool, isn't she? Well, then, a slip, please, Captain.'

Ramsay growled under his breath. But finally he beckoned to the steward with the slotted box.

'Let Ao write her own guess,' he insisted stubbornly.

'Nonsense,' Macduff said. 'Ao's my ward. I'll write it for her. Moreover, if by any miraculous chance she should happen to win the pool, it will be my duty to administer the dough in the best interests of her welfare, which obviously means buying us both tickets to Lesser Vega.'

'Och, why quibble?' Ramsay said suddenly. 'If ye're lucky enough to have a miracle happen, fair enough.'

Macduff, concealing what he wrote, scribbled busily, folded the paper and pushed it through the slot. Ramsay took a permaseal from the steward and ran it across the box-top.

'Personally,' Macduff said, watching him,'I feel slightly degraded by the atmosphere of the *Sutter.* What with condoning smuggling, shyster tactics and pure vicious gambling, I'm forced to the unsavory conclusion, Captain, that you're running a crime ship. Come, Ao, let us seek purer air.'

Ao licked her thumb and thought of something very nice, perhaps the taste of her thumb. No one would ever know.

Time passed, both Bergsonian and Newtonian. On either scale it seemed probable that Macduff's time was running rapidly out.

'Who sups wi' Auld Clootie should hae a long spoon,' Captain Ramsay said to the acting first, on the day of the *Sutter*'s scheduled arrival at Xeria. 'The wonder is that Macduff has evaded Ess Pu's claws this long, the way he's been trying to get at those *sphyghi* plants. What baffles me is what he hopes to accomplish by sneaking around the Algolian's cabin with sodium iodide counters and microwave spectroscopes. Whatever he wrote doon in the lottery box canna be changed. The box is in my safe.'

'Suppose he finds a way to open the safe?' the acting first suggested.

'In addition to the time lock it is keyed to the alpha radiations of my own brain,' Captain Ramsay pointed out. 'He canna possibly – ah, talk of the devil, Mr French, look who's coming.'

The rotund yet agile form of Macduff came scuttling rapidly along the corridor, one jump ahead of the Algolian. Macduff was breathing hard. At sight of the two officers he dived behind them like a quail going to cover. Ess Pu, blind with fury, snapped his claws in the Captain's very face.

'Control yerself, mon!' Ramsay said sharply. The Algolian made a mindless gobbling sound and waved a paper wildly in the air.

'Man, indeed,' Macduff said with some bitterness, from his position of precarious safety. 'He's nothing but an acromegalic lobster. It's getting so any object can be classified as humanoid these days, the way they keep broadening the requirements. Letting in all the riff-raff of the Galaxy. Martians were the opening wedge. Now the deluge. I can see the need for a certain amount of latitude, but we peril the dignity of true humanoids when we apply the proud name of Man to a lobster. Why, the creature isn't even a biped. In fact, there's a certain air of indecent exposure about where he wears his bones.'

'Tush, mon, ye ken the word's a mere figure of speech. What is it, Ess Pu? What's this paper ye keep thrusting at me?'

The Algolian was understood to gibber that Macduff had dropped it while fleeing. He recommended that the Captain read it carefully.

'Later,' Ramsay said, thrusting it in his pocket. 'We're due to land on Xeria vurra soon, and I must be in the control room. Go for-rard, Macduff.'

Macduff obeyed with surprising alacrity, at least until he was out of sight. Ess Pu, muttering thickly, followed. Only then did Ramsay pull the paper from his pocket. He studied it, snorted and handed it to the acting first. Macduff's neat handwriting covered one side of the page, as follows:

Problem: Find out how many seeds in the first ripe sphyghi *fruit. How look inside a sealed fruit in which all seeds may not be formed yet? Ordinary vision useless.*

First day: Attempted to introduce radio-tracer in sphyghi *so I could count radioactivity day by day and work out useful graphs. Failed. Ess Pu installed booby trap, sign of low criminal mentality. No harm done.*

Second day: Attempt to bribe Ess Pu with Immortality Elixir. Ess Pu outraged. Forgot Algolians regard adolescence as despicable. Small minds value size inordinately.

Third day: Tried to focus infrared on sphyghi, *to pick up secondary radiations with acoustical interferometer. Failed. Experimented in long-distance color staining of* sphyghi *cells with light waves. Failed.*

Fourth day: Attempts to introduce chloroform into Ess Pu's quarters failed also. Impossible to get near enough fruit to try analysis through positive ion emissions. Am beginning to suspect Ess Pu was responsible for Captain Masterson's hospitalization back on Aldebaran Tau. Probably crept up from behind in dark alley. All bullies are cowards. Note: try to turn Xerians against Ess Pu on arrival. How?

There the quasi-diary ended. Mr French looked up quizzically.

'I had na realized Macduff was applying science so thoroughly,' Ramsay remarked. 'But this merely confirms what Ess Pu told me weeks ago. He said Macduff was constantly trying to get at the *sphyghi.* But he couldna and he canna and noo we must prepare for landing, Mr French.'

He hurried away, trailed by the acting first. The corridor lay empty and silent for a little while. Then an intercom high in the wall spoke.

'General announcement,' it said. 'Passengers and crew of the *Sutter,* your attention, please. Prepare for landing. Immediately afterwards, passengers will assemble in the grand lounge for the Xerian customs search. The results of the ship's pool will also be announced. Your attendance is compulsory. Thank you.'

There was silence, a sound of heavy breathing and finally a new voice sounded. 'That means you, Macduff,' it said grimly. 'Ye ken? Aye, ye'd better.'

Four minutes later, the *Sutter* landed on Xeria.

Yanked protesting from his cabin, Macduff was dragged to the grand lounge, where everyone else had already assembled. A group of Xerian officials, repressing their joy with some difficulty, was also in evidence, making a rather perfunctory search of the passengers, while other Xerians went through the ship rapidly, testing for contraband.

But it was obvious that the contraband that excited them was the *sphyghi.* A table had been set up in the middle of the big room and upon it, each plant in its own little earthenware pot, the *sphyghi* stood. Plump golden fruit dangled from the branches, the pink glow of ripeness flushing their downy surfaces. An odor of pure delight exhaled from the plants. Ess Pu stood guardian, occasionally exchanging words with a Xerian official, who had already affixed a medal[1] on the Algolian's carapace.

'Outrageous!' Macduff cried, struggling. 'I merely needed another few minutes' work with a vitally important experiment I was –'

'Close your blabber-mouth,' Captain Ramsay told him. 'I shall take great pleasure in kicking you off the *Sutter* myself.'

'Leaving me to the tender mercies of that lobster? He'll kill me! I appeal to our common humanoid –'

Captain Ramsay conferred briefly with the Xerian leader, who nodded.

'Quite right, Captain,' he or it said pedantically. 'Under our laws debtors work out their debts, mayhem is assessed by its results and the aggressor forced to pay full reparations. Homicide naturally always carries the death penalty. Why do you ask?'

'That applies even to Ess Pu?' the Captain persisted.

'Naturally,' the Xerian said.

'Weel, then,' Ramsay said significantly to Macduff.

'Weel, then what? He'll be so rich he won't even mind paying reparations for the privilege of committing mayhem on my person. I bruise very easily.'

'But he wullna kill ye,' Ramsay said comfortingly. 'And it wull be a fine lesson to ye, Macduff.'

'Then at least I intend to get in one good blow,' said Macduff, seizing a stout

1 With suction cups, of course.

Malacca cane from a nearby avian and giving Ess Pu a resounding smack across the carapace. The Algolian let out a steam-whistle shriek of fury and lunged forward while Macduff, brandishing the cane like a rapier, danced pudgily backward, threatening even as he retreated.

'Come on, you overgrown shore dinner,' cried Macduff valiantly. 'We'll have it out now, humanoid to lobster!'

'Lay on, Macduff!' shouted an erudite and enthusiastic Ganymedan.

'Lay off!' bellowed Captain Ramsay, waving his officers to the rescue. But the Xerians were before them. They formed a quick barrier between the combatants and one of them twisted the cane from Macduff's reluctant grasp.

'If he has harmed you, Ess Pu, he will make reparations,' the leader of the Xerians said. 'Law is law. Are you injured?'

Despite Ess Pu's inarticulate gobbles, it was obvious that he was not. And the Xerian jurisprudence takes no notice of injured pride. Termites are humble by nature.

'Let's get this settled,' Captain Ramsay said, annoyed at having his grand lounge turned into a shambles. 'There are only three passengers disembarking here. Ao, Ess Pu and Macduff.'

Macduff looked around for Ao, found her and, scuttling over, tried to hide behind her oblivious back.

'Ah, yes,' the leading Xerian said. 'Ess Pu has already explained the matter of the ship's pool. We will permit the lottery. However, certain conditions must be observed. No non-Xerian will be allowed to approach this table, and I will do the seed counting myself.'

'That wull be satisfactory,' Ramsay said, picking up the sealed ballot box and retreating. 'If ye'll cut open the ripest of the fruit and count the seeds I'll then open this box and announce the winner.'

'Wait!' Macduff cried out but his voice was ignored. The leading Xerian had picked up a silver knife from the table, plucked the largest, ripest *sphyghi*-fruit and cut it neatly in two. The halves rolled apart on the table – to reveal a perfectly empty hollow within the fruit.

The Xerian's shout of dismay echoed through the lounge. The silver knife flashed, chopping the fruit to fragments. But not a single seed glittered in the creamy pulp. 'What's happened?' Macduff demanded. 'No seeds? Obviously a swindle. I never trusted Ess Pu. He's been gloating –'

'Silence,' the Xerian said coldly. In a subdued quiet he used the silver knife again and again in an atmosphere of mounting tension.

'No seeds?' Captain Ramsay asked blankly as the last fruit fell open emptily. The Xerian made no reply. He was toying with the silver knife and regarding Ess Pu.

The Algolian seemed as astounded as anyone else but as Macduff audibly remarked, it was hard to tell, with an Algolian. Captain Ramsay courageously broke the ominous silence by stepping forward to remind the Xerians that he was a representative of the GBI.

'Have no fear,' the Xerian said coldly. 'We have no jurisdiction in your ship, Captain.'

Macduff's voice rose in triumph.

'I never trusted that lobster from the start,' he announced, strutting forward. 'He merely took your money and made a deal for seedless *sphyghi*. He is obviously a criminal. His hasty exit from Aldebaran Tau, plus his known addiction to Lethean dust –'

At that point Ess Pu charged down upon Macduff, raging uncontrollably. At the last moment Macduff's rotund figure shot toward the open port and the thin Xerian sunlight outside. Ess Pu clattered after him, shrieking with fury, mouth membranes flaring crimson in his rage.

At the Xerian leader's quick command, the other Xerians hurried after Macduff. There were distant, cryptic noises from outside. Presently Macduff reappeared, panting and alone.

'Awkward creatures, Algolians,' he said, nodding familiarly to the Xerian leader. 'I see your men have – ah – detained Ess Pu.'

'Yes,' the Xerian said. 'Outside, he is of course under our jurisdiction.'

'The thought had occurred to me,' Macduff murmured, drifting toward Ao.

'Noo wait a minute,' Captain Ramsay said to the Xerians. 'Ye have na –'

'We are not barbarians,' the Xerian said with dignity. 'We gave Ess Pu fifteen million Universal Credits to do a job for us and he has failed. Unless he can return the fifteen million, plus costs, he must work it out. The man-hour' – here Macduff was seen to wince – 'the man-hour on Xeria is the equivalent of one sixty-fifth of a credit.'

'This is highly irregular,' the Captain said. 'However, it's out of my jurisdiction now. You, Macduff – stop looking so smug. You get off at Xeria too, remember. I advise ye to stay out of Ess Pu's way.'

'I expect he'll be busy most of the time,' Macduff said cheerfully. 'I hate to remind a supposedly competent officer of his duties, but haven't you forgotten the slight matter of the ship's pool?'

'What?' Ramsay glanced blankly at the pulped fruit. 'The pool's called off, of course.'

'Nonsense,' Macduff interrupted. 'Let's have no evasions. One might suspect you of trying to avoid a payoff.'

'Mon, ye're daft. How can there be a payoff? The lottery was based on guessing the seed count in a *sphyghi* fruit and it's perfectly obvious the *sphyghi* has no seeds. Vurra weel. If no one has any objections –'

'I object!' Macduff cried. 'On behalf of my ward, I demand that every single guess be counted and tabulated.'

'Be reasonable,' Ramsay urged. 'If ye're merely delaying the evil moment when I kick ye off the *Sutter* –'

'You've got to wind up the pool legally,' Macduff insisted.

'Pah, shut yer clatterin' trap,' Ramsay snapped sourly, picking up the sealed box and attaching a small gadget to it. 'Just as ye like. But I am on to ye, Macduff. Noo, quiet please, everybody.'

He closed his eyes and his lips moved in a soundless mumble. The box flew open, disgorging a clutter of folded papers. At Ramsay's gesture a passenger stepped forward and began to open the slips, reading off names and guesses.

'So ye gain pairhaps five minutes' reprieve,' Ramsay said under his breath to Macduff. 'Then oot ye go after Ess Pu and let me say it is pairfectly obvious ye lured the Algolian out of the *Sutter* on purpose.'

'Nonsense,' Macduff said briskly. 'Am I to blame if Ess Pu focused his ridiculous anti-social emotions on me?'

'Aye,' Ramsay said. 'Ye ken dom well ye are.'

'Male Kor-ze-Kabloom, seven hundred fifty,' called the passenger unfolding another slip. 'Lorma Secundus, two thousand ninety-nine. Ao, *per* –'

There was a pause.

'Well?' Captain Ramsay prompted, collaring Macduff. 'Well, mon?'

'Terence Lao-T'se Macduff –' the passenger continued and again halted.

'What is it? What number did he guess?' Ramsay demanded, pausing at the open port with one foot lifted ready to boot the surprisingly philosophical Macduff down the gangplank. '*I asked ye a question!* What number's on the slip?'

'Zero,' the passenger said faintly.

'Exactly!' Macduff declared, wriggling free. 'And now, Captain Ramsay, I'll thank you to hand over half the ship's pool to me, as Ao's guardian – less, of course, the price of our passage to Lesser Vega. As for Ess Pu's half of the take, send it to him with my compliments.

'Perhaps it will knock a few months off his sentence, which, if my figures are correct, come to nine hundred and forty-six Xerian years. A Macduff forgives even his enemies. Come, Ao, my dear. I must choose a suitable cabin.'

So saying, Macduff lit a fresh cigar and sauntered slowly away, leaving Captain Ramsay staring straight ahead and moving his lips as though in slow prayer. The prayer became audible.

'Macduff,' Ramsay called. '*Macduff!* How did ye do it?'

'I,' said Macduff over his shoulder, 'am a scientist.'

The Lesser Vegan cabaret hummed with festivity. A pair of comedians exchanged quips and banter among the tables. At one table Ao sat between Macduff and Captain Ramsay.

'I am still waiting to hear how ye did it, Macduff,' Ramsay said. 'A bargain's a bargain, ye know. I put my name on yon application, didn't I?'

'I cannot but admit,' Macduff said, 'that your signature facilitated my getting Ao's guardianship, bless her heart. Some champagne, Ao?' But Ao made no response. She was exchanging glances, less blank than usual, with a young Lesser Vegan male at a nearby table.

'Come, noo,' Ramsay insisted.'Remember I wull have to turn over my log at the end of the voyage. I must know what happened concerning yon *sphyghi.* Otherwise, d'ye think I'd hae gone oot on a limb and guaranteed yer tortuous character, even though I carefully added, 'to the best of my knowledge'? No. Ye wrote thot zero when I saw ye do it, long before the fruit ripened.'

'Right,' Macduff said blandly, sipping champagne. 'It was a simple problem in misdirection. I suppose there's no harm in telling you how I did it. Consider the circumstances. You were going to maroon me on Xeria, side by side with that lobster.

'Obviously I had to cut him down to my size by discrediting him with the Xerians. Winning the pool was an unexpected secondary development. Merely a stroke of well-deserved good luck, aided by applied scientific technique.'

'Ye mean that stuff ye wrote down on the paper Ess Pu found – the gibble-gabble aboot interferometers and ion-analyzers? So ye did find some way to count the seeds – och, I'm wrong there, am I?'

'Naturally.' Macduff twirled his glass and preened himself slightly. 'I wrote that paper for Ess Pu's eyes. I had to keep him so busy protecting his *sphyghi* and chasing me that he never had a spare moment to think.'

'I still dinna ken,' Ramsay confessed. 'Even if ye'd known the richt answer in advance, how could ye foresee the pool would be based on *sphyghi?*'

'Oh, that was the simplest thing of all. Consider the odds! What else could it be, with the Aldebaran Lottery fresh in every mind and the whole ship reeking of contraband *sphyghi?* If no one else had suggested it I was prepared to bring it up myself and – what's this? Go away! Get out!'

He was addressing himself to the two comedians, who had worked their way around to Macduff's table. Captain Ramsay glanced up in time to see them commence a new act.

The laugh-getting technique of insult has never basically changed all through the ages, and Galactic expansion has merely broadened and deepened its variety. Derision has naturally expanded to include species as well as races.

The comedians, chattering insanely, began a fairly deft imitation of two apes searching each other for fleas. There was an outburst of laughter, not joined by those customers who had sprung from simian stock.

'Tush!' Ramsay said irately, pushing back his chair. 'Ye dom impudent –'

Macduff lifted a placating palm. 'Tut, tut, Captain. Strive for the objective viewpoint. Merely a matter of semantics, after all.' He chuckled tolerantly. 'Rise above such insularity, as I do, and enjoy the skill of these mummers in the abstract art of impersonation. I was about to explain why I had to keep Ess Pu distracted. I feared he might notice how fast the *sphyghi* were ripening.'

'Pah,' Ramsay said, but relapsed into his chair as the comedians moved on and began a new skit. 'Weel, continue.'

'Misdirection,' Macduff said cheerfully. 'Have you ever had a more incompetent crew member than I?'

'No,' Ramsay said, considering. 'Never in my –'

'Quite so. I was tossed like spindrift from task to task until I finally reached Atmospheric Controls, which was exactly where I wanted to be. Crawling down ventilating pipes has certain advantages. For example, it was the work of a moment to empty a phial of two-four-five-trichlorophenoxyacetic acid' – he rolled the syllables lushly – 'trichlorophenoxyacetic acid into Ess Pu's ventilator. The stuff must have got into everything, including the *sphyghi.*'

'Trichloro – what? Ye mean ye gimmicked the *sphyghi before* the pool?'

'Certainly. I told you the pool was a later by-product. My goal at first was simply to get Ess Pu in trouble on Xeria to save my own valuable person. Luckily I had a fair supply of various hormones with me. This particular one, as the merest child should know, bypasses the need for cross-pollination. Through a law of biology the results will always be seedless fruit. Ask any horticulturist. It's done all the time.'

'Seedless fruit –' Ramsay said blankly. 'Cross-pollin – och, aye! Weel, I'll be dommed.'

A modest disclaimer was no doubt on Macduff's lips, but his eye was caught by the two comedians and he paused, cigar lifted, regarding them. The shorter of the two was now strutting in a wide circle, gesturing like one who smokes a cigar with great self-importance. His companion whooped wildly and beat him over the head.

'Tell me this, brother!' he cried in a shrill falsetto. 'Who was that penguin I seen you with last night?'

'That wasn't no penguin,' the strutter giggled happily. 'That was a Venusian!' Simultaneously he gestured, and a spotlight sprang like a tent over Macduff's shrinking head.

'What! What? *How dare you!*' screamed the outraged Macduff, recovering his voice at last amid ripples of laughter. 'Libellous defamation of – of – I've never been so insulted in my life!' A repressed snort came from the Captain. The ruffled Macduff glared around furiously, rose to his full height and seized Ao's hand.

'Ignore them,' Ramsay suggested in an unsteady voice. 'After all, ye canna deny ye're Venusian by species, Macduff, even though ye insist ye were hatched in Glasga' – Borrn, I mean. Aye, ye're Scots by birth and humanoid by classification, are ye na? And no more a penguin than I'm a monkey.'

But Macduff was already marching toward the door. Ao trailed obediently after, casting back angelic looks at the Lesser Vegan male.

'Outrageous!' said Macduff.

'Come back, mon,' Ramsay called, suppressing a wild whoop. 'Remember the abstract art of impairsonation. 'Tis a mere matter of semantics –'

His voice went unheard. Macduff's back was an indignant ramrod. Towing Ao, his bottle-shaped figure stiff with dignity, Terence Lao-T'se Macduff vanished irrevocably into the Lesser Vegan night, muttering low.

For Macduff, as should be evident by now to the meanest intellect,[1] was not all he claimed to be …

'Tush,' said Captain Ramsay, his face split by a grin, 'that I should ha' seen the day! Waiter! A whusky-and-soda – no more of this nosty champagne. I am celebrating a red-letter occasion, a phenomenon of nature. D'ye ken this is probably the first time in Macduff's life that the unprincipled scoundrel has taken his departure withoot leaving some puir swindled sucker behind?

'D'ye – eh? What's that? What bill, ye daft loon? Pah, it was Macduff who insisted I be his guest tonight. Och, I – ah – eh –

'Dom!'

1 By which we mean the reader who skipped all the science, elementary as it was, in this chronicle.

EXIT THE PROFESSOR

We Hogbens are right exclusive. That Perfesser feller from the city might have known that, but he come busting in without an invite, and I don't figger he had call to complain afterward. In Kaintuck the polite thing is to stick to your own hill of beans and not come nosing around where you're not wanted.

Time we ran off the Haley boys with that shotgun gadget we rigged up – only we never could make out how it worked, somehow – that time, it all started because Rafe Haley come peeking and prying at the shed winder, trying to get a look at Little Sam. Then Rafe went round saying Little Sam had three haids or something.

Can't believe a word them Haley boys say. Three haids! It ain't natcheral, is it? Anyhow, Little Sam's only got two haids, and never had no more since the day he was born.

So Maw and I rigged up that shotgun thing and peppered the Haley boys good. Like I said, we couldn't figger out afterward how it worked. We'd tacked on some dry cells and a lot of coils and wires and stuff and it punched holes in Rafe as neat as anything.

Coroner's verdict was that the Haley boys died real sudden, and Sheriff Abernathy come up and had a drink of corn with us and said for two cents he'd whale the tar outa me. I didn't pay no mind. Only some damyankee reporter musta got wind of it, because a while later a big, fat, serious-looking man come around and begun to ask questions.

Uncle Les was sitting on the porch, with his hat over his face. 'You better get the heck back to your circus, mister,' he just said. 'We had offers from old Barnum hisself and turned 'em down. Ain't that right, Saunk?'

'Sure is,' I said. 'I never trusted Phineas. Called Little Sam a freak, he did.'

The big solemn-looking man, whose name was Perfesser Thomas Galbraith, looked at me. 'How old are you, son?' he said.

'I ain't your son,' I said. 'And I don't know, nohow.'

'You don't look over eighteen,' he said, 'big as you are. You couldn't have known Barnum.'

'Sure I did. Don't go giving me the lie. I'll wham you.'

'I'm not connected with any circus,' Galbraith said. 'I'm a biogeneticist.'

We sure laughed at that. He got kinda mad and wanted to know what the joke was.

'There ain't no such word,' Maw said. And at that point Little Sam started yelling, and Galbraith turned white as a goose wing and shivered all over. He sort of fell down. When we picked him up, he wanted to know what had happened.

'That was Little Sam,' I said. 'Maw's gone in to comfort him. He's stopped now.'

'That was a subsonic,' the Perfesser snapped. 'What is Little Sam – a short-wave transmitter?'

'Little Sam's the baby,' I said, short-like. 'Don't go calling him outa his name, either. Now, s'pose you tell us what you want.'

He pulled out a notebook and started looking through it.

'I'm a – a scientist,' he said. 'Our foundation is studying eugenics, and we've got some reports about you. They sound unbelievable. One of our men has a theory that natural mutations can remain undetected in undeveloped cultural regions, and –' He slowed down and stared at Uncle Les. 'Can you really fly?' he asked.

Well, we don't like to talk about that. The preacher gave us a good dressing-down once. Uncle Les had got likkered up and went sailing over the ridges, scaring a couple of bear hunters outa their senses. And it ain't in the Good Book that men should fly, neither. Uncle Les generally does it only on the sly, when nobody's watching.

So anyhow Uncle Les pulled his hat down further on his face and growled.

'That's plumb silly. Ain't no way a man can fly. These here modern contraptions I hear tell about –'tween ourselves, they don't really fly at all. Just a lot of crazy talk, that's all.'

Galbraith blinked and studied his notebook again.

'But I've got hearsay evidence of a great many unusual things connected with your family. Flying is only one of them. I know it's theoretically impossible – and I'm not talking about planes – but –'

'Oh, shet your trap.'

'The medieval witches' salve used aconite to give an illusion of flight – entirely subjective, of course.'

'Will you stop pestering me?' Uncle Les said, getting mad, on account of he felt embarrassed, I guess. Then he jumped up, threw his hat down on the porch and flew away. After a minute he swooped down for his hat and made a face at the Perfesser. He flew off down the gulch and we didn't see him fer a while.

I got mad, too.

'You got no call to bother us,' I said. 'Next thing Uncle Les will do like Paw, and that'll be an awful nuisance. We ain't seen hide nor hair of Paw since that other city feller was around. He was a census taker, I think.'

Galbraith didn't say anything. He was looking kinda funny. I gave him a drink and he asked about Paw.

'Oh, he's around,' I said. 'Only you don't see him no more. He likes it better that way, he says.'

'Yes,' Galbraith said, taking another drink. 'Oh, God. How old did you say you were?'

'Didn't say nothing about it.'

'Well, what's the earliest thing you can remember?'

'Ain't no use remembering things. Clutters up your haid too much.'

'It's fantastic,' Galbraith said. 'I hadn't expected to send a report like that back to the foundation.'

'We don't want nobody prying around,' I said. 'Go way and leave us alone.'

'But, good Lord!' He looked over the porch rail and got interested in the shotgun gadget. 'What's that?'

'A thing,' I said.

'What does it do?'

'Things,' I said.

'Oh. May I look at it?'

'Sure,' I said. 'I'll give you the dingus if you'll go away.'

He went over and looked at it. Paw got up from where he'd been sitting beside me, told me to get rid of the damyankee and went into the house. The Perfesser came back. 'Extraordinary!' he said. 'I've had training in electronics, and it seems to me you've got something very odd there. What's the principle?'

'The what?' I said. 'It makes holes in things.'

'It can't fire shells. You've got a couple of lenses where the breech should – how did you say it worked?'

'I dunno.'

'Did you make it?'

'Me and Maw.'

He asked a lot more questions.

'I dunno,' I said. 'Trouble with a shotgun is you gotta keep loading it. We sorta thought if we hooked on a few things it wouldn't need loading no more. It don't, neither.'

'Were you serious about giving it to me?'

'If you stop bothering us.'

'Listen,' he said, 'it's miraculous that you Hogbens have stayed out of sight so long.'

'We got our ways.'

'The mutation theory must be right. You must be studied. This is one of the most important discoveries since –' He kept on talking like that. He didn't make much sense.

Finally I decided there was only two ways to handle things, and after what Sheriff Abernathy had said, I didn't feel right about killing nobody till the Sheriff had got over his fit of temper. I don't want to cause no ruckus.

'S'pose I go to New York with you, like you want,' I said. 'Will you leave the family alone?'

He halfway promised, though he didn't want to. But he knuckled under and crossed his heart, on account of I said I'd wake up Little Sam if he didn't. He sure wanted to see Little Sam, but I told him that was no good. Little Sam couldn't go to New York, anyhow. He's got to stay in his tank or he gets awful sick.

Anyway, I satisfied the Perfesser pretty well and he went off, after I'd promised to meet him in town next morning. I felt sick, though, I can tell you. I ain't been away from the folks overnight since that ruckus in the old country, when we had to make tracks fast.

Went to Holland, as I remember. Maw always had a soft spot fer the man that helped us get outa London. Named Little Sam after him. I fergit what his name was. Gwynn or Stuart or Pepys – I get mixed up when I think back beyond the War between the States.

That night we chewed the rag. Paw being invisible, Maw kept thinking he was getting more'n his share of the corn, but pretty soon she mellowed and let him have a demijohn. Everybody told me to mind my p's and q's.

'This here Perfesser's awful smart,' Maw said. 'All perfessers are. Don't go bothering him any. You be a good boy or you'll ketch heck from me.'

'I'll be good, Maw,' I said. Paw whaled me alongside the haid, which wasn't fair, on account of I couldn't see him.

'That's so you won't fergit,' he said.

'We're plain folks,' Uncle Les was growling. 'No good never come of trying to get above yourself.'

'Honest, I ain't trying to do that,' I said. 'I only figgered –'

'You stay outa trouble!' Maw said, and just then we heard Grandpaw moving in the attic. Sometimes Grandpaw don't stir for a month at a time, but tonight he seemed right frisky.

So, natcherally, we went upstairs to see what he wanted.

He was talking about the Perfesser.

'A stranger, eh?' he said. 'Out upon the stinking knave. A set of rare fools I've gathered about me for my dotage! Only Saunk shows any shrewdness, and, dang my eyes, he's the worst fool of all.'

I just shuffled and muttered something, on account of I never like to look at Grandpaw direct. But he wasn't paying me no mind. He raved on.

'So you'd go to this New York? 'Sblood, and hast thou forgot the way we shunned London and Amsterdam – and Nieuw Amsterdam – for fear of questioning? Wouldst thou be put in a freak show? Nor is that the worst danger.'

Grandpaw's the oldest one of us all and he gets kinda mixed up in his language sometimes. I guess the lingo you learned when you're young sorta sticks with you. One thing, he can cuss better than anybody I've ever heard.

'Shucks,' I said. 'I was only trying to help.'

'Thou puling brat,' Grandpaw said. ''Tis thy fault and thy dam's. For building that device, I mean, that slew the Haley tribe. Hadst thou not, this scientist would never have come here.'

'He's a perfesser,' I said. 'Name of Thomas Galbraith.'

'I know. I read his thoughts through Little Sam's mind. A dangerous man. I never knew a sage who wasn't. Except perhaps Roger Bacon, and I had to bribe him to – but Roger was an exceptional man. Hearken:

'None of you may go to this New York. The moment we leave this haven, the moment we are investigated, we are lost. The pack would tear and rend us. Nor could all thy addle-pated flights skyward save thee, Lester – dost thou hear?'

'But what are we to do?' Maw said.

'Aw, heck,' Paw said. 'I'll just fix this Perfesser. I'll drop him down the cistern.'

'An' spoil the water?' Maw screeched. 'You try it!'

'What foul brood is this that has sprung from my seed?' Grandpaw said, real mad. 'Have ye not promised the Sheriff that there will be no more killings – for a while, at least? Is the word of a Hogben naught? Two things have we kept sacred through the centuries – our secret from the world, and the Hogben honor! Kill this man Galbraith and ye'll answer to me for it!'

We all turned white. Little Sam woke up again and started squealing. 'But what'll we do?' Uncle Les said.

'Our secret must be kept,' Grandpaw said. 'Do what ye can, but no killing. I'll consider the problem.'

He seemed to go to sleep then, though it was hard to tell.

The next day I met Galbraith in town, all right, but first I run into Sheriff Abernathy in the street and he gave me a vicious look.

'You stay outa trouble, Saunk,' he said. 'Mind what I tell you, now.' It was right embarrassing.

Anyway, I saw Galbraith and told him Grandpaw wouldn't let me go to New York. He didn't look too happy, but he saw there was nothing that could be done about it.

His hotel room was full of scientific apparatus and kinda frightening. He had the shotgun gadget set up, but it didn't look like he'd changed it any. He started to argue.

'Ain't no use,' I said. 'We ain't leaving the hills. I spoke outa turn yesterday, that's all.'

'Listen, Saunk,' he said. 'I've been inquiring around town about you Hogbens, but I haven't been able to find out much. They're close-mouthed around here. Still, such evidence would be only supporting factors. I know our theories are right. You and your family are mutants and you've got to be studied!'

'We ain't mutants,' I said. 'Scientists are always calling us outa our names. Roger Bacon called us homunculi, only –'

'*What?*' Galbraith shouted. 'Who did you say?'

'Uh – he's a share-cropper over in the next county,' I said hasty-like, but I could see the Perfesser didn't swaller it. He started to walk around the room.

'It's no use,' he said. 'If you won't come to New York, I'll have the foundation send a commission here. You've got to be studied, for the glory of science and the advancement of mankind.'

'Oh, golly,' I said. 'I know what that'd be like. Make a freak show outa us. It'd kill Little Sam. You gotta go away and leave us alone.'

'Leave you alone? When you can create apparatus like this?' He pointed to the shotgun gadget. 'How *does* that work?' he wanted to know, sudden-like.

'I told you, I dunno. We just rigged it up. Listen, Perfesser. There'd be trouble if people came and looked at us. Big trouble. Grandpaw says so.'

Galbraith pulled at his nose.

'Well, maybe – suppose you answered a few questions for me, Saunk.'

'No commission?'

'We'll see.'

'No, sir. I won't –'

Galbraith took a deep breath.

'As long as you tell me what I want to know, I'll keep your whereabouts a secret.'

'I thought this fundation thing of yours knows where you are.'

'Ah – yes,' Galbraith said. 'Naturally they do. But they don't know about *you*.'

That gave me an idea. I coulda killed him easy, but if I had, I knew Grandpaw would of ruined me entire and, besides, there was the Sheriff to think of. So I said, 'Shucks,' and nodded.

My, the questions that man asked! It left me dizzy. And all the while he kept getting more and more excited.

'How old is your grandfather?'

'Gosh, I dunno.'

'Homunculi – mm-m. You mentioned that he was a miner once?'

'No, that was Grandpaw's paw,' I said. 'Tin mines, they were, in England. Only Grandpaw says it was called Britain then. That was during a sorta magic plague they had then. The people had to get the doctors – droons? Droods?'

'Druids?'

'Uh-huh. The Druids was the doctors then, Grandpaw says. Anyhow, all the miners started dying round Cornwall, so they closed up the mines.'

'What sort of plague was it?'

I told him what I remembered from Grandpaw's talk, and the Perfesser got very excited and said something about radioactive emanations, as nearly as I could figger out. It made oncommon bad sense.

'Artificial mutations caused by radioactivity!' he said, getting real pink around the jowls. 'Your grandfather was born a mutant! The genes and chromosomes were rearranged into a new pattern. Why, you may all be supermen!'

'Nope,' I said. 'We're Hogbens. That's all.'

'A dominant, obviously a dominant. All your family were – ah – peculiar?'

'Now, look!' I said.

'I mean, they could all fly?'

'I don't know how yet, myself. I guess we're kinda freakish. Grandpaw was smart. He allus taught us not to show off.'

'Protective camouflage,' Galbraith said. 'Submerged in a rigid social culture, variations from the norm are more easily masked. In a modern, civilized culture, you'd stick out like a sore thumb. But here, in the backwoods, you're practically invisible.'

'Only Paw,' I said.

'Oh, Lord,' he sighed. 'Submerging these incredible natural powers of yours … Do you know the things you might have done?' And then all of a sudden he got even more excited, and I didn't much like the look in his eyes.

'Wonderful things,' he repeated. 'It's like stumbling on Aladdin's lamp.'

'I wish you'd leave us alone,' I said. 'You and your commission!'

'Forget about the commission. I've decided to handle this privately for a while. Provided you'll cooperate. Help me, I mean. Will you do that?'

'Nope,' I said.

'Then I'll bring the commission down from New York,' he said triumphantly.

I thought that over.

'Well,' I said finally, 'what do you want me to do?'

'I don't know yet,' he said slowly. 'My mind hasn't fully grasped the possibilities.'

But he was getting ready to grab. I could tell. I know that look.

I was standing by the window looking out, and all of a sudden I got an idea. I figgered it wouldn't be smart to trust the Perfesser too much, anyhow. So I sort of ambled over to the shotgun gadget and made a few little changes on it.

I knew what I wanted to do, all right, but if Galbraith had asked me why I was twisting a wire here and bending a whozis there I couldn't of told him. I got no eddication. Only now I knew the gadget would do what I wanted it to do.

The Perfesser had been writing in his little notebook. He looked up and saw me.

'What are you doing?' he wanted to know.

'This don't look right to me,' I said. 'I think you monkeyed with them batteries. Try it now.'

'In here?' he said, startled. 'I don't want to pay a bill for damages. It must be tested under safety conditions.'

'See the weathercock out there, on the roof?' I pointed it out to him. 'Won't do no harm to aim at that. You can just stand here by the winder and try it out.'

'It – it isn't dangerous?' He was aching to try the gadget, I could tell. I said it wouldn't kill nobody, and he took a long breath and went to the window and cuddled the stock of the gun against his cheek.

I stayed back aways. I didn't want the Sheriff to see me. I'd already spotted him, sitting on a bench outside the feed-and-grain store across the street.

It happened just like I thought. Galbraith pulled the trigger, aiming at the weathercock on the roof, and rings of light started coming out of the muzzle. There was a fearful noise. Galbraith fell flat on his back, and the commotion was something surprising. People began screaming all over town.

I kinda felt it might be handy if I went invisible for a while. So I did.

Galbraith was examining the shotgun gadget when Sheriff Abernathy busted in. The Sheriff's a hard case. He had his pistol out and handcuffs ready, and he was cussing the Perfesser immediate and rapid.

'I seen you!' he yelled. 'You city fellers think you can get away with anything down here. Well, you can't!'

'Saunk!' Galbraith cried, looking around. But of course he couldn't see me.

Then there was an argument. Sheriff Abernathy had seen Galbraith fire the shotgun gadget and he's no fool. He drug Galbraith down on the street, and I come along, walking soft. People were running around like crazy. Most of them had their hands clapped to their faces.

The Perfesser kept wailing that he didn't understand.

'I seen you!' Abernathy said. 'You aimed that dingus of yours out the window and the next thing everybody in town's got a toothache! Try and tell me you don't understand!'

The Sheriff's smart. He's known us Hogbens long enough so he ain't surprised when funny things happen sometimes. Also, he knew Galbraith was a scientist feller. So there was a ruckus and people heard what was going on and the next thing they was trying to lynch Galbraith.

But Abernathy got him away. I wandered around town for a while. The pastor was out looking at his church windows, which seemed to puzzle him. They was stained glass, and he couldn't figger out why they was hot. I coulda told him that. There's gold in stained-glass windows; they use it to get a certain kind of red.

Finally I went down to the jailhouse. I was still invisible. So I eavesdropped on what Galbraith was saying to the Sheriff.

'It was Saunk Hogben,' the Perfesser kept saying. 'I tell you, he fixed that projector!'

'I saw you,' Abernathy said. 'You done it. Ow!' He put up his hand to his jaw. 'And you better stop it, fast! That crowd outside means business. Half the people in town have got toothaches.'

I guess half the people in town had gold fillings in their teeth.

Then Galbraith said something that didn't surprise me too much. 'I'm having a commission come down from New York; I meant to telephone the foundation tonight, they'll vouch for me.'

So he was intending to cross us up, all along. I kinda felt that had been in his mind.

'You'll cure this toothache of mine – and everybody else's – or I'll open the doors and let in that lynch mob!' the Sheriff howled. Then he went away to put an icebag on his cheek.

I snuck back aways, got visible again and made a lot of noise coming along the passage, so Galbraith could hear me. I waited till he got through cussing me out. I just looked stupid.

'I guess I made a mistake,' I said. 'I can fix it, though.'

'You've done enough fixing!' He stopped. 'Wait a minute. What did you say? You can cure this – what is it?'

'I been looking at that shotgun gadget,' I said. 'I think I know what I did wrong. It's sorta tuned in on gold now, and all the gold in town's shooting out rays or heat or something.'

'Induced selective radioactivity,' Galbraith muttered, which didn't seem to mean much. 'Listen. That crowd outside – do they ever have lynchings in this town?'

'Not more'n once or twice a year,' I said. 'And we already had two this year, so we filled our quota. Wish I could get you up to our place, though. We could hide you easy.'

'You'd better do something!' he said. 'Or I'll get that commission down from New York. You wouldn't like that, would you?'

I never seen such a man fer telling lies and keeping a straight face.

'It's a cinch,' I said. 'I can rig up the gadget so it'll switch off the rays immediate. Only I don't want people to connect us Hogbens with what's going on. We like to live quiet. Look, s'pose I go back to your hotel and change over the gadget, and then all you have to do is get all the people with toothaches together and pull the trigger.'

'But – well, but –'

He was afraid of more trouble. I had to talk him into it. The crowd was yelling outside, so it wasn't too hard. Finally I went away, but I came back, invisible-like, and listened when Galbraith talked to the Sheriff.

They fixed it all up. Everybody with toothaches was going to the Town Hall and set. Then Abernathy would bring the Perfesser over, with the shotgun gadget, and try it out.

'Will it stop the toothaches?' the Sheriff wanted to know. 'For sure?'

'I'm – quite certain it will.'

Abernathy had caught that hesitation.

'Then you better try it on me first. Just to make sure. I don't trust you.'

It seemed like nobody was trusting nobody.

I hiked back to the hotel and made the switch-over in the shotgun gadget. And then I run into trouble. My invisibility was wearing thin. That's the worst part of being just a kid.

After I'm a few hunnerd years older I can stay invisible all the time if I want to. But I ain't right mastered it yet. Thing was, I needed help now because there was something I had to do, and I couldn't do it with people watching.

I went up on the roof and called Little Sam. After I'd tuned in on his haid, I had him put the call through to Paw and Uncle Les. After a while Uncle Les come flying down from the sky, riding mighty heavy on account of he was carrying Paw. Paw was cussing because a hawk had chased them.

'Nobody seen us, though,' Uncle Les said. 'I *think*.'

'People got their own troubles in town today,' I said. 'I need some help. That Perfesser's gonna call down his commission and study us, no matter what he promises.'

'Ain't much we can do, then,' Paw said. 'We cain't kill that feller. Grandpaw said not to.'

So I told 'em my idea. Paw being invisible, he could do it easy. Then we made a little place in the roof so we could see through it, and looked down into Galbraith's room.

We was just in time. The Sheriff was standing there, with his pistol out, just waiting, and the Perfesser, pale around the chops, was pointing the shotgun gadget at Abernathy. It went along without a hitch. Galbraith pulled the trigger, a purple ring of light popped out, and that was all. Except that the Sheriff opened his mouth and gulped.

'You wasn't faking! My toothache's gone!'

Galbraith was sweating, but he put up a good front. 'Sure it works,' he said. 'Naturally. I told you –'

'C'mon down to the Town Hall. Everybody's waiting. You better cure us all, or it'll be just too bad for you.'

They went out. Paw snuck down after them, and Uncle Les picked me up and flew on their trail, keeping low to the roofs, where we wouldn't be spotted. After a while we was fixed outside one of the Town Hall's windows, watching.

I ain't heard so much misery since the great plague of London. The hall was jam-full, and everybody had a toothache and was moaning and yelling. Abernathy come in with the Perfesser, who was carrying the shotgun gadget, and a scream went up.

Galbraith set the gadget on the stage, pointing down at the audience, while the Sheriff pulled out his pistol again and made a speech, telling everybody to shet up and they'd get rid of their toothaches.

I couldn't see Paw, natcherally, but I knew he was up on the platform. Something funny was happening to the shotgun gadget. Nobody noticed, except me, and I was watching for it. Paw – invisible, of course – was making a few changes. I'd told him how, but he knew what to do as well as I did. So pretty soon the shotgun was rigged the way we wanted it.

What happened after that was shocking. Galbraith aimed the gadget and pulled the trigger, and rings of light jumped out, yaller this time. I'd told Paw to fix the range so nobody outside the Town Hall would be bothered. But inside –

Well, it sure fixed them toothaches. Nobody's gold filling can ache if he ain't got a gold filling.

The gadget was fixed now so it worked on everything that wasn't growing. Paw had got the range just right. The seats was gone all of a sudden, and so was part of the chandelier. The audience, being bunched together, got it good. Pegleg Jaffe's glass eye was gone, too. Them that had false teeth lost 'em. Everybody sorta got a once-over-lightly haircut.

Also, the whole audience lost their clothes. Shoes ain't growing things, and no more are pants or shirts or dresses. In a trice everybody in the hall was naked as needles. But, shucks, they'd got rid of their toothaches, hadn't they?

We was back to home an hour later, all but Uncle Les, when the door busted open and in come Uncle Les, with the Perfesser staggering after him. Galbraith was a mess. He sank down and wheezed, looking back at the door in a worried way.

'Funny thing happened,' Uncle Les said. 'I was flying along outside town and there was the Perfesser running away from a big crowd of people, with sheets wrapped around 'em – some of 'em. So I picked him up. I brung him here, like he wanted.' Uncle Les winked at me.

'Ooooh!' Galbraith said. '*Aaaah!* Are they coming?'

Maw went to the door.

'They's a lot of torches moving up the mountain,' she said. 'It looks right bad.'

The Perfesser glared at me.

'You said you could hide me! Well, you'd better! This is your fault!'

'Shucks,' I said.

'You'll hide me or else!' Galbraith squalled. 'I – I'll bring that commission down.'

'Look,' I said, 'if we hide you safe, will you promise to fergit all about that commission and leave us alone?'

The Perfesser promised. 'Hold on a minute,' I said, and went up to the attic to see Grandpaw.

He was awake.

'How about it, Grandpaw?' I asked.

He listened to Little Sam for a second.

'The knave is lying,' he told me pretty soon. 'He means to bring his commission of stinkards here anyway, recking naught of his promise.'

'Should we hide him, then?'

'Aye,' Grandpaw said. 'The Hogbens have given their word – there must be no more killing. And to hide a fugitive from his pursuers would not be an ill deed, surely.'

Maybe he winked. It's hard to tell with Grandpaw. So I went down the ladder. Galbraith was at the door, watching the torches come up the mountain.

He grabbed me.

'Saunk! If you don't hide me –'

'We'll hide you,' I said. 'C'mon.'

So we took him down to the cellar …

When the mob got here, with Sheriff Abernathy in the lead, we played dumb. We let 'em search the house. Little Sam and Grandpaw turned invisible for a bit, so nobody noticed them. And naturally the crowd couldn't find hide nor hair of Galbraith. We'd hid him good, like we promised.

That was a few years ago. The Perfesser's thriving. He ain't studying us, though. Sometimes we take out the bottle we keep him in and study him.

Dang small bottle, too!

THE TWONKY

The turnover at Mideastern Radio was so great that Mickey Lloyd couldn't keep track of his men. Employees kept quitting and going elsewhere, at a higher salary. So when the big-headed little man in overalls wandered vaguely out of a storeroom, Lloyd took one look at the brown dungaree suit – company provided – and said mildly, 'The whistle blew half an hour ago. Hop to work.'

'Work-k-k?' The man seemed to have trouble with the word.

Drunk? Lloyd, in his capacity as foreman, couldn't permit that. He flipped away his cigarette, walked forward and sniffed. No, it wasn't liquor. He peered at the badge on the man's overalls.

'Two-o-four, m-mm. Are you new here?'

'New. Huh?' The man rubbed a rising bump on his forehead. He was an odd-looking little chap, bald as a vacuum tube, with a pinched, pallid face and tiny eyes that held dazed wonder.

'Come on, Joe. Wake up!' Lloyd was beginning to sound impatient. 'You work here, don't you?'

'Joe,' said the man thoughtfully. 'Work. Yes, I work. I make them.' His words ran together oddly, as though he had a cleft palate.

With another glance at the badge, Lloyd gripped Joe's arm and ran him through the assembly room. 'Here's your place. Hop to it. Know what to do?'

The other drew his scrawny body erect. 'I am – expert,' he remarked. 'Make them better than Ponthwank.'

'O.K.,' Lloyd said. 'Make 'em, then.' And he went away.

The man called Joe hesitated, nursing the bruise on his head. The overalls caught his attention, and he examined them wonderingly. Where – oh, yes. They had been hanging in the room from which he had first emerged. His own garments had, naturally, dissipated during the trip – what trip?

Amnesia, he thought. He had fallen from the … the something … when it slowed down and stopped. How odd this huge, machine-filled barn looked! It struck no chord of remembrance.

Amnesia, that was it. He was a worker. He made things. As for the unfamiliarity of his surroundings, that meant nothing. He was still dazed. The clouds would lift from his mind presently. They were beginning to do that already.

Work. Joe scuttled around the room, trying to goad his faulty memory. Men in overalls were doing things. Simple, obvious things. But how childish – how elemental! Perhaps this was a kindergarten.

After a while Joe went out into a stock room and examined some finished models of combination radio-phonographs. So that was it. Awkward and clumsy, but it wasn't his place to say so. No. His job was to make Twonkies.

Twonkies? The name jolted his memory again. Of course he knew how to make Twonkies. He'd made them all his life – had been specially trained for the job. Now they were using a different model of Twonky, but what the hell! Child's play for a clever workman.

Joe went back into the shop and found a vacant bench. He began to build a Twonky. Occasionally he slipped off and stole the material he needed. Once, when he couldn't locate any tungsten, he hastily built a small gadget and made it.

His bench was in a distant corner, badly lighted, though it seemed quite bright to Joe's eyes. Nobody noticed the console that was swiftly growing to completion there. Joe worked very, very fast. He ignored the noon whistle, and, at quitting time, his task was finished. It could, perhaps, stand another coat of paint; it lacked the Shimmertone of a standard Twonky. But none of the others had Shimmertone. Joe sighed, crawled under the bench, looked in vain for a relaxopad, and went to sleep on the floor.

A few hours later he woke up. The factory was empty. Odd! Maybe the working hours had changed. Maybe – Joe's mind felt funny. Sleep had cleared away the mists of amnesia, if such it had been, but he still felt dazed.

Muttering under his breath, he sent the Twonky into the stock room and compared it with the others. Superficially it was identical with a console radio-phonograph combination of the latest model. Following the pattern of the others, Joe had camouflaged and disguised the various organs and reactors.

He went back into the shop. Then the last of the mists cleared from his mind. Joe's shoulders jerked convulsively.

'Great Snell!' he gasped. 'So that was it! I ran into a temporal snag!'

With a startled glance around, he fled to the storeroom from which he had first emerged. The overalls he took off and returned to their hook. After that, Joe went over to a corner, felt around in the air, nodded with satisfaction and seated himself on nothing, three feet above the floor. Then Joe vanished.

'Time,' said Kerry Westerfield, 'is curved. Eventually it gets back to the same place where it started. That's duplication.' He put his feet up on a conveniently outjutting rock of the chimney and stretched luxuriously. From the kitchen Martha made clinking noises with bottles and glasses.

'Yesterday at this time I had a Martini,' Kerry said. 'The time curve indicates that I should have another one now. Are you listening, angel?'

'I'm pouring,' said the angel distantly.

'You get my point, then. Here's another. Time describes a spiral instead of a circle. If you call the first cycle "a", the second one's "a plus I" – see? Which means a double Martini tonight.'

'I knew where that would end,' Martha remarked, coming into the spacious, oak-raftered living room. She was a small, dark-haired woman, with a singularly pretty face and a figure to match. Her tiny gingham apron looked slightly absurd in combination with slacks and silk blouse. 'And they don't make infinity-proof gin. Here's your Martini.' She did things with the shaker and manipulated glasses.

'Stir slowly,' Kerry cautioned. 'Never shake. Ah – that's it.' He accepted the drink and eyed it appreciatively. Black hair, sprinkled with gray, gleamed in the lamplight as he sipped the Martini. 'Good. Very good.'

Martha drank slowly and eyed her husband. A nice guy, Kerry Westerfield. He was forty-odd, pleasantly ugly, with a wide mouth and with an occasional sardonic gleam in his gray eyes as he contemplated life. They had been married for twelve years, and liked it.

From outside, the late, faint glow of sunset came through the windows, picking out the console cabinet that stood against the wall by the door. Kerry peered at it with appreciation.

'A pretty penny,' he remarked. 'Still –'

'What? Oh. The men had a tough time getting it up the stairs. Why don't you try it, Kerry?'

'Didn't you?'

'The old one was complicated enough,' Martha said in a baffled manner. 'Gadgets. They confuse me. I was brought up on an Edison. You wound it up with a crank, and strange noises came out of a horn. That I could understand. But now – you push a button, and extraordinary things happen. Electric eyes, tone selections, records that get played on both sides, to the accompaniment of weird groanings and clickings from inside the console – probably you understand those things. I don't even want to. Whenever I play a Crosby record in a super-duper like that, Bing seems embarrassed.'

Kerry ate his olive. 'I'm going to play some Debussy.' He nodded toward a table. 'There's a new Crosby record for you. The latest.'

Martha wriggled happily. 'Can I, maybe, huh?'

'Uh-huh.'

'But you'll have to show me how.'

'Simple enough,' said Kerry, beaming at the console. 'Those babies are pretty good, you know. They do everything but think.'

'I wish they'd wash the dishes,' Martha remarked. She set down her glass, got up and vanished into the kitchen.

Kerry snapped on a lamp nearby and went over to examine the new radio, Mideastern's latest model, with all the new improvements. It had been expensive – but what the hell? He could afford it. And the old one had been pretty well shot.

It was not, he saw, plugged in. Nor were there any wires in evidence – not even a ground. Something new, perhaps. Built-in antenna and ground. Kerry crouched down, looked for a socket, and plugged the cord into it.

That done, he opened the doors and eyed the dials with every appearance of satisfaction. A beam of bluish light shot out and hit him in the eyes. From the depths of the console a faint, thoughtful clicking proceeded. Abruptly it stopped. Kerry blinked, fiddled with dials and switches, and bit at a fingernail.

The radio said, in a distant voice, 'Psychology pattern checked and recorded.'

'Eh?' Kerry twirled a dial. 'Wonder what that was? Amateur station – no, they're off the air. Hm-m-m.' He shrugged and went over to a chair beside the shelves of albums. His gaze ran swiftly over the titles and composers' names. Where was the *Swan of Tuonela?* There it was, next to *Finlandia.* Kerry took down the album and opened it in his lap. With his free hand he extracted a cigarette from his pocket, put it between his lips and fumbled for the matches on the table beside him. The first match he lit went out.

He tossed it into the fireplace and was about to reach for another when a faint noise caught his attention. The radio was walking across the room toward him. A whiplike tendril flicked out from somewhere, picked up a match, scratched it beneath the table top – as Kerry had done – and held the flame to the man's cigarette.

Automatic reflexes took over. Kerry sucked in his breath, and exploded in smoky, racking coughs. He bent double, gasping and momentarily blind.

When he could see again, the radio was back in its accustomed place.

Kerry caught his lower lip between his teeth. 'Martha,' he called.

'Soup's on,' her voice said.

Kerry didn't answer. He stood up, went over to the radio and looked at it hesitantly. The electric cord had been pulled out of its socket. Kerry gingerly replaced it.

He crouched to examine the console's legs. They looked like finely finished wood. His exploratory hand told him nothing. Wood – hard and brittle.

How in hell –

'Dinner!' Martha called.

Kerry threw his cigarette into the fireplace and slowly walked out of the room. His wife, setting a gravy boat in place, stared at him.

'How many Martinis did you have?'

'Just one,' Kerry said in a vague way. 'I must have dozed off for a minute. Yeah. I must have.'

'Well, fall to,' Martha commanded. 'This is the last chance you'll have to make a pig of yourself on my dumplings, for a week, anyway.'

Kerry absently felt for his wallet, took out an envelope and tossed it at his wife. 'Here's your ticket, angel. Don't lose it.'

'Oh? I rate a compartment!' Martha thrust the pasteboard back into its envelope and gurgled happily. 'You're a pal. Sure you can get along without me?'

'Huh? Hm-m-m – I think so.' Kerry salted his avocado. He shook himself and seemed to come out of a slight daze. 'Sure, I'll be all right. You trot off to Denver and help Carol have her baby. It's all in the family.'

'We-ell, my only sister –' Martha grinned. 'You know how she and Bill are. Quite nuts. They'll need a steadying hand just now.'

There was no reply. Kerry was brooding over a forkful of avocado. He muttered something about the Venerable Bede.

'What about him?'

'Lecture tomorrow. Every term we bog down on the Bede, for some strange reason. Ah, well.'

'Got your lecture ready?'

Kerry nodded. 'Sure.' For eight years he had taught at the University, and he certainly should know the schedule by this time!

Later, over coffee and cigarettes, Martha glanced at her wrist watch. 'Nearly train time. I'd better finish packing. The dishes –'

'I'll do 'em.' Kerry wandered after his wife into the bedroom and made motions of futile helpfulness. After a while, he carried the bags down to the car. Martha joined him, and they headed for the depot.

The train was on time. Half an hour after it had pulled out, Kerry drove the car back into the garage, let himself into the house and yawned mightily. He was tired. Well, the dishes, and then beer and a book in bed.

With a puzzled look at the radio, he entered the kitchen and started on the dishes. The hall phone rang. Kerry wiped his hands on a dish towel and answered it.

It was Mike Fitzgerald, who taught psychology at the University.

'Hiya, Fitz.'

'Hiya. Martha gone?'

'Yeah. I just drove her to the train.'

'Feel like talking, then? I've got some pretty good Scotch. Why not run over and gab a while?'

'Like to,' Kerry said, yawning again, 'but I'm dead. Tomorrow's a big day. Rain check?'

'Sure. I just finished correcting papers, and felt the need of sharpening my mind. What's the matter?'

'Nothing. Wait a minute.' Kerry put down the phone and looked over his shoulder, scowling. Noises were coming from the kitchen. What the hell!

He went along the hall and stopped in the doorway, motionless and staring. The radio was washing the dishes.

After a while he returned to the phone. Fitzgerald said, 'Something?'

'My new radio,' Kerry told him carefully. 'It's washing the dishes.'

Fitz didn't answer for a moment. His laugh was a bit hesitant. 'Oh?'

'I'll call you back,' Kerry said, and hung up. He stood motionless for a while, chewing his lip. Then he walked back to the kitchen and paused to watch.

The radio's back was toward him. Several limber tentacles were manipulating the dishes, expertly sousing them in hot, soapy water, scrubbing them with the little mop, dipping them into the rinse water and then stacking them neatly in the metal rack. Those whip-lashes were the only sign of unusual activity. The legs were apparently solid.

'Hey!' Kerry said.

There was no response.

He sidled around till he could examine the radio more closely. The tentacles emerged from a slot under one of the dials. The electric cord was dangling. No juice, then. But what –

Kerry stepped back and fumbled out a cigarette. Instantly the radio turned, took a match from its container on the stove and walked forward. Kerry blinked, studying the legs. They couldn't be wood. They were bending as the – the thing moved, elastic as rubber. The radio had a peculiar sidling motion unlike anything else on earth.

It lit Kerry's cigarette and went back to the sink, where it resumed the dishwashing.

Kerry phoned Fitzgerald again. 'I wasn't kidding. I'm having hallucinations or something. That damned radio just lit a cigarette for me.'

'Wait a minute.' Fitzgerald's voice sounded undecided. 'This is a gag, eh?'

'No. And I don't think it's a hallucination, either. It's up your alley. Can you run over and test my knee-jerks?'

'All right,' Fitz said. 'Give me ten minutes. Have a drink ready.'

He hung up, and Kerry, laying the phone back into its cradle, turned to see the radio walking out of the kitchen toward the living room. Its square, box-like contour was subtly horrifying, like some bizarre sort of hobgoblin. Kerry shivered.

He followed the radio, to find it in its former place, motionless and impassive. He opened the doors, examining the turntable, the phonograph arm and the other buttons and gadgets. There was nothing apparently unusual. Again he touched the legs. They were not wood, after all. Some plastic, which seemed quite hard. Or – maybe they were wood, after all. It was difficult to make certain, without damaging the finish. Kerry felt a natural reluctance to use a knife on his new console.

He tried the radio, getting local stations without trouble. The tone was good – unusually good, he thought. The phonograph –

He picked up Halvorsen's *Entrance of the Boyars* at random and slipped it into place, closing the lid. No sound emerged. Investigation proved that the needle was moving rhythmically along the groove, but without audible result. Well?

Kerry removed the record as the doorbell rang. It was Fitzgerald, a gangling, saturnine man with a leathery, wrinkled face and a tousled mop of dull gray hair. He extended a large, bony hand.

'Where's my drink?'

'Lo, Fitz. Come in the kitchen. I'll mix. Highball?'

'Highball.'

'O.K.' Kerry led the way. 'Don't drink it just yet, though. I want to show you my new combination.'

'The one that washes dishes?' Fitzgerald asked. 'What else does it do?'

Kerry gave the other a glass. 'It won't play records.'

'Oh, well. A minor matter, if it'll do the housework. Let's take a look at it.' Fitzgerald went into the living room, selected *Afternoon of a Faun* and approached the radio. 'It isn't plugged in.'

'That doesn't matter a bit,' Kerry said wildly.

'Batteries?' Fitzgerald slipped the record in place and adjusted the switches. 'Ten inch – there. Now we'll see.' He beamed triumphantly at Kerry. 'Well? It's playing now.'

It was.

Kerry said, 'Try that Halvorsen piece. Here.' He handed the disk to Fitzgerald, who pushed the reject switch and watched the lever arm lift.

But this time the phonograph refused to play. It didn't like *Entrance of the Boyars*.

'That's funny,' Fitzgerald grunted. 'Probably the trouble's with the record. Let's try another.'

There was no trouble with *Daphnis and Chloë*. But the radio silently rejected the composer's *Bolero*.

Kerry sat down and pointed to a nearby chair. 'That doesn't prove anything. Come over here and watch. Don't drink anything yet. You, uh, you feel perfectly normal?'

'Sure. Well?'

Kerry took out a cigarette. The console walked across the room, picking up a match book on the way and politely held the flame. Then it went back to its place against the wall.

Fitzgerald didn't say anything. After a while he took a cigarette from his pocket and waited. Nothing happened.

'So?' Kerry asked.

'A robot. That's the only possible answer. Where in the name of Petrarch did you get it?'

'You don't seem much surprised.'

'I am, though. But I've seen robots before; Westinghouse tried it, you know. Only this –' Fitzgerald tapped his teeth with a nail. 'Who made it?'

'How the devil should I know?' Kerry demanded. 'The radio people, I suppose.'

Fitzgerald narrowed his eyes. 'Wait a minute. I don't quite understand –'

'There's nothing to understand. I bought this combination a few days ago. Turned in the old one. It was delivered this afternoon, and . . .' Kerry explained what had happened.

'You mean you didn't know it was a robot?'

'Exactly. I bought it as a radio. And – and – the damn thing seems almost alive to me.'

'Nope.' Fitzgerald shook his head, rose and inspected the console carefully. 'It's a new kind of robot. At least –' He hesitated. 'What else is there to think? I suggest you get in touch with the Mideastern people tomorrow and check up.'

'Let's open the cabinet and look inside,' Kerry suggested.

Fitzgerald was willing, but the experiment proved impossible. The presumably wooden panels weren't screwed into place, and there was no apparent way of opening the console. Kerry found a screwdriver and applied it, gingerly at first, then with a sort of repressed fury. He could neither pry free a panel or even scratch the dark, smooth finish of the cabinet.

'Damn!' he said finally. 'Well, your guess is as good as mine. It's a robot. Only I didn't know they could make 'em like this. And why in a radio?'

'Don't ask me.' Fitzgerald shrugged. 'Check up tomorrow. That's the first step. Naturally, I'm pretty baffled. If a new sort of specialized robot has been invented, why put it in a console? And what makes those legs move? There aren't any casters.'

'I've been wondering about that, too.'

'When it moves, the legs look – rubbery. But they're not. They're hard as – as hardwood. Or plastic.'

'I'm afraid of the thing,' Kerry said.

'Want to stay at my place tonight?'

'N-no. No. I guess not. The – robot can't hurt me.'

'I don't think it wants to. It's been helping you, hasn't it?'

'Yeah,' Kerry said, and went off to mix another drink.

The rest of the conversation was inconclusive. Fitzgerald, several hours later, went home rather worried. He wasn't as casual as he had pretended, for the sake of Kerry's nerves. The impingement of something so entirely unexpected on normal life was subtly frightening. And yet, as he had said, the robot didn't seem menacing.

*

Kerry went to bed, with a new detective mystery. The radio followed him into the bedroom and gently took the book out of his hand. Kerry instinctively snatched for it.

'Hey!' he said. 'What the devil –'

The radio went back into the living room. Kerry followed, in time to see the book replaced on the shelf. After a bit Kerry retreated, locking his door, and slept uneasily till dawn.

In dressing gown and slippers, he stumbled out to stare at the console. It was back in its former place, looking as though it had never moved. Kerry, rather white around the gills, made breakfast.

He was allowed only one cup of coffee. The radio appeared, reprovingly took the second cup from his hand and emptied it into the sink.

That was quite enough for Kerry Westerfield. He found his hat and topcoat and almost ran out of the house. He had a horrid feeling that the radio might follow him, but it didn't, luckily for his sanity. He was beginning to be worried.

During the morning he found time to telephone Mideastern. The salesman knew nothing. It was a standard model combination, the latest. If it wasn't giving satisfaction, of course, he'd be glad to –

'It's O.K.,' Kerry said. 'But who made the thing? That's what I want to find out.'

'One moment, sir.' There was a delay. 'It came from Mr Lloyd's department. One of our foremen.'

'Let me speak to him, please.'

But Lloyd wasn't very helpful. After much thought, he remembered that the combination had been placed in the stock room without a serial number. It had been added later.

'But who made it?'

'I just don't know. I can find out for you, I guess. Suppose I ring you back.'

'Don't forget,' Kerry said, and went back to his class. The lecture on the Venerable Bede wasn't too successful.

At lunch he saw Fitzgerald, who seemed relieved when Kerry came over to his table. 'Find out any more about your pet robot?' the psychology professor demanded.

No one else was within hearing. With a sigh Kerry sat down and lit a cigarette. 'Not a thing. It's a pleasure to be able to do this myself.' He drew smoke into his lungs. 'I phoned the company.'

'And?'

'They don't know anything. Except that it didn't have a serial number.'

'That may be significant,' Fitzgerald said.

Kerry told the other about the incidents of the book and the coffee, and

Fitzgerald squinted thoughtfully at his milk. 'I've given you some psych tests. Too much stimulation isn't good for you.'

'A detective yarn!'

'Carrying it a bit to extremes, I'll admit. But I can understand why the robot acted that way, though I dunno how it managed it.' He hesitated. 'Without intelligence, that is.'

'Intelligence?' Kerry licked his lips. 'I'm not so sure that it's just a machine. And I'm not crazy.'

'No, you're not. But you say the robot was in the front room. How could it tell what you were reading?'

'Short of X-ray vision and superfast scanning and assimilative powers, I can't imagine. Perhaps it doesn't want me to read anything.'

'You've said something,' Fitzgerald grunted. 'Know much about theoretical machines of that type?'

'Robots?'

'Purely theoretical. Your brain's a colloid, you know. Compact, complicated – but slow. Suppose you work out a gadget with a multimillion radioatom unit embedded in an insulating material. The result is a brain, Kerry. A brain with a tremendous number of units interacting at light-velocity speeds. A radio tube adjusts current flow when it's operating at forty million separate signals a second. And, theoretically, a radioatomic brain of the type I've mentioned could include perception, recognition, consideration, reaction and adjustment in a hundred-thousandth of a second.'

'Theory.'

'I've thought so. But I'd like to find out where your radio came from.'

A page came over. 'Telephone call for Mr Westerfield.'

Kerry excused himself and left. When he returned, there was a puzzled frown knitting his dark brows. Fitzgerald looked at him inquiringly.

'Guy named Lloyd, at the Mideastern plant. I was talking to him about the radio.'

'Any luck?'

Kerry shook his head. 'No. Well, not much. He didn't know who had built the thing.'

'But it was built in the plant?'

'Yes. About two weeks ago – but there's no record of who worked on it. Lloyd seemed to think that was very, very funny. If a radio's built in the plant, they know who put it together.'

'So?'

'So nothing. I asked him how to open the cabinet, and he said it was easy. Just unscrew the panel in back.'

'There aren't any screws,' Fitzgerald said.

'I know.'

They looked at one another.

Fitzgerald said, 'I'd give fifty bucks to find out whether that robot was really built only two weeks ago.'

'Why?'

'Because a radioatomic brain would need training. Even in such matters as the lighting of a cigarette.'

'It saw me light one.'

'And followed the example. The dishwashing – hm-m-m. Induction, I suppose. If that gadget has been trained, it's a robot. If it hasn't –' Fitzgerald stopped.

Kerry blinked. 'Yes?'

'I don't know what the devil it is. It bears the same relation to a robot that we bear to Eohippus. One thing I do know, Kerry; it's very probable that no scientist today has the knowledge it would take to make a – a thing like that.'

'You're arguing in circles,' Kerry said. 'It was made.'

'Uh-huh. But how – when – and by whom? That's what's got me worried.'

'Well, I've a class in five minutes. Why not come over tonight?'

'Can't. I'm lecturing at the Hall. I'll phone you after, though.'

With a nod Kerry went out, trying to dismiss the matter from his mind. He succeeded pretty well. But dining alone in a restaurant that night, he began to feel a general unwillingness to go home. A hobgoblin was waiting for him.

'Brandy,' he told the waiter. 'Make it double.'

Two hours later a taxi let Kerry out at his door. He was remarkably drunk. Things swam before his eyes. He walked unsteadily toward the porch, mounted the steps with exaggerated care and let himself into the house.

He switched on a lamp.

The radio came forward to meet him. Tentacles, thin but strong as metal, coiled gently around his body, holding him motionless. A pang of violent fear struck through Kerry. He struggled desperately and tried to yell, but his throat was dry.

From the radio panel a beam of yellow light shot out, blinding the man. It swung down, aimed at his chest. Abruptly a queer taste was perceptible under Kerry's tongue.

After a minute or so, the ray clicked out, the tentacles flashed back out of sight and the console returned to its corner. Kerry staggered weakly to a chair and relaxed, gulping.

He was sober. Which was quite impossible. Fourteen brandies infiltrate a definite amount of alcohol into the system. One can't wave a magic wand and instantly reach a state of sobriety. Yet that was exactly what had happened.

The – robot was trying to be helpful. Only Kerry would have preferred to remain drunk.

He got up gingerly and sidled past the radio to the bookshelf. One eye on the combination, he took down the detective novel he had tried to read on the preceding night. As he had expected, the radio took it from his hand and replaced it on the shelf. Kerry, remembering Fitzgerald's words, glanced at his watch. Reaction time, four seconds.

He took down a Chaucer and waited, but the radio didn't stir. However, when Kerry found a history volume, it was gently removed from his fingers. Reaction time, six seconds.

Kerry located a history twice as thick.

Reaction time, ten seconds.

Uh-huh. So the robot did read the books. That meant X-ray vision and superswift reactions. Jumping Jehoshaphat!

Kerry tested more books, wondering what the criterion was. *Alice in Wonderland* was snatched from his hand; Millay's poems were not. He made a list, with two columns, for future reference.

The robot, then, was not merely a servant. It was a censor. But what was the standard of comparison?

After a while he remembered his lecture tomorrow, and thumbed through his notes. Several points needed verification. Rather hesitantly he located the necessary reference book – and the robot took it away from him.

'Wait a minute,' Kerry said. 'I need that.' He tried to pull the volume out of the tentacle's grasp, without success. The console paid no attention. It calmly replaced the book on the shelf.

Kerry stood biting his lip. This was a bit too much. The damned robot was a monitor. He sidled toward the book, snatched it and was out in the hall before the radio could move.

The thing was coming after him. He could hear the soft padding of its – its feet. Kerry scurried into the bedroom and locked the door. He waited, heart thumping, as the knob was tried gently.

A wire-thin cilium crept through the crack of the door and fumbled with the key. Kerry suddenly jumped forward and shoved the auxiliary bolt into position. But that didn't help, either. The robot's precision tools – the specialized antennae – slid it back; and then the console opened the door, walked into the room and came toward Kerry.

He felt a touch of panic. With a little gasp he threw the book at the thing, and it caught it deftly. Apparently that was all that was wanted, for the radio turned and went out, rocking awkwardly on its rubbery legs, carrying the forbidden volume. Kerry cursed quietly.

The phone rang. It was Fitzgerald.

'Well? How'd you make out?'

'Have you got a copy of Cassen's *Social Literature of the Ages?*'

'I don't think so, no. Why?'

'I'll get it in the University library tomorrow, then.' Kerry explained what had happened. Fitzgerald whistled softly.

'Interfering, is it? Hm-m-m. I wonder ...'

'I'm afraid of the thing.'

'I don't think it means you any harm. You say it sobered you up?'

'Yeah. With a light ray. That isn't very logical.'

'It might be. The vibrationary equivalent of thiamine chloride.'

'Light?'

'There's vitamin content in sunlight, you know. That isn't the important point. It's censoring your reading – and apparently it reads the books, with superfast reactions. That gadget, whatever it is, isn't merely a robot.'

'You're telling me,' Kerry said grimly. 'It's a Hitler.'

Fitzgerald didn't laugh. Rather soberly, he suggested, 'Suppose you spend the night at my place?'

'No,' Kerry said, his voice stubborn. 'No so-and-so radio's going to chase me out of my house. I'll take an axe to the thing first.'

'We-ell, you know what you're doing, I suppose. Phone me if – if anything happens.'

'O.K.,' Kerry said, and hung up. He went into the living room and eyed the radio coldly. What the devil was it – and what was it trying to do? Certainly it wasn't merely a robot. Equally certainly, it wasn't alive, in the sense that a colloid brain is alive.

Lips thinned, he went over and fiddled with the dials and switches. A swing band's throbbing, erratic tempo came from the console. He tried the short-wave band – nothing unusual there. So?

So nothing. There was no answer.

After a while he went to bed.

At luncheon the next day he brought Cassen's *Social Literature* to show Fitzgerald.

'What about it?'

'Look here.' Kerry flipped the pages and indicated a passage. 'Does this mean anything to you?'

Fitzgerald read it. 'Yeah. The point seems to be that individualism is necessary for the production of literature. Right?'

Kerry looked at him. 'I don't know.'

'Eh?'

'My mind goes funny.'

Fitzgerald rumpled his gray hair, narrowing his eyes and watching the other man intently. 'Come again. I don't quite –'

With angry patience, Kerry said, 'This morning I went into the library and looked up this reference. I read it all right. But it didn't mean anything to me. Just words. Know how it is when you're fagged out and have been reading a lot? You'll run into a sentence with a lot of subjunctive clauses, and it doesn't percolate. Well, it was like that.'

'Read it now,' Fitzgerald said quietly, thrusting the book across the table.

Kerry obeyed, looking up with a wry smile. 'No good.'

'Read it aloud. I'll go over it with you, step by step.'

But that didn't help. Kerry seemed utterly unable to assimilate the sense of the passage.

'Semantic block, maybe,' Fitzgerald said, scratching his ear. 'Is this the first time it's happened?'

'Yes – no. I don't know.'

'Got any classes this afternoon? Good. Let's run over to your place.'

Kerry thrust away his plate. 'All right. I'm not hungry. Whenever you're ready –'

Half an hour later they were looking at the radio. It seemed quite harmless. Fitzgerald wasted some time trying to pry a panel off, but finally gave it up as a bad job. He found pencil and paper, seated himself opposite Kerry and began to ask questions.

At one point he paused. 'You didn't mention that before.'

'Forgot it, I guess.'

Fitzgerald tapped his teeth with the pencil. 'Hm-m-m. The first time the radio acted up –'

'It hit me in the eye with a blue light.'

'Not that. I mean – what it said.'

Kerry blinked. 'What it said?' He hesitated. '"Psychology pattern checked and noted," or something like that. I thought I'd tuned in on some station and got part of a quiz program or something. You mean –'

'Were the words easy to understand? Good English?'

'No, now that I remember it,' Kerry scowled. 'They were slurred quite a lot. Vowels stressed.'

'Uh-huh. Well, let's get on.' They tried a word-association test.

Finally Fitzgerald leaned back, frowning. 'I want to check this stuff with the last tests I gave you a few months ago. It looks funny to me – damned funny. I'd feel a lot better if I knew exactly what memory was. We've done considerable work on mnemonics – artificial memory. Still, it may not be that at all.'

'Eh?'

'That – machine. Either it's got an artificial memory, has been highly trained or else it's adjusted to a different milieu and culture. It has affected you – quite a lot.'

Kerry licked dry lips. 'How?'

'Implanted blocks in your mind. I haven't correlated them yet. When I do, we may be able to figure out some sort of answer. No, that thing isn't a robot. It's a lot more than that.'

Kerry took out a cigarette; the console walked across the room and lit it for him. The two men watched with a faint shrinking horror.

'You'd better stay with me tonight,' Fitzgerald suggested.

'No,' Kerry said. He shivered.

The next day Fitzgerald looked for Kerry at lunch, but the younger man did not appear. He telephoned the house, and Martha answered the call.

'Hello! When did you get back?'

'Hello, Fitz. About an hour ago. My sister went ahead and had her baby without me – so I came back.' She stopped, and Fitzgerald was alarmed at her tone.

'Where's Kerry?'

'He's here. Can you come over, Fitz? I'm worried.'

'What's the matter with him?'

'I – I don't know. Come right away.'

'O.K.,' Fitzgerald said, and hung up, biting his lips. He was worried. When, a short while later, he rang the Westerfield bell, he discovered that his nerves were badly out of control. But sight of Martha reassured him.

He followed her into the living room. Fitzgerald's glance went at once to the console, which was unchanged, and then to Kerry, seated motionless by a window. Kerry's face had a blank, dazed look. His pupils were dilated, and he seemed to recognize Fitzgerald only slowly.

'Hello, Fitz,' he said.

'How do you feel?'

Martha broke in. 'Fitz, what's wrong? Is he sick? Shall I call the doctor?'

Fitzgerald sat down. 'Have you noticed anything funny about that radio?'

'No. Why?'

'Then listen.' He told the whole story, watching incredulity struggle with reluctant belief on Martha's face. Presently she said, 'I can't quite –'

'If Kerry takes out a cigarette, the thing will light it for him. Want to see how it works?'

'N-no. Yes. I suppose so.' Martha's eyes were wide.

Fitzgerald gave Kerry a cigarette. The expected happened.

Martha didn't say a word. When the console had returned to its place, she shivered and went over to Kerry. He looked at her vaguely.

'He needs a doctor, Fitz.'

'Yes.' Fitzgerald didn't mention that a doctor might be quite useless.

'What is that thing?'

'It's more than a robot. And it's been readjusting Kerry. I told you what's happened. When I checked Kerry's psychology patterns, I found that they'd altered. He's lost most of his initiative.'

'Nobody on earth could have made that –'

Fitzgerald scowled. 'I thought of that. It seems to be the product of a well-developed culture, quite different from ours. Martian, perhaps. It's such a specialized thing that it naturally fits into a complicated culture. But I do not understand why it looks exactly like a Mideastern console radio.'

Martha touched Kerry's hand. 'Camouflage?'

'But why? You were one of my best pupils in psych, Martha. Look at this logically. Imagine a civilization where a gadget like that has its place. Use inductive reasoning.'

'I'm trying to. I can't think very well. Fitz, I'm worried about Kerry.'

'I'm all right,' Kerry said.

Fitzgerald put his finger tips together. 'It isn't a radio so much as a monitor. In this other civilization, perhaps every man has one, or maybe only a few – the ones who need it. It keeps them in line.'

'By destroying initiative?'

Fitzgerald made a helpless gesture. 'I don't know! It worked that way in Kerry's case. In others – I don't know.'

Martha stood up. 'I don't think we should talk any more. Kerry needs a doctor. After that we can decide upon that.' She pointed to the console.

Fitzgerald said, 'It'd be rather a shame to wreck it, but –' His look was significant.

The console moved. It came out from its corner with a sidling, rocking gait and walked toward Fitzgerald. As he sprang up, the whiplike tentacles flashed out and seized him. A pale ray shone into the man's eyes.

Almost instantly it vanished; the tentacles withdrew, and the radio returned to its place. Fitzgerald stood motionless. Martha was on her feet, one hand at her mouth.

'Fitz!' Her voice shook.

He hesitated. 'Yes? What's the matter?'

'Are you hurt? What did it do to you?'

Fitzgerald frowned a little. 'Eh? Hurt? I don't –'

'The radio. What did it do?'

He looked toward the console. 'Something wrong with it? Afraid I'm not much of a repairman, Martha.'

'Fitz.' She came forward and gripped his arm. 'Listen to me.' Quick words spilled from her mouth. The radio. Kerry. Their discussion.

Fitzgerald looked at her blankly, as though he didn't quite understand. 'I guess I'm stupid today. I can't quite understand what you're talking about.'

'The radio – you know! You said it changed Kerry –' Martha paused, staring at the man.

Fitzgerald was definitely puzzled. Martha was acting strangely. Queer! He'd always considered her a pretty level-headed girl. But now she was talking nonsense. At least, he couldn't figure out the meaning of her words; there was no sense to them.

And why was she talking about the radio? Wasn't it satisfactory? Kerry had said it was a good buy, with a fine tone and the latest gadgets in it. Fitzgerald wondered, for a fleeting second, if Martha had gone crazy.

In any case, he was late for his class. He said so. Martha didn't try to stop him when he went out. She was pale as chalk.

Kerry took out a cigarette. The radio walked over and held a match.

'Kerry!'

'Yes, Martha?' His voice was dead.

She stared at the – the radio. Mars? Another world – another civilization? What was it? What did it want? What was it trying to do?

Martha let herself out of the house and went to the garage. When she returned, a small hatchet was gripped tightly in her hand.

Kerry watched. He saw Martha walk over to the radio and lift the hatchet. Then a beam of light shot out, and Martha vanished. A little dust floated up in the afternoon sunlight.

'Destruction of life-form threatening attack,' the radio said, slurring the words together.

Kerry's brain turned over. He felt sick – dazed and horribly empty. Martha –

His mind churned. Instinct and emotion fought with something that smothered them. Abruptly the dams crumbled, and the blocks were gone, the barriers down. Kerry cried out hoarsely, inarticulately, and sprang to his feet.

'Martha!' he yelled.

She was gone. Kerry looked around. Where –

What had happened? He couldn't remember.

He sat down in the chair again, rubbing his forehead. His free hand brought up a cigarette, an automatic reaction that brought instant response. The radio walked forward and held a lighted match ready.

Kerry made a choking, sick sound and flung himself out of the chair. He remembered now. He picked up the hatchet and sprang toward the console, teeth bared in a mirthless rictus.

Again the light beam flashed out.

Kerry vanished. The hatchet thudded on to the carpet.

The radio walked back to its place and stood motionless once more. A faint clicking proceeded from its radioatomic brain.

'Subject basically unsuitable,' it said, after a moment. 'Elimination has been necessary.' Click! 'Preparation for next subject completed.'

Click.

*

'We'll take it,' the boy said.

'You won't be making a mistake,' smiled the rental agent. 'It's quiet, isolated and the price is quite reasonable.'

'Not so very,' the girl put in. 'But it is just what we've been looking for.'

The agent shrugged. 'Of course, an unfurnished place would run less. But –'

'We haven't been married long enough to have any furniture,' the boy grinned. He put an arm around his wife. 'Like it, hon?'

'Hm-m-m. Who lived here before?'

The agent scratched his cheek. 'Let's see. Some people named Westerfield, I think. It was given to me for listing just about a week ago. Nice place. If I didn't own my own house, I'd jump at it myself.'

'Nice radio,' the boy said. 'Late model, isn't it?' He went over to examine the console.

'Come along,' the girl urged. 'Let's look at the kitchen again.'

'O.K., hon.'

They went out of the room. From the hall came the sound of the agent's smooth voice, growing fainter. Warm afternoon sunlight slanted through the windows.

For a moment there was silence. Then –

Click!

A GNOME THERE WAS

Tim Crockett should never have sneaked into the mine on Dornsef Mountain. What is winked at in California may have disastrous results in the coal mines of Pennsylvania. Especially when gnomes are involved.

Not that Tim Crockett knew about the gnomes. He was just investigating conditions among the lower classes, to use his own rather ill-chosen words. He was one of a group of southern Californians who had decided that labor needed them. They were wrong. They needed labor – at least eight hours of it a day.

Crockett, like his colleagues, considered the laborer a combination of a gorilla and The Man with the Hoe, probably numbering the Kallikaks among his ancestors. He spoke fierily of down-trodden minorities, wrote incendiary articles for the group's organ, *Earth,* and deftly maneuvered himself out of entering his father's law office as a clerk. He had, he said, a mission. Unfortunately, he got little sympathy from either the workers or their oppressors.

A psychologist could have analyzed Crockett easily enough. He was a tall, thin, intense-looking young man, with rather beady little eyes, and a nice taste in neckties. All he needed was a vigorous kick in the pants.

But definitely not administered by a gnome!

He was junketing through the country, on his father's money, investigating labor conditions, to the profound annoyance of such laborers as he encountered. It was with this idea in mind that he surreptitiously got into the Ajax coal mine – or, at least, one shaft of it – after disguising himself as a miner and rubbing his face well with black dust. Going down in the lift, he looked singularly untidy in the midst of a group of well-scrubbed faces. Miners look dirty only after a day's work.

Dornsef Mountain is honeycombed, but not with the shafts of the Ajax Company. The gnomes have ways of blocking their tunnels when humans dig too close. The whole place was a complete confusion to Crockett. He let himself drift along with the others, till they began to work. A filled car rumbled past on its tracks. Crockett hesitated, and then sidled over to a husky specimen who seemed to have the marks of a great sorrow stamped on his face.

'Look,' he said, 'I want to talk to you.'

'Inglis?' asked the other inquiringly. 'Viskey. Chin. Vine. Hell.'

Having thus demonstrated his somewhat incomplete command of English, he bellowed hoarsely with laughter and returned to work, ignoring the baffled Crockett, who turned away to find another victim. But this section of the mine seemed deserted. Another loaded car rumbled past, and Crockett decided to see where it came from. He found out, after banging his head painfully and falling flat at least five times.

It came from a hole in the wall. Crockett entered it, and simultaneously heard a hoarse cry from behind him. The unknown requested Crockett to come back.

'So I can break your slab-sided neck,' he promised, adding a stream of sizzling profanity. 'Come outa there!'

Crockett cast one glance back, saw a gorillalike shadow lurching after him, and instantly decided that his stratagem had been discovered. The owners of the Ajax mine had sent a strong-arm man to murder him – or, at least, to beat him to a senseless pulp. Terror lent wings to Crockett's flying feet. He rushed on, frantically searching for a side tunnel in which he might lose himself. The bellowing from behind re-echoed against the walls. Abruptly Crockett caught a significant sentence clearly.

'– before that dynamite goes off!'

It was at that exact moment that the dynamite went off.

Crockett, however, did not know it. He discovered, quite briefly, that he was flying. Then he was halted, with painful suddenness, by the roof. After that he knew nothing at all, till he recovered to find a head regarding him steadfastly.

It was not a comforting sort of head – not one at which you would instinctively clutch for companionship. It was, in fact, a singularly odd, if not actually revolting, head. Crockett was too much engrossed with staring at it to realize that he was actually seeing in the dark.

How long had he been unconscious? For some obscure reason Crockett felt that it had been quite a while. The explosion had – what?

Buried him here behind a fallen roof of rock? Crockett would have felt little better had he known that he was in a used-up shaft, valueless now, which had been abandoned long since. The miners, blasting to open a new shaft, had realized that the old one would be collapsed, but that didn't matter.

Except to Tim Crockett.

He blinked, and when he reopened his eyes, the head had vanished. This was a relief. Crockett immediately decided the unpleasant thing had been a delusion. Indeed, it was difficult to remember what it had looked like. There was only a vague impression of a turnip-shaped outline, large, luminous eyes, and an incredibly broad slit of a mouth.

Crockett sat up, groaning. Where was this curious silvery radiance coming from? It was like daylight on a foggy afternoon, coming from nowhere in particular, and throwing no shadows. 'Radium,' thought Crockett, who knew very little of mineralogy.

He was in a shaft that stretched ahead into dimness till it made a sharp turn perhaps fifty feet away. Behind him – behind him the roof had fallen. Instantly Crockett began to experience difficulty in breathing. He flung himself upon the rubbly mound, tossing rocks frantically here and there, gasping and making hoarse, inarticulate noises.

He became aware, presently, of his hands. His movements slowed till he remained perfectly motionless, in a half-crouching posture, glaring at the large, knobbly, and surprising objects that grew from his wrists. Could he, during his period of unconsciousness, have acquired mittens? Even as the thought came to him, Crockett realized that no mittens ever knitted resembled in the slightest degree what he had a right to believe to be his hands. They twitched slightly.

Possibly they were caked with mud – no. It wasn't that. His hands had – altered. They were huge, gnarled, brown objects, like knotted oak roots. Sparse black hairs sprouted on their backs. The nails were definitely in need of a manicure – preferably with a chisel.

Crockett looked down at himself. He made soft cheeping noises, indicative of disbelief. He had squat bow legs, thick and strong, and no more than two feet long – less, if anything. Uncertain with disbelief, Crockett explored his body. It had changed – certainly not for the better.

He was slightly more than four feet high, and about three feet wide, with a barrel chest, enormous splay feet, stubby thick legs, and no neck whatsoever. He was wearing red sandals, blue shorts, and a red tunic which left his lean but sinewy arms bare. His head –

Turnip-shaped. The mouth – *Yipe!* Crockett had inadvertently put his fist clear into it. He withdrew the offending hand instantly, stared around in a dazed fashion, and collapsed on the ground. It couldn't be happening. It was quite impossible. Hallucinations. He was dying of asphyxiation, and delusions were preceding his death.

Crockett shut his eyes, again convinced that his lungs were laboring for breath. 'I'm dying,' he said. 'I c-can't breathe.'

A contemptuous voice said, 'I hope you don't think you're breathing *air*!'

'I'm n-not –' Crockett didn't finish the sentence. His eyes popped again. He was hearing things.

He heard it again. 'You're a singularly lousy specimen of gnome,' the voice said. 'But under Nid's law we can't pick and choose. Still, you won't be put to digging hard metals, I can see that. Anthracite's about your speed. What're you staring at? You're *very* much uglier than I am.'

Crockett, endeavoring to lick his dry lips, was horrified to discover the end of his moist tongue dragging limply over his eyes. He whipped it back, with a loud smacking noise, and managed to sit up. Then he remained perfectly motionless, staring.

The head had reappeared. This time there was a body under it.

'I'm Gru Magru,' said the head chattily. 'You'll be given a gnomic name, of course, unless your own is guttural enough. What is it?'

'Crockett,' the man responded, in a stunned, automatic manner.

'Hey?'

'Crockett.'

'Stop making noises like a frog and – oh, I see Crockett. Fair enough. Now get up and follow me or I'll kick the pants off you.'

But Crockett did not immediately rise. He was watching Gru Magru – obviously a gnome. Short, squat and stunted, the being's figure resembled a bulging little barrel, topped by an inverted turnip. The hair grew up thickly to a peak – the root, as it were. In the turnip face was a loose, immense slit of a mouth, a button of a nose, and two very large eyes.

'Get *up!*' Gru Magru said.

This time Crockett obeyed, but the effort exhausted him completely. If he moved again, he thought, he would go mad. It would be just as well. Gnomes –

Gru Magru planted a large splay foot where it would do the most good, and Crockett described an arc which ended at a jagged boulder fallen from the roof. 'Get up,' the gnome said, with gratuitous bad temper, 'or I'll kick you again. It's bad enough to have an outlying prospect patrol, where I might run into a man any time, without – *Up!* Or –'

Crockett got up. Gru Magru took his arm and impelled him into the depths of the tunnel.

'Well, you're a gnome now,' he said. 'It's the Nid law. Sometimes I wonder if it's worth the trouble. But I suppose it is – since gnomes can't propagate, and the average population has to be kept up somehow.'

'I want to die,' Crockett said wildly.

Gru Magru laughed. 'Gnomes *can't* die. They're immortal, till the Day. Judgment Day, I mean.'

'You're not logical,' Crockett pointed out, as though by disproving one factor he could automatically disprove the whole fantastic business. 'You're either flesh and blood and have to die eventually, or you're not, and then you're not real.'

'Oh, we're flesh and blood, right enough,' Gru Magru said. 'But we're not mortal. There's a distinction. Not that I've anything against some mortals,' he hastened to explain. 'Bats, now – and owls – they're fine. But men!' He shuddered. 'No gnome can stand the sight of a man.'

Crockett clutched at a straw. 'I'm a man.'

'You were, you mean,' Gru said. 'Not a very good specimen, either, for my ore. But you're a gnome now. It's the Nid law.'

'You keep talking about the Nid law,' Crockett complained.

'Of course you don't understand,' said Gru Magru, in a patronizing fashion. 'It's this way. Back in ancient times, it was decreed that if any humans got lost in underearth, a tithe of them would be transformed into gnomes. The first gnome emperor, Podrang the Third, arranged that. He saw that fairies could kidnap human children and keep them, and spoke to the authorities about it. Said it was unfair. So when miners and such-like are lost underneath, a tithe of them are transformed into gnomes and join us. That's what happened to you. See?'

'No,' Crockett said weakly. 'Look. You said Podrang was the first gnome emperor. Why was he called Podrang the Third?'

'No time for questions,' Gru Magru snapped. 'Hurry!'

He was almost running now, dragging the wretched Crockett after him. The new gnome had not yet mastered his rather unusual limbs, and, due to the extreme wideness of his sandals, he trod heavily on his right hand, but after that learned to keep his arms bent and close to his sides. The walls, illuminated with that queer silvery radiance, spun past dizzily.

'W-what's that light?' Crockett managed to gasp. 'Where's it coming from?'

'Light?' Gru Magru inquired. 'It isn't light.'

'Well, it isn't dark –'

'Of course it's dark,' the gnome snapped. 'How could we see if it wasn't dark?'

There was no possible answer to this, except, Crockett thought wildly, a frantic shriek. And he needed all his breath for running. They were in a labyrinth now, turning and twisting and doubling through innumerable tunnels, and Crockett knew he could never retrace his steps. He regretted having left the scene of the cave-in. But how could he have helped doing so?

'Hurry!' Gru Magru urged. 'Hurry!'

'Why?' Crockett got out breathlessly.

'There's a fight going on!' the gnome said.

Just then they rounded a corner and almost blundered into the fight. A seething mass of gnomes filled the tunnel, battling with frantic fury. Red and blue pants and tunics moved in swift patchwork frenzy; turnip heads popped up and down vigorously. It was apparently a free-for-all.

'See!' Gru gloated. 'A fight! I could smell it six tunnels away. Oh, a beauty!' He ducked as a malicious-looking little gnome sprang out of the huddle to seize a rock and hurl it with vicious accuracy. The missile missed its mark, and Gru, neglecting his captive, immediately hurled himself upon the little gnome, bore him down on the cave floor, and began to beat his head against it. Both parties shrieked at the tops of their voices, which were lost in the deafening din that resounded through the tunnel.

'Oh – my,' Crockett said weakly. He stood staring, which was a mistake. A very large gnome emerged from the pile, seized Crockett by the feet, and threw him away. The terrified inadvertent projectile sailed through the tunnel to crash heavily into something which said, *'Whoo-doof!'* There was a tangle of malformed arms and legs.

Crockett arose to find that he had downed a vicious-looking gnome with flaming red hair and four large diamond buttons on his tunic. This repulsive creature lay motionless, out for the count. Crockett took stock of his injuries – there were none. His new body was hardy, anyway.

'You saved me!' said a new voice. It belonged to a – lady gnome. Crockett decided that if there was anything uglier than a gnome, it was the female of the species. The creature stood crouching just behind him, clutching a large rock in one capable hand.

Crockett ducked.

'I won't hurt you,' the other howled above the din that filled the passage. 'You saved me! Mugza was trying to pull my ears off – oh! He's waking up!'

The red-haired gnome was indeed recovering consciousness. His first act was to draw up his feet and, without rising, kick Crockett clear across the tunnel. The feminine gnome immediately sat on Mugza's chest and pounded his head with the rock till he subsided.

Then she arose. 'You're not hurt? Good! I'm Brockle Buhn ... Oh, look! He'll have his head off in a minute!'

Crockett turned to see that his erstwhile guide, Gru Magru, was gnomefully tugging at the head of an unidentified opponent, attempting, apparently, to twist it clear off. 'What's it all about?' Crockett howled. 'Uh – Brockle Buhn! *Brockle Buhn!*'

She turned unwillingly. 'What?'

'The fight! What started it?'

'I did,' she explained. 'I said, "Let's have a fight."'

'Oh, that was all?'

'Then we started.' Brockle Buhn nodded. 'What's your name?'

'Crockett.'

'You're new here, aren't you? Oh – I know. You were a human being!' Suddenly a new light appeared in her bulging eyes. 'Crockett, maybe you can tell me something. What's a kiss?'

'A – kiss?' Crockett repeated, in a baffled manner.

'Yes. I was listening inside a knoll once, and heard two human beings talking – male and female, by their voices. I didn't dare look at them, of course, but the man asked the woman for a kiss.'

'Oh,' Crockett said, rather blankly. 'He asked for a kiss, eh?'

'And then there was a smacking noise and the woman said it was wonderful. I've wondered ever since. Because if any gnome asked me for a kiss, I wouldn't know what he meant.'

'Gnomes don't kiss?' Crockett asked in a perfunctory way.

'Gnomes dig,' said Brockle Buhn. 'And we eat. I like to eat. Is a kiss like mud soup?'

'Well, not exactly.' Somehow Crockett managed to explain the mechanics of osculation.

The gnome remained silent, pondering deeply. At last she said, with the air of one bestowing mud soup upon a hungry applicant, 'I'll give you a kiss.'

Crockett had a nightmare picture of his whole head being engulfed in that enormous maw. He backed away. 'N-no,' he got out. 'I – I'd rather not.'

'Then let's fight,' said Brockle Buhn, without rancor, and swung a knotted fist which smacked painfully athwart Crockett's ear. 'Oh, no,' she said regretfully, turning away. 'The fight's over. It wasn't very long, was it?'

Crockett, rubbing his mangled ear, saw that in every direction gnomes were picking themselves up and hurrying off about their business. They seemed to have forgotten all about the recent conflict. The tunnel was once more silent, save for the pad-padding of gnomes' feet on the rock. Gru Magru came over, grinning happily.

'Hello, Brockle Buhn,' he greeted. 'A good fight. Who's this?' He looked down at the prostrate body of Mugza, the red-haired gnome.

'Mugza,' said Brockle Buhn. 'He's still out. Let's kick him.'

They proceeded to do it with vast enthusiasm, while Crockett watched and decided never to allow himself to be knocked unconscious. It definitely wasn't safe. At last, however, Gru Magru tired of the sport and took Crockett by the arm again. 'Come along,' he said, and they sauntered along the tunnel, leaving Brockle Buhn jumping up and down on the senseless Mugza's stomach.

'You don't seem to mind hitting people when they're knocked out,' Crockett hazarded.

'It's *much* more fun,' Gru said happily. 'That way you can tell just where you want to hit 'em. Come along. You'll have to be inducted. Another day, another gnome. Keeps the population stable,' he explained, and fell to humming a little song.

'Look,' Crockett said. 'I just thought of something. You say human beings are turned into gnomes to keep the population stable. But if gnomes don't die, doesn't that mean that there are more gnomes now than ever? The population keeps rising, doesn't it?'

'Be still,' Gru Magru commanded. 'I'm singing.'

It was a singularly tuneless song. Crockett, his thoughts veering madly, wondered if the gnomes had a national anthem. Probably 'Rock Me to Sleep.' Oh, well.

'We're going to see the Emperor,' Gru said at last. 'He always sees the new gnomes. You'd better make a good impression, or he'll put you to placer-mining lava.'

'Uh –' Crockett glanced down at his grimy tunic. 'Hadn't I better clean up a bit? That fight made me a mess.'

'It wasn't the fight,' Gru said insultingly. 'What's wrong with you, anyway? I don't see anything amiss.'

'My clothes – they're dirty.'

'Don't worry about that,' said the other. 'It's good filthy dirt, isn't it? Here!' He halted, and, stooping, seized a handful of dust, which he rubbed into Crockett's face and hair. 'That'll fix you up.'

'I – *pffht!* ... Thanks ... *pffh!*' said the newest gnome. 'I hope I'm dreaming. Because if I'm not –' He didn't finish. Crockett was feeling unwell.

They went through a labyrinth, far under Dornsef Mountain, and emerged at last in a bare, huge chamber with a throne of rock at one end of it. A small gnome was sitting on the throne paring his toenails. 'Bottom of the day to you,' Gru said. 'Where's the Emperor?'

'Taking a bath,' said the other. 'I hope he drowns. Mud, mud, mud – morning, noon and night. First it's too hot. Then it's too cold. Then it's too thick. I work my fingers to the bone mixing his mud baths, and all I get is a kick,' the small gnome continued plaintively. 'There's such a thing as being *too* dirty. Three mud baths a day – that's carrying it too far. And never a thought for me! Oh, no. I'm a mud puppy, that's what I am. He called me that today. Said there were lumps in the mud. Well, why not? That damned loam we've been getting is enough to turn a worm's stomach. You'll find His Majesty in there,' the little gnome finished, jerking his foot toward an archway in the wall.

Crockett was dragged into the next room, where, in a sunken bath filled with steaming, brown mud, a very fat gnome sat, only his eyes discernible through the oozy coating that covered him. He was filling his hands with mud and letting it drip over his head, chuckling in a senile sort of way as he did so.

'Mud,' he remarked pleasantly to Gru Magru, in a voice like a lion's bellow. 'Nothing like it. Good rich mud. *Ah!*'

Gru was bumping his head on the floor, his large, capable hand around Crockett's neck forcing the other to follow suit.

'Oh, get up,' said the Emperor. 'What's this? What's this gnome been up to? Out with it.'

'He's new,' Gru explained. 'I found him topside. The Nid law, you know.'

'Yes, of course. Let's have a look at you. Ugh! I'm Podrang the Second, Emperor of the Gnomes. What have you to say to that?'

All Crockett could think of was: 'How – how can you be Podrang the Second? I thought Podrang the Third was the first emperor.'

'A chatterbox,' said Podrang II, disappearing beneath the surface of the mud and spouting as he rose again. 'Take care of him, Gru. Easy work at first. Digging anthracite. Mind you don't eat any while you're on the job,' he cautioned the dazed Crockett. 'After you've been here a century, you're allowed one mud bath a day. Nothing like 'em,' he added, bringing up a gluey handful to smear over his face.

Abruptly he stiffened. His lion's bellow rang out.

'Drook! *Drook!*'

The little gnome Crockett had seen in the throne room scurried in, wringing his hands. 'Your Majesty! Isn't the mud warm enough?'

'You crawling blob!' roared Podrang II. 'You slobbering, offspring of six thousand individual offensive stenches! You mica-eyed, incompetent, draggle-eared, writhing blot on the good name of gnomes! You geological mistake! You – you –'

Drook took advantage of his master's temporary inarticulacy. 'It's the best mud, Your Majesty! I refined it myself. Oh, Your Majesty, what's wrong?'

'There's a worm in it!' His Majesty bellowed, and launched into a stream of profanity so horrendous that it practically made the mud boil. Clutching his singed ears, Crockett allowed Gru Magru to drag him away.

'I'd like to get the old boy in a fight,' Gru remarked, when they were safely in the depths of a tunnel, 'but he'd use magic, of course. That's the way he is. Best emperor we've ever had. Not a scrap of fair play in his bloated body.'

'Oh,' Crockett said blankly. 'Well, what next?'

'You heard Podrang, didn't you? You dig anthracite. And if you eat any, I'll kick your teeth in.'

Brooding over the apparent bad tempers of gnomes, Crockett allowed himself to be conducted to a gallery where dozens of gnomes, both male and female, were using picks and mattocks with furious vigor. 'This is it,' Gru said. 'Now! You dig anthracite. You work twenty hours, and then sleep six.'

'Then what?'

'Then you start digging again,' Gru explained. 'You have a brief rest once every ten hours. You mustn't stop digging in between, unless it's for a fight. Now, here's the way you locate coal. Just think of it.'

'Eh?'

'How do you think I found you?' Gru asked impatiently. 'Gnomes have – certain senses. There's a legend that fairy folk can locate water by using a forked stick. Well, we're attracted to metals. Think of anthracite,' he finished, and Crockett obeyed. Instantly he found himself turning to the wall of the tunnel nearest him.

'See how it works?' Gru grinned. 'It's a natural evolution, I suppose. Functional. We have to know where the underneath deposits are, so the authorities gave us this sense when we were created. Think of ore – or any deposit in the ground – and you'll be attracted to it. Just as there's a repulsion in all gnomes against daylight.'

'Eh?' Crockett started slightly. 'What was that?'

'Negative and positive. We need ores, so we're attracted to them. Daylight is harmful to us, so if we think we're getting too close to the surface, we think of light, and it repels us. Try it!'

Crockett obeyed. Something seemed to be pressing down the top of his head.

'Straight up,' Gru nodded. 'But it's a long way. I saw daylight once. And – a man, too.' He stared at the other. 'I forgot to explain. Gnomes can't stand the sight of human beings. They – well, there's a limit to how much ugliness a gnome can look at. Now you're one of us, you'll feel the same way. Keep away from daylight, and never look at a man. It's as much as your sanity is worth.'

There was a thought stirring in Crockett's mind. He could, then, find his way out of this maze of tunnels, simply by employing his new sense to lead him to daylight. After that – well, at least he would be above ground.

Gru Magru shoved Crockett into a place between two busy gnomes and thrust a pick into his hands. 'There. Get to work.'

'Thanks for –' Crockett began, when Gru suddenly kicked him and then took his departure, humming happily to himself. Another gnome came up, saw Crockett standing motionless, and told him to get busy, accompanying the command with a blow on his already tender ear. Perforce Crockett seized the pick and began to chop anthracite out of the wall.

'Crockett!' said a familiar voice. 'It's you! I thought they'd send you here.'

It was Brockle Buhn, the feminine gnome Crockett had already encountered. She was swinging a pick with the others, but dropped it now to grin at her companion.

'You won't be here long,' she consoled. 'Ten years or so. Unless you run into trouble, and then you'll be put at really hard work.'

Crockett's arms were already aching. '*Hard* work! My arms are going to fall off in a minute.'

He leaned on his pick. 'Is this your regular job?'

'Yes – but I'm seldom here. Usually I'm being punished. I'm a troublemaker, I am. I eat anthracite.'

She demonstrated, and Crockett shuddered at the audible crunching sound. Just then the overseer came up. Brockle Buhn swallowed hastily.

'What's this? he snarled. 'Why aren't you at work?'

'We were just going to fight,' Brockle Buhn explained.

'Oh – just the two of you? Or can I join in?'

'Free for all,' the unladylike gnome offered, and struck the unsuspecting Crockett over the head with her pick. He went out like a light.

Awakening some time later, he investigated bruised ribs and decided Brockle Buhn must have kicked him after he'd lost consciousness. What a gnome! Crockett sat up, finding himself in the same tunnel, dozens of gnomes busily digging anthracite.

The overseer came toward him. 'Awake, eh? Get to work!'

Dazedly Crockett obeyed. Brockle Buhn flashed him a delighted grin. 'You missed it. I got an ear – see?' She exhibited it. Crockett hastily lifted an exploring hand. It wasn't his.

Dig … dig … dig … the hours dragged past. Crockett had never worked so hard in his life. But, he noticed, not a gnome complained. Twenty hours of toil, with one brief rest period – he'd slept through that. Dig … dig … dig …

Without ceasing her work, Brockle Buhn said, 'I think you'll make a good gnome, Crockett. You're toughening up already. Nobody'd ever believe you were once a man.'

'Oh – no?'

'No. What were you, a miner?'

'I was –' Crockett paused suddenly. A curious light came into his eyes. 'I was a labor organizer,' he finished.

'What's that?'

'Ever heard of a union?' Crockett asked, his gaze intent.

'Is it an ore?' Brockle Buhn shook her head. 'No, I've never heard of it. What's a union?'

Crockett explained. No genuine labor organizer would have accepted that explanation. It was, to say the least, biased.

Brockle Buhn seemed puzzled. 'I don't see what you mean, exactly, but I suppose it's all right.'

'Try another tack,' Crockett said. 'Don't you ever get tired of working twenty hours a day?'

'Sure. Who wouldn't?'

'Then why do it?'

'We always have,' Brockle Buhn said indulgently. 'We can't stop.'

'Suppose you did?'

'I'd be punished – beaten with stalactites, or something.'

'Suppose you all did,' Crockett insisted. 'Every damn gnome. Suppose you had a sit-down strike.'

'You're crazy,' Brockle Buhn said. 'Such a thing's never happened. It – it's *human.*'

'Kisses never happened underground, either,' said Crockett. 'No, I don't want one! And I don't want to fight, either. Good heavens, let me get the set-up here. Most of the gnomes work to support the privileged classes.'

'No. We just work.'

'But why?'

'We always have. And the Emperor wants us to.'

'Has the Emperor ever worked?' Crockett demanded, with an air of triumph. 'No! He just takes mud baths! Why shouldn't every gnome have the same privilege? Why –'

He talked on, at great length, as he worked. Brockle Buhn listened with increasing interest. And eventually she swallowed the bait – hook, line and sinker.

An hour later she was nodding agreeably. 'I'll pass the word along. Tonight. In the Roaring Cave. Right after work.'

'Wait a minute,' Crockett objected. 'How many gnomes can we get?'

'Well – not very many. Thirty?'

'We'll have to organize first. We'll need a definite plan.'

Brockle Buhn went off at a tangent. 'Let's fight.'

'No! Will you listen? We need a – a council. Who's the worst trouble-maker here?'

'Mugza, I think,' she said. 'The red-haired gnome you knocked out when he hit me.'

Crockett frowned slightly. Would Mugza hold a grudge? Probably not, he decided. Or, rather, he'd be no more ill tempered than other gnomes. Mugza might attempt to throttle Crockett on sight, but he'd no doubt do the same to any other gnome. Besides, as Brockle Buhn went on to explain, Mugza was the gnomic equivalent of a duke. His support would be valuable.

'And Gru Magru,' she suggested. 'He loves new things, especially if they make trouble.'

'Yeah.' These were not the two Crockett would have chosen, but at least he could think of no other candidates. 'If we could get somebody who's close to the Emperor … What about Drook – the guy who gives Podrang his mud baths?'

'Why not? I'll fix it.' Brockle Buhn lost interest and surreptitiously began to eat anthracite. Since the overseer was watching, this resulted in a violent quarrel, from which Crockett emerged with a black eye. Whispering profanity under his breath, he went back to digging.

But he had time for a few more words with Brockle Buhn. She'd arrange it. That night there would be a secret meeting of the conspirators.

Crockett had been looking forward to exhausted slumber, but this chance was too good to miss. He had no wish to continue his unpleasant job digging anthracite. His body ached fearfully. Besides, if he could induce the gnomes to strike, he might be able to put the squeeze on Podrang II. Gru Magru had said the Emperor was a magician. Couldn't he, then, transform Crockett back into a man?

'He's never done that,' Brockle Buhn said, and Crockett realized he had spoken his thought aloud.

'Couldn't he, though – if he wanted?'

Brockle Buhn merely shuddered, but Crockett had a little gleam of hope. To be human again!

Dig ... dig ... dig ... dig ... with monotonous, deadening regularity. Crockett sank into a stupor. Unless he got the gnomes to strike, he was faced with an eternity of arduous toil. He was scarcely conscious of knocking off, of feeling Brockle Buhn's gnarled hand under his arm, of being led through passages to a tiny cubicle, which was his new home. The gnome left him there, and he crawled into a stony bunk and went to sleep.

Presently a casual kick aroused him. Blinking, Crockett sat up, instinctively dodging the blow Gru Magru was aiming at his head. He had four guests – Gru, Brockle Buhn, Drook and the red-haired Mugza.

'Sorry I woke up too soon,' Crockett said bitterly. 'If I hadn't, you could have got in another kick.'

'There's lots of time,' Gru said. 'Now, what's this all about? I wanted to sleep, but Brockle Buhn here said there was going to be a fight. A *big* one, huh?'

'Eat first,' Brockle Buhn said firmly. 'I'll fix mud soup for everybody.' She bustled away, and presently was busy in a corner, preparing refreshments. The other gnomes squatted on their haunches, and Crockett sat on the edge of his bunk, still dazed with sleep.

But he managed to explain his idea of the union. It was received with interest – chiefly, he felt, because it involved the possibility of a tremendous scrap.

'You mean every Dornsef gnome jumps the Emperor?' Gru asked.

'No, no! Peaceful arbitration. We just refuse to work. All of us.'

'*I* can't,' Drook said. 'Podrang's got to have his mud baths, the bloated old slug. He'd send me to the fumaroles till I was roasted.'

'Who'd take you there?' Crockett asked.

'Oh – the guards, I suppose.'

'But they'd be on strike, too. *Nobody'd* obey Podrang, till he gave in.'

'Then he'd enchant me,' Drook said.

'He can't enchant us all,' Crockett countered.

'But he could enchant *me*,' Drook said with great firmness. 'Besides, he *could* put a spell on every gnome in Dornsef. Turn us into stalactites or something.'

'Then what? He wouldn't have any gnomes at all. Half a loaf is better than none. We'll just use logic on him. Wouldn't he rather have a little less work done than none at all?'

'Not him,' Gru put in. 'He'd rather enchant us. Oh, he's a bad one, he is,' the gnome finished approvingly.

*

But Crockett couldn't quite believe this. It was too alien to his understanding of psychology – human psychology, of course. He turned to Mugza, who was glowering furiously.

'What do you think about it?'

'I want to fight,' the other said rancorously. 'I want to kick somebody.'

'Wouldn't you rather have mud baths three times a day?'

Mugza grunted. 'Sure. But the Emperor won't let me.'

'Why not?'

'Because I want 'em.'

'You can't be contented,' Crockett said desperately. 'There's more to life than – than digging.'

'Sure. There's fighting. Podrang lets us fight whenever we want.'

Crockett had a sudden inspiration. 'But that's just it. He's going to stop all fighting! He's going to pass a new law forbidding fighting except to himself.'

It was an effective shot in the dark. Every gnome jumped.

'Stop – *fighting!*' That was Gru, angry and disbelieving. 'Why, we've always fought.'

'Well, you'll have to stop,' Crockett insisted.

'Won't!'

'Exactly! Why should you? Every gnome's entitled to life, liberty and the pursuit of – of pugilism.'

'Let's go and beat up Podrang,' Mugza offered, accepting a steaming bowl of mud soup from Brockle Buhn.

'No, that's not the way – no, thanks, Brockle Buhn – not the way at all. A strike's the thing. We'll peaceably force Podrang to give us what we want.'

He turned to Drook. 'Just what can Podrang do about it if we all sit down and refuse to work?'

The little gnome considered. 'He'd swear. And kick me.'

'Yeah – and then what?'

'Then he'd go off and enchant everybody, tunnel by tunnel.'

'Uh-huh.' Crockett nodded. 'A good point. Solidarity is what we need. If Podrang finds a few gnomes together, he can scare the hell out of them. But if we're all together – that's it! When the strike's called, we'll all meet in the biggest cave in the joint.'

'That's the Council Chamber,' Gru said. 'Next to Podrang's throne room.'

'O.K. We'll meet there. How many gnomes will join us?'

'All of 'em,' Mugza grunted, throwing his soup bowl at Drook's head. 'The Emperor can't stop us fighting.'

'And what weapons can Podrang use, Drook?'

'He might use the Cockatrice Eggs,' the other said doubtfully.

'What are those?'

'They're not really eggs,' Gru broke in. 'They're magic jewels for wholesale enchantments. Different spells in each one. The green ones, I think, are for turning people into earthworms. Podrang just breaks one, and the spell spreads out for twenty feet or so. The red ones are – let's see. Transforming gnomes into human beings – though that's a bit *too* tough. No … yes. The blue ones –'

'Into *human beings!*' Crockett's eyes widened. 'Where are the eggs kept?'

'Let's fight,' Mugza offered, and hurled himself bodily on Drook, who squeaked frantically and beat his attacker over the head with his soup bowl, which broke. Brockle Buhn added to the excitement by kicking both battlers impartially, till felled by Gru Magru. Within a few moments the room resounded with the excited screams of gnomic battle. Inevitably Crockett was sucked in …

Of all the perverted, incredible forms of life that had ever existed, gnomes were about the oddest. It was impossible to understand their philosophy. Their minds worked along different paths from human intelligences. Self-preservation and survival of the race – these two vital human instincts were lacking in gnomes. They neither died nor propagated. They just worked and fought. Bad-tempered little monsters, Crockett thought irritably. Yet they had existed for – ages. Since the beginning, maybe. Their social organism was the result of evolution far older than man's. It might be well suited to gnomes. Crockett might be throwing the unnecessary monkey wrench in the machinery.

So what? He wasn't going to spend eternity digging anthracite, even though, in retrospect, he remembered feeling a curious thrill of obscure pleasure as he worked. Digging might be fun for gnomes. Certainly it was their *raison d'être.* In time Crockett himself might lose his human affiliations, and be metamorphosed completely into a gnome. What had happened to other humans who had undergone such an – alteration as he had done? All gnomes look alike. But maybe Gru Magru had once been human – or Drook – or Brockle Buhn.

They were gnomes now, at any rate, thinking and existing completely as gnomes. And in time he himself would be exactly like them. Already he had acquired the strange tropism that attracted him to metals and repelled him from daylight. But he didn't *like* to dig!

He tried to recall the little he knew about gnomes – miners, metal-smiths, living underground. There was something about the Picts – dwarfish men who hid underground when invaders came to England, centuries ago. That seemed to tie in vaguely with the gnomes' dread of human beings. But the gnomes themselves were certainly not descended from Picts. Very likely the two separate races and species had become identified through occupying the same habitat.

Well, that was no help. What about the Emperor? He wasn't, apparently, a gnome with a high I.Q., but he *was* a magician. Those jewels – Cockatrice Eggs – were significant. If he could get hold of the ones that transformed gnomes into men …

But obviously he couldn't, at present. Better wait. Till the strike had been called. The strike …

Crockett went to sleep.

He was roused, painfully, by Brockle Buhn, who seemed to have adopted him. Very likely it was her curiosity about the matter of a kiss. From time to time she offered to give Crockett one, but he steadfastly refused. In lieu of it, she supplied him with breakfast. At least, he though grimly, he'd get plenty of iron in his system, even though the rusty chips rather resembled corn flakes. As a special inducement Brockle Buhn sprinkled coal dust over the mess.

Well, no doubt his digestive system had also altered. Crockett wished he could get an X-ray picture of his insides. Then he decided it would be much too disturbing. Better not to know. But he could not help wondering. Gears in his stomach? Small millstones? What would happen if he inadvertently swallowed some emery dust? Maybe he could sabotage the Emperor that way.

Perceiving that his thoughts were beginning to veer wildly, Crockett gulped the last of his meal and followed Brockle Buhn to the anthracite tunnel.

'How about the strike? How's it coming?'

'Fine, Crockett.' She smiled, and Crockett winced at the sight. 'Tonight all the gnomes will meet in the Roaring Cave. Just after work.'

There was no time for more conversation. The overseer appeared, and the gnomes snatched up their picks. Dig … dig … dig … It kept up at the same pace. Crockett sweated and toiled. It wouldn't be for long. His mind slipped a cog, so that he relapsed into a waking slumber, his muscles responding automatically to the need. Dig, dig, dig. Sometimes a fight. Once a rest period. Then dig again.

Five centuries later the day ended. It was time to sleep.

But there was something much more important. The union meeting in the Roaring Cave. Brockle Buhn conducted Crockett there, a huge cavern hung with glittering green stalactites. Gnomes came pouring into it. Gnomes and more gnomes. The turnip heads were everywhere. A dozen fights started. Gru Magru, Mugza and Drook found places near Crockett. During a lull Brockle Buhn urged him to a platform of rock jutting from the floor.

'Now,' she whispered. 'They all know about it. Tell them what you want.'

Crockett was looking out over the bobbing heads, the red and blue garments, all lit by that eerie silver glow. 'Fellow gnomes,' he began weakly.

'*Fellow gnomes!*' The words roared out, magnified by the acoustics of the cavern. That bull bellow gave Crockett courage. He plunged on.

'Why should you work twenty hours a day? Why should you be forbidden to eat the anthracite you dig, while Podrang squats in his bath and laughs at you? Fellow gnomes, the Emperor is only one; you are many! He can't make you work. How would you like mud soup three times a day? The Emperor can't fight you all. If you refuse to work – all of you – he'll have to give in! He'll have to!'

'Tell 'em about the non-fighting edict,' Gru Magru called.

Crockett obeyed. That got 'em. Fighting was dear to every gnomic heart. And Crockett kept on talking.

'Podrang will try to back down, you know. He'll pretend he never intended to forbid fighting. That'll show he's afraid of you! We hold the whip hand! We'll strike – and the Emperor can't do a damn thing about it. When he runs out of mud for his baths, he'll capitulate soon enough.'

'He'll enchant us all,' Drook muttered sadly.

'He won't dare! What good would that do? He knows which side his – ugh – which side his mud is buttered on. Podrang is unfair to gnomes! That's our watchword!'

It ended, of course, in a brawl. But Crockett was satisfied. The gnomes would not go to work tomorrow. They would, instead, meet in the Council Chamber, adjoining Podrang's throne room – and sit down.

That night he slept well.

In the morning Crockett went, with Brockle Buhn, to the Council Chamber, a cavern gigantic enough to hold the thousands of gnomes who thronged it. In the silver light their red and blue garments had a curiously elfin quality. Or, perhaps, naturally enough, Crockett thought. Were gnomes, strictly speaking, elves?

Drook came up. 'I didn't draw Podrang's mud bath,' he confided hoarsely. 'Oh, but he'll be furious. Listen to him.'

And, indeed, a distant crackling of profanity was coming through an archway in one wall of the cavern.

Mugza and Gru Magru joined them. 'He'll be along directly,' the latter said. 'What a fight there'll be!'

'Let's fight now,' Mugza suggested. 'I want to kick somebody. Hard.'

'There's a gnome who's asleep,' Crockett said. 'If you sneak up on him, you can land a good one right in his face.'

Mugza, drooling slightly, departed on his errand, and simultaneously Podrang II, Emperor of the Dornsef Gnomes, stumped into the cavern. It was the first time Crockett had seen the ruler without a coating of mud, and he could not help gulping at the sight. Podrang was *very* ugly. He combined in himself the most repulsive qualities of every gnome Crockett had previously seen. The result was perfectly indescribable.

'Ah,' said Podrang, halting and swaying on his short bow legs. 'I have guests. Drook! Where in the name of the nine steaming hells is my bath?' But Drook had ducked from sight.

The Emperor nodded. 'I see. Well, I won't lose my temper, *I won't lose my temper!* I WON'T –'

He paused as a stalactite was dislodged from the roof and crashed down. In the momentary silence, Crockett stepped forward, cringing slightly.

'W-we're on strike,' he announced. 'It's a sit-down strike. We won't work till –'

'*Yaah!*' screamed the infuriated Emperor. 'You won't work, eh? Why, you boggle-eyed, flap-tongued, drag-bellied offspring of unmentionable algae! You seething little leprous blotch of bat-nibbled fungus! You cringing parasite on the underside of a dwarfish and ignoble worm! *Yaaah!*'

'Fight!' the irrepressible Mugza yelled, and flung himself on Podrang, only to be felled by a well-placed foul blow.

Crockett's throat felt dry. He raised his voice, trying to keep it steady.

'Your Majesty! If you'll just wait a minute –'

'You mushroom-nosed spawn of degenerate black bats,' the enraged Emperor shrieked at the top of his voice. 'I'll enchant you all! I'll turn you into naiads! Strike, will you! Stop me from having my mud bath, will you? By Kronos, Nid, Ymir and Loki, you'll have cause to regret this! *Yah!*' he finished, inarticulate with fury.

'Quick!' Crockett whispered to Gru and Brockle Buhn. 'Get between him and the door, so he can't get hold of the Cockatrice Eggs.'

'They're not in the throne room,' Gru Magru explained unhelpfully. 'Podrang just grabs them out of the air.'

'Oh!' the harassed Crockett groaned. At that strategic moment Brockle Buhn's worst instincts overcame her. With a loud shriek of delight she knocked Crockett down, kicked him twice and sprang for the Emperor.

She got in one good blow before Podrang hammered her atop the head with one gnarled fist, and instantly her turnip-shaped skull seemed to prolapse into her torso. The Emperor, bright purple with fury, reached out – and a yellow crystal appeared in his hand.

It was one of the Cockatrice Eggs.

Bellowing like a *musth* elephant, Podrang hurled it. A circle of twenty feet was instantly cleared among the massed gnomes. But it wasn't vacant. Dozens of bats rose and fluttered about, adding to the confusion.

Confusion became chaos. With yells of delighted fury, the gnomes rolled forward toward their ruler. 'Fight!' the cry thundered out, reverberating from the roof. '*Fight!*'

Podrang snatched another crystal from nothingness – a green one, this time. Thirty-seven gnomes were instantly transformed into earthworms, and were trampled. The Emperor went down under an avalanche of attackers, who abruptly disappeared, turned into mice by another of the Cockatrice Eggs.

Crockett saw one of the crystals sailing toward him, and ran like hell. He found a hiding place behind a stalagmite, and from there watched the carnage. It was definitely a sight worth seeing, though it could not be recommended to a nervous man.

The Cockatrice Eggs exploded in an incessant stream. Whenever that happened, the spell spread out for twenty feet or more before losing its efficacy. Those caught on the fringes of the circle were only partially transformed. Crockett saw one gnome with a mole's head. Another was a worm from the waist down. Another was – *ulp!* Some of the spell patterns were not, apparently, drawn even from known mythology.

The fury of noise that filled the cavern brought stalactites crashing down incessantly from the roof. Every so often Podrang's battered head would reappear, only to go down again as more gnomes sprang to the attack – to be enchanted. Mice, moles, bats and other things filled the Council Chamber. Crockett shut his eyes and prayed.

He opened them in time to see Podrang snatch a red crystal out of the air, pause and then deposit it gently behind him. A purple Cockatrice Egg came next. This crashed against the floor, and thirty gnomes turned into tree toads.

Apparently only Podrang was immune to his own magic. The thousands who had filled the cavern were rapidly thinning, for the Cockatrice Eggs seemed to come from an inexhaustible source of supply. How long would it be before Crockett's own turn came? He couldn't hide here forever.

His gaze riveted to the red crystal Podrang had so carefully put down. He was remembering something – the Cockatrice Egg that would transform gnomes into human beings. Of course! Podrang wouldn't use *that,* since the very sight of men was so distressing to gnomes. If Crockett could get his hands on that red crystal …

He tried it, sneaking through the confusion, sticking close to the wall of the cavern, till he neared Podrang. The Emperor was swept away by another onrush of gnomes, who abruptly changed into dormice, and Crockett got the red jewel. It felt abnormally cold.

He almost broke it at his feet before a thought stopped and chilled him. He was far under Dornsef Mountain, in a labyrinth of caverns. No human being could find his way out. But a gnome could, with the aid of his strange tropism to daylight.

A bat flew against Crockett's face. He was almost certain it squeaked, 'What a fight!' in a parody of Brockle Buhn's voice, but he couldn't be sure. He cast one glance over the cavern before turning to flee.

It was a complete and utter chaos. Bats, moles, worms, ducks, eels and a dozen other species crawled, flew, ran, bit, shrieked, snarled, grunted, whooped and croaked all over the place. From all directions the remaining gnomes – only about a thousand now – were converging on a surging mound of gnomes that marked where the Emperor was. As Crockett stared, the mound dissolved, and a number of gecko lizards ran to safety.

'*Strike, will you!*' Podrang bellowed. '*I'll show you!*'

Crockett turned and fled. The throne room was deserted, and he ducked into the first tunnel. There, he concentrated on thinking of daylight. His left ear felt compressed. He sped on till he saw a side passage on the left, slanting up, and turned into it at top speed. The muffled noise of combat died behind him.

He clutched the red Cockatrice Egg tightly. What had gone wrong? Podrang should have stopped to parley. Only – only he hadn't. A singularly bad-tempered and short-sighted gnome. He probably wouldn't stop till he'd depopulated his entire kingdom. At the thought, Crockett hurried along faster.

The tropism guided him. Sometimes he took the wrong tunnel, but always, whenever he thought of daylight, he would *feel* the nearest daylight pressing against him. His short, bowed legs were surprisingly hardy.

Then he heard someone running after him.

He didn't turn. The sizzling blast of profanity that curled his ears told him the identity of the pursuer. Podrang had no doubt cleared the Council Chamber, to the last gnome, and was now intending to tear Crockett apart pinch by pinch. That was only one of the things he promised.

Crockett ran. He shot along the tunnel like a bullet. The tropism guided him, but he was terrified lest he reach a dead end. The clamor from behind grew louder. If Crockett hadn't known better, he would have imagined that an army of gnomes pursued him.

Faster! Faster! But now Podrang was in sight. His roars shook the very walls. Crockett sprinted, rounded a corner, and saw a wall of flaming light – a circle of it, in the distance. It was daylight, as it appeared to gnomic eyes.

He could not reach it in time. Podrang was too close. A few more seconds, and those gnarled, terrible hands would close on Crockett's throat.

Then Crockett remembered the Cockatrice Egg. If he transformed himself into a man now, Podrang would not dare touch him. And he was almost at the tunnel's mouth.

He stopped, whirling and lifted the jewel. Simultaneously the Emperor, seeing his intention, reached out with both hands, and snatched six or seven of the crystals out of the air. He threw them directly at Crockett, a fusillade of rainbow colors.

But Crockett had already slammed the red gem down on the rock at his feet. There was an ear-splitting crash. Jewels seemed to burst all around Crockett – but the red one had been broken first.

The roof fell in.

A short while later, Crockett dragged himself painfully from the debris. A glance showed him that the way to the outer world was still open. And – thank heaven! – daylight looked normal again, not that flaming blaze of eye-searing white.

He looked toward the depths of the tunnel, and froze. Podrang was emerging, with some difficulty, from a mound of rubble. His low curses had lost none of their fire.

Crockett turned to run, stumbled over a rock, and fell flat. As he sprang up, he saw that Podrang had seen him.

The gnome stood transfixed for a moment. Then he yelled, spun on his heel, and fled into the darkness. He was gone. The sound of his rapid footfalls died.

Crockett swallowed with difficulty. *Gnomes are afraid of men – whew!* That had been a close squeak. But now …

He was more relieved than he had thought. Subconsciously he must have been wondering whether the spell would work, since Podrang had flung six or seven Cockatrice Eggs at him. But he had smashed the red one first. Even the strange, silvery gnome-light was gone. The depths of the cave were utterly black – and silent.

Crockett headed for the entrance. He pulled himself out, luxuriating in the warmth of the afternoon sun. He was near the foot of Dornsef Mountain, in a patch of brambles. A hundred feet away a farmer was plowing one terrace of a field.

Crockett stumbled toward him. As he approached, the man turned.

He stood transfixed for a moment. Then he yelled, spun on his heel, and fled.

His shrieks drifted back up the mountain as Crockett, remembering the Cockatrice Eggs, forced himself to look down at his own body.

Then he screamed too. But the sound was not one that could ever have emerged from a human throat.

Still, that was natural enough – under the circumstances.

THE BIG NIGHT

Chapter 1. Last of the Hyper Ships

She came lumbering up out of the ecliptic plane of the planets like a wallowing space beast, her jet tubes scarred and stained, a molten streak across her middle where Venus's turgid atmosphere had scarred her, and every ancient spot weld in her fat body threatened to rip apart the moment she hit stress again.

The skipper was drunk in his cabin, his maudlin voice echoing through the compartments as he bewailed the unsympathetic harshness of the Interplanetary Trade Commission.

There was a mongrel crew from a dozen worlds, half of them shanghaied. Logger Hilton, the mate, was trying to make sense out of the tattered charts, and *La Cucaracha,* her engines quaking at the suicidal thought, was plunging ahead through space into the Big Night.

In the control room a signal light flared. Hilton grabbed a mike.

'Repair crew!' he yelled. 'Get out on the skin and check jet A-six. Move!'

He turned back to his charts, chewing his lip and glancing at the pilot, a tiny, inhuman Selenite, with his arachnoid multiple limbs and fragile-seeming body. Ts'ss – that was his name, or approximated it – was wearing the awkward audio-converter mask that could make his subsonic voice audible to human ears, but, unlike Hilton, he wasn't wearing space armor. No Lunarian ever needed protection against deep space. In their million years on the Moon, they had got used to airlessness. Nor did the ship's atmosphere bother Ts'ss. He simply didn't trouble to breathe it.

'Blast you, take it easy!' Hilton said. 'Want to tear off our hide?'

Through the mask the Selenite's faceted eyes glittered at the mate.

'No, sir. I'm going as slowly as I can on jet fuel. As soon as I know the warp formulae, things'll ease up a bit.'

'Ride it! Ride it – without jets!'

'We need the acceleration to switch over to warp, sir.'

'Never mind,' Hilton said. 'I've got it now. Somebody must have been breeding fruit-flies all over these charts. Here's the dope.' He dictated a few equations that Ts'ss' photographic memory assimilated at once.

A distant howling came from far off.

'That's the skipper, I suppose,' Hilton said. 'I'll be back in a minute. Get into hyper as soon as you can, or we're apt to fold up like an accordion.'

'Yes, sir. Ah – Mr Hilton?'

'Well?'

'You might look at the fire extinguisher in the Cap'n's room.'

'What for?' Hilton asked.

Several of the Selenite's multiple limbs pantomimed the action of drinking. Hilton grimaced, rose and fought the acceleration down the companionway. He shot a glance at the visio-screens and saw they were past Jupiter already, which was a relief. Going through the giant planet's gravity-pull wouldn't have helped *La Cucaracha*'s aching bones. But they were safely past now. Safely! He grinned wryly as he opened the captain's door and went in.

Captain Sam Danvers was standing on his bunk, making a speech to an imaginary Interplanetary Trade Commission. He was a big man, or rather he had been once, but now the flesh had shrunk and he was beginning to stoop a little. The skin of his wrinkled face was nearly black with space-tan. A stubble of gray hair stood up angrily.

Somehow, though, he looked like Logger Hilton. Both were deep-space men. Hilton was thirty years younger, but he, too, had the same dark tan and the same look in his blue eyes. There's an old saying that when you go out into the Big Night, beyond Pluto's orbit, that enormous emptiness gets into you and looks out through your eyes. Hilton had that. So did Captain Danvers.

Otherwise – Hilton was huge and heavy where Danvers was a little frail now, and the mate's broad chest bulged his white tunic. He hadn't had time yet to change from dress uniform, though he knew that even this cellulose fabric couldn't take the dirt of a space-run without showing it. Not on *La Cucaracha*, anyway.

But this would be his last trip on the old tub.

Captain Danvers interrupted his speech to ask Hilton what the devil he wanted. The mate saluted.

'Routine inspection, sir,' he observed, and took down a fire extinguisher from the wall. Danvers sprang from the bunk, but Hilton moved too fast. Before the captain reached him, Hilton had emptied the tank down the nearest disposal vent.

'Old juice,' he explained. 'I'll refill her.'

'Listen, Mr Hilton,' Danvers said, swaying slightly and stabbing a long forefinger at the mate's nose. 'If you think I had whiskey in there, you're crazy.'

'Sure,' Hilton said. 'I'm crazy as a loon, skipper. How about some caffeine?'

Danvers weaved to the disposal port and peered down it vaguely.

'Caffeine. Huh? Look, if you haven't got sense enough to take *La Cucaracha* into hyper, you ought to resign.'

'Sure, sure. But in hyper it won't take long to get to Fria. You'll have to handle the agent there.'

'Christie? I – I guess so.' Danvers sank down on the bunk and held his head. 'I guess I just got mad, Logger. ITC – what do they know about it? Why, we opened that trading post on Sirius Thirty.'

'Look, skipper, when you come aboard you were so high you forgot to tell me about it,' Hilton said. 'You just said we'd changed our course and to head for Fria. How come?'

'Interplanetary Trade Commission,' Danvers growled. 'They had their crew checking over *La Cucaracha.*'

'I know. Routine inspection.'

'Well, those fat slobs have the brassbound nerve to tell me my ship's unsafe! That the gravity-drag from Sirius is too strong – and that we couldn't go to Sirius Thirty!'

'Could be they're right,' Hilton said thoughtfully. 'We had trouble landing on Venus.'

'She's old.' Danvers' voice was defensive. 'But what of it? I've taken *La Cucaracha* around Betelgeuse and plenty closer to Sirius than Sirius Thirty. The old lady's got what it takes. They built atomic engines in those days.'

'They're not building them now,' Hilton said, and the skipper turned purple.

'Transmission of matter!' he snarled. 'What kind of a crazy set-up is that? You get in a little machine on Earth, pull a switch and there you are on Venus or Bar Canopus or – or Purgatory, if you like! I shipped on a hyper ship when I was thirteen, Logger. I grew up on hyper ships. They're solid. They're dependable. They'll take you where you want to go. Hang it, it isn't safe to space travel without an atmosphere around you, even if it's only in a suit.'

'That reminds me,' Hilton said. 'Where's yours?'

'Ah, I was too hot. The refrigerating unit's haywire.'

The mate found the lightweight armor in a closet and deftly began to repair the broken switch.

'You don't need to keep the helmet closed, but you'd better wear the suit,' he said absently. 'I've issued orders to the crew. All but Ts'ss, and he doesn't need any protection.'

Danvers looked up. 'How's she running?' he asked quickly.

'Well, she could use an overhaul,' Hilton said. 'I want to get into hyperspace fast. This straight running is a strain. I'm afraid of landing, too.'

'Uh. Okay, there'll be an overhaul when we get back – *if* we make a profit. You know how much we made this last trip. Tell you what – you supervise the job and take a bigger cut for it.'

Hilton's fingers slowed on the switch. He didn't look around.

'I'll be looking for a new berth,' he said. 'Sorry, Skipper. But I won't be aboard after this voyage.'

There was silence behind him. Hilton grimaced and began to work again on the spacesuit. He heard Danvers say:

'You won't find many hyper ships needing mates these days.'

'I know. But I've got engineering training. Maybe they would use me on the matter transmitters. Or as an outposter – a trader.'

'Oh, for the love of Pete! Logger, what are you talking about? A – *trader?* A filthy outposter? You're a hyper ship man!'

'In twenty years there won't be a hyper ship running,' Hilton said.

'You're a liar. There'll be one.'

'She'll fall apart in a couple of months!' Hilton said angrily. 'I'm not going to argue. What are we after on Fria, the fungus?'

After a pause Danvers answered.

'What else is there on Fria? Sure, the fungus. It's pushing the season a little. We're not due there for three weeks Earth-time, but Christie always keeps a supply on hand. And that big hotel chain will pay us the regular cut. Blamed if I know why people eat that garbage, but they pay twenty bucks a plate for it.'

'It could mean a profit, then,' Hilton said. 'Provided we land on Fria without falling apart.' He tossed the repaired suit on the bunk beside Danvers. 'There you are, skipper. I'd better get back to controls. We'll be hitting hyper pretty soon.'

Danvers leaned over and touched a button that opened the deadlight. He stared at the star screen.

'You won't get this on a matter transmitter,' he said slowly. 'Look at it, Logger.'

Hilton leaned forward and looked across the Captain's shoulder. The void blazed. To one side a great arc of Jupiter's titan bulk blared coldly bright. Several of the moons were riding in the screen's field, and an asteroid or two caught Jupiter's light in their tenuous atmospheres and hung like shining veiled miniature worlds against that blazing backdrop. And through and beyond the shining stars and moons and planets showed the Big Night, the black emptiness that beats like an ocean on the rim of the Solar System.

'So it's pretty,' Hilton said. 'But it's cold, too.'

'Maybe. Maybe it is. But I like it. Well, get a job as a trader, you jackass. I'll stick to *La Cucaracha.* I know I can trust the old lady.'

For answer the old lady jumped violently and gave a wallowing lurch.

Chapter 2. Bad News

Hilton instantly exploded out of the cabin. The ship was bucking hard. Behind him the mate heard Danvers shouting something about incompetent pilots, but he knew it probably wasn't the Selenite's fault. He was in the control cabin while *La Cucaracha* was still shuddering on the downswing of the last jump. Ts'ss was a tornado of motion, his multiple legs scrabbling frantically at a dozen instruments.

'I'll call the shot!' Hilton snapped, and Ts'ss instantly concentrated on the incredibly complicated controls that were guiding the ship into hyper.

The mate was at the auxiliary board. He jerked down levers.

'Hyper stations!' he shouted. 'Close helmets! Grab the braces, you sun-jumpers! Here we go!'

A needle swung wildly across a gauge, hovering at the mark. Hilton dropped into a seat, sliding his arms under the curved braces and hooking his elbows around them. His ankles found similar supports beneath him. The visor screens blurred and shimmered with crawling colors, flicking back and forth, on and off, as *La Cucaracha* fought the see-saw between hyper and normal space.

Hilton tried another mike. 'Captain Danvers. Hyper stations. All right?'

'Yeah, I'm in my suit,' Danvers' voice said. 'Can you take it? Need me? What's wrong with Ts'ss?'

'The vocor at my board blew out, Cap'n,' Ts'ss said. 'I couldn't reach the auxiliary.'

'We must need an overhaul bad,' Danvers said, and cut off.

Hilton grinned. 'We need a rebuilding job,' he muttered, and let his fingers hang over the control buttons, ready in case Ts'ss slipped.

But the Selenite was like a precision machine; he never slipped. The old *Cucaracha* shook in every brace. The atomic engines channeled fantastic amounts of energy into the dimensional gap. Then, suddenly, the see-saw balanced for an instant, and in that split second the ship slid across its power-bridge and was no longer matter. It no longer existed, in the three-dimensional plane. To an observer, it would have vanished. But to an observer in hyper-space, it would have sprung into existence from white nothingness.

Except that there *were* no hyperspatial observers. In fact, there wasn't anything in hyper – it was, as some scientist had once observed, just stuff, and nobody knew what the stuff was. It was possible to find out some of hyper's properties, but you couldn't go much further than that. It was white, and it must have been energy, of a sort, for it flowed like an inconceivably powerful tide, carrying ships with it at speeds that would have destroyed the crew in normal space. Now, in the grip of the hyper current, *La Cucaracha* was racing toward the Big Night at a velocity that would take it past Pluto's orbit in a matter of seconds.

But you couldn't see Pluto. You had to work blind here, with instruments. And if you got on the wrong level, it was just too bad – for you!

Hastily, Hilton checked the readings. This was Hyper C-758-R. That was right. On different dimensional levels of hyper, the flow ran in various directions. Coming back, they'd alter their atomic structure to ride Hyper M-75-L, which rushed from Fria toward Earth and beyond it.

'That's that,' Hilton said, relaxing and reaching for a cigarette. 'No meteors, no stress-strain problems – just drift till we get close to Fria. Then we drop out of hyper, and probably fall apart.'

An annunciator clicked. Somebody said:

'Mr Hilton, there's some trouble.'

'There is. Okay, Wiggins. What now?'

'One of the new men. He was out skinside making repairs.'

'You had plenty of time to get back inside,' snapped Hilton, who didn't feel quite as sure of that as he sounded. 'I called hyper stations.'

'Yes, sir. But this fella's new. Looks like he never rode a hyper ship before. Anyhow, his leg's broken. He's in sick bay.'

Hilton thought for a moment. *La Cucaracha* was understaffed anyway. Few good men would willingly ship on such an antique.

'I'll come down,' he said, and nodded at Ts'ss. Then he went along the companionway, glancing in at the skipper, who had gone to sleep. He used the handholds to pull himself along, for there was no accelerative gravity in hyper. In sick bay he found the surgeon, who doubled in brass as cook, finishing a traction splint on a pale, sweating youngster who was alternately swearing feebly and groaning.

'What's the matter with him?' Hilton asked.

Bruno, the sawbones, gave a casual soft salute. 'Simple fracture. I'm giving him a walker splint, so he'll be able to get around. And he shot his cookies, so he can't be used to hyper.'

'Looks like it,' Hilton said, studying the patient. The boy opened his eyes, glared at Hilton.

'I was shanghaied!' he yelped. 'I'll sue you for all you're worth!'

The first officer was unperturbed.

'I'm not the skipper, I'm mate,' Hilton said. 'And I can tell you right now that we're not worth much. Ever hear about discipline?'

'I was shanghaied!'

'I know it. That's the only way we can get a full crew to sign articles on *La Cucaracha*. I mentioned discipline. We don't bother much with it here. Just the same, you'd better call me Mister when people are around. Now shut up and relax. Give him a sedative, Bruno.'

'No! I want to send a spacegram!'

'We're in hyper. You can't. What's your name?'

'Saxon. Luther Saxon. I'm one of the consulting engineers on Transmat.'

'The matter-transmission gang? What were you doing around the space docks?'

Saxon gulped. 'Well – uh – I go out with the technical crews to supervise new installations. We'd just finished a Venusian transmission station. I went out for a few drinks – that was all! A few drinks, and –'

'You went to the wrong place,' Hilton said, amused. 'Some crimp gave you a Mickey. Your name's on the articles, anyhow, so you're stuck, unless you jump ship. You can send a message from Fria, but it'd take a thousand years to reach Venus or Earth. Better stick around, and you can ride back with us.'

'On this crate? It isn't safe. She's so old I've got the jitters every time I take a deep breath.'

'Well, stop breathing,' Hilton said curtly. *La Cucaracha* was an old tramp, of course, but he had shipped on her for a good many years. It was all right for this Transmat man to talk; the Transmat crews never ran any risks.

'Ever been on a hyper ship before?' he asked.

'Naturally,' Saxon said. 'As a passenger! We have to get to a planet before we can install a transmission station, don't we?'

'Uh-huh.' Hilton studied the scowling face on the pillow. 'You're not a passenger now, though.'

'My leg's broken.'

'You got an engineering degree?'

Saxon hesitated and finally nodded.

'All right, you'll be assistant pilot. You won't have to walk much to do that. The pilot'll tell you what to do. You can earn your mess that way.'

Saxon spluttered protests.

'One thing,' Hilton said. 'Better not tell the skipper you're a Transmat man. He'd hang you over one of the jets. Send him for'rd when he's fixed up, Bruno.'

'Yessir,' Bruno said, grinning faintly. An old deep-space man, he didn't like Transmat either.

Hilton pulled himself back to the control room. He sat down and watched the white visoscreens. Most of Ts'ss' many arms were idle. This was routine now.

'You're getting an assistant,' Hilton said after a while. 'Train him fast. That'll give us all a break. If that fat-headed Callistan pilot hadn't jumped on Venus, we'd be set.'

'This is a short voyage,' Ts'ss said. 'It's a fast hyper flow on this level.'

'Yeah. This new guy. Don't tell the skipper, but he's a Transmat man.'

Ts'ss laughed a little.

'That will pass, too,' he said. 'We're an old race, Mr Hilton. Earthmen are babies compared to the Selenites. Hyper ships are fading out, and eventually Transmat will fade out too, when something else comes.'

'We won't fade,' Hilton said, rather surprised to find himself defending the skipper's philosophy. '*Your* people haven't – you Selenites.'

'Some of us are left, that's true,' Ts'ss said softly. 'Not many. The great days of the Selenite Empire passed very long ago. But there are still a few Selenites left, like me.'

'You keep going, don't you? You can't kill off a – a race.'

'Not easily. Not at once. But you can, eventually. And you can kill a tradition, too, though it may take a long time. But you know what the end will be.'

'Oh, shut up,' Hilton said. 'You talk too much.'

Ts'ss bent again above the controls. *La Cucaracha* fled on through the white hyper flow, riding as smoothly as the day she had been launched.

But when they reached Fria, it would be rough space and high gravity. Hilton grimaced.

He thought: So what? This is just another voyage. The fate of the universe doesn't depend on it. Nothing depends on it, except, maybe, whether we make enough profit to have the old lady overhauled. And that won't matter to me for it's my last voyage into the Big Night.

He watched the screens. He could not see it, but he knew that it hung beyond the universal whiteness, in a plane invisible to his eyes. The little sparks of worlds and suns glowed in its immensity, but never brightened it. It was too vast, too implacable. And even the giant suns would be quenched in its ocean, in the end. As everything else would be quenched, as everything moved on the tides of time into that huge darkness.

That was progress. A wave was born and gathered itself and grew – and broke. A newer wave was behind it. And the old one slipped back and was lost forever. A few foam-flecks and bubbles remained, like Ts'ss, remnant of the giant wave of the ancient Selenite Empire.

The Empire was gone. It had fought and ruled a hundred worlds, in its day. But, in the end, the Big Night had conquered and swallowed it.

As it would swallow the last hyper ship eventually …

They hit Fria six days later, Earth time. And *hit* was the word. One of Ts'ss' chitin-covered arms was snapped off by the impact, but he didn't seem to mind. He couldn't feel pain, and he could grow another limb in a few weeks. The crew, strapped to their landing braces, survived with minor bruises.

Luther Saxon, the Transmat man, was in the auxiliary pilot's seat – he had enough specialized engineering training so that he learned the ropes fast – and he acquired a blue bump on his forehead, but that was all. *La Cucaracha* had come out of hyper with a jolt that strained her fat old carcass to the limit, and the atmosphere and gravity of Fria was the penultimate straw. Seams ripped, a jet went out, and new molten streaks appeared on the white-hot hull.

The crew had been expecting liberty. There was no time for that. Hilton told off working gangs to relieve each other at six-hour intervals, and he said, rather casually, that Twilight was out of bounds. He knew the crew would ignore that order. There was no way to keep the men aboard, while Twilight sold liquor and even more effective escape mechanisms. Still, there were few women on Fria, and Hilton hoped that enough working stiffs would keep on the job to get *La Cucaracha* repaired and spaceworthy before the fungus cargo was loaded.

He knew that Wiggins, the second mate, would do his best. For himself he went with the skipper in search of Christie, the Fria trader. The way led through Twilight, the roofed settlement, that was shielded from the hot, diamond-bright glare of the primary. It wasn't big. But then Fria was an outpost, with a floating population of a few hundred. They came in and out with the ships and the harvest seasons. If necessary, Hilton thought, some of the bums could be shanghaied. Still, it wasn't too likely that any of the crew would desert. None of them would be paid off till they went back in the Solar System.

They found Christie in his plasticoid cabin, a fat, bald, sweating man puffing at a huge meerschaum pipe. He looked up, startled, and then resignedly leaned back in his chair and waved them to seats.

'Hello, Chris,' Danvers said. 'What's new?'

'Hello, Skipper. Hi, Logger. Have a good trip?'

'The landing wasn't so good,' Hilton said.

'Yeah, I heard about it. Drinks?'

'Afterward,' Danvers said, though his eyes gleamed. 'Let's clean up the business first. Got a good shipment ready?'

Christie smoothed one of his fat, glistening cheeks. 'Well – you're a couple of weeks early.'

'You keep a stockpile.'

The trader grunted. 'Fact is – look, didn't you get my message? No, I guess there wasn't time. I sent a spacemail on the *Blue Sky* last week for you, Skipper.'

Hilton exchanged glances with Danvers.

'You sound like bad news, Chris,' he said. 'What is it?'

Christie said uncomfortably, 'I can't help it. You can't meet competition like Transmat. You can't afford to pay their prices. You got running expenses on *La Cucaracha*. Jet fuel costs dough, and – well, Transmat sets up a transmitting station, pays for it, and the job's done, except for the power outlay. With atomic, what does that amount to?'

Danvers was growing red.

'Is Transmat setting up a station here?' Hilton said hastily.

'Yeah. I can't stop 'em. It'll be ready in a couple of months.'

'But why? The fungus isn't worth it. There isn't enough market. You're pulling a bluff, Chris. What do you want? A bigger cut?'

Christie regarded his meerschaum. 'Nope. Remember the ore tests twelve years ago? There's valuable ores on Fria, Logger. Only it's got to be refined plenty. Otherwise it's too bulky for shipment. And the equipment would cost too much to freight by spaceship. It's big stuff – I mean big.'

Hilton glanced at Danvers. The skipper was purple now, but his mouth was clamped tightly.

'But – hold on, Chris. How can Transmat get around that? By sending the crude ores to Earth in their gadgets?'

'The way I heard it,' Christie said, 'is that they're going to send the refining machines here and set 'em up right on Fria. All they need for that is one of their transmitters. The field can be expanded to take almost anything, you know. Shucks you could move a planet that way if you had the power! They'll do the refining here and transmit the refined ores back Earthside.'

'So they want ores,' Danvers said softly. 'They don't want the fungus, do they?'

Christie nodded. 'It looks like they do. I had an offer. A big one. I can't afford to turn it down, and you can't afford to meet it, Skipper. You know that as well as I do. Thirteen bucks a pound.'

Danvers snorted. Hilton whistled.

'No, we can't meet that,' he said. 'But how can they afford to pay it?'

'Quantity. They channel everything through their transmitters. They set one up on a world, and there's a door right to Earth – or any planet they name. One job won't net them much of a profit, but a million jobs – and they take everything! So what can I do, Logger?'

Hilton shrugged. The captain stood up abruptly.

Christie stared at his pipe.

'Look, Skipper. Why not try the Orion Secondaries? I heard there was a bumper crop of bluewood gum there.'

'I heard that a month ago,' Danvers said. 'So did everybody else. It's cleaned out by now. Besides, the old lady won't stand a trip like that. I've got to get an overhaul fast, and a good one, back in the System.'

There was a silence. Christie was sweating harder than ever. 'What about that drink?' he suggested. 'We can maybe figure a way.'

'I can still pay for my own drinks,' Danvers lashed out. He swung around and was gone.

'Jehoshaphat, Logger!' Christie said. 'What could I do?'

'It's not your fault, Chris,' Hilton said. 'I'll see you later, unless – anyhow, I'd better get after the skipper. Looks like he's heading for Twilight.'

He followed Danvers, but already he had lost hope.

Chapter 3. Danvers Lays the Course

Two days later the skipper was still drunk.

In the half-dusk of Twilight, Hilton went into a huge, cool barn where immense fans kept the hot air in circulation, and found Danvers, as usual, at a back table, a glass in his hand. He was talking to a tiny-headed Canopian, one of that retrovolved race that is only a few degrees above the moron level. The Canopian looked as though he was covered with black plush, and his red eyes glowed startlingly through the fur. He, too, had a glass.

Hilton walked over to the two. 'Skipper,' he said.

'Blow,' Danvers said. 'I'm talking to this guy.'

Hilton looked hard at the Canopian and jerked his thumb. The red-eyed shadow picked up his glass and moved away quickly. Hilton sat down.

'We're ready to jet off,' he said.

Danvers blinked at him blearily. 'You interrupted me, mister. I'm busy.'

'Buy a case and finish your binge aboard,' Hilton said. 'If we don't jet soon, the crew will jump.'

'Let 'em.'

'Okay. Then who'll work *La Cucaracha* back to Earth?'

'If we go back to Earth, the old lady will land on the junkpile,' Danvers said furiously. 'The ITC won't authorize another voyage without a rebuilding job.'

'You can borrow dough.'

'Ha!'

Hilton let out his breath with a sharp, angry sound. 'Are you sober enough to understand me? Then listen. I've talked Saxon around.'

'Who's Saxon?'

'He was shanghaied on Venus. Well – he's a Transmat engineer.' Hilton went on quickly before the skipper could speak. 'That was a mistake. The crimp's mistake and ours. Transmat stands behind its men. Saxon looked up the Transmat crew on Fria, and their superintendent paid me a visit. We're in for trouble. A damage suit. But there's one way out. No hyper ship's due to hit Fria for months and the matter transmitter won't be finished within two months. And it seems Transmat has a shortage of engineers. If we can get Saxon back to Venus or Earth fast, he'll cover. There'll be no suit.'

'Maybe he'll cover. But what about Transmat?'

'If Saxon won't sign a complaint, what can they do?' Hilton shrugged. 'It's our only out now.'

Danvers' brown-splotched fingers played with his glass.

'A Transmat man,' he muttered. 'Ah-h. So we go back Earthside. What then? We're stuck.' He looked under his drooping lids at Hilton. 'I mean *I'm* stuck. I forgot you're jumping after this voyage.'

'I'm not jumping. I sign for one voyage at a time. What do you want me to do, anyhow?'

'Do what you like. Run out on the old lady. You're no deep-space man.' Danvers spat.

'I know when I'm licked,' Hilton said. 'The smart thing then is to fight in your own weight, when you're outclassed on points, not wait for the knock-out. You've had engineering training. You could get on with Transmat, too.'

For a second Hilton thought the skipper was going to throw the glass at him. Then Danvers dropped back in his chair, trying to force a smile.

'I shouldn't blow my top over that,' he said, with effort. 'It's the truth.'

'Yeah. Well – are you coming?'

'The old lady's ready to jet off?' Danvers said. 'I'll come, then. Have a drink with me first.'

'We haven't time.'

With drunken dignity Danvers stood up. 'Don't get too big for your boots, mister. The voyage isn't over yet. I said have a drink! That's an order.'

'Okay, okay!' Hilton said. 'One drink. Then we go?'

'Sure.'

Hilton gulped the liquor without tasting it. Rather too late, he felt the stinging ache on his tongue. But before he could spring to his feet, the great dim room folded down upon him like a collapsing umbrella, and he lost consciousness with the bitter realization that he had been Mickeyed like the rawest greenhorn. But the skipper had poured that drink …

The dreams were confusing. He was fighting something, but he didn't know what. Sometimes it changed its shape, and sometimes it wasn't there at all, but it was always enormous and terribly powerful.

He wasn't always the same, either. Sometimes he was the wide-eyed kid who had shipped on *Starhopper,* twenty-five years ago, to take his first jump into the Big Night. Then he was a little older, in a bos'n's berth, his eye on a master's ticket, studying, through the white, unchangeable days and nights of hyperspace, the intricate logarithms a skilled pilot must know.

He seemed to walk on a treadmill toward a goal that slid away, never quite within reach. But he didn't know what that goal was. It shone like success. Maybe it was success. But the treadmill had started moving before he'd really got started. In the Big Night a disembodied voice was crying thinly:

'You're in the wrong game, Logger. Thirty years ago you'd have a future in hyper ships. Not any more. There's a new wave coming up. Get out, or drown.'

A red-eyed shadow leaned over him. Hilton fought out of his dream. Awkwardly he jerked up his arm and knocked away the glass at his lips. The Canopian let out a shrill, harsh cry. The liquid that had been in the glass was coalescing in midair into a shining sphere.

The glass floated – and the Canopian floated too. They were in hyper. A few lightweight straps held Hilton to his bunk, but this was his own cabin, he saw. Dizzy, drugged weakness swept into his brain.

The Canopian struck a wall, pushed strongly, and the recoil shot him toward Hilton. The mate ripped free from the restraining straps. He reached out and gathered in a handful of furry black plush. The Canopian clawed at his eyes.

'Captain!' he screamed. 'Captain Danvers!'

Pain gouged Hilton's cheek as his opponent's talons drew blood. Hilton roared with fury. He shot a blow at the Canopian's jaw, but now they were floating free, and the punch did no harm. In midair they grappled, the Canopian incessantly screaming in that thin, insane shrilling.

The door handle clicked twice. There was a voice outside – Wiggins, the second. A deep thudding came. Hilton, still weak, tried to keep the Canopian away with jolting blows. Then the door crashed open, and Wiggins pulled himself in.

'Dzann!' he said. 'Stop it!' He drew a jet-pistol and leveled it at the Canopian.

On the threshold was a little group. Hilton saw Saxon, the Transmat man, gaping there, and other crew members, hesitating, unsure. Then, suddenly, Captain Danvers' face appeared behind the others, twisted, strained with tension.

The Canopian had retreated to a corner and was making mewing, frightened noises.

'What happened, Mr Hilton?' Wiggins said. 'Did this tomcat jump you?'

Hilton was so used to wearing deep-space armor that till now he had scarcely realized its presence. His helmet was hooded back, like that of Wiggins and the rest. He pulled a weight from his belt and threw it aside; the reaction pushed him toward a wall where he gripped a brace.

'Does he go in the brig?' Wiggins asked.

'All right, men,' Danvers said quietly. 'Let me through.' He propelled himself into Hilton's cabin. Glances of discomfort and vague distrust were leveled at him. The skipper ignored them.

'Dzann!' he said. 'Why aren't you wearing your armor? Put it on. The rest of you – get to your stations. You too, Mr Wiggins. I'll handle this.'

Still Wiggins hesitated. He started to say something.

'What are you waiting for?' Hilton said. 'Tell Bruno to bring some coffee. Now beat it.' He maneuvered himself into a sitting position on his bunk. From the tail of his eye he saw Wiggins and the others go out. Dzann, the Canopian, had picked up a suit from the corner and was awkwardly getting into it.

Danvers carefully closed the door, testing the broken lock.

'Got to have that fixed,' he murmured. 'It isn't shipshape this way.' He found a brace and stood opposite the mate, his eyes cool and watchful, the strain still showing on his tired face. Hilton reached for a cigarette.

'Next time your tomcat jumps me, I'll burn a hole through him,' he promised.

'I stationed him here to guard you, in case there was trouble,' Danvers said. 'To take care of you if we cracked up or ran into danger. I showed him how to close your helmet and start the oxygen.'

'Expect a half-witted Canopian to remember that?' Hilton said. 'You also told him to keep drugging me.' He reached toward the shining liquid sphere floating near by and pushed a forefinger into it. He tasted the stuff. 'Sure. *Vakheesh.* That's what you slipped in my drink on Fria. Suppose you start talking, skipper. What's this Canopian doing aboard?'

'I signed him,' Danvers said.

'For what? Supercargo?'

Danvers answered that emotionlessly, watching Hilton.

'Cabin boy.'

'Yeah. What did you tell Wiggins? About me, I mean?'

'I said you'd got doped up,' Danvers said, grinning. 'You were doped, too.'

'I'm not now.' Hilton's tone rang hard. 'Suppose you tell me where we are? I can find out. I can get the equations from Ts'ss and run chartlines. Are we on M-75-L?'

'No, we're not. We're riding another level.'

'Where to?'

The Canopian shrilled, 'I don't know name. Has no name. Double sun it has.'

'You crazy!' Hilton glared at the skipper. 'Are you heading us for a double primary?'

Danvers still grinned. 'Yeah. Not only that, but we're going to land on a planet thirty thousand miles from the suns – roughly.'

Hilton flicked on his deadlight and looked at white emptiness.

'Closer than Mercury is to Sol. You can't do it. How big are the primaries?'

Danvers told him.

'All right. It's suicide. You know that. *La Cucaracha* won't take it.'

'The old lady will take anything the Big Night can hand out.'

'Not this. Don't kid yourself. She might have made it back to Earth – with a Lunar landing – but you're riding into a meat grinder.'

'I haven't forgotten my astrogation,' Danvers said. 'We're coming out of hyper with the planet between us and the primaries. The pull will land us.'

'In small pieces,' Hilton agreed. 'Too bad you didn't keep me doped. If you keep your mouth shut, we'll replot our course to Earth and nobody'll get hurt. If you want to start something, it'll be mutiny, and I'll take my chances at Admiralty.'

The captain made a noise that sounded like laughter.

'All right,' he said. 'Suit yourself. Go look at the equations. I'll be in my cabin when you want me. Come on, Dzann.'

He pulled himself into the companionway, the Canopian gliding behind him as silently as a shadow.

Hilton met Bruno with coffee as he followed Danvers. The mate grunted, seized the covered cup, and sucked in the liquid with the deftness of long practice under antigravity conditions. Bruno watched him.

'All right, sir?' the cook-surgeon said.

'Yeah. Why not?'

'Well – the men are wondering.'

'What about?'

'I dunno, sir. You've never – you've always commanded the launchings, sir. And that Canopian – the men don't like him. They think something's wrong.'

'Oh, they do, do they?' Hilton said grimly. 'I'll come and hold their hands when they turn in for night watch. They talk too much.'

He scowled at Bruno and went on toward the control room. Though he had mentioned mutiny to the skipper, he was too old a hand to condone it, except in extremity. And discipline had to be maintained, even though Danvers had apparently gone crazy.

Ts'ss and Saxon were at the panels. The Selenite slanted a glittering stare at him, but the impassive mask under the audio filter showed no expression. Saxon, however, swung around and began talking excitedly.

'What's happened, Mr Hilton? Something's haywire. We should be ready for an Earth landing by now. But we're not. I don't know enough about these equations to chart back, and Ts'ss won't tell me a blamed thing.'

'There's nothing to tell,' Ts'ss said. Hilton reached past the Selenite and picked up a folder of ciphered figures. He said absently to Saxon:

'Pipe down. I want to concentrate on this.'

He studied the equations.

He read death in them.

Chapter 4. Gamble With Death

Logger Hilton went into the skipper's cabin, put his back against the wall, and started cursing fluently and softly. When he had finished, Danvers grinned at him.

'Through?' he asked.

Hilton switched his stare to the Canopian, who was crouched in a corner, furtively loosening the locks of his spacesuit.

'That applies to you, too, tomcat,' he said.

'Dzann won't mind that,' Danvers said. 'He isn't bright enough to resent cussing. And I don't care, as long as I get what we want. Still going to mutiny and head for Earth?'

'No, I'm not,' Hilton said. With angry patience he ticked off his points on his fingers. 'You can't switch from one hyperplane to another without dropping into ordinary space first, for the springboard. If we went back into normal space, the impact might tear *La Cucaracha* into tiny pieces. We'd be in suits, floating free, a hundred million miles from the nearest planet. Right now we're in a fast hyper flow heading for the edge of the universe, apparently.'

'There's one planet within reach,' Danvers said.

'Sure. The one that's thirty thousand miles from a double primary. And nothing else.'

'Well? Suppose we do crack up? We can make repairs once we land on a planet. We can get the materials we need. You can't do that in deep space. I know landing on this world will be a job. But it's that or nothing – now.'

'What are you after?'

Danvers began to explain:

'This Canopian – Dzann – he made a voyage once, six years ago. A tramp hyper ship. The controls froze, and the tub was heading for outside. They made an emergency landing just in time – picked out a planet that had been detected and charted, but never visited. They repaired there, and came back into the trade routes. But there was a guy aboard, an Earthman who was chummy with Dzann. This guy was smart, and he'd been in the drug racket, I think. Not many people know what raw, growing *paraine* looks like, but this fellow knew. He didn't tell anybody. He took samples, intending to raise money, charter a ship and pick up a cargo later. But he was knifed in some dive on Callisto. He didn't die right away, though, and he liked Dzann. So he gave Dzann the information.'

'That halfwit?' Hilton said. 'How could he remember a course?'

'That's one thing the Canopians can remember. They may be morons, but they're fine mathematicians. It's their one talent.'

'It was a good way for him to bum a drink and get a free berth,' Hilton said.

'No. He showed me the samples. I can talk his lingo, a little, and that's why he was willing to let me in on his secret, back on Fria. Okay. Now. We land on this planet – it hasn't been named – and load a cargo of *paraine.* We repair the old lady, if she needs it –'

'She will!'

'And then head back.'

'To Earth?'

'I think Silenus. It's an easier landing.'

'Now you're worrying about landings,' Hilton said bitterly. 'Well, there's nothing I can do about it, I suppose. I'm stepping out after this voyage. What's the current market quotation on *paraine*?'

'Fifty a pound. At Medical Center, if that's what you mean.'

'Big money,' the mate said. 'You can buy a new ship with the profits and still have a pile left for happy days.'

'You'll get your cut.'

'I'm still quitting.'

'Not till this voyage is over,' Danvers said. 'You're mate on *La Cucaracha.*' He chuckled. 'A deep-space man has plenty of tricks up his sleeve – and I've been at it longer than you.'

'Sure,' Hilton said. 'You're smart. But you forgot Saxon. He'll throw that damage suit against you now, with Transmat behind him.'

Danvers merely shrugged. 'I'll think of something. It's your watch. We have about two hundred hours before we come out of hyper. Take it, mister.'

He was laughing as Hilton went out …

In two hundred hours a good deal can happen. It was Hilton's job to see that it didn't. Luckily, his reappearance had reassured the crew, for when masters fight, the crew will hunt for trouble. But with Hilton moving about *La Cucaracha,* apparently as casual and assured as ever, even the second mate, Wiggins, felt better. Still, it was evident that they weren't heading for Earth. It was taking too long.

The only real trouble came from Saxon, and Hilton was able to handle that. Not easily, however. It had almost come to a showdown, but Hilton was used to commanding men, and finally managed to bluff the Transmat engineer. Dissatisfied but somewhat cowed, Saxon grumblingly subsided.

Hilton called him back.

'I'll do my best for you, Saxon. But we're in the Big Night now. You're not in civilized space. Don't forget that the skipper knows you're a Transmat man, and he hates your insides. On a hyper ship, the Old Man's word is law. So – for your own sake – watch your step!'

Saxon caught the implication. He paled slightly, and after that managed to avoid the captain.

Hilton kept busy checking and rechecking *La Cucaracha.* No outside repairs could be done in hyper, for there was no gravity, and ordinary physical laws were inoperative – magnetic shoes, for example, wouldn't work. Only in the ship itself was there safety. And that safety was illusory for the racking jars of the spatial see-saw might disintegrate *La Cucaracha* in seconds.

Hilton called on Saxon. Not only did he want technical aid, but he wanted to keep the man busy. So the pair worked frantically over juryrigged systems that would provide the strongest possible auxiliary bracing for the ship. Torsion, stress and strain were studied, the design of the craft analyzed, and structural alloys X-ray tested.

Some flaws were found – *La Cucaracha* was a very old lady – but fewer than Hilton expected. In the end, it became chiefly a matter of ripping out partitions and bulkheads and using the material for extra bracing.

But Hilton knew, and Saxon agreed with him, that it would not be enough to cushion the ship's inevitable crash.

There was one possible answer. They sacrificed the after section of the craft. It could be done, though they were racing against time. The working crews mercilessly cut away beams from aft and carried them forward and welded them into position, so that, eventually, the forward half of the ship was tremendously strong and cut off, by tough air-tight partitions, from a skeleton after half. And that half Hilton flooded with manufactured water, to aid in the cushioning effect.

Danvers, of course, didn't like it. But he had to give in. After all, Hilton was keeping the ship on the skipper's course, insanely reckless as that was. If *La Cucaracha* survived, it would be because of Hilton. But Captain Danvers shut himself in his cabin and was sullenly silent.

Toward the end, Hilton and Ts'ss were alone in the control room, while Saxon, who had got interested in the work for its own sake, superintended the last-minute jobs of spot bracing. Hilton, trying to find the right hyper space level that would take them back to Earth after they had loaded the *paraine* cargo, misplaced a decimal point and began to curse in a low, furious undertone.

He heard Ts'ss laugh softly and whirled on the Selenite.

'What's so funny?' he demanded.

'It's not really funny, sir,' Ts'ss said. 'There have to be people like Captain Danvers, in any big thing.'

'What are you babbling about now?' he asked curiously.

Ts'ss shrugged. 'The reason *I* keep shipping on *La Cucaracha* is because I can be busy and efficient aboard, and planets aren't for Selenites any more. We've lost our own world. It died long ago. But I still remember the old traditions of our Empire. If a tradition ever becomes great, it's because of the men who dedicate themselves to it. That's why anything ever became great. And it's why hyper ships came to mean something, Mr Hilton. There were men who lived and breathed hyper ships. Men who worshipped hyper ships, as a man worships a god. Gods fall, but a few men will still worship at the old altars. They can't change. If they were capable of changing, they wouldn't have been the type of men to make their gods great.'

'Been burning *paraine*?' Hilton demanded unpleasantly. His head ached, and he didn't want to find excuses for the skipper.

'It's no drug dream,' Ts'ss said. 'What about the chivalric traditions? We had our Chyra Emperor, who fought for –'

'I've read about Chyra,' Hilton said. 'He was a Selenite King Arthur.'

Slowly Ts'ss nodded his head, keeping his great eyes on Hilton.

'Exactly. A tool who was useful in his time, because he served his cause with a single devotion. But when that cause died, there was nothing for Chyra – or Arthur – to do except die too. But until he did die, he continued to serve his broken god, not believing that it had fallen. Captain Danvers will never believe the hyper ships are passing. He will be a hyper-ship man until he dies. Such men make causes great – but when they outlive their cause, they are tragic figures.'

'Well, I'm not that crazy,' Hilton growled. 'I'm going into some other game.

Transmat or something. You're a technician. Why don't you come with me after this voyage?'

'I like the Big Night,' Ts'ss said. 'And I have no world of my own – no living world. There is nothing to – to make me want success, Mr Hilton. On *La Cucaracha* I can do as I want. But away from the ship, I find that people don't like Selenites. We are too few to command respect or friendship any more. And I'm quite old, you know.'

Startled, Hilton stared at the Selenite. There was no way to detect signs of age on the arachnoid beings. But they always knew, infallibly, how long they had to live, and could predict the exact moment of their death.

Well, *he* wasn't old. And he wasn't a deep-space man as Danvers was. He followed no lost causes. There was nothing to keep him with the hyper ships, after this voyage, if he survived.

A signal rang. Hilton's stomach jumped up and turned into ice, though he had been anticipating this for hours. He reached for a mike.

'Hyper stations! Close helmets! Saxon, report!'

'All work completed, Mr Hilton,' said Saxon's voice, strained but steady.

'Come up here. May need you. General call: stand by! Grab the braces. We're coming in.'

Then they hit the see-saw!

Chapter 5. Hilton's Choice

No doubt about it, she was tough – that old lady. She'd knocked around a thousand worlds and ridden hyper for more miles than a man could count. Something had got into her from the Big Night, something stronger than metal bracing and hard alloys. Call it soul, though there never was a machine that had a soul. But since the first log-craft was launched on steaming seas, men have known that a ship gets a soul – from somewhere.

She hopped like a flea. She bucked like a mad horse. Struts and columns snapped and buckled, and the echoing companionways were filled with an erratic crackling and groaning as metal, strained beyond its strength, gave way. Far too much energy rushed through the engines. But the battered old lady took it and staggered on, lurching, grunting, holding together somehow.

The see-saw bridged the gap between two types of space, and *La Cucaracha* yawed wildly down it, an indignity for an old lady who, at her age, should ride sedately through free void – but she was a hyper ship first and a lady second. She leaped into normal space. The skipper had got his figures right. The double sun wasn't visible, for it was eclipsed by the single planet, but the pull of that monstrous twin star clamped down like a giant's titanic fist closing on *La Cucaracha* and yanking her forward irresistibly.

There was no time to do anything except stab a few buttons. The powerful rocket-jets blazed from *La Cucaracha's* hull. The impact stunned every man aboard. No watcher saw, but the automatic recording charts mapped what happened then.

La Cucaracha struck what was, in effect, a stone wall. Not even that could stop her. But it slowed her enough for the minimum of safety, and she flipped her stern down and crashed on the unnamed planet with all her after jets firing gallantly, the flooded compartments cushioning the shock, and a part of her never made of plastic or metal holding her together against even that hammer blow struck at her by a world.

Air hissed out into a thinner atmosphere and dissipated. The hull was half molten. Jet tubes were fused at a dozen spots. The stern was hash.

But she was still – a ship.

The loading of cargo was routine. The men had seen too many alien planets to pay much attention to this one. There was no breathable air, so the crew worked in their suits – except for three who had been injured in the crash, and were in sick-bay, in a replenished atmosphere within the sealed compartments of the ship. But only a few compartments were so sealed. *La Cucaracha* was a sick old lady, and only first aid could be administered here.

Danvers himself superintended that. *La Cucaracha* was his own, and he kept half the crew busy opening the heat-sealed jets, doing jury-rig repairs, and making the vessel comparatively spaceworthy. He let Saxon act as straw-boss, using the engineer's technical knowledge, though his eyes chilled whenever he noticed the Transmat man.

As for Hilton, he went out with the other half of the crew to gather the *paraine* crop. They used strong-vacuum harvesters, running long, flexible carrier tubes back to *La Cucaracha*'s hold, and it took two weeks of hard, driving effort to load a full cargo. But by then the ship was bulging with *paraine*, the repairs were completed, and Danvers had charted the course to Silenus.

Hilton sat in the control room with Ts'ss and Saxon. He opened a wall compartment, glanced in, and closed it again. Then he nodded at Saxon.

'The skipper won't change his mind,' he said. 'Silenus is our next port. I've never been there.'

'I have,' Ts'ss said. 'I'll tell you about it later.'

Saxon drew an irritated breath. 'You know what the gravity pull is, then, Ts'ss. I've never been there either, but I've looked it up in the books. Giant planets, mostly, and you can't come from hyper into normal space after you've reached the radius. There's no plane of the ecliptic in that system. It's crazy. You have to chart an erratic course toward Silenus, fighting varying gravities from a dozen planets all the way, and then you've still got the primary's pull to consider. You know *La Cucaracha* won't do it, Mr Hilton.'

'I know she won't,' Hilton said. 'We pushed our luck this far, but any more would be suicide. She simply won't hold together for another run. We're stranded here. But the skipper won't believe that.'

'He's insane,' Saxon said. 'I know the endurance limits of a machine – that can be found mathematically – and this ship's only a machine. Or do you agree with Captain Danvers? Maybe you think she's alive!'

Saxon was forgetting discipline, but Hilton knew what strain they were all under.

'No, she's a machine all right,' he merely said. 'And we both know she's been pushed too far. If we go to Silenus, it's –' He made a gesture of finality.

'Captain Danvers says – Silenus,' Ts'ss murmured. 'We can't mutiny, Mr Hilton.'

'Here's the best we can do,' Hilton said. 'Get into hyper somehow, ride the flow, and get out again somehow. But then we're stuck. Any planet or sun with a gravity pull would smash us. The trouble is, the only worlds with facilities to overhaul *La Cucaracha* are the big ones. And if we don't get an overhaul fast we're through. Saxon, there's one answer, though. Land on an asteroid.'

'But why?'

'We could manage that. No gravity to fight, worth mentioning. We certainly can't radio for help, as the signals would take years to reach anybody. Only hyper will take us fast enough. Now – has Transmat set up any stations on asteroids?'

Saxon opened his mouth and closed it again.

'Yes. There's one that would do, in the Rigel system. Far out from the primary. But I don't get it. Captain Danvers wouldn't stand for that.'

Hilton opened the wall compartment. Gray smoke seeped out.

'This is *paraine,*' he said. 'The fumes are being blown into the skipper's cabin through his ventilator. Captain Danvers will be para-happy till we land on that Rigel asteroid, Saxon.'

There was a little silence. Hilton suddenly slammed the panel shut.

'Let's do some charting,' he said. 'The sooner we reach the Rigel port, the sooner we can get back to Earth – via Transmat.'

Curiously, it was Saxon who hesitated.

'Mr Hilton. Wait a minute. Transmat – I know I work for the outfit, but they – they're sharp. Business men. You have to pay plenty to use their matter transmitters.'

'They can transmit a hyper ship, can't they? Or is it too big a job?'

'No, they can expand the field enormously. I don't mean that. I mean they'll want payment, and they'll put on the squeeze. You'll have to give up at least half of the cargo.'

'There'll still be enough left to pay for an overhaul job.'

'Except they'll want to know where the *paraine* came from. You'll be over a barrel. You'll *have* to tell them, eventually. And that'll mean a Transmat station will be set up right here, on this world.'

'I suppose so,' Hilton said quietly. 'But the old lady will be spaceworthy again. When the skipper sees her after the overhaul, he'll know it was the only thing to do. So let's get busy.'

'Remind me to tell you about Silenus,' Ts'ss said.

The Lunar Refitting Station is enormous. A crater has been roofed with a transparent dome, and under it the hyper ships rest in their cradles. They come in battered and broken, and leave clean and sleek and strong, ready for the Big Night again. *La Cucaracha* was down there, no longer the groaning wreck that had settled on the Rigel asteroid, but a lovely lady, shining and beautiful.

Far above, Danvers and Hilton leaned on the railing and watched.

'She's ready to jet,' Hilton said idly. 'And she looks good.'

'No thanks to you, mister.'

'Tush for that!' Hilton said. 'If I hadn't doped you, we'd be dead and *La Cucaracha* floating around in space in pieces. Now look at her.'

'Yeah. Well, she does look good. But she won't carry another *paraine* cargo. That strike was mine. If you hadn't told Transmat the location, we'd be set.' Danvers grimaced. 'Now they're setting up a Transmat station there; a hyper ship can't compete with a matter transmitter.'

'There's more than one world in the Galaxy.'

'Sure. Sure.' But Danvers' eyes brightened as he looked down.

'Where are you heading, Skipper?' Hilton said.

'What's it to you? You're taking that Transmat job, aren't you?'

'You bet. I'm meeting Saxon in five minutes. In fact, we're going down to sign the contracts. I'm through with deep space. But – where are you heading?'

'I don't know,' Danvers said. 'I thought I might run up around Arcturus and see what's stirring.'

Hilton did not move for a long time. Then he spoke without looking at the captain.

'You wouldn't be thinking of a stopover at Canis after that, would you?'

'No.'

'You're a liar.'

'Go keep your appointment,' Danvers said.

Hilton eyed the great hyper ship below. 'The old lady's always been a nice, clean craft. She's never got out of line. She's always charted a straight course. It'd be too bad if she had to carry slaves from Arcturus to the Canis market. It's illegal, of course, but that isn't the point. It's a rotten, crooked racket.'

'I didn't ask your advice, mister!' Danvers flared. 'Nobody's talking about slave-running!'

'I suppose you weren't figuring on unloading the *paraine* at Silenus? You can get a good price for *paraine* from Medical Center, but you can get six times the price from the drug ring on Silenus. Yeah, Ts'ss told me. He's been on Silenus.'

'Oh, shut up,' Danvers said.

Hilton tilted back his head to stare through the dome at the vast darkness above. 'Even if you're losing a fight, it's better to fight clean,' he said. 'Know where it'd end?'

Danvers looked up, too, and apparently saw something in the void that he didn't like.

'How can you buck Transmat?' he demanded. 'You've got to make a profit somehow.'

'There's an easy, dirty way, and there's a clean, hard way. The old lady had a fine record.'

'You're not a deep-space man. You never were. Beat it! I've got to get a crew together!'

'Listen –' Hilton said. He paused. 'Ah, the devil with you. I'm through.'

He turned and walked away through the long steel corridor.

Ts'ss and Saxon were drinking highballs at the Quarter Moon. Through the windows they could see the covered way that led to the Refitting Station, and beyond it the crags of a crater-edge, with the star-shot darkness hanging like a backdrop. Saxon looked at his watch.

'He isn't coming,' Ts'ss said.

The Transmat man moved his shoulders impatiently. 'No. You're wrong. Of course, I can understand your wanting to stay with *La Cucaracha*.'

'Yes, I'm old. That's one reason.'

'But Hilton's young, and he's smart. He's got a big future ahead of him. That guff about sticking to an ideal – well, maybe Captain Danvers is that sort of man, but Hilton isn't. He isn't in love with hyper ships.'

Ts'ss turned his goblet slowly in his curious fingers. 'You are wrong about one thing, Saxon. I'm not shipping on *La Cucaracha*.'

Saxon stared. 'But I thought – why not?'

'I will die within a thousand Earth hours,' Ts'ss said softly. 'When that time comes, I shall go down into the Selenite caverns. Not many know they exist, and only a few of us know the secret caves, the holy places of our race. But I know. I shall go there to die, Saxon. Every man has one thing that is strongest – and so it is with me. I must die on my own world. As for Captain Danvers, he follows his cause, as our Chyra Emperor did, and as your King Arthur did. Men like Danvers made hyper ships great. Now the cause is dead, but the type of men who made it great once can't change their allegiance. If they could, they would never have spanned the Galaxy with their ships. So Danvers will stay with *La Cucaracha*. And Hilton –'

'He's not a fanatic! He won't stay. Why should he?'

'In our legends Chyra Emperor was ruined, and his Empire broken,' Ts'ss said. 'But he fought on. There was one who fought on with him, though he did not believe in Chyra's cause. A Selenite named Jailyra. Wasn't there – in your legends – a Sir Lancelot? He didn't believe in Arthur's cause either, but he was Arthur's friend. So he stayed. Yes, Saxon, there are the fanatics who fight for what they believe – but there are also the others, who do not believe, and who fight in the name of a lesser cause. Something called friendship.'

Saxon laughed and pointed out the window. 'You're wrong, Ts'ss,' he said triumphantly. 'Hilton's no fool. For here he comes.'

Hilton's tall form was visible moving quickly along the way. He passed the window and vanished. Saxon turned to the door.

There was a pause.

'Or, perhaps, it isn't a lesser cause,' Ts'ss said. 'For the Selenite Empire passed, and Arthur's court passed, and the hyper ships are passing. Always the Big Night takes them, in the end. But this has gone on since the beginning –'

'What?'

This time Ts'ss pointed.

Saxon leaned forward to look. Through the angle of the window he could see Hilton, standing motionless on the ramp. Passersby streamed about him unnoticed. He was jostled, and he did not know it, Hilton was thinking.

They saw the look of deep uncertainty on his face. They saw his face suddenly clear. Hilton grinned wryly to himself. He had made up his mind. He turned and went rapidly back the way he had come.

Saxon stared after the broad, retreating back, going the way it had come, toward the Refitting Station where Danvers and *La Cucaracha* waited. Hilton – going back where he had come from, back to what he had never really left.

'The crazy fool!' Saxon said. 'He can't be doing this! Nobody turns down jobs with Transmat!'

Ts'ss gave him a wise, impassive glance. 'You believe that,' he said. 'Transmat means much to you. Transmat needs men like you, to make it great – to keep it growing. You're a lucky man, Saxon. You're riding with the tide. A hundred years from now – two hundred – and you might be standing in Hilton's shoes. Then you'd understand.'

Saxon blinked at him. 'What do you mean?'

'Transmat is growing now,' Ts'ss said gently. 'It will be very great – thanks to men like you. But for Transmat too, there will come an end.'

He shrugged, looking out beyond the crater's rim with his inhuman, faceted eyes, at the glittering points of light which, for a little while, seemed to keep the Big Night at bay.

NOTHING BUT GINGERBREAD LEFT

The only way to make people believe this story is to write it in German. And there's no point in doing that, for the German-speaking world is already starting to worry about gingerbread left.

I speak figuratively. It's safer. Very likely Rutherford, whose interests are equally divided between semantics and Basin Street, could create an English equivalent of gingerbread left, God forbid. As it is, the song, with its *reductio ad absurdum* of rhythm and sense, is meaningless in translation. Try translating Jabberwocky into German. So what?

The song, as Rutherford wrote it in German, had nothing to do with gingerbread, but, since the original is obviously unavailable, I'm substituting the closest thing to it that exists in English. It's lacking in that certain compelling perfection on which Rutherford worked for months, but it'll give you an idea.

We'll start, I suppose, with the night Rutherford threw a shoe at his son. He had reason. Phil Rutherford was in charge of semantics at the University, and he was battling a hangover and trying to correct papers at the same time. Physical disabilities had kept him out of the army, and he was brooding over that, wondering if he should gulp some more Sherman units of thiamin, and hating his students. The papers they had handed in were no good. For the most part, they smelled. Rutherford had an almost illicit love for words, and it distressed him to see them kicked around thus. As Humpty Dumpty had said, the question was which was to be the master.

Usually it wasn't the students. Jerry O'Brien had a good paper, though, and Rutherford went over it carefully, pencil in hand. The radio in the living room didn't bother him; the door was closed, anyhow. But, abruptly, the radio stopped.

'Hi,' said Rutherford's thirteen-year-old son, poking his untidy head across the threshold. There was an ink smudge on the end of the youth's nose. 'Hi, pop. Finished my homework. Can I go to the show?'

'It's too late,' Rutherford said, glancing at his wrist watch. 'Sorry. But you've an early class tomorrow.'

'*Nom d'un plume,*' Bill murmured. He was discovering French.

'Out. I've got work to do. Go listen to the radio.'

'They make with corn tonight. Oh, well –' Bill retreated, leaving the door ajar. From the other room came confused, muffled sounds. Rutherford returned to his work.

He became aware, presently, that Bill was repeating a monotonous, rhythmic string of phrases. Automatically Rutherford caught himself listening, straining to catch the words. When he did, they were meaningless – the familiar catch phrases of kids.

'Ibbety zibbety zibbety zam –'

It occurred to Rutherford that he had been hearing this for some time, the mystic doggerel formula for choosing sides – 'and out goes *you!*' One of those things that stick in your mind rather irritatingly.

'Ibbety zibbety –' Bill kept chanting it in an absent-minded monotone, and Rutherford got up to close the door. It didn't quite stop. He could still hear just enough of the rhythmic noises to start his mind moving in a similar rhythm. Ibbety zibbety – the hell with it.

After a while Rutherford discovered that his lips were moving silently, and he shoved the papers back on his desk, muttering darkly. He was tired, that was it. And correcting exams required concentration. He was glad when the bell rang.

It was Jerry O'Brien, his honor student. Jerry was a tall, thin, dark boy with a passion for the same low-down music that attracted Rutherford. Now he came in grinning.

'Hi, prof,' he greeted the older man. 'I'm in. Just got my papers today.'

'Swell. Sit down and tell me.'

There wasn't much to tell, but it lasted quite a while. Bill hung around, listening avidly. Rutherford swung to glare at his son.

'Lay off that ibbety-zibbety stuff, will you?'

'Huh? Oh sure. I didn't know I was –'

'For days he's been at it,' Rutherford said glumly. 'I can hear it in my sleep.'

'Shouldn't bother a semanticist.'

'Papers. Suppose I'd been doing important precision work. I mean really important. A string of words like that gets inside your head and you can't get it out.'

'Especially if you're under any strain, or if you're concentrating a lot. Distracts your attention, doesn't it?'

'It doesn't bother *me*,' Bill said.

Rutherford grunted. 'Wait'll you're older and really have to concentrate, with a mind like a fine-edged tool. Precision's important. Look what the Nazis have done with it.'

'Huh?'

'Integration,' Rutherford said absently. 'Training for complete concentration. The Germans spent years building a machine – well, they make a fetish out of wire-edged alertness. Look at the stimulant drugs they give their raiding pilots. They've ruthlessly cut out all distractions that might interfere with *über alles*.'

Jerry O'Brien lit a pipe. 'They are hard to distract. German morale's a funny thing. They're convinced they're supermen, and that there's no weakness in *them.* I suppose, psychologically speaking, it'd be a nice trick to convince them of personal weakness.'

'Sure. How? Semantics?'

'I dunno how. Probably it can't be done, except by blitzes. Even then, bombs aren't really an argument. Blowing a man to bits won't necessarily convince his comrades that he's a weakling. Nope, it'd be necessary to make Achilles notice he had a heel.'

'Ibbety zibbety,' Bill muttered.

'Like that,' O'Brien said. 'Get some crazy tune going around a guy's skull, and he'll find it difficult to concentrate. I know I do, sometimes, whenever I go for a thing like the Hut-Sut song.'

Rutherford said suddenly, 'Remember the dancing manias of the middle ages?'

'Form of hysteria, wasn't it? People lined up in queues and jitter-bugged till they dropped.'

'Rhythmic nervous exaltation. It's never been satisfactorily explained. Life is based on rhythm – the whole universe is – but I won't go cosmic on you. Keep it low-down, to the Basin Street level. Why do people go nuts about some kinds of music? Why did the "Marseillaise" start a revolution?'

'Well, why?'

'Lord knows.' Rutherford shrugged. 'But certain strings of phrases, not necessarily musical, which possess rhythm, rhyme, or alliteration, do stick with you. You simply can't get 'em out of your mind. And –' He stopped.

O'Brien looked at him. 'What?'

'Imperfect semantics,' Rutherford said slowly. 'I wonder. Look, Jerry. Eventually we forget things like the Hut-Sut. We can thrust 'em out of our minds. But suppose you got a string of phrases you *couldn't* forget? The perverse factor would keep you from erasing it mentally – the very effort to do so would cancel itself. Hm-m-m. Suppose you're carefully warned not to mention Bill Fields' nose. You keep repeating that to yourself "Don't mention the nose." The words, eventually, fail to make sense. If you met Fields, you'd probably say, quite unconsciously, "Hello, Mr Nose." See?'

'I think so. Like the story that if you meet a piebald horse, you'll fall heir to a fortune if you don't think about the horse's tail till you're past.'

'Exactly.' Rutherford looked pleased. 'Get a perfect semantic formula and you can't forget it. And the perfect formula would have everything. It'd have rhythm, and just enough sense to start you wondering what it meant. It wouldn't necessarily mean anything, but –'

'Could such a formula be invented?'

'Yeah. Yeah. Combine language with mathematics and psychology, and something could be worked out. Could be, such a thing was accidentally written in the middle ages. What price the dance manias?'

'I don't think I'd like it.' O'Brien grimaced. 'Too much like hypnosis.'

'If it is, it's self-hypnosis, and unconscious. That's the beauty of it. Just for the hell of it – draw up a chair.' Rutherford reached for a pencil.

'Hey, pop,' Bill said, 'why not write it in German?'

Rutherford and O'Brien looked at each other, startled. Slowly a gleam of diabolic understanding grew in their eyes.

'German?' Rutherford murmured. 'You majored in it, didn't you, Jerry?'

'Yeah. And you're no slouch at it, either. Yeah – we *could* write it in German, couldn't we? The Nazis must be getting plenty sick of the Horst Wessel song.'

'Just for the … uh … fun of it,' Rutherford said, 'let's try. Rhythm first. Catchy rhythm, with a break to avoid monotony. We don't need a tune.' He scribbled for a bit. 'It's quite impossible, of course, and even if we did it, Washington probably wouldn't be interested.'

'My uncle's a senator,' O'Brien said blandly.

LEFT!
LEFT!
LEFT a wife and SEVenteen children in
STARVing condition with NOTHing but gingerbread LEFT
LEFT!
LEFT a wife and SEVenteen children –

'Well, I might know something about it,' said Senator O'Brien.

The officer stared at the envelope he had just opened. 'So? A few weeks ago you gave me this, not to be opened till you gave the word. Now what?'

'You've read it.'

'I've read it. So you've been annoying the Nazi prisoners in that Adirondack hotel. You've got 'em dizzy repeating some German song I can't make head nor tail out of.'

'Naturally. You don't know German. Neither do I. But it seems to have worked on the Nazis.'

'My private report says they're dancing and singing a lot of the time.'

'Not dancing, exactly. Unconscious rhythmic reflexes. And they keep repeating the … er … semantic formula.'

'Got a translation?'

'Sure, but it's meaningless in English. In German it has the necessary rhythm. I've already explained –'

'I know, senator, I know. But the War Department has no time for vague theories.'

'I request simply that the formula be transmitted frequently on broadcasts to Germany. It may be hard on the announcers but they'll get over it. So will the Nazis, but by that time their morale will be shot. Get the Allied radios to cooperate –'

'Do you really believe in this?'

The senator gulped. 'As a matter of fact, no. But my nephew almost convinced me. He helped Professor Rutherford work out the formula.'

'Argued you into it?'

'Not exactly. But he keeps going around muttering in German. So does Rutherford. Anyway – this can do no harm. And I'm backing it to the limit.'

'But –' The officer peered at the formula in German. 'What possible harm can it do for people to repeat a song? How can it help us –'

LEFT!
LEFT!
LEFT a wife and SEVenteen children in
STARVing condition with NOTHing but gingerbread LEFT
LEFT –

'*Aber,*' said Harben, '*aber, aber, aber!*'

'But me no buts,' retorted his superior officer, Eggerth. 'The village must be searched completely. The High Command is quartering troops here tomorrow, on their way to the eastern front, and we must make sure there are no weapons hidden anywhere.'

'*Aber* we search the village regularly.'

'Then search it again,' Eggerth ordered. 'You know how those damned Poles are. Turn your back for a minute and they've snatched a gun out of thin air. We want no bad reports going back to the Führer. Now get out; I must finish *my* report, and it must be accurate.' He thumbed through a sheaf of notes. 'How many cows, how many sheep, the harvest possibilities – *ach*. Go away and let me concentrate. Search carefully.'

'*Heil,*' Harben said glumly, and turned. On the way out his feet found a familiar rhythm. He started to mutter something.

'Captain Harben!'

Harben stopped.

'What the devil are you saying?'

'Oh – the men have a new marching song. Nonsense, but it's catchy. It is excellent to march to.'

'What is it?'

Harben made a deprecating gesture. 'Meaningless. It goes "Left, left, left a wife and seventeen children –" '

Eggerth stopped him. 'That. I've heard it. *Unsinn. Heil.*'

Heiling, Harben went away, his lips moving. Eggerth bent over the report, squinting in the bad light. Ten head of cattle, scarcely worth slaughtering for their meat, but the cows giving little milk ... Hm-m-m. Grain – the situation was bad there, too. How the Poles managed to eat at all – they'd be glad enough to have gingerbread, Eggerth thought. For that matter, gingerbread was nutritious, wasn't it? Why were they in starving condition if there was still gingerbread? Maybe there wasn't *much* –

Still, why nothing *but* gingerbread? Could it be, perhaps, that the family disliked it so much they ate up everything else first? A singularly shortsighted group. Possibly their ration cards allowed them nothing but gingerbread *LEFT*

LEFT

LEFT a wife and SEVenteen children in

STARVing condition –

Eggerth caught himself sharply, and his pencil began to move again. The grain – he figured rather more slowly than usual, because his mind kept skipping back to a ridiculous rhythm. *Verdammt!* He would not –

Inhabitants of the village, thirty families, or was it forty? Forty, yes. Men, women, children – small families mostly. Still, one could seldom expect to find seventeen children. With that many, a *Frau* could be wealthy through bounties alone. Seventeen children. In starving condition. Why didn't *they* eat the gingerbread? Ridiculous. What, in the name of *Gott*, did it matter whether seventeen nonexistent, completely hypothetical children ate gingerbread, or, for that matter, whether they ate nothing but gingerbread LEFT

LEFT

LEFT a wife and SEVenteen children –

'Hell fire and damnation!' exploded Eggerth, looking furiously at his watch. 'I might have finished the report by this time. Seventeen children, *pfui!*'

Once more he bent to his work, determined not to think of ... of – '

But it nibbled at the corners of his mind, like an intrusive mouse. Each time he recognized its presence, he could thrust it away. Unfortunately, Eggerth was repeating to his subconscious, 'Don't think of it. Forget it.'

'Forget what?' asked the subconscious automatically.

'Nothing but gingerbread LEFT –'

'Oh, yeah?' said the subconscious.

The search party wasn't working with its accustomed zeal and accuracy. The men's minds didn't seem entirely on their business. Harben barked orders, conscious of certain distractions – sweat trickling down inside his uniform, the harsh scratchiness of the cloth, the consciousness of the Poles silently watching and waiting. That was the worst of being in an army of occupation. You always felt that the conquered people were waiting. Well –

'Search,' Harben commanded. 'By pairs. Be thorough.'

And they were thorough enough. They marched here and there through the village, to a familiar catchy rhythm, and their lips moved. Which, of course, was harmless. The only untoward incident occurred in an attic which two soldiers were searching. Harben wandered in to supervise. He was astonished to see one of his men open a cupboard, stare directly at a rusty rifle barrel, and then shut the door again. Briefly Harben was at a loss. The soldier moved on.

'Attention!' Harben said. Heels clicked. 'Vogel, I saw that.'

'Sir?' Vogel seemed honestly puzzled, his broad, youthful face blank.

'We are searching for guns. Or, perhaps, the Poles have bribed you to overlook certain matters – eh?'

Vogel's cheeks reddened. 'No, sir.'

Harben opened the cupboard and took out a rusty, antique matchlock. It was obviously useless as a weapon now, but nevertheless it should have been confiscated. Vogel's jaw dropped.

'Well?'

'I … didn't see it, sir.'

Harben blew out his breath angrily. 'I'm not an idiot. I saw you, man! You looked right at that gun. Are you trying to tell me –'

There was a pause. Vogel said stolidly, 'I did not see it, sir.'

'Ah? You are growing absent-minded. You would not take bribes, Vogel; I know you're a good party man. But when you do anything, you must keep your wits about you. Wool-gathering is dangerous business in an occupied village. Resume your search.'

Harben went out, wondering. The men definitely seemed slightly distracted by something. What the devil could be preying on their minds so that Vogel, for example, could look right at a gun and not see it? Nerves? Ridiculous. Nordics were noted for self-control. Look at the way the men moved – their coordinated rhythm that bespoke perfect military training. Only through discipline could anything valuable be attained. The body and the mind were, in fact, machines, and should be controlled. There a squad went down the street, marching left, left, left a wife and –

That absurd song. Harben wondered where it had come from. It had grown like a rumor. Troops stationed in the village had passed it on, but where they had learned it Heaven knew. Harben grinned. When he got leave, he'd remember to tell the lads in Unter den Linden about that ridiculous song – it was just absurd enough to stick in your mind. Left. Left.

LEFT a wife and SEVenteen children in
STARVing condition –

After a while the men reported back; they hadn't found anything. The antique flintlock wasn't worth bothering about, though, as a matter of routine, it must be reported and the Polish owner questioned. Harben marched the men back to their quarters and went to Eggerth's billet. Eggerth, however, was still busy, which was unusual, for he was usually a fast worker. He glowered at Harben.

'Wait. I cannot be interrupted now.' And he returned to his scribbling. The floor was already littered with crumpled papers.

Harben found an old copy of *Jugend* that he hadn't read, and settled himself in a corner. An article on youth training was interesting. Harben turned a page, and then realized that he'd lost the thread. He went back.

He read a paragraph, said, 'Eh?' and skipped back again. The words were there; they entered his mind; they made sense – of course. He was concentrating. He wasn't allowing that damned marching song to interfere, with its gingerbread LEFT

LEFT

LEFT a wife and SEVenteen children –

Harben never did finish that article.

Witter of the Gestapo sipped cognac and looked across the table at Herr Doktor Schneidler. Outside the café, sunlight beat down strongly on the Königstrasse.

'The Russians –' Schneidler said.

'Never mind the Russians,' Witter broke in hastily. 'I am still puzzled by that Polish affair. Guns – machine guns – hidden in that village, after it had been searched time and again. It is ridiculous. There were no raids over that locality recently; there was no way for the Poles to have got those guns in the last few weeks.'

'Then they must have had them hidden for more than a few weeks.'

'Hidden? We search carefully, Herr Doktor. I am going to interview that man Eggerth again. And Harben. Their records are good, but –' Witter fingered his mustache nervously. 'No. We can take nothing for granted. You are a clever man; what do you make of it?'

'That the village was *not* well searched.'

'Yet it was. Eggerth and Harben maintain that, and their men support them. It's ridiculous to suppose that bulky machine guns could have been passed over like little automatics that can be hidden under a board. So. When the troops marched into that village, the Poles killed forty-seven German soldiers by machine gunning them from the rooftops.' Witter's fingers beat on the table top in a jerky rhythm.

Tap.

Tap.

Tap-ta-tap-ta –

'Eh?' Witter said. 'I didn't catch –'

'Nothing. Merely that you will, of course, investigate carefully. You have a regular routine for such investigations, eh? Well, then – it is simply a matter of scientific logic, as in my own work.'

'How is that progressing?' Witter asked, going off at a tangent.

'Soon. Soon.'

'I have heard that before. For some weeks, in fact. Have you run into a snag? Do you need help?'

'*Ach,* no,' Schneidler snapped, with sudden irritation. 'I want no damn fool assistants. This is precision work, Witter. It calls for split-second accuracy. I have been specially trained in thermodynamics, and I know just when a button should be pressed, or an adjustment made. The heat-radiation of disintegrating bodies –' Presently Schneidler stopped, confused. 'Perhaps, though, I need a rest. I'm fagged out. My mind's stale. I concentrate, and suddenly I find I have botched an important experiment. Yesterday I had to add exactly six drops of a ... a fluid to a mixture I'd prepared, and before I knew it the hypo was empty, and I'd spoiled the whole thing.'

Witter scowled. 'Is something worrying you? Preying on your mind? We cannot afford to have that. If it is your nephew –'

'No, no. I am not worried about Franz. He's probably enjoying himself in Paris. I suppose I'm ... *damn!*' Schneidler smashed his fist down on the table. 'It is ridiculous. A crazy song!'

Witter raised an eyebrow and waited.

'I have always prided myself on my mind. It is a beautifully coherent and logical machine. I could understand its failing through a sensible cause – worry, or even madness. But when I can't get an absurd nonsense rhyme out of my head – I broke some valuable apparatus today,' Schneidler confessed, compressing his lips. 'Another spoiled experiment. When I realized what I'd done, I swept the whole mess off the table. I do not want a vacation; it is important that I finish my work quickly.'

'It is important that you finish,' Witter said. 'I advise you to take that vacation. The Bavarian Alps are pleasant. Fish, hunt, relax completely. Do not think about your work. I would not mind going with you, but –' He shrugged.

Storm troopers passed along the Königstrasse. They were repeating words that made Schneidler jerk nervously. Witter's hands resumed their rhythm on the table top.

'I shall take that vacation,' Schneidler said.

'Good. It will fix you up. Now I must get on with my investigation of that Polish affair, and then a check-up on some Luftwaffe pilots –'

The Herr Doktor Schneidler, four hours later, sat alone in a train compartment, already miles out of Berlin. The countryside was green and pleasant outside the windows. Yet, for some reason, Schneidler was not happy.

He lay back on the cushions, relaxing. Think about nothing. That was it. Let the precision tool of his mind rest for a while. Let his mind wander free. Listen to the somnolent rhythm of the wheels, *clickety-clickety* –

CLICK!

CLICK!
CLICK a wife and CLICKenteen children in
STARVing condition with NOTHing but gingerbread
LEFT –

Schneidler cursed thickly, jumped up, and yanked the cord. He was going back to Berlin. But not by train. Not in any conveyance that had wheels. *Gott,* no!

The Herr Doktor walked back to Berlin. At first he walked briskly. Then his face whitened, and he lagged. But the compelling rhythm continued. He went faster, trying to break step. For a while that worked. Not for long. His mind kept slipping his gears, and each time he'd find himself going LEFT –

He started to run. His beard streaming, his eyes aglare, the Herr Doktor Schneidler, great brain and all, went rushing madly back to Berlin, but he couldn't outpace the silent voice that said, faster and faster, LEFT
LEFT
LEFTawifeandSEVenteenchildrenin
STARVingcondition –

'Why did that raid fail?' Witter asked.

The Luftwaffe pilot didn't know. Everything had been planned, as usual, well in advance. Every possible contingency had been allowed for, and the raid certainly shouldn't have failed. The R. A. F. planes should have been taken by surprise. The Luftwaffe should have dropped their bombs on the targets and retreated across the Channel without difficulty.

'You had your shots before going up?'

'Yes, sir.'

'Kurtman, your bombardier, was killed?'

'Yes, sir.'

'Inexcusably?'

There was a pause. Then – 'Yes, sir.'

'He could have shot down that Hurricane that attacked you?'

'I ... yes, sir.'

'Why did he fail?'

'He was ... singing, sir.'

Witter leaned back in his chair. 'He was singing. And I suppose he got so interested in the song that he forgot to fire.'

'Yes, sir.'

'Then, why in the name of ... of – Why didn't you dodge that Hurricane?'

'I was singing, too, sir.'

The R. A. F. were coming over. The man at the antiaircraft whistled between his teeth and waited. The moonlight would help. He settled himself in the padded seat and peered into the eyepiece. All was ready. Tonight there were at least some British ships that would go raiding no more.

It was a minor post in occupied France, and the man wasn't especially important, except that he was a good marksman. He looked up, watching a little cloud luminous in the sky. He was reminded of a photographic negative. The British planes would be dark, unlike the cloud, until the searchlights caught them. Then –

Ah, well. Left. Left. Left a wife and seventeen –

They had sung that at the canteen last night, chanting it in chorus. A catchy piece. When he got back to Berlin – if ever – he must remember the words. How did they go?

In starving condition –

His thoughts ran on independently of the automatic rhythm in his brain. Was he dozing? Startled, he shook himself, and then realized that he was still alert. There was no danger. The song kept him awake, rather than inducing slumber. It had a violent, exciting swing that got into a man's blood with its

LEFT

LEFT

LEFT a wife –

However, he must remain alert. When the R. A. F. bombers came over, he must do what he had to do. And they were coming now. Distantly he could hear the faint drone of their motors, pulsing monotonously like the song, bombers for Germany, starving condition, with nothing but gingerbread

LEFT!

LEFT

LEFT a wife and SEVenteen children in

STARVing condition with –

Remember the bombers, your hand on the trigger, your eye to the eyepiece, with nothing but gingerbread

LEFT!

LEFT

LEFT a wife and –

Bombers are coming, the British are coming, but don't fire too quickly, just wait till they're closer, and LEFT

LEFT

LEFT a wife and there are their motors, and there go the searchlights, and there they come over, in starving condition with nothing but gingerbread

LEFT!

LEFT!

LEFT a wife and SEVenteen children in –

They were gone. The bombers had passed over. He hadn't fired at all. He'd *forgotten!*

They'd passed over. Not one was left. Nothing was left. Nothing but gingerbread

LEFT!

The Minister of Propaganda looked at the report as though it might suddenly turn into Stalin and bite him. 'No,' he said firmly. 'No, Witter. If this is false, it is false. If it is true, we dare not admit it.'

'I don't see why,' Witter argued. 'It's that song. I've been checking up for a long time, and it's the only logical answer. The thing has swept the German-speaking world. Or it soon will.'

'And what harm can a song do?'

Witter tapped the report. 'You read this. The troops breaking ranks and doing ... what is it? ... snake dances! And singing that piece all the while.'

'Forbid them to sing it.' But the minister's voice was dubious.

'*Ja,* but can they be forbidden to think it? They *always* think of what is *verboten.* They can't help it. It's a basic human instinct.'

'That is what I mean when I said we couldn't admit the menace of this – song, Witter. It mustn't be made important to Germans. If they consider it merely as an absurd string of words, they'll forget it. Eventually,' the minister added.

'The Führer –'

'He must not know. He must not hear about this. He is a nervous type, Witter; you realize that. I hope he will not hear the song. But, even if he does, he *must not* realize that it is potentially dangerous.'

'Potentially?'

The minister gestured significantly. 'Men have killed themselves because of that song. The scientist Schneidler was one. A nervous type. A manic-depressive type, in fact. He brooded over the fact that the ginger – that the phrases stuck in his mind. In a depressive mood, he swallowed poison. There have been others. Witter, between ourselves, this is extremely dangerous. Do you know why?'

'Because it's – absurd?'

'Yes. There is a poem, perhaps you know it – life is real, life is earnest. Germany believes that. We are a logical race. We conquer through logic, because Nordics are the superrace. And if supermen discover that they cannot control their minds –'

Witter sighed. 'It seems strange that a song should be so important.'

'There is no weapon against it. If we admit that it is dangerous, we double or triple its menace. At present, many people find it hard to concentrate. Some find rhythmic movements necessary – uncontrollable. Imagine what would happen if we forbade the people to think of the song.'

'Can't we use psychology? Make it ridiculous – explain it away?'

'It is ridiculous already. It makes no pretense at being anything more than an absurd string of nearly meaningless words. And we can't admit it *has* to be explained away. Also, I hear that some are finding treasonable meanings in it, which is the height of nonsense.'

'Oh? How?'

'Famine. The necessity for large families. Even desertion of the Nazi ideal. Er … even the ridiculous idea that gingerbread refers to –' The minister glanced up at the picture on the wall.

Witter looked startled, and, after a hesitant pause, laughed. 'I never thought of that. Silly. What I always wondered was why they were starving when there was still plenty of gingerbread. Is it possible to be allergic to gingerbread?'

'I do not think so. The gingerbread may have been poisoned – a man who would desert his family might have cause to hate them, also. Perhaps hate them enough to – *Captain Witter!*'

There was a blank silence. Presently Witter got up, heiled, and departed, carefully breaking step. The minister looked again at the picture on the wall, tapped the bulky report before him, and shoved it away to examine a typewritten sheaf which was carefully labeled IMPORTANT. It was important. In half an hour the Führer would broadcast a speech, one for which the world had been waiting. It would explain certain things about dubious matters, such as the Russian campaign. And it was a good speech – excellent propaganda. There were to be two broadcasts, the first to Germany, the second to the rest of the world.

The minister rose and walked back and forth on the rich carpet. His lip lifted in a sneer. The way to conquer any enemy was to crush him – face him and smash him. If the rest of Germany had his own mentality, his own self-confidence, that ridiculous song would lose all its force.

'So,' the minister said. 'It goes so. Left. Left. Left a wife and seventeen children – so. It cannot harm me. It can get no hold on my mind. I repeat it, but only when I wish to do so; and I wish to do so to prove that the doggerel is futile – on me, anyway. So. Left. Left. Left a wife –'

Back and forth strode the Minister of Propaganda, his hard, clipped voice snappily intoning the phrases. This wasn't the first time. He often repeated the song aloud – but, of course, merely to prove to himself that he was stronger than it.

Adolf Hitler was thinking about gingerbread and Russia. There were other problems, too. It was difficult being Leader. Eventually, when a better man came along, he would step out, his work done. The well-worn record slipped from its groove, and Hitler pondered the speech he held. Yes, it was good. It explained much – why things had gone wrong in Russia, why the English invasion had failed, why the English were doing the impossible by way of raiding the continent. He had worried about those problems. They were not really problems, but the people might not understand, and might lose confidence in their Führer. However, the speech would explain everything – even Hess. Goebbels had worked for days on the psychological effects of the speech, and it was, therefore, doubly important that it go through without a hitch. Hitler reached for an atomizer and sprayed his throat, though that was really unnecessary. His voice was in top shape.

It would be distressing if –

Pfui! There would be no hitch. The speech was too important. He had made speeches before, swayed people with the weapon of his oratory. The crucial point, of course, was the reference to Russia and the ill-fated spring campaign. Yet Goebbels had a beautiful explanation; it was true, too.

'It is true,' Hitler said aloud.

Well, it was. And sufficiently convincing. From the Russian discussion he would go on to Hess, and then –

But the Russian question – that was vital. He must throw all his power into the microphones at that moment. He rehearsed mentally. A pause. Then, in a conversational voice, he would say, 'At last I may tell you the truth about our Russian campaign, and why it was a triumph of strategy for German arms –'

He'd prove it, too.

But he must not forget for a moment how vitally important this speech was, and especially the crucial point in it. Remember. Remember. Do it exactly as rehearsed. Why, if he failed –

There was no such word.

But *if* he failed –

No. Even if he did –

But he wouldn't. He mustn't. He never had. And this was a crisis. Not an important one, after all, he supposed, though the people were no longer wholeheartedly behind him. Well, what was the worst that could happen? He might be unable to make the speech. It would be postponed. There could be explanations. Goebbels could take care of that. It *wasn't* important.

Don't think about it.

On the contrary, think about it. Rehearse again. The pause. 'At last I may tell you –'

It was time.

All over Germany people were waiting for the speech. Adolf Hitler stood before the microphones, and he was no longer worried. At the back of his mind, he created a tiny phonograph record that said, over and over, 'Russia. Russia. Russia.' It would remind him what to do, at the right moment. Meanwhile, he launched into his speech.

It was good. It was a Hitler speech.

'Now!' said the record.

Hitler paused, taking a deep breath, throwing his head arrogantly back. He looked out at the thousands of faces beneath his balcony. But he wasn't thinking about them. He was thinking of the pause, and the next line; and the pause lengthened.

Important! Remember! Don't fail!

Adolf Hitler opened his mouth. Words came out. Not quite the right words.

Ten seconds later Adolf Hitler was cut off the air.

It wasn't Hitler personally who spoke to the world a few hours later. Goebbels had had a record made, and the transcription, oddly enough, didn't mention Russia. Or any of the vital questions that had been settled so neatly. The Führer simply couldn't talk about those questions. It wasn't mike fright, exactly. Whenever Hitler reached the crucial point in his speech, he turned green, gritted his teeth, and said – the wrong thing. He couldn't get over that semantic block. The more he tried, the less he succeeded. Finally Goebbels saw what was happening and called it off.

The world broadcast was emasculated. At the time there was considerable discussion as to why Hitler hadn't stuck to his announced program. He'd intended to mention Russia. Why, then –

Not many people knew. But more people will know now. In fact, a lot of people in Germany are going to know. Things get around there. Planes go over and drop leaflets, and people whisper, and they'll remember a certain catchy German stanza that's going the rounds.

Yeah. Maybe this particular copy of *Astounding* will find its way to England, and maybe an R. A. F. pilot will drop it near Berlin, or Paris, for that matter. Word will get around. There are lots of men on the continent who can read English.

And they'll talk.

They won't believe, at first. But they'll keep their eyes open. And there's a catchy little rhythm they'll remember. Some day the story will reach Berlin or Berchtesgarten. Some day it'll reach the guy with the little mustache and the big voice.

And, a little while later – days or weeks, it doesn't matter – Goebbels is going to walk into a big room, and there he's going to see Adolf Hitler goose-stepping around and yelling:

LEFT

LEFT

LEFT a wife and SEVenteen children in

STARVing condition with NOTHing but gingerbread

LEFT –

THE IRON STANDARD

Alien races didn't have to be either friendly or unfriendly; they could be stubbornly indifferent – with serious effect.

'So the ghost won't walk for a year – Venusian time,' Thirkell said, spooning up cold beans with a disgusted air.

Rufus Munn, the captain, looked up briefly from his task of de-cockroaching the soup. 'Dunno why we had to import these. A year plus four weeks, Steve. There'll be a month at space before we hit Earth again.'

Thirkell's round, pudgy face grew solemn. 'What happens in the meantime? Do we starve on cold beans?'

Munn sighed, glancing through the open, screened port of the spaceship *Goodwill* to where dim figures moved in the mists outside. But he didn't answer. Barton Underhill, supercargo and handy man, who had wangled his passage by virtue of his father's wealth, grinned tightly and said, 'What d'you expect? We don't dare use fuel. There's just enough to get us home. So it's cold beans or nothing.'

'Soon it will be nothing,' Thirkell said solemnly. 'We have been spendthrifts. Wasting our substance in riotous living.'

'Riotous living!' Munn growled. 'We gave most of our grub to the Venusians.'

'Well,' Underhill murmured, 'they fed us – for a month.'

'Not now. There's an embargo. What do they have against us, anyhow?'

Munn thrust back his stool with sudden decision. 'That's something we'll have to figure out. Things can't go on like this. We simply haven't enough food to last us a year. And we can't live off the land –' He stopped as someone unzipped the valve screen and entered, a squat man with high cheekbones and a beak of a nose in a red-bronze face.

'Find anything, Redskin?' Underhill asked.

Mike Soaring Eagle tossed a plastisac on the table. 'Six mushrooms. No wonder the Venusians use hydroponics. They have to. Only fungi will grow in this sponge of a world, and most of that's poisonous. No use, skipper.'

Munn's mouth tightened. 'Yeah. Where's Bronson?'

'Panhandling. But he won't get a *fal*.' The Navaho nodded towards the port. 'Here he comes now.'

After a moment the others heard Bronson's slow footsteps. The engineer came in, his face red as his hair. 'Don't ask me,' he murmured. 'Don't say a word, anybody. Me, a Kerry man, trying to bum a lousy *fal* from a shagreen-skinned so-and-so with an iron ring in his nose like a Ubangi savage. Think of it! The shame will stay with me forever.'

'My sympathy,' Thirkell said. 'But did you get any *fals*?'

Bronson glared at him. 'Would I have taken his dirty coins if he'd offered them?' the engineer yelled, his eyes bloodshot. 'I'd have flung them in his slimy face, and you can take my word for it. *I* touch their rotten money? Give me some beans.' He seized a plate and morosely began to eat.

Thirkell exchanged glances with Underhill. 'He didn't get any money,' the latter said.

Bronson started back with a snort. 'He asked me if I belonged to the Beggars' Guild! Even tramps have to join a union on this planet!'

Captain Munn scowled thoughtfully. 'No, it isn't a union, Bronson, or even much like the medieval guilds. The *tarkomars* are a lot more powerful and a lot less principled. Unions grew out of a definite social and economic background, and they fill a purpose – a check-and-balance system that keeps building. I'm not talking about unions; on Earth some of 'em are good – like the Air Transport – and some are graft-ridden, like Undersea Dredgers. The *tarkomars* are different. They don't fulfil any productive purpose. They just keep the Venusian system in its backwater.'

'Yes,' Thirkell said, 'and unless we're members, we aren't allowed to work – at anything. And we can't be members till we pay the initiation fee – a thousand *sofals*.'

'Easy on those beans,' Underhill cautioned. 'We've only ten more cans.'

There was silence. Presently Munn passed cigarettes.

'We've got to do something, that's certain,' he said. 'We can't get food except from the Venusians, and they won't give it to us. One thing in our favor: the laws are so arbitrary that they can't refuse to *sell* us grub – it's illegal to refuse legal tender.'

Mike Soaring Eagle glumly sorted his six mushrooms. 'Yeah. *If* we can get our hands on legal tender. We're broke – broke on Venus – and we'll soon be starving to death. If anybody can figure out an answer to that one –'

This was in 1964, three years after the first successful flight to Mars, five years since Dooley and Hastings had brought their ship down in Mare Imbrium. The Moon, of course, was uninhabited, save by active but unintelligent algae. The big-chested, alert Martians, with their high metabolism and their brilliant, erratic minds, had been friendly, and it was certain that the cultures of Mars and Earth would not clash. As for Venus, till now, no ship had landed there.

The *Goodwill* was the ambassador. It was an experiment, like the earlier

Martian voyage, for no one knew whether or not there was intelligent life on Venus. Supplies for more than a year were stowed aboard, dehydrates, plastibulbs, concentrates and vitamin foods, but every man of the crew had a sneaking hunch that food would be found in plenty on Venus.

There was food – yes. The Venusians grew it, in their hydroponic tanks under the cities. But on the surface of the planet grew nothing edible at all. There was little animal or bird life, so hunting was impossible, even had the Earthmen been allowed to retain their weapons. And in the beginning it had seemed like a gala holiday after the arduous space trip – a year-long fete and carnival in an alien, fascinating civilization.

It was alien, all right. The Venusians were conservative. What was good enough for their remote ancestors was quite good enough for them. They didn't *want* changes, it seemed. Their current set-up had worked O.K. for centuries; why alter it now?

The Earthmen meant change – that was obvious.

Result: a boycott of the Earthmen.

It was all quite passive. The first month had brought no trouble; Captain Munn had been presented with the keys of the capital city, Vyring, on the outskirts of which the *Goodwill* now rested, and the Venusians brought food in plenty – odd but tasty dishes from the hydroponic gardens. In return, the Earthmen were lavish with their own stores, depleting them dangerously.

And the Venusian food spoiled quickly. There was no need to preserve it, for the hydroponic tanks turned out a steady, unfailing supply. In the end the Earthmen were left with a few weeks' stock of the food they had brought with them, and a vast pile of garbage that had been lusciously appetizing a few days before.

Then the Venusians stopped bringing their quick-spoiling fruits, vegetables and meat-mushrooms and clamped down. The party was over. They had no intention of harming the Earthmen; they remained carefully friendly. But from now on it was Pay as You're Served – and no checks cashed. A big meat-mushroom, enough for four hungry men, cost ten *fals*.

Since the Earthmen had no *fals*, they got no meat-mushrooms – nor anything else.

In the beginning it hadn't seemed important. Not until they got down to cases and began to wonder exactly how they could get food.

There was no way.

So they sat in the *Goodwill* eating cold beans and looking like five of the Seven Dwarfs, a quintet of stocky, short, husky men, big-boned and muscular, especially chosen for their physiques to stand the rigors of space flight – and their brains, also specially chosen, couldn't help them now.

It was a simple problem – simple and primitive. They, the representatives of Earth's mightiest culture, were hungry. They would soon be hungrier.

And they didn't have a *fal* – nothing but worthless gold, silver and paper currency. There was metal in the ship, but none of the pure metal they needed, except in alloys that couldn't be broken down.

Venus was on the iron standard.

'– there's got to be an answer,' Munn said stubbornly, his hard-bitten, harsh face somber. He pushed back his plate with an angry gesture. 'I'm going to see the Council again.'

'What good will that do?' Thirkell wanted to know. 'We're on the spot, there's no getting around it. Money talks.'

'Just the same, I'm going to talk to Jorust,' the captain growled. 'She's no fool.'

'Exactly,' Thirkell said cryptically.

Munn stared at him, beckoned to Mike Soaring Eagle and turned towards the valve. Underhill jumped up eagerly.

'May I go?'

Bronson gloomily toyed with his beans. 'Why do *you* want to go? You couldn't even play a slot machine in Vyring's skid row – if they had slot machines. Maybe you think if you tell 'em your old man's a Tycoon of Amalgamated Ores, they'll break down and hand out meal tickets – eh?'

But his tone was friendly enough, and Underhill merely grinned. Captain Munn said, 'Come along, if you want, but hurry up.' The three men went out into the steaming mists, their feet sloshing through sticky mud.

It wasn't uncomfortably hot; the high winds of Venus provided for quick evaporation, a natural air conditioning that kept the men from feeling the humidity. Munn referred to his compass. The outskirts of Vyring were half a mile away, but the fog was, as usual, like pea soup. On Venus it is always bird-walking weather. Silently the trio slogged on.

'I thought Indians knew how to live off the land,' Underhill presently remarked to the Navaho. Mike Soaring Eagle looked at him quizzically.

'I'm not a Venusian Indian,' he explained. 'Maybe I could make a bow and arrow and bring down a Venusian – but that wouldn't help, unless he had a lot of *sofals* in his purse.'

'We might eat him,' Underhill murmured. 'Wonder what roast Venusian would taste like?'

'Find out and you can write a best seller when you get back home,' Munn remarked. '*If* you get back home. Vyring's got a police force, chum.'

'Oh, well,' Underhill said, and left it at that. 'Here's the Water Gate. Lord – I smell somebody's dinner!'

'So do I,' the Navaho grunted, 'but I hoped nobody would mention it. Shut up and keep walking.'

The wall around Vyring was in the nature of a dike, not a fortification.

Venus was both civilized and unified; there were, apparently, no wars and no tariffs – a natural development for a world state. Air transports made sizzling noises as they shot past, out of sight in the fog overhead. Mist shrouded the streets, torn into tatters by occasional huge fans. Vyring, shielded from the winds, was unpleasantly hot, except indoors where artificial air conditioning could be brought into use.

Underhill was reminded of Venice: the streets were canals. Water craft of various shapes and sizes drifted, glided or raced past. Even the beggars travelled by water. There were rutted, muddy footpaths beside the canals, but no one with a *fal* to his name ever walked.

The Earthmen walked, cursing fervently as they splashed through the muck. They were, for the most part, ignored.

A water taxi scooted towards the bank, its pilot, wearing the blue badge of his *tarkomar*, hailing them. 'May I escort you?' he wanted to know.

Underhill exhibited a silver dollar. 'If you'll take this – sure.' All the Earthmen had learned Venusian quickly; they were good linguists, having been chosen for this as well as other transplanetary virtues. The phonetic Venusian tongue was far from difficult.

It was no trouble at all to understand the taxi pilot when he said no.

'Toss you for it,' Underhill said hopefully. 'Double or nothing.'

But the Venusians weren't gamblers. 'Double what?' the pilot inquired. 'That coin? It's silver.' He indicated the silver, rococo filigree on the prow of his craft. 'Junk!'

'This would be a swell place for Benjamin Franklin,' Mike Soaring Eagle remarked. 'His false teeth were made of iron, weren't they?'

'If they were, he had a Venusian fortune in his mouth,' Underhill said.

'Not quite.'

'If it could buy a full-course dinner, it's a fortune,' Underhill insisted.

The pilot, eyeing the Earthmen scornfully, drifted off in search of wealthier fares. Munn, doggedly plodding on, wiped sweat from his forehead. Swell place, Vyring, he thought. Swell place to starve to death.

Half an hour of difficult hiking roused Munn to a slow, dull anger. If Jorust refused to see him, he thought, there was going to be trouble, even though they'd taken away his guns. He felt capable of tearing down Vyring with his teeth. And eating the more edible portions.

Luckily, Jorust was available. The Earthmen were ushered into her office, a big, luxurious room high above the city, with windows open to the cooling breezes. Jorust was skittering around the room on a high chair, equipped with wheels and some sort of motor. Along the walls ran a slanting shelf, like a desk and presumably serving the same function. It was shoulder-high, but Jorust's chair raised her to its level. She probably started in one corner in the morning, Munn thought, and worked her way around the room during the day.

Jorust was a slim, gray-haired Venusian woman with a skin the texture of fine shagreen, and alert black eyes that were wary now. She climbed down from her chair, gestured the men to seats, and took one herself. She lit a pipe that looked like an oversized cigarette holder, stuffing it with a cylinder of pressed yellow herbs. Aromatic smoke drifted up. Underhill sniffed wistfully.

'May you be worthy of your fathers,' Jorust said politely, extending her six-fingered hand in greeting. 'What brings you?'

'Hunger,' Munn said bluntly. 'I think it's about time for a show-down.'

Jorust watched him inscrutably. 'Well?'

'We don't like being pushed around.'

'Have we harmed you?' the Council head asked.

Munn looked at her. 'Let's put our cards on the table. We're getting the squeeze play. You're a big shot here, and you're either responsible or you know why. How about it?'

'No,' Jorust said after a pause, 'no, I'm not as powerful as you seem to think. I am one of the administrators. I do not make the laws. I merely see that they are carried out. We are not enemies.'

'That might happen,' Munn said grimly. 'If another expedition comes from Earth and finds us dead –'

'We would not kill you. It is untraditional.'

'You could starve us to death, though.'

Jorust narrowed her eyes. 'Buy food. Any man can do that, no matter what his race.'

'And what do we use for money?' Munn asked. 'You won't take our currency. We haven't any of yours.'

'Your currency is worthless,' Jorust explained. 'We have gold and silver for the mining – it is common here. A *difal* – twelve *fals* – will buy a good deal of food. A *sofal* will buy even more than that.'

She was right, of course, Munn knew. A *sofal* was one thousand seven hundred twenty-eight *fals*. Yeah!

'And how do you expect us to get any of your iron money?' he snapped.

'Work for it, as our own people do. The fact that you are from another world does not dispose of your obligatory duty to create through labor.'

'All right,' Munn pursued, 'we're willing. Get us a job.'

'What kind?'

'Dredging canals! Anything!'

'Are you a member of the canal dredgers' *tarkomar*?'

'No,' Munn said. 'How could I have forgotten to join?'

Jorust ignored the sarcasm. 'You must join. All trades here have their *tarkomars*.'

'Lend me a thousand *sofals* and I'll join one.'

'You have tried that before,' Jorust told him. 'Our moneylenders reported that your collateral was worthless.'

'Worthless! D'you mean to say we've nothing in our ship worth a thousand *sofals* to your race? It's a squeeze play and you know it. Our water purifier alone is worth six times that to you.'

Jorust seemed affronted. 'For a thousand years we have cleansed our water with charcoal. If we changed now, we would be naming our ancestors fools. They were not fools; they were great and wise.'

'What about progress?'

'I see no need for it,' Jorust said. 'Our civilization is a perfect unit as it stands. Even the beggars are well fed. There is no unhappiness on Venus. The ways of our ancestors have been tested and found good. So why change?'

'But –'

'We would merely upset the *status quo* if we altered the balance,' Jorust said decisively, rising. 'May you be worthy of your fathers' names.'

'Listen –' Munn began.

But Jorust was back on her chair, no longer listening.

The three Earthmen looked at one another, shrugged and went out. The answer was definitely no.

'And that,' Munn said, as they descended in the elevator, 'is emphatically that. Jorust plans to have us starve to death. The word's out.'

Underhill was inclined to disagree. 'She's all right. As she said, she's just an administrator. It's the *tarkomars* who are the pressure group here. They're a powerful bloc.'

'They run Venus. I know.' Munn grimaced. 'It's difficult to understand the psychology of these people. They seem unalterably opposed to change. We represent change. So they figure they'll simply ignore us.'

'It won't work,' Underhill said. 'Even if we starve to death, there'll be more Earth ships later.'

'The same gag could work on them, too.'

'Starvation? But –'

'Passive resistance. There's no law compelling Venusians to treat with Earthmen. They can simply adopt a closed-door policy, and there's not a thing we can do about it. There's no welcome mat on Venus.'

Mike Soaring Eagle broke a long silence as they emerged to the canal bank. 'It's a variation of ancestor worship, their psychology. Transferred egotism, perhaps – a racial inferiority complex.'

Munn shook his head. 'You're drawing it a bit fine.'

'All right, maybe I am. But it boils down to worship of the past. And fear. Their present social culture has worked for centuries. They want no intrusions. It's logical. If you had a machine that worked perfectly at the job for which it had been designed, would you want improvements?'

'Why not?' Munn said. 'Certainly I would.'

'Why?'

'Well – to save time. If a new attachment would make the machine double its production, I'd want that.'

The Navaho looked thoughtful. 'Suppose it turned out – say – refrigerators. There'd be repercussions. You'd need less labor, which would upset the economic structure.'

'Microscopically.'

'In that case. But there'd also be a change in the consumer's angle. More people would have refrigerators. More people would make homemade ice cream. Sales on ice cream would drop – retail sales. The wholesalers would buy less milk. The farmers would –'

'I know,' Munn said. 'For want of a nail the kingdom was lost. You're speaking of microcosms. Even if you weren't, there are automatic adjustments – there always are.'

'An experimental, growing civilization is willing to stand for such adjustments,' Mike Soaring Eagle pointed out. 'The Venusians are ultraconservative. They figure they don't need to grow or change any more. Their system has worked for centuries. It's perfectly integrated. Intrusion of anything might upset the apple cart. The *tarkomars* have the power, and they intend to keep it.'

'So we starve,' Underhill put in.

The Indian grinned at him. 'Looks like it. Unless we can dope out some way of making money.'

'We ought to,' Munn said. 'We were chosen for our I.Q., among other things.'

'Our talents aren't too suitable,' Mike Soaring Eagle remarked, kicking a stone into the canal. 'You're a physicist. I'm a naturalist. Bronson's an engineer and Steve Thirkell's a sawbones. You, my useless young friend, are a rich man's son.'

Underhill smiled in an embarrassed fashion. 'Well, Dad came up the hard way. He knew how to make money. That's what we need now, isn't it?'

'How did he clean up?'

'Stock market.'

'That helps a lot,' Munn said. 'I think our best plan is to find some process the Venusians really *need*, and then sell it to them.'

'If we could wireless back to Earth for help –' Underhill began.

'– then we'd have nothing to worry about,' the Navaho ended. 'Unfortunately Venus has a Heaviside layer, so we can't wireless. You'd better try your hand at inventing something, Skipper. But whether or not the Venusians will want it afterwards, *I* don't know.'

Munn brooded. 'The *status quo* can't remain permanently that way. It ain't sensible, as my grandfather used to say about practically everything. There are always inventors. New processes – they've got to be assimilated into the social set-up. I should be able to dope out a gadget. Even a good preservative for foods might do it.'

'Not with the hydroponic gardens producing as they do.'

'Um-m. A better mousetrap – something useless but intriguing. A one-armed bandit –'

'They'd pass a law against it.'

'Well, you suggest something.'

'The Venusians don't seem to know much about genetics. If I could produce some unusual foods by crossbreeding … eh?'

'Maybe,' Munn said. 'Maybe.'

Steve Thirkell's pudgy face looked into the port. The rest of the party were seated at the table, scribbling on stylopads and drinking weak coffee.

'I have an idea,' Thirkell said.

Munn grunted. 'I know your ideas. What is it now?'

'Very simple. A plague strikes the Venusians and I find an antivirus that will save them. They will be grateful –'

'– and you'll marry Jorust and rule the planet,' Munn finished. 'Ha!'

'Not exactly,' Thirkell went on imperturbably. 'If they're not grateful, we'll simply hold out on the antitoxin till they pay up.'

'The only thing wrong with that brainstorm is that the Venusians don't seem to be suffering from a plague,' Mike Soaring Eagle pointed out. 'Otherwise it's perfect.'

Thirkell sighed. 'I was afraid you'd mention that. Maybe we could be unethical – just a little, you know – and start a plague. Typhoid or something.'

'What a man!' the Navaho said admiringly. 'You'd make a grand murderer, Steve.'

'I have often thought so. But I didn't intend to go as far as murder. A painful, incapacitating disease –'

'Such as?' Munn asked.

'Diphtheria?' the murderous physician suggested hopefully.

'A cheerful prospect,' Mike Soaring Eagle muttered. 'You sound like an Apache.'

'Diphtheria, beriberi, leprosy, bubonic plague,' Pat Bronson said violently. 'I vote for all of 'em. Give the nasty little frogs a taste of their own medicine. Wallop 'em good.'

'Suppose we let you start a mild plague,' Munn said. 'Something that couldn't conceivably be fatal – how would you go about it?'

'Pollute the water supply or something … eh?'

'What with?'

Thirkell suddenly looked heartbroken. 'Oh! *Oh!*'

Munn nodded. 'The *Goodwill* isn't stocked for that sort of thing. We're germless. Antiseptic inside and out. Have you forgotten the physical treatment they gave us before we left?'

Bronson cursed. 'Never will I forget that – a hypo every hour! Antitoxins, shots, ultraviolet X-rays, till my bones turned green.'

'Exactly,' Munn said. 'We're practically germless. It's a precaution they had to take, to prevent our starting a plague on Venus.'

'But we *want* to start a plague,' Thirkell said plaintively.

'You couldn't even give a Venusian a head cold,' Munn told him. 'So that's out. What about Venusian anaesthetics? Are they as good as ours?'

'Better,' the physician admitted. 'Not that they need them, except for the children. Their synapses are funny. They've mastered self-hypnosis so they can block pain when it's necessary.'

'Sulfa drugs?'

'I've thought of that. They've got those, too.'

'My idea,' Bronson broke in, 'is water power. Or dams. Whenever it rains, there's a flood.'

'There's good drainage, though,' Munn said. 'The canals take care of that.'

'Now let me finish! Those fish-skinned so-and-sos have hydropower, but it isn't efficient. There's so much fast water all over the place that they build plants wherever it seems best – thousands of them – and half the time they're useless, when the rains concentrate on another district. Half of the plants are inoperable all the time. Which costs money. If they'd build dams, they'd have a steady source of power without the terrific overhead.'

'It's a thought,' Munn acknowledged.

Mike Soaring Eagle said, 'I'll stick to my crossbreeds in the hydroponic gardens. I can raise beefsteak-mushrooms to taste of Worcestershire sauce or something. An appeal to the palate, you know –'

'Fair enough. Steve?'

Thirkell rumpled his hair. 'I'll think of an angle. Don't rush me.'

Munn looked at Underhill. 'Any flashes of intellect, chum?'

The youngster grimaced. 'Not just now. All I can think of is manipulating the stock market.'

'Without money?'

'That's the trouble.'

Munn nodded. 'Well, my own idea is advertising. As a physicist, it's in my line.'

'How?' Bronson wanted to know. 'Demonstrating atom-smashing? A strong-man act?'

'Pipe down. Advertising isn't known on Venus, though commerce is. That's funny. I should think the retailers would jump at the chance.'

'They've got radio commercials.'

'Stylized and ritualistic. Their televisors are ready-made for splash advertising. A visual blurb … yeah. Trick gadgets I could make to demonstrate the products. Why not?'

'I think I'll build an X-ray machine,' Thirkell said suddenly, 'if you'll help me, Skipper.'

Munn said sure. 'We've got the equipment – and the blueprints. Tomorrow we'll start. It must be pretty late.'

It was, though there was no sunset on Venus. The quintet retired, to dream of full-course dinners – all but Thirkell, who dreamed he was eating a roast chicken that abruptly turned into a Venusian and began to devour him, starting at the feet. He woke up sweating and cursing, took some nembutal, and finally slept again.

The next morning they scattered. Mike Soaring Eagle took a microscope and other gadgets to the nearest hydroponic center and went to work. He wasn't allowed to carry spores back to the *Goodwill*, but there was no objection to his experimenting in Vyring itself. He made cultures and used forced-growth vitamin complexes and hoped for the best.

Pat Bronson went to see Skottery, head of Water Power. Skottery was a tall, saturnine Venusian who knew a lot about engineering and insisted on showing Bronson the models in his office before they settled down to a talk.

'How many power stations do you have?' Bronson asked.

'Third power twelve times four dozens. Forty-two dozen in this district.'

Nearly a million altogether, Bronson made it. 'How many in actual operation now?' he carried on.

'About seventeen dozen.'

'That means three hundred idle – twenty-five dozen, that is. Isn't the upkeep a factor?'

'Quite a factor,' Skottery acknowledged. 'Aside from the fact that some of those stations are now permanently inoperable. The terrain changes rapidly. Erosion, you know. We'll build one station on a gorge one year, and the next the water will be taking a different route. We build about a dozen a day. But we salvage something from the old ones, of course.'

Bronson had a brainstorm. 'No watershed?'

'Eh?'

The Earthman explained. Skottery shook his shoulders in negation.

'We have a different type of vegetation here. There's so much water that roots don't have to strike deeply.'

'But they need soil?'

'No. The elements they need are in suspension in the water.'

Bronson described how watersheds worked. 'Suppose you imported Earth plants and trees and forested the mountains. And built dams to retain your water. You'd have power all the time, and you'd need only a few big stations. And they'd be permanent.'

Skottery thought that over. 'We have all the power we need.'

'But look at the expense!'

'Our rates cover that.'

'You could make more money – *difals* and *sofals* –'

'We have made exactly the same profits for three hundred years,' Skottery explained. 'Our net remains constant. It works perfectly. You fail to understand our economic system, I see. Since we have everything we need, there's no use making more money – not even a *fal* more.'

'Your competitors –'

'We have only three, and they are satisfied with their profits.'

'Suppose I interest them in my plan?'

'But you couldn't,' Skottery said patiently. 'They wouldn't be interested any more than I am. I'm glad you dropped in. May you be worthy of your father's name.'

'Ye soulless fish!' Bronson yelled, losing his temper. 'Is there no red blood in your green-skinned carcass? Does no one on this world know what fight means?' He hammered a fist into his palm. 'I wouldn't be worthy of the old Seumas Bronson's name unless I took a poke at that ugly phiz of yours right now –'

Skottery had pressed a button. Two large Venusians appeared. The head of Water Power pointed to Bronson.

'Remove it,' he said.

Captain Rufus Munn was in one of the telecasting studios with Bart Underhill. They were sitting beside Hakkapuy, owner of Veetsy – which might be freely translated as Wet Tingles. They were watching the telecast commercial plug for Hakkapuy's product, on the visor screen high on the wall.

A Venusian faded in, legs wide apart, arms akimbo. He raised one hand, six fingers spread wide.

'All men drink water. Water is good. Life needs water. Veetsy is good also. Four *fals* buys a globe of Veetsy. That is all.'

He vanished. Colors rippled across the screen and music played in off-beat rhythm. Munn turned to Hakkapuy.

'That isn't advertising. You can't get customers that way.'

'Well, it's traditional,' Hakkapuy said weakly.

Munn opened the pack at his feet, brought out a tall glass beaker, and asked for a globe of Veetsy. It was given him, and he emptied the green fluid into his beaker. After that, he dropped in a half dozen colored balls and added a chunk of dry ice, which sank to the bottom. The balls went up and down rapidly.

'See?' Munn said. 'Visual effect. The marbles are only slightly heavier than Veetsy. It's the visual equivalent of Wet Tingles. Show that on the televisor, with a good sales talk, and see how your sales curve jumps.'

Hakkapuy looked interested. 'I'm not sure –'

Munn dragged out a sheaf of papers and hammered at the breach in the wall. After a time a fat Venusian came in and said, 'May you be worthy of your ancestors' names.' Hakkapuy introduced him as Lorish.

'I thought Lorish had better see this. Would you mind going over it again?'

'Sure,' Munn said. 'Now the principle of display windows –'

When he had finished, Hakkapuy looked at Lorish, who shook his shoulders slowly.

'No,' he said.

Hakkapuy blew out his lips. 'It would sell more Veetsy.'

'And upset the economy charts,' Lorish said. 'No.'

Munn glared at him. 'Why not? Hakkapuy owns Veetsy, doesn't he? Who are you, anyhow – a censor?'

'I represent the advertisers' *tarkomar*,' Lorish explained. 'You see, advertising on Venus is strongly ritual. It is never changed. Why should it be? If we let Hakkapuy use your ideas, it would be unfair to other makers of soft drinks.'

'They could do the same thing,' Munn pointed out.

'A pyramiding competition leading to ultimate collapse. Hakkapuy makes enough money. Don't you, Hakkapuy?'

'I suppose so.'

'Are you questioning the motives of the *tarkomars*?'

Hakkapuy gulped. 'No,' he said hastily. 'No, no, no! You're perfectly right.'

Lorish looked at him. 'Very well. As for you, Earthman, you had better not waste your time pursuing this – scheme – further.'

Munn reddened. 'Are you threatening me?'

'Of course not. I simply mean that no advertiser could use your idea without consulting my *tarkomar*, and we would veto it.'

'Sure,' Munn said. 'O.K. Come on, Bert. Let's get out of here.'

They departed, to stroll along a canal bank and confer. Underhill was thoughtful.

'The *tarkomars* have held the balance of power for a long time, it looks like. They want things to stay as they are. That's obvious.'

Munn growled.

Underhill went on, 'We'd have to upset the whole apple cart to get anywhere. There's one thing in our favor, though.'

'What?'

'The laws.'

'How do you figure that out?' Munn asked. 'They're all against us.'

'So far – yes. But they're traditionally rigid and unswerving. A decision made three hundred years ago can't be changed except by a long court process. If we can find a loophole in those laws, they can't touch us.'

'All right, find the loophole,' Munn said grumpily. 'I'm going back to the ship and help Steve build an X-ray machine.'

'I think I'll go down to the stock exchange and snoop,' Underhill said. 'It's just possible –'

After a week, the X-ray device was finished. Munn and Thirkell looked through the Vyring law records and found they were permitted to sell a self-created device without belonging to a *tarkomar*, provided they obeyed certain trivial restrictions. Leaflets were printed and strewed around the city, and the Venusians came to watch Munn and Thirkell demonstrating the merits of Roentgen rays.

Mike Soaring Eagle knocked off work for the day and recklessly smoked a dozen cigarettes from his scanty store, burning with dull fury as he puffed. He had run into trouble with his hydroponic cultures.

'Crazy!' he told Bronson. 'Luther Burbank would have gone nuts – the way I'm going. How the devil can I guess-pollinate those ambiguous specimens of Venusian flora?'

'Well, it doesn't seem exactly fair,' Bronson consoled. 'Eighteen sexes, eh?'

'Eighteen so far. And four varieties that apparently haven't any sex at all. How can you crossbreed those perverted mushrooms? You'd have to exhibit the result in a side show.'

'You're getting nowhere?'

'Oh, I'm getting places,' Mike Soaring Eagle said bitterly. 'I'm getting all sorts of results. The trouble is nothing stays constant. I get a rum-flavored fungus one day, and it doesn't breed true – its spores turn into something that tastes like turpentine. So you see.'

Bronson looked sympathetic. 'Can't you swipe some grub when they're not looking? That way the job wouldn't be a complete washout.'

'They search me,' the Navaho said.

'The dirty skunks,' Bronson yelped. 'What do they think we are? Crooks?'

'Mph. Something's going on outside. Let's take a look.'

They went out of the *Goodwill* to find Munn arguing passionately with Jorust, who had come in person to examine the X-ray machine. A crowd of Venusians watched avidly. Munn's face was crimson.

'I looked it up,' he was saying. 'You can't stop me this time, Jorust. It's perfectly legal to build a machine and sell it outside the city limits.'

'Certainly,' Jorust said. 'I'm not complaining about that.'

'Well? We're not breaking any law.'

The woman beckoned, and a fat Venusian waddled forward. 'Patent three gross squared fourteen two dozen, issued to Metzi-Stang of Mylosh year fourth power twelve, subject sensitized plates.'

'What's that?' Munn asked.

'It's a patent,' Jorust told him. 'It was issued some time ago to a Venusian inventor named Metzi-Stang. A *tarkomar* bought and suppressed the process, but it's still illegal to infringe on it.'

'You mean somebody's already invented an X-ray machine on Venus?'

'No. Merely sensitized film. But that's part of your device, so you can't sell it.'

Thirkell pushed forward. 'I don't need film –'

The fat Venusian said, 'Vibrationary patent three gross two dozen and seven –'

'What now?' Munn broke in.

Jorust smiled. 'Machines employing vibration must not infringe on that patent.'

'This is an X-ray machine,' Thirkell snapped.

'Light is vibration,' Jorust told him. 'You can't sell it without buying permission from the *tarkomar* now owning that patent. It should cost – let's see – five thousand *sofals* or so.'

Thirkell turned abruptly and went into the ship, where he mixed a whisky-and-soda and thought wistfully about diphtheria germs. After a time the others appeared, looking disconsolate.

'Can she do it?' Thirkell asked.

Munn nodded. 'She can do it, chum. She's done it.'

'We're not infringing on their patents.'

'We're not on Earth. The patent laws here are so wide that if a man invents a gun, nobody else can make telescopic sights. We're rooked again.'

Underhill said, 'It's the *tarkomars* again. When they see a new process or invention that might mean change, they buy it up and suppress it. I can't think of any gadget we could make that wouldn't be an infringement on some Venusian patent or other.'

'They stay within the law,' Munn pointed out. '*Their* law. So we can't even challenge them. As long as we're on Venus, we're subject to their jurisprudence.'

'The beans are getting low,' Thirkell said morosely.

'Everything is,' the captain told him. 'Any ideas, somebody?'

There was silence. Presently Underhill took out a globe of Veetsy and put it on the table.

'Where'd you get that?' Bronson asked. 'It costs four *fals*.'

'It's empty,' Underhill said. 'I found it in an ash can. I've been investigating glassite – the stuff they use for things like this.'

'What about it?'

'I found out how they make it. It's a difficult, expensive process. It's no better than our flexiglass, and a lot harder to make. If we had a flexiglass factory here –'

'Well?'

'The bottom would drop out of Amalgamated Glassite.'

'I don't get it,' Bronson said. 'So what?'

'Ever heard of a whispering campaign?' Underhill asked. 'My father wangled many an election that way, the old devil. Suppose we passed the word around that there was a new process for making a cheaper, better substitute for glassite? Wouldn't Amalgamated stock drop?'

'Possibly,' Munn said.

'We could clean up.'

'What with?'

'Oh.' Underhill was silent. 'It takes money to make money.'

'Always.'

'I wonder. Here's another idea. Venus is on the iron standard. Iron's cheap on Earth. Suppose we talked about bringing in iron here – strewing it broadcast. There'd be a panic, wouldn't there?'

'Not without some iron to strew around,' Munn said. 'Counter-propaganda would be telecast; we couldn't compete with it. Our whispering campaign would be squashed before we got it started. The Venusian government – the *tarkomars* – would simply deny that Earth had unlimited iron supplies. We wouldn't profit, anyway.'

'There must be some angle,' Underhill scowled. 'There's got to be. Let's see. What's the basis of the Venusian system?'

'No competition,' Mike Soaring Eagle said. 'Everybody has all he wants.'

'Maybe. At the top. But the competitive instinct is too strong to be suppressed like that. I'll bet plenty of Venusians would like to make a few extra *fals*.'

'Where does that get us?' Munn wanted to know.

'The way my father did it … Hm-m-m. He manipulated, pulled the wires, made people come to him. What's the weak spot in Venusian economy?'

Munn hesitated. 'Nothing we can strike at – we're too handicapped.'

Underhill shut his eyes. 'The basis of an economic and social system is – what?'

'Money,' Bronson said.

'No. Earth's on the radium standard. Years ago it was gold or silver. Venus is on iron. And there's the barter system, too. Money's a variable.'

'Money represents natural resources –' Thirkell began.

'Man-hours,' Munn put in quietly.

Underhill jumped. 'That's it! Of course – man-hours! That's the constant. The amount of production a man can turn out in an hour represents an arbitrary constant – two dollars, a dozen *difals* or whatever it is. That's the base for any economic set-up. And it's the base we've got to hit. The ancestor worship, the power of the *tarkomars* – they're superficial really. Once the basic system is challenged, they'll go down.'

'I don't see where it gets us,' Thirkell said.

'Make the man-hours variable,' Underhill explained. 'Once we do that, anything can happen.'

'Something had better happen,' Bronson said, 'and quick. We've little food left.'

'Shut up,' Munn said. 'I think the kid's got the right angle. Alter the man-hour constant, eh? How can we do that? Specialized training? Train a Venusian to turn out twice as much stuff in the same period of time? Skilled labor?'

'They've got skilled labor,' Underhill said. 'If we could make 'em work faster, or increase their stamina –'

'Benzedrine plus,' Thirkell interrupted. 'With enough caffeine, vitamin complex and riboflavin – I could whip up a speeder-upper, all right.'

Munn nodded slowly. 'Pills, not shots. If this works out, we'll have to do it undercover after a while.'

'What the devil will it get us to make the Venusians work faster?' Bronson asked.

Underhill snapped his fingers. 'Don't you see? Venus is ultra-conservative. The economic system is frozen static. It isn't adapted to change. There'll be hell popping!'

Munn said, 'We'll need advertising to arouse public interest first of all. A practical demonstration.' He looked around the table, his gaze settling on Mike Soaring Eagle. 'Looks like you're elected, Redskin. You've more stamina than any of us, according to the tests we took back on Earth.'

'All right,' the Navaho said. 'What do I do?'

'Work!' Underhill told him. 'Work till you drop!'

It began early the next morning in the main plaza of Vyring. Munn had checked up carefully, determined to make sure nothing would go wrong, and had learned that a recreation building was to be constructed on the site of the plaza. 'Work won't start for several weeks,' Jorust said. 'Why?'

'We want to dig a hole there,' Munn said. 'Is it legal?'

The Venusian smiled. 'Why, of course. That's public domain – until the contractors begin. But a demonstration of your muscular prowess won't help you, I'm afraid.'

'Eh?'

'I'm not a fool. You're trying to land a job. You hope to do that by advertising your abilities. But why do it in just this way? Anybody can dig a hole. It isn't specialized.'

Munn grunted. If Jorust wanted to jump at that conclusion, swell. He said, 'It pays to advertise. Put a steam shovel to work, back on Earth, and a crowd will gather to watch it. We don't have a steam shovel, but –'

'Well, whatever you like. Legally you're within your rights. Nevertheless you can't hold a job without joining a *tarkomar*.'

'Sometimes I think your planet would be a lot better off without the *tarkomars*,' Munn said bluntly.

Jorust moved her shoulders. 'Between ourselves, I have often thought so. I am merely an administrator, however. I have no real power. I do what I'm told to do. If I were permitted, I would be glad to lend you the money you need –'

'What?' Munn looked at her. 'I thought –'

The woman froze. 'It is not permitted. Tradition is not always wisdom, but I can do nothing about it. To defy the *tarkomars* is unthinkable and useless. I am sorry.'

Munn felt a little better after that, somehow. The Venusians weren't all enemies. The all-powerful *tarkomars*, jealous of their power, fanatically desirous of preserving the *status quo*, were responsible for this mess.

When he got back to the plaza, the others were waiting. Bronson had rigged up a scoreboard, in phonetic Venusian, and had laid out mattock, pick, shovel, wheelbarrow and boards for the Navaho, who stood, a brawny, red-bronze figure, stripped to the waist in the cool wind. A few canal-boats had stopped to watch.

Munn looked at his watch. 'O.K., Redskin. Let's go. Steve can start –'

Underhill began to beat a drum. Bronson put figures on the scoreboard: 4:03:00, Venusian Vyring Time. Thirkell went to a nearby camp table, littered with bottles and medical equipment, shook from a vial one of the stimulant pills he had concocted, and gave it to Mike Soaring Eagle. The Indian ate it, heaved up the mattock and went to work.

That was all.

A man digging a hole. Just why the spectacle should be so fascinating no one has ever figured out. The principle remains the same, whether it's a steam shovel scooping out half a ton of earth at a bite, or a sweating, stocky Navaho wielding shovel and pick. The boats grew thicker.

Mike Soaring Eagle kept working. An hour passed. Another. There were regular, brief rest periods, and Mike kept rotating his tools, to get all his muscles into play. After breaking earth for a while with the mattock, he would shovel it into the wheelbarrow, roll his burden up a plank and dump it on an ever growing pile some distance away. Three hours. Four. Mike knocked off for a brief lunch. Bronson kept track of the time on his scoreboard.

Thirkell gave the Navaho another pill. 'How're you doing?'

'Fine. I'm tough enough.'

'I know, but these stimulants – they'll help.'

Underhill was at a typewriter. He had already ground out a tremendous lot of copy, for he had been working since Mike Soaring Eagle started. Bronson had discovered a long-forgotten talent and was juggling makeshift Indian clubs and colored balls. He'd been keeping that up for quite a while, too.

Captain Rufus Munn was working a sewing machine. He didn't especially like the task, but it was precision work, and therefore helpful to the plan. All the party except Thirkell was doing something, and the physician was busy administering pills and trying to look like an alchemist.

Occasionally he visited Munn and Underhill, collected stacks of paper and carefully sewn scraps of cloth, and deposited them in various boxes near the canal, labelled, 'Take One.' On the cloth a legend was machine-embroidered in Venusian: 'A Souvenir from Earth.' The crowds thickened.

The Earthmen worked on. Bronson kept juggling, with pauses for refreshment. Eventually he experimented with coin and card tricks. Mike Soaring Eagle kept digging. Munn sewed. Underhill continued to type – and the Venusians read what his flying fingers turned out.

'Free! Free! Free!' the leaflets said. 'Souvenir pillow-case covers from Earth! A free show! Watch the Earthmen demonstrate stamina, dexterity and precision in four separate ways. How long can they keep it up? With the aid of POWER PILLS – indefinitely! Their output is doubled and their precision increased by POWER PILLS – they pep you up! A medical product of Earth that can make any man worth twice his weight in *sofals!*'

It went on like that. The old army game – with variations. The Venusians couldn't resist. Word got around. The mob thickened. How long could the Earthmen keep up the pace?

They kept it up. Thirkell's stimulant pills – as well as the complex shots he had given his companions that morning – seemed to be working. Mike Soaring Eagle dug like a beaver. Sweat poured from his shining red-bronze torso. He drank prodigiously and ate salt tablets.

Munn kept sewing, without missing a stitch. He knew that his products were being scanned closely for signs of sloppy workmanship. Bronson kept juggling and doing coin tricks, never missing. Underhill typed with aching fingers.

Five hours. Six hours. Even with the rest periods, it was gruelling. They had brought food from the *Goodwill*, but it wasn't too palatable. Still, Thirkell had selected it carefully for caloric.

Seven hours. Eight hours. The crowds made the canals impassable. A policeman came along and argued with Thirkell, who told him to see Jorust.

Jorust must have put a flea in his ear, for he came back to watch, but not to interfere.

Nine hours. *Ten hours.* Ten hours of Herculean effort. The men were exhausted – but they kept going.

They had made their point by then, though, for a few Venusians approached Thirkell and inquired about the Power Pills. What were they? Did they really make you work faster? How could they buy the –

The policeman appeared to stand beside Thirkell. 'I've a message from the medical *tarkomar*,' he announced. 'If you try to sell any of those things, you go to jail.'

'Wouldn't think of it,' Thirkell said. 'We're giving away free samples. Here, buddy.' He dug into a sack and tossed the nearest Venusian a Power Pill. 'Two days' work in that instead of your usual one. Come back for more tomorrow. Want one, pal? Here. You, too. Catch.'

'Wait a minute –' the policeman said.

'Go get a warrant,' Thirkell told him. 'There's no law against making presents.'

Jorust appeared with a burly, intolerant-looking Venusian. She introduced the latter as head of the Vyring *tarkomars*.

'And I'm here to tell you to stop this,' the Venusian said.

Thirkell knew what to say. His companions kept on with their work, but he felt them watching and listening.

'What rule do you invoke?'

'Why ... why, peddling.'

'I'm not selling anything. This is public domain; we're putting on a free show.'

'Those ... ah ... Power Pills –'

'Free gifts,' Thirkell said. 'Listen, pal. When we gave all our food to you Venusian crooks, did you squawk? No, you took it. And then clamped down. When we asked for our grub back, you just told us that we had no legal recourse; possession is nine points of the law, and we had a perfect right to make free gifts. That's what we're doing now – giving presents. So what?'

Jorust's eyes were twinkling, but she hooded them swiftly. 'I fear he speaks the truth. The law protects him. It is no great harm.'

Thirkell, watching her, wondered. Had Jorust guessed the right answer? Was she on their side? The *tarkomar* leader turned dark green, hesitated, swung on his heel and went away. Jorust gave the Earthmen a long, enigmatic look, moved her shoulders and followed.

'I'm still stiff,' Mike Soaring Eagle said a week later in the *Goodwill*. 'Hungry, too. When do we get grub?'

Thirkell, at the valve, handed out a Power Pill to a Venusian and came back rubbing his hands and grinning. 'Wait. Just wait. What's going on, Skipper?'

Munn nodded towards Underhill. 'Ask the kid. He got back from Vyring a few minutes ago.'

Underhill chuckled. 'There was hell popping. All in a week, too. We've certainly struck at the economic base. Every Venusian who labors on a piecework basis wants our pills, so he can speed up his production and make more *fals*. It's the competitive instinct – which is universal.'

'Well?' Bronson asked. 'How do the lizard-faced big shots like that?'

'They don't like it. It's hit the economic set-up they've had for centuries. Till now, one Venusian would make exactly ten *sofals* a week – say – by turning out five thousand bottle caps. With the pills Steve made up, he's turning out eight or ten thousand and making correspondingly more dough. The guy at the next bench says what the hell, and comes to us for a Power Pill for himself. Thus it goes. And the lovely part is that not all the labor is on piecework basis. It can't be. You need tangibles for piecework. Running a weather machine has got to be measured by time – not by how many raindrops you make in a day.'

Munn nodded. 'Jealousy, you mean?'

Underhill said, 'Well, look. A weather-machine operator has been making ten *sofals* a week, the same as a bottle capper on piecework. Now the bottle capper's making twenty *sofals*. The weather-machine man doesn't see the point. He's willing to take Power Pills, too, but that won't step up his production. He asks for a raise. If he gets it, the economy is upset even more. If he doesn't, other weather-machine operators get together with him and figure it's unfair discrimination. They get mad at the *tarkomars*. They strike!'

Mike Soaring Eagle said, 'The *tarkomars* have forbidden work to any Venusian taking Power Pills.'

'And still the Venusians ask us for Power Pills. So what? How can you prove a man's been swallowing them? His production steps up, sure, but the *tarkomars* can't clamp down on everybody with a good turn-out. They tried that, and a lot of guys who never tried the Power Pills got mad. They were fast workers, that was all.'

'The demonstration we put on was a good idea,' Thirkell said. 'It was convincing. I've had to cut down the strength of the pills – we're running low – but the power of suggestion helps us.'

Underhill grinned. 'So the base – the man-hour unit – had gone cock-eyed. One little monkey wrench, thrown where it'll do the most good. It's spreading, too. Not only Vyring. The news is going all over Venus, and the workers in the other cities are asking why half of Vyring's laborers should get better pay. That's where the equal standard of exchange helps us – one monetary system all over Venus. Nothing has ever been off par here for centuries. Now –'

Munn said, 'Now the system's toppling. It's a natural fault in a perfectly integrated, rigid set-up. For want of a nail the *tarkomars* are losing their grip. They've forgotten how to adjust.'

'It'll spread,' Underhill said confidently. 'It'll spread. Steve, here comes another customer.'

Underhill was wrong. Jorust and the Vyring *tarkomar* leader came in. 'May you be worthy of your ancestors' names,' Munn said politely. 'Drag up a chair and have a drink. We've still got a few bulbs of beer left.'

Jorust obeyed, but the Venusian rocked on his feet and glowered. The woman said, 'Malsi is distressed. These Power Pills are causing trouble.'

'I don't know why,' Munn said. 'They increase production, don't they?'

Malsi grimaced. 'This is a trick! A stratagem! You are abusing our hospitality!'

'What hospitality?' Bronson wanted to know.

'You threatened the system,' Malsi plunged on doggedly. 'On Venus there is no change. There must be none.'

'Why not?' Underhill asked. 'There's only one real reason, and you know it. Any advances might upset the *tarkomars* – threaten the power they hold. You racketeers have had the whip hand for centuries. You've suppressed inventions, kept Venus in a backwater, tried to drive initiative out of the race, just so you could stay on top. It can't be done. Changes happen; they always do. If we hadn't come, there'd have been an internal explosion eventually.'

Malsi glared at him. 'You will stop making these Power Pills.'

'Point of law,' Thirkell said softly. 'Show precedent.'

Jorust said, 'The right of free gift is one of the oldest on Venus. That law could be changed, Malsi, but I don't think the people would like it.'

Munn grinned. 'No. They wouldn't. That would be the tipoff. Venusians have learned it's possible to make more money. Take that chance away from them, and the *tarkomars* won't be the benevolent rulers any more.'

Malsi turned darker green. 'We have power –'

'Jorust, you're an administrator. Are we protected by your laws?' Underhill asked.

She moved her shoulders. 'Yes, you are. The laws are sacrosanct. Perhaps because they have always been designed to protect the *tarkomars*.'

Malsi swung towards her. 'Are you siding with the Earthmen?'

'Why, of course not, Malsi. I'm merely upholding the law, according to my oath of office. Without prejudice – that's it, isn't it?'

Munn said, 'We'll stop making the Power Pills if you like, but I warn you that it's only a respite. You can't halt progress.'

Malsi seemed unconvinced. 'You'll stop?'

'Sure. If you pay us.'

'We cannot pay you,' Malsi said stubbornly. 'You belong to no *tarkomar*. It would be illegal.'

Jorust murmured, 'You might give them a free gift of – say – ten thousand *sofals*.'

'Ten thousand!' Malsi yelped. 'Ridiculous!'

'So it is,' Underhill said. 'Fifty thousand is more like it. We can live well for a year on that.'

'No.'

A Venusian came to the valve, peeped in and said: 'I made twice as many *difals* today. May I have another Power Pill?' He saw Malsi and vanished with a small shriek.

Munn shrugged. 'Suit yourself. Pay up, or we go on handing out Power Pills – and you'll have to adjust a rigid social economy. I don't think you can do it.'

Jorust touched Malsi's arm. 'There is no other way.'

'I –' The Venusian by now was almost black with impotent rage. 'All right,' he capitulated, spitting the words between his teeth. 'I won't forget this, Jorust.'

'But I must administer the laws,' the woman said. 'Why, Malsi! The rule of the *tarkomars* has always been unswerving honesty.'

Malsi didn't answer. He scribbled a credit check for fifty thousand *sofals*, validated it and gave the tag to Munn. After that he sent a parting glare around the cabin and stamped out.

'Well!' Bronson said. 'Fifty grand! Tonight we eat!'

'May you be worthy of your fathers' names,' Jorust murmured. At the valve she turned. 'I'm afraid you've upset Malsi.'

'Too bad,' Munn said hypocritically.

Jorust moved her shoulders slightly. 'Yes. You've upset Malsi. And Malsi represents the *tarkomars* –'

'What can he do about it?' Underhill asked.

'Nothing. The laws won't let him. But – it's nice to know the *tarkomars* aren't infallible. I think the word will get around.'

Jorust winked gravely at Munn and departed, looking as innocent as a cat, and as potentially dangerous.

'Well!' Munn said. 'What does that mean? The end of the *tarkomar's* rule, maybe?'

'Maybe,' Bronson said. 'I don't give a damn. I'm hungry and I want a beef-steak-mushroom. Where can we cash a check for fifty grand?'

COLD WAR

Chapter 1. Last of the Pughs

I'll never have a cold in the haid again without I think of little Junior Pugh. Now there was a repulsive brat if ever I saw one. Built like a little gorilla, he was. Fat, pasty face, mean look, eyes so close together you could poke 'em both out at once with one finger. His paw thought the world of him though. Maybe that was natural, seeing as how little Junior was the image of his pappy.

'The last of the Pughs,' the old man used to say stickin' his chest out and beamin' down at the little gorilla. 'Finest little lad that ever stepped.'

It made my blood run cold sometimes to look at the two of 'em together. Kinda sad, now, to think back to those happy days when I didn't know either of 'em. You may not believe it but them two Pughs, father and son, between 'em came within *that* much of conquerin' the world.

Us Hogbens is quiet folks. We like to keep our heads down and lead quiet lives in our own little valley, where nobody comes near withouten we say so. Our neighbors and the folks in the village are used to us by now. They know we try hard not to act conspicuous. They make allowances.

If Paw gets drunk, like last week, and flies down the middle of Main Street in his red underwear most people make out they don't notice, so's not to embarrass Maw. They know he'd walk like a decent Christian if he was sober.

The thing that druv Paw to drink that time was Little Sam, which is our baby we keep in a tank down-cellar, startin' to teethe again. First time since the War Between the States. We'd figgered he was through teething, but with Little Sam you never can tell. He was mighty restless, too.

A perfesser we keep in a bottle told us once Little Sam e-mitted subsonic somethings when he yells but that's just his way of talking. Don't mean a thing. It makes your nerves twiddle, that's all. Paw can't stand it. This time it even woke up Grandpaw in the attic and he hadn't stirred since Christmas. First thing after he got his eyes open he bust out madder'n a wet hen at Paw.

'I see ye, wittold knave that ye are!' he howled. 'Flying again, is it? Oh, sic a reowfule sigte! I'll ground ye, ywis!' There was a far-away thump.

'You made me fall a good ten feet!' Paw hollered from away down the valley. 'It ain't fair. I could of busted something!'

'Ye'll bust us all, with your dronken carelessness,' Grandpaw said. 'Flying in full sight of the neighbors! People get burned at the stake for less. You want mankind to find out all about us? Now shut up and let me tend to Baby.'

Grandpaw can always quiet the baby if nobody else can. This time he sung him a little song in Sanskrit and after a bit they was snoring a duet.

I was fixing up a dingus for Maw to sour up some cream for sour-cream biscuits. I didn't have much to work with but an old sled and some pieces of wire but I didn't need much. I was trying to point the top end of the wire north-northeast when I seen a pair of checked pants rush by in the woods.

It was Uncle Lem. I could hear him thinking. 'It *ain't* me!' he was saying, real loud, inside his haid. 'Git back to yer work, Saunk. I ain't within a mile of you. Yer Uncle Lem's a fine old feller and never tells lies. Think I'd fool ye, Saunkie boy?'

'You shore would,' I thunk back. 'If you could. What's up, Uncle Lem?'

At that he slowed down and started to saunter back in a wide circle.

'Oh, I just had an idy yer Maw might like a mess of blackberries,' he thunk, kicking a pebble very nonchalant. 'If anybody asks you say you ain't seen me. It's no lie. You ain't.'

'Uncle Lem,' I thunk, real loud, 'I gave Maw my bounden word I wouldn't let you out of range without me along, account of the last time you got away –'

'Now, now, my boy,' Uncle Lem thunk fast. 'Let bygones be bygones.'

'You just can't say no to a friend, Uncle Lem,' I reminded him, taking a last turn of the wire around the runner. 'So you wait a shake till I get this cream soured and we'll both go together, wherever it is you have in mind.'

I saw the checked pants among the bushes and he come out in the open and give me a guilty smile. Uncle Lem's a fat little feller. He means well, I guess, but he can be talked into most anything by most anybody, which is why we have to keep a close eye on him.

'How you gonna do it?' he asked me, looking at the creamjug. 'Make the little critters work faster?'

'Uncle Lem!' I said. 'You know better'n that. Cruelty to dumb animals is something I can't abide. Them there little critters work hard enough souring milk the way it is. They're such teentsy-weentsy fellers I kinda feel sorry for 'em. Why, you can't even see 'em without you go kinda crosseyed when you look. Paw says they're enzymes. But they can't be. They're too teeny.'

'Teeny is as teeny does,' Uncle Lem said. 'How you gonna do it, then?'

'This here gadget,' I told him, kinda proud, 'will send Maw's creamjug ahead into next week some time. This weather, don't take cream more'n a couple of days but I'm giving it plenty of time. When I bring it back – bingo, it's sour.' I set the jug on the sled.

'I never seen such a do-lass brat,' Uncle Lem said, stepping forward and bending a wire crosswise. 'You better do it thataway, on account of the thunderstorm next Tuesday. All right now, shoot her off.'

So I shot her off. When she come back, sure enough, the cream was sour enough to walk a mouse. Crawling up the can there was a hornet from next week, which I squashed. Now that was a mistake. I knowed it the minute I touched the jug. Dang Uncle Lem, anyhow.

He jumped back into the underbrush, squealing real happy.

'Fooled you that time, you young stinker,' he yelled back. 'Let's see you get your thumb outa the middle of next week!'

It was the time-lag done it. I mighta knowed. When he crossed that wire he didn't have no thunderstorm in mind at all. Took me nigh onto ten minutes to work myself loose, account of some feller called Inertia, who mixes in if you ain't careful when you fiddle around with time. I don't understand much about it myself. I ain't got my growth yet. Uncle Lem says he's already forgot more'n I'll ever know.

With that head start I almost lost him. Didn't even have time to change into my store-bought clothes and I knowed by the way he was all dressed up fit to kill he was headed for somewheres fancy.

He was worried, too. I kept running into little stray worrisome thoughts he'd left behind him, hanging like teeny little mites of clouds on the bushes. Couldn't make out much on account of they was shredding away by the time I got there but he'd shore done something he shouldn't. That much *anybody* coulda told. They went something like this:

'Worry, worry – wish I hadn't done it – oh, heaven help me if Grandpaw ever finds out – oh, them nasty Pughs, how could I a-been such a fool? Worry, worry – pore ole feller, such a good soul, too, never done nobody no harm and look at me now.

'That Saunk, too big for his britches, teach him a thing or two, ha-ha. Oh, worry, worry – never mind, brace up, you good ole boy, everything's bound to turn out right in the end. You deserve the best, bless you, Lemuel. Grandpaw'll never find out.'

Well, I seen his checkered britches high-tailing through the woods after a bit, but I didn't catch up to him until he was down the hill, across the picnic grounds at the edge of town and pounding on the sill of the ticket-window at the railroad station with a Spanish dubloon he snitched from Paw's seachest.

It didn't surprise me none to hear him asking for a ticket to State Center. I let him think I hadn't caught up. He argued something turrible with the man behind the window but finally he dug down in his britches and fetched up a silver dollar, and the man calmed down.

The train was already puffing up smoke behind the station when Uncle Lem darted around the corner. Didn't leave me much time but I made it too – just. I had to fly a little over the last half-dozen yards but I don't think anybody noticed.

Once when I was just a little shaver there was a Great Plague in London, where we were living at the time, and all us Hogbens had to clear out. I remember the hullabaloo in the city but looking back now it don't seem a patch on the hullabaloo in State Center station when the train pulled in. Times have changed, I guess.

Whistles blowing, horns honking, radios yelling bloody murder – seems like every invention in the last two hundred years had been noisier than the one before it. Made my head ache until I fixed up something Paw once called a raised decibel threshold, which was pure showing-off.

Uncle Lem didn't know I was anywhere around. I took care to think real quiet but he was so wrapped up in his worries he wasn't paying no mind to nothing. I followed him through the crowds in the station and out onto a wide street full of traffic. It was a relief to get away from the trains.

I always hate to think what's going on inside the boiler, with all the little bitty critters so small you can't hardly see 'em, pore things, flying around all hot and excited and bashing their heads together. It seems plumb pitiable.

Of course, it just don't do to think what's happening inside the automobiles that go by.

Uncle Lem knowed right where he was headed. He took off down the street so fast I had to keep reminding myself not to fly, trying to keep up. I kept thinking I ought to get in touch with the folks at home, in case this turned into something I couldn't handle, but I was plumb stopped everywhere I turned. Maw was at the church social that afternoon and she whopped me the last time I spoke to her outa thin air right in front of the Reverend Jones. He ain't used to us Hogbens yet.

Paw was daid drunk. No good trying to wake him up. And I was scared to death I *would* wake the baby if I tried to call on Grandpaw.

Uncle Lem scuttled right along, his checkered legs a-twinkling. He was worrying at the top of his mind, too. He'd caught sight of a crowd in a side-street gathered around a big truck, looking up at a man standing on it and waving bottles in both hands.

He seemed to be making a speech about headaches. I could hear him all the way to the corner. There was big banners tacked along the sides of the truck that said, PUGH HEADACHE CURE.

'Oh, worry, worry!' Uncle Lem thunk. 'Oh, bless my toes, what *am* I going to do? I never *dreamed* anybody'd marry Lily Lou Mutz. Oh, worry!'

Well, I reckon we'd all been surprised when Lily Lou Mutz up and got herself a husband awhile back – around ten years ago, I figgered. But what it had to do with Uncle Lem I couldn't think. Lily Lou was just about the ugliest female that ever walked. Ugly ain't no word for her, pore gal.

Grandpaw said once she put him in mind of a family name of Gorgon he used to know. Not that she wasn't a goodhearted critter. Being so ugly, she put up with a lot in the way of rough acting-up from the folks in the village – the riff-raff lot, I mean.

She lived by herself in a little shack up the mountain and she musta been close onto forty when some feller from the other side of the river come along one day and rocked the whole valley back on its heels by asking her to marry up with him. Never saw the feller myself but I heard tell he wasn't no beauty-prize winner neither.

Come to think of it, I told myself right then, looking at the truck – come to think of it, feller's name was Pugh.

Chapter 2. A Fine Old Feller

Next thing I knowed, Uncle Lem had spotted somebody under a lamp-post on the sidewalk, at the edge of the crowd. He trotted over. It seemed to be a big gorilla and a little gorilla, standing there watching the feller on the truck selling bottles with both hands.

'Come and get it,' he was yelling. 'Come and get your bottle of Pugh's Old Reliable Headache Cure while they last!'

'Well, Pugh, here I am,' Uncle Lem said, looking up at the big gorilla. 'Hello, Junior,' he said right afterward, glancing down at the little gorilla. I seen him shudder a little.

You shore couldn't blame him for that. Two nastier specimens of the human race I never did see in all my born days. If they hadn't been *quite* so pasty-faced or just the least mite slimmer, maybe they wouldn't have put me so much in mind of two well-fed slugs, one growed-up and one baby-sized. The paw was all dressed up in a Sunday-meeting suit with a big gold watch-chain across his front and the way he strutted you'd a thought he'd never had a good look in a mirror.

'Howdy, Lem,' he said, casual-like. 'Right on time, I see. Junior, say howdy to Mister Lem Hogben. You owe Mister Hogben a lot, sonny.' And he laughed a mighty nasty laugh.

Junior paid him no mind. He had his beady little eyes fixed on the crowd across the street. He looked about seven years old and mean as they come.

'Shall I do it now, Paw?' he asked in a squeaky voice. 'Can I let 'em have it now, paw? Huh, Paw?' From the tone he used, I looked to see if he'd got a machine-gun handy. I didn't see none but if looks was ever mean enough to kill Junior Pugh could of mowed the crowd right down.

'Manly little feller, ain't he, Lem?' Paw Pugh said, real smug. 'I tell you, I'm mighty proud of this youngster. Wish his dear grandpaw coulda lived to see him. A fine old family line, the Pughs is. Nothing like it anywhere. Only trouble is, Junior's the last of his race. You see why I got in touch with you, Lem.'

Uncle Lem shuddered again. 'Yep,' he said. 'I see, all right. But you're wasting your breath, Pugh. I ain't a-gonna do it.'

Young Pugh spun around in his tracks.

'Shall I let him have it, Paw?' he squeaked, real eager. 'Shall I, Paw? Now, Paw? Huh?'

'Shaddup, sonny,' the big feller said and he whammed the little feller across the side of the haid. Pugh's hands was like hams. He shore was built like a gorilla.

The way his great big arms swung down from them big hunched shoulders, you'd of thought the kid would go flying across the street when his paw whopped him one. But he was a burly little feller. He just staggered a mite and then shook his haid and went red in the face.

He yelled out, loud and squeaky, 'Paw, I warned you! The last time you whammed me I warned you! Now I'm gonna let you have it!'

He drew a deep breath and his two little teeny eyes got so bright I coulda sworn they was gonna touch each other across the middle of his nose. His pasty face got bright red.

'Okay, Junior,' Paw Pugh said, real hasty. 'The crowd's ready for you. Don't waste your strength on me, sonny. Let the crowd have it!'

Now all this time I was standing at the edge of the crowd, listening and watching Uncle Lem. But just then somebody jiggled my arm and a thin kinda voice said to me, real polite, 'Excuse me, but may I ask a question?'

I looked down. It was a skinny man with a kind-hearted face. He had a notebook in his hand.

'It's all right with me,' I told him, polite. 'Ask away, mister.'

'I just wondered how you feel, that's all,' the skinny man said, holding his pencil over the notebook ready to write down something.

'Why, peart,' I said. 'Right kind of you to inquire. Hope you're feeling well too, mister.'

He shook his head, kind of dazed. 'That's the trouble,' he said. 'I just don't understand it. I feel fine.'

'Why not?' I asked. 'Fine day.'

'Everybody here feels fine,' he went right on, just like I hadn't spoke. 'Barring normal odds, everybody's in average good health in this crowd. But in about five minutes or less, as I figure it –' He looked at his wrist-watch.

Just then somebody hit me right on top of the haid with a red-hot sledge-hammer.

Now you shore can't hurt a Hogben by hitting him on the haid. Anybody's a fool to try. I felt my knees buckle a little but I was all right in a couple of seconds and I looked around to see who'd whammed me.

Wasn't a soul there. But oh my, the moaning and groaning that was going up from that there crowd! People was a-clutching at their foreheads and a-staggering around the street, clawing at each other to get to that truck where the man was handing out the bottles of headache cure as fast as he could take in the dollar bills.

The skinny man with the kind face rolled up his eyes like a duck in thunder.

'Oh, my head!' he groaned. 'What did I tell you? Oh, my head!' Then he sort of tottered away, fishing in his pocket for money.

Well, the family always did say I was slow-witted but you'd have to be downright feeble-minded if you didn't know there was something mighty peculiar going on around here. I'm no ninny, no matter what Maw says. I turned around and looked for Junior Pugh.

There he stood, the fat-faced little varmint, red as a turkey-gobbler, all swole up and his mean little eyes just a-flashing at the crowd.

'It's a hex,' I thought to myself, perfectly calm. 'I'd never have believed it but it's a real hex. Now how in the world –'

Then I remembered Lily Lou Mutz and what Uncle Lem had been thinking to himself. And I began to see the light.

The crowd had gone plumb crazy, fighting to get at the headache cure. I purty near had to bash my way over toward Uncle Lem. I figgered it was past time I took a hand, on account of him being so soft in the heart and likewise just about as soft in the haid.

'Nosirree,' he was saying, firm-like. 'I won't do it. Not by no manner of means I won't.'

'Uncle Lem,' I said.

I bet he jumped a yard into the air.

'Saunk!' he squeaked. He flushed up and grinned sheepish and then he looked mad, but I could tell he was kinda relieved, too. 'I told you not to foller me,' he said.

'Maw told me not to let you out of my sight,' I said. 'I promised Maw and us Hogbens never break a promise. What's going on here, Uncle Lem?'

'Oh, Saunk, everything's gone dead wrong!' Uncle Lem wailed out. 'Here I am with a heart of gold and I'd just as soon be dead! Meet Mister Ed Pugh, Saunk. He's trying to get me kilt.'

'Now Lem,' Ed Pugh said. 'You know that ain't so. I just want my rights, that's all. Pleased to meet you, young fellow. Another Hogben, I take it. Maybe you can talk your uncle into –'

'Excuse me for interrupting, Mister Pugh,' I said, real polite. 'But maybe you'd better explain. All this is purely a mystery to me.'

He cleared his throat and threw his chest out, important-like. I could tell this was something he liked to talk about. Made him feel pretty big, I could see.

'I don't know if you was acquainted with my dear departed wife, Lily Lou Mutz that was,' he said. 'This here's our little child, Junior. A fine little lad he is too. What a pity we didn't have eight or ten more just like him.' He sighed real deep.

'Well, that's life. I'd hoped to marry young and be blessed with a whole passel of younguns, being as how I'm the last of a fine old line. I don't mean to let it die out, neither.' Here he gave Uncle Lem a mean look. Uncle Lem sorta whimpered.

'I ain't a-gonna do it,' he said. 'You can't make me do it.'

'We'll see about that,' Ed Pugh said, threatening. 'Maybe your young relative here will be more reasonable. I'll have you know I'm getting to be a power in this state and what I says goes.'

'Paw,' little Junior squeaked out just then, 'Paw, they're kinda slowing down. Kin I give it to 'em double-strength this time, Paw? Betcha I could kill a few if I let myself go. Hey, Paw –'

Ed Pugh made as if he was gonna clonk the little varmint again, but I guess he thought better of it.

'Don't interrupt your elders, sonny,' he said. 'Paw's busy. Just tend to your job and shut up.' He glanced out over the moaning crowd. 'Give that bunch over beyond the truck a little more treatment,' he said. 'They ain't buying fast enough. But no double-strength, Junior. You gotta save your energy. You're a growing boy.'

He turned back to me. 'Junior's a talented child,' he said, very proud. 'As you can see. He inherited it from his dear dead-and-gone mother, Lily Lou. I was telling you about Lily Lou. It was my hope to marry young, like I said, but the way things worked out, somehow I just didn't get around to wifin' till I'd got well along into the prime of life.'

He blew out his chest like a toadfrog, looking down admiring. I never did see a man that thought better of himself. 'Never found a woman who'd look at – I mean, never found the right woman,' he went on, 'till the day I met Lily Lou Mutz.'

'I know what you mean,' I said, polite. I did, too. He musta searched a long, long ways before he found somebody ugly enough herself to look twice at him. Even Lily Lou, pore soul, musta thunk a long time afore she said yes.

'And that,' Ed Pugh went on, 'is where your Uncle Lem comes in. It seems like he'd give Lily Lou a bewitchment quite some while back.'

'I never!' Uncle Lem squealed. 'And anyway, how'd I know she'd get married and pass it on to her child? Who'd ever think Lily Lou would –'

'He gave her a bewitchment,' Ed Pugh went right on talking. 'Only she never told me till she was a-layin' on her death-bed a year ago. Lordy, I sure woulda whopped her good if I'd knowed how she held out on me all them years! It was the hex Lemuel gave her and she inherited it on to her little child.'

'I only done it to protect her,' Uncle Lem said, right quick. 'You know I'm speaking the truth, Saunk boy. Pore Lily Lou was so pizon ugly, people used to up and heave a clod at her now and then afore they could help themselves. Just automatic-like. Couldn't blame 'em. I often fought down the impulse myself.

'But pore Lily Lou, I shore felt sorry for her. You'll never know how long I fought down my good impulses, Saunk. But my heart of gold does get me into messes. One day I felt so sorry for the pore hideous critter I gave her the hexpower. Anybody'd have done the same, Saunk.'

'How'd you do it?' I asked, real interested, thinking it might come in handy someday to know. I'm young yet, and I got lots to learn.

Well, he started to tell me and it was kinda mixed up. Right at first I got a notion some furrin feller named Gene Chromosome had done it for him and after I got straight on that part he'd gone cantering off into a rigamarole about the alpha waves of the brain.

Shucks, I knowed that much my own self. Everybody musta noticed the way them little waves go a-sweeping over the tops of people's haids when they're thinking. I've watched Grandpaw sometimes when he had as many as six hundred different thoughts follering each other up and down them little paths where his brain is. Hurts my eyes to look too close when Grandpaw's thinking.

'So that's how it is, Saunk,' Uncle Lem wound up. 'And this here little rattlesnake's inherited the whole shebang.'

'Well, why don't you get this here Gene Chromosome feller to unscramble Junior and put him back the way other people are?' I asked. 'I can see how easy you could do it. Look here, Uncle Lem.' I focused down real sharp on Junior and made my eyes go funny the way you have to when you want to look inside a person.

Sure enough, I seen just what Uncle Lem meant. There was teensy-weensy little chains of fellers, all hanging onto each other for dear life, and skinny little rods jiggling around inside them awful teensy cells everybody's made of – except maybe Little Sam, our baby.

'Look here, Uncle Lem,' I said. 'All you did when you gave Lily Lou the hex was to twitch these here little rods over *that-away* and patch 'em onto them little chains that wiggle so fast. Now why can't you switch 'em back again and make Junior behave himself? It oughta be easy.'

'It would be easy,' Uncle Lem kinda sighed at me. 'Saunk, you're a scatterbrain. You wasn't listening to what I said. I can't switch 'em back without I kill Junior.'

'The world would be a better place,' I said.

'I know it would. But you know what we promised Grandpaw? No more killings.'

'But Uncle Lem!' I bust out. 'This is turrible! You mean this nasty little rattlesnake's gonna go on all his life hexing people?'

'Worse than that, Saunk,' pore Uncle Lem said, almost crying. 'He's gonna pass the power on to his descendants, just like Lily Lou passed it on to him.'

For a minute it sure did look like a dark prospect for the human race. Then I laughed.

'Cheer up, Uncle Lem,' I said. 'Nothing to worry about. Look at the little toad. There ain't a female critter alive who'd come within a mile of him. Already he's as repulsive as his daddy. And remember, he's Lily Lou Mutz's child, too. Maybe he'll get even horribler as he grows up. One thing's sure – he ain't never gonna get married.'

'Now there's where you're wrong,' Ed Pugh busted in, talking real loud. He was red in the face and he looked mad. 'Don't think I ain't been listening,' he said. 'And don't think I'm gonna forget what you said about my child. I told you I was a power in this town. Junior and me can go a long way, using his talent to help us.

'Already I've got on to the board of aldermen here and there's gonna be a vacancy in the state senate come next week – unless the old coot I have in mind's a lot tougher than he looks. So I'm warning you, young Hogben, you and your family's gonna pay for them insults.'

'Nobody oughta get mad when he hears the gospel truth about himself,' I said. 'Junior *is* a repulsive specimen.'

'He just takes getting used to,' his paw said. 'All us Pughs is hard to understand. Deep, I guess. But we got our pride. And I'm gonna make sure the family line never dies out. Never, do you hear that, Lemuel?'

Uncle Lem just shut his eyes up tight and shook his head fast. 'Nosirree,' he said. 'I'll never do it. Never, never, never, never –'

'Lemuel,' Ed Pugh said, real sinister. 'Lemuel, do you want me to set Junior on you?'

'Oh, there ain't no use in that,' I said. 'You seen him try to hex me along with the crowd, didn't you? No manner of use, Mister Pugh. Can't hex a Hogben.'

'Well –' He looked around, searching his mind. 'Hm-m. I'll think of something. I'll – soft-hearted, aren't you? Promised your Grandpappy you wouldn't kill nobody, hey? Lemuel, open your eyes and look over there across the street. See that sweet old lady walking with the cane? How'd you like it if I had Junior drop her dead in her tracks?'

Uncle Lemuel just squeezed his eyes tighter shut.

'I won't look. I don't know the sweet old thing. If she's that old, she ain't got much longer anyhow. Maybe she'd be better off dead. Probably got rheumatiz something fierce.'

'All right, then, how about that purty young girl with the baby in her arms? Look, Lemuel. Mighty sweet-looking little baby. Pink ribbon in its bonnet, see? Look at them dimples. Junior, get ready to blight them where they stand. Bubonic plague to start with maybe. And after that –'

'Uncle Lem,' I said, feeling uneasy. 'I dunno what Grandpaw would say to this. Maybe –'

Uncle Lem popped his eyes wide open for just a second. He glared at me, frantic.

'I can't help it if I've got a heart of gold,' he said. 'I'm a fine old feller and everybody picks on me. Well, I won't stand for it. You can push me just so far. Now I don't care if Ed Pugh kills off the whole human race. I don't care if Grandpaw *does* find out what I done. I don't care a hoot about nothing no more.' He gave a kind of wild laugh.

'I'm gonna get out from under. I won't know nothing about nothing. I'm gonna snatch me a few winks, Saunk.'

And with that he went rigid all over and fell flat on his face on the sidewalk, stiff as a poker.

Chapter 3. Over a Barrel

Well, worried as I was, I had to smile. Uncle Lem's kinda cute sometimes. I knowed he'd put hisself to sleep again, the way he always does when trouble catches up with him. Paw says it's catalepsy but cats sleep a lot lighter than that.

Uncle Lem hit the sidewalk flat and kinda bounced a little. Junior give a howl of joy. I guess maybe he figgered he'd had something to do with Uncle Lem falling over. Anyhow, seeing somebody down and helpless, Junior naturally rushed over and pulled his foot back and kicked Uncle Lem in the side of the haid.

Well, like I said, us Hogbens have got pretty tough haids. Junior let out a howl. He started dancing around nursing his foot in both hands.

'I'll hex you good!' he yelled at Uncle Lem. 'I'll hex you good, you – you ole Hogben, you!' He drew a deep breath and turned purple in the face and –

And then it happened.

It was like a flash of lightning. I don't take no stock in hexes, and I had a fair idea of what was happening, but it took me by surprise. Paw tried to explain to me later how it worked and he said it just stimulated the latent toxins inherent in the organism. It made Junior into a catalytoxic agent on account of the way the rearrangement of the desoxyribonucleic acid his genes was made of worked on the kappa waves of his nasty little brain, stepping them up as much as thirty microvolts. But shucks, you know Paw. He's too lazy to figger the thing out in English. He just steals them fool words out of other folks' brains when he needs 'em.

What really happened was that all the pizon that little varmint had bottled up in him, ready to let go on the crowd, somehow seemed to r'ar back and smack Uncle Lem right in the face. I never seen such a hex. And the awful part was – it worked.

Because Uncle Lem wasn't resisting a mite now he was asleep. Redhot pokers wouldn't have waked him up and I wouldn't put red-hot pokers past little Junior Pugh. But he didn't need 'em this time. The hex hit Uncle Lem like a thunderbolt.

He turned pale green right before our eyes.

Somehow it seemed to me a turrible silence fell as Uncle Lem went green. I looked up, surprised. Then I realized what was happening. All that pitiful moaning and groaning from the crowd had stopped.

People was swigging away at their bottles of headache cure, rubbing their foreheads and kinda laughing weak-like with relief. Junior's whole complete hex had gone into Uncle Lem and the crowd's headaches had naturally stopped right off.

'What's happened here?' somebody called out in a kinda familiar voice. 'Has that man fainted? Why don't you help him? Here, let me by – I'm a doctor.'

It was the skinny man with the kind-looking face. He was still drinking out of the headache bottle as he pushed his way through the crowd toward us but he'd put his notebook away. When he saw Ed Pugh he flushed up angrylike.

'So it's you, is it, Alderman Pugh?' he said. 'How is it you're always around when trouble starts? What did you do to this poor man, anyhow? Maybe this time you've gone too far.'

'I didn't do a thing,' Ed Pugh said. 'Never touched him. You watch your tongue, Dr Brown, or you'll regret it. I'm a powerful man in this here town.'

'Look at that!' Dr Brown yells, his voice going kinda squeaky as he stares down at Uncle Lem. 'The man's dying! Call an ambulance, somebody, quick!'

Uncle Lem was changing color again. I had to laugh a little, inside my haid. I knowed what was happening and it was kinda funny. Everybody's got a whole herd of germs and viruses and suchlike critters swarming through them all the time, of course.

When Junior's hex hit Uncle Lem it stimulated the entire herd something turrible, and a flock of little bitty critters Paw calls antibodies had to get to work pronto. They ain't really as sick as they look, being white by nature.

Whenever a pizon starts chawing on you these pale little fellers grab up their shooting-irons and run like crazy to the battlefield in your insides. Such fighting and yelling and swearing you never seen. It's a regular Bull Run.

That was going on right then inside Uncle Lem. Only us Hogbens have got a special militia of our own inside us. And they got called up real fast.

They was swearing and kicking and whopping the enemy so hard Uncle Lem had gone from pale green to a sort of purplish color, and big yeller and blue spots was beginning to bug out all over him where it showed. He looked oncommon sick. Course it didn't do him no real harm. The Hogbens militia can lick any germ that breathes.

But he sure looked revolting.

The skinny doctor crouched down beside Uncle Lem and felt his pulse.

'Now you've done it,' he said, looking up at Ed Pugh. 'I don't know how you've worked this, but for once you've gone too far. This man seems to have bubonic plague. I'll see you're put under control this time and that young Kallikak of yours, too.'

Ed Pugh just laughed a little. But I could see he was mad.

'Don't you worry about me, Dr Brown,' he said, mean. 'When I get to be governor – and I got my plans all made – that there hospital you're so proud of ain't gonna operate on state funds no more. A fine thing!

'Folks laying around in hospitals eating their fool heads off! Make 'em get out and plough, that's what I say. Us Pughs never gets sick. I got lots of better uses for state money than paying folks to lay around in bed when I'm governor.'

All the doctor said was, 'Where's that ambulance?'

'If you mean that big long car making such a noise,' I said, 'it's about three miles off but coming fast. Uncle Lem don't need no help, though. He's just having an attack. We get 'em in the family all the time. It don't mean nothing.'

'Good heavens!' the doc said, staring down at Uncle Lem. 'You mean he's had this before and lived?' Then he looked up at me and smiled all of a sudden. 'Oh, I see,' he said. 'Afraid of hospitals, are you? Well, don't worry. We won't hurt him.'

That surprised me some. He was a smart man. I'd fibbed a little for just that reason. Hospitals is no place for Hogbens. People in hospitals are too danged nosy. So I called Uncle Lem real loud, inside my head.

'Uncle Lem,' I hollered, only thinking it, not out loud. 'Uncle Lem, wake up quick! Grandpaw'll nail your hide to the barn door if'n you let yourself get took to a hospital. You want 'em to find out about them two hearts you got in your chest? And the way your bones are fixed and the shape of your gizzard? Uncle Lem! Wake up!'

It wasn't no manner of use. He never even twitched.

Right then I began to get really scared. Uncle Lem had sure landed me in the soup. There I was with all that responsibility on my shoulders and I didn't have the least idea how to handle it. I'm just a young feller after all. I can hardly remember much farther back than the great fire of London, when Charles II was king, with all them long curls a-hanging on his shoulders. On him, though, they looked good.

'Mister Pugh,' I said, 'you've got to call off Junior. I can't let Uncle Lem get took to the hospital. You know I can't.'

'Junior, pour it on,' Mister Pugh said, grinning real nasty. 'I want a little talk with young Hogben here.' The doctor looked up, puzzled, and Ed Pugh said, 'Step over here a mite, Hogben. I want a private word with you. Junior, bear down!'

Uncle Lem's yellow and blue spots got green rings around their outside edges. The doctor sorta gasped and Ed Pugh took my arm and pulled me back. When we was out of earshot he said to me, confidential, fixing me with his tiny little eyes:

'I reckon you know what I want, Hogben. Lem never did say he *couldn't*, he only said he wouldn't, so I know you folks can do it for me.'

'Just exactly what is it you want, Mister Pugh?' I asked him.

'You know. I want to make sure our fine old family line goes on. I want there should always be Pughs. I had so much trouble getting married off myself and I know Junior ain't going to be easy to wife. Women don't have no taste nowadays.

'Since Lily Lou went to glory there hasn't been a woman on earth ugly enough to marry a Pugh and I'm skeered Junior'll be the last of a great line. With his talent I can't bear the thought. You just fix it so our family won't never die out and I'll have Junior take the hex off Lemuel.'

'If I fixed it so your line didn't die out,' I said, 'I'd be fixing it so everybody else's line *would* die out, just as soon as there was enough Pughs around.'

'What's wrong with that?' Ed Pugh asked, grinning. 'Way I see it we're good strong stock.' He flexed his gorilla arms. He was taller than me, even. 'No harm in populatin' the world with good stock, is there? I figger given time enough us Pughs could conquer the whole danged world. And you're gonna help us do it, young Hogben.'

'Oh, no,' I said. 'Oh, no! Even if I knowed how –'

There was a turrible noise at the end of the street and the crowd scattered to make way for the ambulance, which drawed up at the curb beside Uncle Lem. A couple of fellers in white coats jumped out with a sort of pallet on sticks. Dr Brown stood up, looking real relieved.

'Thought you'd never get here,' he said. 'This man's a quarantine case, I think. Heaven knows what kind of results we'll find when we start running tests on him. Hand me my bag out of the back there, will you? I want my stethoscope. There's something funny about this man's heart.'

*

Well, *my* heart sunk right down into my boots. We was goners and I knowed it – the whole Hogben tribe. Once them doctors and scientists find out about us we'll never know a moment's peace again as long as we live. We won't have no more privacy than a corncob.

Ed Pugh was watching me with a nasty grin on his pasty face.

'Worried, huh?' he said. 'You gotta right to be worried. I know about you Hogbens. All witches. Once they get Lem in the hospital, no telling what they'll find out. Against the law to be witches, probably. You've got about half a minute to make up your mind, young Hogben. What do you say?'

Well, what could I say? I couldn't give him a promise like he was asking, could I? Not and let the whole world be overrun by hexing Pughs. Us Hogbens live a long time. We've got some pretty important plans for the future when the rest of the world begins to catch up with us. But if by that time the rest of the world is all Pughs, it won't hardly seem worth while, somehow. I couldn't say yes.

But if I said no Uncle Lem was a goner. Us Hogbens was doomed either way, it seemed to me.

Looked like there was only one thing to do. I took a deep breath, shut my eyes, and let out a desperate yell inside my head.

'Grandpaw!' I hollered.

'Yes, my boy?' said a big deep voice in the middle of my brain. You'd athought he'd been right alongside me all the time, just waiting to be called. He was a hundred-odd miles off, and sound asleep. But when a Hogben calls in the tone of voice *I* called in he's got a right to expect an answer – quick. I got it.

Mostly Grandpaw woulda dithered around for fifteen minutes, asking cross questions and not listening to the answers, and talking in all kinds of queer old-fashioned dialects, like Sanskrit, he's picked up through the years. But this time he seen it was serious.

'Yes, my boy?' was all he said.

I flapped my mind wide open like a school-book in front of him. There wasn't no time for questions and answers. The doc was getting out his dingus to listen to Uncle Lem's two hearts beating out of tune and once he heard that the jig would be up for us Hogbens.

'Unless you let me kill 'em, Grandpaw,' I added. Because by that time I knowed he'd read the whole situation from start to finish in one fast glance.

It seemed to me he was quiet an awful long time after that. The doc had got the dingus out and he was fitting its little black arms into his ears. Ed Pugh was watching me like a hawk. Junior stood there all swole up with pizon, blinking his mean little eyes around for somebody to shoot it at. I was half hoping he'd pick on me. I'd worked out a way to make it bounce back in his face and there was a chance it might even kill him.

I heard Grandpaw give a sorta sigh in my mind.

'They've got us over a barrel, Saunk,' he said. I remember being a little surprised he could speak right plain English when he wanted to. 'Tell Pugh we'll do it.'

'But Grandpaw –' I said.

'Do as I say!' It gave me a headache, he spoke so firm. 'Quick, Saunk! Tell Pugh we'll give him what he wants.'

Well, I didn't dare disobey. But this once I really came close to defying Grandpaw.

It stands to reason even a Hogben has got to get senile someday, and I thought maybe old age had finally set in with Grandpaw at last.

What I thunk at him was, 'All right, if you say so, but I sure hate to do it. Seems like if they've got us going and coming, the least we can do is take our medicine like Hogbens and keep all that pizon bottled up in Junior stead of spreading it around the world.' But out loud I spoke to Mister Pugh.

'All right, Mister Pugh,' I said, real humble. 'You win. Only, call off your hex. Quick, before it's too late.'

Chapter 4. Pughs A-Coming

Mister Pugh had a great big yellow automobile, low-slung, without no top. It went awful fast. And it was sure awful noisy. Once I'm pretty sure we run over a small boy in the road but Mister Pugh paid him no mind and I didn't dare say nothing. Like Grandpaw said, the Pughs had us over a barrel.

It took quite a lot of palaver before I convinced 'em they'd have to come back to the homestead with me. That was part of Grandpaw's orders.

'How do I know you won't murder us in cold blood once you get us out there in the wilderness?' Mister Pugh asked.

'I could kill you right here if I wanted,' I told him. 'I would too but Grandpaw says no. You're safe if Grandpaw says so, Mister Pugh. The word of a Hogben ain't never been broken yet.'

So he agreed, mostly because I said we couldn't work the spells except on home territory. We loaded Uncle Lem into the back of the car and took off for the hills. Had quite an argument with the doc, of course. Uncle Lem sure was stubborn.

He wouldn't wake up nohow but once Junior took the hex off Uncle Lem faded out fast to a good healthy color again. The doc just didn't believe it coulda happened, even when he saw it. Mister Pugh had to threaten quite a lot before we got away. We left the doc sitting on the curb, muttering to himself and rubbing his haid dazed like.

I could feel Grandpaw a-studying the Pughs through my mind all the way home. He seemed to be sighing and kinda shaking his haid – such as it is – and working out problems that didn't make no manner of sense to me.

When we drawed up in front of the house there wasn't a soul in sight. I could hear Grandpaw stirring and muttering on his gunnysack in the attic but Paw seemed to have went invisible and he was too drunk to tell me where he was when I asked. The baby was asleep. Maw was still at the church sociable and Grandpaw said to leave her be.

'We can work this out together, Saunk,' he said as soon as I got outa the car. 'I've been thinking. You know that sled you fixed up to sour your Maw's cream this morning? Drag it out, son. Drag it out.'

I seen in a flash what he had in mind. 'Oh, no, Grandpaw!' I said, right out loud.

'Who you talking to?' Ed Pugh asked, lumbering down outa the car. 'I don't see nobody. This your homestead? Ratty old dump, ain't it? Stay close to me, Junior. I don't trust these folks any farther'n I can see 'em.'

'Get the sled, Saunk,' Grandpaw said, very firm. 'I got it all worked out. We're gonna send these two gorillas right back through time, to a place they'll really fit.'

'But Grandpaw!' I hollered, only inside my head this time. 'Let's talk this over. Lemme get Maw in on it anyhow. Paw's right smart when he's sober. Why not wait till he wakes up? I think we oughta get the Baby in on it too. I don't think sending 'em back through time's a good idea at all, Grandpaw.'

'The Baby's asleep,' Grandpaw said. 'You leave him be. He read himself to sleep over his Einstein, bless his little soul.'

I think the thing that worried me most was the way Grandpaw was talking plain English. He never does when he's feeling normal. I thought maybe his old age had all caught up with him at one bank, and knocked all the sense outa his – so to speak – haid.

'Grandpaw,' I said, trying to keep calm. 'Don't you see? If we send 'em back through time and give 'em what we promised it'll make everything a million times worse than before. You gonna strand 'em back there in the year one and break your promise to 'em?'

'Saunk!' Grandpaw said.

'I know. If we promised we'd make sure the Pugh line won't die out, then we gotta make sure. But if we send 'em back to the year one that'll mean all the time between then and now they'll spend spreading out and spreading out. More Pughs every generation.

'Grandpaw, five seconds after they hit the year one, I'm liable to feel my two eyes rush together in my haid and my face go all fat and pasty like Junior. Grandpaw, everybody in the world may be Pughs if we give 'em that much time to spread out in!'

'Cease thy chirming, thou chilce dolt,' Grandpaw hollered. 'Do my bidding, young fool!'

That made me feel a little better but not much. I went and dragged out the sled. Mister Pugh put up quite a argument about that.

'I ain't rid on a sled since I was so high,' he said. 'Why should I git on one now? This is some trick. I won't do it.'

Junior tried to bite me.

'Now Mister Pugh,' I said, 'you gotta cooperate or we won't get nowheres. I know what I'm doing. Just step up here and set down. Junior, there's room for you in front. That's fine.'

If he hadn't seen how worried I was I don't think he'd a-done it. But I couldn't hide how I was feeling.

'Where's your Grandpaw?' he asked, uneasy. 'You're not going to do this whole trick by yourself, are you? Young ignorant feller like you? I don't like it. Suppose you made a mistake?'

'We give our word,' I reminded him. 'Now just kindly shut up and let me concentrate. Or maybe you don't want the Pugh line to last forever?'

'That was the promise,' he says, settling himself down. 'You gotta do it. Lemme know when you commence.'

'All right, Saunk,' Grandpaw says from the attic, right brisk. 'Now you watch. Maybe you'll learn a thing or two. Look sharp. Focus your eyes down and pick out a gene. Any gene.'

Bad as I felt about the whole thing I couldn't help being interested. When Grandpaw does a thing he does it up brown. Genes are mighty slippery little critters, spindle-shaped and awful teensy. They're partners with some skinny guys called chromosomes, and the two of 'em show up everywhere you look, once you've got your eyes focused just right.

'A good dose of ultraviolet ought to do the trick,' Grandpaw muttered. 'Saunk, you're closer.'

I said, 'All right, Grandpaw,' and sort of twiddled the light as it sifted down through the pines above the Pughs. Ultraviolet's the color at the *other* end of the line, where the colors stop having names for most people.

Grandpaw said, 'Thanks, son. Hold it for a minute.'

The genes began to twiddle right in time with the light waves. Junior said, 'Paw, something's tickling me.'

Ed Pugh said, 'Shut up.'

Grandpaw was muttering to himself. I'm pretty sure he stole the words from that perfesser we keep in the bottle, but you can't tell, with Grandpaw. Maybe he was the first person to make 'em up in the beginning.

'The euchromatin,' he kept muttering. 'That ought to fix it. Ultraviolet gives us hereditary mutation and the euchromatin contains the genes that transmit heredity. Now that other stuff's heterochromatin and *that* produces evolutionary change of the cataclysmic variety.

'Very good, very good. We can always use a new species. Hum-m-m.

About six bursts of heterochromatinic activity ought to do it.' He was quiet for a minute. Then he said, 'Ich am eldre and ek magti! Okay, Saunk, take it away.'

I let the ultraviolet go back where it came from.

'The year one, Grandpaw?' I asked, very doubtful.

'That's close enough,' he said. 'Wite thou the way?'

'Oh yes, Grandpaw,' I said. And I bent over and give them the necessary push.

The last thing I heard was Mister Pugh's howl.

'What's that you're doin'?' he hollered at me. 'What's the idea? Look out, there, young Hogben or – what's this? Where we goin'? Young Saunk, I warn you, if this is some trick I'll set Junior on you! I'll send you such a hex as even you-u ...'

Then the howl got real thin and small and far away until it wasn't no more than the noise a mosquito makes. After that it was mighty quiet in the dooryard.

I stood there all braced, ready to stop myself from turning into a Pugh if I could. Them little genes is tricky fellers.

I knowed Grandpaw had made a turrible mistake.

The minute them Pughs hit the year one and started to bounce back through time toward now I knowed what would happen.

I ain't sure how long ago the year one was, but there was plenty of time for the Pughs to populate the whole planet. I put two fingers against my nose to keep my eyes from banging each other when they started to rush together in the middle like all us Pughs' eyes do –

'You ain't a Pugh yet, son,' Grandpaw said, chuckling. 'Kin ye see 'em?'

'No,' I said. 'What's happening?'

'The sled's starting to slow down,' he said. 'Now it's stopped. Yep, it's the year one, all right. Look at all them men and women flockin' outa the caves to greet their new company! My, my, what great big shoulders the men have got. Bigger even than Paw Pugh's.

'An' ugh – just look at the women! I declare, little Junior's positively handsome alongside them folks! He won't have no trouble finding a wife when the time comes.'

'But Grandpaw, that's turrible!' I said.

'Don't sass your elders, Saunk,' Grandpaw chuckled. 'Looka there now. Junior's just pulled a hex. Another little child fell over flat on his ugly face. Now the little child's mother is knocking Junior endwise. Now his pappy's sailing into Paw Pugh. Look at that fight! Just look at it! Oh, I guess the Pugh family's well took care of, Saunk.'

'But what about our family?' I said, almost wailing.

'Don't you worry,' Grandpaw said. 'Time'll take care of that. Wait a minute, let me watch. Hm-m. A generation don't take long when you know how to look. My, my, what ugly little critters the ten baby Pughs was! They was just like their pappy and their grandpappy.

'I wish Lily Lou Mutz could see her grandbabies. I shorely do. Well, now, ain't that cute? Every one of them babies growed up in a flash, seems like, and each of 'em has got ten babies of their own. I like to see my promises working out, Saunk. I said I'd do this, and I done it.'

I just moaned.

'All right,' Grandpaw said. 'Let's jump ahead a couple of centuries. Yep, still there and spreading like crazy. Family likeness is still strong, too. Hum-m. Another thousand years and – well, I declare! If it ain't Ancient Greece! Hasn't changed a bit, neither. What do you know, Saunk!' He cackled right out, tickled pink.

'Remember what I said once about Lily Lou putting me in mind of an old friend of mine named Gorgon? No wonder! Perfectly natural. You ought to see Lily Lou's great-great-great-grandbabies! No, on second thought, it's lucky you can't. Well, well, this is shore interesting.'

He was still about three minutes. Then I heard him laugh.

'Bang,' he said. 'First heterochromatinic burst. Now the changes start.'

'What changes, Grandpaw?' I asked, feeling pretty miserable.

'The changes,' he said, 'that show your old Grandpaw ain't such a fool as you thought. I know what I'm doing. They go fast, once they start. Look there now, that's the second change. Look at them little genes mutate!'

'You mean,' I said, 'I ain't gonna turn into a Pugh after all? But Grandpaw, I thought we'd promised the Pughs their line wouldn't die out.'

'I'm keeping my promise,' Grandpaw said, dignified. 'The genes will carry the Pugh likeness right on to the toot of the judgment horn, just like I said. And the hex power goes right along with it.'

Then he laughed.

'You better brace yourself, Saunk,' he said. 'When Paw Pugh went sailing off into the year one seems like he uttered a hex threat, didn't he? Well, he wasn't fooling. It's a-coming at you right now.'

'Oh, Lordy!' I said. 'There'll be a million of 'em by the time they get here! Grandpaw! What'll I do?'

'Just brace yourself,' Grandpaw said, real unsympathetic. 'A million, you think? Oh, no, lots more than a million.'

'How many?' I asked him.

He started in to tell me. You may not believe it but he's *still* telling me. It takes that long. There's that many of 'em.

You see, it was like with that there Jukes family that lived down south of here. The bad ones was always a mite worse than their children and the same dang thing happened to Gene Chromosome and his kin, so to speak. The Pughs stayed Pughs and they kept the hex power – and I guess you might say the Pughs conquered the whole world, after all.

But it could of been worse. The Pughs could of stayed the same size down through the generations. Instead they got smaller – a whole lot smaller. When I knowed 'em they was bigger than most folks – Paw Pugh, anyhow.

But by the time they'd done filtering the generations from the year one, they'd shrunk so much them little pale fellers in the blood was about their size. And many a knock-down drag-out fight they have with 'em, too.

Them Pugh genes took such a beating from the heterochromatinic bursts Grandpaw told me about that they got whopped all outa their proper form. You might call 'em a virus now – and of course a virus is exactly the same thing as a gene, except the virus is friskier. But heavens above, that's like saying the Jukes boys is exactly the same as George Washington!

The hex hit me – hard.

I sneezed something turrible. Then I heard Uncle Lem sneezing in his sleep, lying back there in the yaller car. Grandpaw was still droning on about how many Pughs was a-coming at me right that minute, so there wasn't no use asking questions. I fixed my eyes different and looked right down into the middle of that sneeze to see what had tickled me –

Well, you never seen so many Junior Pughs in all your born days! It was the hex, all right. Likewise, them Pughs is still busy, hexing everybody on earth, off and on. They'll do it for quite a time, too, since the Pugh line has got to go on forever, account of Grandpaw's promise.

They tell me even the microscopes ain't never yet got a good look at certain viruses. The scientists are sure in for a surprise someday when they focus down real close and see all them pasty-faced little devils, ugly as sin, with their eyes set real close together, wiggling around hexing everybody in sight.

It took a long time – since the year one, that is – but Gene Chromosome fixed it up, with Grandpaw's help. So Junior Pugh ain't a pain in the neck no more, so to speak.

But I got to admit he's an awful cold in the haid.

OR ELSE

Miguel and Fernandez were shooting inaccurately at each other across the valley when the flying saucer landed. They wasted a few bullets on the strange airship. The pilot appeared and began to walk across the valley and up the slope toward Miguel, who lay in the uncertain shade of a cholla, swearing and working the bolt of his rifle as rapidly as he could. His aim, never good, grew worse as the stranger approached. Finally, at the last minute, Miguel dropped his rifle, seized the machete beside him, and sprang to his feet.

'Die then,' he said, and swung the blade. The steel blazed in the hot Mexican sun. The machete rebounded elastically from the stranger's neck and flew high in the air, while Miguel's arm tingled as though from an electric shock. A bullet came from across the valley, making the kind of sound a wasp's sting might make if you heard it instead of feeling it. Miguel dropped and rolled into the shelter of a large rock. Another bullet shrieked thinly, and a brief blue flash sparkled on the stranger's left shoulder.

'Estoy perdido,' Miguel said, giving himself up for lost. Flat on his stomach, he lifted his head and snarled at his enemy.

The stranger, however, made no inimical moves. Moreover, he seemed to be unarmed. Miguel's sharp eyes searched him. The man was unusually dressed. He wore a cap made of short, shiny blue feathers. Under it his face was hard, ascetic and intolerant. He was very thin, and nearly seven feet tall. But he did seem to be unarmed. That gave Miguel courage. He wondered where his machete had fallen. He did not see it, but his rifle was only a few feet away.

The stranger came and stood above Miguel.

'Stand up,' he said. 'Let us talk.'

He spoke excellent Spanish, except that his voice seemed to be coming from inside Miguel's head.

'I will not stand up,' Miguel said. 'If I stand up, Fernandez will shoot me. He is a very bad shot, but I would be a fool to take such a chance. Besides, this is very unfair. How much is Fernandez paying you?'

The stranger looked austerely at Miguel.

'Do you know where I came from?' he asked.

'I don't care a centavo where you came from,' Miguel said, wiping sweat from his forehead. He glanced toward a nearby rock where he had cached a goatskin of wine. 'From *los estados unidos*, no doubt, you and your machine of flight. The Mexican government will hear of this.'

'Does the Mexican government approve of murder?'

'This is a private matter,' Miguel said. 'A matter of water rights, which are very important. Besides, it is self-defense. That *cabrón* across the valley is trying to kill me. And you are his hired assassin. God will punish you both.' A new thought came to him. 'How much will you take to kill Fernandez?' he inquired. 'I will give you three pesos and a fine kid.'

'There will be no more fighting at all,' the stranger said. 'Do you hear that?'

'Then go and tell Fernandez,' Miguel said. 'Inform him that the water rights are mine. I will gladly allow him to go in peace.' His neck ached from staring up at the tall man. He moved a little, and a bullet shrieked through the still, hot air and dug with a vicious splash into a nearby cactus.

The stranger smoothed the blue feathers on his head.

'First I will finish talking with you. Listen to me, Miguel.'

'How do you know my name?' Miguel demanded, rolling over and sitting up cautiously behind the rock. 'It is as I thought. Fernandez has hired you to assassinate me.'

'I know your name because I can read your mind a little. Not much, because it is so cloudy.'

'Your mother was a dog,' Miguel said.

The stranger's nostrils pinched together slightly, but he ignored the remark. 'I come from another world,' he said. 'My name is –' In Miguel's mind it sounded like Quetzalcoatl.

'Quetzalcoatl?' Miguel repeated, with fine irony. 'Oh, I have no doubt of that. And mine is Saint Peter, who has the keys to heaven.'

Quetzalcoatl's thin, pale face flushed slightly, but his voice was determinedly calm. 'Listen, Miguel. Look at my lips. They are not moving. I am speaking inside your head, by telepathy, and you translate my thoughts into words that have meaning to you. Evidently my name is too difficult for you. Your own mind has translated it as Quetzalcoatl. That is not my real name at all.'

'*De veras*,' Miguel said. 'It is not your name at all, and you do not come from another world. I would not believe a *norteamericano* if he swore on the bones of ten thousand highly placed saints.'

Quetzalcoatl's long, austere face flushed again.

'I am here to give orders,' he said. 'Not to bandy words with – Look here, Miguel. Why do you suppose you couldn't kill me with your machete? Why can't bullets touch me?'

'Why does your machine of flight fly?' Miguel riposted. He took out a sack of tobacco and began to roll a cigarette. He squinted around the rock. 'Fernandez is probably trying to creep up on me. I had better get my rifle.'

'Leave it alone,' Quetzalcoatl said. 'Fernandez will not harm you.'

Miguel laughed harshly.

'And you must not harm him,' Quetzalcoatl added firmly.

'I will, then, turn the other cheek,' Miguel said, 'so that he can shoot me through the side of my head. I will believe Fernandez wishes peace, *Señor* Quetzalcoatl, when I see him walking across the valley with his hands over his head. Even then I will not let him come close, because of the knife he wears down his back.'

Quetzalcoatl smoothed his blue steel feathers again. His bony face was frowning.

'You must stop fighting forever, both of you,' he said. 'My race polices the universe and our responsibility is to bring peace to every planet we visit.'

'It is as I thought,' Miguel said with satisfaction. 'You come from *los estados unidos*. Why do you not bring peace to your own country? I have seen *los señores* Humphrey Bogart and Edward Robinson in *las películas*. Why, all over Nueva York gangsters shoot at each other from one skyscraper to another. And what do you do about it? You dance all over the place with *la señora* Betty Grable. Ah yes, I understand very well. First you will bring peace, and then you will take our oil and our precious minerals.'

Quetzalcoatl kicked angrily at a pebble beside his shiny steel toe.

'I must make you understand,' he said. He looked at the unlighted cigarette dangling from Miguel's lips. Suddenly he raised his hand, and a white-hot ray shot from a ring on his finger and kindled the end of the cigarette. Miguel jerked away, startled. Then he inhaled the smoke and nodded. The white-hot ray disappeared.

'Muchas gracias, señor,' Miguel said.

Quetzalcoatl's colorless lips pressed together thinly. 'Miguel,' he said, 'could a *norteamericano* do that?'

'Quién sabe?'

'No one living on your planet could do that, and you know it.'

Miguel shrugged.

'Do you see that cactus over there?' Quetzalcoatl demanded. 'I could destroy it in two seconds.'

'I have no doubt of it, *señor*.'

'I could, for that matter, destroy this whole planet.'

'Yes, I have heard of the atomic bombs,' Miguel said politely. 'Why, then, do you trouble to interfere with a quiet private little argument between Fernandez and me, over a small water hole of no importance to anybody but –'

A bullet sang past.

Quetzalcoatl rubbed the ring on his finger with an angry gesture.

'Because the world is going to stop fighting,' he said ominously. 'If it doesn't we will destroy it. There is no reason at all why men should not live together in peace and brotherhood.'

'There is one reason, *señor*.'

'What is that?'

'Fernandez,' Miguel said.

'I will destroy you both if you do not stop fighting.'

'*El señor* is a great peacemaker,' Miguel said courteously. 'I will gladly stop fighting if you will tell me how to avoid being killed when I do.'

'Fernandez will stop fighting too.'

Miguel removed his somewhat battered sombrero, reached for a stick, and carefully raised the hat above the rock. There was a nasty crack. The hat jumped away, and Miguel caught it as it fell.

'Very well,' he said. 'Since you insist, *señor*, I will stop fighting. But I will not come out from behind this rock. I am perfectly willing to stop fighting. But it seems to me that you demand I do something which you do not tell me how to do. You could as well require that I fly through the air like your machine of flight.'

Quetzalcoatl frowned more deeply. Finally he said, 'Miguel, tell me how this fight started.'

'Fernandez wishes to kill me and enslave my family.'

'Why should he want to do that?'

'Because he is evil,' Miguel said.

'How do you know he is evil?'

'Because,' Miguel pointed out logically, 'he wishes to kill me and enslave my family.'

There was a pause. A road runner darted past and paused to peck at the gleaming barrel of Miguel's rifle. Miguel sighed.

'There is a skin of good wine not twenty feet away –' he began, but Quetzalcoatl interrupted him.

'What was it you said about the water rights?'

'Oh, that,' Miguel said. 'This is a poor country, *señor*. Water is precious here. We have had a dry year and there is no longer water enough for two families. The water hole is mine. Fernandez wishes to kill me and enslave –'

'Are there no courts of law in your country?'

'For such as us?' Miguel demanded, and smiled politely.

'Has Fernandez a family too?' Quetzalcoatl asked.

'Yes, the poors,' Miguel said. 'He beats them when they do not work until they drop.'

'Do you beat your family?'

'Only when they need it,' Miguel said, surprised. 'My wife is very fat and lazy. And my oldest, Chico, talks back. It is my duty to beat them when they need it, for their own good. It is also my duty to protect our water rights, since the evil Fernandez is determined to kill me and –'

Quetzalcoatl said impatiently, 'This is a waste of time. Let me consider.' He rubbed the ring on his finger again. He looked around. The road runner had found a more appetizing morsel than the rifle. He was now to be seen trotting away with the writhing tail of a lizard dangling from his beak.

Overhead the sun was hot in a clear blue sky. The dry air smelled of mesquite. Below, in the valley, the flying saucer's perfection of shape and texture looked incongruous and unreal.

'Wait here,' Quetzalcoatl said at last. 'I will talk to Fernandez. When I call, come to my machine of flight. Fernandez and I will meet you there presently.'

'As you say, *señor*,' Miguel agreed. His eyes strayed.

'And do not touch your rifle,' Quetzalcoatl added with great firmness.

'Why, no, *señor*,' Miguel said. He waited until the tall man had gone. Then he crawled cautiously across the dry ground until he had recaptured his rifle. After that, with a little searching, he found his machete. Only then did he turn to the skin of wine. He was very thirsty indeed. But he did not drink heavily. He put a full clip in the rifle, leaned against a rock, and sipped a little from time to time from the wineskin as he waited.

In the meantime the stranger, ignoring fresh bullets that occasionally splashed blue from his steely person, approached Fernandez' hiding place. The sound of shots stopped. A long time passed, and finally the tall form reappeared and waved to Miguel.

'*Yo voy, señor*,' Miguel shouted agreeably. He put his rifle conveniently on the rock and rose very cautiously, ready to duck at the first hostile move. There was no such move.

Fernandez appeared beside the stranger. Immediately Miguel bent down, seized his rifle and lifted it for a snap shot.

Something thin and hissing burned across the valley. The rifle turned red-hot in Miguel's grasp. He squealed and dropped it, and the next moment his mind went perfectly blank.

'I die with honor,' he thought, and then thought no more.

... When he woke, he was standing under the shadow of the great flying saucer. Quetzalcoatl was lowering his hand from before Miguel's face. Sunlight sparkled on the tall man's ring. Miguel shook his head dizzily.

'I live?' he inquired.

But Quetzalcoatl paid no attention. He had turned to Fernandez, who was standing beside him, and was making gestures before Fernandez' masklike face. A light flashed from Quetzalcoatl's ring into Fernandez' glassy eyes. Fernandez shook his head and muttered thickly. Miguel looked for his rifle or machete, but they were gone. He slipped his hand into his shirt, but his good little knife had vanished too.

He met Fernandez' eyes.

'We are both doomed, Don Fernandez,' he said. 'This *señor* Quetzalcoatl will kill us both. In a way I am sorry that you will go to hell and I to heaven, for we shall not meet again.'

'You are mistaken,' Fernandez replied, vainly searching for his own knife. 'You will never see heaven. Nor is this tall *norteamericano* named Quetzalcoatl. For his own lying purposes he has assumed the name of Cortés.'

'You will tell lies to the devil himself,' Miguel said.

'Be quiet, both of you,' Quetzalcoatl (or Cortés) said sharply. 'You have seen a little of my power. Now listen to me. My race has assumed the high duty of seeing that the entire solar system lives in peace. We are a very advanced race, with power such as you do not yet dream of. We have solved problems which your people have no answer for, and it is now our duty to apply our power for the good of all. If you wish to keep on living, you will stop fighting immediately and forever, and from now on live in peace and brotherhood. Do you understand me?'

'That is all I have ever wished,' Fernandez said, shocked. 'But this offspring of a goat wishes to kill me.'

'There will be no more killing,' Quetzalcoatl said. 'You will live in brotherhood, or you will die.'

Miguel and Fernandez looked at each other and then at Quetzalcoatl.

'The *señor* is a great peacemaker,' Miguel murmured. 'I have said it before. The way you mention is surely the best way of all to insure peace. But to us it is not so simple. To live in peace is good. Very well, *señor*. Tell us how.'

'Simply stop fighting,' Quetzalcoatl said impatiently.

'Now that is easy to say,' Fernandez pointed out. 'But life here in Sonora is not a simple business. Perhaps it is where you come from –'

'Naturally,' Miguel put in. 'In *los estados unidos* everyone is rich.'

'– but it is not simple with us. Perhaps in your country, *señor*, the snake does not eat the rat, and the bird eat the snake. Perhaps in your country there is food and water for all, and a man need not fight to keep his family alive. Here it is not so simple.'

Miguel nodded. 'We shall certainly all be brothers some day,' he agreed. 'We try to do as the good God commands us. It is not easy, but little by little we learn to be better. It would be very fine if we could all become brothers at a word of magic, such as you command us. Unfortunately –' He shrugged.

'You must not use force to solve your problems,' Quetzalcoatl said with great firmness. 'Force is evil. *You will make peace now*.'

'Or else you will destroy us,' Miguel said. He shrugged again and met Fernandez' eyes. 'Very well, *señor*. You have an argument I do not care to resist. *Al fin*, I agree. What must we do?'

Quetzalcoatl turned to Fernandez.

'I too, *señor*,' the latter said, with a sigh. 'You are, no doubt, right. Let us have peace.'

'You will take hands,' Quetzalcoatl said, his eyes gleaming. 'You will swear brotherhood.'

Miguel held out his hand. Fernandez took it firmly and the two men grinned at each other.

'You see?' Quetzalcoatl said, giving them his austere smile. 'It is not hard at all. Now you are friends. Stay friends.'

He turned away and walked toward the flying saucer. A door opened smoothly in the sleek hull. On the threshold Quetzalcoatl turned.

'Remember,' he said. 'I shall be watching.'

'Without a doubt,' Fernandez said. '*Adiós, señor*.'

'*Vaya con Dios*,' Miguel added.

The smooth surface of the hull closed after Quetzalcoatl. A moment later the flying saucer lifted smoothly and rose until it was a hundred feet above the ground. Then it shot off to the north like a sudden flash of lightning and was gone.

'As I thought,' Miguel said. 'He was from *los estados unidos*.'

Fernandez shrugged.

'There was a moment when I thought he might tell us something sensible,' he said. 'No doubt he had great wisdom. Truly, life is not easy.'

'Oh, it is easy enough for him,' Miguel said. 'But he does not live in Sonora. We, however, do. Fortunately, I and my family have a good water hole to rely on. For those without one, life is indeed hard.'

'It is a very poor water hole,' Fernandez said. 'Such as it is, however, it is mine.' He was rolling a cigarette as he spoke. He handed it to Miguel and rolled another for himself. The two men smoked for a while in silence. Then, still silent, they parted.

Miguel went back to the wineskin on the hill. He took a long drink, grunted with pleasure, and looked around him. His knife, machete and rifle were carelessly flung down not far away. He recovered them and made sure he had a full clip.

Then he peered cautiously around the rock barricade. A bullet splashed on the stone near his face. He returned the shot.

After that, there was silence for a while. Miguel sat back and took another drink. His eye was caught by a road runner scuttling past, with the tail of a lizard dangling from his beak. It was probably the same road runner as before, and perhaps the same lizard, slowly progressing toward digestion.

Miguel called softly, '*Señor* Bird! It is wrong to eat lizards. It is very wrong.'

The road runner cocked a beady eye at him and ran on.

Miguel raised and aimed his rifle.

'Stop eating lizards, *Señor* Bird. Stop, or I must kill you.'

The road runner ran on across the rifle sights.

'Don't you understand how to stop?' Miguel called gently. 'Must I explain how?'

The road runner paused. The tail of the lizard disappeared completely.

'Oh, very well,' Miguel said. 'When I find out how a road runner can stop eating lizards and still live, then I will tell you, *amigo*. But until then, go with God.'

He turned and aimed the rifle across the valley again.

ENDOWMENT POLICY

When Denny Holt checked in at the telephone box, there was a call for him. Denny wasn't enthusiastic. On a rainy night like this it was easy to pick up fares, and now he'd have to edge his cab uptown to Columbus Circle.

'Nuts,' he said into the mouthpiece. 'Why me? Send one of the other boys; the guy won't know the difference. I'm way down in the Village.'

'He wants you, Holt. Asked for you by name and number. Probably a friend of yours. He'll be at the monument – black overcoat and a cane.'

'Who is he?'

'How should I know? He didn't say. Now get going.'

Holt disconsolately hung up and went back to his cab. Water trickled from the visor of his cap; rain streaked the windshield. Through the dimout he could see faintly lighted doorways and hear jukebox music. It was a good night to be indoors. Holt considered the advisability of dropping into the Cellar for a quick rye. Oh, well. He meshed the gears and headed up Greenwich Avenue, feeling low.

Pedestrians were difficult to avoid these days; New Yorkers never paid any attention to traffic signals, anyway, and the dimout made the streets dark, shadowy canyons. Holt drove uptown, ignoring cries of 'Taxi.' The street was wet and slippery. His tires weren't too good, either.

The damp cold seeped into Holt's bones. The rattling in the engine wasn't comforting. Some time soon the old bus would break down completely. After that – well, it was easy to get jobs, but Holt had an aversion to hard work. Defense factories – *hm-m-m-m*.

Brooding, he swung slowly around the traffic circle at Columbus, keeping an eye open for his fare. There he was – the only figure standing motionless in the rain. Other pedestrians were scuttling across the street in a hurry, dodging the trolleys and automobiles.

Holt pulled in and opened the door. The man came forward. He had a cane but no umbrella, and water glistened on his dark overcoat. A shapeless slouch hat shielded his head, and keen dark eyes peered sharply at Holt.

The man was old – rather surprisingly old. His features were obscured by wrinkles and folds of sagging, tallowy skin.

'Dennis Holt?' he asked harshly.

'That's me, buddy. Hop in and dry off.'

The old man complied. Holt said, 'Where to?'

'Eh? Go through the park.'

'Up to Harlem?'

'Why – yes, yes.'

Shrugging, Holt turned the taxicab into Central Park. A screwball. And nobody he'd ever seen before. In the rear mirror he stole a glance at his fare. The man was intently examining Holt's photograph and number on the card. Apparently satisfied, he leaned back and took a copy of the *Times* from his pocket.

'Want the light, mister?' Holt asked.

'The light? Yes, thank you.' But he did not use it for long. A glance at the paper satisfied him, and the man settled back, switched off the panel lamp and studied his wristwatch.

'What time is it?' he inquired.

'Seven, about.'

'Seven. And this is 10 January 1943.'

Holt didn't answer. His fare turned and peered out of the rear window. He kept doing that. After a time he leaned forward and spoke to Holt again.

'Would you like to earn a thousand dollars?'

'Are you joking?'

'This is no joke,' the man said, and Holt realized abruptly that his accent was odd – a soft slurring of consonants, as in Castilian Spanish. 'I have the money – your current currency. There is some danger involved, so I will not be overpaying you.'

Holt kept his eyes straight ahead. 'Yeah?'

'I need a bodyguard, that is all. Some men are trying to abduct or even kill me.'

'Count me out,' Holt said. 'I'll drive you to the police station. That's what you need, mister.'

Something fell softly on the front seat. Looking down, Holt felt his back tighten. Driving with one hand, he picked up the bundle of bank-notes and thumbed through them. A thousand bucks – one grand.

They smelled musty.

The old man said, 'Believe me, Denny, it is your help I need. I can't tell you the story – you'd think me insane – but I'll pay you that amount for your services tonight.'

'Including murder?' Holt hazarded. 'Where do you get off calling me Denny? I never saw you before in my life.'

'I have investigated you – I know a great deal about you. That's why I chose you for this task. And nothing illegal is involved. If you have reason to think differently, you are free to withdraw at any time, keeping the money.'

Holt thought that over. It sounded fishy but enticing. Anyhow, it gave him an out. And a thousand bucks –

'Well, spill it. What am I supposed to do?'

The old man said, 'I am trying to evade certain enemies of mine. I need your help for that. You are young and strong.'

'Somebody's trying to rub you out?'

'Rub me … oh. I don't think it will come to that. Murder is frowned upon, except as a last resort. But they have followed me here; I saw them. I believe I shook them off my trail. No cabs are following us –'

'Wrong,' Holt said.

There was a silence. The old man looked out the rear window again.

Holt grinned crookedly. 'If you're trying to duck, Central Park isn't the place. I can lose your friends in traffic easier. O.K., mister, I'm taking the job. But I got the privilege of stepping out if I don't like the smell.'

'Very well, Denny.'

Holt cut left at the level of Seventy-second. 'You know me, but I don't know you. What's the angle, checking up on me? You a detective?'

'No. My name's Smith.'

'Naturally.'

'And you – Denny – are twenty years old, and unavailable for military duty in this war because of cardiac trouble.'

Holt grunted. 'What about it?'

'I do not want you to drop dead.'

'I won't. My heart's O.K. for most things. The medical examiner just didn't think so.'

Smith nodded. 'I know that. Now, Denny –'

'Well?'

'We must be sure we aren't followed.'

Holt said slowly, 'Suppose I stopped at F.B.I. headquarters? They don't like spies.'

'As you like. I can prove to them I am not an enemy agent. My business has nothing to do with this war, Denny. I merely wish to prevent a crime. Unless I can stop it, a house will be burned tonight and a valuable formula destroyed.'

'That's a job for the fire department.'

'You and I are the only ones who can perform this task. I can't tell you why. A thousand dollars, remember.'

Holt was remembering. A thousand dollars meant a lot to him at the moment. He had never had that much money in his life. It meant a stake; capital on which to build. He hadn't had a real education. Until now, he'd figured he'd continue in a dull, plodding job forever. But with a stake – well, he had ideas. These were boom times. He could go in business for himself; that was the way to make dough. One grand. Yeah. It might mean a future.

He emerged from the park at Seventy-second Street and turned south on

Central Park West. From the corner of his eye he saw another taxi swing toward him. It was trying to pocket his cab. Holt heard his passenger gasp and cry something. He jammed on the brakes, saw the other car go by and swung the steering wheel hard, pushing his foot down on the accelerator. He made a U-turn, fast, and was headed north.

'Take it easy,' he said to Smith.

There had been four men in the other taxicab; he had got only a brief glimpse. They were clean-shaven and wore dark clothes. They might have been holding weapons; Holt couldn't be certain of that. They were swinging around, too, now, having difficulties with the traffic but intent on pursuit.

At the first convenient street Holt turned left, crossed Broadway, took the cloverleaf into the Henry Hudson Parkway, and then, instead of heading south on the drive, made a complete circle and returned his route as far as West End Avenue. He went south on West End Avenue. He went south on West End, cutting across to Eighth Avenue presently. There was more traffic now. The following cab wasn't visible.

'What now?' he asked Smith.

'I … I don't know. We must be sure we're not followed.'

'O.K.,' Holt said. 'They'll be cruising around looking for us. We'd better get off the street. I'll show you.' He turned into a parking garage, got a ticket and hurried Smith out of the cab. 'We kill time now, till it's safe to start again.'

'Where –'

'What about a quiet bar? I could stand a drink. It's a lousy night.'

Smith seemed to have put himself completely in Holt's hands. They turned into Forty-second Street, with its dimly lit honky tonks, burlesque shows, dark theater marquees and penny arcades. Holt shouldered his way through the crowd, dragging Smith with him. They went through swinging doors into a gin mill, but it wasn't especially quiet. A jukebox was going full blast in a corner.

An unoccupied booth near the back attracted Holt. Seated there, he signaled the waiter and demanded a rye. Smith, after hesitating, took the same.

'I know this place,' Holt said. 'There's a back door. If we're traced, we can go out fast.'

Smith shivered.

'Forget it,' Holt comforted. He exhibited a set of brass knuckles. 'I carry these with me, just in case. So relax. Here's our liquor.' He downed the rye at a gulp and asked for another. Since Smith made no attempt to pay, Holt did. He could afford it, with a thousand bucks in his pocket.

Now, shielding the bills with his body, he took them out for a closer examination. They looked all right. They weren't counterfeit; the serial numbers were O.K.; and they had the same odd musty smell Holt had noticed before.

'You must have been hoarding these,' he hazarded.

Smith said absently, 'They've been on exhibit for sixty years –' He caught himself and drank rye.

Holt scowled. These weren't the old-fashioned large-sized bills. Sixty years, nuts! Not but what Smith looked that old; his wrinkled, sexless face might have been that of a nonagenarian. Holt wondered what the guy had looked like when he was young. When would that have been? During the Civil War, most likely!

He stowed the money away again, conscious of a glow of pleasure that wasn't due entirely to the liquor. This was the beginning for Denny Holt. With a thousand dollars he'd buy in somewhere and go to town. No more cabbing, that was certain.

On the postage-stamp floor dancers swayed and jitterbugged. The din was constant, loud conversation from the bar vying with the jukebox music. Holt, with a paper napkin, idly swabbed a beer stain on the table before him.

'You wouldn't like to tell me what this is all about, would you?' he said finally.

Smith's incredibly old face might have held some expression; it was difficult to tell. 'I can't, Denny. You wouldn't believe me. What time is it now?'

'Nearly eight.'

'Eastern Standard Time, old reckoning – and January tenth. We must be at our destination before eleven.'

'Where's that?'

Smith took out a map, unfolded it and gave an address in Brooklyn. Holt located it.

'Near the beach. Pretty lonely place, isn't it?'

'I don't know. I've never been there.'

'What's going to happen at eleven?'

Smith shook his head but did not answer directly. He unfolded a paper napkin.

'Do you have a stylo?'

Holt hesitated and then extended a pack of cigarettes.

'No, a … a pencil. Thank you. I want you to study this plan, Denny. It's the ground floor of the house we're going to in Brooklyn. Keaton's laboratory is in the basement.'

'Keaton?'

'Yes,' Smith said, after a pause. 'He's a physicist. He's working on a rather important invention. It's supposed to be a secret.'

'O.K. What now?'

Smith sketched hastily. 'There should be spacious grounds around the house, which has three stories. Here's the library. You can get into it by these windows, and the safe should be beneath a curtain about – here.' The pencil point stabbed down.

Holt's brows drew together. 'I'm starting to smell fish.'

'Eh?' Smith's hand clenched nervously. 'Wait till I've finished. That safe will be unlocked. In it you will find a brown notebook. I want you to get that notebook –'

'– and send it air mail to Hitler,' Holt finished, his mouth twisting in a sneer.

'– and turn it over to the War Department,' Smith said imperturbably. 'Does that satisfy you?'

'Well – that sounds more like it. But why don't you do the job yourself?'

'I can't,' Smith said. 'Don't ask me why; I simply can't. My hands are tied.' The sharp eyes were glistening. 'That notebook, Denny, contains a tremendously important secret.'

'Military?'

'It isn't written in code; it's easy to read. And apply. That's the beauty of it. Any man could –'

'You said a guy named Keaton owned that place in Brooklyn. What's happened to him?'

'Nothing,' Smith said, 'yet.' He covered up hastily. 'The formula mustn't be lost, that's why we've got to get there just before eleven.'

'If it's that important, why don't we go out there now and get the notebook?'

'The formula won't be completed until a few minutes before eleven. Keaton is working out the final stages now.'

'It's screwy,' Holt complained. He had another rye. 'Is this Keaton a Nazi?'

'No.'

'Well, isn't he the one who needs a bodyguard, not you?'

Smith shook his head. 'It doesn't work out that way, Denny. Believe me, I know what I'm doing. It's vitally, intensely important that you get that formula.'

'Hm-m-m.'

'There's a danger. My – enemies – may be waiting for us there. But I'll draw them off and give you a chance to enter the house.'

'You said they might kill you.'

'They might, but I doubt it. Murder is the last recourse, though euthanasia is always available. But I'm not a candidate for that.'

Holt didn't try to understand Smith's viewpoint on euthanasia; he decided it was a place name and implied taking a powder.

'For a thousand bucks,' he said, 'I'll risk my skin.'

'How long will it take us to get to Brooklyn?'

'Say an hour, in the dimout.' Holt got up quickly. 'Come on. Your friends are here.'

Panic showed in Smith's dark eyes. He seemed to shrink into the capacious overcoat. 'What'll we do?'

'The back way. They haven't seen us yet. If we're separated, go to the garage where I left the cab.'

'Y-yes. All right.'

They pushed through the dancers and into the kitchen, past that into a bare corridor. Opening a door, Smith came out in an alley. A tall figure loomed before him, nebulous in the dark. Smith gave a shrill, frightened squeak.

'Beat it,' Holt ordered. He pushed the old man away. The dark figure made some movement, and Holt struck swiftly at a half-seen jaw. His fist didn't connect. His opponent had shifted rapidly.

Smith was scuttling off, already lost in shadows. The sound of his racing footsteps died.

Holt, his heart pounding reasonlessly, took a step forward. 'Get out of my way,' he said, so deep in his throat that the words came out as a purring snarl.

'Sorry,' his antagonist said. 'You mustn't go to Brooklyn tonight.'

'Why not?' Holt was listening for sounds that would mean more of the enemy. But as yet he heard nothing, only distant honking of automobile horns and the low mingled tumult from Times Square, a half block away.

'I'm afraid you wouldn't believe me if I told you.'

There was the same accent, the same Castilian slurring of consonants that Holt had noticed when Smith spoke. He strained to make out the other man's face. But it was too dark.

Surreptitiously, Holt slipped his hand into his pocket and felt the comforting coldness of the brass knuckles. He said, 'If you pull a gun on me –'

'We do not use guns. Listen, Dennis Holt. Keaton's formula must be destroyed with him.'

'Why, you –' Holt struck without warning. This time he didn't miss. He felt the brass knuckles hit solidly and then slide, slippery on bloody, torn flesh. The half-seen figure went down, a shout muffled in his throat. Holt looked around, saw no one and went at a loping run along the alley. Good enough, so far.

Five minutes later he was at the parking garage. Smith was waiting for him, a withered crow in a huge overcoat. The old man's fingers were tapping nervously on the cane.

'Come on,' Holt said. 'We'd better move fast now.'

'Did you –'

'I knocked him cold. He didn't have a gun – or else he didn't want to use it. Lucky for me.'

Smith grimaced. Holt recovered his taxi and maneuvered down the ramp, handling the car gingerly and keeping on the alert. A cab was plenty easy to spot. The dimout helped.

He kept south and east to the Bowery, but at Essex Street, by the subway station, the pursuers caught up. Holt swung into a side street. His left elbow, resting on the window frame, went numb and icy cold.

He steered with his right hand until the feeling wore off. The Williamsburg Bridge took him into Kings, and he dodged and alternately speeded and backtracked until he'd lost the shadows again. That took time. And there was still a long distance to go, by this circuitous route.

Holt, turning right, worked his way south to Prospect Park and then east, toward the lonely beach section between Brighton Beach and Canarsie. Smith, huddled in back, had made no sound.

'So far, so good,' Holt said over his shoulder. 'My arm's in shape again, anyhow.'

'What happened to it?'

'Must have hit my funny-bone.'

'No,' Smith said, 'that was a paralyzer. Like this.' He exhibited the cane.

Holt didn't get it. He kept driving until they were nearly at their destination. He pulled up around the corner from a liquor store.

'I'm getting a bottle,' he said. 'It's too cold and rainy without a shot of something to pep me up.'

'We haven't time.'

'Sure we have.'

Smith bit his lip but made no further objection. Holt bought a pint of rye and, back in the cab, took a swig, after offering his fare a drink and getting a shake of the head for answer.

The rye definitely helped. The night was intensely cold and miserable; squalls of rain swept across the street, sluicing down the windshield. The worn wipers didn't help much. The wind screamed like a banshee.

'We're close enough,' Smith suggested. 'Better stop here. Find a place to hide the taxicab.'

'Where? These are all private houses.'

'A driveway … eh?'

'O.K.,' Holt said, and found one shielded by overhanging trees and rank bushes. He turned off lights and motor and got out, hunching his chin down and turning up the collar of his slicker. The rain instantly drenched him. It came down with a steady, torrential pour, pattering noisily staccato in the puddles. Underfoot was sandy, slippery mud.

'Wait a sec,' Holt said, and returned to the cab for his flashlight. 'All set. Now what?'

'Keaton's house.' Smith was shivering convulsively. 'It isn't eleven yet. We'll have to wait.'

They waited, concealed in the bushes on Keaton's grounds. The house was a looming shadow against the fluctuating curtain of drenched darkness. A lighted window on the ground floor showed part of what seemed to be a library. The sound of breakers, throbbing heavily, came from their left.

Water trickled down inside Holt's collar. He cursed quietly. He was earning his thousand bucks, all right. But Smith was going through the same discomfort and not complaining about it.

'Isn't it –'

'*Sh-h!*' Smith warned. 'The – others – may be here.'

Obediently, Holt lowered his voice. 'Then they'll be drowned, too. Are they after the notebook? Why don't they go in and get it?'

Smith bit his nails. 'They want it destroyed.'

'That's what the guy in the alley said, come to think of it.' Holt nodded, startled. 'Who are they, anyhow?'

'Never mind. They don't belong here. Do you remember what I told you, Denny?'

'About getting the notebook? What'll I do if the safe isn't open?'

'It will be,' Smith said confidently. 'Soon, now. Keaton is in his cellar laboratory, finishing his experiment.'

Through the lighted window a shadow flickered. Holt leaned forward; he felt Smith go tense as wire beside him. A tiny gasp ripped from the old man's throat.

A man had entered the library. He went to the wall, swung aside a curtain, and stood there, his back to Holt. Presently he stepped back, opening the door of a safe.

'Ready!' Smith said. 'This is it! He's writing down the final step of the formula. The explosion will come in a minute now. When it does, Denny, give me a minute to get away and cause a disturbance, if the others are here.'

'I don't think they are.'

Smith shook his head. 'Do as I say. Run for the house and get the notebook.'

'Then what?'

'Then get out of here as fast as you can. Don't let them catch you, whatever you do.'

'What about you?'

Smith's eyes blazed with intense, violent command, shining out of the windy dark. 'Forget me, Denny! I'll be safe.'

'You hired me as a bodyguard.'

'I'm discharging you, then. This is vitally important, more important than my life. That notebook must be in your hands –'

'For the War Department?'

'For … oh yes. You'll do that, now, Denny?'

Holt hesitated. 'If it's that important –'

'It is. It is!'

'O.K., then.'

The man in the house was at a desk, writing. Suddenly the window blew out. The sound of the blast was muffled, as though its source was underground, but Holt felt the ground shake beneath him. He saw Keaton spring up, take a half step away and return, snatching up the notebook. The physicist ran to the wall safe, threw the book into it, swung the door shut and paused there briefly, his back to Holt. Then he darted out of Holt's range of vision and was gone.

Smith said, his voice coming out in excited spurts, 'He didn't have time to lock it. Wait till you hear me, Denny, and then *get that notebook!*'

Holt said, 'O.K.,' but Smith was already gone, running through the bushes. A yell from the house heralded red flames sweeping out a distant, ground-floor window. Something fell crashingly – masonry, Holt thought.

He heard Smith's voice. He could not see the man in the rain, but there was the noise of a scuffle. Briefly Holt hesitated. Blue pencils of light streaked through the rain, wan and vague in the distance.

He ought to help Smith –

He'd promised, though, and there was the notebook. The pursuers had wanted it destroyed. And now, quite obviously, the house was going up in flames. Of Keaton there was no trace.

He ran for the lighted window. There was plenty of time to get the notebook before the fire became dangerous.

From the corner of his eye he saw a dark figure cutting in toward him. Holt slipped on his brass knuckles. If the guy had a gun it would be unfortunate; otherwise, fair enough.

The man – the same one Holt had encountered in the Forty-second Street alley – raised a cane and aimed it. A wan blue pencil of light streaked out. Holt felt his legs go dead and crashed down heavily.

The other man kept running. Holt, struggling to his feet, threw himself desperately forward. No use.

The flames were brightening the night now. The tall, dark figure loomed for an instant against the library window; then the man had clambered over the sill. Holt, his legs stiff, managed to keep his balance and lurch forward. It was agony: like pins and needles a thousand times intensified.

He made it to the window, and, clinging to the sill, stared into the room. His opponent was busy at the safe. Holt swung himself through the window and hobbled toward the man.

His brass-knuckled fist was ready.

The unknown sprang lightly away, swinging his cane. Dried blood stained his chin.

'I've locked the safe,' he said. 'Better get out of here before the fire catches you, Denny.'

Holt mouthed a curse. He tried to reach the man but could not. Before he had covered more than two halting steps, the tall figure was gone, springing lightly out through the window and racing away into the rain.

Holt turned to the safe. He could hear the crackling of flames. Smoke was pouring through a doorway on his left.

He tested the safe; it was locked. He didn't know the combination – so he couldn't open it.

But Holt tried. He searched the desk, hoping Keaton might have scribbled the key on a paper somewhere. He fought his way to the laboratory steps and stood looking down into the inferno of the cellar, where Keaton's burning, motionless body lay. Yes, Holt tried. And he failed.

Finally the heat drove him from the house. Fire trucks were screaming closer. There was no sign of Smith or anyone else.

Holt stayed, amid the crowds, to search, but Smith and his trackers had disappeared as though they had vanished into thin air.

'We caught him, Administrator,' said the tall man with the dried blood on his chin. 'I came here directly on our return to inform you.'

The administrator blew out his breath in a sigh of deep relief.

'Any trouble, Jorus?'

'Not to speak of.'

'Well, bring him in,' the administrator said. 'I suppose we'd better get this over with.'

Smith entered the office. His heavy overcoat looked incongruous against the celoflex garments of the others.

He kept his eyes cast down.

The administrator picked up a memo roll and read: 'Sol 21, in the year of our Lord 2016. Subject: interference with probability factors. The accused has been detected in the act of attempting to tamper with the current probability-present by altering the past, thus creating a variable alternative present. Use of time machines is forbidden except by authorized officials. Accused will answer.'

Smith mumbled, 'I wasn't trying to change things, Administrator –'

Jorus looked up and said, 'Objection. Certain key time-place periods are forbidden. Brooklyn, especially the area about Keaton's house, in the time near 11 P.M., 10 January 1943, is absolutely forbidden to time travellers. The prisoner knows why.'

'I knew nothing about it, Ser Jorus. You must believe me.'

Jorus went on relentlessly, 'Administrator, here are the facts. The accused, having stolen a time traveller, set the controls manually for a forbidden space-time sector. Such sectors are restricted, as you know, because they are keys to the future; interference with such key spots will automatically alter the future and create a different line of probability. Keaton, in 1943, in his cellar laboratory, succeeded in working out the formula for what we know now as M-Power. He hurried upstairs, opened his safe, and noted down the formula in his book, in such a form that it could very easily have been deciphered and applied even by a layman. At that time there was an explosion in Keaton's laboratory and he replaced the notebook in the safe and went downstairs, neglecting, however, to relock the safe. Keaton was killed; he had not known the necessity of keeping M-Power away from radium, and the atomic synthesis caused the explosion. The subsequent fire destroyed Keaton's notebook, even though it had been within the safe. It was charred into illegibility, nor was its value suspected. Not until the first year of the twenty-first century was M-Power rediscovered.'

Smith said, 'I didn't know all that, Ser Jorus.'

'You are lying. Our organization does not make mistakes. You found a key spot in the past and decided to change it, thus altering our present. Had you succeeded, Dennis Holt of 1943 would have taken Keaton's notebook out of the burning house and read it. His curiosity would have made him open the notebook. He would have found the key to M-Power. And, because of the very nature of M-Power, Dennis Holt would have become the most powerful man in his world time. According to the variant probability line you were aiming at, Dennis Holt, had he got that notebook, would have been dictator of the world now. This world, as we know it, would not exist, though its equivalent would – a brutal, ruthless civilization ruled by an autocratic Dennis Holt, the sole possessor of M-Power. In striving for that end, the prisoner has committed a serious crime.'

Smith lifted his head. 'I demand euthanasia,' he said. 'If you want to blame me for trying to get out of this damned routine life of mine, very well. I never had a chance, that's all.'

The administrator raised his eyebrows. 'Your record shows you have had many chances. You are incapable of succeeding through your own abilities; you are in the only job you can do well. But your crime is, as Jorus says, serious. You have tried to create a new probability-present, destroying this one by tampering with a key spot in the past. And, had you succeeded, Dennis Holt would now be dictator of a race of slaves. Euthanasia is no longer your privilege; your crime is too serious. You must continue to live, at your appointed task, until the day of your natural death.'

Smith choked. 'It was *his* fault – if he'd got that notebook in time –'

Jorus looked quizzical. '*His?* Dennis Holt, at the age of twenty, in 1943 ... his fault? No, it is yours, I think – for trying to change your past and your present.'

The administrator said, 'Sentence has been passed. It is ended.'

And Dennis Holt, at the age of ninety-three, in the year of our Lord 2016, turned obediently and went slowly back to his job, the same one he would fill now until he died.

And Dennis Holt, at the age of twenty, in the year of our Lord 1943, drove his taxi home from Brooklyn, wondering what it had all been about. The veils of rain swept slanting across the windshield. Denny took another drink out of the bottle and felt the rye steal comfortingly through his body.

What had it all been about?

Banknotes rustled crisply in his pocket. Denny grinned. A thousand smackeroos! His stake. His capital. With that, now, he could do plenty – and he would, too. All a guy needed was a little ready money, and he could go places.

'You bet!' Dennis Holt said emphatically. 'I'm not going to hold down the same dull job all my life. Not with a thousand bucks – not me!'

HOUSING PROBLEM

Jacqueline said it was a canary, but I contended that there were a couple of lovebirds in the covered cage. One canary could never make that much fuss. Besides, I liked to think of crusty old Mr Henchard keeping lovebirds; it was so completely inappropriate. But whatever our roomer kept in that cage by his window, he shielded it – or them – jealously from prying eyes. All we had to go by were the noises.

And they weren't too simple to figure out. From under the cretonne cloth came shufflings, rustlings, occasional faint and inexplicable pops, and once or twice a tiny thump that made the whole hidden cage shake on its redwood pedestal-stand. Mr Henchard must have known that we were curious. But all he said when Jackie remarked that birds were nice to have around, was 'Clap-trap! Leave that cage alone, d'ya hear?'

That made us a little mad. We're not snoopers, and after that brush-off, we coldly refused to even look at the shrouded cretonne shape. We didn't want to lose Mr Henchard, either. Roomers were surprisingly hard to get. Our little house was on the coast highway; the town was a couple of dozen homes, a grocery, a liquor store, the post office and Terry's restaurant. That was about all. Every morning Jackie and I hopped the bus and rode in to the factory, an hour away. By the time we got home, we were pretty tired. We couldn't get any household help – war jobs paid a lot better – so we both pitched in and cleaned. As for cooking, we were Terry's best customers.

The wages were good, but before the war we'd run up too many debts, so we needed extra dough. And that's why we rented a room to Mr Henchard. Off the beaten track with transportation difficult, and with the coast dimout every night, it wasn't too easy to get a roomer. Mr Henchard looked like a natural. He was, we figured, too old to get into mischief.

One day he wandered in, paid a deposit; presently he showed up with a huge Gladstone and a square canvas grip with leather handles. He was a creaking little old man with a bristling tonsure of stiff hair and a face like Popeye's father, only more human. He wasn't sour; he was just crusty. I had a feeling he'd spent most of his life in furnished rooms, minding his own business and puffing innumerable cigarettes through a long black holder. But he wasn't one of those lonely old men you could safely feel sorry for – far from it! He wasn't poor and he was completely self-sufficient. We loved him.

I called him grandpa once, in an outburst of affection, and my skin blistered at the resultant remarks.

Some people are born under lucky stars. Mr Henchard was like that. He was always finding money in the street. The few times we shot craps or played poker, he made passes and held straights without even trying. No question of sharp dealing – he was just lucky.

I remember the time we were all going down the long wooden stairway that leads from the cliff-top to the beach. Mr Henchard kicked at a pretty big rock that was on one of the steps. The stone bounced down a little way, and then went right through one of the treads. The wood was completely rotten. We felt fairly certain that if Mr Henchard, who was leading, had stepped on that rotten section, the whole thing would have collapsed.

And then there was the time I was riding up with him in the bus. The motor stopped a few minutes after we'd boarded the bus; the driver pulled over. A car was coming toward us along the highway and, as we stopped, one of its front tires blew out. It skidded into the ditch. If we hadn't stopped when we did, there would have been a head-on collision. Not a soul was hurt.

Mr Henchard wasn't lonely; he went out by day, I think, and at night he sat in his room near the window most of the time. We knocked, of course, before coming in to clean, and sometimes he'd say, 'Wait a minute.' There'd be a hasty rustling and the sound of that cretonne cover going on his bird cage. We wondered what sort of bird he had, and theorized on the possibility of a phoenix. The creature never sang. It made noises. Soft, odd, not-always-birdlike noises. By the time we got home from work, Mr Henchard was always in his room. He stayed there while we cleaned. On week-ends, he never went out.

As for the cage …

One night Mr Henchard came out, stuffing a cigarette into his holder, and looked us over.

'Mph,' said Mr Henchard. 'Listen, I've got some property to 'tend to up north, and I'll be away for a week or so. I'll still pay the rent.'

'Oh, well,' Jackie said. 'We can –'

'Claptrap,' he growled. 'It's my room. I'll keep it if I like. How about that, hey?'

We agreed, and he smoked half his cigarette in one gasp. 'Mm-m. Well, look here, now. Always before I've had my own car. So I've taken my bird cage with me. This time I've got to travel on the bus, so I can't take it. You've been pretty nice – not peepers or pryers. You got sense. I'm going to leave my bird cage here, but *don't you touch that cover!*'

'The canary –' Jackie gulped. 'It'll starve.'

'Canary, hmm?' Mr Henchard said, fixing her with a beady, wicked eye. 'Never you mind. I left plenty o' food *and* water. You just keep your hands off. Clean my room when it needs it, if you want, but don't you dare touch the bird cage. What do you say?'

'Okay with us,' I said.

'Well, you mind what I say,' he snapped.

That next night, when we got home, Mr Henchard was gone. We went into his room and there was a note pinned to the cretonne cover. It said, 'Mind, now!' Inside the cage something went *rustle-whirr*. And then there was a faint pop.

'Hell with it,' I said. 'Want the shower first?'

'Yes,' Jackie said.

Whirr-r went the cage. But it wasn't wings. *Thump!*

The next night I said, 'Maybe he left enough food, but I bet the water's getting low.'

'Eddie!' Jackie remarked.

'All right, I'm curious. But I don't like the idea of birds dying of thirst, either.'

'Mr Henchard said –'

'All right, again. Let's go down to Terry's and see what the lamb chop situation is.'

The next night – Oh, well. We lifted the cretonne. I still think we were less curious than worried. Jackie said she once knew somebody who used to beat his canary.

'We'll find the poor beast cowering in chains,' she remarked flicking her dust-cloth at the windowsill, behind the cage. I turned off the vacuum. *Whish – trot-trot-trot* went something under the cretonne.

'Yeah –' I said. 'Listen, Jackie. Mr Henchard's all right, but he's a crackpot. That bird or birds may be thirsty now. I'm going to take a look.'

'No. Uh – yes. We both will, Eddie. We'll split the responsibility.'

I reached for the cover, and Jackie ducked under my arm and put her hand over mine.

Then we lifted a corner of the cloth. Something had been rustling around inside, but the instant we touched the cretonne, the sound stopped. I meant to take only one swift glance. My hand continued to lift the cover, though. I could see my arm moving and I couldn't stop it. I was too busy looking.

Inside the cage was a – well, a little house. It seemed complete in every detail. A tiny house painted white, with green shutters – ornamental, not meant to close – for the cottage was strictly modern. It was the sort of comfortable, well-built house you see all the time in the suburbs. The tiny windows had chintz curtains; they were lighted up, on the ground floor. The moment we lifted the cloth, each window suddenly blacked out. The lights didn't go off, but shades snapped down with an irritated jerk. It happened fast. Neither of us saw who or what pulled down those shades.

I let go of the cover and stepped back, pulling Jackie with me.

'A d-doll house, Eddie!'

'With dolls in it?'

I stared past her at the hooded cage. 'Could you, maybe, do you think, perhaps, train a canary to pull down shades?'

'Oh, my! Eddie, listen.'

Faint sounds were coming from the cage. Rustles, and an almost inaudible pop. Then a scraping.

I went over and took the cretonne cloth clear off. This time I was ready; I watched the windows. But the shades flicked down as I blinked.

Jackie touched my arm and pointed. On the sloping roof was a miniature brick chimney; a wisp of pale smoke was rising from it. The smoke kept coming up, but it was so thin I couldn't smell it.

'The c-canaries are c-cooking,' Jackie gurgled.

We stood there for a while, expecting almost anything. If a little green man had popped out of the front door and offered us three wishes, we shouldn't have been much surprised. Only nothing happened.

There wasn't a sound, now, from the wee house in the bird cage.

And the blinds were down. I could see that the whole affair was a masterpiece of detail. The little front porch had a tiny mat on it. There was a doorbell, too.

Most cages have removable bottoms. This one didn't. Resin stains and dull gray metal showed where soldering had been done. The door was soldered shut, too. I could put my forefinger between the bars, but my thumb was too thick.

'It's a nice little cottage, isn't it?' Jackie said, her voice quavering. 'They must be such *little* guys –'

'Guys?'

'Birds. Eddie, who lives in that house?'

'Well,' I said. I took out my automatic pencil, gently inserted it between the bars of the cage, and poked at an open window, where the shade snapped up. From within the house something like the needle-beam of a miniature flashlight shot into my eye, blinding me with its brilliance. As I grunted and jerked back, I heard a window slam and the shade come down again.

'Did you see what happened?'

'No, your head was in the way. But –'

As we looked, the lights went out. Only the thin smoke curling from the chimney indicated that anything was going on.

'Mr Henchard's a mad scientist,' Jackie muttered. 'He shrinks people.'

'Not without an atom-smasher,' I said. 'Every mad scientist's got to have an atom-smasher to make artificial lightning.'

I put my pencil between the bars again. I aimed carefully, pressed the point against the doorbell, and rang. A thin shrilling was heard.

The shade at one of the windows by the door was twitched aside hastily, and something probably looked at me. I don't know. I wasn't quick enough to see it. The shade fell back in place, and there was no more movement. I rang the bell till I got tired of it. Then I stopped.

'I could take the cage apart,' I said.

'Oh *no!* Mr Henchard –'

'Well,' I said, 'when he comes back, I'm going to ask him what the hell. He can't keep pixies. It isn't in the lease.'

'He doesn't have a lease,' Jackie countered.

I examined the little house in the bird cage. No sound, no movement. Smoke coming from the chimney.

After all, we had no right to break into the cage. Housebreaking? I had visions of a little green man with wings flourishing a night stick, arresting me for burglary. Did pixies have cops? What sort of crimes …

I put the cover back on the cage. After a while, vague noises emerged. *Scrape. Thump. Rustle, rustle, rustle. Pop.* And an unbirdlike trilling that broke off short.

'Oh, my,' Jackie said. 'Let's go away quick.'

We went right to bed. I dreamed of a horde of little green guys in Mack Sennett cop uniforms, dancing on a bilious rainbow and singing gaily.

The alarm clock woke me. I showered, shaved and dressed, thinking of the same thing Jackie was thinking of. As we put on our coats, I met her eyes and said, 'Shall we?'

'Yes. Oh, golly, Eddie! D-do you suppose they'll be leaving for work, too?'

'What sort of work?' I inquired angrily. 'Painting buttercups?'

There wasn't a sound from beneath the cretonne when we tiptoed into Mr Henchard's room. Morning sunlight blazed through the window. I jerked the cover off. There was the house. One of the blinds was up; all the rest were tightly firm. I put my head close to the cage and stared through the bars into the open window, where scraps of chintz curtains were blowing in the breeze.

I saw a great big eye looking back at me.

This time Jackie was certain I'd got my mortal wound. The breath went out of her with a whoosh as I caromed back, yelling about a horrible blood-shot eye that wasn't human. We clutched each other for a while and then I looked again.

'Oh,' I said, rather faintly. 'It's a mirror.'

'A *mirror*?' she gasped.

'Yeah, a big one, on the opposite wall. That's all I can see. I can't get close enough to the window.'

'Look on the porch,' Jackie said.

I looked. There was a milk bottle standing by the door – you can guess the size of it. It was purple. Beside it was a folded postage stamp.

'Purple milk?' I said.

'From a purple cow. Or else the bottle's colored. Eddie, is that a newspaper?'

It was. I strained my eyes to read the headlines. EXTRA was splashed redly across the sheet, in huge letters nearly a sixteenth of an inch high. EXTRA – FOTZPA MOVES ON TUR! That was all we could make out.

I put the cretonne gently back over the cage. We went down to Terry's for breakfast while we waited for the bus.

When we rode home that night, we knew what our first job would be. We let ourselves into the house, discovered that Mr Henchard hadn't come back yet, switched on the light in his room, and listened to the noise from the bird cage.

'Music,' Jackie said.

It was so faint I scarcely heard it, and, in any case, it wasn't real music. I can't begin to describe it. And it died away immediately. *Thump, scrape, pop, buzz*. Then silence, and I pulled off the cover.

The house was dark, the windows were shut, the blinds were down. Paper and milk bottle were gone from the porch. On the front door was a sign that said – after I used a magnifying glass: QUARANTINE! SCOPPY FEVER!

'Why, the little liars,' I said. 'I bet they haven't got scoppy fever at all.'

Jackie giggled wildly. 'You only get scoppy fever in April, don't you?'

'April and Christmas. That's when the bread-and-butter flies carry it. Where's my pencil?'

I rang the bell. A shade twitched aside, flipped back; neither of us had seen the – hand? – that moved it. Silence; no smoke coming out of the chimney.

'Scared?' I asked.

'No. It's funny, but I'm not. They're such standoffish little guys. The Cabots speak only to –'

'Where the pixies speak only to goblins, you mean,' I said. 'They can't snoot us this way. It's our house their house is in, if you follow me.'

'What can we do?'

I manipulated the pencil, and, with considerable difficulty, wrote LET US IN on the white panel of the door. There wasn't room for more than that. Jackie tsked.

'Maybe you shouldn't have written that. We don't want to get *in*. We just want to see them.'

'Too late now. Besides, they'll know what we mean.'

We stood watching the house in the bird cage, and it watched us, in a sullen and faintly annoyed fashion. SCOPPY FEVER, indeed!

That was all that happened that night.

The next morning we found that the tiny front door had been scrubbed clean of my pencil marks, that the quarantine sign was still there, and that there was a bottle of green milk and another paper on the porch. This time the headline said. EXTRA – FOTZPA OVER-SHOOTS TUR!

Smoke was idling from the chimney. I rang the bell again. No answer. I noticed a domino of a mailbox by the door, chiefly because I could see through the slot that there were letters inside. But the thing was locked.

'If we could see whom they were addressed to –' Jackie suggested.

'Or whom they're from. That's what interests me.'

Finally, we went to work. I was preoccupied all day, and nearly welded my thumb onto a boogie-arm. When I met Jackie that night, I could see that she'd been bothered, too.

'Let's ignore them,' she said as we bounced home on the bus. 'We know when we're not wanted, don't we?'

'I'm not going to be high-hatted by a – by a critter. Besides, we'll both go quietly nuts if we don't find out what's inside that house. Do you suppose Mr Henchard's a wizard?'

'He's a louse,' Jackie said bitterly. 'Going off and leaving ambiguous pixies on our hands!'

When we got home, the little house in the bird cage took alarm, as usual, and by the time we'd yanked off the cover, the distant, soft noises had faded into silence. Lights shone through the drawn blinds. The porch had only the mat on it. In the mailbox we could see the yellow envelope of a telegram.

Jackie turned pale. 'It's the last straw,' she insisted. 'A telegram!'

'It may not be.'

'It is, it is, I know it is. Aunt Tinker Bell's dead. Or Iolanthe's coming for a visit.'

'The quarantine sign's off the door,' I said. 'There's a new one. It says 'wet paint.''

'Well, you will scribble all over their nice clean door.'

I put the cretonne back, turned off the light switch, and took Jackie's hand. We stood waiting. After a time something went *bump-bump-bump*, and then there was a singing, like a tea-kettle. I heard a tiny clatter.

Next morning there were twenty-six bottles of yellow milk – bright yellow – on the tiny porch, and the Lilliputian headline announced: EXTRA – TUR SLIDES TOWARD FOTZPA!

There was mail in the box, too, but the telegram was gone.

That night things continued much as before. When I pulled the cloth off there was a sudden, furious silence. We felt that we were being watched around the corners of the miniature shades. We finally went to bed, but in the middle of the night I got up and took another look at our mysterious tenants. Not that I saw *them*, of course. But they must have been throwing a party, for bizarre, small music and wild thumps and pops died into silence as I peeked.

In the morning there was a red bottle and a newspaper on the little porch. The headline said: EXTRA – FOTZPA GOES UP!

'My work's going to the dogs,' I said. 'I can't concentrate for thinking about this business – and wondering ...'

'Me, too. We've *got* to find out somehow.'

I peeked. A shade came down so sharply that it almost tore free from its roller.

'Do you think they're mad?' I asked.

'Yes,' Jackie said, 'I do. We must be bothering the very devil out of 'em. Look – I'll bet they're sitting inside by the windows, boiling mad, waiting for us to go away. Maybe we'd better go. It's time for the bus anyway.'

I looked at the house, and the house, I felt, looked at me with an air of irritated and resentful fury. Oh, well. We went to work.

We were tired and hungry when we got back that night, but even before removing our coats we went into Mr Henchard's room. Silence. I switched on the light while Jackie pulled off the cretonne cover from the cage.

I heard her gasp. Instantly I jumped forward, expecting to see a little green guy on that absurd porch – or anything, for that matter. I saw nothing unusual. There was no smoke coming from the chimney.

But Jackie was pointing to the front door. There was a neat, painted sign tacked to the panel. It said, very sedately, simply, and finally: TO LET.

'Oh, oh, oh!' Jackie said.

I gulped. All the shades were up in the tiny windows and the chintz curtains were gone. We could see into the house for the first time. It was completely and awfully empty.

No furniture, anywhere. Nothing at all but a few scrapes and scratches on the polished hardwood floor. The wallpaper was scrupulously clean; the patterns, in the various rooms, were subdued and in good taste. The tenants had left their house in order.

'They moved,' I said.

'Yes,' Jackie murmured. 'They moved out.'

All of a sudden I felt lousy. The house – not the tiny one in the cage, but our own – was awfully empty. You know how it is when you've been on a visit, and come home into a place that's full of nothing and nobody?

I grabbed Jackie and held her tight. She felt pretty bad, too. You wouldn't think that a tiny TO LET sign could make so much difference.

'What'll Mr Henchard say?' Jackie asked, watching me with big eyes.

Mr Henchard came home two nights later. We were sitting by the fire when he walked in, his Gladstone swinging, the black cigarette holder jutting from below his beak. 'Mph,' he greeted us.

'Hello,' I said weakly. 'Glad you're back.'

'Claptrap!' said Mr Henchard firmly as he headed for his room. Jackie and I looked at one another.

Mr Henchard squalled in sheer fury. His twisted face appeared around the door.

'Busybodies!' he snarled. 'I *told* you –'

'Wait a minute,' I said.

'I'm moving out!' Mr Henchard barked. 'Now!' His head popped back out of sight; the door slammed and locked. Jackie and I waited, half expecting to be spanked.

Mr Henchard bounced out of his room, Gladstone suspended from one hand. He whirled past us toward the door.

I tried to stop him. 'Mr Henchard –'

'Claptrap!'

Jackie pulled at one arm, I got a grip on the other. Between us, we managed to bring him to a stop.

'Wait,' I said. 'You've forgotten your – uh – bird cage.'

'That's what you think,' he snarled at me. 'You can have it. Meddlers! It took me months to build that little house just right, and months more to coax 'em to live in it. Now you've spoiled it. They won't be back.'

'Who?' Jackie gulped.

His beady eyes were fixed malignantly on us. 'My tenants. I'll have to build a new house now – ha! But this time I won't leave it within reach of meddlers.'

'Wait,' I said. 'Are – are you a m-magician?'

Mr Henchard snorted. 'I'm a good craftsman. That's all it takes. You treat them right, and they'll treat you right. Still –' And he gleamed a bit with pride. '– it isn't everybody who knows how to build the right sort of house for *them!*'

He seemed to be softening, but my next question roused him again.

'What were they?' he snapped. 'The Little Folk, of course. Call 'em what you like. Nixie, pixie, leprechaun, brownie – they've had lots of names. But they want a quiet, respectable neighborhood to live in, not a lot of peeping and prying. Gives the property a bad name. No wonder they moved out! And – mph! – they paid their rent on time, too. Still, the Little Folk always do,' he added.

'Rent?' Jackie said faintly.

'Luck,' Mr Henchard said. 'Good luck. What did you expect they'd pay in – money? Now I'll have to build another house to get my special luck back.'

He gave us one parting glare, jerked open the door, and stamped out. We stood looking after him. The bus was pulling into the gas station down the slope, and Mr Henchard broke into a run.

He caught the bus, all right, but only after he'd fallen flat on his face.

I put my arm around Jackie.

'Oh, gosh,' she said. 'His bad luck's working already.'

'Not *bad*,' I pointed out. 'Just normal. When you rent a little house to pixies, you get a lot of extra good luck.'

We sat in silence, watching each other. Finally without saying a word, we went into Mr Henchard's vacated room. The bird cage was still there. So was the house. So was the TO LET sign.

'Let's go to Terry's,' I said.

We stayed later than usual. Anybody would have thought we didn't want to go home because we lived in a haunted house. Except that in our case the exact opposite was true. Our house wasn't haunted any more. It was horribly, desolately, coldly vacant.

I didn't say anything till we'd crossed the highway, climbed the slope, and unlocked our front door. We went, I don't know why, for a final look at the empty house. The cover was back on the cage, where I'd replaced it, but – *thump, rustle, pop!* The house was tenanted again!

We backed out and closed the door before we breathed.

'No,' Jackie said. 'We mustn't look. We mustn't ever, *ever*, look under that cover.'

'Never,' I said. 'Who do you suppose ...'

We caught a very faint murmur of what seemed to be boisterous singing. That was fine. The happier they were, the longer they'd stay. When we went to bed, I dreamed that I was drinking beer with Rip Van Winkle and the dwarfs. I drank 'em all under the table.

It was unimportant that the next morning was rainy. We were convinced that bright yellow sunlight was blazing in through the windows. I sang under the shower. Jackie burbled inarticulately and joyously. We didn't open Mr Henchard's door.

'Maybe they want to sleep late,' I said.

It's always noisy in the machine-shop, and a hand-truckload of rough cylinder casings going past doesn't increase the din noticeably. At three o'clock that afternoon, one of the boys was rolling the stuff along toward the storeroom, and I didn't hear it or see it until I'd stepped back from my planer, cocking my eye at its adjustment.

Those big planers are minor juggernauts. They have to be bedded in concrete, in heavy thigh-high cradles on which a heavily weighted metal monster – the planer itself – slides back and forth.

I stepped back, saw the hand-truck coming, and made a neat waltz turn to get out of its way. The boy with the hand-truck swerved, the cylinders began to fall out, and I took an unbalanced waltz step that ended with my smacking my thighs against the edge of the cradle and doing a neat, suicidal half-somersault. When I landed, I was jammed into the metal cradle, looking at the planer as it zoomed down on me. I've never in my life seen anything move so fast.

It was all over before I knew it. I was struggling to bounce myself out, men were yelling, the planer was bellowing with bloodthirsty triumph, and the cylinder heads were rolling around underfoot all over the place. Then there was the crackling, tortured crash of gears and cams going to pieces. The planer stopped. My heart started.

After I'd changed my clothes, I waited for Jackie to knock off. Rolling home on the bus, I told her about it. 'Pure dumb luck. Or else a miracle. One of those cylinders bounced into the planer in just the right place. The planer's a mess, but I'm not. I think we ought to write a note of thanks to our – uh – tenants.'

Jackie nodded with profound conviction. 'It's the luck they pay their rent in, Eddie. I'm glad they paid in advance, too!'

'Except that I'm off the payroll till the planer's fixed,' I said.

We went home through a storm. We could hear a banging in Mr Henchard's room, louder than any noise that had ever come from the bird cage. We rushed upstairs and found the casement window had come open. I closed it. The cretonne cover had been half blown off the cage, and I started to pull it back in place. Jackie was beside me. We looked at the tiny house; my hand didn't complete its gesture.

The TO LET sign had been removed from the door. The chimney was smoking greasily. The blinds were tightly down, as usual, but there were other changes.

There was a small smell of cooking – corned beef and skunk cabbage, I thought wildly. Unmistakably it came from the pixie house. On the formerly immaculate porch was a slopping-over garbage can, and a minuscule orange crate with unwashed, atom-sized tin cans and what were indubitably empty liquor bottles. There was a milk bottle by the door, too, filled with a biliously lavender liquid. It hadn't been taken in yet, nor had the morning paper. It was certainly a different paper. The lurid size of the headlines indicated that it was a yellow tabloid.

A clothesline, without any clothes hanging on it at the moment, had been tacked up from one pillar of the porch to a corner of the house.

I jerked down the cover, and fled after Jackie into the kitchen. 'My God!' I said.

'We should have asked for references,' she gasped. 'Those aren't *our* tenants!'

'Not the tenants we used to have,' I agreed. 'I mean the ones Mr Henchard used to have. Did you see that garbage pail on the porch!'

'And the clothesline,' Jackie added. 'How – how sloppy.'

'Jukes, Kallikaks and Jeeter Lesters. This isn't Tobacco Road.'

Jackie gulped. 'Mr Henchard said they wouldn't be back, you know.'

'Yeah, but, well –'

She nodded slowly, as though beginning to understand. I said, 'Give.'

'I don't know. Only Mr Henchard said the Little Folk wanted a quiet, respectable neighborhood. And we drove them out. I'll bet we gave the bird cage – the location – a bad reputation. The better-class pixies won't live there. It's – oh, dear – maybe it's a slum.'

'You're very nuts,' I said.

'I'm not. It must be that. Mr Henchard said as much. He told us he'd have to build a new house. Desirable tenants won't move into a bad neighborhood. We've got sloppy pixies, that's all.'

My mouth opened. I stared at her.

'Uh-huh. The tenement type. I'll bet they keep a pixilated goat in the kitchen,' Jackie babbled.

'Well,' I said, 'we're not going to stand for it. I'll evict 'em. I – I'll pour water down their chimney. Where's the teakettle?'

Jackie grabbed me. 'No, you don't! We can't evict them, Eddie. We mustn't. They pay their rent,' she said.

And then I remembered. 'The planer –'

'Just that,' Jackie emphasized, digging her fingers into my biceps. 'You'd have been killed today if you hadn't had some extra good luck. Those pixies may be sloppy, but they pay their rent.'

I got the angle. 'Mr Henchard's luck worked differently, though. Remember when he kicked that rock down the beach steps, and they started to cave in? Me, I do it the hard way. I fall in the planer, sure, and a cylinder bounces after me and stops the machine but I'll be out of a job till the planer's fixed. Nothing like that ever happened to Mr Henchard.'

'He had a better class of tenant,' Jackie explained, with a wild gleam in her eye. 'If Mr Henchard had fallen in the planer, a fuse would have blown, I'll bet. Our tenants are sloppy pixies, so we get sloppy luck.'

'They stay,' I said. 'We own a slum. Let's get out of here and go down to Terry's for a drink.'

We buttoned our raincoats and departed, breathing the fresh, wet air. The storm was slashing down as furiously as ever. I'd forgotten my flashlight, but I didn't want to go back for it. We headed down the slope, toward Terry's faintly visible lights.

It was dark. We couldn't see much through the storm. Probably that was why we didn't notice the bus until it was bearing down on us, headlights almost invisible in the dimout.

I started to pull Jackie aside, out of the way, but my foot slipped on the wet concrete, and we took a nosedive. I felt Jackie's body hurtle against me, and the next moment we were floundering in the muddy ditch beside the highway while the bus roared past us and was gone.

We crawled out and made for Terry's. The barman stared at us, said, 'Whew!' and set up drinks without being asked.

'Unquestionably,' I said, 'our lives have just been saved.'

'Yes,' Jackie agreed, scraping mud from her ears. 'But it wouldn't have happened this way to Mr Henchard.'

The barman shook his head. 'Fall in the ditch, Eddie? And you too? Bad luck!'

'Not bad,' Jackie told him feebly. 'Good. But sloppy.' She lifted her drink and eyed me with muddy misery. I clinked my glass against hers.

'Well,' I said. 'Here's luck.'

WHAT YOU NEED
WE HAVE WHAT YOU NEED

That's what the sign said. Tim Carmichael, who worked for a trade paper that specialized in economics, and eked out a meager salary by selling sensational and untrue articles to the tabloids, failed to sense a story in the reversed sign. He thought it was a cheap publicity gag, something one seldom encounters on Park Avenue, where the shop fronts are noted for their classic dignity. And he was irritated.

He growled silently, walked on, then suddenly turned and came back. He wasn't quite strong enough to resist the temptation to unscramble the sentence, though his annoyance grew. He stood before the window, staring up, and said to himself, '"We have what you need." Yeah?'

The sign was in prim, small letters on a black painted ribbon that stretched across a narrow glass pane. Below it was one of those curved, invisible-glass windows. Through the window Carmichael could see an expanse of white velvet, with a few objects carefully arranged there. A rusty nail, a snowshoe and a diamond tiara. It looked like a Dali décor for Cartier or Tiffany.

'Jewelers?' Carmichael asked silently. 'But why *what you need?*' He pictured millionaires miserably despondent for lack of a matched pearl necklace, heiresses weeping inconsolably because they needed a few star sapphires. The principle of luxury merchandising was to deal with the whipped cream of supply and demand; few people needed diamonds. They merely wanted them and could afford them.

'Or the place might sell jinni flasks,' Carmichael decided. 'Or magic wands. Same principle as a Coney carny, though. A sucker trap. Bill the Whatzit outside and people will pay their dimes and flock in. For two cents –'

He was dyspeptic this morning, and generally disliked the world. Prospect of a scapegoat was attractive, and his press card gave him a certain advantage. He opened the door and walked into the shop.

It was Park Avenue, all right. There were no showcases or counters. It might be an art gallery, for a few good oils were displayed on the walls. An air of overpowering luxury, with the bleakness of an unlived-in place, struck Carmichael.

Through a curtain at the back came a very tall man with carefully combed white hair, a ruddy, healthy face and sharp blue eyes. He might have been sixty. He wore expensive but careless tweeds, which somehow jarred with the décor.

'Good morning,' the man said, with a quick glance at Carmichael's clothes. He seemed slightly surprised. 'May I help you?'

'Maybe.' Carmichael introduced himself and showed his press card.

'Oh? My name is Talley. Peter Talley.'

'I saw your sign.'

'Oh?'

'Our paper is always on the lookout for possible writeups. I've never noticed your shop before –'

'I've been here for years,' Talley said.

'This is an art gallery?'

'Well – no.'

The door opened. A florid man came in and greeted Talley cordially. Carmichael, recognizing the client, felt his opinion of the shop swing rapidly upward. The florid man was a Name – a big one.

'It's a bit early, Mr Talley,' he said, 'but I didn't want to delay. Have you had time to get – what I needed?'

'Oh, yes. I have it. One moment.' Talley hurried through the draperies and returned with a small, neatly wrapped parcel, which he gave to the florid man. The latter forked over a check – Carmichael caught a glimpse of the amount and gulped – and departed. His town car was at the curb outside.

Carmichael moved toward the door, where he could watch. The florid man seemed anxious. His chauffeur waited stolidly as the parcel was unwrapped with hurried fingers.

'I'm not sure I'd want publicity, Mr Carmichael,' Talley said. 'I've a select clientele – carefully chosen.'

'Perhaps our weekly economic bulletins might interest you.'

Talley tried not to laugh. 'Oh, I don't think so. It really isn't in my line.'

The florid man had finally unwrapped the parcel and taken out an egg. As far as Carmichael could see from his post near the door, it was merely an ordinary egg. But its possessor regarded it almost with awe. Had Earth's last hen died ten years before, the man could have been no more pleased. Something like deep relief showed on the Florida-tanned face.

He said something to the chauffeur, and the car rolled smoothly forward and was gone.

'Are you in the dairy business?' Carmichael asked abruptly.

'No.'

'Do you mind telling me what your business is?'

'I'm afraid I do, rather,' Talley said.

Carmichael was beginning to scent a story. 'Of course, I could find out through the Better Business Bureau –'

'You couldn't.'

'No? They might be interested in knowing why an egg is worth five thousand dollars to one of your customers.'

Talley said, 'My clientele is so small I must charge high fees. You – ah – know that a Chinese mandarin has been known to pay thousands of taels for eggs of proved antiquity.'

'That guy wasn't a Chinese mandarin,' Carmichael said.

'Oh, well. As I say, I don't welcome publicity –'

'I think you do. I was in the advertising game for a while. Spelling your sign backwards is an obvious baited hook.'

'Then you're no psychologist,' Talley said. 'It's just that I can afford to indulge my whims. For five years I looked at that window every day and read the sign backwards – from inside my shop. It annoyed me. You know how a word will begin to look funny if you keep staring at it? Any word. It turns into something in no human tongue. Well, I discovered I was getting a neurosis about that sign. It makes no sense backwards, but I kept finding myself trying to read sense into it. When I started to say 'Deen uoy tahw evah ew' to myself and looking for philological derivations, I called in a sign painter. People who are interested enough still drop in.'

'Not many,' Carmichael said shrewdly. 'This is Park Avenue. And you've got the place fixed up too expensively. Nobody in the low-income brackets – or the middle brackets – would come in here. So you run an upper-bracket business.'

'Well,' Talley said, 'yes, I do.'

'And you won't tell me what it is?'

'I'd rather not.'

'I can find out, you know. It might be dope, pornography, high-class fencing –'

'Very likely,' Mr Talley said smoothly. 'I buy stolen jewels, conceal them in eggs and sell them to my customers. Or perhaps that egg was loaded with microscopic French postcards. Good morning, Mr Carmichael.'

'Good morning,' Carmichael said, and went out. He was overdue at the office, but annoyance was the stronger motivation. He played sleuth for a while, keeping an eye on Talley's shop, and the results were thoroughly satisfactory – to a certain extent. He learned everything but why.

Late in the afternoon, he sought out Mr Talley again.

'Wait a minute,' he said, at sight of the proprietor's discouraging face. 'For all you know, I may be a customer.'

Talley laughed.

'Well, why not?' Carmichael compressed his lips. 'How do you know the size of my bank account? Or maybe you've got a restricted clientele?'

'No. But –'

Carmichael said quickly, 'I've been doing some investigating. I've been noticing your customers. In fact, following them. And finding out what they buy from you.'

Talley's face changed. 'Indeed?'

'In*deed*. They're all in a hurry to unwrap their little bundles. So that gave me my chance to find out. I missed a few, but – I saw enough to apply a couple of rules of logic, Mr Talley. *Item:* your customers don't know what they're buying from you. It's a sort of grab bag. A couple of times they were plenty surprised. The man who opened his parcel and found an old newspaper clipping. What about the sunglasses? And the revolver? Probably illegal, by the way – no license. And the diamond – it must have been paste, it was so big.'

'M-mmm,' Mr Talley said.

'I'm no smart apple, but I can smell a screwy set-up. Most of your clients are big shots, in one way or another. And why didn't any of 'em pay you, like the first man – the guy who came in when I was here this morning?'

'It's chiefly a credit business,' Talley said. 'I've my ethics. I have to, for my own conscience. It's responsibility. You see, I sell – my goods – with a guarantee. Payment is made only if the product proves satisfactory.'

'So. An egg. Sunglasses. A pair of asbestos gloves – I think they were. A newspaper clipping. A gun. And a diamond. How do you take inventory?'

Talley said nothing.

Carmichael grinned. 'You've an errand boy. You send him out and he comes back with bundles. Maybe he goes to a grocery on Madison and buys an egg. Or a pawnshop on Sixth for a revolver. Or – well, anyhow, I told you I'd find out what your business is.'

'And have you?' Talley asked.

'"We have what you need,"' Carmichael said. 'But how do you *know*?'

'You're jumping to conclusions.'

'I've got a headache – I didn't have sunglasses! – and I don't believe in magic. Listen, Mr Talley, I'm fed up to the eyebrows and way beyond on queer little shops that sell peculiar things. I know too much about 'em – I've written about 'em. A guy walks along the street and sees a funny sort of store and the proprietor won't serve him – he sells only to pixies – or else he *does* sell him a magic charm with a double edge. Well – *pfui!*'

'Mph,' Talley said.

'"Mph" as much as you like. But you can't get away from logic. Either you've got a sound, sensible racket here, or else it's one of those funny, magic-shop set-ups – and I don't believe that. For it isn't logical.'

'Why not?'

'Because of economics,' Carmichael said flatly. 'Grant the idea that you've got certain mysterious powers – let's say you can make telepathic gadgets. All right. Why the devil would you start a business so you could sell the gadgets so you could make money so you could live? You'd simply put on one of your gadgets, read a stockbroker's mind and buy the right stocks. That's the intrinsic fallacy in these crazy-shop things – if you've got enough stuff on the ball to be able to stock and run such a shop, you wouldn't need a business in the first place. Why go round Robin Hood's barn?'

Talley said nothing.

Carmichael smiled crookedly. '"I often wonder what the vintners buy one half so precious as the stuff they sell,"' he quoted. 'Well – what do *you* buy? I know what you sell – eggs and sunglasses.'

'You're an inquisitive man, Mr Carmichael,' Talley murmured. 'Has it ever occurred to you that this is none of your business?'

'I may be a customer,' Carmichael repeated. 'How about that?'

Talley's cool blue eyes were intent. A new light dawned in them; Talley pursed his lips and scowled. 'I hadn't thought of that,' he admitted. 'You might be. Under the circumstances. Will you excuse me for a moment?'

'Sure,' Carmichael said. Talley went through the curtains.

Outside, traffic drifted idly along Park. As the sun slid down beyond the Hudson, the street lay in a blue shadow that crept imperceptibly up the barricades of the buildings. Carmichael stared at the sign – WE HAVE WHAT YOU NEED – and smiled.

In a back room, Talley put his eye to a binocular plate and moved a calibrated dial. He did this several times. Then, biting his lip – for he was a gentle man – he called his errand boy and gave him directions. After that he returned to Carmichael.

'You're a customer,' he said. 'Under certain conditions.'

'The condition of my bank account, you mean?'

'No,' Talley said. 'I'll give you reduced rates. Understand one thing. I really do have what you need. You don't *know* what you need, but I know. And as it happens – well, I'll sell you what you need for, let's say, five dollars.'

Carmichael reached for his wallet. Talley held up a hand.

'Pay me after you're satisfied. And the money's the nominal part of the fee. There's another part. If you're satisfied, I want you to promise that you'll never come near this shop again and never mention it to anyone.'

'I see,' Carmichael said slowly. His theories had changed slightly.

'It won't be long before – ah, here he is now.' A buzzing from the back indicated the return of the errand boy. Talley said, 'Excuse me,' and vanished. Soon he returned with a neatly wrapped parcel, which he thrust into Carmichael's hands.

'Keep this on your person,' Talley said. 'Good afternoon.'

Carmichael nodded, pocketed the parcel and went out. Feeling affluent, he hailed a taxi and went to a cocktail bar he knew. There, in the dim light of a booth, he unwrapped the bundle.

Protection money, he decided. Talley was paying him off to keep his mouth shut about the racket, whatever it was. O.K., live and let live. How much would be –

Ten thousand? Fifty thousand? How big was the racket?

He opened an oblong cardboard box. Within, nestling upon tissue paper, was a pair of shears, the blades protected by a sheath of folded, glued cardboard.

Carmichael said something softly. He drank his highball and ordered another, but left it untasted. Glancing at his wrist watch, he decided that the Park Avenue shop would be closed by now and Mr Peter Talley gone.

'"... one half so precious as the stuff they sell."' Carmichael said. 'Maybe it's the scissors of Atropos. Blah.' He unsheathed the blades and snipped experimentally at the air. Nothing happened. Slightly crimson around the cheekbones, Carmichael reholstered the shears and dropped them into the side pocket of his topcoat. Quite a gag!

He decided to call on Peter Talley tomorrow.

Meanwhile, what? He remembered he had a dinner date with one of the girls at the office, and hastily paid his bill and left. The streets were darkening, and a cold wind blew southward from the Park. Carmichael wound his scarf tighter around his throat and made gestures toward passing taxis.

He was considerably annoyed.

Half an hour later a thin man with sad eyes – Jerry Worth, one of the copy writers from his office – greeted him at the bar where Carmichael was killing time. 'Waiting for Betsy?' Worth said, nodding toward the restaurant annex. 'She sent me to tell you she couldn't make it. A rush deadline. Apologies and stuff. Where were you today? Things got gummed up a bit. Have a drink with me.'

They worked on a rye. Carmichael was already slightly stiff. The dull crimson around his cheekbones had deepened, and his frown had become set. 'What you need,' he remarked. 'Double crossing little –'

'Huh?' Worth said.

'Nothing. Drink up. I've just decided to get a guy in trouble. If I can.'

'You almost got in trouble yourself today. That trend analysis of ores –'

'Eggs. Sunglasses!'

'I got you out of a jam –'

'Shut up,' Carmichael said, and ordered another round. Every time he felt the weight of the shears in his pocket he found his lips moving.

Five shots later Worth said plaintively, 'I don't mind doing good deeds, but I do like to mention them. And you won't let me. All I want is a little gratitude.'

'All right, mention them,' Carmichael said. 'Brag your head off. Who cares?'

Worth showed satisfaction. 'That ore analysis – it was that. You weren't at the office today, but I caught it. I checked with our records and you had Trans-Steel all wrong. If I hadn't altered the figures, it would have gone down to the printer –'

'What?'

'The Trans-Steel. They –'

'Oh, you fool,' Carmichael groaned. 'I know it didn't check with the office figures. I meant to put in a notice to have them changed. I got my dope from the source. Why don't you mind your own business?'

Worth blinked. 'I was trying to help.'

'It would have been good for a five-buck raise,' Carmichael said. 'After all the research I did to uncover the real dope – Listen, has the stuff gone to bed yet?'

'I dunno. Maybe not. Croft was still checking the copy –'

'O.K.!' Carmichael said. 'Next time –' He jerked at his scarf, jumped off the stool and headed for the door, trailed by the protesting Worth. Ten minutes later he was at the office, listening to Croft's bland explanation that the copy had already been dispatched to the printer.

'Does it matter? Was there – Incidentally, where were you today?'

'Dancing on the rainbow,' Carmichael snapped, and departed. He had switched over from rye to whisky sours, and the cold night air naturally did not sober him. Swaying slightly, watching the sidewalk move a little as he blinked at it, he stood on the curb and pondered.

'I'm sorry, Tim,' Worth said. 'It's too late now, though. There won't be any trouble. You've got a right to go by our office records.'

'Stop me now,' Carmichael said. 'Lousy little –' He was angry and drunk. On impulse he got another taxi and sped to the printer's, still trailing a somewhat confused Jerry Worth.

There was rhythmic thunder in the building. The swift movement of the taxi had given Carmichael a slight nausea; his head ached, and alcohol was in solution in his blood. The hot, inky air was unpleasant. The great Linotypes thumped and growled. Men were moving about. It was all slightly nightmarish, and Carmichael doggedly hunched his shoulders and lurched on until something jerked him back and began to strangle him.

Worth started yelling. His face showed drunken terror. He made ineffectual gestures.

But this was all part of the nightmare. Carmichael saw what had happened. The ends of his scarf had caught in the moving gears somewhere and he was being drawn inexorably into meshing metal cogs. Men were running. The clanking, thumping, rolling sounds were deafening. He pulled at the scarf.

Worth screamed, '... knife! Cut it!'

The warping of relative values that intoxication gives saved Carmichael. Sober, he would have been helpless with panic. As it was, each thought was hard to capture, but clear and lucid when he finally got it. He remembered the shears, and he put his hand in his pocket. The blades slipped out of their cardboard sheath, and he snipped through the scarf with fumbling, hasty movements.

The white silk disappeared. Carmichael fingered the ragged edge at his throat and smiled stiffly.

Mr Peter Talley had been hoping that Carmichael would not come back. The probability lines had shown two possible variants; in one, all was well; in the other …

Carmichael walked into the shop the next morning and held out a five-dollar bill. Talley took it.

'Thank you. But you could have mailed me a check.'

'I could have. Only that wouldn't have told me what I wanted to know.'

'No,' Talley said, and sighed. 'You've decided, haven't you?'

'Do you blame me?' Carmichael asked. 'Last night – do you know what happened?'

'Yes.'

'How?'

'I might as well tell you,' Talley said. 'You'd find out anyway. That's certain, anyhow.'

Carmichael sat down, lit a cigarette and nodded. 'Logic. You couldn't have arranged that little accident, by any manner of means. Betsy Hoag decided to break our date early yesterday morning. Before I saw you. That was the beginning of the chain of incidents that led up to the accident. *Ergo*, you must have known what was going to happen.'

'I did know.'

'Prescience?'

'Mechanical. I saw that you would be crushed in the machine –'

'Which implies an alterable future.'

'Certainly,' Talley said, his shoulders slumping. 'There are innumerable possible variants to the future. Different lines of probability. All depending on the outcome of various crises as they arise. I happen to be skilled in certain branches of electronics. Some years ago, almost by accident, I stumbled on the principle of seeing the future.'

'How?'

'Chiefly it involes a personal focus on the individual. The moment you enter this place' – he gestured – 'you're in the beam of my scanner. In my back room I have the machine itself. By turning a calibrated dial, I check the possible futures. Sometimes there are many. Sometimes only a few. As though at times certain stations weren't broadcasting. I look into my scanner and see what you need – and supply it.'

Carmichael let smoke drift from his nostrils. He watched the blue coils through narrowed eyes.

'You follow a man's whole life – in triplicate or quadruplicate or whatever?'

'No,' Talley said. 'I've got my device focused so it's sensitive to crisis curves. When those occur, I follow them farther and see what probability paths involve the man's safe and happy survival.'

'The sunglasses, the egg and the gloves –'

Talley said, 'Mr – uh – Smith is one of my regular clients. Whenever he passes a crisis successfully, with my aid, he comes back for another checkup. I locate his next crisis and supply him with what he needs to meet it. I gave him the asbestos gloves. In about a month, a situation will arise where he must – under the circumstances – move a red-hot bar of metal. He's an artist. His hands –'

'I see. So it isn't always saving a man's life.'

'Of course not,' Talley said. 'Life isn't the only vital factor. An apparently minor crisis may lead to – well, a divorce, a neurosis, a wrong decision and the loss of hundreds of lives indirectly. I insure life, health and happiness.'

'You're an altruist. Only why doesn't the world storm your doors? Why limit your trade to a few?'

'I haven't got the time or the equipment.'

'More machines could be built.'

'Well,' Talley said, 'most of my customers are wealthy. I must live.'

'You could read tomorrow's stock-market reports if you wanted dough,' Carmichael said. 'We get back to that old question. If a guy has miraculous powers, why is he satisfied to run a hole-in-the-wall store?'

'Economic reasons. I – ah – I'm averse to gambling.'

'It wouldn't be gambling,' Carmichael pointed out. '"I often wonder what the vintners buy …" Just what *do* you get out of this?'

'Satisfaction,' Talley said. 'Call it that.'

But Carmichael wasn't satisfied. His mind veered from the question and turned to the possibilities. Insurance, eh? Life, health and happiness.

'What about me? Won't there be another crisis in my life sometime?'

'Probably. Not necessarily one involving personal danger.'

'Then I'm a permanent customer.'

'I – don't –'

'Listen,' Carmichael said, 'I'm not trying to shake you down. I'll pay. I'll pay plenty. I'm not rich, but I know exactly what a service like this would be worth to me. No worries –'

'It couldn't be –'

'Oh, come off it. I'm not a blackmailer or anything. I'm not threatening you with publicity, if that's what you're afraid of. I'm an ordinary guy, not a melodramatic villain. Do I look dangerous? What are you afraid of?'

'You're an ordinary guy, yes,' Talley admitted. 'Only –'

'Why not?' Carmichael argued. 'I won't bother you. I passed one crisis successfully, with your help. There'll be another one due sometime. Give me what I need for that. Charge me anything you like. I'll get the dough somehow. Borrow it, if necessary. I won't disturb you at all. All I ask is that you let me come in whenever I've passed a crisis, and get ammunition for the next one. What's wrong with that?'

'Nothing,' Talley said soberly.

'Well, then. I'm an ordinary guy. There's a girl – it's Betsy Hoag. I want to marry her. Settle down somewhere in the country, raise kids and have security. There's nothing wrong with that either, is there?'

Talley said, 'It was too late the moment you entered this shop today.'

Carmichael looked up. 'Why?' he asked sharply.

A buzzer rang in the back. Talley went through the curtains and came back almost immediately with a wrapped parcel. He gave it to Carmichael.

Carmichael smiled. 'Thanks,' he said. 'Thanks a lot. Do you have any idea when my next crisis will come?'

'In a week.'

'Mind if I –' Carmichael was unwrapping the package. He took out a pair of plastic-soled shoes and looked at Talley, bewildered.

'Like that, eh? I'll need – shoes?'

'Yes.'

'I suppose –' Carmichael hesitated. 'I guess you wouldn't tell me why?'

'No, I won't do that. But be sure to wear them whenever you go out.'

'Don't worry about that. And – I'll mail you a check. It may take me a few days to scrape up the dough, but I'll do it. How much?'

'Five hundred dollars.'

'I'll mail a check today.'

'I prefer not to accept a fee until the client has been satisfied,' Talley said. He had grown more reserved, his blue eyes cool and withdrawn.

'Suit yourself,' Carmichael said. 'I'm going out and celebrate. You – don't drink?'

'I can't leave the shop.'

'Well, goodbye. And thanks again. I won't be any trouble to you, you know. I promise that!' He turned away.

Looking after him, Talley smiled a wry, unhappy smile. He did not answer Carmichael's goodbye. Not then.

When the door had closed behind him, Talley turned to the back of his shop and went through the door where the scanner was.

The lapse of ten years can cover a multitude of changes. A man with the possibility of tremendous power almost within his grasp can alter, in that time, from a man who will not reach for it to a man who will – and moral values be damned.

The change did not come quickly to Carmichael. It speaks well for his integrity that it took ten years to work such an alteration in all he had been taught. On the day he first went into Talley's shop there was little evil in him. But the temptation grew stronger week by week, visit by visit. Talley, for reasons of his own, was content to sit idly by, waiting for customers, smothering the inconceivable potentialities of his machine under a blanket of trivial functions. But Carmichael was not content.

It took him ten years to reach the day, but the day came at last.

Talley sat in the inner room, his back to the door. He was slumped low in an ancient rocker, facing the machine. It had changed little in the space of a decade. It still covered most of two walls, and the eyepiece of its scanner glittered under amber fluorescents.

Carmichael looked covetously at the eyepiece. It was window and doorway to a power beyond any man's dreams. Wealth beyond imagining lay just within that tiny opening. The rights over the life and death of every man alive. And nothing between that fabulous future and himself except the man who sat looking at the machine.

Talley did not seem to hear the careful footsteps or the creak of the door behind him. He did not stir as Carmichael lifted the gun slowly. One might think that he never guessed what was coming, or why, or from whom, as Carmichael shot him through the head.

Talley sighed and shivered a little, and twisted the scanner dial. It was not the first time that the eyepiece had shown him his own lifeless body, glimpsed down some vista of probability, but he never saw the slumping of that familiar figure without feeling a breath of indescribable coolness blow backwards upon him out of the future.

He straightened from the eyepiece and sat back in his chair, looking thoughtfully at a pair of rough-soled shoes lying beside him on a table. He sat quietly for a while, his eyes upon the shoes, his mind following Carmichael down the street and into the evening, and the morrow, and on toward that coming crisis which would depend on his secure footing on a subway platform as a train thundered by the place where Carmichael would be standing one day next week.

Talley had sent his messenger boy out this time for two pairs of shoes. He had hesitated long, an hour ago, between the rough-soled pair and the smooth. For Talley was a humane man, and there were many times when his job was distasteful to him. But in the end, this time, it had been the smooth-soled pair he had wrapped for Carmichael.

Now he sighed and bent to the scanner again, twisting the dial to bring into view a scene he had watched before.

Carmichael, standing on a crowded subway platform, glittering with oily wetness from some overflow. Carmichael, in the slick-soled shoes Talley had chosen for him. A commotion in the crowd, a surge toward the platform edge. Carmichael's feet slipping frantically as the train roared by.

'Goodbye, Mr Carmichael,' Talley murmured. It was the farewell he had not spoken when Carmichael left the shop. He spoke it regretfully, and the regret was for the Carmichael of today, who did not yet deserve that end. He was not now a melodramatic villain whose death one could watch unmoved. But the Tim Carmichael of today had atonement to make for the Carmichael of ten years ahead, and the payment must be exacted.

It is not a good thing to have the power of life and death over one's fellow humans. Peter Talley knew it was not a good thing – but the power had been put into his hands. He had not sought it. It seemed to him that the machine had grown almost by accident to its tremendous completion under his trained fingers and trained mind.

At first it had puzzled him. How ought such a device to be used? What dangers, what terrible potentialities, lay in that Eye that could see through the veil of tomorrow? His was the responsibility, and it had weighed heavily upon him until the answer came. And after he knew the answer – well, the weight was heavier still. For Talley was a mild man.

He could not have told anyone the real reason why he was a shop-keeper. Satisfaction, he had said to Carmichael. And sometimes, indeed, there was deep satisfaction. But at other times – at times like this – there was only dismay and humility. Especially humility.

We have what you need. Only Talley knew that message was not for the individuals who came to his shop. The pronoun was plural, not singular. It was a message for the world – the world whose future was being carefully, lovingly reshaped under Peter Talley's guidance.

The main line of the future was not easy to alter. The future is a pyramid shaping slowly, brick by brick, and brick by brick Talley had to change it. There were some men who were necessary – men who would create and build – men who should be saved.

Talley gave them what they needed.

But inevitably there were others whose ends were evil. Talley gave them, too, what the world needed – death.

Peter Talley had not asked for this terrible power. But the key had been put in his hands, and he dared not delegate such authority as this to any other man alive. Sometimes he made mistakes.

He had felt a little surer since the simile of the key had occurred to him. The key to the future. A key that had been laid in his hands.

Remembering that, he leaned back in his chair and reached for an old and well-worn book. It fell open easily at a familiar passage. Peter Talley's lips moved as he read the passage once again, in his room behind the shop on Park Avenue.

'And I say also unto thee, that thou art Peter ... And I will give unto thee the keys of the Kingdom of Heaven ...'

ABSALOM

At dusk Joel Locke came home from the university where he held the chair of psychonamics. He came quietly into the house, by a side door, and stood listening, a tall, tight-lipped man of forty with a faintly sardonic mouth and cool gray eyes. He could hear the precipitron humming. That meant that Abigail Schuler, the housekeeper, was busy with her duties. Locke smiled slightly and turned toward a panel in the wall that opened at his approach.

The small elevator took him noiselessly upstairs.

There, he moved with curious stealth. He went directly to a door at the end of the hall and paused before it, his head bent, his eyes unfocused. He heard nothing. Presently he opened the door and stepped into the room.

Instantly the feeling of unsureness jolted back, freezing him where he stood. He made no sign, though his mouth tightened. He forced himself to remain quiet as he glanced around.

It could have been the room of a normal twenty-year-old, not a boy of eight. Tennis racquets were heaped in a disorderly fashion against a pile of book records. The thiaminizer was turned on, and Locke automatically clicked the switch over. Abruptly he turned. The televisor screen was blank, yet he could have sworn that eyes had been watching him from it.

This wasn't the first time it had happened.

After a while Locke turned again and squatted to examine the book reels. He picked out one labeled BRIAFF ON ENTROPIC LOGIC and turned the cylinder over in his hands, scowling. Then he replaced it and went out of the room, with a last, considering look at the televisor.

Downstairs Abigail Schuler was fingering the Mastermaid switchboard. Her prim mouth was as tight as the severe bun of gray-shot hair at the back of her neck.

'Good evening,' Locke said. 'Where's Absalom?'

'Out playing, Brother Locke,' the housekeeper said formally. 'You're home early. I haven't finished the living room yet.'

'Well, turn on the ions and let 'em play,' Locke said. 'It won't take long. I've got some papers to correct, anyway.'

He started out, but Abigail coughed significantly.

'Well?'

'He's looking peaked.'

'Then outdoor exercise is what he needs,' Locke said shortly. 'I'm going to send him to a summer camp.'

'Brother Locke,' Abigail said, 'I don't see why you don't let him go to Baja California. He's set his heart on it. You let him study all the hard subjects he wanted before. Now you put your foot down. It's none of my affair, but I can tell he's pining.'

'He'd pine worse if I said yes. I've my reasons for not wanting him to study entropic logic. Do you know what it involves?'

'I don't – you know I don't. I'm not an educated woman, Brother Locke. But Absalom is bright as a button.'

Locke made an impatient gesture.

'You have a genius for understatement,' he said. 'Bright as a button!'

Then he shrugged and moved to the window, looking down at the play court below where his eight-year-old son played handball. Absalom did not look up. He seemed engrossed in his game. But Locke, watching, felt a cool, stealthy terror steal through his mind, and behind his back his hands clenched together.

A boy who looked ten, whose maturity level was twenty, and yet who was still a child of eight. Not easy to handle. There were many parents just now with the same problem – something was happening to the graph curve that charts the percentage of child geniuses born in recent times. Something had begun to stir lazily far back in the brains of the coming generations and a new species, of a sort, was coming slowly into being. Locke knew that well. In his own time he, too, had been a child genius.

Other parents might meet the problem in other ways, he thought stubbornly. Not himself. He *knew* what was best for Absalom. Other parents might send their genius children to one of the crèches where they could develop among their own kind. Not Locke.

'Absalom's place is here,' he said aloud. 'With me, where I can –' He caught the housekeeper's eye and shrugged again, irritably, going back to the conversation that had broken off. 'Of course he's bright. But not bright enough yet to go to Baja California and study entropic logic. Entropic logic! It's too advanced for the boy. Even you ought to realize that. It isn't like a lollypop you can hand the kid – first making sure there's castor oil in the bathroom closet. Absalom's immature. It would actually be dangerous to send him to the Baja California University now to study with men three times his age. It would involve mental strain he isn't fit for yet. I don't want him turned into a psychopath.'

Abigail's prim mouth pursed up sourly.

'You let him take calculus.'

'Oh, leave me alone.' Locke glanced down again at the small boy on the play court. 'I think,' he said slowly, 'that it's time for another rapport with Absalom.'

The housekeeper looked at him sharply, opened her thin lips to speak, and then closed them with an almost audible snap of disapproval. She didn't understand entirely, of course, how a rapport worked or what it accomplished. She only knew that in these days there were ways in which it was possible to enforce hypnosis, to pry open a mind willy-nilly and search it for contraband thoughts. She shook her head, lips pressed tight.

'Don't try to interfere in things you don't understand,' Locke said. 'I tell you, I know what's best for Absalom. He's in the same place I was thirty-odd years ago. Who could know better? Call him in, will you? I'll be in my study.'

Abigail watched his retreating back, a pucker between her brows. It was hard to know what was best. The mores of the day demanded rigid good conduct, but sometimes a person had trouble deciding in her own mind what was the right thing to do. In the old days, now, after the atomic wars, when license ran riot and anybody could do anything he pleased, life must have been easier. Nowadays, in the violent back-swing to a Puritan culture, you were expected to think twice and search your soul before you did a doubtful thing.

Well, Abigail had no choice this time. She clicked over the wall microphone and spoke into it.

'Absalom?'

'Yes, Sister Schuler?'

'Come in. Your father wants you.'

In his study Locke stood quiet for a moment, considering. Then he reached for the house microphone.

'Sister Schuler, I'm using the televisor. Ask Absalom to wait.'

He sat down before his private visor. His hands moved deftly.

'Get me Dr Ryan, the Wyoming Quizkid Crèche. Joel Locke calling.'

Idly as he waited he reached out to take an old-fashioned cloth-bound book from a shelf of antique curiosa. He read:

> But Absalom sent spies throughout all the tribes of Israel, saying, As soon as ye hear the sound of the trumpet, then ye shall say, Absalom reigneth in Hebron …

'Brother Locke?' the televisor asked.

The face of a white-haired, pleasant-featured man showed on the screen. Locke replaced the book and raised his hand in greeting.

'Dr Ryan. I'm sorry to keep bothering you.'

'That's all right,' Ryan said. 'I've plenty of time. I'm supposed to be supervisor at the Crèche, but the kids are running it to suit themselves.' He chuckled. 'How's Absalom?'

'There's a limit,' Locke said sourly. 'I've given the kid his head, out-lined a broad curriculum, and now he wants to study entropic logic. There are only two universities that handle the subject, and the nearest's in Baja California.'

'He could commute by copter, couldn't he?' Ryan asked, but Locke grunted disapproval.

'Take too long. Besides, one of the requirements is inboarding, under a strict regime. The discipline, mental and physical, is supposed to be necessary in order to master entropic logic. Which is spinach. I got the rudiments at home, though I had to use the tri-disney to visualize it.'

Ryan laughed.

'The kids here are taking it up. Uh – are you sure you understood it?'

'Enough, yeah. Enough to realize it's nothing for a kid to study until his horizons have expanded.'

'We're having no trouble with it,' the doctor said. 'Don't forget that Absalom's a genius, not an ordinary youngster.'

'I know. I know my responsibility, too. A normal home environment has to be maintained to give Absalom some sense of security – which is one reason I don't want the boy to live in Baja California just now. I want to be able to protect him.'

'We've disagreed on that point before. All the quizkids are pretty self-sufficient, Locke.'

'Absalom's a genius, and a child. Therefore he's lacking in a sense of proportion. There are more dangers for him to avoid. I think it's a grave mistake to give the quizkids their heads and let them do what they like. I refused to send Absalom to a Crèche for an excellent reason. Putting all the boy geniuses in a batch and letting them fight it out. Completely artificial environment.'

'I'm not arguing,' Ryan said. 'It's your business. Apparently you'll never admit that there's a sine curve of geniuses these days. A steady increase. In another generation –'

'I was a child genius myself, but I got over it,' Locke said irritably. 'I had enough trouble with my father. He was a tyrant, and if I hadn't been lucky, he'd have managed to warp me psychologically way out of line. I adjusted, but I had trouble. I don't want Absalom to have that trouble. That's why I'm using psychonamics.'

'Narcosynthesis? Enforced hypnotism?'

'It's not enforced,' Locke snapped. 'It's a valuable mental catharsis. Under hypnosis, he tells me everything that's on his mind, and I can help him.'

'I didn't know you were doing that,' Ryan said slowly. 'I'm not at all sure it's a good idea.'

'I don't tell you how to run your Crèche.'

'No. But the kids do. A lot of them are smarter than I am.'

'Immature intelligence is dangerous. A kid will skate on thin ice without making a test first. Don't think I'm holding Absalom back. I'm just running tests for him first. I make sure the ice will hold him. Entropic logic I can understand, but he can't, yet. So he'll have to wait on that.'

'Well?'

Locke hesitated. 'Uh – do you know if your boys have been communicating with Absalom?'

'I don't know,' Ryan said. 'I don't interfere with their lives.'

'All right, I don't want them interfering with mine, or with Absalom's. I wish you'd find out if they're getting in touch with him.'

There was a long pause. Then Ryan said slowly:

'I'll try. But if I were you, Brother Locke, I'd let Absalom go to Baja California if he wants to.'

'I know what I'm doing,' Locke said, and broke the beam. His gaze went toward the Bible again.

Entropic logic!

Once the boy reached maturity, his somatic and physiological symptoms would settle toward the norm, but meanwhile the pendulum still swung wildly. Absalom needed strict control, for his own good.

And, for some reason, the boy had been trying to evade the hypnotic rapports lately. There was something going on.

Thoughts moved chaotically through Locke's mind. He forgot that Absalom was waiting for him, and remembered only when Abigail's voice, on the wall transmitter, announced the evening meal.

At dinner Abigail Schuler sat like Atropos between father and son, ready to clip the conversation whenever it did not suit her. Locke felt the beginnings of a long-standing irritation at Abigail's attitude that she had to protect Absalom against his father. Perhaps conscious of that, Locke himself finally brought up the subject of Baja California.

'You've apparently been studying the entropic logic thesis.' Absalom did not seem startled. 'Are you convinced yet that it's too advanced for you?'

'No, Dad,' Absalom said. 'I'm not convinced of that.'

'The rudiments of calculus might seem easy to a youngster. But when he got far enough into it … I went over that entropic logic, son, through the entire book, and it was difficult enough for me. And I've a mature mind.'

'I know you have. And I know I haven't, yet. But I still don't think it would be beyond me.'

'Here's the thing,' Locke said. 'You might develop psychotic symptoms if you studied that thing, and you might not be able to recognize them in time. If we could have a rapport every night, or every other night, while you were studying –'

'But it's in Baja California!'

'That's the trouble. If you want to wait for my Sabbatical, I can go there with you. Or one of the nearer universities may start the course. I don't want to be unreasonable. Logic should show you my motive.'

'It does,' Absalom said. 'That part's all right. The only difficulty's an intangible, isn't it? I mean, you think my mind couldn't assimilate entropic logic safely, and I'm convinced that it could.'

'Exactly,' Locke said. 'You've the advantage of knowing yourself better than I could know you. You're handicapped by immaturity, lack of a sense of proportion. And I've had the advantage of more experience.'

'Your own, though, Dad. How much would such values apply to me?'

'You must let me be the judge of that, son.'

'Maybe,' Absalom said. 'I wish I'd gone to a quizkid crèche, though.'

'Aren't you happy here?' Abigail asked, hurt, and the boy gave her a quick, warm look of affection.

'Sure I am, Abbie. You know that.'

'You'd be a lot less happy with dementia praecox,' Locke said sardonically. 'Entropic logic, for instance, presupposes a grasp of temporal variations being assumed for problems involving relativity.'

'Oh, that gives me a headache,' Abigail said. 'And if you're so worried about Absalom's overtraining his mind, you shouldn't talk to him like that.' She pressed buttons and slid the cloisonné metal dishes into the compartment. 'Coffee, Brother Locke … milk, Absalom … and I'll take tea.'

Locke winked at his son, who merely looked solemn. Abigail rose with her teacup and headed toward the fireplace. Seizing the little hearth broom, she whisked away a few ashes, relaxed amid cushions, and warmed her skinny ankles by the wood fire. Locke patted back a yawn.

'Until we settle this argument, son, matters must stand. Don't tackle that book on entropic logic again. Or anything else on the subject. Right?'

There was no answer.

'Right?' Locke insisted.

'I'm not sure,' Absalom said after a pause. 'As a matter of fact, the book's already given me a few ideas.'

Looking across the table, Locke was struck by the incongruity of that incredibly developed mind in the childish body.

'You're still young,' he said. 'A few days won't matter. Don't forget that legally I exercise control over you, though I'll never do that without your agreement that I'm acting justly.'

'Justice for you may not be justice for me,' Absalom said, drawing designs on the tablecloth with his fingernail.

Locke stood up and laid his hand on the boy's shoulder.

'We'll discuss it again, until we've thrashed it out right. Now I've some papers to correct.'

He went out.

'He's acting for the best, Absalom,' Abigail said.

'Of course he is, Abbie,' the boy agreed. But he remained thoughtful.

The next day Locke went through his classes in an absent-minded fashion and, at noon, he televised Dr Ryan at the Wyoming Quizkid Crèche. Ryan seemed entirely too casual and noncommittal. He said he had asked the quizkids if they had been communicating with Absalom, and they had said no.

'But they'll lie at the drop of a hat, of course, if they think it advisable,' Ryan added, with inexplicable amusement.

'What's so funny?' Locke inquired.

'I don't know,' Ryan said. 'The way the kids tolerate me. I'm useful to them at times, but – originally I was supposed to be supervisor here. Now the boys supervise me.'

'Are you serious?'

Ryan sobered.

'I've a tremendous respect for the quizkids. And I think you're making a very grave mistake in the way you're handling your son. I was in your house once, a year ago. It's *your* house. Only one room belongs to Absalom. He can't leave any of his possessions around anywhere else. You're dominating him tremendously.'

'I'm trying to help him.'

'Are you sure you know the right way?'

'Certainly,' Locke snapped. 'Even if I'm wrong, does that mean I'm committing fil – filio –'

'That's an interesting point,' Ryan said casually. 'You could have thought of the right words for matricide, parricide, or fratricide easily enough. But it's seldom one kills his son. The word doesn't come to the tongue quite as instantly.'

Locke glared at the screen. 'What the devil do you mean?'

'Just be careful,' Ryan said. 'I believe in the mutant theory, after running this Crèche for fifteen years.'

'I was a child genius myself,' Locke repeated.

'Uh-huh,' Ryan said, his eyes intent. 'I wonder if you know that the mutation's supposed to be cumulative? Three generations ago, two percent of the population were child geniuses. Two generations ago, five percent. One generation – a sine curve, Brother Locke. And the I.Q. mounts proportionately. Wasn't your father a genius too?'

'He was,' Locke admitted. 'But a maladjusted one.'

'I thought so. Mutations take time. The theory is that the transition is taking place right now, from homo sapiens to homo superior.'

'I know. It's logical enough. Each generation of mutations – this dominant mutation at least – taking another step forward till homo superior is reached. What that will be –'

'I don't think we'll ever know,' Ryan said quietly. 'I don't think we'd understand. How long will it take, I wonder? The next generation? I don't think so. Five more generations, or ten or twenty? And each one taking another step, realizing another buried potentiality of homo, until the summit is reached. Superman, Joel.'

'Absalom isn't a superman,' Locke said practically. 'Or a superchild, for that matter.'

'Are you sure?'

'Good Lord! Don't you suppose I know my own son?'

'I won't answer that,' Ryan said. 'I'm certain that I don't know all there is to know about the quizkids in my Crèche. Beltram, the Denver Crèche supervisor, tells me the same thing. These quizkids are the next step in the mutation. You and I are members of a dying species, Brother Locke.'

Locke's face changed. Without a word he clicked off the televisor.

The bell was ringing for his next class. But Locke stayed motionless, his cheeks and forehead slightly damp.

Presently, his mouth twisted in a curiously unpleasant smile, he nodded and turned from the televisor …

He got home at five. He came in quietly, by the side entrance, and took the elevator upstairs. Absalom's door was closed, but voices were coming through it faintly. Locke listened for a time. Then he rapped sharply on the panel.

'Absalom. Come downstairs. I want to talk to you.'

In the living room he told Abigail to stay out for a while. With his back to the fireplace, he waited until Absalom came.

> The enemies of my lord the king, and all that rise against thee to do thee hurt, be as that young man is …

The boy entered without obvious embarrassment. He came forward and he faced his father, the boy-face calm and untroubled. He had poise, Locke saw, no doubt of that.

'I overheard some of your conversation, Absalom,' Locke said.

'It's just as well,' Absalom said coolly. 'I'd have told you tonight anyway. I've got to go on with that entropic course.'

Locke ignored that. 'Who were you vising?'

'A boy I know. Malcolm Roberts, in the Denver Quizkid Crèche.'

'Discussing entropic logic with him, eh? After what I'd told you?'

'You'll remember that I didn't agree.'

Locke put his hands behind him and interlaced his fingers.

'Then you'll also remember that I mentioned I had legal control over you.'

'Legal,' Absalom said, 'yes. Moral, no.'

'This has nothing to do with morals.'

'It has, though. And with ethics. Many of the youngsters – younger than I – at the quizkid crèches are studying entropic logic. It hasn't harmed them. I must go to a crèche, or to Baja California. I must.'

Locke bent his head thoughtfully.

'Wait a minute,' he said. 'Sorry, son. I got emotionally tangled for a moment. Let's go back on the plane of pure logic.'

'All right,' Absalom said, with a quiet, imperceptible withdrawal.

'I'm convinced that that particular study might be dangerous for you. I don't want you to be hurt. I want you to have every possible opportunity, especially the ones I never had.'

'No,' Absalom said, a curious note of maturity in his high voice. 'It wasn't lack of opportunity. It was incapability.'

'What?' Locke said.

'You could never allow yourself to be convinced I could safely study entropic logic. I've learned that. I've talked to other quizkids.'

'Of private matters?'

'They're of my race,' Absalom said. 'You're not. And please don't talk about filial love. You broke that law yourself long ago.'

'Keep talking,' Locke said quietly, his mouth tight. 'But make sure it's logical.'

'It is. I didn't think I'd ever have to do this for a long time, but I've got to now. You're holding me back from what I've got to do.'

'The step mutation. Cumulative. I see.'

The fire was too hot. Locke took a step forward from the hearth. Absalom made a slight movement of withdrawal. Locke looked at him intently.

'It is a mutation,' the boy said. 'Not the complete one, but Grandfather was one of the first steps. You, too – further along than he did. And I'm further than you. My children will be closer toward the ultimate mutation. The only psychonamic experts worth anything are the child geniuses of your generation.'

'Thanks.'

'You're afraid of me,' Absalom said. 'You're afraid of me and jealous of me.'

Locke started to laugh. 'What about logic now?'

The boy swallowed. 'It is logic. Once you were convinced that the mutation was cumulative, you couldn't bear to think I'd displace you. It's a basic psychological warp in you. You had the same thing with Grandfather, in a different way. That's why you turned to psychonamics, where you were a small god, dragging out the secret minds of your students, molding their brains as Adam was molded. You're afraid that I'll outstrip you. And I will.'

'That's why I let you study anything you wanted, I suppose?' Locke asked. 'With this exception?'

'Yes, it is. A lot of child geniuses work so hard they burn themselves out and lose their mental capacities entirely. You wouldn't have talked so much about the danger if – under these circumstances – it hadn't been the one thing paramount in your mind. Sure you gave me my head. And, subconsciously, you were hoping I *would* burn myself out, so I wouldn't be a possible rival any more.'

'I see.'

'You let me study math, plane geometry, calculus, non-Euclidean, but you kept pace with me. If you didn't know the subject already, you were careful to bone up on it, to assure yourself that it was something you *could* grasp. You made sure I couldn't outstrip you, that I wouldn't get any knowledge you couldn't get. And that's why you wouldn't let me take entropic logic.'

There was no expression on Locke's face.

'Why?' he asked coldly.

'You couldn't understand it yourself,' Absalom said. 'You tried it, and it was beyond you. You're not flexible. Your logic isn't flexible. It's founded on the fact that a second-hand registers sixty seconds. You've lost the sense of wonder. You've translated too much from abstract to concrete. I *can* understand entropic logic. I can understand it!'

'You've picked this up in the last week,' Locke said.

'No. You mean the rapports. A long time ago I learned to keep part of my mind blanked off under your probing.'

'That's impossible!' Locke said, startled.

'It is for you. I'm a further step in the mutation. I have a lot of talents you don't know anything about. And I know this – I'm not far enough advanced for my age. The boys in the crèches are ahead of me. Their parents followed natural laws – it's the role of any parent to protect its young. Only the immature parents are out of step – like you.'

Locke was still quite impassive.

'I'm immature? And I hate you? I'm jealous of you? You've quite settled on that?'

'Is it true or not?'

Locke didn't answer. 'You're still inferior to me mentally,' he said, 'and you will be for some years to come. Let's say, if you want it that way, that your superiority lies in your – flexibility – and your homo superior talents. Whatever they are. Against that, balance the fact that I'm a physically mature adult and you weigh less than half of what I do. I'm legally your guardian. And I'm stronger than you are.'

Absalom swallowed again, but said nothing. Locke rose a little higher, looking down at the boy. His hand went to his middle, but found only a lightweight zipper.

He walked to the door. He turned.

'I'm going to prove to you that you're my inferior,' he said coldly and quietly. 'You're going to admit it to me.'

Absalom said nothing.

Locke went upstairs. He touched the switch on his bureau, reached into the drawer, and withdrew an elastic lucite belt. He drew its cool, smooth length through his fingers once. Then he turned to the dropper again.

His lips were white and bloodless by now.

At the door of the living room he stopped, holding the belt. Absalom had not moved, but Abigail Schuler was standing beside the boy.

'Get out, Sister Schuler,' Locke said.

'You're not going to whip him,' Abigail said, her head held high, her lips purse-string tight.

'Get out.'

'I won't. I heard every word. And it's true, all of it.'

'Get out, I tell you!' Locke screamed.

He ran forward, the belt uncoiled in his hand. Absalom's nerve broke at last. He gasped with panic and dashed away, blindly seeking escape where there was none.

Locke plunged after him.

Abigail snatched up the little hearth broom and thrust it at Locke's legs. The man yelled something inarticulate as he lost his balance. He came down heavily, trying to brace himself against the fall with stiff arms.

His head struck the edge of a chair seat. He lay motionless.

Over his still body, Abigail and Absalom looked at each other. Suddenly the woman dropped to her knees and began sobbing.

'I've killed him,' she forced out painfully. 'I've killed him – but I couldn't let him whip you, Absalom! I couldn't!'

The boy caught his lower lip between his teeth. He came forward slowly to examine his father.

'He's not dead.'

Abigail's breath came out in a long, shuddering sigh.

'Go on upstairs, Abbie,' Absalom said, frowning a little. 'I'll give him first aid. I know how.'

'I can't let you –'

'Please, Abbie,' he coaxed. 'You'll faint or something. Lie down for a bit. It's all right, really.'

At last she took the dropper upstairs. Absalom, with a thoughtful glance at his father, went to the televisor.

He called the Denver Crèche. Briefly he outlined the situation.

'What had I better do, Malcolm?'

'Wait a minute.' There was a pause. Another young face showed on the screen. 'Do this,' an assured, high-pitched voice said, and there followed certain intricate instructions. 'Got that straight, Absalom?'

'I have it. It won't hurt him?'

'He'll live. He's psychotically warped already. This will just give it a different twist, one that's safe for you. It's projection. He'll externalize all his wishes, feelings, and so forth. On you. He'll get his pleasure only out of what *you* do, but he won't be able to control you. You know the psychonamic key of his brain. Work with the frontal lobe chiefly. Be careful of Broca's area. We don't want aphasia. He must be made harmless to you, that's all. Any killing would be awkward to handle. Besides, I suppose you wouldn't want that.'

'No,' Absalom said. 'H-he's my father.'

'All right,' the young voice said. 'Leave the screen on. I'll watch and help.'

Absalom turned toward the unconscious figure on the floor.

For a long time the world had been shadowy now. Locke was used to it. He could still fulfill his ordinary functions, so he was not insane, in any sense of the word.

Nor could he tell the truth to anyone. They had created a psychic block. Day after day he went to the university and taught psychonamics and came home and ate and waited in hopes that Absalom would call him on the televisor.

And when Absalom called, he might condescend to tell something of what he was doing in Baja California. What he had accomplished. What he had achieved. For those things mattered now. They were the only things that mattered. The projection was complete.

Absalom was seldom forgetful. He was a good son. He called daily, though sometimes, when work was pressing, he had to make the call short. But Joel Locke could always work at his immense scrapbooks, filled with clippings and photographs about Absalom. He was writing Absalom's biography, too.

He walked otherwise through a shadow world, existing in flesh and blood, in realized happiness, only when Absalom's face appeared on the televisor screen. But he had not forgotten anything. He hated Absalom, and hated the horrible, unbreakable bond that would forever chain him to his own flesh – the flesh that was not quite his own, but one step further up the ladder of the new mutation.

Sitting there in the twilight of unreality, his scrapbooks spread before him, the televisor set never used except when Absalom called, but standing ready before his chair, Joel Locke nursed his hatred and a quiet, secret satisfaction that had come to him.

Some day Absalom would have a son. Some day. Some day.

If you've enjoyed these books and would like to read more, you'll find literally thousands of classic Science Fiction & Fantasy titles through the **SF Gateway**

✶

For the new home of Science Fiction & Fantasy . . .

✶

For the most comprehensive collection of classic SF on the internet . . .

✶

Visit the SF Gateway

www.sfgateway.com

Henry Kuttner (1915–1958)

Henry Kuttner was born in Los Angeles, in 1915. As a young man he worked for the literary agency of his uncle, Laurence D'Orsay, before selling his first story, 'The Graveyard Rats', to *Weird Tales* in early 1936. In 1940 Kuttner married fellow writer C. L. Moore, whom he met through the 'Lovecraft Circle', a group of writers and fans who corresponded with H. P. Lovecraft. During the Second World War, they were regular contributors to John W. Campbell's *Astounding Science-Fiction*, and collaborated for most of the 40s and 50s, publishing primarily under the pseudonyms Lewis Padgett and Lawrence O'Donnell. In 1950 he began studying at the University of Southern California, graduating in 1954. He was working towards his Master's degree but died of a heart attack in 1958, before it was completed.